BLACK LIGHT: VALENTINE ROULETTE

AN ANTHOLOGY OF THE BLACK LIGHT SERIES

RENEE ROSE   LIVIA GRANT   MAREN SMITH

JENNIFER BENE   ADDISON CAIN   LEE SAVINO

SOPHIE KISKER   MEASHA STONE

Published by Black Collar Press

Black Light: Valentine Roulette
Renee Rose, Livia Grant, Maren Smith, Jennifer Bene,
Addison Cain, Lee Savino, Sophie Kisker, Measha Stone

e-book ISBN: 978-0-998219-13-4
paperback ISBN: 978-1-947559-13-4

Cover Art by Eris Adderly, http://erisadderly.com/

First Electronic Publish Date, February 2017

❀ Created with Vellum

THREE HOURS. FOUR HARD LIMITS.

EIGHT SEXY STORIES.

What's inside this anthology?

Valentine Roulette Introduction

Jaxson Davidson, Chase Cartwright, and Emma Fischer have turned Runway into the premier dance club in Washington, D.C. but the ultra-exclusive BDSM club hiding beneath its floors has been slow to grow membership.

As Valentine's Day closes in the staff of Runway and Black Light work hard to make their separate events the talk of the town – and a pair of roulette wheels and fifteen dominants and submissives seems to be just what Black Light needs.

What are the rules of this unique event? Who will participate? Start your night here so you know just what you're signing up for before you spin the wheel!

* * *

Broken by Renee Rose

When the sub known as Slave to Pain spins ageplay, she rolls her eyes. Major Jennifer Riggs doesn't do fluffy, or pigtails, or baby talk. Doesn't need to be cuddled or held. She likes to get in and get out, where only her body gets hurt. And she already has the perfect dom - a sadist who gives it hard.

Derek, aka Master D, has been trying to break through his sub's tough walls for months. When someone else lands her for the Roulette event, he takes matters into his own hands and swaps for his girl. Ageplay isn't his thing, but this may be the perfect time to get past her defenses and give her the support she always shoves away. But when he pushes her past the breaking point, and she comes up swinging, Derek realizes he may have just lost the one sub who was the perfect match for him.

RENEE ROSE is a *USA Today* bestselling author and a naughty wordsmith who writes BDSM and spanking romance novels. She's hit #1 on Amazon in multiple categories in the U.S. and U.K., is often found on the list of Amazon's Top 100 Erotic Authors.

* * *

Revealed by Livia Grant

Actress Khloe Monroe's life is spinning out of control. Surrounded by millions of fans, but she's never felt more alone. When she seeks out an old friend, Chase Cartwright, she doesn't expect his advice to be signing up for a daring game of Valentine Roulette in his secretive BDSM club.

CIA agent Ryder Helms doesn't play at anything in life, especially sex. He's a sadist and a dominant to his core, so when the roulette wheel pairs him with the stunning actress, Khloe Monroe, a BDSM newbie, he's surprised to find she's the best gift he's received in a long time. Dominating an experienced submissive was fun. Dominating an innocent was delicious.

The confidentiality of Black Light may protect Khloe from the paparazzi, but who will protect her from the devastatingly handsome, yet dangerous, Dom she's been paired with?

LIVIA GRANT is a *USA Today* bestselling author who lives in Chicago with her husband and furry rescue dog named Max. Livia's readers appreciate her riveting stories filled with deep, character driven plots, often spiced with elements of BDSM.

* * *

Wet by Jennifer Bene

Sienna doesn't like to talk when she plays at a club. She likes to escape, to be treated like an object so she doesn't have to think. It's nice, it's easy, and she can do it with just about anyone... or so she thought.

When she gets paired with Alexander, a Daddy Dom who insists on calling her 'little girl' and making her talk, she realizes that spinning a giant water tank for breath play is the least of her worries. Now, with every unanswered question, she's plunged into icy water – but the tank isn't the only reason she's wet.

Pleasure and pain give Sienna's temper a voice, but will it force her to connect with herself and the man whose talented hands she's beginning to crave - or will she break under his touch? And if she does shatter, will Alexander be able to put his little girl back together?

JENNIFER BENE is a *USA Today* bestselling author of dangerously sexy and deviously dark romance. From BDSM, to Suspense, Dark Romance, and Thrillers—she writes it all. Always delivering a twisty, spine-tingling journey with the promise of a happily-ever-after.

* * *

Unmasked by Lee Savino

A ruthless master. A reluctant submissive.

Chessie hasn't had an orgasm in a really, really long time, so when her roommate talks her into joining the Roulette game at a local BDSM club, she figures it's worth a shot. What she doesn't expect is to be paired with the handsome Senator Kane — a man she's all too familiar with.

Can Chessie get over her prejudice against him — and her reluctance to submit to her inner desires — to achieve the pleasure she craves at the hands of Master Kane?

LEE SAVINO is a *USA Today* bestselling author of sexy, sexy romance living in Virginia with her husband and little boy. No matter what genre she writes in she loves to write books about strong women and the sexy men who love them.

* * *

Unraveled by Addison Cain

Spencer Cook, Black Light's Dungeon Master, doesn't tolerate impudence from anyone, especially not the Swedish ballbuster brought in to manage the club's floundering bar. Klara Eriksson is a distraction, a vanilla outsider who has no place smiling at and chatting to the guests of D.C.'s elite BDSM club—especially when she has never once smiled at him.

Sending her packing escalates the issue. Klara finds her way back into Black Light as a last-minute participant in the Valentine Roulette party. Desperate to regain her job, Klara offers her ex-boss a wager. If she makes it through the night submitting to a stranger, he rehires her on the spot.

Whipping, breath play... Spencer is forced to watch as a well-known Sadist has his hands, his mouth, and his body all over the BDSM virgin he unwillingly craves. He wants Klara for himself. And Klara, well, she wants to understand why Spencer fills her thoughts each time her dom pushes her past pain and right into pleasure.

ADDISON CAIN is the *USA Today* bestselling author of the international bestselling Alpha's Claim series. She has a penchant for dark themes and unrepentant lust. Heroes are villains, wrong is right, and concepts of obsession color her tales beyond simple black & white.

* * *

Unbroken by Maren Smith

Abby didn't know what she'd first done to get on club dominant Newton's bad side, but she went out of her way to earn the dark glowering looks he so loved to give her. Newton had no idea what he'd done to deserve it, but for two long years mischievous sub Abby had gone out of her way to make his life at the clubs a living hell.

Imagine her surprise when Newton also showed up with playbag in hand for Black Light's first annual event. Imagine his dismay when he spun Abby's name, attaching himself to her for the duration of the night.

If he thought for one second he could break her... If she thought for one second he was going to put up with it...

Valentine Roulette... let the games begin.

MAREN SMITH is a *USA Today* bestselling author with more than 20 years' worth of books in print. She is well known for both her slightly twisted sense of humor and her unhealthy love affair with coffee.

* * *

Bared by Measha Stone

Riley can't remember the last time she played with a Top she couldn't manipulate. That's the problem. She wants something more than topping from the bottom, and she's convinced herself that the Valentine Roulette event is the place to find it.

But when she's paired up with her ex, her confidence waivers. Dane knows her too well, has been watching her for months, and he's not going to give up this time. Will he be able to breach that wall she's been building since she ran out on him all those years ago? Or will she run again, lose the game, and her chance at love?

MEASHA STONE is a *USA Today* bestselling author from the western suburbs of Chicago where she lives with her husband and children, who are just as creative and crazy as her. Her vanilla writing has been published in numerous literary magazines, but she's found her passion in erotic romance.

* * *

Stripped by Sophie Kisker

Adam Quinn and Sari Friesen have been matched for Valentine Roulette. He likes her curves and her smile. She likes his dark eyes and his self-assured dominance. But life hasn't been easy for either of them, and trust comes slowly.

If they can work together for three hours as dom and sub, through a hot wax scene, a whipping, and a capture fantasy, they'll win the prize.

But the secret that one of them is keeping threatens to strip away the tenuous attraction that's growing with every spank, whimper, and moan. At the end of the night, will there be anything left to salvage for a future?

SOPHIE KISKER is a *USA Today* bestselling author of erotic romance full of dominance and submission. They're almost always dark, and sometimes uncomfortable, but they will always have a happy ending. She's a true believer that romantic love and a riding crop make a great combination.

* * *

A Note From the Publisher:

Every book you are about to read happens on the same night, during the same event at the Black Light BDSM club. Valentine Roulette has its own set of rules outside of normal play, and the eight daring couples in these books were brave enough to sign-up.

But before you can decide if *you* are brave enough to spin the wheel, continue reading to find out how the Valentine Roulette event came to be...

VALENTINE ROULETTE
INTRODUCTION

Livia Grant & Jennifer Bene

EARLY JANUARY

"*A*ll right. We've been at this for two hours and need to wrap things up." Jaxson Davidson tried his hardest to wrangle the vocal group of managers gathered around the conference table into some semblance of order. He'd purposefully hired strong leaders when he'd opened Runway a month ago, because after spending most of his adult life in front of cameras he knew he didn't know enough about the dance club and bar industry, even with Chase and Emma at his side.

The good news was that his new business was off to an overwhelming success.

The bad news was that having all of these strong personalities in the same space was not working as the well-oiled machine he'd hoped for, *yet*, which meant he was staying more involved in the day to day decisions than he'd planned.

"I'm sorry, but we still haven't nailed down the Valentine's Day ideas and since we're only five weeks out, we need to finish those plans, even if it takes another two hours." Maxine Torres, Runway's general manager, was the antithesis of Jaxson's style, but although he wanted to strangle her most of the time, he was grateful he'd hired her. He and Chase might pony up the bankroll and name recognition for the club, but he knew Maxine was the reason it was a runaway success. She was a damn fine bar manager.

"Fine. What's still outstanding?" He impatiently tried to push her along.

Maxine clicked away on the tablet she carried with her everywhere.

"We still need to decide on door prizes and gifts to be passed out to all attendees." Carrie Fung, their publicist and media specialist, rarely got a word in edgewise, but she sat at attention, ready to be heard. "It needs to be something we can put the Runway logo on and that people will want to keep and see often."

"How about packets of condoms with our logo? We could add a comment wishing them a 'Happy and Safe Valentine's Day.'" Their DJ, Marvin Washington, better known as DJ Elixxir, had made the same suggestion at their last staff meeting.

As expected, Blake Howard, the head of security, shot the idea down. "I keep telling you that we have to break up enough couples having sex on the premises already without encouraging it by passing out rubbers."

DJ Elixxir grinned. "I know, but it's so fun to look down from my balcony and watch people going at it like rabbits to the beat of my music."

Blake shot back, "There's a place for that shit in this building, and the dance floor isn't it."

Jaxson shot his head of security a warning glare. Most of the people crowded in around the table were not privy to the fact that a top-secret BDSM club was one floor below the dance floor and Jaxson wanted to keep it that way. Knowledge of the secret club was on a need-to-know basis, and blabbermouth Elixxir certainly did *not* need to know.

Carrie interjected with a thankfully better idea. "I was thinking we could buy small tins of breath mints with our Runway logo on it and pass those out. And maybe for the women… long-stemmed roses with a Runway ribbon. And as always, we'll have the step and repeat with the red carpet where the photographer will take commemorative photos – at a hefty profit for us of course."

Jaxson jumped in, "I love those ideas. Let's make it happen."

Maxine glared at him for his continued rush job, but didn't interrupt.

Blake gave a warning, "We've been turning people away at the door every night since we opened so I know it will be a madhouse on the weekend before Valentine's Day. Just a reminder that I'm gonna be riding my boys at the door hard to avoid getting dinged by the fire marshal again. We've already had one warning that we were over our approved capacity, the next one's going to come with a big ass fine."

"Well that's your department so you'd better watch that closely. I'm gonna kick your ass if you get us shutdown." Jaxson meant the warning.

Sensing the meeting was wrapping, Maxine took charge as she always did to recap action items and decisions. She ran a tight ship and as annoying as it was, he knew they needed her.

"So to recap, we'll have the Crushing Stones back again for a concert on that Saturday night. The show will start at 8pm. Doors will open at 6pm and we'll be selling limited VIP tickets in advance at six times the door ticket price."

"Holy shit, that would be $120 bucks," the stage manager, Arianna Esposito, squeaked.

"Yes, and a bargain. Their big arena shows have tickets going for twice that and they'll get an up close and personal view of Cash and the boys here at Runway," Maxine countered before continuing. "We'll pass out the roses to the women and the breath mints to the men as they arrive. Noah, remind us again what you've got planned."

Their head bartender, Noah Garner, piped up, "I've got two thousand glasses ordered for that night with the Runway logo on it. We'll be serving a new drink I've created called a Runway Love Potion and they'll keep the glass as a souvenir."

Jaxson had almost forgotten Chase was in the room, sitting on the couches behind him with Emma, until he piped in, "They are fucking awesome. I think we should keep them on the menu year round."

Jaxson hadn't tasted the drink yet, but he'd been the beneficiary of a pretty tipsy Chase and Emma the week before, when they'd come home frisky as hell after acting as guinea pigs for Noah's experiments for just the right recipe. He could attest that the cocktails had worked as a *very* effective love potion that night.

"Alright, that's it for now. We'll have one more staff meeting in two weeks to nail down any last minute items. Everyone have a great day and get back to work." Jaxson dismissed them, anxious to get on to the second and more important meeting of the day.

Most of the occupants of the room stood and headed for the door, chatting amicably. As expected, the head of his security – and the only man who had sat completely silent in the first meeting – Spencer Cook, remained behind. Unfortunately, so did Maxine.

As soon as the door closed on the office, Maxine spoke up, "Okay, it's time I find out what the hell is going on around here."

Jaxson had known this day was coming. He'd been dodging her prying questions for weeks. "Maxine, it's best if you just get back to work. It's getting late and I know you have to pick up your kids after school soon."

She grinned triumphantly. "Not today. I told Eric he had to pick them up because I had to stay late for a meeting."

Blake piped in, "Your meeting wrapped on time."

"Not that meeting. *THIS* meeting. The one you guys always have without me," she glowered.

The serious looking man in the sharp suit, who'd sat silently for two hours, finally spoke. "You're not invited. Out." Jaxson's friend, Spencer, had always been a man of few words. He was used to dealing with women who were the antithesis of Maxine Torres. As a result, Jaxson's top two employees were like two sheets of sand paper when they got close enough to rub each other.

Maxine didn't back down, instead she put her high-heeled shoes up on the now vacant chair next to her as if to convey she was settling in for the long haul. She stared Spencer down with her best glare before responding, "I'm the manager of this club. That means I need to know everything that goes on here."

"You know everything you need to know."

"Apparently not, since I don't have a clue what the hell you guys are up to."

Spencer broke into a threatening smile that Jaxson had seen many times before. "You couldn't handle it."

"I'm a married mother of three kids; one a teenager. We have three dogs, two cats, and one rabbit. My seventy-three year old mother lives next door and I'm the president of the PTA. Not to mention, I put in fifty hours a week making Runway the premier club east of the Mississippi. I can handle anything," Maxine countered with confidence.

"Well, this meeting has nothing to do with Runway, pets, or families, so you are excused," Spencer answered in his condescending way.

Maxine crossed her arms with a humph, showing no sign of backing down and Jaxson wasn't surprised.

"Maxine, Spencer is right. It is best if you head to your own office now."

She changed tactics, turning to look back at Chase and Emma still sitting on the couch to the side. "Why do they get to stay and I don't? I'm the manager."

"Of Runway, yes. The following meeting is about another venture we have invested in that is not under your control," Jaxson argued more sternly.

He saw her eyes widen a sliver, excited she had him talking. "But it *is* under the same roof, which means I need to know about it. Don't think I don't notice you all disappearing down the back hallway every night around ten when you think I've gone home for the night."

She'd hit a sore spot with Jaxson. He hated to admit it, but he'd been trying to sneak down to Black Light without Maxine noticing and it was quite frankly pissing him off. He resented having to curtail his movements in his own club because he didn't want to make waves with an employee.

I'm the boss, dammit.

"Maxine, don't forget that you work here. We own the place. Chase, Emma, and I can come and go as we please."

"That's not what I'm talking about and you know it. There is something fishy going on around here and I don't like it. If you guys are selling drugs or running some other secretive underground illegal business, I better damn well know about it. I didn't sign up to be involved with anything like that."

Spencer barked an annoyed laugh. "Oh for Christ's sake, there is nothing illegal going on here."

"Prove it," Maxine shouted back.

"I don't need to prove shit to you. You have your job. I have mine and God willing, never the two shall meet," Spencer's voice was rising. Jaxson knew his friend would blow soon if he didn't get Maxine under control.

She barged ahead with her next argument. "Then why is he even here during the Runway meetings? If I don't get to come to his meetings, he shouldn't be at mine," the manager reasoned.

Jaxson had wondered himself why Spencer chose to come. His friend's answer only increased the tension in the room.

"I need to know everything that goes on in this building."

"And I don't?" Maxine countered. "And what's with that anyway. Blake here is head of security. If anyone needs to know what is going on everywhere in the building, it's him, not you."

"Which is why he is allowed to stay." Spencer's normally unreadable face was turning a bit red as Maxine continued to challenge him.

"Just tell me what is downstairs and I'll leave."

"You couldn't handle five minutes down there."

"What, you have a built-in torture chamber?" Maxine chuckled.

"Something like that." His reply startled her into silence.

Jaxson had had enough. "All right you two. You are both important to our success here. I think Spencer is right, though, Maxine. I can assure you there is nothing illegal going on. I think you'll be happier staying in the dark."

"And I know I won't rest until I know." She changed tactics. "He sat silently for my meeting. All I'm asking for is the same courtesy. I want to sit silently during his meeting."

Tit-for-tat. That was the game she was playing. Spencer's eyes lit up with a dangerous twinkle at the thought of shocking his counterpart.

Jaxson relented. They were barely a month in and Maxine was

already acting like a sleuth. They might as well cut her in on their little secret. "Not one word out of you, got it?"

Maxine made a show out of pretend zipping her mouth and then turning an imaginary key before tossing it over her left shoulder and then returning her arms into their defensive crossed position.

Spencer glared at her for a few long seconds before turning his attention to Jaxson at the other end of the long table. He didn't bother getting up to move closer to the other occupants in the room, instead electing to remain removed as he often did.

"You're really gonna put up with her shit?" he challenged Jaxson.

For some reason, Spencer's aggression bothered him more than Maxine's. "She's no more of a prima donna than you are. You both can be a pain in my ass, but I hired each of you because you are experienced and the best. So the answer to your question is, yes. Yes, I'm putting up with her shit because she's right. While Black Light is a secret, as the manager of Runway, Maxine has the right to know what is going on below her club." He paused, turning to pin Maxine with a threatening glare. "But she better keep in mind that what she is about to hear is one-hundred percent confidential. It is not to be discussed with anyone outside of this room. Not her hairdresser, the other employees... not even her husband. She's a smart lady. I don't need to remind her of the NDA she signed when she took the job."

Keeping her mouth closed tightly, she nodded her agreement to Jaxson's warning.

Spencer didn't like it, but he proceeded. "Fine. We've wasted enough time. If she loses her shit over this, it's not on me."

"Duly noted," Jaxson reassured him. "Continue. What have you and the guys cooked up for Valentine's Day?"

"Hold on." Spencer pulled his cell phone out of his pocket and punched in what looked like a short text message. Within ten seconds, the door to the office opened and four men in leather pants and black T-shirts shuffled in. They halted briefly at the sight of Maxine in the room, but recovered quickly, taking the seats around the table recently vacated by the managers of the Runway teams.

Jaxson saw Maxine's eyes fill with surprise, but to her credit, she held her tongue.

Spencer opened the plain manila folder in front of him, taking the top sheet out, and began to fill them in. "We've come up with an excellent idea that's going to get the place packed on Valentine's night. We're going to setup a mixer game of Valentine Roulette."

The dungeon master paused dramatically giving the occupants of the room time to assimilate what he'd said.

Chase stood and pulled out the chair next to Jaxson at the table, taking a seat as he questioned Spencer. "Roulette. As in Russian Roulette?"

Blake looked at him, annoyance in his eyes. "Yeah, we're gonna off the participants until the last man is standing. Nothing like killing participants to drive up membership."

The newest men in the room broke into snickers at Chase's expense, which annoyed Jaxson.

"Explain. Now." He knew how to talk to Spencer. The snickers ended abruptly.

"We'll have a private sign-up period starting next week. Dominant and submissive club members will be able to read the rules and decide if they want to sign up and consent on-line in advance. The night of the party they will be randomly paired up to scene with one person. They won't know who they will play with in advance and they can't refuse their play partner without using their safeword which will disqualify them."

Jaxson was intrigued, but he had a lot of questions. "So, how do they get paired up?"

"We'll have two large roulette wheels, just like in a casino only the first one will have the names of the submissives on it. The Doms will draw numbers to see who goes first and one by one, they will go up and take their chances spinning the wheel. They play with whomever the wheel names and then we take her name off the wheel and the next guy spins. Rinse and repeat until they are all paired up."

Chase interrupted. "So, is it just a singles night?"

"Not at all. If couples want to play, they can, but they are committing to most likely playing with other partners. Couples not wanting to play will be spectators... voyeurs... We'll have small cocktail tables setup throughout the club and we'll serve top-end champagne and appetizers. We'll sell tickets over and above membership fees as a special event since the club is normally closed on Tuesdays."

Jaxson suspected he knew what the other roulette wheel was for. "And the second wheel? They spin for their scene?"

Owen, the dungeon's Master Shibarist answered him. "Exactly. Each participant will be allowed to put three things from the wheel on their hard limit list when they sign up. If they roll something on either of their hard limit list, they can spin again. If not, they have to play the scene they roll for a minimum of thirty minutes before they can take their chances by spinning again."

Chase asked, "How many activities are on the wheel?"

"We brainstormed over twenty activities so far. I think we could come up with a few more ideas, too," Owen replied.

"What kind of stuff are we talking about here?" Jaxson pressed, curious.

Spencer picked up the top piece of paper from the open manila folder and started reading the list. "Bondage, Anal Play, Pet Play, Water Sports, Electrical Play, Suspension, Whipping Post, Medical Play, High Protocol, Pain Play, Humiliation, Water/Tub, Sybian-Orgasm Torture, Latex Encasement, Fire Play, Age Play, Oral Sex, Breath Play, Blood Play, and Needle Play. We also decided we could put several role-play options on for things like principal/naughty student, royalty, law enforcement. We've accumulated a pretty extensive wardrobe for scenes already and will continue to add to the costume options over time. We could even throw a Dom's choice role-play in there for fun; like a wild card."

Maxine fidgeted in the chair next to him. He suspected she might be regretting promising to remain silent.

Jaxson's cock was expanding in his jeans at the mental image of the sexy scenes that could play out on Valentine's night. He had to admit, the plan was appealing for several reasons.

"I like it. We've wanted to introduce more of a variety of activities and try to get the current members to come out of their shell a bit. This could help with that, but some of those activities are heavy duty. What if we get a novice Dom who has to do a complex fetish like

Blood Play or Suspension? If they fuck it up, it could go south quickly."

Spencer reassured him, "That's the greatest part of the plan. Between my four dungeon monitors, and me, we have all of those activities covered. We'll each be assigned stations that we will monitor, but also act as a trainer for Doms who are learning new activities. Safety first."

Jaxson nodded, relieved they had a plan to keep the submissives safe.

Chase challenged Spencer next. "This seems pretty risky for both the Doms and the subs who participate. What incentive is there to get people to sign up?"

"The prize at the end of the night will be one month's dues free for anyone who finishes the night and who played by the rules. Then the monitors and I can give out extra comp days or weeks for extra good scenes, and we'll choose one couple to award the grand prize of two months free membership."

Jaxson wasn't too crazy about that. "That's a lot of free membership cash to be giving away."

"We plan on maxing out at fifteen couples, and don't forget, I'm sure some of them will drop out when it gets too intense for them. And we'll more than make up for it by selling the VIP tickets for the observers that night. I think what's most important is that we continue to distinguish ourselves as the premium BDSM club on the east coast. Black Light is not only secure and confidential, but also focused on providing safe, sane, and consensual play. We'll be offering training for Doms and subs both."

Garreth, one of the most hardcore Doms of the group spoke up next. "Don't forget, I'm also an EMT. I'll come prepared in case anything gets out of hand with the needle or fire play."

"Well, you'd better make damn sure nothing gets out of control. It's great we are prepared for an emergency, but we can't put subs in danger intentionally."

Spencer spoke up, out of patience. "I'm counting on the sign up process to weed out anyone who isn't going to be able to handle it."

Chase challenged him, "And why is that?"

"Because, it will be a legal document that will scare away anyone not fully committed."

Up until now, Emma had been sitting quietly through both meetings, but Jaxson heard the quaver in her voice when she spoke up softly to question the plan. "So if I were to sign up, I could only say no to three of those things? What if I wanted to say no to more than three?"

Jaxson turned and could see the fear in her eyes. He rushed to help her relax. "You don't have anything to worry about, sweetheart. We'll be observers that night. I have zero desire to play with anyone other than you and Chase, angel."

Visible relief passed across her face before she pressed forward with another question. "And what about sex? Are they expected to have sex with their partner who will most likely be a stranger to them?"

Garreth answered her and Jaxson was relieved to hear the respect in his voice as he recognized he was talking to the boss's submissive. "Intercourse will be one of the things on the list that they can put on their hard list, but if they refuse to have sex then that will leave only two other picks for their limit list."

Emma glanced his way and Jax could see concern in her beautiful violet eyes. "What is it, sweetheart?"

"I don't think that's enough options for hard limits. There are a lot of scary things on that list."

Jaxson gave her a reassuring nod. He trusted her instincts. "You heard the lady, gentlemen. We bump the hard list choices from three to four."

"Now, wait a minute. We're gonna be spinning all night long because there are so many free passes," Spencer grumbled, careful not to direct his anger directly at Emma.

Jaxson closed the discussion. "There will be four options for submissives to put on their hard limits. Next topic."

Chase thought of the next controversial question. "What happens if a male Dom gets paired with a male submissive and they don't bend that way?" As the only switch in the room, Chase had a unique view into the D/s dynamics at play with an event like this.

Jaxson wasn't thrilled to see the surprise on Spencer's face. It told him the others in the room hadn't considered this obstacle, which annoyed him. Just because his employees were strictly male dominants who topped female submissives didn't mean there weren't many other D/s combinations. Jaxson, Chase and Emma were proof of that.

Spencer reluctantly answered, "I don't think we have a large enough membership pool yet to offer anything other than male on female options this year. Maybe by next year, assuming this is a success, we can be more inclusive during the sign up process and try to accommodate our gay and bisexual members, as well as our female Dommes and male submissives."

"I agree with you for this year, but let's make it more inclusive going forward."

Spencer nodded his agreement.

Jaxson glanced at Maxine who was still sitting silently at the table. He had to stifle his grin as he realized she was turning beet red in her attempt at holding her silence. She looked as if a rant was literally bubbling up, ready to spew from her mouth at any moment.

Moving to a more tactical discussion, Jaxson spoke, "So talk to me about the legalities. This obviously goes over and above our normal contract for membership. What are we doing to protect ourselves from lawsuits when one of the participants isn't happy with the way things turn out for them on the wheel?"

Owen answered, "We had the same law firm you used to buy the building and do all of the contracting for Runway and Black Light write up the contract for participants. As they also wrote up the membership agreement for Black Light, we figured they were setup for this as well."

"Yeah, good thinking. How much is that gonna cost us?" Jaxson hadn't been thrilled with the bill they'd got from Lambert, Urbanski and Reed's law firm their last go-round. They'd luckily been able to work out a discount membership, and a set of free months, for the partners of the firm to reduce the billable hours.

Spencer grinned. "They did it pro-bono. I just had to offer Alexander a free pass to participate."

"Excellent."

Maxine shifted in her seat, sitting bolt upright as she took her feet from the chair next to her. She looked as if she were about to spring out of her chair. Jaxson couldn't hide his grin any longer.

"Would you like to be excused now, Maxine?" he prodded.

She hesitated, unsure if she was allowed to speak to respond. He was being an ass since he knew Maxine didn't have a single ounce of submissiveness in her body, but he just couldn't resist. "You may speak."

Her eyes flashed angry at his condescending approval. "Let me get this straight. You barbarians are running a sex club beneath my Runway?"

Spencer looked like he wanted to throttle her, but Jaxson waved him off before responding. "We are running an exclusive BDSM club beneath *my* Runway." He stopped and looked at Chase and rephrased. "Correction. My, Chase, and Emma's Runway. Yes, there is sex involved, but it is way more complicated than that."

"Listen, I'm no prude, but I'm not entirely sure I'm comfortable with this," she objected.

"Which part? The sex or the BDSM part?"

"All of it. Particularly the fact that young women are going to be used and possibly abused for men's satisfaction."

Jaxson leaned forward, placing his hands on the table and leaning closer to her to make sure he was getting his point across as he answered her as best he could. "Emma," he didn't take his eyes off Maxine as he waited for his lover to answer from behind him.

"Yes, sir."

"Have you been to Black Light?"

"Of course. Many times."

"Have you ever seen anyone, man or woman, being abused against their will?"

"No, sir."

"As my submissive, have you ever felt abused by our lifestyle?"

He could hear the humor in her voice as she answered. "Abused? Goodness, no. More like pampered and loved."

"Even when you've been punished?"

She hesitated before answering this question. He suspected she didn't care admitting it, but he knew her answer was the truth. "Especially when I've been punished."

"Good girl," Jaxson praised.

"Good girl? Seriously? She's not a fucking puppy!" Maxine's anger was bubbling up.

"That's enough. We asked you to leave. You insisted on staying. You said you could handle it."

"That was before I knew what was going on," she countered. "I'm not sure I can deal with this."

Jaxson pressed her hard. "Then I'm sorry to see you go. Accept it, or I'll be expecting your resignation before you leave today."

Her eyes widened at his threat. He prayed she'd back down. He really didn't want to lose her. She was a damn fine manager for Runway, but he also knew he wouldn't put up with her giving them shit for their lifestyle or running Black Light.

An awkward silence hung in the air as he and the bossy woman in the room squared off. He could see indecision flitting through her eyes as she weighed her options. He was a bit surprised when Emma came into his peripheral view, coming to sit in the chair next to Maxine, recently vacated by her propped up feet.

"It really is okay, Maxine. I remember not understanding the whole lifestyle at all when I met Jaxson and Chase. It confused me too. After all, I'd been raised to be a Type-A career woman. I never would have dreamed I'd enjoy being a sexual submissive, but honestly, I've never been happier. I've met so many submissives in the club and I can assure you, everything that I've seen has been consensual. It may not be for you, but please don't quit over this. We need you and you're great at your job."

Jaxson could have kissed Emma. She was saying exactly what needed to be said, and with a credibility that only a woman could pull off in this situation.

Maxine glanced back up at Jaxson and hesitated only a few seconds before giving her answer. "Fine. As long as you all keep it private, I'll back off. I'm not sure I understand it all, but it's none of my business."

Spencer couldn't contain his response. "That's what I said in the beginning."

She glared at him and then went to work. "So, who do you have designing the website sign-up for the event?"

Spencer glanced at his four employees for support, but all five men got a deer in the headlights look on their face.

Maxine continued on. "That's what I thought. I assume you have a food and beverage operation down there? Where are you getting your liquor? Are you doing any product ordering that we could combine with Runway to get volume discounts? How about your scheduling, memberships, accounting?"

The more tactical things Maxine rattled off, the more sheepish the Master of the Dungeon looked. Jaxson had to hide a new grin – this time at his friend's expense. He was enjoying Spencer being schooled by the real outlet manager in the room.

"Maxine, you bring up excellent points. I'm sure there are some scales of economy we could gain by combining some of the resources between the two clubs." He paused to pin Spencer with a glare. "You are an excellent Master Dom, Spencer, but you don't know shit about running a club. Effective immediately, I'd like you two to work together on the non-BDSM components of Black Light."

"You have to be shitting me. You want me to work with *her*? You told me Black Light was all mine to run."

"And it is. You have complete creative control over the BDSM components, but Maxine can help with the F&B and purchasing. Let her help you with the website setup for the event. Keep in mind, it has to be 100% confidential and have a login/password setup to protect identities."

Maxine did her best to ignore the grumbling at the other end of the table as she turned back to Jaxson. "I understand the need for confidentiality, but I'd like to let Noah in on the secret. He does all of our ordering of supplies and liquor. Trying to add anything to orders without him knowing will be impossible, and I've put him in charge of inventory control."

Jaxson and Spencer answered, "Agreed", and, "No fucking way", simultaneously.

Spencer grumbled. "I already hired my own bartenders for Black Light. We don't need his help."

Maxine rounded on him. "Let me guess. Old friends of yours?" When Spencer sat silently, she had her affirmation. "I'm not suggesting Noah work downstairs. I'm only saying he helps with inventory control and purchasing. Don't worry. He won't interfere with your boys' club."

"All right, I think we've had enough for today. Getting the website setup is a top priority and then sending out a confidential email to all of our membership with the invitation to participate or attend as observers comes next. Let's get back together in two weeks at our next staff meeting. I'll expect to hear how we are doing with participation. And Spencer?" He pinned his friend with a glare. He knew the Dom wasn't going to like his next request any more than he'd liked the rest of the meeting. "Emma is our accountant. I'd like her to run the numbers with the planned participation and ticket sales to understand where our breakeven number is. We need to set target sales thresholds to make sure we aren't losing money."

"For Christ's sake. You act like you're running a huge corporation or something. I thought you wanted to have a private place for the BDSM elite to play safely here in D.C. without fear of being outed with the media or public."

"Yes, but I never once said I wanted to open Black Light to lose money. It's a business. Just like Runway. I'm willing to give it a few months to get things rolling, particularly since we can't do any wide advertising and keep our anonymity. We'll only get business through private referrals, which will take time to happen, but let me be clear. We either figure out a way to start making a profit within the next few months or we'll shut it down. I'm not running a charity here, particularly since almost every Dominant member we've signed up so far is a millionaire."

"That's the problem. We are heavy on Doms and since many of them already have regular subs, they pay the couple rate. It is single submissives we are short on. Many of them don't have the money for the hefty membership fees."

"Well then, this is a great opportunity for many of them to come and play with the possibility of winning a month's free membership. Just be careful who you invite. Even if they are a guest, they have to still agree to all of the confidentiality clauses."

Terry, the burliest of the four dungeon monitors, had sat quietly in the meeting up until that moment. Jaxson always thought he'd earned his nickname, Muscles, honestly.

"I'm still doing part-time security over at the Overtime BDSM club next to the Capitol Building. Been there a couple of years now. I can get together a short list of submissives I think would be a good fit if you'd like. Most couldn't afford the monthly fee for Black Light, but I think they'd love to participate in the Valentine Roulette event, especially if they had a chance to win a month or two of regular membership to come and play."

Spencer cautioned, "That's a good idea, but just be careful. Confidentiality is a top priority."

Jaxson had worried about this. "We are in a bit of a bind, though. We can let the subs in for free for the event to get the interest up. We'll never have enough members to make the business work if we don't widen our invitations a little bit." As his dungeon master started to argue back, he closed the meeting with, "I'm not suggesting we take out a full page ad in The Post, but we need to get a buzz going among the known BDSM community if we plan on getting enough members."

In the brief silence that hung in the air, he heard Emma's tummy growling. The blush across the bridge of her nose was adorable. As their eyes met, he knew they needed to wrap up so he could take care of filling her tummy. His growing cock wanted to feed her an appetizer of cum before taking her out for a proper dinner.

"So we have a plan. Let's close this meeting. We'll get back together in two weeks for our next meeting. Don't wait until then if you need to run anything past me. Have a good evening, everyone." The tone in his voice didn't leave room for uncertainty. Everyone around the table knew they'd just been dismissed.

Maxine grabbed up her tablet and cell phone and almost sprinted from the room to avoid further interaction with the men of Black Light. Spencer hesitated as if he wanted to stay to debate something with Jaxson, but eventually left, trailing behind the four dungeon monitors, and Blake.

Once the three lovers were alone, the atmosphere switched in a flash from business to pleasure. Chase almost attacked him, sliding to his knees and crawling under the table to start grasping at Jaxson's pants zipper.

"I fucking love watching you dominate the meeting like that. Watching you keep even Spencer and his boys in check is the hottest thing ever. I've been like steel for the last thirty minutes."

Jaxson chuckled until he felt his lover's warm hand pulling his own hardening cock free from the confines of his underwear. His touch was the perfect aphrodisiac to add to the growing sexual need hanging in the air. Jaxson reached his hand out as an invitation to Emma who sat nearby watching her lovers starting without her.

"Come here, sweetheart. I want to give you a big kiss. You were perfect in the meeting."

"Are we really going to have front row seats that night for the Valentine Roulette?" He saw excitement in her eyes.

"That was the plan."

Emma rushed to stand next to his chair where he could pull her down into an urgent kiss. Jaxson let the pleasure of the two mouths connecting with him intimately wash over him. Within seconds, his cock was rock hard and ready for the next phase of their tryst. As tempted as he was to let his lovers finish him off, he knew they deserved to come too and he really did want to feed Emma his growing load.

He broke out of the kiss and pushed his rolling executive chair away from the table, leaving a panting Chase on his knees under the table.

"Get on up here, Chase. You're gonna pound our Emma while she kneels on the chair. Come here, sweetheart."

He pushed to his feet so she could place her knees on the seat his ass had just vacated. She faced the back of the chair. "That's it. Lean over the back of the chair and I'll feed you while Chase services your hot little pussy. Don't forget. We all come together."

Chase was already on his feet, freeing his own manhood from his pants and stepping up to bare Emma's core. Jaxson waited until Chase's eyes met his own, telling him all was ready. The only indication to Chase it was time was a small nod. The men both entered Emma, one in her mouth and the other in her pussy, in one strong push. Jaxson felt her gagging as the tip of his engorged penis hit the back of her throat. Her gurgling cry as Chase went equally deep at the other end of her enhanced Jaxson's pleasure. She was holding onto the back of the chair for stability, which meant he had complete control over the speed and depth he fucked her mouth. The sound of bodies slapping together was joined by the slurping of wet channels being plundered front and back on their submissive.

The soundtrack of the room was too fucking sexy to let any of them last for long. He could feel Emma trying to pull off his cock as she attempted to ask permission to come. He was too close to allow her to stop, even for a second. Instead, he wrapped his fingers through her long dark hair and used her wet orifice to chase his own pleasure.

Jaxson was so focused on plunging into Emma's throat he missed Chase leaning in, seeking his own intimate connection to his Dom. The men's mouths connected in an open mouth kiss, completing their favorite triangle of connection for the trio.

Within seconds, they all tipped into a loud orgasm with the men depositing their loads into Emma's warm body.

Chase grinned his lopsided smile as they began to peel apart from each other. "That should tide us over for a few hours. I'm starving. I vote we go to dinner before we head down to Black Light for round two."

Jaxson pulled one of the cloth hankies he always carried with him out of his pocket to start cleaning up Emma's spunk filled mouth where she'd dribbled drops of sticky cum she couldn't quite swallow.

"That's one idea. I kinda thought we could order up a pizza and start round two while we waited."

Emma giggled as Chase got to work stripping her. "Perfect plan. You order the pizza."

VALENTINE'S DAY, EVENING, AT BLACK LIGHT

*C*hase was going to be late to his own event if he didn't get moving. Watching a few couples enter Black Light, he pulled up the cuff up on his tuxedo shirt, baring his invisible tattoo and holding it under the black light scanner on the desk in front of him. The beeping acknowledgement coincided with a locker springing open to his left.

"You know the drill, Mr. Cartwright," the security guard added.

"Danny, for crying out loud. When the hell are you going to start calling me Chase?"

The guard grinned. "When you're no longer my boss."

They'd had this discussion before, too many times, so Chase knew to let it go and simply sighed as he stepped out of the way of the next guest. More patrons were arriving by the time he'd finished depositing all of his electronics in his locker. Several people he'd never seen before had pieces of paper printed with a QR code that allowed them entrance for the one-night special event. Still, Danny asked for photo ID every time.

Chase breathed a sigh of relief at the strict security measures. God willing, no one unauthorized would be entering Black Light ever again. Not after they'd had a breach like Madeline O'Neill's so early in their history. If it weren't for Thomas Hathaway, they probably would have been exposed as front-page news before they'd even been able to identify the gaps in their policies. The experience from just a few weeks before had taught them all to be extra vigilant, and was a solid reminder of why Black Light had the membership it did.

Security was paramount.

The vibe in the club was exciting from the minute he walked through the door. The lighting was not quite as dim as usual, allowing spectators to view several of the nearby scenes that would be surrounding them throughout the evening. As a result, Chase could see across the massive expanse of the club, his eyes honing in on his lovers as they slow danced on the area of floor in front of the bar. The winding, sexy beat of the music set the perfect tone for the night's upcoming event.

"Hello, sir. Would you like some champagne?" One of the bartenders greeted him in a skimpy outfit, offering the tray of sparkling glasses.

"Well, of course. Thanks."

"You'll let me know if there is anything else I can do for you tonight, won't you?" she flirted.

"Thanks, darling, but champagne is all I'll need tonight."

Her lips formed a pretty pout. "Yes, sir."

Chase downed the glass of bubbly and put the empty back on her tray quickly, hoping Jaxson hadn't noticed his arrival. He'd sure like a second glass later before he got on stage to settle his nerves, but his Dom had made it clear that both Chase and Emma were restricted to only one cocktail tonight since they'd each overindulged the Saturday night before. Jaxson hadn't been happy that his submissives had both spent that night on the cold tile of their bathroom paying homage to the porcelain gods.

He didn't even make it halfway across the space before he was met by an uncharacteristically animated Dungeon Master. Spencer Cook stopped him just in front of the table they were setting up for blood and fire play.

"I just saw the final list of contestants, Chase. You have to disqualify her. She's no longer allowed on the premises."

His friend never said a name. He didn't need to. Chase knew full well that the cause of the DM's current angst was the head bartender he'd just fired the week before, Klara Eriksson. The two of them had been setting off fireworks when in the same room together since the moment they'd met and tonight would likely be no different.

Chase wasn't privy to everything that had happened between the two, but the one thing he did know was that it took a lot to pique the jaded DM's interests these days, but Klara had done it easily. Spencer could bitch about her all he wanted; Chase knew the root of his annoyance with the bossy bartender was his deep-seated desire to tame her. Watching her, the untouchable object of his desire, playing as a submissive with some other Dom was sure to cause new drama for the audience tonight, which was exactly why Chase knew what he needed to do.

"She signed up fair and square. We are allowing non-members to participate in hopes of drumming up more members."

"That's just it. She's not a submissive, and even if she was, she can't afford the membership," Spencer objected.

"Well, that's why she would appreciate the month of free membership for completing the challenge."

"Did you hear me? She's not a submissive."

"And she told you this?" Chase stared him down, knowing the answer.

"You've met her! You can see as much as I can that she's a total pitbull. A bitch on wheels. She's cut from the same cloth as Maxine for Christ's sake. This is not the place for her."

Chase grinned. "Apparently, she doesn't agree. The sign-up procedure was extremely clear on what tonight would entail, and she worked here for over a month. There is absolutely no chance of her not understanding exactly what she's signed up for. We have just enough participants to fulfill all fifteen couples so I'm sorry, but your request is denied. Klara plays."

"You sonofabitch..."

"Is there a problem here?" Jaxson had stepped up behind Chase. He could feel his Dom's power emitting from his tense body. Spencer had dared challenge Jaxson's submissive and it wasn't going over well.

Spencer's eyes widened slightly, but he didn't back down. "Chase needs to strike Klara from the players list. We'll just have to cancel one of the fifteen couples. Whatever man draws number fifteen..."

He didn't finish his sentence. Jaxson had lifted his hand like a stop sign, stepping closer until the dungeon master stopped talking.

Jaxson's voice was soft, but deadly clear. "Klara is an adult. She signed up of her own free will and she'll participate until she chooses to remove herself by use of her safeword and not a moment before. If her presence is going to bother you so much, perhaps you should stay behind the bar tonight and cover her old job."

The men stood silently, chest to chest in their showdown. Spencer finally backed down, taking a slight step back to signal his surrender. "For the record, this is bullshit. She is an ex-employee. She shouldn't be on the premises."

Jaxson pressed him. "Noted, but overruled."

After Spencer stomped off, Jaxson turned to Chase. "You okay?"

"Sure, but I do love it when you come riding in to save me like my knight in shining armor."

Jaxson grinned his sexiest smile. "I'll be showing you later exactly how I like to be repaid for my chivalry."

"Ah, so it's not free then?" Chase flirted with his Dom, more than grateful that Jaxson had backed him up and supported what he'd told their employee.

Jaxson pulled him closer, leaning in to whisper in his ear with a hint of a growl, "I'll make sure you enjoy the payment as much as I do."

Chase's blood heated, rushing to his cock at the naughty promise. He suspected he'd have blue balls by the end of the night being a spectator and not a participant in the night's events. There probably wouldn't even be time for a little bit of play with him at the roulette wheels. "Yes, sir."

"Let's go see Emma before you have to go on stage." Jaxson reluctantly peeled apart from him, grabbing Chase's hand and weaving them through the small cocktail tables and chairs they'd brought in for the event. As they neared the main stage, the tables were almost full with spectators and club members who had paid the high price to be voyeurs for the evening.

Chase stopped to chat and welcome couples in risqué evening wear, running into the occasional submissive, naked on their knees or collared and on their master's leash. The sight of a submissive kitty-cat, furry tail and all, got Chase's eager mind thinking of where he might buy such an adorable outfit for his Emma.

Would she be willing to try a bit of pet play after seeing the kinks tonight?

"Chase!" Samantha Carter pulled away from her new husband, Jonah, weaving through the growing crowd to give Chase a huge hug.

"Now this is a welcome surprise! I thought you two were headed back up to New York after last Saturday night." He laughed as he leaned back from her.

Jonah 'Cash' Carter caught up with his wife and joined them with a grin on his face. "I confess. Sami wanted to stay and spend a bit more time with Emma, and, well... I didn't want to miss tonight's event. I think it'll be a great way to introduce Samantha to some new kinks without having her try them herself first."

Chase reached out to shake his friend's hand. "Smart man. I'm pretty sure even Emma will be picking up a few new things tonight. I'm just hoping they are kinks that will go on our play list and not our hard limit list."

Samantha, a relative novice to the lifestyle, giggled self-consciously. Chase put her at ease with a warm smile, "Emma is going to be so excited to see you. We have a table right over there in front of the main stage. I'm sure we can find a spot for you two near us so you girls can visit some when your Doms are busy."

As a group they turned and pushed their way through the last of the mingling crowd until they settled into seats at the table, and Chase parted ways. It was time to get the party started. At the foot of the stairs to the stage he found Spencer's right-hand man, Owen, waiting for him. With Spencer trying to lose his shit over Klara's recent arrival, Owen seemed to be stepping up and Chase was grateful that one of the dungeon monitors was filling the gap.

"All but two of the participants have arrived, Chase. Luckily, it's one Dom and one sub missing, so if they don't make it here in the next few minutes, we could technically start without them, I guess. Candy is phoning them now to see if they're close."

"Sounds good. Any new info you can tell me about the contestants that I should know before we start?"

Owen leaned in closer, keeping his voice down. "Well, the Russian Ambassador arrived with several subs with him already and had intended for them to all play with the sub he rolls. He wasn't happy to find out he'd need to leave them out of the play. We didn't put multiple partners on the wheel or the hard limit list. We'll have to see who he gets and see if it will be a problem."

"Got it."

"And, that last minute Dom addition, Spencer's friend, scares the bejesus out of me, so I feel sorry for whoever ends up with him. He seems hardcore with a capital H. I'll let the guys know to keep an eye on him to make sure he doesn't push too hard."

"Sounds good. There are a few of these subs who won't be able to handle that kind of intense."

"No shit, but then again, that's what kinda makes tonight fun."

"Tell that to the sub who ends up with him."

A commotion near the entrance interrupted the men's discussion. They turned in time to see Congressman Masterson trying to drag his ex-wife, Veronica, back towards the exit.

Owen cursed under his breath. "Shit. I was worried that might happen. Excuse me." He peeled off toward the yelling couple looking determined to quiet them down.

Alone once more, Chase pulled out his prompt sheet and made a few notes with the pen he always carried, refreshing his memory of each of the participants once more. He was just finishing when Spencer appeared next to him.

"It's just after eight and the final participants just arrived. Let's get this show on the road," the dungeon master grumbled, clearly still holding a grudge.

Chase slipped the name and limits cards he'd be passing out to the contestants into his side pocket. He grabbed the wireless microphone from the nearby table next, glad to see it was still there after that afternoon's sound check. After he'd flicked it on, he hesitated as the nerves caught up to him again, glancing back to the table where Jaxson and Emma sat with Cash and Samantha. He felt heat rising on his face to find Jaxson and Emma both staring at him, but there was a supportive smile on each of their faces. Jaxson's slight nod was the sign he'd been waiting for from his Dom to proceed with the event.

Here we go.

A few seconds later, Chase was center stage as the lights in the room dimmed slightly and spotlights lit up the portion of the stage they would be using for roulette. There were still many conversations happening around the expanse as Chase opened the show.

"Ladies and gentlemen, welcome to Black Light." Random applause and cheers broke out, settling the last of the conversations. He turned on his bright smile, the one that had booked him so many gigs as a model, and continued. "I'd like to introduce myself first. I'm Chase Cartwright, and I'm one of the owners here. Jaxson, Emma, and I would like to wish you all a very happy Valentine's Day, and to thank you for choosing to spend the night here with us - enjoying the first of what we hope will become an annual event, Valentine Roulette."

The room that had hushed as his introduction began broke out into a round of excited applause. When the clapping ebbed, Chase glanced to the participants on either side of the stage. "I would like to start by thanking those of you who have come here tonight as participants. I'm sure it must be a bit nerve wracking signing up to play a game where you don't know exactly who you'll be playing with, or even what activities you'll be asked to participate in. Our hope is that you'll look at the evening as an adventure where you'll hopefully learn something about yourself and your limits, all in a safe environment. You're all brave as hell, and we definitely look forward to enjoying all of your efforts."

Supportive cheers came up from the attendees at the tables, several crying out names in support of friends. Several of the submissives glanced out into the crowd of tables before returning their eyes to him.

"For those of you here as observers, I want to remind you of the rules our participants have agreed to when they signed up for Roulette. In a couple of minutes, fifteen Dominants will join me on the stage. They will be drawing numbers for their turn at the first of two roulette wheels. On the first wheel are the names of fifteen submissives. I will spin the wheel and each Dom will take their turn dropping the ball to choose their submissive for the night."

Chase took a break and glanced to his left at the group of nervous looking women grouped together on the floor. "Ladies, when you hear your name called, Garreth will be waiting to help you up these stairs so you can join your Dominant and me center stage. After you're together, I'll spin the second wheel and you'll drop the ball, this time into the wheel that will choose your first activity."

Chase looked up to address the rest of the audience again. "There are twenty-five activities on the wheel and each participant was allowed to choose up to four activities to place on their hard-limit list. I'll check my master list after each roll, and assuming the submissive rolls an action that is not on either limit list, they will spend at least thirty minutes participating in that event. After thirty minutes, couples can either continue with that activity, or, if they so choose, they may come back up to the stage and the sub can roll again to get another random kink to play."

The room was abuzz with excited conversations on the variety of possibilities. Chase waited until the din died down to continue. "I know everyone is excited, but there are just a few more rules to go through before we get started. The event will continue until eleven this evening. Couples who stay together and complete one or more of their rolled kinks will each receive one month of free membership to Black Light, worth $2,500 each. There will be dungeon monitors available throughout the dungeon. They are there to keep everyone safe and are also available for coaching Doms who may need assistance with scenes they are less familiar with. Just speak up if you need help at any time and we will connect you to the right monitor."

"And finally, I have to mention that every participant can use either the house safeword of 'red', or an otherwise negotiated safe-word you choose as a couple, to immediately end play at any time. I will remind you, however, that if one of you safewords, you both will be out of the contest. So, it's in your best interest to work together as a team. Doms, it's okay to push your submissives to the edge. Just try not to push them over the line, because if they safeword – you're done for the night, too."

Taking a slow breath, he steadied himself. "So, before we begin, does anyone have any questions?"

One of the Doms called out, "What about time for aftercare? Do we have any time between scenes for that?"

Chase hadn't discussed the exact rules for this with Spencer, but he knew the right answer to the important question. "Great question. Of course, Doms should be watching out for the health and welfare of their submissive and providing aftercare within reason is more than acceptable. We also have some light snacks and non-alcoholic drinks at the bar if you need them, which are available to participants and attendees alike."

The next question was quieter, coming from the submissive group. "What happens if we... like... you know... need to take a bit of a break?"

Chase smiled. "Talk to your Dom. Maybe use 'yellow' to let him know you need to slow down." He turned to the men. "I'm sure your Doms are going to want to win as much as you do and won't want to push you beyond your limit unless they can't help it."

When no more questions surfaced, Chase reached out to the table holding both roulette wheels. Between the wheels was a box that held fifteen wooden popsicle-type sticks. Each had a number from one to fifteen on the end, which Chase hid in his palm.

"Gentlemen, it's time for you to join me here on the stage please." Chase motioned to the set of stairs just to the right side of the stage. "Please watch your step."

It took a few minutes for all fifteen men to shuffle one at a time up the stairs and line up on the stage. He observed each man as they walked up, putting names with each of the faces from the sheet he'd studied before, noting how most looked like they were trying way too hard to hide how nervous they were.

He started at the end of the line farthest from him, stepping in front of each man and allowing him to draw one wooden stick from his hand as he moved down the line, passing out all fifteen sticks. Along the way, he heard several men curse their number, either unhappy with the low or high number they hadn't wanted.

"Alright, then. Let's begin. Would the dominant with number one step forward?" For a brief moment, Chase thought they'd screwed up the numbers on the sticks because no one moved. Finally, Antonio Stavros, the Greek hotelier stepped up – charming, handsome, but clearly nervous. He shot the man a supportive smile, because of all Doms to go first, Stavros would have been his last choice. In fact, being a switch himself, Chase wondered if Mr. Stavros might have been a bit more comfortable on the submissive side of the room if they'd allowed male subs this year. Regardless, he waved him forward.

"Alright, ladies and gentlemen. Our first Dom has elected to simply go by the nickname 'The Traveler' tonight. I'll spin the wheel and then you can drop the ball in whenever you're ready." Chase had to grab the man's hand to give him the heavy marble. As he glanced down at the fifteen names spread out on the wheel, he tried to think who might be the best match for the non-dominant Dom. He wasn't sure who might be *best*, but he knew who would be worst.

As soon as the marble rested on a name, it was as if Chase's thought had willed the ball to find the woman he'd been thinking of. "Marty, the wheel has chosen you."

All eyes watched the group of submissives until one of the tallest in the group stepped forward towards the second set of stairs. Chase had seen her at the club before and knew that no matter what kink they spun, Marty would be the one in control. The irony of two people who wanted to play on the other side of the D/s equation getting each other was not lost on Chase. He glanced down at his cheat sheet and grinned.

"Well, our first couple is very compatible. They have chosen the exact same hard limits. Well done." He handed the marble to Marty who stepped closer as he gave the activity wheel a spin. "Anytime you're ready, Marty, release the ball to choose your activity."

She dropped the marble without hesitation, and after a moment it clattered into place. "Electrical Play! And that's not on your lists. If you two would be so kind as to step over to the side. Please wait until we have everyone's assignments figured out before you start."

Chase reached in and took the paper with Marty's name on it off the wheel, leaving a hole where her name had been. They'd created different length cards for the submissive names to keep the chances fair as each roll progressed.

Chase moved on. "Will the Dom with number two step forward?" This time, Ryan 'River' Trubach jumped forward excitedly. As the men were friends, Chase knew Ryan loved to get down and dirty with his subs, and didn't consider the night complete unless it included anal sex. For a moment, he thought Ryan might be a good match for his old girlfriend, Khloe, but then he remembered she'd hated anal sex. For that matter, many of the subs had put it on their hard limits.

Chase had barely spun the wheel when River released the heavy marble. It spun around the wheel before eventually bouncing around several times, finally landing on Paris Charleston. River looked at Chase, looking for his reaction to the pairing. Chase glanced down at his cheat sheet, and gave Ryan an encouraging smile. "River has drawn Daddy's Girl to play with tonight. Would Daddy's Girl join us?"

As the young blonde with a wispy haircut advanced on the stage, Chase saw her excitement at being paired with the popular musician. River looked like he appreciated the petite package she'd squeezed into a corset dress.

She seemed eager to get going, dropping the marble quickly, and while it jumped around, Chase looked up their hard limits. When the marble fell on Blood Play, he called it out to the room. "Blood Play! But... both of our players listed that on their hard limit list so Daddy's Girl, let's spin again."

This time the marble came to rest in the suspension slot on the wheel. "Alright, River is gonna get some practice with his rope skills tonight! They've rolled suspension as their first activity."

Once the wheel was ready, he called for the next Dom, "Number three, please step forward."

Chase's eyes scanned the line of alpha men, watching until the extremely handsome, yet definitely intimidating, friend of Spencer's took one reluctant step forward as if he were stepping up for a firing squad. It was worrisome enough that he was a badass Dom, but from the looks of things he was a not-too-happy badass Dom.

"I'll need you to come a bit closer," Chase glanced down at his cheat sheet. "Mr. Helms." The silver haired Dom had neglected to provide an alias, and there was no way he planned on calling this guy by his first name. In fact, he was tempted to call the smooth, James Bondish looking man, *sir*.

Chase thrust the marble into the Dom's hand as he gave the wheel a spin, not even attempting to tell the man what to do. The Dom held the marble so long Chase wondered if he'd need to respin, but Mr. Helms finally let go. By the time the ball dropped in, the wheel was barely spinning at all and the marble came to rest next to...

Oh, fuck. She's gonna kill me.

Chase hesitated, glancing up first at Ryder Helms. From the look on his face, he wasn't any happier with his spin than Chase was, but he couldn't delay any longer. Turning to the submissives, his eyes searched out his ex-girlfriend and announced to the room, "Mr. Helms has rolled The Princess."

Immediately, Khloe started glancing around at the other women in shock. She even inquired with an exasperated laugh, "Oh, come on. Surely one of you put The Princess as your name too, right? I mean, he couldn't have rolled me. He just... couldn't."

Chase easily heard her comment and therefore so did her Dom-for-the-night. His reaction to her outburst was about what Chase would expect. "I'd get on up here now if you know what's good for you, Miss Monroe."

"Hey! He can't use my real name!"

Chase sent him a dirty look, but considering it was impossible that anyone in the room didn't recognize one of America's A-list celebrities, he found it hard to fault the man. In fact, with the prima donna theatrics Khloe was currently employing, Chase started to feel sorry for the guy, because badass or not, a sub could still be a nightmare.

Khloe refused to climb the stairs, instead demanding they re-roll to choose another submissive for the Dom, shaking her head as Chase motioned to her to get moving.

It wasn't until Ryder Helms stalked to the stairs as if he were going to go collect her himself that she started moving – only it was in the wrong direction. Chase couldn't hide his smile as his pain-in-the-ass ex-girlfriend started rushing towards the exit, her silver-haired Dominant fast on her heels. The entire room held their breath, waiting to see what would happen when he finally caught up to her, pulling her to a stop. His right hand thrust into her signature, long, flowing hair, holding her head immobile as he leaned in to whisper God-only-knew-what into her ear. A full minute went by as the room held their breath, waiting to see the outcome of the fireworks underway.

Knowing what a prima donna Khloe could be, he put his money on her walking out the door the second the Dom released her. So, when Ryder stepped away from his sub and reached his hand out to her, no one in the room was more surprised than Chase when Khloe slowly slipped her hand in his and allowed herself to be pulled back towards the stage. As they got closer, Chase could see the satisfaction in Ryder Helms eyes as they approached.

What on earth had he said to her?

When she was finally in place, Khloe slowly reached out to take the marble, acting as if she were in a trance. If he didn't know better, he'd swear she had been hypnotized. The wheel spun, but she stood frozen. The light touch of Ryder's hand at the small of her back set her into motion, dropping the marble from up high and watching it bounce around. When it landed on medical play, Ryder Helms broke into his first smile of the night. That smile did not bode well for Khloe.

Chase glanced at his cheat sheet, almost hoping to find medical play on Khloe's hard list, but it wasn't to be. With a nod, he announced to the crowd, "Mr. Helms and his Princess will be starting at the medical play station this evening." The crowd buzzed at the news, and Chase was sure they'd have plenty of voyeurs interested in watching their play.

Next up was one of their original members who played with the same submissive almost every weekend. They had seemed so perfect together that Chase had been a bit surprised to see they'd each signed up for roulette, but assumed they were looking to experiment with new partners. "Master D, you're up next," Chase announced.

The big man strode up to the wheel in silence, throwing his ball in too hard just after Chase started the spin.

"Easy, big guy," Chase joked. When the wheel chose an unfamiliar name, he realized he'd assumed wrong. Anyone could see Master D had not spun the sub he'd wanted, although his normal sub didn't seem to mind at all. "Ms. Jones! Her hard limits are electrical pain play, blood play, needle play, and water sports."

When she joined them on the stage, he could see she looked terrified, so he softened his voice as he handed her the marble, "Ms. Jones, toss your ball in."

She released it, and it spun with the wheel before dropping into, "Sybian Orgasm Torture!" The new sub to the club followed Master D away from the wheels, and Chase could only shake his head and hope the night worked out for them.

Senator Kane joined him next, looking as affable as he always did in his suit. "Good luck, Kane," Chase whispered as he handed him the marble and set the spin. It landed on the name that made his eyes dart over to Master D, sure that the wheels and the gods of chance were having way too much fun. "Slave to Pain," he called out and handed over the little card with her complete lack of limits on it.

The intense painslut moved onto the stage in stilettos and stared him down as she took the marble. *At least Master D wasn't the only one disappointed with his spin.* "Let's see what the lovely lady gets."

Just like D, she dropped the marble barely an instant after he spun it, and a moment later it clattered into Ageplay. The sub didn't even try to hide her disgusted eyeroll, and he laughed. "Slave to Pain doesn't look impressed. Perhaps she'll say *red*."

Chase was taunting her, but she just shook her head, and he shrugged as she moved to follow Kane off stage.

Numbers six and seven went off without a hitch with the Russian Ambassador looking pretty happy to be playing with most likely the only woman submissive in the field, the FBI linguist who seemed more than happy that he came with an entourage. Even the playboy of the group, Flyer, seemed content with his shy 'Babygirl'.

Number eight was a Dom Chase knew well.

"Alright, looks like Alexander is up next." As Chase's lawyer came closer, the men shook hands and the other man smiled as he leaned closer.

"Roll me a winner, will ya, Chase?"

"They're all winners," Chase replied under his breath.

The marble bounced, clattered, before finally landing on Sienna

Davis, a sub Chase knew next to nothing about except that Terry had recommended her from Overtime, another BDSM club in the city. "Would Sienna please join her Dominant on the stage?"

He scanned the group of subs until a rather small, plain looking girl peeled herself apart from the dwindling group of submissives and started up the stairs. Alexander met her at the top to greet her, always the gentlemanly Daddy Dom, but she pulled out of his hand as soon as she was center stage.

Sienna was silent, and her fingers trembled as she took the marble. When it dropped into Needle Play, the couple before him startled him, and the audience, by both exclaiming, "Hard list!" almost in unison. From the looks of things, they'd surprised each other too as they both broke out in nervous laughter.

"Looks like we'll roll again." He offered a reassuring smile, and plucked the ball out for her. This time they came up with one of the most intense options for the night, the activity they had almost pulled from the list... but they'd already rented the equipment. His eyes found the petite brunette's and he questioned for a moment if she'd panic – or faint. Both looked possible as he announced to the crowd, "Water-based breath play!"

Alexander grinned like a wolf and quickly guided the wide-eyed girl off the stage. They were going to need guidance, and luck, but if anyone could handle the intensity of that activity with care, it was their lawyer – and he looked like he planned on having a lot of fun with her. Chase didn't even need to call on number nine. Newton Isaacs had already stepped forward to take his spot at the wheel.

"Let's see who Sir Newton will be playing with tonight." While the marble jumped around, Chase looked up at the seven remaining submissives and smiled at the alarm he saw on Abby's face. He had no idea what had transpired in their past, but both Newton and Abby were Black Light regulars and they got along like opposite ends of the same magnet. Sure enough, when the gods of chance mocked them once again and the ball dropped into Abby's slot, Chase looked up to see Newton's normally neutral expression tugged into a frown.

"Abby," Chase announced, seeking her out through the bright stage lights. She didn't look happy at all as she stared up at the ceiling like

God might intervene and move the little white ball away from her name. Sighing, he beckoned her onto the stage. "Abby? Come on. You're holding up the line."

Crooking his finger, he waited until she joined Newton by the wheel, and then he spoke quietly, trying to avoid more drama as the two petulant participants avoided each other. "There is no swapping partners without one hell of a damned good reason, and that reason is approved only by the DMs." He sighed, and spoke fast to remind them of the rules and to make sure they understood. "I want verbal acknowledgement that you both understand the terms of this event."

"I understand," Abby muttered.

"So do I," Newton managed to force the words out.

"Do you plan to proceed?" he asked, wondering if either would even make it ten minutes before they blew up at each other. *Maybe the audience will like the show.*

"I do," the reluctant Dom answered, and Abby simply nodded.

"Take your spin." Handing the white ball to her, Chase spun the wheel and glanced into the audience to seek Emma's reassuring smile, and the heat of Jaxson's pride glowing in his eyes. As the wheel slowed he tried to ignore the buzzing argument in front of him, and finally announced, "Tickling!"

"When?" Newton demanded, suddenly loud enough to hear over the din of the audience.

"Now?" Chase answered, but Newton held up a finger as if *he* were interrupting them. As the two dissolved into another argument, he sought Garreth's eyes at the stairs, the DM grimacing at the squabble taking place center stage. The whole room seemed to be caught up in their back and forth exchange, and even though Chase tried to cut them off several times, they ignored him.

As their bickering escalated, Chase looked for Spencer who was standing too close to Klara and not paying near enough attention to the drama unfolding in front of him, holding up the event and delaying the start. With a sudden shout, Abby stared at Newton incredulously, "What?"

"What?" he echoed back, and Chase rolled his eyes, done with their antics.

"And a one, and a two, and..." he sang out, conducting the room with two fingers as the audience echoed back, "WHAT!"

The two finally seemed to remember where they were, and he sighed, reminding them of their activity with a gesture to the wheel, "Tickling. You want to take your place with everyone else so we can continue this?"

When they finally cleared center stage, he wondered if they should have brought in more monitors for the night. With this many odd pairings, it was definitely going to be an interesting night. But, Chase was grateful that the next pairing of Cecil, the tech security guru, and Marcy, a nurse from the VA, went off without an interruption. And their match-up would still be fun to watch. Marcy had the reputation of being a crier, and Cecil had a reputation of loving to deliver a good mind-fuck to his subs, which should make for an entertaining twist.

Prominent L.A. businessman, and multi-millionaire, Will Coleman was finally up. Congressman Masterson's ex-wife almost sprang out of her shoes in anticipation, hyper-focused as Will took his turn at the wheel. As the groups got smaller and smaller, the chances of the Mastersons ending up with each other were increasing. Coleman didn't hesitate to set his ball to spinning, and when Chase called out, "Klara!" as Will's partner, Mrs. Masterson wasn't the only one to make an audible sound at the news as both the audience and participants recognized the pretty blonde ex-bartender.

Chase glanced stage right in time to see their Dungeon Master, Spencer Cook, standing with his arms crossed and his face cold behind the soon-to-be-sub. He apparently didn't approve of Klara's play partner, but Chase had to squelch his smile because he suspected his friend Spencer wouldn't like anyone, other than himself of course, playing with Klara Eriksson.

Klara flashed a quick smile at Chase as she took her spot next to the wheel. To his knowledge, she'd never played in the lifestyle and as he handed over the ball he watched her eyes narrow on the wheel. Then he started the spin, and she let go.

"Whipping!" he called out to the crowd, watching as Will Coleman claimed Klara for the night and pressed her back from the wheels. Her

Dom led her to the side as Chase caught a glimpse of Spencer's now stony face waiting in the wings.

You snooze, you lose, man.

Next up was Adam Quinn. He was new to the club and about all Chase knew about him was that he was had been divorced, but had played frequently before his marriage. He was friends with Colin, a club regular and they'd accepted his referral for the man. When the wheel chose Sari as his play partner, Chase called out, "Sari, will you join your Dom on the stage?"

None of the dwindling group of submissives moved into motion, but Chase knew who she was by process of elimination. She was the only sub who had been one of the later entries and was new to Black Light as well.

Sari looked lost in thought until Chase repeated, "Sari?" The sub gave a tentative wave until she saw Adam crook a finger at her, and then she moved forward, almost tripping on the stairs as Garreth helped her up.

"Sorry, sir! I wasn't listening!" Even her voice sounded nervous as she stared up at Adam. Chase grinned, watching the man slowly raise an eyebrow.

"I see that. Are you fully present now?"

Sari swallowed. "Yes, sir, I am." With her confirmation Chase handed her the ball and spun the wheel. It landed on wax play, but there were no theatrics from either of them. They held a brief, quiet discussion before Adam led her away to the side of the stage, and Chase inwardly wished them well.

Veronica Masterson was nearly in a meltdown when The Judge stepped forward as the thirteenth Dom to pick a submissive. The Mastersons were down to a one in three chance they'd get stuck together, and it was clear that Veronica was about to rush up the stage to take her place next to the judge when Chase had to disappoint her and call out, "Katie, please join The Judge on the stage."

As the sub rolled their kink of role-playing a naughty schoolgirl scene, Chase watched Congressman Masterson gloating the more upset his ex-wife got. They were now down to a fifty-fifty chance of playing together.

Dane, a Black Light member, stepped forward, making the congressman the last Dom waiting. Only the congressman's ex and another Black Light member, Riley, were left to choose from. A crowd of friends for the two remaining contestants gathered around them and it looked to Chase as if Riley wasn't even paying attention any longer.

"Riley!" The second Chase announced the sub as Dane's partner, all hell broke loose. Scott Masterson burst out laughing, his ex burst out crying, and Chase had to repeat Riley's name a little louder because she still had not responded. "Riley!"

She seemed to need prodding to take the steps, but eventually moved. The dungeon monitor, Garreth, stepped closer to her, helping her up the steps to join Dane.

When she got face to face with her Dom, she muttered, "You?"

Chase grinned. "So, I see you two have met. Let's give the wheel another roll, shall we?"

Pointing to the wheel, he handed her the ball and re-explained the directions since she'd clearly not been paying attention. "I'll spin, you drop the ball when you're ready. If the ball lands on an activity that either of you have deemed a hard limit, we'll spin again. Okay?"

"Yes, I understand."

"Then here we go." He gave her a wicked smile, trying to encourage her to smile as he set the wheel to spinning. Except she seemed to have zoned out again, and Chase sighed, whispering, "Riley, you have to drop the ball."

With a nod she finally set the thing spinning in the track, shifting self-consciously as she awaited the roulette wheel's decision. She tensed when it landed on... "Humiliation!" he called. Glancing down at his list, he asked, "Not on either of your lists, is it?"

"No," Riley spoke softly.

"No," Dane confirmed. "We're good with this."

"Yeah. Good." She confirmed as Dane took her hand, pulling his shell-shocked submissive stage left.

"I won't do it. I quit!" Veronica Masterson was making a scene. "This was rigged. You did this to me on purpose, you bastard."

"Oh, please, stop being so melodramatic. At least sex and dominance is something we've always done well. It was the other parts of the marriage you suck at." The congressman got in a jab.

"Oh, right. And you're such a prince."

Chase tried to get things under control, not interested in fielding another argument before the event could start. "Alrighty then. Looks like we'll have some entertainment here tonight, folks. Mrs. Masterson, if you'd..."

Chase was interrupted by her correcting him. "I'm no longer his Mrs."

He corrected himself. "Sorry. Veronica, if you'd be so kind as to join us on the stage. You can roll for your kink. That is unless you are dropping out before you begin."

Congressman Masterson was being a real dick. "Yeah, Ronnie. You always have been a quitter, doing everything half-ass and then abandoning things before you finish."

His words acted as a challenge... a dare. His ex-wife stomped up the stairs in her heels, pushing aside Garreth's helping hand to grab the marble from Chase defiantly.

Only when the marble landed on Pet Play, did her hard-as-nails facade start to crumble again.

"And the Mastersons will be starting out with Pet Play this evening." He fought to keep the laughter from his voice. "That concludes our pairing ceremony. I thank all of you who are participating and also, those of you here to observe. You may all get started with your first kink."

Keep reading, it's time to spin the wheel and join Valentine Roulette...

BROKEN

A Black Light: Valentine Roulette Novella

by

Renee Rose

CHAPTER 1

*S*ee-through leather and mesh dress: check.

Fuck-me pumps: in the bag.

Push up bra that didn't really hold anything up anyway: already on.

G-string panties so she didn't show her twat in front of the entire crowd: also already in place.

What else? Jennifer rifled through the small duffel bag of her things for the Valentine Roulette event one last time before leaving her one-bedroom brownstone.

She would change when she got there. Riding the Metro in that outfit would get her arrested at best. Not to mention the fact she'd be hoofing it across the Key Bridge to Black Light from the Rosslyn Station Metro stop. At least she'd had time to stop at home and change out of her Army uniform. She preferred no one at Black Light see her in her service uniform. If anyone at the Pentagon found out Major Dibbs, daughter of General Dyson Dibbs, liked to have her ass whipped at a BDSM club, she'd never again successfully command the men underneath her.

She locked her door and walked to Union Station, blood humming with the happy buzz of anticipation, knowing she soon would receive the oh-so-coveted pain—her drug of choice.

She needed it, craved it. Every weekend since it opened found her at the elite club, Black Light, the only place she could release the pent-up stress of exceeding everyone's expectations as the most perfect female soldier.

She'd spent her career proving women deserved equal treatment in the ranks. The irony that she needed to spend time on her knees in front of a man to let all that go wasn't lost on her.

She slipped onto a crowded Metro train and grabbed the overhead handrail. Couples were out in droves for their Valentine's dates, fingers and lips tangled together in juicy public displays of affection.

She didn't need any of that. Roses and chocolate had never been part of romance to her. Just give her a long, hard whipping, and she'd find Jesus.

Every freaking time.

The Metro pulled up at Rosslyn station, and she climbed out, then took off at a brisk pace down the darkened streets. She kept her gaze alert and her demeanor confident.

Never show fear.

It was one of the many lessons her father had drilled into his only child from the time she was old enough to understand his lectures, along with *never quit, don't let them see you cry,* and *hard work pays off.* He may have been a hard-ass, but he'd taught her skills that had allowed her to fast-track into a level 4 position of major at the tender age of twenty-nine.

Not that she was afraid to walk alone at night. If the Army had taught her anything, it was how to defend herself, but there was no reason to invite trouble.

She passed Runway, the wildly popular new nightclub where, on weekends, teams of beautiful twenty and thirty-somethings lined up to get in at street level. But it was what went on below Runway she'd come for—Black Light.

She walked around the block to the paranormal store, entered, and walked through to the back where a security guard leaned up against the wall beside a door. She flashed a plain white plastic card that appeared blank, but when the guard held it under a black light, the words Black Light appeared in bold letters. Without looking, he reached behind himself and grasped the doorknob, twisting it and opening the door for her. She headed down the stairs and through a tunnel. It was dank and chilly, but at least there wasn't any wind like there had been outside. At the end of the tunnel, she pushed open a door and stepped into the security/locker room bathed in a pale purple hue from a combination of black light and recessed LEDs.

"Hi, Danny." She presented her card once again to the security guard who sat behind the desk.

He grinned. "Hey, doll." A locker popped open automatically to her right. "That one's yours. You know the drill."

"I sure do." She put her phone in the locker. All electronics had to be checked here, to prevent anyone from filming or recording anything that happened. Which was one of the reasons she trusted this place enough to come. Heh. All puns intended. But yeah, it was risky enough that she came here anonymously. If it ever got out she liked to be tied up and whipped until she trembled, her career would be over.

Tonight, she'd be earning herself a month's free membership, which she would use to its full extent. Membership to Black Light cost a fortune, basically accounting for half her entire monthly budget.

But it was worth it. She needed it like she needed food and water and exercise, which was why she was there every weekend, without fail. Always to see one dom.

Only one dom.

God, she hoped Master D got her name on the roulette wheel. No one else would take care of her needs like he did.

The odds were slim, though. There were fifteen doms who would draw numbers to spin for one of fifteen submissives participating in the roulette.

Please let it be Master D.

She headed out of the locker room. Another security guy opened the door to the club, and she stepped in, breathing the addictive scent of leather and vanilla-scented candles. The place was packed, but the energy was completely different from the nightclub above.

They were closed tonight, but usually when she came, party-goers were imbibing too much, letting alcohol spur their libidos and lower their inhibitions. In Black Light, customers didn't get sloppy. There was a sharp awareness to the way people interacted. Energy crackled and charged in readiness, like bowstrings drawn taut and aimed to fire.

Spectators had staked out their seats for the night's entertainment, filling all the front rows around the stage. Or gathered in seats around the stations they most wanted to observe, such as the spanking benches or fire play area.

She stepped into the main room. Bells went off. Her hyper-tuned awareness had sensed him, and she shifted her gaze, scanning. There —across the crowded floor, standing with his back against the wall and his arms folded across his massive chest—*Master D.*

She'd served on five tours to Iraq, had been in life and death situations more times than she could count, jumped out of planes, rappelled from bridges. But that ice-blue gaze made her tummy flip and sent shivers down her spine at the same time a warm flush sped across her skin.

My master.

He was her dominant. Not that they'd ever agreed upon anything. They didn't have any arrangement—she'd refused that, in fact. They hardly talked, and she liked it that way, but she found him here, every Friday or Saturday night, and he gave her what she needed.

Too bad she'd probably have to suffer under another dominant's whip tonight. She just hoped he wasn't a bumbling idiot. Hoped he gave it to her hard enough, gave her what she craved.

Nothing changed on Master D's face. He didn't lift his chin or wave or wink to show he'd seen her, but his gaze seared like a laser, burning her up from the inside out. He wore that keen, assessing expression, taking in everything, showing nothing. She wondered if he'd ever worked in interrogation when he'd served in the armed forces.

Because he was definitely military. Even if she hadn't spied him in passing last week at the Pentagon, she would've known by the way he carried himself, the set of his shoulders and the lift of his chest. The build of his body and his quiet presence. He had the look of a Navy

SEAL or Army Special Forces or Marine Special Ops—alert. Ready. Deadly. Which totally wound her crank. Yeah—he was her type, if she ever had one. To fuck, not to date.

The familiar fluster she experienced with him almost made her blush, but she shoved it back down, lifting her chin even higher as she marched to the women's locker room, her clit already beginning to pulse between her legs.

* * *

DEREK WATCHED his little pain slut emerge from the women's locker room dressed in the hottest shreds of fabric—leather and see-through mesh stitched together in horizontal stripes, somehow suggesting both prisoner and slave. His cock stirred in his jeans.

She was a dream sub for a sadist like him.

Her sandy-blonde hair was down, as he always demanded. Otherwise, how could he bury his fist in it and pull?

Had she bought that sexy little number for him? No. She'd dressed for the audience watching tonight. She probably wouldn't be his partner, which made him want to storm across the floor, throw her over his shoulder, and carry her out of there before the damn event got started.

But she'd never allowed him to lay claim to her. In the scene, yes. But not outside of it. And damn if he didn't want to find out if they had something beyond the magic they made here.

Her gaze flicked over to him, and she feigned disinterest. He knew better. Her body responded to him like a violin to a master. She looked tough, and she played a rough game, but he knew how to make Major Jennifer Dibbs come like a freight train.

He didn't call her that, of course. She went simply by 'Slave to Pain' at Black Light.

He wasn't supposed to know her name, but he'd seen her last week at the Pentagon. He'd barely dared a glance in her direction, but it had been enough to memorize her name and rank, to research the beautiful blonde who rocked his world every weekend.

The youngest female ever to achieve the rank of major, she came from a military family. Her father was a general in the Army. She'd been instrumental behind the scenes in the landmark 2015 decision to allow women in the same combat roles as men. She spent all week proving herself tough enough to fight beside men.

And, every weekend, surrendered to him.

He'd been scening with her since Black Light opened in November. He'd asked around, but no one knew much about her other than that she'd shown up the first night as a guest of Senator Kane's. Apparently they had scened together in the past but had no romantic attachments.

Lord, he'd never forget the night they met.

He had a sub on the St. Andrew's cross and had just finished working her over. The sub had come with her own dom—her husband, who had arranged the scene with Derek—who'd taken her down and provided aftercare, leaving Derek free to clean the equipment.

Jennifer stepped forward from where she'd been watching in the shadows. He'd seen her there, of course. His training as a SEAL made him hyper aware of all activity around him at all times. She carried herself like a domme—spine starched, chin up. She walked right up to him in six-inch stilettos, her long, slender legs giving him a hard on, and dropped to her knees at his feet.

He tangled his fingers in her hair and tugged it back to lift her beautiful face. "You want on this cross, baby?"

She licked her lips and nodded. He knew then he was a goner. She was his perfect match. Beautiful. Poised. Experienced. He figured she had to be batshit crazy because all the good ones were.

He stripped her down to a G-string and the stilettos, fastened her on the cross, and warmed her up with a flexible leather paddle. She actually sighed —not a contented sigh, but a sigh of impatience.

He gripped her hair and yanked her head back. "Did you just fucking sigh, little sub?"

Her ass tightened. Christ, he loved that submissive reaction to dominance. It was like a dog tucking its tail. A sub afraid of what he'd do to that pretty posterior. And she should be.

"I'm sorry, sir," she said breathlessly.

"You're sorry." He made his voice hard and disappointed, as if the sigh had been the hugest violation in the history of BDSM scenes. "What's the problem, exactly?" He gripped one of her thighs, which had begun to tremble. It was muscular, like the rest of her. She was fit—but not like yoga fit. More like CrossFit built. Military, he knew now.

She licked her lips, which looked dry. "Nothing, sir."

He lifted a bottle of water to her lips. "Drink." It spilled down her chin and neck when he poured it too fast on purpose. "Are you feeling impatient, little sub? Can't wait for me to get down to it?"

She hesitated, and he knew she was debating the wisdom of telling him the truth.

"I punish for lies, baby."

"Yes, sir." The breathy quality of her voice made his cock swell uncomfortably in his jeans.

He softened the grip of his fingers on her thigh, smoothed up and down her leg in a caress. "Good girl. I like it when you tell your master the truth."

Cheek pressed against the cross, she blinked her long, thick lashes while her chest rose and fell in short beats.

"I get it. It's the first time we've scened together. You're not sure I'm going to give you what you need. I'm telling you right now, baby, I will never leave you wanting. But I'm in charge of timing around here."

"Yes, sir," she said immediately, as if still hoping to hurry him up to the good part.

He had to stifle a laugh. Poor girl needed it badly.

"I'll have to give you a lesson in patience tonight, little sub."

She showed nothing on her face, accepting that pronouncement quietly.

He went to his bag and rummaged around until he found a bullet vibe. "This has been sterilized," he told her, to head off any fears, sliding his finger under the gusset of her tiny G-string to find her...fucking drenched.

He almost growled with the desire to just fuck her senseless right there, but somehow managed to hold back. Slipping the bullet vibe inside her, he turned it on, watching her face as he slowly slid his belt out of the buckles.

Her blue eyes rolled back in her head, cheeks flushed with the fever of desire.

"This should teach you patience, my dear." He wrapped the buckle end of *the belt around his fist and snapped it across her tightened buttocks. Not holding back.*

She made an oomph sound and squeezed her buns even tighter.

Another time he'd give her a lesson in keeping them soft. Not that night, though. He wanted to see how much the beautiful, impatient sub could take.

He whipped her fast and hard, taking care with his aim so he hit only the lower half of her buttocks and the backs of her thighs. By the time he finished, she was glassy eyed, panting, and dripping wet.

He stopped and let stillness reverberate. It made its own music after the fast rhythm of an intense whipping. Her body would be twitching, tingling, and pulsing now. The pain would set in even more fiercely in the moments that followed.

She wriggled on the cross.

He strolled casually to her side and shoved her hair back from her eyes. "Yes?"

Her gaze held confusion and need.

He pressed the water bottle to her lips. "Say it."

She licked the spilled water from her lips. "What?" Her voice came as no more than a croak.

"Beg me for it."

"For what?" she whispered.

He didn't answer, letting the spaciousness of silence give birth to whatever she needed.

She orgasmed right then. Right there. A shudder rocked her entire body, her head flopped back, eyes rolled.

When it passed, and her pretty eyelashes fluttered open, he shook his head, making his face appear disappointed. "Bad girl."

Her dazed look faded and a little notch of worry ticked between her brows.

"Did I say you could come?"

"N-no, sir. I'm sorry."

"I told you to beg me for it. I told you this was an exercise in patience. Did you exercise patience tonight?"

She fucking orgasmed again.

Jesus Christ, he'd never seen such a beautiful, responsive sub in his life.

He wanted this girl. Needed her. This was what he'd been dreaming of, all the years of playing the BDSM scene. She was what he'd been looking for.

After the second orgasm passed, she hung from the restraints, broken and limp.

He shook his head again and flicked one brow in a threatening way. "Looks like you're getting the cane now."

The vibrator was still buzzing inside her, probably torturing the hell out of her. He picked up his meanest rattan cane and positioned himself by her side, tapping her ass once to take aim.

Swish-whack.

She choked on a gasp then clamped her lips together, as if determined not to cry out again.

"Bad. Girl." He sliced the cane through the air again, leaving a second welt, just below the first. "You don't fucking orgasm without permission." He whipped her again.

"I'm sorry!" Her gasp held a ring of panic.

"You will be." Again and again, he whipped her, laying neat lines down her ass to her thighs, ten in all.

The poor girl was trembling like a leaf when he let her off the cross. He wasn't sure if she could take any more, or if he should end the scene, but he pushed her to her knees at his feet and unbuttoned his jeans.

She lunged for his cock, like a greedy little sub, used her hands and mouth with an enthusiasm he'd rarely seen before. All the time, the vibrator buzzed inside her.

Sucking hard, bobbing her head in and out along his length, she lifted her eyes to his face, pleading.

She wanted to come. Again. She dared take her mouth off to ask. "Please, sir? May I—" she didn't finish the sentence, because he'd frowned when she came off, and she returned to her frantic sucking.

"I come first." His fingers twisted in her hair, forcing her head faster. "And when I'm done, and you've licked me clean, I'll let you finish."

She hummed her assent, the vibration bringing him to the precipice.

As she worked, he distracted himself with learning her beauty—the gloss of her thick blond hair, the curve of her slender but muscular shoulders, the long column of her neck. He found one nipple and tortured it, squeezing and rolling it between his thumb and forefinger. Pinching it tight and pulling hard the moment he came like a fucking rocket down her throat.

She took all of it. Swallowed him down. Licked him clean. And then he pulled her to her feet, spun her around to face away from him, and brought his fingers between her legs. Three flicks of her clit was all it took, and she went off again, gripping his wrist to pull his hand over her mons, throwing her head back on his shoulder.

She smelled of a fruity soap, the leather of the cross, and of him.

He bit her neck and pulled up on her mons, his undulating fingers covering the whole of it while she shook and shuddered.

He removed the vibe, draped her in a blanket, and held her on a couch for a while after, giving her sips of water while she returned to the planet. "What's your name?" he asked when she started to go stiff on him.

"I go by Slave to Pain."

For once, he didn't want her damn scene name. He wanted her real name. Wanted her address. Her phone number. But that wasn't the way things worked.

"I'm Master D."

She got up and picked up her clothes. He cleaned the equipment quickly, not wanting her to leave before he talked to her.

"Well, thanks doesn't exactly cover it, but..." she said, an awkwardness marring the confidence with which she'd previously held herself.

"I'd like to see you again."

"Next Friday night? Same time, same place?" she suggested.

Yeah. He hadn't meant at Black Light, but he'd take what he could get.

"For sure. May I give you my number?"

She shook her head quickly, as if she'd prepared for this question. "No, I don't see men outside of here."

He nodded. He may be a dom, but he didn't get pushy when it came to making arrangements. A sub needed to feel safe. If she had a personal rule about keeping it at the club, he would respect that. For the time being.

THAT HAD BEEN two months ago.

They'd scened together almost every weekend since, but he still hadn't managed to bust her security wall down and get a date.

Tonight. Dammit, tonight he needed her digits because this Valentine Roulette thing had him about ready to hogtie her, pick her up, and march the fuck out.

He didn't want her to play with another dom.

Not even for a second.

* * *

JENNIFER SWALLOWED, eyes flicking over to Master D. He didn't pretend not to see her. He stared a hole right through her—his gaze hot, dark, and demanding.

She resisted the urge to wipe her clammy hands on her dress.

Never show fear.

She wasn't afraid, not really. No dom here could do anything to her she couldn't handle. She was Army-tough, for God's sake. But an underlying anxiety had her buzzing. Her father always said the best way to address fear was to name it and blow it up with a hand grenade. So what was she afraid of?

It had something to do with Master D. Her fear of *not* being with him. Was that the same thing as being afraid of another dom? No, it wasn't.

Did she feel disloyal?

That thought registered like a punch in the gut.

Yeah. She did. She was actually afraid of Master D's reaction to her scening with someone else. He'd been offering his number, asking for hers for weeks now. She'd steadfastly refused, following her ironclad rule of keeping BDSM at Black Light and her personal life personal.

She didn't date. It just didn't work. Period. She'd tried—Lord, she had tried. During Basic, she'd fallen in love. Sal had been a hot alpha male from New Jersey. He'd turned her on with his strong, decisive personality. But the same thing that made him attractive ended up breaking them apart. He was protective and possessive to a fault. He became controlling. Jealous. And when she'd been promoted quickly, he couldn't take it. It drove him nuts that she had a higher rank than he did. He'd ended up hating her—doing everything he could to tear her down.

She'd been sent to Iraq, and Sal had been sent to Afghanistan, and that had been the end of it. Later, she found out the separation had been her father's doing. Which figured, since he was the original controlling man in her life.

No. What turned her on sexually didn't work in real life. It just didn't. She was a career woman who needed to be strong. The kind of man she liked—an alpha male, not a beta—couldn't take that.

She jerked when, suddenly, Master D appeared in front of her, his barrel chest clearly defined with muscles beneath his tight black T-shirt.

"Jesus, where'd you come from?"

Damn, he was stealthy for such a big guy.

He shoved her up against the wall, pinning her wrists above her head with one hand, the other gripping her jaw to hold her face in place. His thigh wedged between her legs, forcing her feet apart and giving her something to grind down on. "Did you wear that dress for them?" he growled.

A wave of knowing washed over her. Yep. He was going to see this as a betrayal. Something in her stomach knotted. She opted for a truth that wouldn't piss him off.

"I bought it for you."

The thumb of the hand gripping her jaw eased and slid over her skin, stroking her cheek. "Did you?" His voice was a purr now.

"Yeah." She'd lost her breath. It always seemed to happen when he dominated her. Sometimes she hated herself for it—she wasn't allowed to feel fear, after all. But, at some point, she'd drawn a line. The sub she became in Black Light was someone else. Someone who liked to surrender. Liked to get scared and excited by a man bigger than she was. It didn't reflect on Major Jennifer Dibbs. It wasn't a personality flaw—it was a kink. Just about sex and the way she liked to do it. Another reason to keep things separate and clean. She didn't need her headspace to get fucked up by her kink.

He yanked the neckline of her dress down under her breasts. If the fabric hadn't been so stretchy, it would've torn. He shoved the cups of her bra down next. "Are you going to let them see these pretty little boobies?"

Ouch. Yeah, they were little. She knew it. They weren't her best asset. But she still didn't love hearing them called *little boobies*. He probably guessed that, like he guessed everything about her. His hand cupped one, somehow making it seem bigger than it was by wrapping around to hold her muscle on the side, too. Bless the man.

"I- I don't know."

He arched a brow. "You don't know?" His voice sounded incredulous. "Well, you'd better decide, little slave, or the decision will be made for you."

Her head wobbled on her neck. "Probably," she whispered.

His face turned stony. He pinched her nipple and twisted.

She shrieked and tried to rise up on her tiptoes, but he had her pinned too tightly.

"You will be punished for any and all transgressions I see tonight."

What the fuck? They didn't have any rules or arrangements for her to transgress against. But her pussy had just turned molten at his words, the idea of punishment at his hands so terribly exciting she didn't care how unfair the statement had been.

He continued to hold her nipple in a tight twist, sending shards of pain sprinting out through her breast.

"Yes, sir," she squeaked.

He waited one beat. Two. Then his grip on her breast and wrists eased, his palm massaging her wounded breast as he leaned over and bit her ear. "I'll be watching," he growled against her neck, then kissed it, his lips suddenly soft, the gesture oddly tender.

It made her knees go weak.

Good thing he was still holding her up.

CHAPTER 2

*D*erek took some small satisfaction in knowing he'd just turned his beautiful sub on.

For some other asshole.

He eased away from her, putting her breasts back in their padded push-up cups and making sure she was steady on her feet before he let go completely. The subs and doms were gathering beside the stage, getting ready for their pairings.

"It's showtime. Don't forget—I'll be watching you." He made the 'eyes on you' gesture, which was so over the top they both grinned.

He knew the possessive thing both turned her on and made her uncomfortable. It came too close to getting personal, and she didn't do that with him.

"Let's go." He hooked a palm through her elbow and guided her over to the stage. As if she needed his help. No, his girl could take care of herself. He knew that. But protecting was in his blood. He couldn't stop the desire to be at her side or back at all times, ready to defend her safety or honor.

Turns out he'd been wrong about her having to be nuts. She was that perfect. No cray cray had ever reared its head. In fact, he found in her the perfect playmate—intelligent, greedy for his commands, impossibly obedient, and always ready to go off like a firecracker once she'd had her punishment. She wanted more pain than any sub he'd encountered and required zero emotional support, not that he hadn't tried to offer it. He wasn't a fuzzy warm dom, but he understood the dynamic enough to know a sub was vulnerable after a scene and required care.

She let him take care of her physical needs after a particularly rough session—let him wrap her up in a blanket and hold her on a couch until the shaking stopped, but she never cried. Never wanted to talk. Always got up and walked out alone at the end.

So she might not be crazy, but he thought something was off with her. She had a secret. He'd figured she must be married. Or famous.

When he'd seen her at the Pentagon, the pieces had fallen into place. She had a career to protect. An extremely impressive career. He admired the hell out of what she'd done in the Army.

And that just made her even more desirable.

The fact was, Jennifer fascinated the hell out him. He wanted more from her but hadn't figured out how to break the rigid boundaries she set up for herself.

Which didn't mean they hadn't had sex. She sucked him off when he demanded it, and he'd even fucked her on a few occasions.

But, bizarre though it was for him—the sadist who didn't do happy endings—he craved a deeper connection. He wanted to take her for coffee, or to make her laugh. He wanted to share something more than what they already exchanged.

But tonight that probably wouldn't happen. And that pissed him the fuck off.

He almost hadn't signed up to participate in the stupid roulette. He wouldn't have, if Jaxson hadn't asked him personally because they needed one more dom. How in the fuck would he keep an eye on Jennifer to be sure nothing bad happened to her? To be sure she got what she needed if he was scening with someone else? What if she got some asshole show-off who didn't know what he was doing?

Christ, if any guy did wrong by her, he would rip him to shreds. With his bare hands. And so...yeah. He was in a quandary about how to scene with someone else without losing his shit over what was going on with his sub. Yes, *his* sub.

Because Jennifer belonged to him. They fit together. She knew it on some level, even if she wasn't ready to admit it to herself.

They reached the stage and joined the other doms and subs gathered there.

Chase, one of the kinky pretty-boy co-owners of both Runway upstairs and Black Light, took the mic and explained to the audience how the evening would work. Each dom would spin the roulette wheel to choose a sub. Then the sub would spin to pick the activity. Both had been given the opportunity to declare four hard limits. He hadn't declared any. If he knew Jennifer, she hadn't, either. And he sure as hell didn't want her getting something dangerous with some jerkoff who didn't know what he was doing.

He ground his molars. The only solution was for him to land on Slave to Pain when he spun that fucking roulette wheel. He *had* to be her dom tonight. If ever he needed a little luck, it was right now.

He stuck his hand in the bucket Chase was passing around and drew his number. Four.

Fuck. He needed number one. Needed to reduce the odds he could get his girl. Fingernails punching holes in his palms, he lined up on the side of the stage.

Jennifer sent another quick glance his way, and this time he glimpsed the flash of anxiety in it. She needed him just as desperately as he wanted to be the one to take care of her.

"You hoping for your usual sub or looking for someone new?" the dom beside him asked in a Southern drawl. A senator who had long been on the scene in the most private of circles, Derek had seen him at Black Light a few times. Tall and fair, Senator Kane looked like 'money' with patrician blue-blood good looks. He had his eye on a very nervous sub in a black mask and dress who appeared to be hiding behind the other subs but couldn't stop craning her neck to openly stare back at the senator.

"Yes."

"This whole roulette thing is annoying as hell. I'd rather just do what I want to do."

Derek chuckled. "Spoken like a true dom. Looks like that one in the mask recognizes you."

The senator's lips curved into a smirk. "Yes," he drawled. "I think she might. And I believe she's more than a little out of her element."

"Well, let's hope you get her, rather than me." Derek knew the senator to be a precise and intense, but very caring Dom. He'd be a good for a beginner, unlike Derek. Patting newbie subs' asses wasn't Derek's thing. He liked to scene with someone he didn't have to baby.

"Master D, you're up next," Chase announced.

Derek strode up to the wheel and threw his ball in too hard after Chase gave it a spin.

"Easy, big guy," Chase joked.

The ball spun around, finally bouncing and landing on...*Ms. Jones.*

The senator's girl in the black dress and mask tottered forward.

"Ms. Jones!" Chase called out. He handed Derek her card with the hard limits listed on the back. *Electrical pain play, blood play, needle play, and water sports.*

"Ms. Jones, toss your ball in."

The sub, who looked terrified but actually not very submissive, stepped up to the activity wheel and threw her ball in after Chase spun it.

"Sybian Orgasm Torture!"

Ms. Jones's shoulders hiked up a half inch.

He crooked a finger at Ms. Jones, but it took all his resistance to keep from looking over at Jennifer.

Sorry, sweetheart. I wanted you.

Senator Kane stepped up to the wheel. And landed on...*Slave to Pain.*

The gods were laughing their asses off at him. That was the only explanation, because why in the fuck would he and the senator each get the other's girl? On one hand, he didn't need to worry about Jennifer—she'd partnered with the senator before, and they'd be fine together. But if the man put his cock anywhere near her, Derek would have to cut his balls off. Seriously.

He sought her out with his gaze. If Jennifer's eyes hadn't darted to meet his, he might have been able to let things stand. But she hadn't looked at Senator Kane—she'd gazed at him. She wanted him—needed him. She shouldn't be scening with anyone else.

"Slave to Pain," Chase cried and handed her card to the senator.

Derek wondered if she'd listed any hard limits at all. Probably not —that girl never shrank from a challenge.

"Let's see what the lovely lady gets."

She stepped forward, impossibly balanced and comfortable in stiletto heels, even though he could just as easily see her in combat boots. Chase spun the wheel, and she threw her ball in.

Senator Kane stepped over and claimed her, holding her hand as they both watched the arrow spin. She stiffened and glanced down at their connected palms as if confused about why he would do such a thing. It almost made Derek smile. *Almost.*

The arrow stopped on *Ageplay.*

Jennifer didn't hide an eye roll.

Chase laughed. "Slave to Pain doesn't look impressed. Perhaps she'll say *red.*"

Jennifer shook her head.

The woman didn't ever safeword, and he had a feeling it was both out of pride and a high pain tolerance. Obviously she didn't think ageplay would even come close to scratching her itch. Because they both knew how hard she needed it.

He stood and waited while the rest of the couples were matched up and chose their activities, but the entire time his mind was on his problem—how to swap partners with the senator. He could try asking, but he knew Chase and Jaxson would never go for it. The game was the game, no matter how stupid he and the senator thought it was.

No, better to take matters into his own hands...

The couple supposed to be up at the wheel were bickering so much they didn't hear Chase prompting them.

"What?" the dom answered the sub glaring up at him.

"And a one, and a two, and..." Chase sang out, conducting the crowded room as if they were an orchestra. The entire room echoed, "What?"

The couple jumped, startled, and the audience chuckled.

When the last pairing had been made, he took Ms. Jones's elbow and led her off the stage, choosing a single seat in the crowd with no empty chairs near it. He sat and pointed at his feet.

She adjusted her mask, though it was already on straight, and shifted on her feet.

"*Kneel*, Ms. Jones."

Her lips took on a doubtful angle. "Um…"

He gave her a cold, disapproving stare. "Little sub, if you don't want me to start your orgasm torture with the worst caning of your life, you need to kneel at my feet. *Now*."

Okay, maybe he was trying to scare her off. He could've shown a little more sympathy for the girl who was obviously so completely out of her depth. But when she toddled back and whispered, "Red," all he could do was laugh.

* * *

JENNIFER HAD zero desire for an ageplay scene. Senator Kane appeared amused, and she had a feeling he'd probably make a great daddy dom, but it just wasn't her thing. She didn't need to be coddled by a dom. In fact, she craved the opposite—delicious, cold cruelty. The way Master D gave it to her.

She sighed, holding the senator's hand as he led her through the crowd to a plush sofa. He sat down and pulled her onto his lap.

Yuck.

Totally not her thing. She shot a glance across the room, where her spidey sense alerted her to Master D's presence. He wore that hard, dominating look she loved so well as he pointed to the space at his feet.

She almost laughed. His poor sub had no idea what she was in for.

"So what was that eye rolling up there all about, little miss?"

"Come on, Senator. You know ageplay isn't exactly my cup of tea."

"Right. You like to keep things clean of all emotion."

Ouch. While it might be true, she didn't like hearing it out loud. "What's wrong with that?" she asked a little too defensively.

He gripped her ear and tugged it like she was a naughty child, although she could see humor in his eyes. "Watch your tone, little miss."

She refrained from another eye roll with great effort. But then her heart lurched.

There, looming imposingly in front of her, stood Master D. His unhappy sub was in tow, looking ready to scream for help.

"We're swapping subs." He reached for Jennifer's hand while thrusting the frightened sub toward the senator.

Kane shoved her ass off his lap and stood, throwing a protective arm out to encircle Ms. Jones's waist. They knew each other, somehow, but she'd bet her last dollar they'd never scened together, because Ms. Jones was a BDSM virgin if she'd ever seen one.

D pulled her up against his hard muscled body, and her temperature rose by at least four degrees.

"What's going on?" spluttered Ms. Jones.

"She safeworded," Master D explained, "but I don't want her to flunk out so quickly. She just needs a different dom."

"Sounds like you're mine, now," the senator drawled. "Unless you want to safeword out of the whole thing."

"You're going to get us all disqualified," Jennifer said, but without much conviction. Yes, she could really use the free month's membership, but she'd also much rather play with Master D.

"I'll run it by the Dungeon Master. Besides, the senator will cover our fees if that happens." He winked at the senator, who grimaced but didn't deny it.

Jennifer had to bite down on the laugh bubbling up. Both Master D and the senator were take-charge sort of men—obviously. Following the contrived rules of the roulette game didn't work for them. They had their own ideas of who they wanted to scene with, and it seems D had just ensured they both achieved those desires.

Master D and the senator traded sub cards, not that hers had any limits listed. "Say 'bye to the senator," her dom growled in her ear.

She smiled, the anticipation of pleasure sending endorphins coursing through her body. "Have fun." She waved at the senator and Ms. Jones as Master D tugged her away.

"Thank God," she said in an undertone. "I should have listed ageplay as a hard limit."

Master D stopped and twirled her around to face him. "Thank God you're scening with me or thank God you're not doing ageplay?"

Oh please. Sometimes the male egos around there were just too much.

"Both," she answered diplomatically.

"Oh, we're still doing ageplay, baby girl."

She threw her hands on her hips. "Really?" He must be out of his mind—he was about the furthest thing from a daddy dom she'd ever encountered.

A gleam appeared in D's eye—one she didn't love.

"What? You think I can't break you as your daddy? Afraid to go over my knee for a bare bottom spanking?"

She snorted. The idea was ludicrous. D never used the over-the-lap position. For one thing, he wasn't a touchy-feely daddy dom. For another, he gave it hard, which required the full swing of his arm with his chosen implement, most often a rattan cane. So, yeah, the thought of an over-the-lap spanking from him was so un-scary, it was laughable.

"I believe this requires a change of costume." His lips quirked up like he was thoroughly enjoying himself, and he tugged her toward the costume room.

When he looked back, she gave him a roll of her eyes.

"Uh uh." He pulled her up alongside him, guiding her through the tangle of tables and chairs, sofas and kneeling pillows. "One more eye roll, and Daddy will put you in diapers. And I'm quite certain *that* would be a real punishment for you."

Ugh. Seriously?

Her stomach tightened. A flush of heat spread across her chest and up her neck, and her nostrils flared with distaste.

"I'm sorry, Daddy," he prompted, giving her ass a pat.

She pressed her lips together, feeling mutinous. This wasn't the way they played. He didn't *pat* her ass, he whipped it, and he never got cutesy.

His grin broadened.

He stopped dead in the middle of the floor and spun her to face him. Although couples were starting their scenes in the various areas throughout Black Light, they drew a fair amount of attention from the seated spectators in their vicinity.

Without a word, he gripped her dress at the back and tore it off, fabric ripping as it went.

Damn. She'd just bought the thing, and it hadn't been cheap.

A few females nearby gasped. The push-up bra went next. "Shoes off," he barked, tapping one of her calves.

She slipped out of her stilettos, which he picked up, along with the ripped dress. She now stood in nothing but her lace-topped black thigh-high stockings and a tiny G-string, annoyed, but more than a little turned on by his sudden and unexpected show of dominance.

He surveyed her critically, eyes traveling over her small breasts, down her tummy and the length of her legs. To her shock, he bent and ripped her stockings off, too.

Her belly quivered with excitement. This was the master she knew. Hard and demanding. Unbending, unwavering in his domination of her. His firm hand both steadied and unmoored her, because while she liked his control, she hated screwing up. Hated the way he viewed her with thin-lipped displeasure now.

"Sorry...*Daddy*," she whispered when his ice-blue eyes met hers.

Something gleamed in his gaze, whether it was that he liked her apologizing or liked hearing her call him *Daddy*, she wasn't sure.

All she knew was that it was going to cost her to act like a baby girl. She liked to play slave. She would've licked his boot if he'd demanded it. Would've crouched down and served as his footstool without a moment's hesitation. But this—this daddy thing—was uncharted territory for her.

It was too cozy. Implied a closeness and emotional attachment, which they didn't do. Not even as a child had she acted like a little girl. Her mother's death when she was just six had ended her babyhood. She'd had to grow up fast and start performing for her father, the highly undemonstrative and exacting General Dibbs.

D touched her nose. "You will be sorry, baby. When Daddy gives you an order, you obey it the first time he asks. Got it?"

It surprised her how well the daddy dom talk rolled off his tongue. She'd thought he would sound more out of character, but he didn't.

Her heart picked up speed at his continued displeasure. She wasn't afraid of his punishment—she liked that part—she just didn't like getting things wrong. She didn't like failure.

He put a finger under her chin. "Answer with words, baby girl."

She blinked rapidly. "Yes, Daddy." She cursed her voice for failing her, her words dropping with no more than a whisper.

His face softened. He usually wore either an impassive expression or a stern scowl when he dommed. She hadn't seen this one before. "Good girl."

She blinked, surprised at the way butterflies flopped and fluttered in her belly at those words, her pussy growing even more moist for him.

It seemed he could reduce her to surrendered mush with any form of domination—even daddy domination.

He threaded his fingers through her hair. It started as a caress, but she knew to expect pain, and sure enough, he bunched his digits when they reached the back of her head, tugged her hair. "I fucking love that look on you," he growled.

Her pussy clenched and released, excitement at both his dominance and his words sending heat pouring down her legs.

"Wh-what look?" She hated when she sounded so wobbly.

"Submission. Those beautiful blue eyes go wide, your chest and shoulders go soft, and you have eyes only for me." He pulled her forward against his body. The hard bulge of his cock pressed into her belly, and she caught her breath, his obvious interest boosting her excitement. "Daddy's already hard for you, baby girl."

He released her hair abruptly and stepped back. With a hand on her elbow, he laid a single loud smack on her ass and led her, barefooted and almost completely naked, through the crowd to the costume room.

Jennifer's heart pitter-pattered against her ribs like a hummingbird on cocaine. Her lips buzzed, face felt too tight. The combination of public humiliation and Master D's scolding had her fucking falling apart. And he hadn't even spanked her yet.

Not that she thought an over-the-lap spanking would do anything for her. She had an ass of steel. She rarely marked, even with the cruelest of implements. It usually took the St. Andrew's cross and a cane to push her over the edge and into subspace.

This daddy thing was new territory, though. She'd always thought ageplay stupid and fluffy. For subs who liked to feel submissive but didn't really enjoy pain. The kind who needed to be coddled and cuddled and treated like a princess before and after their spankings. That wasn't her. Not by a long shot. She could take anything a dom handed her.

But she hadn't expected the rush of emotion she'd experienced when Master D had stripped her and taken her shoes. Such a simple punishment. Somehow he'd known just how to dent her armor and, now, she suddenly didn't feel quite so confident or content about what they had to do up there on stage for everyone to see.

Master D led her past the hot tub area to the costume room, but he stopped before they entered, pushing her up against the wall with a hand at her throat, his eyes glittering.

She smirked, breaking character. "I don't think daddy doms pin their girls against walls."

His slow smile was feral, but his grip at her throat relaxed. "You're probably right, baby doll." He stroked a hand down her neck to one bare breast, pinched her erect nipple between his thumb and forefinger, and rubbed. "Are these little nipples hard for me, little girl?"

Just the deep rumble of his voice had her creaming her tiny G-string. "Always," she admitted.

He rewarded her with a satisfied smirk that made her chest grow warm. "Good girl." His hand traveled lower, down her side to her hip, which he squeezed possessively.

"It's a good thing the senator and his sub wanted to switch."
Mmm...that voice!

"Why is that?" She sounded out of breath.

"I was going to throat punch him if he fucked you tonight."

She sucked in her breath, a simultaneous rush of pleasure and anxiety coursing through her. He'd shown possessiveness once before. A month ago, they'd finished a scene, and he'd tugged her hair back and kissed her throat. "Your master's going to be out of the country for a week or two," he said. "I don't want you coming here without me."

Her tummy had flopped. She needed him. Not seeing him for two weeks would kill her. But she wasn't going to let him dictate terms like that. "I'm sorry, Master, but I have to. I can't go two weeks without my fix."

His eyes had narrowed to dangerous slits. "I see." He'd released her. She'd expected him to argue or say more. It was worse—he went silent. He cleaned their equipment, packed his bag up, and gave a little salute as he walked out, confirming her suspicion he was military.

She hadn't gone the next week. She'd tried to tell herself it wasn't because Master D had told her not to, but she couldn't dredge up any enthusiasm about scening with someone else. She'd gone the following week, and he'd been back. He must have asked around because he'd known she hadn't gone without him, and had been downright gleeful, rewarding her with five incredible orgasms over the course of the night. That night had been the closest he'd come to being affectionate. But even that wasn't daddy-style.

It was exactly that possessiveness that firmed her decision not to date Master D—or someone like him—in real life. Their relationship needed to remain limited to where it was now—anonymous weekend hookups at Black Light. No exchange of numbers. No meeting outside of this safe place. Period. Because while his possessiveness was flattering, it wouldn't work with the way she needed to live her life.

But her thoughts scattered as he kneaded her ass, squeezing roughly before his mouth descended on hers.

The room swooped around her before she closed her eyes and surrendered fully, his lips commanding hers, tongue invading. He tasted of mint, and his skin smelled of a light soap. He dominated her, cupping the back of her head to hold her still as he made his ownership clear. When he pulled back, he leaned his forehead against hers and slid his fingers between her legs, under the gusset of her panties.

"That's right, baby." His voice sounded low and guttural. Sparks shot through her entire body as he stroked his finger along her juicy slit. "You're always wet for Daddy, aren't you?"

She caught her lower lip between her teeth to keep from moaning.

He drew his hand away and kicked her legs apart. "Aren't you?" He delivered a sharp slap between her legs, nearly sending her into climax.

She blinked, trying to clear her lust-addled brain. What had he asked? Oh yeah. "Yes, Daddy," she said, because it was true. If he touched her, she got wet. It was pretty much a rule. Hell, she probably got wet just being in the same room as him.

"That's because this hot little body belongs to me," he growled and spanked her pussy again. "Doesn't it?"

God, just one or two more slaps and she'd be there. She had to lean her head against the wall to hold it up. "Again, Daddy," she whispered.

His lips quirked, but instead of giving her the satisfaction she desired, he gripped her elbow and tugged her into the costume room.

Thwarted lust made her dizzy, and she barely took in the bright, ordered room. It was fully stocked with costumes—racks and racks of every kinky role-play outfit ever dreamed of.

"I need a baby girl outfit," Master D said to the pretty little kitty sub who toddled out from behind the counter on patent leather platform boots.

She smiled warmly at Jennifer, who didn't smile back. "That's fun! I have some really cute ones over here. What age are you thinking?" She beckoned them over to a rack of adult-sized onesies, ruffled Alice in Wonderland style dresses, and Catholic schoolgirl outfits.

Jennifer scowled and cocked a hip, trying to ignore how vulnerable she felt naked.

"Hmm." Master D tapped his lips, and she couldn't help but stare. They were sensual and soft, which on another man might look feminine, but against his square jaw, tough, manly scars, and close-cropped hair, just made him look damn sexy.

"Definitely not these—unless she really misbehaves." He shoved the onesie pajamas down the rack.

Thank God. At least he knew her. He always seemed to know what floated her boat and what didn't.

"And even these are a little young." He dismissed the frilly Alice in Wonderland tea-party dresses. "Maybe something like this. He held up a tiny fur-trimmed mini skirt, made fluffy by a layer of crinoline.

Only the memory of his diaper threat kept her from rolling her eyes again.

He took it off the hanger and thrust it at her. "Put this on, baby."

It was a simple skirt that tied in the back, making it a one-size-fits-all. The kitty lady scurried around behind her to help her tie it.

Okay, maybe it wasn't one-size-fits-all, because it didn't come around to cover her ass in the back. Or it was supposed to be an apron?

She whirled around, craning her neck to see behind her.

"Mmm," Master D said appreciatively. "That's nice. Everyone will see your rosy red ass—I mean, bottom—when I'm through with you."

His correction forced a smile from her and their eyes met. His, ice-blue and beautiful, crinkling at the corners. Had they ever crinkled before? Had she seen him smile before tonight? If she had, it hadn't struck her the way it did in this moment.

Something fluttered in her chest—the desire to earn that smile again. Well, that was weird. While she always wanted to get things 'right' with a dom—especially him—she didn't ever get personal with it.

"For the top, I'd love something simple. Maybe that schoolgirl blouse left unbuttoned and tied at the waist so I can play with these pretty little boobies." He cupped one of her too-small breasts and squeezed.

No. She was *not* experiencing a flush of pleasure at hearing him describe her breasts that way. Somehow she no longer felt like a sexy, savvy submissive, but more like an awkward teenager, unsure of her body, her desires, and how to act.

Damn him—he was doing this on purpose.

Kitty Girl brought the blouse and helped her slip it on. Jennifer batted her hands away to tie it herself, but Master D smacked her ass

—hard. "Naughty, baby girl. Let the nice kitty help you or Daddy will have to spank you."

As if a spanking scared her.

"Over *her* lap."

Okay, that was weird. And awkward. And definitely not something she wanted to try.

She swallowed and dropped her hands, looking pointedly away, over Kitty Girl's shoulder. "Sorry, Daddy," she mumbled.

The eyes crinkled again. He was enjoying this far too much.

Kitty Girl finished tying her blouse. "She needs pigtails," she announced.

Jennifer barely managed not to show her some hand to hand combat moves she'd perfected in the service.

"For sure," Master D agreed.

Kitty girl scurried behind the counter and produced a brush and elastic bands. She beckoned Jennifer over to a chair and pulled her hair into two high pigtails.

"Do you want bows?"

D tilted his head to the side, considering. "Nah, this is good."

Kitty Girl stood back and surveyed her with a self-satisfied smile. "Adorable."

Not a word she would ever elect to be called of her own accord.

"Yes," Master D drawled. "Isn't she?" His long arm reached out, and he cupped her nape and pulled her out of the chair and flush against his body.

The bulge of his rock-hard cock pressed against her bare belly, and something in her flared back to life, the awkwardness melting away as heat swirled in her core.

His mouth descended on hers with another demanding, open-mouthed kiss. They hadn't kissed before tonight. Not ever. She hadn't thought it was his style. It certainly wasn't hers.

But as his tongue swept into her mouth, and his lips twisted over hers, punishing her, owning her, her knees went weak and moisture soaked her little G-string.

"Daddy's going to teach his little girl a long hard lesson tonight," he growled when he pulled away.

Her belly flipped.

Even though, rationally, she still doubted he'd bring her to the place she needed to go, her body reacted to his words, the thrill of fear coursing into her bloodstream. And she fucking loved that he knew how to do this. How to say just the right things to make her go cross-eyed and weak with submission.

Even as a daddy dom.

CHAPTER 3

erek turned to the costume attendant and indicated the pile of Jennifer's clothing and shoes. "Will you put her things in a bag for me to pick up later?"

"Of course." The girl beamed a megawatt smile, and Jennifer looked like she wanted to poke her eyes out.

He hid his grin and tucked both hands under Jennifer's armpits. "Up, baby girl."

Alarm comically flashed across her face. "What?"

He didn't suppress his amusement. "You heard me. Daddies carry their Littles."

"Oh God," she moaned but took his lead, jumping to straddle him when he jerked up on her armpits.

"Oh fuck, yeah," he growled when the smooth bare skin between her breasts landed in front of his face. He dragged his tongue up the length of her breastbone to the hollow of her throat. "Baby girl, you're making your daddy so fucking hard for you."

A reluctant smile tugged at Jennifer's lips.

Out in the middle of the club, a kerfuffle was happening. A sub yelled, "Red!" and stood up. She wore a collar around her neck, and her dom held the leash. Apparently pet play wasn't her thing.

He threw Jennifer into the air and shifted so she came down on his right hip, just like a little girl. "Let's go for a ride, pumpkin."

She shrieked when he took off running, zooming through around the edges of the club where he could move without hindrance. Jennifer clung to his neck, giggles erupting from her lips, unable to remain dignified or stoic. Spectators pointed and laughed at his antics.

He liked making her laugh, his little Jennifer. She was far too serious normally. It wasn't his style, but the role playing helped them both break out of their norm. And hell, considering he hadn't been able to get a date out of her in two months, maybe they needed to bust the mold.

He hadn't been planning on taking center stage, but he noticed the main stage was empty, and he didn't require anything more than a chair for the scene he had in mind. He caught Chase's eye as he jogged near and lifted his chin in the direction of the stage with his eyebrows raised.

Chase grinned and waved a hand toward the floor, as if to usher them up.

He held up one finger and eased Jennifer to her feet so they could both catch their breaths. He wanted to get in tune with her before they headed up there. Sending a sub into submission was something similar to hypnosis. There were certain signs he looked for, to know if they were under his spell, ready for anything he asked of them. And it would be easier to send her there in private than it would be on the stage.

"Do I get to wear something else for our next round?" Jennifer didn't hide her distaste for the baby girl outfit he'd put her in. And that was why he wouldn't let her out of it.

"No, baby girl. You'll be spending the rest of the evening as my Little." He touched her lightly on the nose with his forefinger.

She wrinkled her nose, which made her look exactly like a petulant child.

"You see," he said, wrapping an arm around her back and pulling her soft form against his hard one. "You could use a heavy dose of daddy time. I know you don't want to accept it—and frankly, I can't believe I'm offering it. This is probably a once-in-a-lifetime chance for you, doll, so you should soak it up while you can."

"Right, because it's so enjoyable." Sarcasm dripped from her lips.

He cocked his head and issued a stern warning look, his hand wrapping over her throat in a distinctly un-daddy way. "Careful, baby."

He knew he sounded dangerous. He had his cool, manicured dom mode and, to back that up, he had Deadly D. He didn't usually show that side—except in his line of work, when he really meant business. But some women loved to hear it, and Jennifer was one of them.

She shivered beneath his palms.

Without removing the hand from her throat, he stroked his thumb along her jaw. His other hand wandered to cup her ass, which he gripped with enough force on her cheek to make her gasp. "Are you going to be a good girl for Daddy?" He kept the sinister warning tone in place.

Her eyes dilated, body went soft beneath his hands. He had her submission. "Yes, sir," she breathed.

He knew she loved every minute of his threat, even before he moved the hand on her ass around front to cup her mons under the fluffy skirt, slipping one finger under the gusset of her panties.

Dripping wet.

His blood surged, cock stiffened, rising against the zipper of his black jeans.

He slid his digit back and forth over her glossy slit before penetrating her.

Her eyes flew open in alarm, and she rose to her tiptoes, following his upward thrust. He used the hand at her throat to hold in her place as he pumped his finger in and out of her.

She mewled, expression turning pleading and needy.

He pulled his finger out and slapped her ass. "You want Daddy to fuck that tight little pussy, don't you?"

She swallowed and nodded.

"Do you want him to do it on stage?"

He watched the turmoil on her face. On one hand, his little sub never backed down, not from a challenge or an order. On the other, she wasn't the exhibitionist type. If he had to guess, he'd say she only entered the roulette for the month's free membership. Black Light cost a fucking fortune, and the military didn't make you rich. That was why he'd retired and gone private contractor. He made three times now what he'd made as a SEAL.

She shrugged, and answered with her eyes lowered. "Whatever Daddy wants."

"Mmm." He rewarded her surrender by stroking his hands over her body, cupping both cheeks and kneading them. "You're such a good girl. Always such a good girl for Daddy."

With her ass so delectably bare, he insinuated one finger between her cheeks, seeking out her most private hole and rubbing a tight circle over it. At the same time, he brought the opposite hand around front, delving once more into her moist heat. "Do you want Daddy to fuck you here?" He vibrated the finger over her anus.

Her pussy clenched, muscles tightening around his finger. A scrambled, panicked look scurried across her face. "N-not really...?"

With a sharp thrust, he buried two fingers up to the knuckle in her pussy, making her fall forward, hands flying to his biceps. "Don't lie to me, little girl, or I will spank you so hard you'll remember me every time you sit for a week."

Color bloomed up her neck and across her lovely face.

"I will spank you all night long, until your ass is worn out and you're limp with surrender. And then I'll fuck your tight little ass and show you how much you'll like it."

Her pussy spasmed around his fingers again, and she flushed even deeper.

"Jesus, D," she whispered.

He eased his fingers out, giving her a feral smile. "Are you ready for your lesson?"

Uncertainty flickered over her face, but she drew a breath and nodded. "Yes, sir—I mean, Daddy."

His lips stretched into a wolfish grin. It was so fucking cute when she called him that, especially because it wasn't her style. He kind of loved the intimacy it conveyed.

"Daddy's going to spank you so hard you won't be able to sit for a week. Or at least a day," he modified, dropping out of character to shoot her a conspiratorial grin.

The quick, grateful smile she flashed back made his heart double pump.

"You don't believe I'm going to be able to break you as a daddy dom, do you?"

She hesitated. "No, s—Daddy."

"You think I can't make you cry like the little girl you're playing?" He'd never seen her cry—not in all the times he'd punished her until she was falling down and shaking. Knowing her non-submissive side was as competitive as he was, he said, "I'll bet you I can."

She turned and looked him square in the face. "What will you bet?"

Bait taken. He had her number. To make it where she'd made it in the Army meant she had a type A personality. She was ambitious, probably a perfectionist, and certainly driven. She went after her release with those qualities—asking for more, needing to be taken far beyond what others could take.

He stopped and turned her to face him. "A date. Outside of Black Light. You and me."

Her challenging smile faded, shutters slammed down over her face.

"I know you don't like to get personal, baby. But I think I deserve a chance. One chance to see you outside of this place."

She lifted her chin, her mouth firmed. "I don't date."

"Afraid you'll lose the bet?" he taunted.

Her nostrils flared. "No."

He arched a brow.

"Fine. I'll take that bet."

She wasn't agreeing to a date. No, Jennifer was sure she would win. Well, she had no idea how determined a man like him could be. He would make her cry tonight. And he'd have that goddamn date.

Chase spoke from the stage. "Next up on the main stage is our ageplay couple—known here at Black Light as Master D and Slave to Pain. D and Slave, please come on up."

"Good." He grabbed a chair from the audience and slung his duffel bag over his shoulder before he started walking again, propelling her up to the stage. He led Jennifer to the center, sat down in the chair, and dropped his dom-duffel of toys beside him. "Stand in front of me, legs wide, back to the audience." He unzipped his bag and fished out a wooden hairbrush and the item he'd bought impulsively from a market on the way. It must have been divine inspiration, because it seemed quite perfect right now—a piece of ginger root.

"Hold open your skirt in the back, baby girl. Show them that perfect a—bottom." Using the hunting knife he kept on him, he quickly peeled the ginger and carved a thick finger with a bulbous end.

She lifted her eyebrows, but obeyed, pulling the edges of the poufy skirt forward to increase the gap in the back, showing her muscular ass, threaded by the tiny G-string.

He tugged her panties down until they dropped at her ankles. "Daddy needs your bottom bare for this spanking, angel."

He knew he'd pushed her limits by the way she'd frozen, jaw tightening. But her back was to the audience—they couldn't see her twat— only he could. And while she set firm personal limits, he knew she wouldn't safeword. No—his Jennifer would take just about anything he threw her way within a scene. Delicious experience had taught him that.

He patted his lap.

Jennifer started to roll her eyes then quickly dived over his lap to hide it.

He collected both her pigtails and wrapped them up in his fist to tip her head back. "Don't think I didn't see that, little girl," he growled.

She actually giggled.

It was so odd to see his serious sub laugh that he chuckled out loud, too. "Laugh now, babygirl. You won't be laughing when I'm through with you."

"Okay, Daddy," she mocked, clearly unimpressed.

"Reach back and hold open your butt cheeks."

She obeyed. He hadn't punished her anally before, even though he was a big fan of plugs and anal sex as a means of showing a sub who is in charge. It just hadn't seemed right for her—she needed pain and lots of it, not so much the humiliation. But, tonight, she'd be getting the full treatment.

He picked up the ginger finger and sucked on it to coat it with saliva. No lube for figging—it ruined the effect. He touched the end of the root to her anus and pushed lightly.

"Open for it."

She squeezed instead.

He kept steady, gentle pressure on the tight ring of muscles. "Exhale, baby."

The muscles relaxed as she blew out her breath and he slid the root in. "You earned yourself a figging, baby girl, with all that eye rolling." He pumped the ginger finger in and out, twirling it to make sure the ginger juice touched all her membranes. "So here's the deal. I need you to keep this ginger in your little bottom hole for the entire spanking. It must stay in until I take it out, understand?"

He saw her pelvic floor lift, as if she was squeezing her pussy. Good—it turned her on as much as it did him.

"Yes, Daddy." He could tell the word *daddy* still didn't come easily to her, and he loved watching her suffer with it.

* * *

MAYBE SHE WAS out of her depth. Damn, she'd always prided herself on being able to take anything a dom threw at her. Anything. She would've been okay with ball gags and hoods, blood play, breath play, even. But calling Master D *Daddy* was just…

What? *Weird. Bizarre.* Yes, all of those things. But what about it made her so uncomfortable? It was the affection.

It *hurt* her. Made her chest ache.

Fucking hurt her worse than any beating he'd ever given—and he definitely knew how to give it hard. Yes, Master D, with his rippling muscles, quick reflexes, and physical prowess, knew exactly how to hurt her in all the right ways. His whip never wrapped to her hip; he never beat one cheek harder than the other. He ramped up the intensity, delivering pain in measured doses, always taking her a little further than she thought possible. He knew when to pause, when to let her catch her breath, when to whip her relentlessly.

He normally didn't say much. She'd considered him the strong, silent type. Tonight, she'd heard more words from him than in the entirety of their other scenes. And hearing sweet words from him instead of cool, tight orders unmoored her.

She didn't want affection from him. Didn't want to laugh, to share in secret conspiratorial glances or giggles. And she sure as hell didn't want to be babied.

The ginger hadn't kicked in yet. She'd never been figged before but had certainly researched it, as she relentlessly studied everything in the BDSM lifestyle. It may take up to thirty minutes to activate and then would create a burning sensation in her anus.

No problem. She could handle pain, even when it came mixed with a heavy dose of humiliation. She could handle humiliation, too, although she didn't love it. But hell, she'd made it through basic training. She'd had her fair share of being humbled in front of a crowd.

Master D spanked her with his hand, warming her ass for the hairbrush. He was considerate like that, even though he knew she wouldn't complain if he went straight to the hard stuff.

"A warm-up prevents bruising, little slave," he'd said once, after she'd acted antsy for him to get on with the show. He'd punished her for her impatience, of course.

"You're in big trouble, little girl." Master D's deep growl reverberated in her entire body, seeming to speak within her, the only voice or sound she heard. She'd gone into submission that fast, even with the audience and the unusual position. His hand beat at a steady pace, right buttock, left buttock, his left arm wrapped snuggly around her waist, holding her tight, though she'd never struggle or kick.

She wasn't the kind of sub who liked to pretend she hated it, not that she judged. She didn't need to be tied down or cuffed or strapped to a spanking bench. She prided herself on following her dom's instructions explicitly.

Even so, she found the tight, intimate hold pleasurable. The heat of his lap and the wrap of his arm felt almost like an embrace. A tender spanking—a completely foreign experience for her.

"Do you know why?"

He paused.

Oh dear lord. Was this going to be one of those question and answer scenes? She'd very much prefer a ball gag and hood—keep it anonymous and silent.

"No, Daddy."

He picked up the intensity, and she lifted her ass to meet the punishing blows. As usual, her cheeks had reached the perfect level of sting, so that the increased force he used didn't shock her system but came as delicious pain.

She breathed into the fire, endorphins flooding her system, the early stages of bliss already creeping to the edge of her state.

"You've been holding yourself away from me, little girl."

She hadn't thought it possible with just his hand, but he spanked even harder. She absorbed the sensation, sharpening her experience to nothing more than his voice. His hand. Her body, which belonged to him. His words didn't make sense to her—*holding herself away from him* in what way? But she wasn't the type to question or argue. Whatever he said was truth in that moment.

"You show up here, take your punishment, and leave. Week after week, since Black Light opened. It's not good enough, little girl."

Not good enough.

She gritted her teeth. She was never not good enough. Or at least she spent every minute of her life making sure she measured up. What in the hell more did he want from her?

He paused the spanking and pumped the ginger root in and out of her ass, twisting it. A slight warmth tingled everywhere it touched, a prelude of the burning that was sure to follow.

She felt needy, but for more than just pain. The foreign longing irritated her like a scratchy sweater. She'd thought she'd figured things out in this place. She submitted, received pain, found release. But this new craving—this blinding desire for approval, the need to be right in her master's eyes?

Ugh.

When he resumed spanking, it was with the smooth, flat side of a wooden hairbrush.

She sucked in her breath to keep herself from wriggling away from it, her eyes watering from the pain. "What do you want?" she gasped, knowing she sounded disrespectful, shocked at her own breakage of protocol.

"I want you to give me everything, sunshine. I want you. All of you."

She didn't answer, not knowing what to say. Not wanting to speak as every part of her body tuned into the steady beat of the hard brush on her tender ass.

A moan escaped her lips.

"Bad girl."

He didn't usually use words like that, and they struck her like a javelin to the chest. Usually her pain was for his pleasure—a sadist enjoying his torture. But to hear disapproval from him caused her more discomfort than the spanking, which was getting intense. The pain had built, her ass becoming a heated, throbbing mass of nerve endings that screamed in protest at the thuddy, insistent smack of the hairbrush.

"No."

Shit. Had she actually just whimpered *no*? What the hell? She wasn't the sort of sub to beg, certainly not one to ever tell her dom *no*.

"No?" His voice rang sharp and cruel, and he brought the hairbrush down with even more force.

She had to close her throat to keep another whimper from tumbling out.

"Have you given yourself to me, little girl? Do you let me see beyond the perfect obedience, sub?"

"No."

Why in the hell were actual tears in her eyes? Not the kind that just came from her eyes watering, but real emotional ones. Her throat closed, and she held her breath.

"Why is that, baby girl? Are you afraid of breaking protocol?"

Why was he asking her these questions? Of course she was afraid of breaking protocol! She never broke fucking protocol!

"What happens if you screw up?"

She shifted on his lap, violating her own vow to always hold still for her dom. She wanted the damn scene to be over. This wasn't her thing. Not in the slightest. To make matters worse, the ginger in her anus had begun to seriously burn, the discomfort making her itchy to move—to get up and walk away—no—*run* away from this whole crazy event.

Her master went on relentlessly, spanking with too much force now—it was all too much. When he spoke, his voice sounded harsh and angry. "I asked you a question. What happens if you screw up?"

"You beat my ass!" she shouted, angry now.

"*Language*, little girl. This isn't a dungeon scene." This time the rebuke was cold and tight.

It had the effect of lassoing in her errant emotions, drawing her up tight to toe the line he drew for her.

"Apologize and try again."

Oh God. She hated screwing up. Hated it more than anything in the world. Her face burned, pressure building behind her eyes and nose. "Sorry...Daddy. You beat my *bottom*." Her voice choked, but she still managed to inflict a little sarcasm into the last word.

"That's right, baby. So is that any different than when you don't screw up?"

What kind of mind fuck is this?

She really didn't want to play this game anymore.

"Is it?" His voice snapped like a whip.

"No, sir." A tear dropped onto the stage floor.

Jesus fucking Christ. This wasn't her. She didn't cry.

He didn't correct her.

"So why isn't it okay to screw up?"

Stop. Just stop. She needed him to stop this interrogation.

As usual, her dom seemed to know exactly where she was, because he didn't force an answer this time.

"Who needed you to be perfect, angel?" His voice came softer now, a caress after the sharpness, though the incredible, steady beating of the hairbrush never paused, never stopped.

It took her a moment to understand the question. Was he asking about her childhood?

"Was it your father?"

Oh, fuck no.

Something inside her ripped. She was a child again, the one who never measured up. She had never been physically punished—no. That would've been a relief compared to the withdrawal of love she experienced any time she misstepped. The general had extremely high expectations for his only child, the daughter he reminded over and over again she must be a good reflection on him.

"Did he need you to be perfect?"

A sob crested her throat and erupted. Tears poured from her eyes, dripping in a mess on the black stage floor.

With just one stupid question, she cowered and crouched in the shadow of *not good enough.* Of *wrong.* Of the place she always suspected she belonged and had worked her whole life to avoid.

Her back shook with sobs—real crying with genuine tears, not just panting through pain. Oh God, she was a total mess.

It flew out of her in a torrent, choking her.

Breaking her.

* * *

DEREK LIGHTENED up on the spanks but didn't break the rhythm, giving Jennifer a chance to release everything that was coming up.

He hadn't been sure he could do it. Most of his questioning had been guesswork, since he and Jennifer hardly spoke more than necessary in a scene. But he'd busted a wall, and the real Jennifer was leaking out in the most beautiful, messy sort of way.

Yeah, ageplay wasn't his thing, but he wouldn't trade this moment for anything. Getting through to Jennifer, finding out what she kept hidden so well, and helping her to release her demons meant more to him than he'd known.

And while messy emotional stuff wasn't usually his gig, he actually welcomed the opportunity to hold his sweet sub and provide every level of comfort she needed.

Her sobs gradually subsided, and he stopped spanking, laying the brush down on the floor beside his chair. He eased the ginger finger out of her anus and dropped it back into the plastic baggie he'd brought it in.

Smoothing Jennifer's skirt back down, he lifted her to her feet, rising from the chair so he could take her into his arms.

The audience broke into applause.

And then she swung at him.

Fuck.

He dodged her flying fist, and the clapping stopped abruptly, morphing into a tight silence punctuated by several gasps and whispers.

"Whoa—out of line," one female cried out, indignant on his behalf. "That's what a safeword is for!"

His heart jammed up in his throat. He'd taken it too far. Or not far enough. Either way, his sub was furious with him, and if he didn't fix the situation quickly, he might lose her.

Unacceptable.

He raised his hand to shut up the crowd, never taking his gaze from Jennifer's flushed face. Her eyes and nose were red, mascara smudged under her eyes. Fists balled at her sides, her chest heaved with rapid breath.

His chest tightened to see her this way, even though he'd been the one to cause her pain. Sadism was like that—with the desire to hurt also came the equal desire to comfort, to protect.

"It's okay. I get it. I hurt you. You want to hurt me back?" He beckoned to her. "Come on, throw another one. I promise I won't duck this time."

Her knuckles slammed into his jaw, not with enough force to knock him off balance, but definitely with enough to bruise.

He rubbed his jaw as the crowd muttered again. "That's a beautiful right hook, baby. Now—"

But Jennifer was walking swiftly away, and if he didn't catch her, he feared he'd never see her again.

She headed straight for the door out of the club then seemed to remember how she was dressed and made a sharp right turn, beelining it for the women's locker room. Thank God she wasn't in streetworthy clothing.

He jogged to catch her. Chase had taken the stage, introducing the next couple, thankfully shifting the attention away from his drama. Accelerating his speed, he caught her right before she went in, darting in front of her to block her way.

The security guy, Terry, came over, frowning.

Jennifer sidestepped to get by him, but Derek shifted as well.

"Okay, maybe she just needs a little break," Terry said.

Derek had to work very hard to keep his hands from forming fists. "Just give us some space, here. I'm not touching her, and she hasn't safeworded. There's no need for you to be involved."

Jennifer's lips pressed into a thin line, her tear-streaked face completely closed and angry.

He caught her eye and tried to hold it, but she glared resolutely over his shoulder. "Listen to me"—*Baby* didn't sound right— "Jennifer."

Her eyes flashed wide when she heard her name, but her face turned even stormier.

"We had a bad scene. You're upset. I'm not letting you walk out of here without aftercare."

A glimpse of surprise flickered on her face, but then she visibly hardened again.

"You don't have to talk to me about what's going on inside your head. You don't even have to say a goddamn word, but I need to make sure you're taken care of."

She drew herself up, an effect that was lost by the way her lips still trembled and defeat still shadowed her eyes. "I don't need anyone to take care of me."

"Baby." He said the word softly, infusing it with his regret. He wanted to argue with her, to tell her he knew damn well that wasn't true, but seeing the firmness in the set of her mouth, he abandoned that tack. "*I* need it."

Her eyes flashed. "I don't give a shit what you need."

Somewhere across the club, a sub screamed as she dropped into the water tank.

The fucking security guy still hovered nearby, waiting to get involved. Derek chose to use it to his advantage. "Fine." He flicked a glance toward Terry. "If you won't accept it from me, Terry will find someone else to give it to you, but you're not leaving this building without aftercare." He honestly didn't want to trust her fragile state to anyone else's care, but if came down to that or nothing, he cared more about her than about his own need to be her man.

They both turned to look at Terry, who appeared startled to be put in the middle of it. Derek prayed they had enough brotherly trust between them for him to back him up.

Terry considered for a moment then gave a single nod. "That's right."

Jennifer rolled her eyes, but he could see the signs of another break—tears starting to swim, lips quivering.

He moved in quickly, slipping an arm around her waist with the lightest touch. "Come on, angel," he murmured encouragingly. "I'll give you a whipping, if you still need it."

The offer was the carrot for her, not the stick. Only in this upside down world of Black Light was that a treat rather than a punishment.

Her shoulders relaxed slightly, and her lips twitched.

"I'll even let you punch me again."

She gave a choked snort but allowed him to lead her away from the locker room. He picked up his duffel bag of dom equipment on the way and escorted her into a safe room where people went to chill out and be away from scenes when they'd had too much. It had red leather couches and warm lighting. No one else was in there.

"Just you and me, the way it's supposed to be." He pulled a blanket from his bag and wrapped her up in it, scooping under her knees and lifting her into his arms. "I know we don't usually do things this way, but tonight's unusual."

She leaned her forehead against his jaw, and the gesture nearly broke him. He hated to see her so fragile, but the honor of comforting her in this moment was priceless.

Sinking to sit on the loveseat, he tucked her up against his chest.

"Baby, I know I pushed your buttons tonight." He tugged the elastic bands out of her hair to release the pigtails. "I won't say I didn't mean to, because we both know I did." He combed his fingers through her silky blonde hair, watching the strands feather out over her shoulders. "I wasn't trying to humiliate you, at least not in a way that's not sexy."

He rubbed her back and kissed the top of her head.

Her eyes lifted.

Yeah, he knew. The affectionate dom thing wasn't usually his gig, but that didn't mean he didn't know how to do it. And with her, it felt right.

"It wasn't about winning the bet, either." He held his breath, praying she wasn't going to tell him that bet was off, because he knew how close he was to having her sever all ties.

She stilled, clearly listening, but didn't speak.

"It came from the deepest connection with you. I don't want you to work so goddamn hard to please me, week after week. And that's something you'll probably never hear from a dom's lips again."

She gave a shaky chuckle.

He brushed some hair back from her face and cupped her cheek. "You *are* the perfect sub." He smiled when a slight blush of pleasure bloomed on her cheeks. "I think we have something together. Something that could go beyond Black Light."

She made a restless move.

"No, wait—I know you've been keeping your walls high. You like to keep things separate and neat and clean. But life isn't fucking clean. And I want to be part of your messiness."

Her nostrils flared, eyes widened in alarm.

He tightened his arms around her, afraid she'd try to bolt. "Don't you fucking run from me," he growled.

She liked the dominant threat. Her pupils dilated, breath sucked in over her berry lips.

"You think I can't handle you in real life, too?"

"I don't do this in real life." She jerked again, in a clear attempt to get off his lap.

"I know you outrank me, angel."

She stilled. Swiveled on his lap to look him square in the face, measuring him.

"I saw the insignia on your uniform, baby. Did you really think I'd fail to notice the sexiest officer in the entire fucking Army when she passed me?"

A reluctant smile tugged at Jennifer's lips. "You were in civilian clothes."

"Retired Navy SEAL doing contract work. And you're a major already, turning the military on its head. Your career far outshines mine." He attempted to show in his expression and tone that his respect was genuine, in fact, it went beyond respect. He was down-right proud of what she'd accomplished. "Yeah, I'm beneath you. You might be impressed by my security clearance level, though." He winked.

"Navy SEAL is impressive enough," she muttered, blushing.

He brushed a kiss across the bridge of her nose. "What I'm trying to say is that I know who you are. In here and out there. And I want both."

She shook her head. "That doesn't work."

"Don't fucking tell a SEAL he can't make something work."

She rolled her eyes, and he was glad to see the return of humor. "I don't even know your name."

"No? It's Derek. Derek King."

He leaned his forehead against hers. "So, are you going to let me have that date?"

"I don't...think..." she whispered, but he heard the longing in her voice.

"I *did* win the bet." He made his voice teasing, hoping it wouldn't piss her off. "Come on, just one date. To see what else is possible between us." When she didn't answer, he prompted, "So, we have a date?"

She searched his face.

He held his breath, not sure what she was looking for.

Dragging her lower lip between her teeth, she drew a breath and let it out slowly then nodded.

He had to restrain himself from fist-pumping. "Good." He kissed her forehead. "You won't be sorry." He stroked his hands up and down her body. "You ready to spin again? Or do you want to accept Dom's Choice this time?"

She blinked, clearly adjusting to the idea of scening again. "Dom's Choice," she murmured.

His heart swelled. She trusted him. They'd clicked from day one because she let him lead without question or hesitation. Considering who she was in her day life, that meant everything.

CHAPTER 4

*J*ennifer didn't actually need the promised whipping. Despite the fact she'd been angry as hell at the time, she'd still received the same endorphin rush from the hairbrush paddling, and now that her emotions had been wrung out and restored as well, she didn't need anything more.

Well, an orgasm or two might be nice. But even that wasn't necessary. She had a tenuous peace in her heart she'd never felt before. Or was it just exhaustion? No, it was peace. She felt more relaxed with Derek, but it also seemed fragile—like someone might come and take it from her at any moment.

And, honestly, if she hadn't made the bet, she never would've agreed to a date. Master D—Derek—thought he wanted to date her, but what did he know about her other than that she could take a good beating? She wasn't submissive in real life—couldn't be. She had to be tough. Strong.

When he figured that out, he'd turn mean and try to tear her down, the way Sal had. And she couldn't take losing him. Not when she needed him to be her weekend dom to keep her sane.

Derek led her toward the roulette wheel, but Chase hailed him from the stage before they arrived. A dom and his sub stood there. The tall, clean-shaven dom, who she didn't recognize, looked smart in a red shirt, black trousers, and a red-and-black striped tie. He leaned his head close to Chase's.

"Master D, can you give Adam a quick refresher on using a whip?"

"A bullwhip?"

A shiver ran down Jennifer's spine just hearing the implement named. Derek had used one on her the third time they'd scened together, and it had been amazing—fulfilling all her dungeon fantasies. He'd been masterful with it, which she knew from her research was a challenge.

"Wait here, baby, I'll be right back," Derek murmured, squeezing her hip before he left her side. The other dom placed his sub, a tall, curvy woman with long, chestnut curls, in a cage. Derek conferred with him for a few moments then they taped a pillow to the center of the St. Andrew's cross for the dom to practice with. She couldn't hear what was said, but it seemed like Derek offered a few pointers then shook hands with the dom and returned to her.

Seeing her interest in the scene, he bit her ear. "Maybe I'll put you on the cross next, baby girl."

"Mmm," was all she could manage.

Derek propelled her to the roulette wheel. She dropped her ball into the spinning wheel, not really caring what she landed on. It landed on *whipping.*

Derek's dark chuckle sent frissons of pleasure shooting through her. "Looks like the wheel knows just what you need, baby," he murmured, his deep voice plunging straight to her core. "Why don't you spin it once more so we don't have to come back?"

She obeyed, landing this time on anal penetration with condom.

"Now that's what I'm talking about," Derek growled, the satisfied smirk on his face positively wolfish.

She shivered. He hadn't fucked her ass before, although he'd threatened it. Usually the pain play took up most of their time together.

"Let's go, baby." Derek ducked and picked her up in a fireman's carry—throwing her over his shoulder so her ass flew up in the air, the miniscule skirt fluttering down to show her bare bottom and probably more to the entire place.

She smacked his back. "This isn't ageplay, this is Viking capture fantasy."

His deep laugh shook his whole torso. He smacked her ass. "This is whatever I say it is, pumpkin." He took off, zooming around the room like he had before, sending her into shrieks of laughter.

Damn, she didn't want to have this much fun with him. She was starting to feel...*close* to him.

Some of the nearby audience twittered.

He circled the room then pulled up and dropped her in front of the spanking bench.

"Kneel, little girl."

So it was still "little girl"? Funny, it didn't bug her as much as it had before. She certainly had become that little girl, with the tears and tantrum to match, but it had turned out all right. The world hadn't collapsed because she'd shown weakness.

It was a good thing Derek had stopped her from leaving, though. Because if he hadn't talked her down, she probably would've hated him forever. Never returned to Black Light, too embarrassed to show her face again.

Now, anger had been replaced with a warm glow. The whole event seemed different somehow—less stressful, more welcoming. She knelt on the padded leather knee rests of the spanking bench, folding her torso over the body rest and placing her forearms on the second set of narrow padded leather rests.

Derek buckled her with the efficiency she'd come to expect from him. Lord, she valued an experienced dom. No, not just any experienced dom, because she'd had the chance to scene with Senator Kane tonight, who she'd played with in the past, and it hadn't excited her in the least.

Derek stroked her ass. "So...a whipping and then an ass-fucking."

"Language, Daddy," she sang out in a fake baby girl voice.

He smacked her ass with his palm, hard. Her flesh was still tenderized from the hairbrushing earlier, and it stung and made her gasp. "Bottom-fucking, then."

She giggled.

He kneaded and stroked her twitching ass. "I mean...Daddy's

going to teach his baby girl a long, hard lesson with his strap and then he's going to punish this naughty little ass some more with his cock."

That tweaked her. Her pussy clenched, pelvic floor lifting and fluttering.

He stopped stroking and rummaged in his duffel bag, producing a thick leather strop.

She shivered, knowing it was a serious instrument, especially considering how sore she already was.

"You're in big trouble, baby girl." He whapped the leather into his open palm. "Do you know why?"

Oh lordy. More question and answering? "No, Daddy," she said brightly, letting the perkiness of her voice serve as subtle rebellion.

He chuckled, but before the deep reverberation had stopped, a line of fire exploded across her ass.

She jerked, the ankle and wrist cuffs biting into her flesh and she cursed herself for the instinctive lurch away. She prided herself on being able to hold a position during a whipping. Drawing a long, slow breath, she counseled herself to remain still. It was only the surprise of the first stroke that had made her struggle.

He struck again, and this time she'd prepared for it, opening up for the pain, welcoming it. That was the trick. If you braced against it, the pleasure took longer to arrive. She liked to think of each stinging weal as another stroke toward her orgasm—already framing it in her mind as pleasure, even though it hurt.

"You don't *ever* run away from me, baby girl." His voice was low and dangerous. He sounded like he meant business, and she fucking loved it when he used that tone with her. Except this time it was about something real that had just happened. Which made this punishment versus pleasure.

He whipped her again, and her momentary distraction caused her once more to flinch. *Dammit.* She was really off her game tonight. Another line of fire fell, and another.

She drew measured breaths across her teeth, found her eyes watering.

What in the hell? Maybe once the dam opened, the water ran free?

"If you're mad at me"—he laid another stroke and she sank her teeth into her lower lip— "you stay and tell me about it."

Damn, the man could wield a strop. A sheen of sweat broke out across her back and chest.

"Preferably with respect, but if you can't manage that, you tell me anyway. I'll deal with your naughtiness later."

Aaand that made her pussy wet.

"But you don't ever run away." He struck the backs of her thighs, and she tossed her head back, squeezing her eyes closed and holding her breath to keep from crying out. "Answer me." The cold command drew her out of the pain and into the present. Had he asked a question? No.

"Yes, sir. Daddy. Sir."

He whipped again. "Apologize."

It made her heart explode into a gallop. The feeling of being wrong, being held accountable. She hated it but sort of loved him for forcing her into this place. And definitely hated him.

"I'm sorry I ran off." Her voice warbled a little.

Derek must have heard it because his face suddenly appeared beside hers, blue eyes assessing but warm. He'd crouched beside her, and his big hand dropped onto the back of her head, fingers burrowing into her hair and massaging her scalp. "I'm sorry you thought you had to." His voice came low enough that only she could hear. "You're always safe with me, baby. Even when you crack."

Oh damn him.

She turned her face away, but his grip on her hair immediately turned brutal, lifting and turning her head back. Tears blurred her vision. "S-stop," she quavered.

"Nope." He said it quickly and with complete determination.

A tear dribbled across her nose. He thumbed it away.

"You think I'd break you and then let you fall? No fucking way, baby."

"Shut up," she croaked.

He kissed her temple and leaned his forehead against hers. "I'm not a daddy dom. Not even close. But I do know how to take care of you. And I will. I promise you that."

She wanted out of the scene again. Her emotions scrabbled all over the place, the primary one being fear.

As usual, her perceptive dom sensed it. He released her and switched the strop from his left hand to his right as he stood. It was his look of disappointment that did her in.

She didn't expect him to be merciful, and he wasn't. The thick leather fell with hard blows, filling the air with loud cracks as it struck her raw flesh.

Her back shook with threatened sobs, but she shoved them back down. She wasn't going to fail this again.

"Stop!" she screamed.

Stop wasn't a safeword, and most doms would demand her to use one or shut up, but Derek returned to crouch beside her.

"Yes?"

Tears ran across her face in messy lines, dripping into her mouth and nose. "What do you want from me?" she sobbed.

He mopped her tears with his palm, though the gesture wasn't particularly tender. More matter-of-fact.

"I want you to stop holding back from me. Give me a chance." He stroked her hair back and this time his touch was a caress.

"I... can't," she croaked. She expected more anger. More whipping, but his expression didn't change, and he didn't move.

"Tell me what you're afraid of."

She closed her eyes, letting more tears run. "You," she whispered. "Everything. I just *can't*."

* * *

DEREK'S CHEST felt like an anvil had dropped on it. Jennifer's resistance was so much more than he'd expected. But he'd made his play, and he wasn't going to back down or stop until he succeeded.

Jennifer was his, dammit. She'd been his since the first night she walked up to him and dropped to her knees. He just needed to make her realize it.

Something had her terrified of relationships, and he needed to figure out what it was.

"Who hurt you, baby?"

Her face slackened slightly, eyes going wider. She licked her lips.

"What happened? What are you afraid I'll do?"

She made a restless motion. "Master..." She swallowed. "Derek, please. Let me out of this thing."

He shook his head. "Nope. There's only two ways out. One is to safeword. You know I'd let you out immediately, but I'd be pretty fucking disappointed. The other is to wade through this shit until we get to the other side. You're a soldier, angel—are you really going to quit when things get tough?"

It was a low blow, to invoke her military pride, but he'd taken the gloves off quite a bit earlier in the evening.

Her gaze turned defiant. If she'd been standing, her chin would've lifted.

He grinned. "That's what I thought." He stood again. "I'm going to finish this whipping. And then I'm going to take your ass—I mean, your naughty little bottom hole—and when I'm finished, you'd better be ready to talk to your daddy about what you need."

He saw confusion flit across her face before he walked back. She looked so beautiful, buckled and spread for him on the bench. Her flimsy skirt was flipped up on her back, leaving her delectable ass and pussy bare and presented for all to see. She'd already taken a lot. Her cheeks were swollen and red from the hairbrushing and now marked with stripes from the belt. Her backside would definitely be too sore for sitting the next day.

"Ten more for refusing to talk to Daddy."

Her head twisted around, but he started in on the whipping before she could protest.

He brought the strap down across her quivering cheeks. "Count them."

"One, sir," she shouted in perfect military cadence. He whipped her again. "Two, sir."

"It's *Daddy*." Another strike.

"Three, Daddy." She sounded out of breath.

He struck a fourth time, a fifth. Six times. His cock pressed painfully against his fly. He shouldn't love hurting women, but he'd long since given up trying to defend against the eroticism of it. As long as his partner loved it, too, it had to be okay.

Jennifer's voice grew more hoarse, choked.

Seven, eight, nine strokes.

He heard tears behind the words. His poor baby. She'd never cried before tonight. This had to be killing her—not the pain part but actually losing the war to tears.

"Ten, Daddy!"

He dropped the strap and ran his palm up the beautiful slope of her back. "Good girl," he soothed her, noting the tremble running through her and the fine sheen of perspiration coating her back. "Sweet girl. Daddy forgives you."

She sagged, probably only semi-coherent at this point. That was part of the cruelty of requiring a sub to count their last strokes—to ask them to speak when they wanted to fly away.

On to her reward, then.

And his.

On the other side of the dungeon, a dom fucked his sub in the stockade, and her wanton sounds filled the entire floor.

From his duffel bag, he pulled out a small bullet vibrator and turned it on. Jennifer jumped when he brought it to her labia, her pelvic floor contracting, inner thighs flexing against her bonds. He dragged it slowly up and down her slit, teasing her opening, not quite reaching her clit. Jennifer's toes curled.

Adorable.

He did a swift drive-by of her clit, and she made a choking sound. Another fleeting touch. The third time he kept the vibe there and circled her swollen nub as he massaged her anus with the thumb of his other hand.

She mewled.

He removed the vibe, to her moan of protest, and slid it inside her, pushing it up until it bumped the G-spot area on the high front wall. He left it there and applied a generous amount of lube to her anus then unbuttoned his black jeans and let his raging hard-on spring free.

Without taking his eyes from the fucking *amazing* sight of his sub presented and quivering for him, he rolled on a condom and lubed his sheathed cock. "Okay, beautiful girl." He released her wrist cuffs and pulled her hips back two inches, away from the bench. "You're going to hold perfectly still right here, got it, baby?"

"Yes, si—Daddy."

He knew she would, too. Give her an order, she followed. He reached around the front of her hips, now that there was room, and lightly grazed her clit.

Her groan was all wanton. Fitting his cock against her back entrance, he pushed gently. "Take a breath, beautiful."

Her back stretched as she complied.

"Now, blow it out." As she exhaled, he eased forward, breaching the tight ring of muscles. "Good girl," he praised, moving slowly, giving her time to relax and breathe through the shock of intrusion.

"You know why Daddy's fucking your ass, baby girl?"

She shook her head. "Because I landed on it?"

He slapped her clit. "Don't get smart, little one." He slapped again. "Or Daddy will have to punish you again before we're through."

Her breath shuddered audibly when she sucked it in.

"No, Daddy is fucking his baby girl's ass because he *owns* it." He waited for her to deny it, but she didn't. "When you've been naughty, your ass will get fucked. When you've been good, your ass will get fucked. When you need to be reminded of who's in charge, your ass will get fucked. And mostly your ass will get fucked just because Daddy wants to." He reached forward with his free hand and gripped her hair, lifting her head straight up. "Isn't that right, baby?"

"Yes, Daddy," she gasped.

"Good girl." He gripped her waist and shoved deep, moving in and out faster but keeping his strokes smooth and direct.

Her breath came in short pants now; a high pitched whine keened from her throat.

"Does my baby need to come?"

"Yes, master," she gasped. "I mean, Daddy...oh God, *please!*"

His thighs shook with need, balls tightened. "Fuck, yeah," he growled and snapped his hips, barely keeping his mind enough to keep from pounding her into oblivion. "You...take...Daddy's...cock...like a...good girl." He spoke on each thrust, burying deep on the last one and assaulting her clit with rapid slaps. "Come, baby!"

She screamed, body shaking. He managed to shove the tips of a few fingers into her pussy, wanting to feel the squeezing of those muscles as she came all over them.

"That's my good girl," he murmured, rubbing the pads of his fingers up and down over her swollen, glossy slit. "Such a good girl."

She let out a sob and collapsed completely, muscles going slack beneath him.

He waited to catch his breath, the intensity of the moment making it hard to return to a thinking state. Eventually, he eased out of her and removed the condom before tossing a blanket over Jennifer's back.

He was torn between wanting to give her all the care she needed and being responsible for cleaning the equipment so another couple could move on. He unbuckled her ankles and helped her to stand, wrapping the blanket more snugly around her. "Close your eyes. Stand here and count to thirty. I'm going to wipe down the bench and then we'll go to the chill room," he murmured.

She obeyed, closing her eyes and nodding.

He patted her bottom. "Good girl."

* * *

JEN HAD NEVER BEEN SO WORKED over in her life. Her body felt boneless, made of rubber. She wasn't even sure how she managed to stand. Derek's command to close her eyes had been a godsend because she definitely didn't want to take in the audience around them, nor the other couples nor...anything but him.

Her pussy still pulsed with the incredible climax, and her anus burned. Her ass throbbed in time with her heartbeat. Bliss poured through her, swirled in her chest, her belly, her core. She might actually be floating an inch off the floor.

But Derek still wanted to talk. What had he said?

When I'm finished, you'd better be ready to talk to your daddy about what you need.

She didn't even know what he meant by that. She didn't need anything except for things to remain the same between them. She needed him to be her weekend dungeon master, nothing more, nothing less.

One of Derek's strong arms looped around her waist. "Okay, baby." In a quick swoop, he had her up in his arms, cradled like an infant. She hadn't liked all the carrying earlier, but this time, it felt both necessary and right.

He made it seem easy, like she weighed nothing, and giving herself to him seemed easier this time, too.

He carried her to the chill-out room and sat down on one of the red leather couches.

"Ready to talk?"

She shook her head.

He didn't turn stern, but, rather, the corners of his lips quirked and he touched her nose. "Too bad. You gotta tell me why you're so sure we can't have a relationship."

She thought about arguing that they *did* have a relationship—one that worked perfectly as it was, but she didn't want to annoy him. Not when she was feeling so good.

"Who hurt you? What did he do?"

She tried to swallow over the stiff band that had tightened around her throat.

"Did he cheat on you?"

She shook her head.

"Leave you?"

"No, sir," she whispered, hoping he wouldn't correct her. She really preferred sir to daddy. She tried to think of the words to explain to Derek, but the thought of bringing Sal—insignificant, petty, small Sal —into a discussion about *their* relationship seemed wrong. But wasn't that what she was doing anyway? Letting Sal dictate the current terms of her relationship status? She'd broken up with him but still let him mean so much. Was Derek like him?

In this light, they seemed completely different. Of course they both were years older than she and Sal had been then. They brought maturity to the table.

"I just—" She wanted to explain it to him, didn't want him to think it was about him, specifically. "I can't be submissive in my real life. I just can't. It's hard enough to try to lead men who hate answering to a female officer. I feel like I'm always trying to prove myself. I don't have the energy to do that in a relationship, too."

Derek's gaze turned sympathetic. "Baby," he said softly, "I would never stand in your way. You know I have complete respect for you— out there and in here. That's how this works. You say *yellow*, I pay close attention. You say *red*, I stop. You're always in control of me and my actions." He stroked her cheek. "I know a submissive isn't a doormat. I don't expect to control your life. Is that what you're afraid of?"

She watched him carefully, looking for a trap. "Yes." She left the *sir* off as a test. They were talking about real life. Would they be equals out there?

"Baby, I'm actually a pretty laid-back guy. I take orders well. I also lead well. I'm open to negotiating when and how you allow me to lead. And I would never, ever take your submission for granted. I know it's a gift."

It sounded too good to be true, but she couldn't stop the fireworks exploding in her chest, in her heart.

"I would support your career one hundred percent. When you came home, wound tighter than a spring, I'd make you dinner and whip your ass until you went soft again. Until your pussy's dripping wet for me and you're willing to give me anything I ask for."

Her laugh came out shaky. "Yeah?"

He leaned his forehead against hers. "Yeah."

"I just...can't deal with controlling."

He chuckled. "Oh, you deal with controlling magnificently. You just need to negotiate boundaries—areas of life where you won't tolerate it."

She nodded, relief sweeping through her. He made it sound so easy. "Yes," she breathed.

"I get it. And I'm still in." He picked up her hand and kissed the inside of her wrist, his lips impossibly soft for such a tough man.

"Me too."

Surprise and pleasure sparked in his expression. "You're in?"

She nodded. "Yes, I'm in."

He stood up, abruptly, still holding her. "Come on, let's go."

She kicked her feet playfully. "Where are we going?"

"We're getting out of here. I'm taking you home. My place or yours?"

"Wait—what about the event? We might win a prize!"

He shook his head. "I won the prize I came for."

Her heart did a double backflip and landed with its arms in a victory V. By the time she'd recovered her breath to laugh or protest, he'd made it to the costume room, where he demanded her bag of ripped clothing and shoes.

"Derek—Daddy—do you still want me to call you that?"

He grinned. "Master, sir, Daddy, Derek. Any of those will do. Depends on the moment, I guess. We'll figure it out, won't we?"

She seriously couldn't wipe the goofy grin from her face.

He dropped her in front of the women's locker room. "Get changed. You have exactly"—he looked at his watch—"two-point-five minutes."

She laughed and went inside. She had to force her muscles to move because hurrying wasn't in their repertoire at the moment. As she dressed, Derek filled her every thought—the idea of going home with him thrilling now, instead of non-negotiable.

She stepped out to find him clocking her on his watch.

"Two-point-two-three. You never back down from a challenge, do you, baby?"

She laughed. "Never."

He winked. "That's why I'm signing up for your team. I don't want to ever go against you, beautiful."

And with that, the last fear left from Sal exploded with a puff and drifted away. Derek hooked an arm around her waist and pulled her against his side, leaning over to kiss the top of her head.

"I never thought you'd be the head-kissing type."

"Is it a letdown?"

She laughed. "No...just unexpected."

"There's a lot you're going to find out about me, baby." When she looked up, he winked. "All good, I swear."

Her heart had already soared on ahead, through the tunnel and up the stairs, gliding into their future. For the moment, all she could do was lean her head against his shoulder, allow herself to be tucked against his side, and sigh. "I can't wait to find out."

THE END

ABOUT THE AUTHOR

USA TODAY BESTSELLING AUTHOR RENEE ROSE loves a dominant, dirty-talking alpha hero! She's sold over a half million copies of steamy romance with varying levels of kink. Her books have been featured in USA Today's Happily Ever After and Popsugar. Named Eroticon USA's Next Top Erotic Author in 2013, she has also won Spunky and Sassy's Favorite Sci-Fi and Anthology author, The Romance Reviews Best Historical Romance, and Spanking Romance Reviews' Best Sci-fi, Paranormal, Historical, Erotic, Ageplay and favorite couple and author. She's hit the USA Today list five times with various anthologies.

WHERE TO FIND RENEE ROSE:

- Visit her blog at www.reneeroseromance.com
- Follow Renee at www.facebook.com/ReneeRoseRomance
- Follow her on Twitter @ReneeRoseAuthor
- Follow her on Instagram @reneeroseromance

http://reneeroseromance.com/

OTHER BOOKS BY RENEE ROSE

Dark Mafia Romance

The Don's Daughter, Mob Mistress, The Bossman

Contemporary

Owned by the Marine, *Theirs to Punish, Punishing Portia, The Professor's Girl, Safe in his Arms, Saved, The Elusive "O" (FREE)*

Sci-Fi

The Hand of Vengeance, His Human Slave, His Human Prisoner, Training His Human

Paranormal

The Alpha's Promise, His Captive Mortal, The Alpha's Punishment, The Alpha's Hunger, Deathless Love, Deathless Discipline, The Winter Storm: An Ever After Chronicle

Regency

The Darlington Incident, Humbled, The Reddington Scandal, The Westerfield Affair, Pleasing the Colonel

Western

His Little Lapis, The Devil of Whiskey Row, The Outlaw's Bride

Medieval

Mercenary, Medieval Discipline, Lords and Ladies, The Knight's Prisoner, Betrothed, Held for Ransom, The Knight's Seduction, The Conquered Brides (5 book box set)

Renaissance

Renaissance Discipline

Ageplay

Stepbrother's Rules, Her Hollywood Daddy, His Little Lapis

REVEALED

A BLACK LIGHT: VALENTINE ROULETTE NOVELLA

by

Livia Grant

CHAPTER 1

"$\mathcal{M}$iss Monroe, I'm sorry to wake you, but we're about to land. I need you to put your seat in an upright position and stow your belongings. We'll be landing at LaGuardia in about twenty minutes."

She flew this red-eye transcontinental trip often between Los Angeles and New York City. The first-class flight attendant knew her well, waking her to ensure she'd have enough time to put on her face as well as choke down at least one energy drink, a tall cup of coffee and a granola bar. Today, however, when Khloe pulled off the soft eye mask she wore when sleeping, she was also greeted with a decorated chocolate cupcake with an unlit candle in the middle.

"I wish we could light it, but that's against regulations. The crew and I would like to wish you a happy birthday." Several other flight attendants had gathered to wish her well. It was a very nice thought, but she'd be lying if she said she was excited about turning twenty-five while she'd been sleeping at thirty thousand feet.

Khloe plastered on her default smile. "Thank you so much, Wendy. Everyone. I really appreciate it." As the attendant reached to place the cupcake on the small table next to her seat, Khloe complained. "Oh no you don't! Someone else needs to eat that."

Wendy didn't look surprised at all at her refusal to eat the fattening food, yet she ignored her customer's wish completely, setting the cupcake down next to her already waiting coffee and low-fat breakfast bar. "I knew you'd say that, but it's your birthday. If you can't splurge on one small cupcake on your birthday, then when can you? Live dangerously."

Khloe wasn't sure if the off-handed comment made her want to laugh or cry. Wendy's broad smile told her the older woman only had her best wishes in mind, but she couldn't possibly know the struggle Khloe fought every single day to stay thin enough. Pretty enough. Young enough.

Working in a business that prized physical perfection took its toll.

If she felt like this on her twenty-fifth birthday, she couldn't even imagine what it would be like turning thirty or God-forbid, forty. Each year that passed went faster than the last. What alarmed her most was that life seemed to be getting harder instead of easier. She'd poured everything she had into her Plan A: becoming an A-list actress and model. Everything she ate, wore, worked-on, and even thought about revolved around making that happen.

And eating cupcakes didn't help her cause.

Khloe spent ten minutes freshening up in the tiny inflight lavatory, pulling her signature long sandy-blonde hair into a high pony-tail and applying just enough make-up to not look like she'd just taken the red-eye. The only good thing about arriving in NYC at seven-thirty on a Friday morning was that the business travelers rushing through the airport were more worried about catching their flights home than looking for celebrities.

Wendy had her designer winter coat and Rimowa carryon bag waiting for her as she deplaned. She'd be the first off the 747. "I hope you have a wonderful birthday today, Miss Monroe, and also a Happy Valentine's Day. We'll see you the next time."

Shit. She'd almost forgotten about that joyful occasion. She hid her anxiety, hoping her sixth sense was wrong. "Thanks, Wendy. Next time."

Pulling her large sunglasses from the side-pocket of her leather bag, Khloe took off down the long jet way. She pushed down the flutter of butterflies she always got just before stepping into public;

always aware she was on display. Unflattering pictures taken when she'd been caught off-guard weren't going to make her dream come true. She'd learned the more success she had, the more careful she had to be.

With each step she took, she raised her chin a bit more, added a bit more sass to her swagger, neutralized her face into her superior, unapproachable glare she liked to carry when traveling without her bodyguard or publicist.

That was another side effect of her success; attracting the crazies.

By the time she shot out of the doorway into the terminal, she was in her celebrity zone. It was what let her ignore the whispers of people recognizing her as she walked by, pointing or even yelling out to try to get her attention. It also allowed her not to panic when she saw people with their cell phones out, taking photos as she passed by.

She'd texted her car service while they'd taxied to the gate and she was grateful to see the driver in a black suit holding the small whiteboard with MONROE splashed across it. She didn't recognize the driver, but it didn't matter. He recognized her, and he reached out to take her bag as soon as she reached him.

"Good morning, Miss Monroe. I'm Johnson. It's my pleasure to drive you into Manhattan this morning. The weather is a balmy thirty degrees and the sun is even out to welcome you home this morning."

"Thank you, Johnson."

Polite, but removed. Her mantra.

Once settled into the back of the black Lincoln Town Car, Khloe relaxed slightly. The tinted windows protected her from the paparazzi and allowed her to take off her sunglasses. Her stomach growled, always hungry. This morning felt worse, as if her tummy was angry with her for passing up on the chance to eat a cupcake.

Hell. It was her birthday. She should splurge.

"Can you run through a Starbucks drive-through for me? I'd kill for a skinny latte."

"Of course, Miss Monroe."

It was eight-fifteen by the time they hit the Chelsea neighborhood where she'd rented a loft for the last four years. What her apartment lacked in size, it more than made up for with a combination of famous neighbors and tight building security. Most of the shops on 10th Avenue weren't open yet, but Johnson ran in to collect the venti skinny latte she'd ordered from her phone app.

As she waited in the car, she allowed herself to feel a bit of excitement for the upcoming weekend. She had pissed off her producers in L.A. by demanding they worked around her starting her one-week hiatus a day early so she could fly to NYC in time to surprise Dean. She was arriving twenty-four hours early, just in time to surprise her famous boyfriend at the opening night of the newest Broadway play that his best friend just happened to be starring in.

Khloe looked forward to seeing the boyfriend she'd been apart from for five weeks. She'd been horny as hell lately and God knows her vibrator would appreciate a break. She glanced at her watch as they pulled up in front of her building. Eight-thirty. He would be arriving from London in about two hours. She had just enough time to work out and take a shower before he got to her apartment.

"Welcome home, Miss Monroe." Patrick, their primary doorman, held open the car door for her, helping her out while the driver gathered up her belongings and brought them to her on the curb.

"Thanks, Patrick. It's good to be home."

"You gonna be in town for long this visit?"

"A whole week! Can you believe it?"

"That's great. I'm happy for you. You just let me know if there is anything you need. Anything at all." She'd given her doorman a handsome bonus during the holidays. It sounded like he was still appreciative.

"Sounds good."

The lobby was small, but opulent. The elevator tiny, but fast. She enjoyed thinking about her coming evening while she rode to her twenty-third story apartment. It wasn't exactly the penthouse. Not yet, but it was only two floors below. So close.

And yet so far. I'm always coming in second.

She pushed down the constant temptation to wallow in self-doubt, focusing on mind-over-matter. She knew she'd enjoy the show that night, but it was the red-carpet opportunity that had got her on the plane a day early. It wasn't every day she'd get to be photographed alongside so many other celebrities and she just couldn't pass up the opportunity. She considered it her birthday present to herself.

Her key stuck in the old door, making her wrestle with the second dead-bolt before it finally sprang free, allowing her entrance into the small but open living space. Khloe flicked on the light switch next to the entrance. The line of decorative lamps hanging down above the large eat-in island illuminated, separating the upscale kitchen from the living room. She stopped to lock the door behind her before crossing to the blackout drapes hiding the wall of windows to her right. She swished them open, letting the bright sunlight bathe the apartment as she gazed west to the Hudson River just a few blocks away.

God, she was tired. It was so tempting to just go back to her bedroom and take a nap, but the health club on the mezzanine level of the building was calling to her. Before she could back out, she grabbed her latte and headed down the hallway to the left, dragging her suitcase behind. She'd change and go workout first.

The slapping sounds followed by feminine laughter hit her ears a split second too late. She'd already turned the knob on the bedroom door, letting not only the offending sounds, but heartbreaking pictures burn into her memory the split-second the door was open.

Unlucky for her, the two occupants of her bedroom hadn't heard Khloe enter. No. That would have been too merciful. Instead, she stood frozen, doomed to watch her boyfriend of five months fucking the very married actress who'd be starring in that night's grand opening on Broadway.

Looks like she'd got an early jump on her opening night celebration.

It was insane that the very next thing that crossed Khloe's mind wasn't *how could the bastard cheat on me?* No. It wasn't even *how could she cheat on her extremely handsome husband?* It was a crushing disappointment that not once in all of their time together had Dean looked that excited to be with her. Their sex life was like a watered down version of the glorious fuckfest happening in front of her.

Gloria Mining's perfect body was stretched taut, her hands

secured in Khloe's very own leather cuffs from a boyfriend past. The carabiner connecting them attached to a new hook she'd never seen in her ceiling. Both traitors were buck naked, with boyfriend's hands dug into the bony hips of his lover, easily lifting her body to the perfect angle to accommodate his pounding thrusts.

"Holy love of Jesus, I'm gonna come again!" Gloria screamed just before Dean's glistening, perfect body began grunting, his own ejaculation mere seconds away.

In the throes of her own emotional thrashing, Khloe's latte slipped through her fingers, crashing to the floor and exploding out into a six-foot radius of hot coffee, blanketing even the copulating couple. She took small pleasure in seeing the pained grimace on his face as he turned toward her, although she suspected it was the burn of the liquid and agony of pinching off his own release that accounted for his discomfort more than being caught with his dick where it didn't belong.

"Khloe! What the fuck?"

"You took the words right out of my mouth, Dean." A forced calm she didn't dare abandon came over her. "Nice to see you too, Gloria. I wasn't expecting to see you until after the show tonight."

The three occupants of the room froze, unsure exactly how to undo the current mess. Khloe, having been down this particular road once before, had the perfect idea.

Grabbing her cell phone from her back pocket, she quickly unlocked the screen and raised it up to start snapping away. It took the adulterers in the room a few seconds to realize what was happening.

"Goddammit, Khloe. That's enough! Put the phone away!"

She flipped into video mode just in time to capture the wet mess of Dean's withdrawal from the now struggling-to-be-free woman in front of him. The same woman screaming for him to release her trapped arms as she wriggled like a fish hooked at the end of a line. Had it been happening to someone else, the scene might have been funny. The cheater ran towards the bed to grab a throw blanket to wrap around his waist to hide his fast deflating cock.

"You would be more interested in hiding your too-small dick

before helping me down, you bastard." Seems Gloria wasn't as big of a fan of his tool as she'd appeared just moments before. Maybe she was a better actress than Khloe had given her credit for.

Khloe rubbed it in. "Uh-oh, Dean. Looks like trouble in paradise."

He threw her a dirty glare as he finally approached Gloria to begin loosening her restraints. Something snapped inside her in that surreal moment, standing in her own bedroom filming her now ex-boyfriend releasing his married lover from the very bonds she longed to be in. It wasn't that his betrayal left her heartbroken. They hadn't been in love. It was deeper than that, if that were possible. Standing there as an outsider to an intimacy she craved, Khloe's insecurities closed in, reminding her that yet again, she was second best in someone's life. Replaceable. Interchangeable.

The ringing in her ears was a warning sign. She'd pushed herself too far. Too little sleep. Too much caffeine. Strenuous exercise and too-few calories mixed a dangerous cocktail on a normal day. The poisonous kick of adrenaline brought on by betrayal could be her knockout blow. Tears pricked her eyes. If she didn't hurry, they'd get to see her cry.

I need to get the fuck out of here.

She couldn't stay here. Not now. Maybe never again. Without a word, she turned to retreat, pulling her carryon bag behind her. She hadn't unpacked a thing, so all she had to do was pick up her leather travel bag near the door. The last thing she heard before she walked out was both lovers screaming at her to erase the photos.

"Are you hungry Miss Monroe? I could stop and pick you up something to eat."

Johnson was a saint. Truly. She'd called him from the lobby of her building, begging him to rush back to pick her up. Desperate to get away before Dean tried to follow her. She was smart enough to know not to catch a taxi. It wouldn't have been safe to lose it in a public cab.

But the back of Johnson's private livery car had been the perfect place for a meltdown. An hour-long, screaming, crying, cussing melt-down. To his credit, the driver only tried to help in the beginning minutes, concerned for her. He eventually caught on that his passenger just needed to get something out of her system and had patiently been driving her around the streets of Manhattan for the last two hours.

It was about an hour into the drive that her phone had started to light up with calls from Dean. The same Dean who rarely called her when they were apart, leaving it up to her to try to track him down when she wanted to chat. The same Dean who was presently not worried about her wellbeing, but rather what she planned to do with the damning evidence she carried on her iPhone. Seems he was to be auditioning with Gloria's talented director of a husband for a part in an upcoming project. She guessed fucking the director's wife wouldn't gain him many brownie points.

For the first time in a long time, Khloe was tempted to direct the driver to the Bronx. The only thing that stopped her from running home to visit mom and dad was knowing that there was virtually no chance they could make her feel any better and a greater than average shot they'd make her feel worse.

Her ultra religious parents didn't approve of her lifestyle.

"I'm so sorry, Miss Monroe, but I have another ride chartered in about an hour. Are you ready for me to take you back to your apartment yet or would you prefer I take you to a hotel instead?"

Their eyes met briefly in the rear-view mirror. She saw pity staring back at her and she hated it.

Where to go? Not to her apartment. Not the Bronx. In fact, nowhere in NYC.

"Take me back to the airport."

"Yes, ma'am."

She had the thirty-minute drive to figure out where she would fly. It was a bit overwhelming. She had nine days off and literally the ability to fly anywhere in the world her U.S. passport would allow. A Caribbean island? Too romantic to go alone. Europe? Back to L.A.?

Who could she call to go with her? How sad that in five minutes she couldn't come up with a single name of a travel companion, other than staff who worked for her. This wasn't the first time in her life a crushing loneliness hit her. She had thousands of acquaintances in her contact list. Maybe millions of fans, yet in times like this, she had to face how truly alone she was in the world.

She thought back to one of the only times in her life she'd felt like she belonged. Like she'd been wanted. Like she was with real friends.

Familiar regret pressed in, offering to suffocate her and put her out of her misery. She'd had something special just once, four years before when she'd been younger… dumber. Naive enough to think the love she'd felt would be easy to find. She'd tried to trade it up for the next bigger size and in the process, had lost it all.

"Which airline, Miss Monroe?" Johnson asked. They were entering the airport property.

"American, please."

Her mind raced as he dropped her at the curb and she walked through the sliding door, keeping her sunglasses on, this time to hide her red eyes. There was no line at the premier passenger line. She had her ID and credit card in her hand by the time the airline employee smiled and asked, "Good morning. How can I assist you?"

She pushed her butterflies down and held her credit card out as she replied, "I need a one-way first-class ticket on your next flight to Washington National Airport in D.C."

"Of course, Miss Monroe."

She'd seen his photo all over the press lately. For the first time in years, she actually knew where to find him. She just prayed she wouldn't chicken out when she got there.

She needed to talk to Chase Cartwright.

CHAPTER 2

"*T*his is complete bullshit. I've been on the sidelines long enough. I'm as ready as I am gonna be. I need to get back on assignment." Ryder Helms was talking too loud. He knew the drill. His boss set a public meeting place to break the bad news, knowing Ryder wouldn't be able to make a scene.

Well, his boss was in for a rude awakening if he thought Ryder would lie down and let the agency walk all over him.

"I talked to your doctors. You're not cleared for action. Period. Be glad we're letting you take light duty. I'd rather you take a vacation, get some R&R, but I know better than to think you'd do something as sensible as that," his boss deadpanned.

"Listen, I can golf as good as the next guy, and I'm not opposed to some dirty downtime on a private beach, preferably with a naked woman beside me, but I digress. You need me back in Moscow. The longer I'm gone, the harder it's gonna be to regain my cover. We've invested too many fucking years to just throw my connections down the drain." Ryder had lowered his voice, leaning in to avoid the group of women lunching nearby from hearing the details of their private conversation.

Ryder's commanding officer, Brandon Webster, took a bite of his rare steak as if he hadn't a care in the world before answering.

Every second that ticked by, Ryder's blood pressure rose another point.

"This is not the time, nor the place, for this discussion," was Webster's only response.

"Which is exactly why I told you it was a bullshit move." He took a deep breath and laid his cards on the table. "I'm not gonna let this drop just because you choose to have lunch with the garden club. We're gonna talk about this. It's up to you if you want to do it here or somewhere more private."

His superior officer grimaced as if he'd eaten something bitter. "You can be a real pain in my ass, you know that?"

Ryder grinned. "Yeah, but you need me, and you know it."

The balding man took another bite of steak before waving down the nearby waiter to ask for their check. Ten minutes later, the men stepped out into the frigid February winter in the nation's capital. They'd been eating in an upscale restaurant not far from the capitol so he wasn't surprised to bump into a sitting U.S. Senator as they left.

"Let's take a walk, shall we?" Brandon suggested.

The men took a silent stroll towards the nearby small park. Children's playground equipment stood buried under a soft blanket of snow and the men had the space to themselves. They'd found the privacy needed for the conversation Ryder was desperate to have.

He waited for his commanding officer to restart the exchange as the men walked side-by-side along the snow-covered path. He didn't have to wait long.

"Now, let's get this straight. I don't want to fuck things up in Moscow any more than you do, but my hands are tied. You've had three medical incidents in the last two years. You've been red flagged. You aren't going back undercover until you get a clean bill of health. Period." The balding man didn't bother glancing sideways at him.

Ryder pulled him to a stop so they could see each other as he delivered his retort. "Listen, we both know damn well my three *medical* incidents are only because of my assignment. I'm in excellent health, despite being abducted and tortured for a week over two years ago. Despite jumping from the back of a moving truck at forty miles per hour last year. And yes, even in spite of being shot twice at close range four months ago. I'm a fucking machine to be in the shape I'm in considering all I've been through in the last two years."

"You've just proven their point. It's getting too dangerous." Ryder didn't like the look in Webster's eye as he finished his thought. "We're considering not sending you back in."

"Now wait a fucking minute. It's bad enough my return to duty is being delayed. You've lost your mind if you think I'm walking away from this. We're getting close. I can feel it. Igor Romanovski's brigade is going to fall and when it does, I'll be there with the Volkov's to step into the void. We're this close to having connections sitting directly on the Bratva council. We can't abandon the mission."

Brandon Webster gave his full attention to his pissed off agent, finally raising his own voice in frustration. "You don't need to tell me what's at stake here. Don't forget that the Soviet block was where I did my active duty years. The stakes are as high as ever right now with global violence at an all-time high. With the Russian government dabbling in politics around the globe. Don't think for one minute that I don't know how many American lives I'll be putting at risk if I lose out on the chance to have an insider sitting at the table with some of the world's biggest crime lords. It's just…" His voice trailed off.

"It's just what?" Ryder pressed.

"You're almost forty, Ryder. You were less than an inch away from having a bullet turn you into a paraplegic. It's okay to let it affect you. Hell, I'd be worried if it didn't make you pause."

Fuck. So much for doctor-patient confidentiality.

"I see Dr. Albright has been shooting off at the mouth again. What the hell ever happened to patient privacy?"

"Give me a break. You aren't a schoolteacher or an office worker. You're a deep-cover agent. A highly trained killing machine. A multi-lingual intelligence officer with years of experience. If you think you're entitled to privacy, you're not nearly as smart as I'd given you credit for."

Ryder recognized the backhanded compliment. He also knew his boss was right. Physically, his body was healing. Mentally, he'd been struggling to get back to his A-game and going back into the Volkov Bratva before he was ready was like a suicide mission.

"So where does this leave me?" he pressed, not sure he wanted to hear the answer.

"Right now, it leaves you on light duty. Instead of fighting it, try to enjoy it. We need your help at Langley with the influx of intel translations. When you're not there, I know you have a few friends here in D.C. from your Marine days. Call them. Maybe go out for a beer. Play poker. Visit the local BDSM club and take out some of your built up aggression on one of the pain sluts you like to play with."

Ryder had never discussed his sexual proclivities with his boss. He raised his eyebrow in surprise causing Webster to chuckle. "What? You don't think word of your kinky shit hasn't made it back to me? Just keep it legal, will ya? And remember you aren't in Russia. The agency doesn't need any new scandals and you sure as shit don't need to have your face plastered on the front page of The Post. There's no faster way to get yourself sidelined for good."

Ryder pulled the collar of his wool winter coat up higher to keep out the brisk wind. Shit, he hated his options.

"Fine. I'll keep coming out to Langley and helping with the intel, but I'm on record. One more month. That's all. I need to be back in Moscow by the end of March."

"Why don't we wait and see how the next few weeks go?" his boss offered.

"Great. Now all I need to do is find some friends to invite me out for a beer."

* * *

"If you're gonna be this sour, you should have just stayed home. We don't need you scaring all of the subs away. We're already short on 'em as it is," his old friend Spencer Cook warned. Ryder consciously tried to stop scowling as he sipped his scotch.

Being limited to only two drinks was yet another argument he'd had with the dungeon master. Sure, it was nice to be an invited guest to D.C.'s premier BDSM club, but he wasn't really a 'club' kinda guy. He preferred his flavor of domination to be more on the down and dirty end of the continuum over what was practiced at the safe, sane, and consensual Black Light.

Spencer didn't seem impressed. "Like I was saying. We just had someone drop out of the Valentine Roulette event next Tuesday night. You'd really be doing me a favor if you'd step up and you'd get something valuable in return. Besides getting to play with a willing sub for the night, you'll get a one-month free membership worth $2,500. You said you might be stuck in town another month or two. I'm sure it would be easier to blow off some of that steam you seem to have pent up by having a place to come that specializes in your kind of kink."

Ryder had to admit, he was tempted. Not that the club scene was really his thing, but he sure as hell wasn't up for dating or, God forbid, getting into any kind of a relationship. He'd had no problems at all finding willing sex partners in Moscow. Women who craved the darker dominance he provided were easy to find there.

Not so much in D.C.

If he was going to be stuck on the sidelines for a few more months, something needed to change. His left hand was starting to get a workout.

Yep. Kinky sex with nameless strangers was exactly what the doctor ordered and Black Light, while still too tame for his tastes, was light years ahead of any other club in town. Not to mention it came with a built in benefit of being one-hundred percent confidential, something of great value for an undercover agent.

"Fine. How do I sign up?" he finally relented.

"Really?" Spencer seemed genuinely surprised. "I never thought you'd say yes."

"Well, do you want me to or not? I don't like bullshit games."

"Yeah, yeah. Settle down. Let me go get you a card with all of the details. You can sign up online from home later."

Ryder didn't answer. He didn't have anything new to say. He instead turned away from the bar to take another look around the club. Being the Saturday night before Valentine's Day, the place was busy, despite it being only seven o'clock. He suspected a few members would be heading upstairs in an hour to catch the Crushing Stones concert playing at Runway. He wondered if he'd see Cash Carter after the show, that is if he stuck around that long. He had it on good authority Cash was into the lifestyle.

The more he took in his surroundings, the more uncomfortable he got. Most likely due to the early hour, there was too much foreplay and socializing going on to suit him; people mingling, chatting, flirting. He could mingle with the best of them when his job called for it. Hell, he could literally charm the clothes off women if he put his mind to it. Single women. Married women. Tall. Short. Curvy. Skinny. Rich. Poor. Didn't matter. It was one of the helpful side effects of his deep psychological training. Of course, the intention was to be able to get inside the heads of the world's most dangerous criminals; to figure out what made them tick and then find the best way to neutralize them before they could endanger American lives. The fact that the skill also benefited him with the ladies was just a bonus.

Spencer had returned and placed a small card next to Ryder's rocks glass.

"Don't lose this. The info is confidential."

Ryder swung back towards the bar, picking up the small card with just a website URL printed on it. He didn't bother looking at his old friend to deadpan, "You forget what I do for a living?"

They'd served together years before. Even Spencer didn't know what Ryder did exactly these days, or even for which branch of the government, but he was sure his old friend had a pretty good idea.

"Naw." Spencer smirked. "I guess the secret is safe with you."

"Damn straight." Ryder picked up the card and slid it into the pocket of his black pants. "I'll check it out, but you better promise me I won't get stuck with some sugar-pop kinkster who's only in it for a good-girl spanking from their 'daddy.'"

Spencer chuckled. "I can't promise anything. The wheel will pick your partner and your kink. If it's too risky for you, maybe you should stay home and knit instead."

"Smartass." He downed the last of his drink before standing. "I'm gonna take a piss. I'll try not to make anyone cry while I'm gone."

CHAPTER 3

"Can you circle around the block again, driver?" Shit, she forgot his name.

"Of course, Miss Monroe."

Runway dance club was only five minutes from the Hyatt hotel Khloe had been holed up in for over twenty-four hours, yet she'd been riding around in the hotel's limousine for over twenty minutes.

I can't chicken out now.

She peered down at the phone in her lap. Chase Cartwright's contact info was already pulled up. She even had the text typed.

"Just hit *SEND* already," she chastised herself out loud. The driver gave her an odd look in the rearview mirror. She finally pressed the button. Now she'd wait and hope. She wasn't entirely sure he'd answer, not considering how she'd ended things between them years before.

As she waited, they turned the block to drive past the front of the club again. It was getting late enough that there was now a line of patrons lining up to get into the club. She hadn't known when she'd booked the flight to come to D.C. that the Crushing Stones would be playing live at the club tonight. She suspected the venue would be packed and if she didn't get in there soon, she might miss her chance.

"It's looking pretty hectic, Miss Monroe. Shouldn't you have a security detail with you?" The elderly driver was kind to be concerned.

"I'm sure it'll be fine." She wished she believed that herself. She was supposed to be at home in NYC where she didn't need her detail with her. She'd given them the week off. She tried to convince herself while she answered the driver. "The club will have good security."

In the ten minutes she waited for Chase to respond to her text, the crowd kept growing and now wrapped around the side of the building. She could see they were now letting VIP's in the side entrance so she instructed the driver to get in the line of limos.

Too soon, it was her turn to exit her car.

Dammit Chase, why didn't you answer me?

She pushed down her insecurities and put on her celebrity face that she promptly hid behind her sunglasses, despite it being dark outside. The door next to her opened and a Runway doorman held his gloved hand out to assist her from the car. Only when he'd already closed the limo door and her driver had driven away did he speak.

"May I see your invitation, miss?"

They were walking towards the revolving door marked VIP Entrance, but when she failed to answer him, her escort pulled them to a stop about a dozen feet short of the door.

"You do have a ticket for tonight's closed event, right?"

Khloe took a deep breath and put on her best bitch tone. "I'm a close, personal friend of Mr. Cartwright's. I'm sure he'll be happy to invite me in for the show."

The doorman appeared uncomfortable. "I'm sorry, ma'am, but the show has been sold out for weeks. If you'd like, I can flag you down a cab since your driver already left."

She pushed down her panic. Despite what the gossip rags said about her, she hated confrontation. "Are you deaf? I told you Chase will be happy to see me."

"Okay, let's go see if your name is on the list at the door," he offered, unwilling to deny her without checking.

They passed by a long line of people waiting to get into the main entrance around the corner. Each person gave her the evil eye as she was escorted past them to the front of the line.

"Jerry, this young lady says she's a friend of Mr. Cartwright. Can you see if she's on the entry sheet for tonight?"

Jerry looked skeptical. "Everyone I've been expecting already checked in for the pre-party. I'm sorry miss..."

While he'd been talking, Khloe took her sunglasses off and pinned the overweight guard with an expectant smile.

He finished his sentence. "Miss Monroe. One second please." He turned away from her slightly and pressed the button on the microphone clipped to his coat lapel. "Blake, I need you at the VIP entrance, please. Blake to VIP entrance."

While they waited in the blustery cold, patrons wearing all kinds of Crushing Stones shirts, sweatshirts and hats moved slowly by, now gawking at the recognized celebrity in their midst. Several paparazzi caught wind of her arrival and moved closer, calling out to her. She smiled, making the best of the situation and letting them snap their photos.

"Miss Monroe. We weren't expecting you this evening."

She turned to greet the tall man who must be Blake. "I didn't realize it would be like trying to get into Fort Knox tonight. I'm just trying to see my old friend Chase Cartwright." When she sensed he wasn't going to be swayed, she pressed. "I wanted to surprise him."

"Well we don't care much for surprises, especially on concert nights," he countered.

She contemplated leaving, but the thought of going back to the hotel room she'd spent the last twenty-four hours crying her eyes out in depressed her. She didn't want to be alone with her gloomy thoughts again tonight.

She waited long enough for Blake to relent. "Okay, it's crowded inside. Stick close."

He led her through the revolving door. She noticed he didn't stop to have her take her coat off at the coat check, but instead weaved through the socializing crowd, around tall cocktail tables and chairs and to the edge of the already crowded dance floor.

The music was pounding a heavy beat and the dancers were grinding to the DJ's mix. She couldn't hear what he said, but Blake shouted into the ear of a passing server who immediately weaved out to the center of the dance floor.

Through the gyrating bodies, Khloe caught her first glimpse of Chase. He had his back to her, but when he turned to stare in her general direction, she could see he and Jaxson had been sandwiching the curvy brunette she'd seen photographed with the men many times over the last year. Khloe stood by as the three of them conversed on the floor and when they all three turned to glare at her, she could see the irritation on the men's faces. She also saw an emotion kin to fear emanating from their girlfriend.

Jaxson leaned in to talk into Chase's ear and then finally Chase was moving towards her.

He was even more handsome than she remembered, all except the scowl on his face as he approached her. He leaned close to shout over the music.

"Khloe. What are you doing here?"

Not exactly the welcome she had imagined. "I was in town. I just wanted to see an old friend."

"Bullshit. Why are you really here?" he pressed her.

An unexpected ache pressed on her chest, remembering how close they'd been at one time and knowing she'd been the one who'd rashly thrown it away. Maybe she should have stayed at the hotel. At least there no one would see her cry.

She swallowed the lump in her throat. She didn't know how to verbalize why she was there. She didn't really know herself. She just knew one thing.

"I'm sorry, Chase. I just… needed to see… a friend." He blurred in front of her and it pissed her off. She needed to keep her cool.

"Since when are you and I friends, Khloe?" He paused, his trademark happy smile wiped away, a frown in its place. "Don't you remember? You traded me in on the next bigger and better version many boyfriends ago. Why are you here slumming it with me, a mere model?"

She tried to rouse her anger. "Don't be such a dick."

"Don't lie to me. Why me? Why now?"

Unexpected rage rolled off the man who never got angry. The crowd was pressing in on them and she felt Blake's hand now on her right elbow as if he were ready to drag her out of the club. The paparazzi would have a field day photographing Khloe Monroe being thrown out of Runway, but that wasn't even the main reason she wanted to stay.

She peered past Chase, back out to the dance floor and saw Jaxson and Emma were standing still in the middle of the dancing crowd, watching their lover with worry. Loving concern.

No one ever looked at her like that. Ever.

Blake had started to pull her away by the time she answered her ex-boyfriend in a rush. "Please, Chase. I have nowhere else to go. I just need..." She paused, and he waited. "I just need to be with real people tonight. Just one night."

His eyes widened at her exclamation, staring at her until Blake started pulling her away again. She fought to maintain eye contact with Chase as they got farther apart. She was relieved when he took off after them.

"Blake! Hold up." When he'd caught up, he shouted at them. "Wait here," before turning and weaving through couples back out to the dance floor. The three lovers got close together, Chase talking to them before all three of them turned to stare at her. She held her breath until she saw Jaxson nod. The chill of his glare made her shiver.

Chase returned and addressed Blake. "Miss Monroe will be my guest tonight, Blake." The rest of his comments were sent her way. "But let me be clear, Khloe. It's one night, and if you do or say anything to upset Jaxson or Emma, you're out of here. Got it?"

His eyes danced with a hypnotic passion as he talked of his lovers. She recognized it as love. An emotion she'd never seen in his eyes when he had spoken of her. She pressed down the depressing jealousy to answer with a simple, "Thanks."

They weaved through the crowd back towards the coat check, stopping several times for Khloe to sign autographs and take selfies with fans excited to see one of their favorite actresses. Chase then led her towards the grand circular staircase that led to the second floor of the club. Her stiletto heeled boots clinked on the glass stairs, the neon lighting marking the way.

As they neared the top, the music grew a bit softer and the space was much less crowded. Rather than close-together tables and chairs, the second story was comprised of about a dozen seating arrangements where couches and comfortable chairs were organized for small groups of friends to gather together and enjoy each other's company. Chase led her to the railing overlooking the huge stage and runway below.

"This is the VIP floor. We don't allow photographers or the press up here without an invitation and escort."

She relaxed slightly at the news, happy to have some privacy with Chase. But the privacy was short lived when she saw Jaxson and Emma arriving at the top of the stairs and heading their way. Khloe leaned in to talk softly to Chase. "I thought we could maybe go somewhere private to talk."

He cut her off, "Well, you thought wrong. You're welcome to join our table, Khloe. Cash Carter's wife will be here soon and will sit with us to watch the show. I'll introduce you around, but let me be clear. You are a guest of *ours*, not *mine*. Understand?"

She nodded just as Jaxson and Emma arrived. The four of them stood awkwardly studying each other until Jaxson finally spoke. "Hello again, Khloe. Kind of an unexpected surprise seeing you again."

She caught the annoyed peek Emma sent his way before the curvy woman stepped closer and stuck her hand out. "Don't mind him. Nice to meet you, Miss Monroe. I'm Emma."

"Khloe." She answered as they shook hands. "Nice to meet you."

"Emma!" They all swung to look at the woman shouting Emma's name.

"Samantha!" Emma ripped her hand away quickly and took off running towards the brunette heading their way. It was easy to figure out it was Mrs. Cash Carter since the singer himself was following along behind his wife, a huge grin on his face.

Jaxson and Chase followed Emma, all of them leaving Khloe to stand awkwardly alone, deserted. As she watched the friends hugging and laughing good-naturedly, a fresh pang of loneliness invaded. She might be surrounded by crowds of people everyday, yet witnessing the warmth of what was clearly love and close friendship, it only brought her own life into focus that much clearer.

I shouldn't have come here. I feel worse, not better.

She suspected they wouldn't miss her if she left. Khloe moved in the direction she'd come in and was almost to the stairs when she felt a hand on her arm, holding her back.

"Where are you going so soon?" Chase swung her around. He looked worried.

"You were right, Chase. I shouldn't have come here tonight."

He looked like he might agree, but he instead tried to convince her to stay. "You're here now. Stay. Meet Cash and Sam. Enjoy the show."

"I can't. I don't belong here." Her voice hitched with emotion. She needed to leave.

He pinned her with a serious glare. "Why did you really come?"

How could she explain it to him? She didn't really understand it herself. He pressed her. "What happened to Dean? I thought you guys were hot and heavy?"

An emotional bark of laughter escaped as she tried to hold it together. "He slipped and fell." She paused, "And his dick accidentally fell into our good friend Gloria."

His eyes widened as he whistled in surprise.

She continued, "I was lucky enough to come home just in time to watch the finale from the door of *my* bedroom. In *my* apartment. On *my* birthday. Some kinda present, eh?"

A familiar softness she'd always loved slipped into his eyes. "I'm really sorry, Khloe. That sucks."

"Yeah, it really does." She looked away, embarrassed. Jaxson and Emma kept glancing their way, distracted by Chase being away from them. That's when it hit her. All this time, she'd thought she'd had them figured out, but now she wasn't so sure. "So what's with you taking Jaxson's seconds? I know you two are friends, but I was kinda hoping you'd be wanting to have someone of your own by now, instead of sharing with him."

She half expected him to be angry at her words, but she never expected him to smile. "You haven't been paying very close attention to the gossip rags."

"Who believes anything they print?"

"Well, this time they got it right. Come on. You'll see." He took her elbow and pulled her back in the direction of the group of friends.

"Cash and Samantha, I'd like to introduce you to an old friend of mine, Khloe Monroe. Khloe, this is Cash and Samantha Carter."

She shook the singer's hand first and then his wife's. "Nice to meet you both."

"Well, I'm off. Take good care of my lady while I'm gone. I'll catch you guys after the show. Your stage manager will have a heart attack if I don't get backstage in the next few minutes."

He stopped just long enough to plant a big kiss on his wife before swatting her ass playfully and turning to leave. The group headed to the couches in the middle that would have the best view of the show about to begin. Emma and Samantha sat together on one couch and Jaxson and Chase on another leaving the only chair for her to sit alone. The women were talking excitedly about their plans for Valentine's Day the coming Tuesday.

Another day Khloe was dreading.

Jaxson interrupted them. "Ladies, do I need to remind you that you're talking about a private event with non-members present?"

Both women's eyes widened, worry seeping in.

Chase injected, "Hey, I have an idea. We're down one woman for Roulette, aren't we?"

Jaxson sent a glare his way, "Not you too?"

Chase was unfazed. "I'm serious. Just think about it for a minute. This might be a great solution."

"It's a terrible solution all the way around. She's only here one night." Jaxson was adamant.

She felt like an outsider. "What the hell are you guys talking about?"

Jaxson's, "Nothing," coincided with Chase's, "A Valentine's Day party we're throwing."

Khloe snorted. "I don't think I'll be celebrating Valentine's this year. I'd rather stay in and eat a tub of ice cream."

Chase wouldn't let it drop, only he was talking to Jaxson about it as if she wasn't even there. It kinda pissed her off.

"Think about it. Security is tight. She'll have privacy from the press and I really think she could benefit from a bit of exploration."

She wasn't sure why Jaxson seemed so pissed off, but he was. "Since when does she need our help finding men? She burns through them faster than the ink in magazines can dry."

The press was never kind to ambitious women like Khloe, but she wasn't used to having people be hostile to her face. "What the hell is your problem, Jax?"

"Chase may be nice and try to forget how you used him, but I have a better memory than he does."

Chase leaned in closer, reaching out to hold Jaxson's hand. "You're making too big of an issue about this, baby. It was years ago."

Jaxson tore his eyes away from her to look at Chase. Time stood still as the two men leaned closer, locking lips in a heated kiss that went on so long it felt like the temperature of the room was heating up. Khloe sat transfixed, shocked at the passion between the men.

When they separated, she blurted, "Wait a minute. You mean... the tabloids... that public kiss... you two really are together?"

Chase turned to look her way, his lips slightly swollen from his kiss. "No." He paused before adding. "Us *three* really are together."

It blew her mind.

Before she could recover Emma spoke to the men from her couch. "Now that we've shocked her, I'm going to agree with Chase. I think her attending is a good idea."

Chase globbed on. "It would give her the protection from the press she needs. Privacy to explore."

Emma added, "I saw the list of participants and I think she'd fit right in." Chase and Jaxson were both listening to her every word.

"Well, thanks Emma, but I don't think I need a blind date to a lame Valentine's Day party," Khloe protested.

All four of them started chuckling at her description of the event just as the house lights started to dim. Intro music had begun and someone announced the Crushing Stones were about to begin their show.

Jaxson closed the topic. "I'll think about it and we can talk about it more after the concert. I think it's time we head over to the railing so we can see Cash and the boys better. "

Khloe had the distinct feeling they were hiding something big from her, but she didn't have a chance to press them for answers before the first sounds of the Crushing Stones opening song pounded through the club. Khloe joined them at the railing, grateful for the fun distraction to help her forget about how messed up her life felt.

CHAPTER 4

"*A*re you sure this is the right address?" The same Hyatt driver from last Saturday night was dropping her off at a Georgetown psychic shop just around the corner from Runway.

She didn't think it was possible, but she was even more nervous tonight than she had been three days earlier. That was because now she was privy to the details of exactly what she'd signed up for.

Not for the first time did she chastise herself for being so reckless.

"Yes, this is the right place. I'll text you when I'm ready to leave." She waited while the driver got out and came around to her side of the luxury car, opening the door and holding out his hand to help her avoid falling on the icy sidewalk. As she was ready to walk into the shop, she turned and added nervously. "I'll either be ready to leave just after eleven or in fifteen minutes if it's a disaster."

The older driver smiled indulgently. "I'll come back for you whenever you need me, ma'am."

Khloe pushed through the door before she could second-guess her decision. The jingling bell on the entry announced her arrival in the dimly lit space. A gypsy looking woman moved to greet her with a smile.

"Hello, may I help you this evening?"

Khloe fumbled with her petite purse, pulling out a sheet of paper with a QR code on it.

"Ah, you're looking for Luis. He's right through the curtain at the back of the shop." She motioned her arm in a sweeping welcome.

"Thanks," she answered robotically. She felt like she was in a trance, inside someone else's body. She was going through the motions, determined to live dangerously despite the anxiety nipping at her.

Behind the curtain a large Hispanic man stood guard. The only thing more remarkable than his bulging muscles was the long scar on his cheek.

"Invitation paperwork please, miss." She held out the slip of paper with the QR code. He reviewed her paperwork, before speaking. "Welcome, Miss Monroe. At your request, once you are inside the club, you'll be referred to as The Princess." He opened a door and motioned to her. "Please step down these stairs and follow the tunnel until you get to the next door. Danny will be there to assist you."

She felt wobbly on her high-heels. The steps were concrete and the walls of the tunnel were lit with the occasional lamp that cast eerie shadows. The space was cold and creepy, reminding her of the over-the-top activities she might be asked to participate in tonight.

She was a novice at best in the BDSM lifestyle, having dabbled with a boyfriend or two over the years. Going online to sign up for the event had been an eye opener for her. She'd had to Google several times to even figure out what activities would be offered. Then, she'd found there weren't nearly enough opportunities to put hard limits in the sign-up process. There was a very good possibility she'd be using her safeword tonight. She'd listed blood, needle, and fire play on her absolutely no-fucking-way list, but there had been at least six more kinks she'd wanted to list, but finally settled on putting cell popping, knowing she couldn't have someone mark her body, even temporarily. She needed to be back on set the following Sunday and the hard-ass director wouldn't take kindly to her having visible marks on her body that he'd have to shoot around.

She was grateful to finally get to a heavy, nondescript door. A welcome rush of warm air greeted her as she pulled the door open to find herself in a large room lit with glowing recessed lights. More than one wall was covered with small lockers. A cute guy stood in the center of the room behind a tall counter.

"Good evening. May I help you?"

"Em, I think so." Khloe handed him the now crumpled paper she'd been clutching nervously on her walk.

The guard scanned her paper. "Welcome to Black Light, Miss Monroe. I'm afraid I'll need to see a photo identification, please."

His request caught her off guard. Sure the website had warned her to bring her ID, but as a celebrity, most people tended to let her pass. Still, she presented her New York driver's license.

"Thank you." After he assured himself she was indeed Khloe Monroe, he reached to an iPad and within seconds she heard a locker to her left pop as it sprung open. "Please take off your coat and leave it here in your locker along with your purse and all electronics including your cell phone. No cameras or recording devices are allowed on the floor."

She didn't like being separated from her cell phone. It was her lifeline out of here if she needed to bug out.

"I'm sure Chase and Jaxson won't mind if I…"

He held up his hand like a stop sign. "No exceptions. Not even for Mr. Cartwright and Mr. Davidson."

Khloe hesitated, briefly considering leaving, but knowing she'd regret not going in to at least check out the club, even if she did leave before the event started.

After she reluctantly had everything secured, she headed towards the door marked Black Light. She was about to enter when two handsome men arrived and were greeted by the security guy.

"Welcome back Congressman Masterson. Senator Kane."

Chase had assured her there would be many high-profile members in attendance and that she wouldn't stand out. She was relieved to find it might be the truth. Still, when she caught the men staring at her, she fled through the door, too nervous to strike up a conversation.

By the time she was ten feet inside the club, though, she knew she'd just jumped from the frying pan into the fire.

Everywhere she looked, debauchery greeted her. She stood rooted to her spot, gawking at the sexy environment so long that the two politicians entered and caught up to her.

"Well, look what we have here. I sure hope you were waiting for me to join you, darling." The two men wore business suits as if they'd just come from starring in a C-span special. The younger of the two dared touch her arm, attaching himself to her without her permission.

She felt the heat creeping up her neck. Before she could react to send them on their way, a roving server stopped to offer champagne. "Hello, sir. Happy to have you back at Black Light."

"Thanks, darling." He grabbed a flute and handed it to Khloe who wasted no time in downing the drink. She'd finished before he brought his own flute to his lips. She yanked free with enough velocity that his bubbly sloshed down onto his boring grey tie. "Shit." He pulled his arm free of her elbow to swish at the spill.

Khloe jumped at the chance to scurry away from the men, ignoring his cursing as she pushed forward into the crowd. Only when she was away from them did it occur to her that the man she'd just pissed off might be playing Roulette tonight.

My luck he'll roll me and take out his anger on my ass.

It took all her bravery to keep putting one foot in front of the other, weaving through the provocative scenes and socializing couples towards the main stage across the room. Snippets of tantalizing interludes already in progress were the sound track to the salacious event about to be underway.

If she'd been horrified or even frightened, she would have spun and left, but there was no denying the atmosphere had her heart pounding hard enough to make her feel light headed. A nameless need pulsed inside her, partly centered in her panties, but if she were honest with herself, it went deeper than that. She didn't know what to call this longing and she had absolutely no clue how to quench it. All she knew was it had been building for months, and spending the last few days holed up in her hotel room, researching all of the diabolical activities that would be on the roulette wheel that night, the need had magnified until she could think of little else.

Like it or not, Black Light was like a homing beacon, drawing her deeper like a magnetic pull. She just prayed she'd be brave enough to see it through.

Three hours. You can do anything for three hours.

Khloe took a couple of deep breaths as she approached the stage and caught her first peek of Chase. He looked amazing in his tuxedo. Happy. Relaxed. She also couldn't miss the love shining from him as he leaned in to talk privately to Jaxson, the two men sharing a private moment in the otherwise crowded room.

"Good evening, Princess. Please make your way to stage right near the steps to the stage. All of the submissives are congregating there." It was a man full of muscles wearing a staff T-shirt directing participants.

She managed to nod, catching sight of a group of nervous looking women, and suspecting she looked as anxious as they did. While a few chatted with friends, the majority stood silently as Chase climbed the set of stairs on the opposite side of the stage, knowing Roulette was about to begin. Khloe said a small prayer that she didn't end up being a pawn in the game about to begin, easily sacrificed by a dominant too impatient to put up with her inexperience.

A woman yelling profanity had everyone spinning towards the exit where she saw the congressman who'd tried to talk with her physically dragging the screaming woman out of the club. Two employees stepped in to arbitrate the scene. More interested in the internal turmoil happening, Khloe tried to focus on Chase and the coming event. Only when the very woman who'd been screaming stepped into the middle of the group of submissives, still cursing her ex-husband, did she start to understand the dynamics at play.

A few seconds later, Chase was center stage as the lights in the room dimmed and spotlights lit up the portion of the stage they would be using for roulette.

"Ladies and gentlemen, welcome to Black Light. I'd like to introduce myself first. I'm Chase Cartwright, and I'm one of the owners here. Jaxson, Emma, and I would like to wish you all a very happy Valentine's Day, and to thank you for choosing to spend the night here with us — enjoying the first of what we hope will become an annual event, Valentine Roulette."

The room that had hushed as his introduction began broke out into a round of excited applause. When the clapping ebbed, Chase continued. "I would like to start by thanking those of you who have come here tonight as participants. I'm sure it must be a bit nerve wracking signing up to play a game where you don't know exactly who you'll be playing with or even what activities you'll be asked to participate in."

She tried to pay attention to his words, but she was too nervous. Bits and pieces of his instructions of when to come forward and how to roll got through, but the majority of her attention was on the group of men gathered at the other set of stairs, trying to read them.

One of the dominants she was watching called out, "What about time for aftercare? Do we have any time between scenes for that?"

She liked that he was concerned for the submissive's safety and made a mental note to be relieved if he rolled her as his partner.

Too soon, Chase called the men to the stage, motioning for them to join him via the stairs. Her heart rate went up with each minute that passed as her ex-boyfriend had the men first line up and then draw numbers to decide the order of the game.

She had a better look at the dominants now that they were in the light. She quickly put the men into three categories with River Trubach from the Crushing Stones and a handsome guy who looked a bit like a Greek god in her most hopeful play-partner pile. The vast majority of the men she couldn't tell enough to know which end of the continuum they belonged in, but there were two men who absolutely scared the shit out of her. They didn't break a smile. They didn't look nervous. They simply looked like predators.

The scariest of them had actually started staring at her as if she would be his next meal. She made up her mind to safeword immediately if the wheel was cruel enough to pair them together.

"Alright, then. Let's begin. Would the dominant with number one step forward?" Mr. Greek-god himself stepped forward. Khloe wasn't crazy about the idea of being chosen first, but she held her breath, hoping Chase would call out 'The Princess' when the ball stopped on the wheel. She exhaled in disappointment when he announced, "Marty, the wheel has chosen you."

The tallest among them separated herself from the women and started towards the stairs.

It's okay. There are plenty others left for you.

Her hope renewed when River jumped forward to take the second roll of the night. When the wheel chose Daddy's Girl instead of Princess, a real panic started to settle into Khloe's chest. She forced herself to take deep breaths to stay calm.

Her resolve went out the window the second the scariest looking guy on the stage stepped forward to roll third. As he moved into the direct spotlight, she caught a glimpse of his steely eyes staring directly at her. His hair was cut short and the streaks of silver at his temples gave him a distinguished and authoritative aura.

Chase called him Mr. Helms as he thrust the marble into the Dom's hand, giving the wheel a spin. Time seemed to stand still, until Chase started looking through the group of women, searching for someone. Her heart lurched when his gaze stopped on her. There was a buzz in her ears almost preventing her from hearing his announcement. "Mr. Helms has rolled The Princess."

Khloe panicked. There had to be a mistake. She turned to the other women, glancing around in shock. "Oh, come on. Surely one of you put The Princess as your name too, right? I mean, he couldn't have rolled me. He just… couldn't… have…" Her voice trailed off when it was clear every woman was staring at her with relief in their eyes that they hadn't drawn the guy who could win the 'scariest dom' award for the night.

"I'd get on up here now, if you know what's good for you, Miss Monroe." His authoritative voice carried easily across the space between them, sounding as uncompromising as he looked.

She spun to face him, anger flaring. "Hey! He can't use my real name!" she protested.

Chase sent him a dirty look, but didn't come to her defense. She shot him a look that could kill a lesser man, shaking her head in disbelief, as she stood grounded, refusing to move forward.

The word 'red' sat at the end of her tongue, ready to fly out of her mouth. Before she used it, she instead demanded they re-roll to choose another submissive for the Dom. Chase shook his head apologetically, refusing to accommodate her wish.

When Mr. Helms stalked towards to the stairs as if he were going to drag her up on the stage with force, her feet finally moved. Khloe spun and started racing towards the exit, which was easier said than done. Cocktail tables full of spectators were in the walkway, slowing her down. She heard the commotion behind her and knew instinctively he was chasing after her. In a brief moment of clarity, she felt like Little Red Riding Hood, being chased by the big bad wolf through the dense woods.

She didn't even make it half way to the door before muscular arms snatched her. One arm wrapped around her waist, yanking her to an abrupt stop. His other hand jammed into her long hair, snapping her head back so far it hurt. He squeezed her so hard that the last pockets of air left her, leaving her gasping while he ground his hips against her lower back, pressing his steely erection against her so hard she couldn't have ignored it if she tried.

She'd expected him to yell at her, but he instead placed his lips against the shell of her left ear, his gravelly voice low enough for her ears only. "You're not getting away from me, Miss Monroe. I won you fair and square. You may not know me, but believe me when I tell you you'll be glad we met in three hours. I may not know why you're here yet, but I'm gonna make it my mission to find out and give you exactly what you need before you leave here tonight." He paused, releasing her slightly. "Take a deep breath." When she didn't comply he barked. "Now."

Her body obeyed, gasping for precious air as he continued on.

"That's it. I feel you squirming against me. You've got an itch that needs to be scratched, don't you? Well, I'm your man. Just so you know, if you leave now, you'll be walking away from the best sex of your life."

Khloe fought to think. Fear warred with curiosity, turning her into a jumbled mess. Who was this guy? So conceited. So sure of himself. So strong. He smelled amazing and his hard appendage grinding against her promised a one-way ride to heaven.

His hand against her stomach moved higher, molding against her right breast, massaging her. He squeezed so hard pain shot through her body, making her feel more alive than she'd possibly ever felt.

"Be brave." He finally closed the deal with his promise. "Let me take care of you tonight, baby."

No one was more surprised than her when he suddenly released her. She gasped for another breath, keeping her eye on the door in the distance.

She could leave. She'd never have to see anyone in this room ever again, including Chase Cartwright. She could chalk the whole night up to a failed experiment and drag herself back to New York and lick her wounds there until she had to leave for L.A. on Sunday.

A tanned hand came into view. He was offering the chance to choose him. To choose adventure. To pursue the nebulous desire draining her daily as she chased after something she couldn't name.

She didn't remember making the decision. All she knew was her hand reached for his, locking them together just before he gently pulled her back into motion, this time back towards the stage where the roulette wheel would decide how they would spend the next three hours.

CHAPTER 5

*R*yder was stunned she'd followed him back to the stage. He hadn't had nearly enough time yet to study her to understand what made her tick. He'd taken a hell of a chance, hoping to push the right buttons to make her want to stay. She could have just as easily screamed 'red' and be half way back to her hotel by now.

He'd wanted her from the moment he saw her in the small crowd of subs congregating near the stage. It wasn't because she was famous. He could give a shit about that. It wasn't even because she was easily the most beautiful woman in attendance that night, but she was.

No. What had caught his attention was her complete lack of protocol while she looked around the BDSM club, clearly out of her element. Most of the subs wore skimpy outfits he suspected lured in play partners on a normal basis. They fought to look cool, like they had things under control.

One look at Khloe Monroe, and he knew she was completely in over her head. He was curious how she'd found herself a participant in the night's entertainment. She emanated fear mingled with an almost palpable desperation he found himself anxious to explore. Screw winning a month's free membership. *She* was too sweet of a prize to turn down. He looked forward to playing hard with his trophy for the evening. As they walked back to the stage, he made it his personal challenge to push her as hard as possible without making her safeword.

Khloe wore a tight-fitted sweater dress, just modest enough to hide all of her best bits, but dipping low enough to show the ample swell of her breasts. She'd filled his palm perfectly when he'd clamped down to stop her from leaving. It had taken all of his self-control to keep from biting her neck as he'd held her stationary. There would be time for biting later.

Once on stage, she took the marble from the emcee, but then froze staring at the spinning wheel in a trance. He placed his hand at the small of her back with the lightest touch, urging her to drop the ball that would shape the next three hours. She responded beautifully. He stepped closer to watch the marble spin and fall into the absolute best slot he could hope for.

"Mr. Helms and his Princess will be starting at the medical play station this evening." The crowd buzzed at the news as Khloe visibly shivered. Of course she had no way of knowing how much real life practice he'd had with the very activity they were about to play out. If she'd known, he had no doubt she'd be running for the door again.

They took their place waiting with the other couples. There were still many couples to be paired up, but Ryder didn't waste time waiting to start his dominance over his prize. When she tried to shuffle away from him towards the stairs, he grabbed her by her hips and yanked her back against his chest. He felt her bones protruding, making sharp handles he used to subdue her. She was too thin.

If she were mine, I'd see that she put on some weight. I prefer soft handles to grab onto as I fuck.

Still, she molded to him as if they were puzzle pieces locking together. He felt her wobbling on her too-high heels, fighting to keep her distance from him, but falling helplessly against his chest instead. He spoke against her ear again. "Stay still. Eyes forward. Think about how I'm going to examine every inch of your body as soon as they get through assigning activities."

Khloe released a distressed gurgle as she tried to pull away, but he easily held her stationary. He listened impatiently as couples were matched up and assigned their first sexual activity for the night, but the second the ceremony portion of the night was complete, he started pushing his captive ahead of him towards his bag of goodies waiting near the exit of the stage. She half-heartedly tried to pull away from him, but he held her tighter. Despite her lame protests, she trembled, no doubt in part due to fear, but he was equally sure she had a deep-seated need she was suppressing.

He released her hip to grab his leather duffle bag, but she took the opportunity to wrench away. He needed to nip her skittish behavior in the bud right away. They only had three hours and he didn't want to spend it continuously convincing her to turn herself over to him. The sooner she realized he owned her for the next three hours, the better off they would both be.

Ryder dropped his bag and moved into action. They were only a few feet from the back wall of the stage. She was wafer-thin. Despite her trying to dig her heels in, it was too easy to propel forward until her chest pressed against the unforgiving wall. He applied all his weight to her body to sandwich her as he delivered his message. "If you came here for a polite Dom who would baby you, Princess, and check in on you every thirty seconds, you're going to be disappointed. You might as well safeword now." He stepped back, spinning her before pushing her back against the wall so he could look into her wide doe-like eyes. She was drowning in fear. Had he been under-cover, he'd have congratulated himself on a job well done, but tonight he was playing a delicate game of cat and mouse. He didn't want to lose his prey just yet. He needed to sweeten the deal.

He towered over her by at least six inches, despite her stupidly tall heels. Her pupils were dilated. Her breathing uneven. She opened and closed her mouth like a guppy; unable to speak the word he suspected was on her tongue.

He took action. His mouth crashed over hers in a passionate kiss meant to steal the word 'red.' It worked like a charm. Maybe too well. As his sub-for-the-night melted into his arms, he found himself equally affected by her responsive body. Even the taste of her cherry lipstick and minty breath turned him on until he lost sight of his end goal.

When she broke the kiss to gasp for air, he moved lower. His mouth sought out the tender spot where her neck met her shoulder blade, using his tongue to first taste her before biting down just hard enough to seal his possession further. He felt her collapse against him when he started sucking her neck, hopefully leaving his mark while turning Khloe into a pile of putty in his hands. He could smell the evidence of her arousal wafting up between them.

Yes, Miss Monroe is in desperate need of a good hard fuck. Lucky for her, I'm just the man for the job.

Time was wasting, but before he moved them towards the medical section, he wanted to seal her cooperation. Ryder cupped her flushed face, holding her stationary so she couldn't look away. "I want you to trust me, Princess. I know it's hard since we just met, but I promise you a few things." He paused to make sure she was listening. "If you submit to me, you'll be rewarded. Obey and I'll deliver more pleasure than you even thought possible." He pressed against her harder to deliver the remainder of his promise. "But fight me, and you'll find I know how to deliver pain equally well. Defiance will be punished. Swiftly and thoroughly. Understand?"

She tried to turn her head away, but he was too strong. She resorted to slamming her eyes closed to shut him out while her breathing became ragged. He gave her a few long seconds to contemplate before pressing her again.

"One final promise." He waited until she opened her expressive eyes. They drew him in. He could lose himself in them if he let it happen. "I hope you'll turn yourself over to me for the next three hours. I'll help you explore parts of yourself you've never confronted before, and push you to do things you never dreamed possible. But I promise to honor your safeword. You say red and it all stops. You believe me, don't you, Khloe?"

Her eyes widened at his use of her real name. He got the feeling few people took the time to see the real woman who was Khloe Monroe, instead choosing to see just another public persona.

Her words were so soft he almost missed them. "What if you scare me?"

Ryder chuckled, genuinely surprised at her question. "Baby, I'd be disappointed if you weren't at least a little afraid. I'll let you in on a little secret. That's part of the turn on for me."

"But, what if I can't handle it? I've never… I mean… I'm not… shit." She was flustered.

It must be the club setting. There was no other explanation for his sudden urge to hug her closer and comfort her until she calmed. That wouldn't help with their first scene at all. Instead, Ryder settled on reassuring her verbally. "You've never scened before. I know. Do you have any experience at all in the lifestyle?"

She shook her head from side to side slowly.

"How the hell did you end up in the Roulette event?"

She glanced around as if she'd just remembered something, finally returning her gaze to him. "I'm an old friend of Chase and Jaxson's."

That explained a lot. "Well then, you should be able to trust they won't let anything too bad happen to you, now would they?" She didn't look very convinced, telling him they hadn't been that close of friends after all. "Are you ready to turn yourself over?"

He waited almost a full minute for her answer. "Don't do any damage to my face or my hair. I have to be on camera in less than a week."

He'd take it as her consent. "Deal."

Only when he turned to head down the stairs towards their first scene did he realize they'd had a large audience waiting for the outcome of their private conversation. As they moved away from the stage, he could see pockets of observers spread out throughout the club floor, congregating around scenes getting underway. The group following behind him and Khloe was substantially larger, he was sure due to her star power. The crowd would work to his favor, adding a deeper level of embarrassed humiliation for his novice submissive.

Ryder had admired the medical setup the weekend before when his friend Spencer had given him a short tour of the club. He'd been impressed that Black Light had purchased all the right equipment and then some. He was no expert on the BDSM club scene, but to him, they'd earned their enormous fees and reputation as *the* place to play for discriminating dominants and submissives.

He led her by the hand to the medical room where an ominous

padded table waited for them. He doubted an inexperienced sub like Khloe picked up on the hidden amenities of the setting, but to the trained operative, he couldn't wait to get started.

First things first. He reached into his bag and pulled out a bottle of water, thrusting it into her trembling hands. "Drink. All of it."

"Excuse me?" She looked disoriented, exactly how he wanted her.

"I don't want you dehydrated. I'm gonna push you hard. Don't move. Just drink."

He waited for her to unscrew the top and take a tentative first swig before he turned, returning to his bag of goodies and pulling out a few items he would be using soon. He looked back to nod silent encouragement for her to keep drinking while he went to a rolling cabinet against the back wall of the room. He found everything he'd hoped they would stock.

When he returned to his Princess, she had only drank half the bottle. "You don't listen very well. I said all of it."

"I don't want…"

"I don't give a shit what you want, Khloe. I give orders. You follow them or are punished. Understand?"

Her eyes flared, anger and fear warring. He reached out to grab her upper arms and shake her slightly. "Answer me. Understood?"

She whispered, "Yes."

"Yes, sir. Repeat again, properly," he coached sternly.

"Yes, sir."

"Good girl. We'll get you trained yet. Drink."

This time he let his hands fall lower to grab around her waist, holding her, watching her while she struggled to drink the last half of the bottle of water. She was wasting precious time, but he did have a method to his madness. He knew she'd be protesting harder if she had any clue of his plans.

He took the empty bottle and tossed it towards his own bag of goodies when she finished.

"Hair and face, right?" He pressed her.

"Yes, but…"

He pulled the small set of scissors from his pocket and before she could pull away, cut a one-inch slit in the low-cut bodice of her sweater dress. He grabbed each half of the opening and yanked hard, ripping the fabric all the way down to her navel in one pull. As tempting as it was to get his first glimpse of her nude flesh, Ryder kept his eyes trained on her eyes, enjoying first her surprise and then anger finishing on fear shining back at him.

While she stood in shock, he ripped the remaining fabric, using the scissors again to cut where the hem of her dress refused to tear. He spread the material wide, finally glancing down for his first peek at her perfect body.

Christ, she had fucking Barbie-doll proportions; ample breasts, a wafer thin waist spreading to wide hips. An hourglass of perfection for those who liked that sort of thing. He'd personally prefer a bit more flesh to hold on to, but that was just him.

"You can't do this," she protested lamely.

"I just did."

"I mean, there have to be some rules..."

His hands clamped down on her bare waist to hold her immobile before cutting her off. "There are only a few rules I give a shit about. One, I'm your Dom. You're my submissive for the next few hours and that means I can do whatever the hell I want with you, when I want and how I want. You obey, you'll be rewarded in ways you never even knew were possible. You don't, you'll regret it. It's that simple."

She snorted a nervous chuckle, but he watched her body language carefully, using his extensive training to read her as if she were spouting out her inner most desires. He briefly remembered she was an actress by trade and wondered if perhaps she was playing him, but for three hours, he honestly didn't care. He was having the most fun he'd had in years.

Her eyes spoke volumes. It was almost too easy. "It's okay. I know why you're here, Princess."

She had a bit of fight left in her and he adored her all the more for it. "That's rich, since I don't have the first fucking clue on that myself."

He knew she told the truth and something he didn't want to name pulled at his conscience. "Then let me help you." When she didn't protest, he pushed on. "You're desperate for someone to actually look *inside* you. Not at you. Not like all your fans do, barely scratching the surface. No, what you want more than anything is to be the center of someone's entire universe."

Her eyes widened, sparking with a longing he'd seen many times on women over the years. A longing he normally fed just long enough to get what he wanted out of them before moving on. He felt obliged to warn her. "I'm going to be that person for the next three hours. You'll be the center of my universe, but be warned. I'll give you a taste, but that's all I have to give."

She broke their visual connection to look around wildly. He suspected he'd struck a chord and she was panicking at his direct hit. Not for the first time, he sensed she was lost. Floundering. His methods may be unconventional, but he knew he could help her, if only she'd turn herself over to him. It was a positive sign that she'd held off calling red.

His thumb caressed her flat stomach as he pulled her closer again, moving one hand to her hair, yanking her head back so she had no choice but to look him in the eyes. "Ready, Princess?"

Her nod was minuscule, but was enough to move him back into action. His hands moved to her dress, pushing the now two pieces over her shoulders, letting the heavy winter fabric fall to a pool at her feet.

"Have you ever been a Victoria's Secret model?" He saw a slight shake of her head. "Too bad." His hand cupped her mounds camouflaged by the lacy black bra, letting his thumbs tease the peaks. "I'll get a closer look in a minute. For now, let's get you up on the examination table."

He grabbed the fabric at the valley of her breasts, yanking her to follow behind him as he moved to the center of the room. She almost ran to keep up with him in her spiked heels. As soon as they were close enough, he turned to scoop her up, his arms under her knees and back to lift her so she lay prone on the leather padded top.

Before she could protest, he moved to the head of the table, pulling the leather wrist cuffs from under the table and making quick work of securing her arms above her head. By the time she understood she was now his captive, he had already pulled the two-inch wide leather strap from under the table and was buckling it across her tummy. The water hadn't made it through her system yet, but soon enough, the strap would be pressing her, demanding she expel the excess liquid.

When he reached under the table to pull the stirrups into her line of sight, Khloe moved into full meltdown mode, kicking wildly to avoid him capturing her ankles, trying her best to buck her hips off the table to escape and tiring herself out in the process. He worked silently, knowing his silence would be more intimidating than words. He moved with purpose, methodically unzipping her left fashion boot and removing it and the small sock she'd worn. When she continued to try to kick free, Ryder slapped the inside of her bare thigh. It wasn't a particularly hard spank, but it subdued her nonetheless.

"That's it. Be a good girl. You have no choice in the matter. I will examine you. All you have to do is lay back and submit."

Her eyes searched the space, too frantic to appreciate the possibilities of her position yet.

Once he had both legs bared and secured, Ryder stepped back to admire his captive. He watched her reaction as he spread the stirrups wider, splitting her open uncomfortably. Khloe's chest heaved up and down from the table as she gasped for calming breaths.

"Now that I have you where I want you, I have a few questions for you. You'll answer or be punished. Understand?"

He knew she wasn't really listening. She wasn't focused enough yet. His palm landing on her other inner thigh helped. "Answer yes, sir if you understand."

Her small "yes, sir" went straight to his aching cock. She was fucking perfect.

"Very good. Now, tell me Princess. I assume you've read all of the Disney classics? Did you choose your nickname tonight because you wanted to be like a princess?" He could see her confusion. "Well I've got news for you. The only princess I'll be treating you as tonight will be Sleeping Beauty." Her eyes widened telling him what he wanted to know. "I see you've read Anne Rice's version, haven't you? It's okay, you don't need to answer. I see it in your eyes. You know exactly what kind of royalty you'll be treated like tonight, don't you?"

Beautiful tears pooled in her pleading eyes. This was where he differed from every other man in the room. The other BDSM play partners would read her fear and back down from it. But he didn't dabble in the BDSM lifestyle. He didn't play. He fucking owned it. He lived on the edge and tonight, he'd be taking Khloe Monroe to the edge with him.

"What if I can't do it?" Her voice was surprisingly calm for a captive.

He hesitated, not wanting to push too hard too fast. "Then do us both a favor and safeword right now." She was tempted, but pushed down her fear.

"Ready Princess?"

"What should I call you?"

"My name is Ryder, but tonight, just call me Master."

CHAPTER 6

hloe had never felt so alive. It was like every cell of her body was on high alert, ready to do her master's bidding. It was ridiculous, really. Who the fuck did he think he was? They'd known each other all of thirty minutes, so it was ridiculous to recognize she hadn't felt this level of intimacy with anyone ever before. The novelty of it made her brave enough to see where it would take her.

He'd assured her he'd stop if she cried out red and, despite his harsh treatment, she believed him. And while she was under no delusion that Chase had any romantic feelings for her, she knew he wouldn't let anything truly dangerous happen to her. Those were the only reasons she was able to get her excited breathing under control.

His name was Ryder. Her eyes tracked him as he moved around the perimeter of the room, collecting up any number of diabolical items he planned to use on her body. There was something about him that fascinated her. She couldn't put her finger on it, but she suspected it had to do with the fact that he was the first person in a long time whom she felt wasn't interested in her as an actress. He didn't seem to care about how much money she made or how famous she was. As fucked up as the game they were playing was, it felt real.

There were very few things in her life that she could say that about.

Before they really got started, a loud commotion could be heard across the club as a woman screamed, "Red!" at the top of her lungs. She turned, trying to see what was happening. Even from the distance, she recognized the last couple to be matched. Congressman Masterson and his ex-wife were not doing too well with their Pet Play kink.

Ryder raised an eyebrow when she looked back at him. "I'd stay focused on your own predicament if I were you, little girl."

She suspected that was good advice.

Khloe tugged at her restraints, testing to see if she had any wiggle room and strangely relieved when she found little. He'd left her lying flat, thankfully, as she didn't want to see the growing crowd that had gathered around inside the doorway and even the cutout window, supplied so voyeurs could watch the famous actress be dominated by the scariest of the roulette dominants.

Her bubble of self-confidence burst when he approached between her legs and held up what looked like a sharp scalpel. Survival instincts kicked in and she did her best to flail in her bonds, fighting to be free.

"That's it, baby. Try to fight me. I love it." Holy shit if she didn't see the truth in his eyes as he held the sharp implement closer for her to get a good look.

"Sonofabitch," she cried out.

"That's one. I'm Master or Sir. Any other names will earn you a punishment. Now, I'd hold still if I were you."

"I don't like this!" she countered.

"There are no rules that say you have to like anything. You just have to obey."

Her struggles were fruitless, but she didn't stop until he volleyed a few sharp swats to her exposed inner thighs with his palm. The embarrassment was worse than the pain.

"You're a real prince, you know that?"

"Oh baby, don't I know it." He moved around next to her and reached out to pull up the fabric of her bra between her boobs. He waited until she looked into his eyes to reply. "Here's the thing. You have princes chasing you daily, yet you're at Black Light, looking for something you can't even name. Now, hold perfectly still unless you want to turn this into a blood play scene."

Khloe held her breath while she felt him brush the dull edge of the scalpel across her skin just before situating it at her bra and pulling up to let the blade slice through the lace. The tension now released, the fabric flew apart, exposing her mounds and protruding nipples to her captor. He took his time admiring her, reaching to cup her bare breast, pinching the tight tip between his thumb and middle finger until she moaned.

She knew her panties would come off next, but the Dom used the electronic controls on the diabolical table to first move the head of the table upright, bending her at the tummy and also allowing the crowd to now witness her expressions. The only saving grace was that the spotlight above the table was bright enough to make it difficult to see out into the audience. She needed to pretend they weren't there. Instead, she turned her attention back to the man now standing between her widely spread legs. There was open lust in his eyes that made her feel powerful.

"Hold still," he ordered. She complied, wanting him to draw blood even less than he did.

Her panties fell away, ruined, leaving her completely bare. A palpable electric charge zinged in the air as his gaze devoured her bare pussy.

"What a shame. You're already bald. I was looking forward to shaving you before your examination." He let his fingers brush through her folds, coming into the lightest of contact with her clit. Christ, if only he'd pay attention there a bit longer, she'd be a puddle of goo. Instead, he yanked his hand away before she could enjoy it. She groaned in frustration.

"Lucky for you, I have extensive experience with medical examinations. Well, medical torture to be more precise."

It was as if the restraints had a way of dulling her brain as sure as they subdued her body. His words sunk in too late. Ryder had already sat down on a rolling stool as if he were preparing to stay there a while when the word torture registered. His next words were worse. "I've learned that unless I want to get pissed on halfway through the exam, I need to insert a catheter now to get you nice and cleaned out."

Humor danced in his eyes and she hated him in that moment. He was enjoying her humiliation entirely too much.

"Are you nuts? That isn't sexy!" she cried out.

"Oh, baby, I beg to differ. I'll tell you what. Why don't we ask the spectators gathering around us and see what they think?"

She gurgled in frustration as he wheeled closer.

"But you aren't a doctor!" she countered.

"Oh, and you know that, do you?" He was donning latex gloves and she had to admit, looking rather doctorly in a hot kind of way.

Like most warm-blooded women, she'd had naughty fantasies of a diabolical doctor taking liberties with her while she was spread help-lessly before him. It was supposed to be fodder for masturbating, not something that happened in real life.

She hated that he'd inclined the table to give her a front row seat to what he had planned. She watched as he touched her pussy, lightly caressing her slick lips and drawing an involuntary groan. She was stretched taut, unable to stop him when his thumb circled her nubbin, pressing hard enough to light her up with an electric energy, but not near hard enough to get her off. He inserted two fingers next, curling with her body as he pressed on her lower tummy exactly like her own OBGYN did in her annual exam.

She watched in fascination as he pulled a small tray on wheels closer. He opened a sterilized package containing a long stick with a medicated swab at the end. She supposed she should be grateful that the soft tip was cool as he used it to clean her lady bits where he planned to insert the catheter, ensuring she wouldn't be exposed to an infection.

He unwrapped the catheter next, stopping to dip it in lubrication before placing the tip against her urethra opening. Only then did he look up to pin her with a dominant glare. His steel-grey eyes danced with an excitement that made him even more handsome.

He didn't need to tell her to hold still. She couldn't have moved if she wanted to. He waited long enough that the sounds of the crowd surrounding them broke through their private connection, reminding Khloe she was about to be catheterized in front of dozens of strangers.

Khloe felt the unforgiving tube pinch as Ryder pushed it inside her. She'd expected pain, but found it didn't hurt per se, but she was aware of it invading her body. She watched enthralled as Ryder fed the tubing deeper into her body until yellow urine filled the tube to the stopper. Still, he pressed forward another few inches.

It was as he was attaching the collection bag and hanging it on a metal hook near her left arm that she felt the first burn where the tubing sat inside her. It was as if he'd warmed the catheter before inserting it, which she knew hadn't happened. With each passing second, the burning grew more uncomfortable until she was wiggling her ass as if she could somehow get away from the sensation, which of course was ridiculous.

Khloe turned her attention on the bag hanging beside her, watching it fill with her bright yellow urine, trying to keep her mind off the growing discomfort of the slow burn.

"I see the warming jelly is doing its job," he added with a sadistic grin. "Let's see how it does with the speculum."

He added a new dollop of the gel to the metal instrument that looked more heavy duty than any she'd seen at her own doctor's office. He inserted the cold implement fast and deep and then pulled it out. In again. Out. Slowly fucking her with the diabolical device. If he was trying to upset her, he was failing. Even with the burning gel, it felt fucking fantastic. He must have realized it, too, because he finally left the metal buried inside her just before using its design to splay her open uncomfortably for his examination.

"It's too much!"

The doctor-wanna-be ignored her complaint. "Very nice. Very nice, indeed." The heat was worse with the speculum as he'd used much more of the wicked gel. She couldn't help but thrust her hips up and down the few inches of movement she had available as warmth turned to heat turned to burn.

"Ooh. Owie. It's too hot!" she protested. Instead of removing the offending device, he instead dabbed a quarter-sized glob directly on his gloved finger and without warning, inserted his digit as deep into her bowels as it would go.

"Noooo!" She wiggled as much as the restraints allowed, which wasn't much. She'd never been into anal play, so having his finger shoved where the sun didn't shine unhinged her.

"That's it, baby. Buck for me. It turns me on big time."

"You sonofabitch!"

"Tsk. Tsk. I warned you about being disrespectful. I'm afraid I'll need to punish you to help you remember to call me Master or Sir. I was going to just do a quick exam. Instead, we'll have to take it to the next level, won't we?" His words were harsh, but she could swear he was almost smiling with glee at the thought of punishing her.

She had no idea what the hell that meant, but she didn't want to know. She slammed her eyes closed, trying her best to breathe through the not entirely bad sensations bombarding her body. The first moments of panic coincided with the insertion of a long, thin plug in her ass. She opened her eyes just in time to see the final inches disappear inside her.

The burn was intensifying in all of her private parts. Her clit, pussy, and anus throbbed in beat with her heart. Despite how she wanted to feel about his rough treatment, her body had a mind of its own. Her Dom for the night stood, taking off his latex gloves and leaving her to suffer in silence while he returned to the cabinet for new supplies.

His form no longer shielded her naked body from the growing crowd pressing in around the openings to the room, anxious to watch the actress and sadist square off. Most of the crowd was just a blob of shadows in the distance, but the spotlight illuminating the medical table sprayed wide enough that she could make out a few faces in the front rows. One submissive was on her knees, sucking off her Dom while he watched with interest. Another sub was folded over a cocktail table, her ass bared as her Dom pounded her from behind while they both watched the medical torture in progress.

Khloe's eyes met the sub being plowed. They held their connection with Khloe getting more jealous with each pounding second that passed. Her own pussy throbbed with heated need and neglect.

"Don't worry, Princess. If you're a good girl, you'll get pounded exactly like her before the night is over. That's what you want, isn't it?"

He'd startled her, leaning in to whisper in her ear as they both watched the show in progress. She couldn't form words her need was so intense.

"That's okay. You'll be screaming for me to fuck you before too long. But first, I can't trust you to be respectful. Your punishment will be to be gagged so you can't slip up again. If you're a good girl, I'll only leave it in for ten minutes this first time. The next time you call me something other than Master or Sir, I'll leave in for twenty minutes. I sure hope you're a fast learner."

He thrust a squishy red ball into her restrained hand above her head. Her fingers tingled from being raised and held immobile for so long.

It wasn't until the huge dildo in a harness came into view that Khloe understood his intention. One of the only parts of her body left relatively unrestrained was her head. She fought like a wildcat, thrashing her head from side to side, trying her best to avoid the inevitable. Unfortunately, her Master wasn't afraid to grab her by her hair, subduing her long enough to get the thick tip of the rubber gag against her lips.

"I'm gonna count to three. I expect you to open wide before I hit three or you will regret it. One way or another, the penis gag is going in. The only question will be if you want this small one or the extra large one I have in my own bag. I'll be happy to retrieve it if you'd prefer."

Their eyes locked in a stand off. She wanted to hate him for the depraved things he was doing to her body, but she'd never been as turned on in her entire life. He had hooked her. Now he was reeling her in. She would see the night through if for no other reason than to have the devastatingly handsome man currently controlling her fate scratch her needy itch.

"One." She looked down at the gag he held at her lips. The diameter of the thick penis shaped rubber was at least two inches across and easily that long. It would fill her mouth completely.

"Two." Fuck. It would be uncomfortable enough. Anything bigger would be hell.

She opened her mouth wide at the exact moment he said, "Three." His eyes filled with a gleeful satisfaction at her obedience. She hated herself just a little bit for liking how it felt to make the sadistic bastard happy.

As she expected, the rubber filled her mouth, pressing her jaw open uncomfortably while the hard object touched the back of her tongue, bringing out her gag reflex. She had to force herself to relax to make the gagging stop. She tried not to panic when he lifted her head, pulling the leather straps around to the back of her head and tightening the contraption so there would be no escaping it until he released her.

"You can deny it all you want, but I know you're enjoying everything I've done to you so far, Khloe. Still, I want you to know the red ball in your hand is your new safeword. Until I take the gag out, just drop the ball if you want to bail out on me. Understand?"

She could only gurgle from behind the gag. Already wetness was pooling in her mouth as she was unable to swallow around the intruder. She prayed she'd be able to avoid drooling like an idiot before it was time to take out the gag.

He left her alone again and she used his time away to take some deep breaths through her nose, trying not to think about the throbbing need building deep inside her. She was relieved when he returned to remove the catheter, but was disappointed when he didn't remove the dildo in her ass, too.

"I'm going to continue my examination, now." His hands worked like magic, massaging the kinks in her taut muscles, mixing pleasure with the occasional pinch of pain. He took his time, truly looking at every inch of her body as if he were inspecting her. Her toes, ankles and calves spread wide in the stirrups. On to her thighs, stopping to thrust the anal plug in and out several times before moving to massage her breasts.

His first touch was clinical. Small circular massages exactly like she did to herself in the shower once a month. Only when the inspection was done, Ryder took it to the next level. Squeezing first her left and then her right orbs before turning all of his attention onto her protruding tips.

She was helpless to stop his mouth from crashing down to her nipple, sucking it into his mouth and nipping her lightly with his teeth. Pleasure and pain burst bright. She'd closed her eyes to enjoy the sensations so when the unforgiving nipple clamp pinched hard, she howled into her penis gag. White-hot pain seared through her left tit and for the first time of the day, her eyes filled with unshed tears. It was a race to let the pain settle in before drops actually fell. The tears won, streaming down her cheeks to mingle with the drool that had slipped out from around the damn gag.

The second his warm mouth enclosed her right tit, she yowled harder. There was no way she could enjoy the heavenly warmth of his mouth sucking her to bliss when she knew the agony that was coming on its heels. He pinched her pebbled tip, yanking it up to make a better target for the fucking clamp that tortured her a few seconds later.

Only when he pulled away from her body did she see the nipple clamps were linked by a long chain. She recognized a glee in his eyes as he flamed her agony by lifting the chain up towards the dildo thrust down her throat. He attached the chain to the leather strap holding it to her head. Now, each time she moved her head more than an inch, pressure pulled her nips, shooting a renewed jolt of pain through her breasts.

He stopped to stroke her hair in an oddly comforting way. She got the impression he was impressed by her stamina and it made her proud in a sick way.

"You're doing well. Only five more minutes with the gag. Honestly, you'll be happy you can't talk when you see the final examination of the day."

Khloe couldn't even fathom what devious torture he could come up with next that could be worse than all he'd done to her already. He'd literally examined every inch of her body. There was no place left to invade.

Oh how wrong she was.

The second he hung the bulging red enema bag on the hook previously occupied by her catheter bag, Khloe lost it. She flailed against her restraints with all her strength, ignoring the shooting pain in her nipples as she jerked again and again, frantic to loosen the hold of the leather. True panic consumed her at the thought of Ryder doing something so personal... so invasive... so humiliating... to her at all, even in private. But in front of an audience was simply unacceptable. She was Khloe Monroe. She'd pushed her public persona down in order to participate in Roulette, but it came crashing back with a vengeance.

She screamed into the gag, thrashing hard enough that the clamp on her right tit flew off, snapping up to hit her in the face with the velocity of her distraught struggles. She felt the red ball in her hand and knew it was time to drop it. The dangerous game she'd been playing just got too ugly for her see to the end. Her hand cramped as she loosened her grip on the ball.

But then Ryder was there, blanketing her with the weight of his body. He'd stepped between her legs, held high and wide at the end of the table. Instead of continuing his medical torture, he leaned into her body, holding her head in his hands to keep her from her continued thrashing.

She heard the sobs and knew they were her own. His comforting shushing felt out of place, but had the desired effect. As she slowly calmed, she found herself gasping for breath. Her nose was running, blocking the only avenue of breathing she had left. Panic returned.

Ryder took action, loosening the buckle behind her head and removing the gag shoved down her throat, throwing the device to the floor with a loud clunk.

She was desperate to have her hands free. She struggled, but he maintained control. "That's enough. Calm down, Khloe. Take a deep breath for me, baby." She fought to obey, sucking in uneven breaths between continued sobs.

Relief mingled with debilitating humiliation, mixing a strange cocktail of emotions for the BDSM novice. As the hard-ass Dom pulled an old fashioned hankie from his pocket and started dabbing at her tears and snot, someone stepped next to the table and tried to pull Ryder away from her.

"That's enough. She's done. This was a mistake." It was Chase. She should feel relieved. He'd cared enough to step in to rescue her. So why did his intervention feel like too little, too late?

Ryder ignored him, instead leaning in to cup her chin in his hand as he held the hankie to her nose, instructing her, "Blow for me, baby."

Through her tears, she saw his genuine concern for her wellbeing. It shocked her. He'd played the role of hard-ass so convincingly that she was having trouble reconciling this new, softer version of the man standing in front of her.

"That's my girl. You scared me there for a minute." Something close to a smile graced his lips, turning him into his own version of a sex-god.

Chase had stepped closer again and was reaching to release her hands from the restraints. Ryder's smile was gone in a heartbeat as he pushed Chase away from Khloe with force. She couldn't turn her head completely, but out of the corner of her eye, she saw Jaxson catch Chase before he fell against the medical cabinet along the far wall of the room.

If she thought Chase looked angry, Jaxson looked murderous. She'd never seen him like this and prayed she never would again. As the tall man stalked forward, Khloe actually feared for Ryder's safety.

But her Dom-for-the-night didn't back down at all. He stalked towards Jaxson and the two men bumped chests a few feet away from her prone body.

"You need to pack it in here, Helms."

"I don't think so. I still have almost two hours with my sub."

"Wrong. She safeworded. You're done here."

Only when she heard his words did Khloe realize that in her fight to be free, she had indeed dropped the red ball she'd been clutching since he'd gagged her.

All three men turned towards her expectantly. She should be relieved. Chase and Jaxson had come to her rescue. Just minutes before she'd been desperate to be free of Ryder. He'd gone too far. He was too hard-core for her.

So why did the disappointment in his eyes bother her so much? She didn't owe him anything. Hell they barely knew each other. That was the whole problem. Valentine Roulette was a dangerous game to play with a complete stranger. She'd learned that lesson the hard way.

He didn't take his eyes off her as he stepped away from Jaxson and turned back towards her. As he approached, Ryder's gaze burned hotter with each step he took closer. She'd expected him to release her when he got close enough so she was totally shocked when he gripped her hair and yanked her head forward, stopping just inches from his own face.

The intensity in his eyes revived the embers of their attraction. "Did I lose you, baby, or are you still with me?"

Jaxson had followed him and tried to push Ryder away from her, but he didn't give up that easy. "Back off, Davidson. If Khloe wants to be done, I'll respect her wishes. But we need a minute."

The men were in a showdown. The only thing good about it was it gave her a few moments to get her breathing back under control. When Jaxson and Ryder each turned to pin her with a concerned glare, she felt heat on her cheeks.

God, I wish he'd undone my arms.

"It's up to you, Khloe. Say the word and we'll release you and make sure you make it back to your hotel safe and sound. You don't have to finish tonight if you want to safeword," Jaxson reassured her.

The mention of her hotel jarred her. She'd spent four miserable days there, feeling utterly alone and sorry for herself. As afraid as she'd been a few minutes before, she'd at least felt alive. As alone as she'd felt on display, she'd been acutely aware that she wasn't alone at all. Ryder had made her the center of his world, and as fucked up as it had been, it had still felt good.

She looked up into her Dom's eyes and saw the same intensity that had scared her at the start of the event. Truth be told, it still did. But that was the whole point, wasn't it? In a moment of clarity, she wasn't sure if she'd be happy at the end of the night if she stayed, but she knew without a shadow of a doubt, she'd regret it if she left.

She didn't break her visual connection with her Dom as she answered Jaxson. "Thank you for checking on me, Jaxson and Chase. Really, I do appreciate it, but my hand cramped. I accidentally dropped the ball. I didn't mean to safeword."

Ryder's lips almost formed a smile. As handsome as he was, she suspected he could woo the hardest of hearts if only he smiled more.

Chase didn't believe her. "This is bullshit, Khloe. You were frantic. You absolutely safeworded. You don't owe this guy anything. It was a mistake asking you to sign up."

Ryder looked like he wanted to punch Chase. Jaxson stepped sideways to put himself between his lover and her Dom. Pangs of jealousy poked at her as she realized Chase had found the kind of love most people only dream of, yet never find. She hoped the men and Emma knew how lucky they were to have each other.

Jaxson and Ryder stood in a showdown until Jaxson backed down. "Khloe, we'll be watching from afar. And Helms, no more gags. She needs to be able to talk and safeword if she wants to. Got it?"

Ryder looked like he was going to pick a fight with the taller man, but finally backed down. "Fine. I agree we don't know each other well enough yet. No more gags."

Jaxson seemed satisfied. Chase did not. It didn't matter. Jaxson took charge, pulling his lover away and out of the room.

Ryder was back at her side, unbuckling her arms and wrists, giving her a minute to lower her hands and shake them out to bring circulation back again.

"Thanks. Can you undo my legs too?" Her voice quavered.

She never expected him to say no, but he did. "Not yet."

She glanced up at the bulging bag that still hung next to them and panicked. "You can't... I won't..."

He held his finger to her lips to quiet her. "Shhh. Under normal circumstances, I don't take kindly to a sub saying no to an activity I've chosen, but let's face it. There's nothing normal about tonight's event. Strangers paired together doing hard-core activities. I admit I want to push you to the edge, but I'm sorry if I pushed you too far too fast. I've decided to put the enema on hold for tonight."

Relief coursed through her until he added, "But, if we play again another night, I reserve the right to change your mind."

Khloe bit her tongue. She was tempted to tell him she'd never change her mind, but then he grinned the world's sexiest smile that lit up his eyes with a fun mischief she'd do just about anything to see again.

"Now, where were we before we ran off the tracks there for a little bit? Ah yes, I remember. I was just about ready to reward you for being such a good girl."

"Yeah, well I pretty much blew that, didn't I?" she snapped back.

He got serious again. "No, Khloe. I blew it. There's nothing wrong with having limits. In my line of work, I sometimes tend to forget that." He stopped short of actually apologizing. She suspected that was something Ryder Helms didn't do often. It made her curious about what kind of work he was in.

"Now, I'll tie your hands again if I need to, but if you promise to behave, I'll leave them loose. I want you to grip the handles at the edge of the table." He moved her hands, positioning them the way he wanted. "Yep, just like that. Now, don't let go until I give you permission. Can you do that?"

He waited expectantly for her answer. Her quiet, "Yes, Sir," felt foreign, but she liked the approval she saw in his eyes.

Ryder Helms was a complicated man.

CHAPTER 7

*R*yder knew he was working on borrowed time. He didn't often admit it, but he'd fucked up royally tonight. As he observed the vulnerability in Khloe's eyes as she quietly agreed to obey him, he knew he didn't deserve her trust.

She'd been so responsive. Perfectly submissive. He'd allowed himself to forget she was a newbie to the scene. He'd treated her like the pain-sluts he loved to play with in Moscow. Women who were so jaded that they'd accept any degrading act his perverted mind could dream up. He was under no delusion. Even if they enjoyed some of what he delivered, they did it for the money and gifts.

Khloe Monroe was the antithesis of them and he'd let himself forget that. He couldn't remember the last time he'd mastered a sub even half as beautiful, or a fraction as unique as the actress.

He reached up to caress the red mark on her left cheek where the nipple clamp had flung and hit her. It could have put her eye out.

Stop being such a pussy, Helms. She's fine.

He pushed his guilt down. It was a useless emotion he'd learned to purge long ago. Agents who felt guilt got dead fast. Only he wasn't on a mission and as much as he wanted to pretend he was, the special woman staring back at him expectantly made it impossible to pretend. This was real. *She* was real.

He had many diabolical kinks he'd love to introduce his novice sub to, but he needed to rebuild the precarious thread of trust he'd managed to weave and then sever in just over an hour. He hated the awkward rift that had built up between them.

Luckily, he knew how to fix it.

He started at her cheek, kissing the red mark softly, hoping to make her unintended boo-boo better. She shivered as his light kisses trailed down her neck, her shoulder, stopping to remove the one remaining nipple clamp before lathing her tender nipples with licks and light sucking that served to bring relief to any lingering pain. He luxuriated in cupping her ample globes, loving how she filled his large hands and then some. Her soft sigh as she started to relax urged him on.

His lips trailed lower, kissing and nibbling her tummy and rib cage until his captive broke into a fit of giggles. He pulled back to grin at her. "Looks like I've learned something else about you. You're ticklish. I bet you'd just love it if we rolled tickling as our next activity."

"Don't quote me on this, but I think I'd rather try the damn enema."

His bark of laughter sounded foreign to his own ears. He couldn't remember the last time he'd genuinely laughed. It felt good... and odd. Very un-dom-like. He fought to regain the upper hand.

"I'll remember you said that. Now, close your eyes." The humor in her eyes doused slightly as she sized him up.

Get control, Helms.

"Now, Princess. Closed."

She complied, snapping her eyes closed. He took a moment to study her. Being the sick bastard that he was, he especially adored the black lines of mascara marking the paths of her tears. Tears he'd caused. Tears he'd enjoyed swiping away.

Ryder leaned down again, letting his lips resume their trail across her body, nipping and licking lower. She wiggled, but he remained patient, moving ever-so-slowly, stoking the fire he'd built in her earlier. She'd literally been ready to self-combust with sexual need and he wanted to drive her there again.

The first swipe of his tongue through her soaking folds tasted like fucking heaven. She was his new favorite meal, which could be a problem since he wasn't sure he'd ever see her again after tonight. He used the tip of his tongue to tease her swollen clit poking out from its soft hood. Khloe was perfectly pink and wonderfully wet as he increased his pressure, circling, swirling and sucking until he had to wrap his arms around her splayed open legs in order to hold her steady enough to keep from jerking away from him as she gyrated her hips.

The erotic sounds coming from her were a turn-on. The fact that she wasn't formulating real words, but instead had devolved into a hot mess of sexual desire turned him on more than he cared to admit. Her raw, animalistic groans of bliss as she chased her orgasm had blood rushing to his already hard cock like water to a fire hose; fast and high-pressured.

He estimated their three hours was half over, and that bummed him out. He wanted to drag out their time together. There were so many things he didn't know yet. He backed off with his tongue, frustrating his submissive when her orgasm proved just out of reach. She had no clue that it was taking every ounce of his self-control to keep from pulling out his cock and pounding her as hard and fast as his body could deliver.

He sucked and licked until his tongue grew tired, taking her to the edge again and again. She had long ago stopped stringing intelligent words together let alone verbalizing what she wanted. He didn't need her words. Her body screamed its need.

Ryder closed the deal by grabbing the end of the butt-plug he'd inserted almost a half hour before. Without warning, he pulled the plug out of her ass in one stroke and shoved it back in the following second. Khloe bucked her ass up off the padded table, dislodging his tongue.

He latched on again, sucking her sex into his mouth before fucking her ass harder. He had to wrap his left arm around her leg to hold her still enough to finally ride her to her climax.

Her guttural howl was truly the sexiest sound he'd heard in his whole life. He had succeeded in so much more than just getting her off. Khloe Monroe had just come unhinged... in public... with an audience. He suspected she'd be embarrassed later, but he leaned back on the rolling stool to just gaze at her perfect body now covered in a thin sheen of perspiration. He was glad he'd left her in a sitting position so he, and all the other spectators, could enjoy the vision of the sexually satiated star.

She is fucking amazing.

He knew they'd spent too much time at this one kink and should probably pack it up and head back to the roulette wheel to take their chances on another scene, but Ryder had no desire to nurse his hard-on for another hour before getting his own release. And anyway, once would never be enough. Not with his Princess. He was greedy. He needed her now.

Ryder stood and moved to the opposite end of the medical table. His captive was distracted and didn't seem to care when he grabbed the electronic control and reclined her, leaving her legs spread, giving their spectators a nice view of her recovering girly bits.

He had to hand it to Davidson. Black Light had the best toys. Ryder fiddled with the controller until he got the table arranged the way he wanted. The end closest to him had just folded towards the floor, leaving Khloe's head at the very tip of table, her long messy hair dangling down almost to the floor.

Her eyes were closed so she didn't see the reposition coming. He grabbed a handful of that glorious mane of hers and held her head up just as his other hand hooked her armpit and yanked her closer to his body. Her head now dangled above the floor, held up by his grasp of her hair. Her caramel-brown eyes shone with surprise and only opened wider when he used his free hand to wrestle with his belt buckle. When it was taking too long, he released her hair, letting her head fall back to an almost ninety-degree angle.

Both hands fumbled faster to get his zipper down, finally springing his tortured cock from the prison of his boxer briefs. Even upside down, his submissive-for-the-night was exceptional. Her eyes were glazed over with a lusty trance while her pink tongue licked her lips as if she were looking forward to devouring the meal in front of her.

Ryder nursed his erection while he enjoyed his view. He was so turned on, a dollop of pre-cum not only formed, but splashed to the floor in his excitement.

"Open that beautiful mouth of yours, Princess. It's my turn to take the edge off."

Her face was flushed. He wasn't sure if it was excitement, embarrassment, or just that her head dangled towards the floor. He didn't care the reason, but he fucking loved it.

She spread her delicate lips to form a small O.

"Oh baby, you're gonna have to open wider than that."

He knew he was being a dick, but he'd let the BDSM dynamics of their session get out of whack since he'd pushed her too far. He needed to reestablish who was in charge.

Ryder clamped his hands on either side of Khloe's upside-down face and stepped closer until the wet tip of his rod was at her now closed lips. Nervous, she wiggled to try to get away from his grasp, but it only made him keep her in a tighter headlock.

"Khloe, that's enough. You have a job to do, darling. Open. Now."

She might be inexperienced, but she had an instinctual submissive streak because she responded beautifully to his dominant instructions. Her lips spread wide and he shoved home, into her warm and wet mouth.

Fuck, she felt perfect. She'd taken three-quarters of his length in his first thrust, no small feat for a submissive. He'd looked forward to her gagging as she struggled to take his full length. He let his thumb stroke her cheek as his hips rocked, his form of an olive branch to keep his novice calm through her adorable struggle.

The height of the table was perfect for him to angle her neck in a way that allowed him to thrust so deep that his cock snaked down her throat. It was a tight fit, but she surrendered herself, letting him completely control his speed, angle, and depth. Khloe only protested when Ryder paused, buried to the hilt, cutting off her oxygen for several seconds.

Her teeth nicked his shaft as she coughed with his next withdrawal, but it only added to his pleasure. She gasped for several deep breaths before taking him deep again. This time she swallowed around him and he almost lost his load. The only way he managed to last more than thirty seconds was through his disciplined cadence of self-control, stalling deep inside her so often she was struggling to push him away.

Memories of pushing her too far earlier brought a fresh dose of that emotion he so rarely felt; guilt. He didn't like it at all.

Ryder pulled out to the tip and gave Khloe long enough to catch her breath. He held her head up so he could see her eyes and the second he did, he was a goner. Tears swam in her expressive gaze, spilling towards the floor in a puddle. Despite his rough use of her, lust and excitement warred in her gaze. He saw no fear. No anger. Just desire.

It only took three more strokes down her throat to get his eruption started. She tried to jerk away from him when she tasted the first spurt of his ejaculation, but he renewed his hold on her head. It excited him to know his cum would be filling her stomach.

They were both out of breath by the time he tucked his now flaccid shaft back in his pants. He lifted the table to support her head first before moving to the opposite end of the table where he started to unbuckle her legs from the stirrups. Knowing she'd been in the awkward position for awhile, Ryder spent a few minutes gently massaging her right foot, ankle and calf before letting it rest on his shoulder while he repeated the treatment on her other leg.

Khloe watched him intently as he cared for her. He didn't miss the fresh tears in her eyes and suspected she was crashing emotionally after the intense scene they'd shared. They still had other challenges ahead and Ryder wasn't willing to pass up spending a minute of that time with his Princess.

He scooped her up into his arms after all restraints were removed. Ryder was glad he'd gotten the tour from Spencer so he knew where he wanted to take Khloe for a bit of aftercare and privacy. He liked the way she snuggled closer to him placing her head on his shoulder and wrapping her arms around his neck.

As they left the room, he noticed the crowd that had been watching was breaking up; looking for their next kinky scene to witness, which suited him just fine. As helpful as the spectators were to adding to the ambiance of the scene, he was anxious to be alone with his Roulette partner.

It only took a minute to weave his way to the small quiet space at the edge of the room. There was one other couple in the far corner, but they looked self-absorbed. Ryder crossed to the long red couch opposite them and plunked down, settling Khloe in his lap.

He'd snagged up his duffle bag before they'd left medical and he juggled his limp submissive in his lap as he searched his bag until he came out with another bottle of water. He hugged Khloe closer so he could use his hands to unscrew the top of the bottle before holding it to her lips.

"Drink for me, baby. I don't want you to get dehydrated." She opened enough for him to tilt the bottle, managing to get most of the water into her mouth, but spilling several drops down her chin and onto her breasts.

Ryder wished he could see her face, but she'd buried it in the crook of his neck. He heard the sounds of her crying before he felt her first shudder. She was coming down emotionally and it felt odd to recognize that he actually wanted to be exactly where he was in that moment. One advantage of playing with club subs in Moscow was they rarely, if ever, wanted or needed his aftercare. They approached domination and submission as a business where money was to be made.

As he rocked the actress in his arms, he caressed her softly, letting her come down at her own pace. When she'd stopped crying and was instead sniffling against his shirt, Ryder pulled his hankie out and helped her clean up again.

Their eyes met as he asked her to blow her nose and the innocent blush that graced her cheeks was so out of place considering the raunchy shit he'd just done to her body. Her voice quavered when she finally spoke.

"No one has ever done anything like that to me before. Ever."

"That doesn't surprise me, Princess. What did surprise me is that you sure seemed to like it."

"No I didn't," she protested too quickly.

"Oh no you don't. Don't you dare start fucking lying to me now."

He pulled her away from him so they could see each other. He saw the conflict in her eyes. "Own it. It's okay."

"What is?"

"To admit that you like it rough. That you love being dominated."

"Love is a strong word," she protested.

"Fine. Do you like the word crave better?"

It took her several long seconds to answer with a soft, "Maybe."

Ryder reached into this bag again, this time to grab an energy bar. He hugged her closer so he could get his hands together to unwrap it before he held it to her lips. Khloe shook her head, trying to get away from the food.

"I can't eat."

"Like hell you can't. You're skin and bones, for Christ's sake."

"I'm overweight according to my agent."

"Well then your agent is an asshole."

That brought a smile to her face and he noticed she didn't defend the jerk. He wouldn't back down and when she accepted it, she opened her mouth to bite off the end of the bar. As he watched her struggle to finish eating, he admired the dichotomy of strength and submission that was Khloe Monroe.

I can't get attached.

"You ready to go roll again?"

She hesitated, looking nervous all over again. "Can I put a robe on until after we roll?" she asked hopefully.

"Nope. Not until after 11:01pm."

Despite looking dejected at his denial, she answered with a quiet, "Yes, Sir."

Shit. She's perfect.

CHAPTER 8

"*A*re you okay?" Chase leaned in to question to her as they stood next to the activity roulette wheel.

Before she could even answer, Ryder stepped between them and was pushing Chase back. "Did I give you permission to talk to my sub?"

"Your sub is my old friend so fuck off," her ex countered.

Khloe knew it was shallow, but she kinda liked having two smoking hot men arguing over her.

"Chase, it's okay. Really." He didn't look like he believed her, but he shook his head slightly before resuming his emcee duties by begrudgingly giving the activity wheel a spin and reaching out to hand her the white marble.

She was nervous as she watched the small ball swirl and bounce around, waiting to see what fate would deliver to her next. A part of her wished the night would have just ended after their first scene. Not only because she was emotionally and physically drained, but more because Ryder had been right. She did crave it rough. Something had always been missing from her relationships. She'd assumed it was love. Now she suspected what she'd really been waiting for was a man strong enough to take what he wanted.

A man like Ryder Helms.

The only drawback was he scared the shit out of her. What if they rolled an activity that ruined the whole night?

"Mr. Helms and The Princess have rolled Dom's Choice," Chase announced.

Her "Fuck," slipped out.

Ryder leaned closer to talk against her ear as he gripped her hips. "Oh yes, you can count on fucking, Princess."

Chase wasn't backing down. "Khloe, just safeword already. It's okay. I'm sorry I conned you into doing this."

Both dominant men waited for her to respond to Chase's apology. As handsome as Chase was, it was Ryder who held her attention. No one had ever looked at her with the hungry glare he held in his eyes.

"I'll keep going." Her answer was barely more than a whisper, but it brought a curse from her old friend and a sexy smile from her Dom for the night.

"Good girl, Princess." In an odd move, he held out his crooked arm for her to put her left hand through. It felt like he was formally escorting her, but courtesans rarely paraded around naked. He led her back down the steps, away from the stage. Away from the safety net of her friends. She felt the eyes tracking them as they weaved through the sexy scenes already in progress on the club floor as they headed to an empty platform in the middle of the room. While it wasn't as high compared to the stage where the roulette wheels were set up as a main attraction, this platform was completely surrounded by the club meaning there would be absolutely no privacy for its occupant.

Her heart rate doubled as she looked at the extraordinary furniture and props available. What she'd seen of Black Light so far, while sexy and extreme, paled when compared to the diabolical things surrounding her.

Dungeon was the word she was looking for. While it may not have the same historical ambience as a medieval torture chamber, the evil props promised to scare the bejesus out of her. A heavy metal cage hung from the ceiling, restraints visible where a naughty sub would be punished. A St. Andrew's cross with leather straps stood near one edge, its sturdy base sure to hold any captive steady while strapped to it. An old fashioned stockade stood to one side and a whipping post, rings and ropes for restraints, on the other.

Dozens of punishment implements could be seen through the glass doors of the rolling supply cabinet, available for masters to use on errant slaves. Paddles, whips, chains, rope, straps, canes and items she didn't even recognize ratcheted up her adrenaline until she felt light headed.

Ryder had stayed near the steps, letting her stand alone at the edge of the stage, taking it all in. She could feel his warmth at her back he was so close, yet he didn't reach out to touch her. Her mind was screaming at her to run as far away as fast as possible. This was hardcore. She was in over her head and she didn't particularly want to drown. Yet while her mind tried to reason through her options, her body had already begun heating up, ready for round two with the sex-god she'd been assigned.

"We have just about an hour left, Princess. What's it gonna be? You brave enough to stick with me or you want to pack it in?"

She heard the challenge in his voice. He was goading her.

In the distance, she heard a guttural scream from one of her fellow submissives. The feminist in her should be rushing to the woman's aid, but instead, she felt jealous. She didn't have a clue how to reconcile the things she'd learned about herself in the last few hours. She suspected thinking about it all would consume her over the next few days. But now, she only had one hour. She didn't know exactly what she wanted, but she knew what she didn't want, and that was to go back to her hotel room, alone and regretting missing out on a final scene with her one-night Master.

It was as if he was in her brain, listening to her internal debate because within seconds of her silent decision, Ryder pulled her back into a hug with a condescending, "Good girl. Now stay."

She watched him go to work, dragging what looked like a heavy-duty sawhorse from the other side of the rolling cabinet that she hadn't been able to see before. From the open cabinet, he grabbed up a long length of white rope and a few other smaller items she couldn't see before heading back in her direction.

Khloe shivered despite the club being extra warm.

She had no doubt that Ryder was a sadist, but watching him mentally prepare for the scene, his glare dominant, his lips a straight line, seemed oddly familiar. It wasn't unlike how she prepared for an acting role. She relaxed slightly realizing in this scene, he might be in control, but she was the ultimate director. She could cry the BDSM version of 'cut', *red*, at any time if he pushed her too far.

When he had things ready for her, her silver fox crooked his finger in a sexy come hither motion. As her bare feet moved forward, she again felt like Little Red Riding hood being sucked into the wolf's trap.

He twined their fingers together as he escorted her to the center of the platform where he'd left his supplies. He reached to grab what looked like leather cuffs before demanding, "Hold out your hands for me, baby."

She complied and within two minutes, he had her wrists buckled into the tight-fitting restraints that were linked by a one-foot heavy-duty chain, thick enough to tow a car out of a snow bank. Only when he had her bound did he pull the remote control out of his back pocket. Within seconds a large metal hook started lowering from the ceiling above her until it stopped at eye level.

Ryder worked silently to connect the center of her chain to the hook and then start the hook's ascension to the ceiling again. With each inch it moved up, Khloe's pulse increased. There was a brief moment of panic when the hook had stretched her arms high that she worried he might raise it until her feet left the ground, but he stopped well before that.

Khloe didn't expect him to pull a hairbrush from his back pocket next, but he did. She caught his small smile at her surprise as he walked behind her. Like other times that night, Ryder jammed his hand into her signature hair and yanked her head back. He held her head immobile while she felt the hairbrush starting to yank through the knots that had formed during their adventure. Tears welled as sharp pangs of pain in her scalp warred with the ache of desire in her deepest core. He eventually gave up with the brush and just yanked her mane into one messy ponytail. She felt him tie rope around her hair, and then wrap the rope around the hook with her arms.

Only when the hook moved higher did she feel the tug against her head and arms warring for her attention. He stopped the mechanism just before she would have moved to her tippy-toes to keep contact with the floor.

With her immobilized, Ryder took a minute to step closer, letting his warm hand caress her taut body, laid out for him like a gift. He spent extra time pinching her still tender nipples until they protruded embarrassingly from her globes.

"No! Please!" She tried to pull away when she saw him pull a fresh set of nipple clamps from his pocket. The last pair had been agony. Her body couldn't handle that again so soon.

"Shhh, Princess. These are much kinder. They'll just give you an extra zing."

Khloe was skeptical, but she settled down, letting the dominant pull her left tit away from her body first before letting the tweezer-like end latch onto her left tit. True to his word, he played with the tension until it was fastened just tight enough to stay attached before repeating on the other side.

She wasn't surprised when the chain connecting the two ends was raised and attached to the same hook above her head, connecting her arms, hair, and tits in an erotic way.

She'd been standing facing the St. Andrew's cross, but Ryder grabbed her hips, picking her up to temporarily relieve the pull on her arms, only to spin them around in a one-eighty that now had her facing the largest part of the crowd of spectators, once again following the famous movie star as if she were meant to be their personal live stage show.

Embarrassment at her naked display had her wanting to shrink away, but Ryder had stepped up against her back, his hands digging into her hips to ensure she was immobile as he once again whispered against the shell of her ear, his words meant only for his captive.

"Look at them all, Princess. For the rest of their lives, every time these people see you in a magazine or on a movie screen – hell, even as they're masturbating in the privacy of their own homes, every single kinkster out there watching you will remember the night they got to witness how beautiful you are up close and personal. They'll remember the rapture on your face as you come, your guttural cries as you let your body finally admit what it craves."

His words excited her and a part of her hated herself for it.

"Let's give 'em a good show, baby."

Seconds later the sound of him dragging the sawhorse closer broke the hushed silence of the dungeon. As he positioned it directly in front of her, she glanced down for her first close look at the diabolical piece of furniture. It was made of heavy wooden blocks, polished smooth with heavy metal rings positioned at odd locations along the legs and each end where they met in the V. It was the top tip of the V that held her attention.

"It's a called a wooden pony." He answered her unasked question.

It took a few seconds for the words to sink in. "Christ. No!" She tried to shrink backwards, but all she managed to do was pull her hair and nipples painfully. "But, I don't ride!"

Ryder chuckled. He fucking laughed at her. "Princess, today you do." He was at the far end of the contraption, the horse between them. He waited until she tore her eyes from the torture device to look into his. She'd expected to find him gloating with sadistic glee, but was shocked to find him smiling at her in a comforting way. His back was to their audience so they couldn't see his mouth deliver the low message meant only for her.

"Trust me, baby. I've been paying attention. Let me prove to you that when it comes to sex, I know you better than you know yourself."

He was so confident. Conceited really. Hollywood was chock-full of conceited assholes, so why did he feel so different? He gave her time to sort it out. Ryder might be a cocky bastard, but unlike any other man she'd met, he'd made her believe to her core that she was the only thing he was thinking about in their time together. He'd made Khloe the center of his universe, at least for their dangerous game of Roulette.

His eyes flamed with barely contained dominance, just waiting for her permission to unleash it on her. That he even stopped to confirm he had her approval was reason enough to trust him. Her small nod was what he'd been waiting for.

"Open your legs as far as you can and still keep your toes on the ground." When she stood stock still, he barked a stern, "Now."

As soon as she had separated her legs even a few inches, he started shoving the wood forward, moving between her legs. It was too tall, forcing her to stand on her tippy toes to keep from putting her weight on the slightly rounded, but nonetheless, pointed top ridge. Only when he had her positioned in the middle did he stop and reach out to roughly pull at her labia, spreading her lower lips wide around the hard surface.

His fingers grazed her clit, bringing an unexpected zing. When he pulled away, he lifted his glistening fingers to her mouth. "Lick me clean. You're dripping all over the wood already."

He didn't wait for her tongue to lick. Instead, he shoved his wet digits into her mouth, forcing them deep enough to make her gag. She tasted her own juice and hated how turned on she felt by his rough treatment.

Still, it wasn't until he started cranking a wheel she couldn't see that she realized the true danger of her predicament. The horse's legs started moving farther apart from each other, forcing her legs apart until they were spread so wide that her feet left the ground completely.

The bulk of her weight now crushed her girly parts down against the unforgiving wood. The surprised scream she heard was her own. The pain wasn't sharp. It was more like an uncompromising pressure that started to build. Khloe instinctively tried to pull herself up, using her restrained arms. It worked for a less than a minute. She was able to almost pull herself completely off the pony, but then the muscles in her arms started to burn from the effort of holding her frame off the torture device.

Ryder stood directly in front of her, enthralled by her predicament. "Eyes. Don't look away from me, Khloe. If you do, I'll make it worse." She saw the sick glee in his gaze, almost daring her to glance away, before adding. "If you can keep your eyes on me until I tell you to stop, I'll reward you."

She somehow doubted his idea of a reward was the same as hers, but she knew without a doubt she didn't want to find out what his perverted mind could come up with that would be worse.

Their showdown was hypnotic. Focusing on holding his glare actually helped her keep her mind off the growing pain in her shoulders and arms, off the cramping in her splayed legs and even off thinking about what was happening in the audience. She could hear sounds of sex and submission, but she didn't dare let it distract her from her mission.

She had no idea how long it lasted. All she knew was she could barely hold her body weight up by her arms for more than a few seconds before she would come crashing down on her pussy, each time harder than last. She finally gave up trying to pull herself up, resigning that as bad as the pain was in her cunt, she was doing herself no favors by crashing down on it again and again.

Khloe saw approval in Ryder's eyes as she bit the inside of her cheek and the pain settled deeper. She hadn't realized she was crying until she felt the wet tears splashing down onto her breasts being pulled up to the ceiling by the still attached nipple tweezers. It was then that his approval turned to pride.

Ryder Helms was proud of her and the knowledge filled her with a strange gratification. It made her heart pound harder, almost anxious for his next test so she could prove to him again she was worthy.

Her master took slow steps forward, stalking closer like he was circling his prey, properly trapped and unable to escape. When he was close enough, he reached out to cup her boob, tweaking the tip lightly.

"Such a good girl." His hand roamed her body, caressing, pinching, and even tickling. A full-body shudder consumed her. She felt on fire, ready to combust into flames. Instead of focusing on the pain, all she could think about was having his cock inside her.

His slap to her ass made her jerk, jarring her pain points.

"Stay," he ordered as he pulled away from her.

It was on the tip of her tongue to answer 'where the hell would I go', but she bit the words back. She didn't want to see his reaction to her sass.

He was back quickly, kneeling next to her right leg. When he lifted her foot and bent it back so that her toes almost touched her butt, the weight on her girly parts shifted, rubbing her clit hard against the rolled top of the pony and zinging her with a bolt of hot agony.

Her muscles were fatigued so she had no fight left in her to try to stop him from wrapping the soft, white rope around her ankle and thigh, now brought together. He was exceptionally thorough, arranging the rope in a perfect line, encasing her entire leg until he reached her bent knee with the hugging rope. She watched him artfully tie it off in an impossibly tight knot that ensured she would not be stretching her leg out until he wanted her to.

By the time he'd repeated the rope treatment on her left side, her legs were beginning to tingle. The change in position of her legs also changed how she was balancing on the top of the pony, making her torso lean forward slightly and putting greater pressure directly on her swollen clit. As if he wanted to prove he knew her torment, Ryder placed his fingers directly on her button, mastering her completely and effectively launching her into another stratosphere.

Her orgasm lit like a rocket. It was as if he'd created an on/off switch on her body that only he controlled. Through the pleasure, she felt the bite of pain as she completely relaxed her body until her shoulders, arms, scalp, and tits all felt on fire. Her chin had dropped to her chest and she felt the drool on her chin, dripping down.

Ryder was there, his arm wrapped around her waist, lifting her just enough to take the weight off, bringing her a few precious moments of reprieve.

"You are so fucking beautiful. In case I don't have the chance to tell you later, I want you to know I feel lucky that the wheel matched us up tonight, Khloe."

It felt like he was telling her goodbye. A few hours ago, she wouldn't have bet any money that she could have made it ten minutes with the terrifying Dom on the stage with her. Now, a blanket of sadness threatened to ruin their final time together as she realized she would most likely never see the older Dominant after she left Black Light.

His voice against her ear brought her back to the present. "How would you like a little help with holding up your weight, Princess?"

"Yes, please," she begged.

"Your wish is my command." It got worse when he walked away, forcing her pussy to bear her weight again. She heard the sound of the mechanical motor at the same time that she felt the tension on her shoulders, arms, and boobs lesson slightly. Unfortunately, what relief they felt seemed to quadruple the pain as the pony felt like it was about to split her down the middle. Her body was leaning forward, dragged down by gravity she was too tired to fight. Her tears turned to open crying as she let the pain consume her.

His hands were massaging her ass, now sticking out as she almost lay on the top of the pony. He lulled her into compliance so when she felt the slick wetness being spread across her anus, she bucked, trying to get away from the dirty invasion of Ryder's digits being thrust in and out of her body.

"Dammit!" she protested.

"Patience, Princess. You asked for relief."

His finger fucking did distract her. With him now behind her, she had a direct view of the crowd of spectators gathered around to witness her debasing. She saw women, and a few men, with jealousy in their glare. Others looked on with shock and awe. More than one couple was in the middle of fucking while they enjoyed the show.

She'd just started to relax into his invasion, opening her bottom wider to surrender to his dominance, when she felt the cold hardness at her opening. She didn't have time to clench before a piercing pain pinched her bottom hole as what felt like a tennis ball sized metal sphere was pressed home, deep inside her bowels. Once the ball got past the entrance, the searing pain eased slightly.

She could feel it shoved inside her, yet she still felt as if her back passage were completely filled, the puckered opening stretched uncomfortably wide to accommodate whatever the hell it was her Dom had shoved inside her.

It had been worth it. Once he'd plugged her butt, he lowered the hook above even more, letting her torso fall forward on top of the pony. She was far from comfortable, but the hardest edge had been taken off and she was grateful. Unfortunately, the chain of the nipple clamps was now pressing against her neck and shoulder in the forward position she found herself in. She allowed herself several deep, cleansing breaths, mistakenly thinking the worst was over.

How wrong she was. Her ass, now thrust up in the air at the back end of the pony, was to become target practice for his implement of pain. It struck her bare skin with a loud splat just below where the plug protruded from her body.

"Ow!" she screamed.

The second strike came quickly, feeling much harder than the first. Panic closed in. She wasn't sure if he'd struck harder or if it was just worse because she knew what was coming.

"Stop! Please."

The next paddle struck lower, hitting fresh flesh. She lurched forward trying to get away and only succeeding in renewing the pain in her pussy, ass, and shoulders.

Tears blurred her vision as her bottom felt on fire. Still, she'd dreamed of being spanked. She'd even begged Dean to try a little hanky-spanky, but he'd denied her. Memories of him doing something not terribly different than what was happening to Khloe with Ryder, only with the married Gloria, jarred Khloe back to reality. The spanking hurt way worse than she'd ever thought it would, yet the empty ache at her core now throbbed with need.

"Take a look at it, Princess." He'd stepped closer, thrusting a crimson red leather paddle in her line of sight. "I know you'll feel cheated if I don't light up your ass before I send you on your way tonight. I'm gonna paddle you until your butt is as red as the implement."

She groaned through her tears. Overwhelmed... consumed by the emotions the sexy dominant evoked in every inch of her body. Ironically, his use of the word red had reminded her she had the ability to stop things immediately. She held the real control. The word sat on the end of her tongue, tempted to spill out as he delivered the next strong swat to her ass. When she opened her mouth, she surprised herself by screaming his name instead of red.

"Ryder!"

"I'm here, baby. You're fighting it. Don't think about it. Just feel."

The leather fell again... and again... until she sobbed. Everything she'd been worrying about before Roulette fell away. The pain settled in, pushing away her hunger. Ryder's presence dominated her, pressing away her loneliness, her self-doubt, even her fear. All that was left was need. The need to please him. The need to make him proud. The need to have him inside her.

He stood close enough to brush her naked body as he exerted himself delivering the discipline he'd somehow known she craved. He stopped to caress her hot globes tenderly between strikes.

Relief invaded when she heard his implement crash to the floor, but panic returned when she felt him move away from her body. He left her collapsed over the pony until the sound of the hook above her head moving jarred her back to reality. He was raising the hook back up again, but this time, the greatest pressure pulling up was centered at her bottom hole as she was physically lifted by her tits, arms, hair, shoulders, and now ass.

The new pain was exquisite, encircling her completely and threatening to overwhelm her. Ryder didn't stop when she was merely upright. She rose higher until she felt the first real relief in her private parts since the scene had started. Once he stopped raising her up, he kicked the pony hard, sliding it forward and away from them. Her body was now dangling from the hook in the ceiling.

He was in front of her again, this time an unreadable glare in his eyes. What she now recognized was a hook in her pucker felt like it was splitting her back passage open. The only thing that helped her forget about the pain was watching Ryder unbuckle his leather belt and unzip his black fitted pants, letting them fall to the floor where he stepped out of them, kicking them aside.

She'd swallowed his cock in their first scene, but she hadn't been able to get a good look at it. She knew she was gawking at him with a stupid look on her face, but she couldn't help it. She couldn't believe she'd been able to take that shaft down her throat. She'd never been very good at giving blowjobs so she was seriously proud of herself for getting him off earlier now that she saw his impressive length.

He was nursing the flesh-covered steel in his hand as his gaze devoured her.

"Please..."

"Beg me. Tell me exactly what you want, baby."

He was such a cocky sonofabitch, yet he seemed to have the playbook to her body so she didn't bother resisting.

"You. I want you, dammit."

"You have me. I'm right here."

"Please... Ryder..."

He glared dangerously. "Tsk, tsk. You're supposed to call me Master or Sir." His words didn't match his gaze. She just knew he liked hearing his name on her lips.

"Ryder!" This time she screamed his name and he moved into action, unable to deny her another minute.

Her body registered relief as he lifted her by her hips, taking some of the pressure off her shoulders, hair, tits, and especially her anal cavity, although she was still unaccustomed to the uncomfortable fullness.

"Ready, baby?" She felt the tip of his cock sliding through her tender folds and knew the ride he was about to take her on would be a strange mix of pleasure and pain. She held her breath, strangely wanting the moment to last forever.

CHAPTER 9

*R*yder froze, wanting to sear the scene into his memory. Khloe Monroe was unexpected perfection. What a treat she'd turned out to be. He'd avoided looking at his watch, not wanting to acknowledge how little time they had left together. He was under no delusion. They would almost certainly not be seeing each other again after they said goodbye tonight.

"Master!" Christ, she'd done it. Surprised him again.

He couldn't wait any more. He buried himself deep inside her in one stroke, dragging a scream like none other. Over her shoulder, he watched the heads in the crowd turn towards them to watch the grand finale.

Her tunnel was impossibly tight. He could feel the ball of the stainless steel anal hook shoved up her ass rubbing against his shaft as he pummeled her pussy hard and fast. He didn't have the patience for finesse. Raw passion drove their coupling.

He had trouble formulating words, but managed to speak into her jostling ear held in front of him by the hook from the ceiling. "Keep your eyes open. Watch the crowd while they enjoy watching me fuck you, Princess."

She gurgled that sexy growl of hers that showed up when she lost control. He almost regretted taking her from behind because he hated to miss watching her expression when he pushed her over the edge to freefall into her *la petite mort,* yet he knew the spectators would appreciate the memory.

He shifted his grip from her hips to grab where her roped legs met her torso, giving him a much better grasp to lift her body to the perfect angle for his deep drilling.

Thank God he'd fucked her mouth earlier or he would have already spent. The fire building in his balls felt like an inferno. The wet slapping sounds their bodies made as they crashed together only made it harder to hold back from exploding.

As tight as she was, she squeezed him with rhythmic contractions as she howled her orgasm for the entire club to hear. He didn't let up the pace at all, pounding her hard and fast through one orgasm and building for her next one. The next time she yowled like that, they'd be coming together.

She mewed through her pounding, the perfect receptacle for his aggression, feeding his lusty dominance.

He felt his eruption building. He'd been a dick and had broken the game's rules by doing something he never did. He was riding her bareback. Their attraction was too primal to be separated by a latex barrier. He may not be able to keep her, but he would mark her as his own for at least tonight. She'd feel his seed dripping down her leg in her limo on the way back to the hotel and smell the evidence of their coupling on her tiny panties in the morning after it seeped out while she was sleeping that night.

He needed her to catch up. He reached around her body to go to work with his fingers, teasing and stroking her swollen clit as his hips kept up the thunderous pace.

"Come with me, baby." As he felt the first spurt of cum jutting out of his shaft and into her core, he demanded, "Now!"

It was a toss up who came harder. As he came down from the ultimate high, he felt his own legs getting wobbly from the exertion of holding them both up through their coupling. He hated to pull out, but he knew she'd been hanging longer than a newbie really should have. He let his wet cock swing in the air as he started undoing the ropes holding her legs bent.

The crowd of spectators actually broke out into a smattering of applause, appreciating the show they'd been lucky enough to witness. He was glad the majority of the group broke up, retreating to find another scene before the event ended.

Out of the corner of his eye, he detected someone approaching from across the stage. One of the dungeon monitors advanced warily, holding out his hands as a sign of non-aggression. It told Ryder the crowd really had witnessed him at his most unbridled if even the hard-ass Dom in front of him didn't want to cross him.

That Khloe Monroe hadn't shirked away from him even when he had shown her the most controlling version of himself was amazing.

"I'd like to help you get Miss Monroe out of her restraints," the employee offered.

"Back off. No one touches her but me," he warned. He saw the guy looking like he might challenge him so Ryder tacked on a request. "What you could do is find a robe that she'll be able to wear back to her hotel. Bring us a cold bottle of water too. Put it on my account."

The monitor didn't look happy at being turned into an errand boy, but Ryder didn't really give a shit. He turned his attention back to releasing his captive, helping to massage out her muscles as each restraint was removed. She was too wobbly to hold herself up fully so the second the final leather cuff fell from her wrist, Ryder scooped her into his arms.

She was feather light as he moved towards the stairs. It was only then that he realized he hadn't put his own pants back on and while he wasn't modest, he knew he needed to grab them and at least shove them into his bag, yet he knew Khloe was in no condition to stand on her own.

He looked out into the crowd, hoping to find an empty couch to lay her down while he cleaned up their little mess. Instead of a couch, he found Jaxson Davidson standing alone, his arms crossing his chest, staring at them. The men sized each other up for a few long seconds before Ryder made up his mind.

He moved down the steps in the direction of Jaxson. He stopped a few inches away from the only man in the club Ryder felt might be a bigger hard-ass than himself if the occasion called for it. He wasn't sure how he felt about Khloe being old friends with a man he suddenly saw as a rival. Had they fucked?

Are you fucking jealous, asshole?

As if to prove to himself that he wasn't, he made his request. "Can you hold her while I get my stuff gathered up?"

Jaxson's eyes widened, surprise registering at Ryder's request. He reached out and the men completed the transfer of the wet-noodle of a submissive. Only after his arms were empty did he add on, "Don't you dare fucking leave with her. I'm going to take her for a shower and help her come down, but I just need a minute."

Jaxson nodded a short assent and Ryder went to work dressing and gathering up his belongings. He glanced back a few times to make sure Davidson wasn't taking her away. He wasn't too crazy to see them talking softly, but he was too far away to hear what was being said.

By the time Ryder returned and held out his arms to take Khloe back, the look on Jaxson's face had softened. As soon as he held her, his sub snuggled into his arms, pressing her face into the crook of his neck, her head resting on his shoulder while the men stood in a showdown.

"Well…" he started to thank Davidson, but was cut off.

"You surprised me tonight, Helms."

"How so?" he countered, not really sure he gave a shit.

"I didn't think you were the kind of Dom who took the time to figure out what their submissive really needed. I took you more for the, 'my way or the highway' kinda guy."

Damned if Jaxson hadn't pegged him perfectly. He wasn't sure if it pissed him off more that he'd been that obvious when he'd shown up for Roulette or that he'd allowed Khloe Monroe to soften him.

Her soft mew against his neck helped push down his aggression towards the club owner. "Yeah, well I'm not stupid. I can recognize a gift when I see it."

Jaxson Davidson fucking smiled at his confession. He should have kept his mouth shut. Ryder felt foolish, like some kind of lovesick puppy stupid enough to be affected by a piece of ass. Only the second he thought of the woman in his arms that way, he regretted it. She was so much more.

Davidson leaned in closer, as if he was about to share a secret. "It's confusing, isn't it?"

Ryder suspected the younger man knew exactly how he was feeling in that moment. Still, he was done talking. He didn't prod Jaxson to expound, yet the taller man did anyway. "We're a lot alike, you and me, Helms. I don't know much about you, but I know a shit ton about Khloe." The younger man had been talking softly, but he leaned closer to deliver his final message directly into his ear. "She's had a rough time of it lately, so you'd better be fucking careful not to hurt her. Spencer's told me just enough about you to know you're not gonna be around for long. If you can't give her what she needs long term, do her a favor and walk away. Let tonight just be a great memory."

Jaxson didn't stick around long enough to hear Ryder's response. It was just as well because all he really wanted to do was punch the asshole for sticking his nose into matters that were none of his business. Even more, he would string Spencer up if he'd shared anything that could compromise his undercover status.

"Ryder?" The sexy woman in his arms was stirring, finally coming out of the haze he'd pushed her into. He struggled to hold her while swishing the messy hair out of her face so he could see her better. Her caramel-brown eyes stared at him with an expectation that made him feel uncomfortable.

"Let's get you cleaned up why don't we?" he countered.

"Is it over?" The disappointment in her voice bolstered his ego.

"Not quite. We have just enough time to spend some time showering."

"But what if they disqualify us for not spinning another activity?"

"Baby, I don't give a shit about the free month of membership." He cut himself off before he added that he didn't care since she'd already told him she'd be leaving soon. Had she been hanging around D.C. for the next month, he'd have been sorely tempted to make tonight a regular thing. Jaxson's warning replayed, reminding him he might be in over his head.

Khloe snuggled into his neck again with a sigh. Ryder ignored the smiles and atta-boys thrown their way as he weaved them away from the stage, across the main floor of Black Light towards the locker rooms. There were still several scenes in action, but the clock on the wall behind the bar as he passed told him it was ten-fifty. They'd spend their last ten minutes together showering.

He passed a living room style pit group where several couples were enjoying a down and dirty orgy, trying to take the sexual edge off that had built up watching the evening's entertainment. As he entered the co-ed bathroom facilities, he was greeted with an edgy scene that turned him on and that he suspected would freak Khloe out.

The room was completely open, but broken up into a few areas. To his left were several sinks and mirrors. In the far left corner was a seating area with plastic covered furniture. Small lockers lined the walls for members to use. Straight ahead was a raised hot tub with a door next to it labeled 'steam room.' To his direct right was a row of three toilets, open to the room. And in the far right corner were the communal showers they would be headed towards.

The room was surprisingly empty except for the scene in the very middle of the room. A curvy sub was restrained backwards over a bolster with her front facing the ceiling. Leather straps held her immobile, and her mouth was stretched wide by a ring gag. Above her, not one but two men were just finishing pissing on her. The older guy was aiming haphazardly, spraying her body but the younger Dom took the time to aim his spray directly into the funnel that deposited the hot liquid into her mouth.

The sub gurgled and sputtered, trying to swallow around the gag holding her mouth open. The scene was pretty common for the men's rooms in the clubs in Moscow. He just hoped the guys pissing were watching the bottom carefully. He'd found it wasn't always easy for the sub in the receiving position to swallow fast enough. He moved past them, sure they could handle their own safety.

He headed to the sitting area first, laying Khloe down long enough to strip himself naked and head to the showers to get the water warmed up. Once again, he had to hand it to Davidson and

Cartwright. They'd spared no expense, supplying the room with every amenity their patrons might need.

When he got back to Khloe, she was more alert and staring across the room entranced by the watersports scene in progress. He watched for her reaction to one of the Doms reaching down to pull the funnel out of the piss-sub's mouth before walking away to wash his hands as if he'd just finished at a normal urinal. The man hadn't even finished washing his hands when a new Dom came in and whipped out his dick, spraying his piss across the woman's body haphazardly as if he were watering his garden, the excess liquid falling to the floor and down the drain in the floor.

Khloe didn't take her eyes off the spectacle. Ryder watched her instead, trying to gauge her reaction to the edgy play. He suspected from the blush creeping up her neck and across the bridge of her nose and cheeks that she liked it more than she would admit.

"See something you like?" he prodded.

She protested a bit too much, "Oh hell no. I was just curious. I mean, that's just gross."

"Uh-ha. If you say so, Princess." He knew she was gearing up for a fight so he changed the subject. "I have the water hot. Let's go shower."

She protested. "It's okay. I can just shower back at the…"

He cut her off, holding two fingers to her lips to shush her. "We played hard. I still have ten more minutes as your Master. I intend to use them wisely."

Before heading to the shower, he reached to grab the cold bottle of water the dungeon monitor had supplied him on the way to the locker room. He held it to her lips and Khloe took several long drags.

He scooped her up into his arms and for the first time, she protested the royal treatment. "It's okay, I can walk now."

He ignored her objection, stalking to the shower area where three shower spouts rained water down on them. The room was thankfully warm enough that he didn't need to worry about her catching a chill. For someone who'd tried to walk on her own, once in his arms, she acted like she didn't want him to let her go.

He knew how she felt.

Ryder put his back against the tiled wall and slid down until he sat with Khloe in his lap, the water spraying down on his legs and splashing her back, but leaving them able to see each other.

They'd been through so much together over the last three hours. In some ways he felt so close to the woman in his arms, but the awkward silence that fell between them reminded him they were near strangers.

"Hi there."

Hi there? What the fuck, Helms? You're acting like a goddamn teenager on a first date.

Khloe grinned at him.

"What?"

She teased him. "You just smiled."

Her observation didn't make him feel any better. "Yeah, well don't tell anyone. You'll ruin my reputation." He was only half kidding.

"Who are you, really?"

"Ryder."

"Yeah, but where are you from?"

"Does it matter?" He saw disappointment in her eyes at his brisk answer and knew he was being a dick.

"Fine," she snapped growing shorter with him as well. "You know what I do for a living. How about you?"

He tried to lighten things up with a flip, yet unfortunately close to truthful answer. "I could tell you, but then I'd have to kill you."

She responded to his smile. "Seriously. Just give me something. Anything."

"I just gave you the best orgasms of your life. Being a bit greedy, don't you think?"

She challenged him. "I never said those were the best orgasms of my life."

"Baby, you don't need to tell me anything. I know the truth."

"Kinda sure of yourself, aren't you?" she teased.

But he got serious. "Always, but especially where you're concerned. Tell me it's a lie," he challenged. He watched her eyes dilate.

She whispered, "It's not a lie. It was... you were... amazing."

The invisible thread he'd felt tying him to her from the moment he'd set eyes on her was still at work. It was a novelty and he suspected he'd be sad when he had to sever it in the near future, which was exactly why he needed to keep from falling further under her spell.

"Let's get you cleaned up, young lady. I can't very well send you back to your hotel looking like you've been rode hard and put away wet."

He didn't miss the sadness in her eyes at the mention of returning to her hotel. He pushed to his feet and spent the next ten minutes enjoying soaping every inch of her body, massaging away her aches and even washing her hair, being careful to massage her scalp and pull his fingers through her wild mane until he'd got the tangles out. That he was caring for his sub in a rather non-sexual way was surprising enough, but that he was thoroughly enjoying himself was astonishing. Each minute of his aftercare made him regret that they were getting closer to never seeing each other again.

"Let's get you dried off." He knew the event had officially ended. It was time to finish up.

"Yeah, we need to hurry. I need to pee bad."

He'd reached to turn off the water, but her words stopped him. He was tempted. How would she respond if he pressed her? There was only one way to find out. On the one hand, he hoped he didn't fuck things up between them and then he reminded himself, he might be doing her a favor if he made her hate him.

Ryder reached out and grabbed her upper arms, pulling her close and delivering his command in his best Dom voice. "Squat. Right here. Right now."

"What?" She was genuinely confused. He knew she thought their scene was over.

"You heard me. Our last roll of the wheel was Dom's Choice. The night isn't over yet. I choose to watch you squat down and piss right there." He pointed to the drain about three feet away.

"But…" She stood frozen, fear and temptation warring in her eyes.

He pinned her with his best glare. He knew from experience it was effective on even the sassiest of submissives. That Khloe didn't shrink back from it or burst into tears was a novelty.

They had a stand off going. Neither backed down. A rowdy couple came in and headed towards the hot tub. He had his back to them, but Khloe broke his stare to glance nervously at them and then back to the submissive still playing the role as the community urinal over the drain in the middle of the room. He could see her turning her options over in her head. He watched her, enjoying her struggle like the sonofabitch that he was. When she finally raised her eyes to meet his gaze, the heat of her desire singed him.

She was ready. She just needed his final push.

"Now, Khloe. Piss for me like the dirty girl you are." Her eyes widened. He was pushing her. Would she break?

She didn't take her eyes off his as she slowly shuffled to her right towards the drain. The move put her directly under the overhead shower of water again. She struggled to keep her eyes open with water splashing everywhere.

She hesitated. "I don't think I can."

He moved into the water in front of her, cupping her face in his hands roughly. "You can do anything, baby. You are fearless, do you hear me?" He hated the vulnerable doubt he saw in her eyes. He may not be able to protect her from the tabloids and the bullshit that no doubt would dog her once she left Black Light, but tonight he would push her where he knew she needed to go.

"Spread your legs wider, sub." He felt her move to obey him. "Good girl. Now squat down." He released her face and nodded. It took her longer to obey this time, but she slowly moved towards the floor, her eyes never looking away from his.

Christ, she was amazing. They both held their breath, waiting. He barked the final order. "Piss. Now."

He finally broke their visual connection to look lower. For the first time, she had not obeyed him. He saw her struggling to submit, but her body wasn't cooperating. He added some incentive.

"I'm gonna count. If you don't start pissing by the count of three, you'll have to hold it until you get back to your hotel and as an added punishment, I'll send you off with ten lashes from my leather belt."

He saw the brief flash of anger in her eyes at his threat, but it was quickly replaced with longing. He might have made a tactical mistake with this strategy. Seems Miss Monroe might have enjoyed her paddling in the dungeon even more than he'd believed she had.

"One." Her internal struggle was beautiful. As a sadist, he loved a good mind-fuck as much as the real thing. And he was fucking with her big time.

"Two." The first signs of panic graced her eyes. She was afraid of his belt. She should be. Part of him hoped she'd fail.

The yellow stream mixed with the water showering down on them exactly as his "Three" hung in the air. He didn't know which part turned him on more, her submissive act of peeing in front of everyone in the room or her humiliation tinted glare as she refused to look away.

In the end, Khloe Monroe proved she had his number every bit as much as he had hers. Just as her stream of piss came to an end, she reached out and grabbed his filling erection. Despite two high-powered orgasms in the last two hours, his dick was ready to go for round three.

Khloe fell onto her knees to steady herself just before lunging forward to suck his wet cock into her mouth. For the first time in a long time, he was truly caught off guard. He was no longer in control and it rocked his world. The submissive in front of him got bolder, reaching around to grab his ass with both hands to help leverage her rocking up and down on his rod. With each thrust, she took him deeper until she was gagging on almost every insertion. Still, she didn't back down.

It was when she returned her gaze to his from her knees, pausing with his manhood obscenely filling her wide mouth and throat that he had to reach out and steady himself with the tiled wall. He could swear the naughty submissive at his feet had tried to smile around his cock as she'd recognized her effect on him.

"Christ, Khloe, baby. You feel so warm and wet." When he was close to spurting, he knew he needed to take back control. Ryder released the wall, wrapping his fingers through her wet mane to grab her in a headlock. He held her stationary and took over thrusting his erection down her throat again and again until she sputtered. He watched her eyes carefully, knowing when she was panicking and needing air. He gave her a hit of oxygen, just enough to take the edge off and then resumed his face-fucking of the gorgeous woman at his feet.

He squirted the first shot of cum down her throat, holding them together until the second spurt filled her mouth and then finally pulling out to let her breathe while he deposited the rest of his load onto her chest. Each of them took deep breaths after their impromptu exertion. He could see the exhaustion returning to Khloe as she came down from the high their scene had given her.

Ryder held out his hand and helped her to her feet. He pushed down the regret of the night coming to an end to turn off the water before grabbing a couple of the blanket-sized towels. They were silent as he dried her from head to toe before wrapping her up to keep her from getting chilled. He quickly patted himself dry and wrapped the towel around his waist before reaching for her hand and pulling her back towards his bag in the seating area.

The room had several more couples now, cleaning up after their Valentine's fun. Ryder wished they could be alone again and then felt relief that they couldn't, afraid he'd make an ass out of himself by saying something nice.

He wrapped her in the oversized robe and then dressed.

"I can't go back to the hotel in a robe. The photographers will go crazy. I can see the headlines now."

He hadn't really thought about that when he'd enjoyed cutting off her dress at the start of the night. "Let's check with Davidson and see if you can borrow something from his girlfriend."

Ryder wasn't crazy about having to talk to the owner again, but Khloe looked like she wanted that even less than he did.

"It's okay. I have a long coat in the locker at the entrance. And I have my shoes so I don't think they'll have a clue as long as I keep my coat closed tight."

When they exited the co-ed locker room, the main floor of Black Light was almost empty. The background music that had been playing all night was off and the lights had been raised. Employees were working to clean things up and a few final couples were lingering, acting like they didn't want the night to end.

He was happy to see that Khloe wanted to steer clear of the trio of owners and their famous friends just as much as he did, yet that left only the direction of the exit. She was taking shorter steps the closer they got to the final door where their magic would have to come to an end. Ryder powered through, pulling Khloe the final few feet until his hand rested on the doorknob.

She pulled her hand from his and took a step back, defiance in her eyes.

"You know everything about me, but I know nothing about you except your name. It's not fair."

He couldn't help but smile at her petulant tantrum. "Careful, Princess. I'd hate to end the night with you over my knee for your sass."

She took it as a dare. "Fuck you. I'm not leaving until you tell me something. And not some bullshit. Something real." She folded her arms across her chest for good measure.

"Baby, every minute of tonight, you had the real me."

She didn't back down. "At least tell me where you live. What you do for a living."

"Why, so you can schedule a visit? It doesn't work like that with me, Princess."

"So how does it work? You just fuck strangers, spend the night doing all kinds of intimate things with them and then you walk away, never to see each other again?" Tears floated in her eyes. He saw her struggle with her emotions.

"Khloe, you've had an emotional night. You need a good night's rest."

"Bullshit. I need you to level with me. Was tonight just a game? Something you do with a different woman every week?"

Her inquisition pissed him off. This, right here, was why the Moscow subs were perfect for him. Not one of them expected anything emotional from him. He didn't have room for emotional attachments in his life. The worst part was that tonight he was already having to push down his own crazy inclination to drive her back to her hotel, and spend the next three days holed up, fucking like rabbits. He didn't need her tempting him further.

He hardened his heart, knowing tonight was all they were meant to have. She had her glamorous, very public life to return to—and Ryder, well he had to stay in the shadows. He couldn't afford to be splashed all over newspapers and social media as the mysterious man in Khloe Monroe's life.

He took a deep breath and said the words he needed to say. "Tonight *was* a game, Khloe. A game called Valentine Roulette. I'm sorry if you thought it was something more than that. Don't get me wrong. I had an amazing time and I'll admit I hate to say goodbye too, but we each need to go our own way, baby. I don't have the kind of life you would fit into."

His words hurt her. For once, the sadist in him hated to see the pain cross her face. He wanted to reach out and hold her to him and take back his harsh words, but he was too disciplined for that. He allowed himself one weakness.

He leaned down, capturing her lips in a farewell kiss. He still felt the incredible electricity coursing between them. He luxuriated in sliding his tongue into her mouth, tasting the toothpaste she'd used just minutes before as they'd cleaned up together.

In the end, Khloe was stronger than him. He felt her hands on his chest just before she yanked back, pushing him away so hard he almost fell backwards.

Christ, she was amazing. Not a stitch of makeup. Her hair still wet, hanging down the back of the oversized robe. Yet she was the most beautiful woman he'd ever seen. She reached up to touch her swollen lips as a tear spilled down her cheek.

When he reached out to swipe it away, she flinched away from him.

She fought for control of her voice, quietly whispering, "Goodbye, Ryder."

She turned and almost ran through the exit. He panicked, second-guessing wanting it to end like this. He had just started to chase after her when he felt the clamp of a hand on his shoulder.

Ryder spun, more than ready to take out his frustration on anyone who dared pick a fight with him. A concerned Jaxson held up his hands as if to surrender.

"Whoa there, Helms."

"I need to leave," he swung around to chase after Khloe, but Jaxson's words at his back stopped him.

"Don't fuck it up now. You're doing the right thing in letting her go, and you know it."

He swung around to argue. "But I hurt her."

"Of course you did. You were her Dom."

"Not like that. I mean I really hurt her."

Jaxson took a bit longer to answer this time. "Like I said, of course you hurt her. How did you see this playing out? You planning on retiring and following her around the globe from movie set to photo shoot watching men try to get in her pants?" Jaxson paused before adding more quietly, "Or maybe you think she'll retire and move to Moscow with you."

"I'm gonna fucking kill Spencer."

"Don't bother. He's already in a world of hurt with his own woman problems tonight. And anyway, I can be very persuasive when I want to be."

He hated it, but Davidson was saying exactly what he needed to hear. They were better off making a clean break tonight. It had been an amazing night that he'd never forget and that would just have to be enough.

The men stood grounded until things got awkward. A few of the last couples to leave moved past them looking like they wanted to say goodbye to the owner, but seeing the intense showdown in progress, thought better of it and headed out.

Ryder had nothing new to say. He picked his duffle up again and started for the door. Davidson called out to him.

"You're welcome at Black Light whenever you're in town."

Ryder paused long enough to lift his right hand in an acknowledgement and then walked through the exit.

He wouldn't be back.

THE END ... FOR NOW

* * *

COMING **in the Spring of 2017! A full-length book in the Black Light Series!**

Ryder and Khloe's chemistry is too hot to ignore. Neither of them wants to let go of the memories of their Valentine's Day game, but it takes a rabid fan putting Khloe's life in danger to move Ryder into action.

No one gets to hurt Khloe but him.

ABOUT LIVIA GRANT

USA Today bestselling author Livia Grant lives in Chicago with her husband and furry rescue dog named Max. She is fortunate to have been able to travel extensively and as much as she loves to visit places around the globe, the Midwest and its changing seasons will always be home. Livia's readers appreciate her riveting stories filled with deep, character driven plots, often spiced with elements of BDSM.

Sign up for Livia's newsletter to make sure you never miss a new release.

* * *

Livia wants to share a FREE book with her readers. Grab your copy of *Infamous Love* today. https://dl.bookfunnel.com/79tvw4b2cz

* * *

Did you know Livia has a private Facebook reader group? If you'd like to hear about her upcoming projects and talk about the BDSM lifestyle, please check out Livia's Passion Vault at: https://www.facebook.com/groups/296689347184223

* * *

Livia's Website
Facebook Author Page
BookBub

facebook.com/lb.grant.9

instagram.com/liviagrantauthor

bookbub.com/profile/livia-grant

twitter.com/LBGrantAuthor

tiktok.com/@liviagrant

ALSO BY LIVIA GRANT

Dark Pen Series

Devil's Contract

Dirty Ledger

Dangerous Notes

* * *

Black Light Series

Infamous Love, A Black Light Prequel

Black Light: Rocked

Black Light: Valentine Roulette

Black Light: Rescued

Black Light: Roulette Redux

Complicated Love

Black Light: Celebrity Roulette

Black Light: Purged

Black Light: Scandalized

Black Light: Roulette War

Black Light: The Beginning

Black Light: Roulette Rematch

Infamous Trio Boxed Set

Black Light: Gamble - coming Summer 2022

Black Light: Discipline - coming Fall 2022

Black Light: Roulette Swap - coming February 2023

Black Light: Rolled - coming Summer 2023

* * *

Punishment Pit Series

Wanting it All

Securing it All

Having it All

Balancing it All

Defending it All

Protecting it All

Expecting it All

Celebrating it All

Punishment Pit Series Volume One (Books 1-3)

Punishment Pit Series Volume Two (Books 4-6)

Deceiving it All - Coming 2023

Stand Alone Books

Blessed Betrayal

Royalty, American Style

Alpha's Capture (as Livia Bourne)

Blinding Salvation (as Livia Bourne)

Out of Print Books

Psychology of Submission, Corbin's Bend Series

Life's Unexpected Gifts, Corbin's Bend Series

Melting Silver, Red Petticoat Series

Bite Me – Vampire Anthology

Just Breathe – Anthology

Royally Mine – Anthology - *USA Today Bestseller*

Heroes to Obey – Anthology - *USA Today Bestseller*

A Lovely Meal – RWA Anthology

I Have Lived & I Have Loved - Charity Anthology

Dirty Daddies: 2021 Anniversary Anthology - *USA Today Bestseller*

Christmas at the Club Anthology

WET

A Black Light: Valentine Roulette Novella

by

Jennifer Bene

CHAPTER 1

*S*ienna focused on keeping her back perfectly straight as the Dom above her shifted in his seat, the heels of his shoes digging into her ribs. Master Kent, as he preferred to be called, was busy talking to another Dom while she served as his footstool. It had been at least an hour, probably more, and her knees were aching, her wrists were sore, but nothing could beat the quiet inside her head whenever she served.

Submission was the dream she got to step inside between long drags in the waking world, where there was nothing but responsibility. Just jobs, bills, and disappointment. For this pure moment she only had one thing to think about as the men's conversation blurred into white noise in her ears – *keep your back straight, be quiet, and don't move.* The way he'd commanded it, pushing her to her knees in front of him, had made everything instantly simple, easy to fulfill, easy to get right.

It was why she kept coming back here week after week.

The sound of a feminine voice, and low male laughter, pulled Sienna out of her headspace a little. Glancing up through her hair, she saw the five-inch stilettos first, and then the long line of smooth leg, before the red dress started high on the woman's thighs. Swallowing, Sienna dropped her head back down and let her brown hair curtain her face again.

She didn't pay attention to the conversation, furniture wasn't *able* to listen to conversations, and that was another way that everything was simpler inside the club. All she ever had to do was what she was told. *Exactly* what she was told.

"Up," Master Kent ordered as he lifted his feet from her back, just before he shoved her over with a shoe in her side. She caught herself with one shaky arm, landing on her hip.

"Yes, sir," Sienna whispered as she reformed into a kneel at his feet. With a quick movement he ripped her head back, his fist tight in her hair, and that's when she saw the blonde at his side. The red dress was stunning, and Sienna was pretty sure the woman had extensions to have such perfect, platinum blonde waves, but she forced her eyes low again to focus on the bit of worn leather between Master Kent's thighs.

"You like being my footstool, don't you slut?"

"Yes, Master Kent." She nodded as much as she could with his hand holding her head still, and he chuckled before pressing the edge of his glass to her chin, tilting it so that she had no choice but to part her lips for the burn of the liquor. Even opening her mouth, and swallowing as much as she could, some still spilled out the sides of her lips.

"Dammit. Look what a mess you made," he growled and released her, and she struggled not to cough as the harsh burn made its way to her stomach. Master Kent snapped his fingers in front of her face and then pointed down to the floor. "You spilled some of my drink on my shoes, lick it off."

"I'm sorry, sir." Sienna felt that surge of twisted satisfaction inside as she scooted back to kneel in front of him, leaning forward so she could trace her tongue over the shining leather of his black shoes. There really wasn't much alcohol on them, maybe a few drops, but she gave him the show he wanted, and the low groan of the Dom behind her in the other chair almost made her smile. After a few minutes of licking his shoes until the thin sheen of her saliva made them glint with the lights in the club, she sat back on her heels to see the blonde kissing him.

The woman broke the kiss first, her eyes meeting Sienna's for a second before she returned them to the floor, cursing herself for staring. "That was pretty," the woman cooed, and Master Kent chuckled.

"It absolutely was. You're a good whore, aren't you?" He leaned forward to cup Sienna's chin, running his thumb over her damp lips.

"Yes, Master Kent."

Smiling, he gripped her chin a little harder. "What do you say for getting the opportunity to lick my shoes?"

"Thank you, sir."

"Good, slut." The words made her skin tingle all over, a strange little buzz that was so strong she could almost hear it. "I'm done with you for the night, go get yourself something to drink. I told the bar that you could have one on my tab."

Sienna finally lifted her eyes to his, and he gave her a little smile and a wink before he let go and sat back in his seat. He was handsome, early-forties, with dark hair, and he was completely uncomplicated. Her favorite kind when it came to play. "Thank you, Master Kent."

"Bye bye," the blonde waved her fingers as Sienna stood slowly, but they were already making out again by the time she was upright. She nodded to the other Dom, and he raised his glass in her direction before turning his eyes to the scene before him.

Just another day in paradise.

Winding her way to the bar between the various equipment set-ups, she let her eyes wander while she rolled her wrists at her sides, working to ease the strain. There was a pretty intense caning happening on one of the spanking benches, and there was a Dom flogging his sub as she rode a wooden pony. Those were the only interesting scenes happening inside Overtime tonight, but she wasn't sure if she wanted to stay and watch or go home and sleep.

"Hey, what would you like?" T-Baby smiled at her as she adjusted the oversized pink bow on one of the afro puffs on either side of her head.

"Just a glass of wine? Cabernet if you have it?"

"Of course, and I'll give you the good stuff since Master Kent told me it's on *his* tab." She giggled, walking to the narrow shelves of alcohol to grab a bottle and pour. T-Baby was in an obscenely short and frilly pink skirt, with a white corset on top that had pink ribbon as the backing. A stark contrast to her mocha skin, which made her the picture of innocence.

Littles...

Sienna shook her head and smiled to herself, not really getting the allure of dressing and acting like a kid, but – to be fair – a lot of people didn't understand her craving for humiliation and service. Taking a slow breath she repeated one of the community's many mantras in her head, '*Your kink is not my kink, and that's okay*.' It was a good reminder, because consenting adults or not, there were some much stranger kinks in the world than the littles – and she'd tried several of them.

"Here you go, sweetie. You feeling okay?" T-Baby leaned forward on the short bar, baring all of her cleavage.

"I'm good, thank you." Sienna spoke softly.

"If you're sure." T-Baby shrugged and walked away to keep cleaning. The woman never bothered her, never tried to make her talk, and it was why she often retreated to the bar at the end of the night. When whoever she'd played with had long since left.

Taking her first sip of the wine she moaned softly, grateful to wash the acrid taste of whatever hard liquor Master Kent had been drinking out of her mouth. His shoes had been more pleasant.

"Sienna." A rough voice made her jump a little, and she turned before looking *way* up to meet one of the dungeon monitors in the eye. It was the one they all referred to as 'Muscles', because he looked like he took steroids at breakfast while he ate an entire cow. He was massive, with muscles where Sienna hadn't even been sure there *should* be muscles.

Realizing he was waiting for her to respond in some way, she cleared her throat. "Um, yes?"

"What just happened over there? I saw you with that guy for the last couple of hours, and then that blonde shows up and he's leaving with her. Right now." Muscles looked agitated, glancing back at the door to the exit. "Did he cross a line?"

"No, no, we were just playing together tonight." Sienna tried to explain, but speaking was not a natural talent for her, and the DM was only getting more irritated.

"Exactly, that fucker doesn't just get to do some pick-up play and then literally kick you to the side when he sees something else he wants. Aftercare is a minimal expectation." He growled, actually growled like some large beast, and then he held up a finger between them. "I'm going to go have a conversation with him about club expectations."

"Wait!" She grabbed onto his arm when he turned to walk away, but she may as well have tried to stop a moving car. Sienna almost spilled her wine as he pulled her with him for a step, and then he looked down at her. Being 5' 2" on a good day, this was one of those times she really hated being short, because Muscles was easily a foot taller and about a million times stronger.

"I'm not waiting, he just walked out the door with her! You don't deserve this, Sienna, you –"

"That's his girlfriend!" Almost shouting it, she felt her eyes go wide as he stilled, and then he turned to face her completely and she took a step back so it was easier to see him. "She, the girl I mean, she's his girlfriend. Bombshell Life, or something like that, is her username on FetLife."

"Explain," Muscles demanded and Sienna took a large drink of her wine, trying to fortify her voice so she could answer him.

"It's a thing they have, I've served Master Kent before for it."

"A thing." The huge man in front of her looked doubtful, and she sighed.

"He didn't do anything wrong. She likes to pretend they don't know each other, that she distracts him from some other sub he's playing with, and then he chooses her over the sub." Sienna shrugged, feeling an inkling of shame as Muscles stared down at her, irritation still etched into his features. "I think it's how they first met, but we discussed it all online. He knows what I like, and I knew the deal."

"That's no excuse to ignore aftercare," Muscles grumbled.

Sienna shrugged. "Being ignored is part of it."

"Your kink?" The man asked, wiping his face free of the irritation he'd been broadcasting.

"I like it," she confessed in a whisper, but instead of judgment she saw him physically relax.

"Okay, I just –" Muscles rubbed his hand over his short-cropped hair. "I was worried about you, but I'm glad it was all arranged."

Smiling a little at him, she tried to show him she felt fine – because she *did* feel fine. Good. Peaceful, actually. Serving as a footstool for the last however-long had been the quietest her head had been since the *last* time she was at the club, but all of that was too much to explain. "Thanks for checking on me."

"Of course. It's the job and all that." He seemed suddenly awkward, which was a challenge since he took up about twice the physical space that she did, and his bare chest was a veritable monument to strength and the benefits of weight lifting. "I see you here a lot, you know."

"Really?" She snuck a sip of her wine, bringing her eyes up from the dark tattoo covering his shoulder and the upper part of his bicep. "I'm really only here once or twice a week."

"That's pretty consistent considering I rarely see you play with the same person."

Sienna blushed, wishing he would just walk away now that he knew about the arrangement she'd had with Master Kent and his girl-friend. She didn't need to evaluate her life choices while standing in a BDSM club, and definitely didn't want to discuss them with a stranger. The heat was scalding her cheeks as she tried to speak, "I didn't – I mean I don't –"

"Hey, I don't care that you play here a lot. I think that's great. You know what you like, and you seek it out, but it would be nice to see one of them stick around long enough to see you to the fucking door." Muscles sounded like he was lecturing in a Dom 101 class, which Overtime held once a month, but while some of the Doms may need a few tips in basic protocol for play, *she* definitely didn't need to hear it.

"I'm fine. I promise." *Seriously. He didn't even take any of my clothes off.*

"Right…" He turned to sweep his eyes across the floor, and she studied his face while he wasn't focused on her. The man clearly had a passion for this, a real dedication to the community, and she respected him for it. It would just be nice if his attentions were applied to someone else.

This was the kind of torture she hated. Socializing.

If she were a more talkative person she'd explain that she wasn't upset in the least by her evening. It wasn't like she was new to the community, she'd had several Doms since college, it was just none of them lasted. She was too busy, they were too busy, and the relationships usually dissolved without a lot of drama. Pick-up play suited her; it worked because it was uncomplicated. Planned out. Organized, without the convoluted expectations that came from anything *more*. Sienna spent most of her life quiet, she spent her life listening and watching. Well, except for her second job as a waitress where she had to make casual conversation with customers before putting in their orders – but that was easy. It was like reading from a pre-written script. Spontaneous discussions like this? *Real* conversations? That's where she usually panicked.

Why couldn't she just be a footstool for another thirty minutes?

"Muscles?" she asked, trying to get his attention, but he turned back to her with a laugh.

"Terry. You can call me Terry. That's just what all these assholes call me because they don't hit the gym as hard as I do." *That's the truth.*

"Okay, Terry then. Listen, I'm really okay. I got to – you know, *relax.* Get into my headspace for the night. So, I'm fine, and I promise you Master Kent didn't do anything wrong. Please don't say anything, sir?"

"I get it, I won't talk to him about it." He nodded, suddenly looking animated as he brought his hands together in front of him, making his biceps bulge. "You know, I actually have an idea. There's another club that just opened a couple of months ago that's looking for more subs. I work there on the nights I'm not here, and I think you'd be an interesting addition to the mix."

She almost laughed out loud, but it came out as just a huff of breath. "Interesting?"

Her?

"Absolutely. You're into service submission, right? And humiliation? I know you did the watersports thing towards the end of last year with that blond guy, and at the Halloween Masque you were at one of the blowjob stations." Terry said the words so casually, but she felt the tickle of shame again. Too many people talked trash about her kinks for it not to faze her.

"Yes, I am, and I did that." It had taken years for her to be able to admit to her kinks aloud, and even feeling dizzy from the strain of saying it to him, she wasn't going to be shamed inside the club. "But, really, it's fine. I barely have enough free time to come here, and I –"

"Look, this new club is exclusive. Super private, *very* expensive, but they've got an event coming up and they're short on the roster for submissives so you'd get in free. I think you'd be a fun wrench to throw in their gears."

"Why?" Sienna asked, looking up at him as he chuckled and rolled his shoulders, making his pecs do a little dance, and his washboard abs rise and fall.

"Because you're real, and a lot of the people there have forgotten what real people are like. The guy who owns the place asked me to see who I could find here, and I'm pretty sure that's why." He tilted his head at her. "Interested?"

"Maybe," she admitted. A new club with new people might be nice. Especially since she knew most of the people here, and she'd somehow developed a reputation as the sub who was a 'use-at-club-and-leave' type. No one had asked her out after play in a long time.

A year at least, which was a depressing realization.

"Okay, let me give you my email address and I'll send you the details, along with the website for the application. It just opened so I'm sure you'll get in."

"Wait, an application?" Sienna took another drink of her wine before she set it on the bar as Terry reached over the top to snag a napkin, waving at T-Baby to get her attention.

"Yeah, they're crazy about security." Terry smiled as T-Baby walked over and he got a pen from her, scratching out something on the napkin in front of him. When he finished he held it out to her, leaning down slightly to meet her eyes easier. "Just send me an email so I can get you the link, and then apply. Do it as a favor to me, alright?"

"A favor?" she asked as she took the napkin, craning her neck to look back up at him as he stood upright.

"I always look out for you." He shrugged like it was obvious. "And I'll be there that night to look out for you too."

"What night?"

Terry smiled, tapping the bar as he turned away from her. "Valentine's."

"Wait – what kind of event is this?" Sienna raised her voice as he walked away, a nervous tension making her heart race.

He turned around, walking backwards for a few steps. "A fun one. Sign-up, Sienna. I think you'll thank me later."

Watching as Terry 'Muscles' the dungeon monitor walked away to take up his usual post near the St. Andrew's Cross, Sienna sighed and stared down at the napkin. His handwriting was terrible, but she was able to make out the email address.

A Valentine's Day event?

When she looked up at the club, her eyes passed over the various members in attendance, ticking them off one by one and categorizing them appropriately: taken and unavailable, taken and played with as a couple, unattached and played with. There were maybe a few people she didn't immediately recognize, but it was a serious comment on how long she'd been playing at Overtime – and how *many* people she'd played with.

Having a second club to go to wouldn't be a bad idea, and if Terry thought she was a good fit – she probably was. Hell, it was a compliment that he'd even cared enough to approach her. Short, and small, with dull brown hair, and boring brown eyes – Sienna was someone that got overlooked a lot. At work, on the street, and at Overtime.

With a steadying breath, she stared at the email address for a long minute, adjusting her skirt and blouse as she toyed with the edge of the paper. The decision to sign up and at least *try* to get a space at the event seemed to be unavoidable, as if it were destiny. Or at least, she *would* have thought it was destiny if she believed in that stuff.

As long as this isn't some BDSM version of speed-dating.

Finding a dry, clean space on the bar she set the napkin down, turning to watch T-Baby giggle and flirt her way through another drink pour. When she glanced towards her, Sienna raised a hand to ask her to come back, because if she was really going to do this – she needed another glass of wine before she asked for a ride home.

CHAPTER 2

FEBRUARY 14TH – BLACK LIGHT

*A*lexander walked slowly behind a couple through the chilly tunnel from the psychic shop, tugging his coat tighter around him. The man and woman were dressed well, and clearly heading to watch the Valentine Roulette event that Jaxson Davidson had put together. Watch, *not* participate, which made Alexander slow his steps even further so he wouldn't catch up.

It was an interesting concept, one that had caught his attention enough to sign up, but as he listened to the couple laughing and chatting about what they might see that night – he felt a lot more like an actor about to step on stage than a Dom about to play with a new sub for the evening. He liked his kink, but he didn't need to be the center of attention. Especially not with how he liked to play.

Not sure this was your brightest idea, Alexander...

Unfortunately, the man from the couple held the door into the security room for him as they got to it, and Alexander had to pick up his pace to avoid being rude. "Hey," the man said, nodding at him as he stepped past.

"Evening," Alexander replied, avoiding a conversation by turning away once inside like he might be meeting someone.

Meeting someone? Ha. That was a joke.

He'd have to find someone able to handle him to have that.

Fidgeting, he pulled off his coat and took out his wallet, waiting for a few of the couples that had been milling around to go ahead and enter Black Light. Daniel, the desk security in the locker room, was scanning people in as they lined up in front of him. Most had the membership cards, sleek white plastic with text only visible under black light, but one person scanned in with a tattoo on the inside of his forearm. *Interesting.* Alexander tried to get a good look at the man who had a lifetime membership to the club, but he wasn't able to before it was his turn.

"Evening, Daniel."

"Happy Valentine's, Mr..." Daniel waited until the scanner read his name, and then he smiled at him. "Reed. I see you're a participant, so I'll just remind you of the one drink rule once you're inside."

"Not a problem." He smiled before taking the card back.

"Good, you'll be locker thirty-one tonight. All technology in, no exceptions."

"I know the routine." Alexander chuckled internally at the confusion on the security guard's face. He clearly didn't remember him, but since Alexander had helped Jaxson Davidson review the security protocols, the security staff, and the non-disclosure agreement his law firm had drawn up for them – he was intimately familiar with all of the safeguards in place. Especially since he'd spent the end of January going over everything *again* after an issue with one of the guests had almost turned into a liability for the club and all its members.

'Reporters,' Alexander grumbled in his head as he tucked his phone in the locker and shut it tight. Wallet away, coat dropped off through the window, he followed a couple into Black Light.

Walking into the club was like breathing fresh air, because it was the one place in his life he didn't have to watch every word he said. Every move he made. Becoming partner at a law firm had been his goal in life, but while he loved almost everything about being a lawyer, it also meant curbing certain aspects of his personality.

Not *every* aspect; being dominant had never been a weakness in a courtroom.

An attractive young woman in a very tiny dress approached him carrying a tray of champagne, "Would you like a drink, sir?"

"No, thank you." He gave her a smile, and then stepped past to scan the small crowd. There were tables lining the edges of the main floor, and a tighter grouping of them up near the stage. Even near the entrance he could see the roulette wheels set up, and he took a slow breath.

You've signed up, you're here, you may as well have some fun with it.

Just as he started to let his eyes roam again, he caught sight of Jaxson laughing at a table near the front. Alexander headed in the man's direction, looking around to get a feel for the people in attendance. Who were the participants, and who were the couples? In some places the answer was obvious, in others... not so much.

"Jaxson," Alexander smiled when the man turned around, still mid-laugh at something the others at the table had said.

"Alexander! I was starting to worry you might have had cold feet. You're cutting it a little close." There was a question in Jaxson's voice that Alexander was not in the mood to answer so publically, so he simply shrugged.

"I had work to wrap-up at the office. I do have *other* clients, you know."

"I'm guessing that's why you're dressed so well?" Jaxson asked.

Straightening his suit jacket, Alexander grinned. "When do I *not* dress well, Jaxson?"

"Cocky bastard," Jaxson laughed before turning back to the table. "I don't think you've met Cash Carter, and his new wife Samantha."

Raising his eyes to the rock star at the table, Alexander gave a small smile and nodded, but he spent his days around too many high-profile individuals to be star struck by the lead singer. "Nice to meet you, Cash, and it's quite lovely to meet you, Samantha." Reaching over he offered Samantha his hand and when she took it, he squeezed lightly. "You look beautiful. Marriage clearly suits you well."

"She is beautiful." Cash draped an arm over the woman's shoulders and leaned back with her, an unnecessary claim of possession since she was married, which meant completely off-limits to Alexander – but he had to admit that, otherwise, she would have been just his type. Brown hair, an innocent face, a slight flush to her cheeks that summoned all sorts of thoughts. "And I go by Jonah around my friends... but you can call me Cash."

Samantha shoved at Jonah's chest and then smiled up at him. "I think the appropriate answer is actually 'thank you'." She laughed a little. "So, you work for the law firm Jaxson uses?"

"He's a partner, actually, and all three of those jerks have memberships to Black Light as part of their fees. Only Alexander has taken us up on the offer though," Jaxson answered Samantha for him.

"It's true, my partners aren't into this scene at all, and I'm sure they'd have a little trouble looking me in the eye on Monday if they came by."

"And here you are trying to get *another* month free out of me? Wasn't six enough?"

Alexander grinned. "I'm here for the challenge, you can keep the month if it hurts your pocket book so much."

"Right," Jaxson rolled his eyes, laughing again.

"Go ahead, I'll just bill you for the hours we talked on the phone last month and I'm sure I can cover the membership fees here."

"Asshole."

"Yes." Alexander laughed as he agreed, feeling the tension ease a bit inside him. It was true he was there for a challenge, a sub he didn't know, the potential to spin activities he wasn't familiar with – it was what had drawn him to the event in the first place. "But, let's be honest, Jaxson. There's nowhere else in the city I'd really like to play. After all, I know how secure this club is compared to the others, and my firm has seen more than one issue appear for our clients when poor decisions were made." He glanced back to the stage, still feeling an edge of concern that he'd be one of the points of interest for the audience members slowly taking their seats at the tables. Normally, everyone would be busy playing – tonight he'd be part of the main attractions.

One of the waitstaff walked by again with a tray of champagne, and he was tempted to snag one. A drink would definitely make him *feel* better, but he was getting a new sub tonight, and that meant he needed his head completely clear.

How else could he figure out which buttons to push?

Jaxson lowered his voice a little, leaning back in his seat. "You know, I checked the sub roster and based on what we know of the participants, there's only one little in the group."

"Not surprising," Alexander muttered, and looked over the women in the crowd. He'd played with a variety of different submissives in his life, and while he definitely had a 'Daddy Dom' persona when he played, he also liked to break them down. Get them to snap, to cry, all so he could pick up the pieces when it was over – and *that* he could do with any sub he drew that night. "It won't be an issue either way."

"I'm sure it won't." Jaxson smiled and glanced towards the stage where people were starting to gather near the stairs. "Looks like it's almost time for you to take your place."

"Lights, camera, action." With a sigh, Alexander stepped past Jaxson to catch Emma's hand, leaning down to press a kiss to her knuckles. "I hope you enjoy your evening, Emma."

"I will. Good luck, Alexander!" She gave him a perky little smile, her shoulders lifting with her sincere cheer, and he winked at her before releasing her hand to move towards the stage. It was good to see her more confident, more *herself* sitting next to Jaxson Davidson. When he'd first met the girl, she'd still seemed to be in a bit of shell shock that the two models had chosen her – but Alexander knew why. Emma was the antithesis of shallow, she was pure, and caring, and all of that showed in her natural beauty. They had a relationship to envy, but one thing had become very clear to Alexander in the last few years.

Relationships didn't work out for him.

As he stopped near the grouping of men, he noticed that most of them were in suits as well, dressing to make an impression, and that's when he noticed the women gathering on the other side. There were outfits ranging from what could best be described as creative lingerie, to full dresses that covered enough to be considered modest in this room.

Which one would he spin? His cock twitched in his pants as he traced feminine curves with his eyes, thinking of all kinds of things he could do to bring one of them to tears.

There was a commotion near the exit and Alexander's ears perked up, watching as a man tried to lead a woman towards the door, and they were clearly arguing. He had an urge to step in, but one of the dungeon monitors was already closing in. What surprised him more than anything was that both parties split and started walking towards opposite sides of the stage.

Interesting, had a couple signed up to play with others and one was backing out?

Chase stepped onto the stage then, the lights coming down, and Alexander couldn't help but smile as the blond turned on his charm and started to explain the idea of Black Light's Valentine Roulette. It was a pity that Chase didn't speak up in more of the meetings at the firm, because he had a talent with language. He was quick-witted, smart, and approachable.

Jaxson, on the other hand, had almost made several of the paralegals piss themselves.

When Chase called for the dominants to join him on stage, he followed the queue of other Doms to walk up the steps, feeling a bit awkward as he stood near the heat of the spotlights. Chase walked by with wooden sticks, and he drew number eight. As he stared down at the little number, Alexander couldn't tell how he felt about it. The middle was better than the end, but he really just wanted to know who he had so he could start to get to know them.

And figure out what makes her tick, his mind added, and it made him smile a little. Looking across the stage to see the collection of submissives gathered at the base of the other set of stairs, he tried to keep himself from hoping for a specific one. There were some of the women dressed loud and provocatively, and he immediately pulled back from them.

They were probably brats, and brats grated his nerves.

He wanted someone who *wanted* to play. Someone who would be a challenge. Alexander slipped deep into thought as the first few draws went off without a problem, but then Khloe Monroe threw a hissy fit over the Dom that drew her name. It was impressive to see that serious looking man stalk her down and bring her back to the stage to spin her scene. While it was entertaining, Alexander was just grateful he hadn't drawn the actress – but it seemed like *she* could be in over her head with this guy.

Another few names went by, and then Chase was smiling at him. "Alright, looks like Alexander is up next."

Stepping forward, he smiled and shook Chase's hand, leaning in to speak under his breath, "Roll me a winner, will ya, Chase?"

"They're all winners," Chase replied and handed him the small, white marble. As soon as the wheel started spinning, Alexander felt the same nerves he always did just before he stood up from his table in a courtroom. That worry that based on the words he said, the actions he took, everything could go south – but the rush of adrenaline that filled him along with the nerves was exactly why he was a lawyer, and it was the same reason he dropped the ball with a grin.

Time for a challenge, Alexander.

* * *

"WOULD Sienna please join her Dominant on the stage?" Chase Cartwright called out her name, but she felt frozen to the spot for an instant. Lifting her eyes to the stage she almost gawked at the man standing before the wheel.

Gorgeous.

He had a suit on that fit to his body like it was custom-made, dark hair in a clean cut, and even from the floor she could see baby blue eyes. He narrowed his gaze to see past the spotlights and she knew she needed to move, forcing herself to step out of the group of women to walk towards the stairs. Her heels were the nicest pair she owned, as was the sleek black dress she'd bought for a New Year's party three years before. However, the short steps to the stage were not *nearly* enough to prepare herself, especially when she lifted her gaze and found the Dom waiting for her at the top, smiling like some charming prince. "Good evening, Sienna."

"Hi," she squeaked, and he offered his hand to guide her back to the roulette wheel. Her heart was pounding in her chest, and she slipped free of his hand as soon as she could, offering her shaking fingers to Chase so he could give her the little white ball. The idea that an audience of people were at her back, along with the heat of the spotlight, made her feel a little dizzy.

Why on earth had she let Terry convince her to do this? This was a nightmare.

The wheel started to spin and she released the ball without a thought, wanting it over. None of the segments made any sense as they whirled, but then the wheel started to slow and the ball clunked into a slot.

Needle play.

"That's on my hard list!" Sienna gasped.

"Hard list!" Alexander called out beside her, and then they both looked at each other, breaking into nervous laughter. His name had returned to her memory just as he'd spoken, and she was still stunned that *this* guy felt like attending an event to get paired up for kink. Surely he had a list of women at his door, ready and willing to kneel at his feet?

Get your mind back in the game, Sienna.

Chase was smiling, and she had no doubts that he had been a model. He was gorgeous, and when he met her eyes to hand her the ball again, she had to swallow. "Looks like we'll roll again!" he announced for the benefit of the crowd. Another spin, and she prayed silently that she'd get something on the wheel that would let her leave the damn stage.

Spin, spin, spin, clatter.

"Water based breath play!" Chase called out, and she knew her eyes went wide. *What the fuck is that?* Glancing up at Alexander to see his reaction, she saw a wolfish grin that was more than enough confirmation that he was happy with the results.

"Come on, little girl," he purred against her ear, a hand in the small of her back as he led her to the stairs on the Dom's side.

Letting him lead her, she obediently followed until they stood outside the sea of tables focused towards the stage. "I'm Alexander," he was smiling again, offering his hand and she took it, but he immediately adjusted their touch so he could lean down to brush his lips across the back of her hand.

"Sienna," she whispered, and he chuckled as he stood upright, towering over her. He *had* to be close to six feet tall.

"Yes. That's a beautiful name for a lovely little girl." He went still as he stared at her, and she knew she'd flinched when he had used the term again. Lifting her chin with a finger, those blue eyes bored into her. "What? Don't like being called little girl?"

"It's... silly."

"Excuse me?" he asked, and there was a bite to his tone that made her submissive streak shiver.

"I just, um –" Her voice trailed off, slinking away to some place inside her that she couldn't reach.

"You're here to play, correct?"

Sienna nodded, unable to make a sound as he held onto her chin, his eyes tracing over her lips before finding their way back to her gaze.

"Then I think I can call you anything I like." There was a force in him, a distracting power that already had her melting.

"Yes, sir," she whispered.

"That's my girl." Smiling, Alexander released her chin and turned to look back at the stage. A man and a woman were bickering in front of the roulette wheels to the complete amazement of the crowd, and the obvious irritation of their MC.

After several moments the woman shouted, "What?"

"What?" The man echoed, sounding confused.

With a sigh, Chase raised his hands and sang out, "And a one, and a two, and..." when the audience shouted back with a resounding 'WHAT', the pair seemed to become aware of their location, and shuffle to the side of the stage. Sienna swallowed, a nervous tension tickling up her spine as she watched the last few participants get paired off. It was peaceful until the very last couple, and the angry shouting match on stage as they were paired was only capped with the spin of pet play.

For an instant, Sienna felt jealous of the other woman, wished she could swap, because pet play would have been easy for her. Crawling, serving, obeying – it took no thought. It was simple. But she had *no* idea what water based breath play would be, and a cold shiver rushed over her skin as she looked across the room and her eyes landed on an oversized tank of water.

Oh God. No way.

CHAPTER 3

*A*lexander was smiling as the last couple left the stage and Chase signaled the official start of the event, but Sienna couldn't think straight. Her eyes were dancing between the water tank and the Dom standing beside her, wondering what in the hell she'd signed up for.

"Give me a moment, I'm going to locate someone to help us get setup properly." He spoke with the kind of confidence that *should* have calmed her, but she wasn't sure how she felt. Tracking the dark haired demi-god through the room, she saw him stop at one monitor, and get pointed towards another man. Sienna wasn't sure what they said, but they both looked back at her with predatory gleams.

Fuck.

Alexander summoned her with a crook of his finger, and her feet started moving before she'd given them permission – but *he* was the one in charge tonight, so that shouldn't have been a surprise. As she approached, they kept their eyes on her, but it was the dungeon monitor who spoke, "I'm Garreth, I'm a dungeon monitor here and I'll be observing your activity to make sure you're safe. Do you have any medical conditions we should know about?"

"No, sir."

"Nothing that would interfere with breath play or submersion in water?"

His words created a nervous energy inside her, and she shifted her weight between her feet, looking up at the water tank again. *That's where I'm going to be.*

She knew it before they'd even confirmed it. *Submersion in water.* Even imagining it was making her ears buzz in a funny way, her stomach twisting into tight knots of anxious energy.

"Sienna?" Alexander prompted. "He asked you a question, little girl. You need to pay attention."

"No. Nothing will interfere, sir." Pointedly keeping her gaze locked to the DM, she ignored Alexander's use of the term again, and then Garreth turned to speak to her Dom for the night.

"Alright, let me walk you through the set-up, how it works, and some things to watch for." Garreth had started to walk towards the tank, but he paused when Alexander didn't move.

Because he was staring at her.

"I want you to strip, underwear too, leave your clothes against the wall by the tank, and then kneel at the bottom of the stairs. Understand, little one?" He was smiling as she lifted her eyes to his and nodded once, fighting the urge to argue at his continued use of the *little* language.

"Yes, sir."

"Good." Alexander walked away to accompany the DM to the tank, and she uncharacteristically felt like stomping her feet and throwing a damn temper tantrum so it would at least make sense. Why was he *insisting* on calling her little girl? She had given a brief description of her style of submission in the application, had been clear in her kinks and experiences – but maybe he didn't know.

Reassuring herself that it was just a mistake, she slowly unzipped the dress and stepped out of it, carrying it past the hot tub, and what looked like massage tables, over to the tank where she could hear the two men talking. Their voices were like a low hum amidst the soft instrumental music and the other discussions happening around the room. Within eyesight of both men she slid her underwear down first, drawing her heels through, before she slipped them off as well.

Even shorter. Great.

Sienna was used to feeling short though, and if Alexander was hoping to throw her off her game in making her strip – he was going to be surprised. She wasn't concerned about being naked in front of club members. Especially with their activity being one of the farthest removed from the gathering of tables.

Her main interest was in what she had spun on the damn wheel.

With a silent sigh she took the bra off, drawing it down her arms and moving to kneel at the edge of the steps leading up to the raised platform the tank sat on. It was gigantic. Alexander could have laid down in it without touching either end, but she was completely focused on the strange chair that seemed to be a part of the tank. It was missing the front legs, the metal seat dangling out over the water.

"Just watch your time, and it will be fine." Garreth said, and then she realized both men were looking at her, and Sienna dropped her eyes to the tiled floor.

Alexander took the steps slowly, each of his shining shoes landing heavily before he continued. Once he was on the floor, he paced around her slowly, and she shifted her posture to ensure she was presenting in a proper kneel. "You are beautiful, little girl."

Her teeth clenched, but she stayed silent, only letting out a gasp when he eased his fingers into her hair, gliding down to the back of her head before he gripped hard and made her look up at him.

"I want to know more about you." He smiled slowly, a look that she was sure charmed most of his submissives. "Tell me something."

"What would you like me to say, sir?" It was a plea for him to give her direction, to make it so she didn't have to think, but he seemed determined to make her come up with her own answers.

"I want to know *you*, little one. Tell me something you like or don't like."

"I don't like being called little girl, sir." Sienna muttered, and he chuckled, tightening his fingers in her hair until little pinpricks of pain rushed over her skin.

"I already know that, and I'm enjoying it very much, *little girl.*" Pulling her to her feet, he pushed her to the stairs so that she climbed them in front of him, the angle of her neck growing uncomfortable. "Tell me something I *don't* know."

"Like what, sir?" she whispered, unsure what he was looking for as he planted her in the odd chair. Garreth had clearly slid it backwards on its track, because she was still able to put her feet on the floor for now, her toes just able to touch the damp edge of the cold tank.

Alexander leaned down to brush his lips across her shoulder, nudging her hair out of the way as his mouth grazed her neck before stopping beside the shell of her ear. "Tell me anything. I want to get to know you."

Sienna found herself mute, because his intimate touch had sent her thoughts somewhere else, and it was hard enough to speak even when she was fully aware. No matter what he called her, Alexander was a Dom in the truest sense. It was evident in the sophisticated rumble of his voice, the commanding way he held his fist in her hair, and the possessive way he nipped at the skin just below her ear.

"Speak," he growled, and her lips parted at his command, but she couldn't make words form.

What would she even say? What could he possibly want to know about her? About her boring life?

"You're a quiet one, aren't you?" he asked rhetorically, releasing her hair to walk around her. With a firm grip he captured one ankle, lifting it to attach it to the cuff on the seat of the chair. "There's only one problem with that..." Alexander came back to the other ankle, repeating the process so that her legs were folded in such a way that she seemed to be kneeling, thighs stretched wide, over the chair.

"Sir?" she managed to ask, and he chuckled behind her.

"I like to hear my subs talk, and you're mine for the evening." Capturing her wrists from where she'd been bracing on her legs, he pulled them to the back of the chair, cuffing them separately to either side so she couldn't budge forward at all. "That means you're going to talk, little girl. Even if I have to make you scream first."

The words plucked at the heat inside her, making her pussy clench with the promise of his dominance. Sienna shifted on the seat, testing her new bonds, and heard the metal links clatter against the chair. Each leather cuff was lined with silk, and not painful in the least, but as she stared down into the water she felt her breathing pick up in her lungs again. Panic teasing her.

Submerged. Fuck.

"Have you played long?" he asked, combing his fingers through her hair, drawing it back into a small ponytail. Far too short for much else.

"Yes, sir."

Alexander jerked her back against the chair by the ponytail he'd just tied off. "How long, little girl?"

Sienna clenched her teeth, counting silently in her head, way too much thinking for play. "Nine or ten years. *Sir.*"

"Then you know the rules, you answer your dominant when he asks you a question." He leaned close to her ear, now on the other side. "Next time you fail to respond to me, that will result in a consequence, little girl. Understand?"

Despite her issue with his language, her body responded with a rush of arousal, heat coiling in-between her spread thighs. "Yes, sir."

"That's my good girl," he purred. Alexander wound a thick, broad strap just under her breasts, his thumbs grazing her nipples as he brought it around to buckle it in place, tightening it so she was securely held to the back of the chair.

Fuck. I'm definitely going in the water.

How long can I hold my breath?

As if it would help she took in a slow breath, and held it, trying to count to see how long she'd last.

"Garreth," Alexander called and she turned to see the DM only a few steps away. They whispered for a moment, and then Garreth chuckled and walked down the stairs, disappearing into the main floor. Her Dom, the man who had drawn her name for the evening, to own her for the night, was still there – and she released the held breath from her lungs on a whine.

She'd only counted to eighteen.

Alexander was handsome, and devious in a way that she would normally be attracted to, and if he'd just stop calling her little girl she could slip into her role. Fade, disappear inside it. She could sense him even now, standing just behind her, and she wondered how she looked tethered to the chair with the dark straps folding her into position. Yes, *this* was something she could enjoy. The silence, the slightly uncomfortable positioning, it was more in line with how she normally played.

But then Alexander drew her back with his voice, "I haven't seen you at Black Light before, do you play somewhere else? With someone else? I mean, do you have a Dom?"

"Overtime, sir, and no, I do not have a Dom."

A quiet huff left his lips, and then he walked to the edge of the tank where she could see him. Tall, dark, and handsome. "Why are you here tonight, little one?"

Why? Sienna rolled her neck, testing her movement at the ankles and wrists, but found that she was so securely attached to the chair that the *only* thing she could move was her head. "I signed up, sir?"

"Obviously." He sighed, looking down at her again. "You have such a lovely voice, I want to hear you speak. Just tell me about yourself."

"What do you want to know, sir?"

The question seemed to frustrate him, and he pulled out an index card from a pocket on his suit jacket, glancing over it before he tossed it into the tank. Sienna was drawn to the way it floated on the surface for a moment, before it sunk and floated down to the bottom like a leaf falling from a tree. "Let's start with what I know about you. Your hard limits for tonight were anal, fisting, blood play, and – of course – needle play, which we both had. "

"Yes, sir."

"I also had blood play, but I included fire play as well. Tell me, does fire play interest you?"

"No, sir," she answered, staring somewhere around his forehead to avoid his intense eyes, wondering what *else* he had on his limit list.

"Does the water scare you?" he asked, moving a little closer. That predatory edge showing in each gesture.

Scared? That word made sense. It was a word that matched the tense fluttering in her belly, but she'd felt it before. She'd done scary things before, which meant she could handle this, right?

Sienna stared down at the water just as a set of lights lit up where they were. Overhead ones, embedded in the ceiling, and she groaned because now they might as well have been a main attraction on the floor.

It was worse than standing on the damn stage.

"Answer me, little girl," Alexander purred behind her, and she turned as she heard Garreth climbing the steps behind them. "Ah, perfect."

"Sorry, I had to interrupt someone to get to the costume box. Thanks for waiting for me to get back."

"You should be here," Alexander acknowledged, but Sienna was still focused on the reference to a *costume box*. That is, until he took a bright, silk, baby-blue bow from Garreth and held it in front of her. "This will complete the look I think."

Sienna bit down on her cheek as she felt him working the clip of the bow into her hair, positioning it just above her ponytail. The *click* of it locking in place bothered her more than she expected. She liked humiliation, liked being shoved around, slapped, spat on, pissed on, talked down to – but *this?* This felt like someone trying to turn her into something she wasn't.

A Little.

A charming, baby girl. Ready to giggle and smile for her Daddy Dom.

Sienna did *not* giggle.

For the first time in her years as a sub, Sienna wanted to argue with her dominant, wanted to storm off like one of those prima-donna submissives she'd seen in the past. And it was over a fucking bow.

Just as she was about to speak up, there was a scream from somewhere on the floor. Followed by a very loud, very clear, "RED!"

Alexander went stiff, and so did she, both of them turning to look across the main play space to see the couple who had matched last facing off. The woman had a collar and leash around her neck, draping down over her bra and underwear, and she was screaming at the Dom in front of her as a pair of monitors appeared to separate them.

"I guess they're out of the game early," Alexander laughed, and she bit down on the complaints she'd been about to make. "So, little girl, answer me. Are you scared of the water?"

"No," she pushed the word through gritted teeth, and he stepped behind her. There was a distinct metal *clink* and the chair slid forward until it locked in place with the seat hanging over the water. To think she wasn't scared was ridiculous, but she wasn't admitting it to *him.*

"Good." He tilted his head as he watched her from the side. "The bow looks lovely on you, little one. So, why don't you tell me what you do for a living?"

While he slowly took off his suit jacket, she tried to steady her mind enough to ignore the bow she could feel brushing her scalp, the shining glint of the water in front of her, and somehow form language. "I have two jobs," she muttered, and he paused rolling up one sleeve to listen to her.

"Speak up, little one. I want to hear you loud and clear."

"I have two jobs, sir," she said a bit louder, struggling to retain the honorific.

"Really? What are your jobs?" Alexander asked the question like he was at a dinner party, walking to the steps to hang his coat on the railing before he wandered back. He started on his second sleeve as he waited.

"I'm a stenographer, and I waitress a few nights a week. A stenographer is –"

"I know what a stenographer is, I work at a law firm." He chuckled, but she stilled instantly.

Alexander was a lawyer? How in the hell had she managed to nab one of those assholes?

"That means you're good at listening, right?" he asked, and she almost snapped at him. How was he getting under her skin so easily? Where was the usual comfort she had when she played?

"Yes, sir," she answered through clenched teeth.

"Wonderful," he purred. "Then this should be very easy for you to remember. Every time you refuse to answer me, I'm going to put you in the tank." He lifted a metal remote from the floor which had two simplistic buttons on it, connected by a thick cable to the floor. Then he held out his hand and Garreth approached to offer a sleek looking vibrator to him. "But, if you answer me, I'll reward you with this like the good little girl I know you're going to be. However, there will be no coming without permission. I want you to have plenty of incentive to tell me about yourself. Understand?"

Sienna was stunned for a moment, trying to process what he'd said, and then she watched him sigh, and press the button in his hand. The chair pivoted forward smoothly, and she barely managed to gasp in air before she was under the water. It was cold, and her arms and legs immediately tugged at the cuffs, but there was no give.

Shit, shit, shit.

Before she could really panic, the chair lifted, and she found herself gasping as chilly water ran over her entire body. Naked skin forming goose bumps in the air of the room while she tried to recover. Alexander was still standing in the same spot, only now he was smiling. "Sienna, do you understand the rules of this game?"

"Yes, sir," she hissed, and for some unknown reason she felt the rush of submission inside her. The thrill of obeying, even though she still wanted to shout at him.

"Good. Now, little one, tell me why you have two jobs."

"Because," she answered, and he waited for a moment, and then shrugged and pressed the button. Sienna drew in air just before she hit the water again, jerking against the chair once she was under the surface, frantically fighting her body's urge to breathe.

Son of a bitch, this son of a bitch.

It was longer than the first dunk, she was sure, but when the chair lifted her out of the water she almost choked trying to draw in air. "Sir!" she called out as the rear legs of the chair met the floor.

"Yes, little girl?" Alexander raised an eyebrow at her, toying with the controls in his hand, his expression placid. "I'm waiting..."

Sienna whined, trying to think of what he wanted to hear – but the problem was he wanted to hear about *her*. There was no script for this interaction, no easy answers, she had to fucking talk to him, and that was the problem. "I need the money?" she offered and instantly flinched, waiting for the chair to pivot, but instead he moved close and brushed the stray strands of her hair off her cheeks.

"Good, girl." He had swapped the items in his hands, and the dull hum of the vibrator made her open her eyes just before it slipped between her legs. Alexander nestled it in her folds until it was flush with her clit, and she bucked against the restraints as he found his mark and a zing of pleasure shot up her spine, making her stiffen. "Does that feel good, little one?" he purred.

"Yes, sir." Nodding, she twisted her wrists in the cuffs, trying desperately to hold herself still so the pleasure would continue, but his damnable voice kept pulling her focus away.

"Tell me why you need the money. Is the stenographer position not enough?"

Sienna moaned softly, too well acquainted with the teasing buzz of a vibrator not to respond, but she didn't want to answer his question. Didn't want to talk about the personal details of her life. This was supposed to be play, one night of kinky fun with a random partner. It was *supposed* to be perfect for her.

Why was this asshole even asking about her job?

The delightful buzz of the vibrator left her suddenly, and as soon as he stepped back the chair pivoted, forcing her under the chilly water once more.

* * *

ALEXANDER WATCHED SIENNA STRUGGLE, keeping an eye on the second hand of his watch. This was dangerous, a kind of play he'd never dare do on his own, but with an EMT at his back, he felt secure. When the second hand hit the mark, he pressed the raise button, and she lifted out of the water.

Her body was sparkling, the swell of her breasts glistening in the lights. Rivulets of water flowed between them to pool between her thighs, and he let his eyes enjoy the sight. Sienna was shaved smooth, and he wanted to explore her further, wanted to watch her come – but she was locked down tight. Refusing to speak about even the smallest of things, and *that* had to change.

There was an easy solution, though.

He just needed to break her first, and then he could get her back. Put her together in a way that would bring them both pleasure.

"Want to tell me why you need a second job?" he asked.

Sienna turned towards him, her short brown hair mostly pulled back in the ponytail, the baby blue bow damp and limp against the top of her head, and she looked beautiful in her disarray. The quiet little girl fighting to bite her tongue, to hold back whatever words she *really* wanted to say. There was a fire behind her brown eyes, and it was something he wanted to prod at, to bring forth.

"Little one," he threatened, holding up the remote, and the way her eyes widened made his cock swell in his pants.

Pretty, pink lips parted, and her tongue flicked out to catch a bead of water. "I –" She looked distressed, but she wasn't near breaking yet as her soft voice continued, "I don't get enough hours as a court reporter, sir."

"So, you supplement your income waitressing?" Alexander asked, stepping close to flip on the vibrator, but he held the buzzing implement in front of her. Tempting her. Waiting for her to respond.

Come on beautiful, come out of your shell.

"Yes, sir." She nodded, keeping her eyes on the water. Part of him wanted to force her to look at him, to turn those warm, brown eyes to his, but physical interactions were clearly what she was used to. He had seen her relax as he'd held her chin, as he'd forced her up the stairs, and it was becoming clear that the only way to *really* push her was to make her speak.

Which meant, unfortunately for her, that he had found the button to push.

"Explain," he demanded, and she shifted in the chair, her hips wiggling in the most enticing of ways.

"What do you want from me, sir?" Sienna sounded tense, exasperated, but that just meant she was one minute closer to breaking down.

"I *want* you to answer me without me having to ask you twenty questions."

Her jaw clenched, eyes flicking up to his face for just a moment before she glared back at the water. *So stubborn.*

"Last chance, little girl. You want a reward or a punishment?"

"Punishment." The word came out as almost a hiss between her teeth, and he couldn't even stifle his laugh as he turned off the vibrator and stepped back.

"Alright then." With a single press of the down button, he watched the chair swing forward into the water, her body submerging along with the metal of the chair. Lifting his watch he counted to the maximum time Garreth had provided him, watching the second hand tick by. At first she was still, he could see her in his peripheral vision, but then she started to really fight, and as soon as the time was up he lifted her out.

Sienna was coughing, gasping, whining loudly as she struggled against the cuffs binding her so marvelously exposed to the chair, and Alexander was grateful she'd spun this. Having a soaking wet little girl so frustrated was a veritable gift to him.

And Jaxson had questioned why he'd want to sign up.

For the first time since he'd drawn her name, she lifted those brown eyes to him with heat behind them, growling at him. "Why are you doing this? Why won't you just play with me?"

"I *am* playing with you, little one. You just aren't submitting to it." He grinned when she let out a groan of frustration, a *real* noise from her. Things were progressing nicely. "Ready to tell me about yourself, yet?"

"What do you want to know?" Sienna raised her voice at him, and he noticed she'd dropped the *sir* from her language altogether.

Naughty little girl.

"What did you forget?" he asked.

"I have no idea!"

Pressing the button, he dunked her again, but it was more for shock value than punishment this time, so he let her back up almost immediately. She came up cursing under her breath, more animated than he'd seen her all night. Gone was the small, quiet girl who had seemed stunned to meet him on stage – *this* was a girl he could have some fun with. "You'll refer to me as sir as you answer my questions, or we can keep playing the dunk tank game all night."

"What do you want to know, *sir*?" she snapped, glaring up at him as she shivered in the cooler air of the room.

His cock strained inside his pants, the defiant expression on her face making him imagine what it would be like to make her cry. To push her until she snapped and became his, completely. "Tell me why you need to have two jobs."

"Because it's expensive to live in D.C. and not all of us were lucky enough to end up as lawyers!" Sienna stared at him, her expression hard, and he rested the controls for the chair against the tank to move close. Unconsciously, she leaned back against the seat, trying her best to keep him in her line of sight, but he was happy to keep his gaze on hers as he slid the vibrator between her pussy lips and flipped it on.

The reaction was instantaneous. Her hips jerked, her eyes clenched tight, and she pressed her lips together to stifle the whine as he focused the highest setting on her clit. She was splendid. So contained, so controlled, so full of mindless obedience – and he was forcing her to let go of all of it.

For him. In front of him.

Alexander reached up to catch her soaking wet ponytail, angling her neck back over the top of the chair so her throat was exposed to his lips. He kissed and licked and nipped as she writhed in the seat, and he felt the moment when she stopped fighting and started to ride the little toy. Grinding herself down against it, seeking her completion.

How he wished that were his cock...

Her skin was soaking his shirt, but he didn't care as he leaned closer to whisper in her ear. "Tell me the truth, little girl, do you like working two jobs?"

"No, sir!" Sienna answered, almost shouting the words as her back arched away from the chair, lifting her breasts in such a tempting way that he couldn't ignore it. With a low sound, he drew one of her nipples into his mouth, and when she tried to pull away in her surprise he followed, locking her against the hard metal of the chair so he could tease her to the edge.

Just as her hips picked up a rhythm, soft sounds of satisfaction leaving her lips, he stepped back completely, bringing the vibrator with him so he could see her undone. *And she was.* Sienna's knees were even wider than the bondage of the chair demanded, her back arched, her head braced against the top of the chair so that every inch of her body was available to look at.

Beautiful.

"Sienna," he called out to her, and she whined. "Do you want to come, little girl?"

"Yes, sir," she mumbled, nodding as she rolled her hips against the seat. Temptation embodied.

"Then tell me something new. Tell me why you don't have a Dom." Alexander couldn't hide his excitement as she sat up in the chair, cheeks flushed, wet hair a mess, and glared at him.

"Why don't *you* have a sub, sir?" Sienna had tried to make the question polite with the addition of *sir*, but it decidedly wasn't.

"Want to try that again, little girl?" He offered her the chance, but she barely glanced at the water before those warm, chocolate brown eyes found his – all kinds of fire present now that he'd woken her up a little.

"Afraid to answer the question?" she taunted, and he picked up the remote and dunked her without another word. It was clear from her wild movements in the water that she was furious, but he started unbuttoning his dress shirt one handed as he watched the time.

When the second hand found its place, he pressed the up button, and let go of the remote again to finish unbuttoning his shirt. "Now, are you ready to try answering me?"

Sienna screamed, full of frustration and raw anger, and he smiled at her as he let his shirt fall open. He gave her a few seconds to relax, but instead she turned to him, meeting his eyes full-force, and shouted, "Go fuck yourself!"

Alexander's eyes went wide before he licked his lips and moved close to her, well-aware of the sudden gathering of people drawing closer to the tank so they could see what was happening. He kept his voice low, just for the two of them, and her breath caught as he reached her, halting the angry panting. "I plan on fucking you, little one. I plan on fucking you until you scream for me, just like that, but you have absolutely *not* earned it yet."

"You're an asshole," she hissed, also quiet enough that their audience couldn't hear her, but all he wanted to do in that moment was kiss her. Sienna was so much more than she appeared. A veritable firestorm underneath her cool, calm exterior.

How long had she hidden this from the world?

Had anyone else managed to draw it out of her, or was he the first?

Stepping back, he tugged his damp shirt off and tossed it to the floor, taking a bit of satisfaction in the way her eyes skipped down over his chest and abs. "You're a naughty, little girl, Sienna. Take a big breath."

She gasped in air as he pressed the button on the remote. Another splash, another lingering sight of her struggles as the seconds ticked by, and then he brought her back up. There was a whine to her scream that time, interspersed with coughs, as she hung her head down. Water flooded the deck he stood on, but she was clearly still recovering. Her chest heaving in the most distracting of ways.

Alexander was *definitely* gaining an appreciation for breath play.

Checking his watch just for show, since he knew exactly what time it was, he looked back up at her and lifted the remote for the tank. "We still have almost two hours if you want to keep going. Ready to talk, little girl?"

Sienna shivered, breathing hard, soaking wet as she jerked her head up and stared at him. "No, sir."

CHAPTER 4

*S*he was under the water again, but even the cold wasn't enough to push back the heat coiling low in her belly. Never in her life had she felt like this, so out of control. Her mind was a whirlwind of thoughts, things she wanted to scream at him, words she wanted to call him – and some of them she'd actually *said.*

It was just about getting her tongue to work.

She'd spent too many years quiet, too many years stifled and pushed to the boundaries of the world, and she had made a nest out of that place. A refuge in obscurity.

But fucking Alexander was tearing it all to shreds. Pushing her to the edge like all lawyers did, as if she were some hostile witness.

Breaching the water this time she gasped for air, but bit her tongue on the string of curses she wanted to release. There were people nearby, the glass of their drinks catching the light in the shadows beside the water tank, and if she'd had enough energy to feel self-conscious she would have blushed. As it was, she was flushed enough from sheer anger.

The chair settled back on the platform with a jerk, and Alexander's sleek, fit form filled her vision. This time, it was his hand between her thighs, swiping at the slick wetness of her lips that had *nothing* to do with the fucking water tank. "Tell me why you don't have a Dom, Sienna."

"I don't need one, sir," she snarled, but it was half-hearted as his other hand jerked her hips forward on the seat enough to slide two fingers inside her. With a deft touch, he found the place inside her that sent her head reeling, her wrists tugging at the cuffs as she tried to ground herself, to focus on anything but the waves of pleasure pulsing out from his strokes. Despite her attempts, little pants and hushed moans escaped her, unable to clear her head enough to stop them.

"What happened to your last Dom?" he asked, leaning forward to block her body from the view of the people gathered, his tongue tracing her collar bone.

Sienna whined, angling for just a little more friction from his fingers, just a little *more* so she could fall over the edge and drop into bliss where his antagonizing remarks, the water tank, *all* of it would be easier to take. Alexander bit down on the flesh of her shoulder, a sharp nip that made her gasp.

"Tell me," he commanded, and the submissive streak inside her overwhelmed her reluctance to speak.

"He was busy, and I barely had any free time. He found someone new." She moaned as he adjusted his touch and slid a third finger inside her, stretching her in a battle of pleasure and pain until she made her hips ache with how she twisted away from the chair.

"There is no way he found someone as delightful as you." The low growl in his tone did nothing to change the impact of his words, early tears springing to the edges of her eyes as he said things that he couldn't possibly know. "When? When did he leave?"

Sienna wanted to scream, or cry, *anything* to avoid answering him, but he was teasing her to the edge of oblivion and she wanted to fall over. Wanted to tumble into the boiling pleasure that promised her escape from having to talk anymore. She just had to answer him once more. Just once more. "A little over a year ago!" she shouted.

"Idiot," Alexander said it like a curse against her neck, and then he captured her lips, his tongue parting hers so that he could own her completely. The kiss was explosive, upending her universe on its axis, and making gravity non-existent for a brief moment. *This* was what she needed. To let go, to submit, to belong to someone else so fully that she ceased to exist.

But it only lasted a moment before he slid his fingers from her and grabbed the vibrator from atop his soaked shirt. "Please!" she shouted as he turned it on, but Alexander ignored her pleas and pressed it to her clit.

Her body was painfully taut, her body arched so far off the chair that the cuffs at her ankles and wrists were taking most of her weight, and she knew she was going to lose it soon. One way or another, she was going to snap – but whether it would be into the pain, or the pleasure, she couldn't tell.

"Do you want to come, little girl?" he asked, and she could hear the roughness in his voice. Alexander wanted her just as much as she wanted him.

"Yes, sir!" she cried out, not even trying to be quiet anymore, but he forced her hips back to the chair, relieving the strain as he kept the vibrator on her clit. Summoning crippling waves of pleasure that made her muscles taut, her body reaching for what only he could give her.

"How much do you want to come?" The tease in his tone should have been warning enough, but she couldn't think straight enough to evaluate it.

"I want it, sir! Very much, sir, please!"

Alexander stood up beside her and ripped the promise of bliss away so suddenly that she almost sobbed. He was holding the buzzing vibrator at his side, the lean lines of his frame standing out in the lights with the dim club as a backdrop behind him. Sienna panted as she stared at him, the terrible buzzing in her veins making her whine. He was enjoying this, loving her tortured cries, and she tried to silence them as he smiled slowly. "I'll let you come, little girl. I'll make you come so much you'll scream. But you have to speak for me."

"I am speaking," she said it with exasperation, unable to even explain how hard it was for her, but he just shook his head.

"No, I want you to say... 'Please, Daddy, I want to come.' Look me in the eyes, say it, and then I'll let you."

Groaning she fought against the restraints, trying frantically to come, but she couldn't even bring her thighs together. The low sound of laughter from beside the tank pushed back the hazy desperation, the powerful storm inside her calming enough for her to breathe, and she leveled her gaze at him. Some semblance of self-control returning with a single thought – *I am not a little.* "I won't say it, sir."

"You sure?" he taunted.

Instead of answering, Sienna tried to breathe, tried to capture enough air for what she knew was coming, but the frigid splash of water as her world tilted was still a shock. Her skin was too hot, she was sweating from the stress he was putting her through, and the sudden cold of the tank was borderline vicious. Just as her lungs were threatening to boycott her command not to breathe, the chair lifted out of the water and she coughed and growled, cursing in a stream of obscenities Sienna was quite sure she'd never said in her *life* – much less to a Dom.

Alexander was on her as soon as the chair settled into place, fist tightly wrapped in her soaked ponytail to force her head back hard against the seat. "Who do you belong to tonight, little one?"

Glaring at him, she gulped air, trying to come up with a response that would display just how angry she was with him for making her talk, how frustrated she was with him for edging her like this. She *wanted* their gathered audience to understand that *this wasn't her.*

"Answer me. Now." His voice had a darker edge, a strength to it that called to the submissive buried underneath all her raw emotion – the things that should have been calm and quiet when she played. One hand landed on her thigh, squeezing hard enough to leave bruises, while the hand in her hair shook her slightly before tightening. "Who do you belong to tonight?"

"You!" Sienna answered, and she hated the surge of frustrated tears in her eyes, burning as they tried to fall.

"That's right," he growled. "And are you supposed to be an obedient little girl?"

"Yes, sir," she forced the words between her teeth, straining to lean closer to him even though it pulled her hair.

"Then say it, say 'I want to come, Daddy'. Do it."

"No," she answered, and she watched his blue eyes go wide in surprise, before they narrowed and he released her, returning a second later with the vibrator. The first brush of it against her clit was cataclysmic, and the scream she released was pure fury, but he grabbed her hip and held her firmly to the chair so that she had no choice but to take it. Flickers of sparks wound their way up her spine, tightening every muscle in her body as he dragged her to the edge. Hanging her over it with only his hand to decide whether she felt grace or damnation.

Bastard.

There was nowhere to move, no way to avoid the onslaught of pleasure – and she knew in that moment that he intended to break her. The shift in him was clear. Something new. Threatening. But the damn vibrator made it so fucking hard to think, to focus.

"You're so strong, Sienna," Alexander purred against her ear as she whined. "You're always so strong, aren't you?"

She shook her head hard. *Not strong, never strong. Meek, quiet, unimportant.*

"I think you have those two jobs so you don't have to ask for help from anyone. I think you've always been like that, always alone even if you're with someone. Afraid to *need* anyone."

"Stop," she whimpered, and she wasn't sure what she was begging for more. For him to stop teasing her, or to stop speaking the words that she realized she couldn't quite deny.

"You know what else your card said about you, little one?" He waited just a beat, not long enough for her to actually answer as she tried to arch away from the chair. "It said you were into service and humiliation, and I think that's true. I think you get off on it, from letting men use you. But I think you submit because you like to feel the connection to another person when you let them take you, let them do whatever degrading thing they choose." Alexander pulled back and met her eyes, but she squeezed them shut. "You don't want to let anyone in, little girl. You don't want to let anyone close enough to hurt you, but you still want to feel *some* connection, don't you?"

Sienna released a wordless cry, an unintelligible plea for him to stop before he continued. To let her go, to let her come, to let the lightning running under her skin find its mark. She needed to come, she needed to fall apart, she needed to escape him and his damning words. For the first time in her years of play, she contemplated her safeword. The tongue-based shape of the 'R' in *'red'* forming inside her mouth, but he spoke first.

"I think it's because you don't want to be anything more than an object, little one. Some *thing* for them to abuse, because as long as you're not a person you don't ever have to feel, ever have to connect, ever have to risk being rejected." Alexander's words felt like a knife sliding between her ribs to reach her heart, twisting at just the right moment to stop it between one beat and the next.

It's not true. That's not it. It's not it. It's just what I like.

"NO!" she screamed, hating that she was so close to an orgasm that her body was a network of live wires, too tense to fully feel the agony that had tears rolling down her cheeks as he rolled the devious little toy around her swollen clit. Fresh waves of heat making her forget the chill in her skin. "Stop, please stop," she begged, shaking her head and jerking at the cuffs, but he wasn't going to stop.

"You want to be an object, little one, but here's the thing – you *deserve* to be taken care of. You *deserve* to be treated like a person, Sienna. To be cared for, supported, and I can do that. I can give you the connection you crave. I can degrade you like a little whore until you beg me to stop, but when it's all over..." Alexander's voice was hushed, and she opened her eyes to see him waiting, staring, and then he spoke the words that threatened to crush her. "I'll be there to pick you up, little girl. I'll remind you that even tied down, spread wide for all of these people to stare at, to enjoy your screams, your choking – you are still a person. You are still beautiful."

It felt like lies. Pretty lies, but lies all the same.

And her body was strung too taut for him to be playing with her mind too.

Hot tears rolled down her cheeks, a sniffle breaking her shaking breaths as she stared into blue eyes. Endless and steady.

"That's what a Daddy does, little one." Alexander slipped a hand between her thighs, just beneath the agonizing touch of the vibrator, and pushed two fingers deep. "I can feel you squeezing. I know you want to come. Just admit it all. Say it, and it's yours."

"I don't want it," she groaned. Wincing in her efforts to stop the orgasm, to hold back, to find some center that could keep it at bay. Being an object was what she'd always craved, mindless and easy. Giving herself over so she disappeared. How could being a person do that? Being a person meant having responsibilities, thoughts, distractions. That's what she came to clubs like this to escape, and no *Daddy Dom* could change that.

"That's a lie, little girl."

"No, sir." Her head was muddled, mixed-up, but she knew herself. "I don't want to be a person."

"You're wrong. But if I have to force you to see it, if I have to break you down, use you, so you'll listen to me, so you'll admit you need a real connection – I'm happy to do it." The pressure of the vibrator bordered on painful just before he pulled it away, and she actually gasped in relief, light-headed from the sudden absence of stimulation.

Alexander was intense again, moving with clear purpose – and she envied his clarity.

But he'd promised to use her.

He pressed a button on the chair and the back started to drop. It clicked several times until finally locking in a position that had her flat, her head angled down over the top, tears reversing their paths to roll up her cheeks towards her temples. "You're going to realize you need a Daddy before the end of the night, little one."

Sienna's muscles were quaking, her mind had been tossed into a blender, and her emotions wrapped inside a hurricane. Everything was shaking as she watched Alexander take position just behind her, his hands plucking at the buckle of his belt. It left his slacks on a whisper, and she wanted the pain of it, wanted something to distract her from his words, but he dropped the shining leather to the floor.

"Please, just stop," she pleaded, and he crouched down so he was beside her head.

"That's not how you make this stop, little girl. Say the word if you really want me to stop, otherwise I'm about to fuck your throat and make you listen to me." Alexander slid his hand under her jaw, angling her chin up until she let go and let her head hang over the back of the chair. "Last chance," he growled as he stood slowly, but she stayed silent.

The truth was that as his hand went back to the button and zipper on his slacks, she wanted him to use her – no matter what he *thought* that would bring about. His words had been like razorblades inside her, and this was the answer. This was absolution from his accusations, distraction from the impossible tension between her thighs. He thought this would be some kind of illuminating punishment, but it was just freedom from speaking.

"Say the word, or open your mouth, little one." Alexander pushed his boxers out of the way, stroking his cock and she stayed silent. Focusing all of her attention, her distress, on the hard shaft running between his fingers.

Sienna wet her lips, tracing her tongue across them, and then she opened gratefully and he moved into her mouth. She moaned as he slid between her lips, and in this position he had a direct line to her throat, which he took full advantage of. On his next thrust he was testing her, seeing if she would panic, but she swallowed around him and he leaned forward to lay one hand gently across her neck. Drawing back, he pushed forward hard, slipping into the tight confines of her throat, and her air supply was instantly cut-off. Just like the water, but so much hotter. He held still, gripping her neck from the outside as she ignored the urge to fight.

This was so much easier than talking.

"You like it when I use you?" he asked as he pulled from her throat, allowing her the briefest of breaths through her nose before he slid forward again, beginning a rhythm that was merciless, bruising, and kept her on the dizzying edge of being breathless. "Do you like it when I take your throat like it's mine, little girl?"

Moaning her affirmation, she reveled in the way she nearly choked as he took what he wanted from her. Everything else fell away. Her own need, the chill of her skin, the too true words he'd spoken aloud – there was nothing but him, his cock deep in her throat, the warm, male taste of him on her tongue.

"Does this make you happy? Having me fuck your face? Treating you like just another hole to use?" The words should have been comforting. It was the language she was used to, the stuff that the Doms at Overtime said as she knelt on the floor between their knees, or on the tile in the shower. But for some reason, it brought the tears back, and she gagged the next time he thrust deep and held still in her throat.

Using her like a piece of meat. Like an object. Just like she wanted, right?

* * *

Alexander had to focus, the tight grip of Sienna's throat threatening to make him come too soon, but he had a reason behind this. A reason behind feeling the warm, wet, confines wrapped around his cock.

Fuck. Think, Alexander.

Opening his eyes only made things worse. Her beautiful body was laid out before him, breasts angled high from having her arms cuffed underneath her, nipples hard from the chill on her skin, her thighs spread wide, the pink lips of her pussy swollen and shining from her arousal.

He wanted to taste her, wanted to fuck her, wanted to feel her come.

"Dammit," he growled and pulled himself free of her mouth, a thick strand of saliva connecting them for just a moment. *What had he been saying?*

It was important.

"Tell me what you want, little girl." He fisted her hair, very aware that his cock was jutting out from his hips with an audience to stare, and she looked about as dazed as he did.

"You, sir," she whispered, hoarse from the hard throat fucking where he'd almost lost track of himself.

"Then be honest. What does being used provide you? What does a Dom give you when he treats you like nothing more than an object?" The moment he finished speaking, he saw the tears in her eyes. That warm, brown gaze tinted with pain.

"I can't," she groaned and closed her eyes to him.

Alexander growled, tucking his very frustrated cock back into his boxers to force the seat back into the upright position. Turning on his most aggressive voice, he put his face right in front of hers. "Tell me."

Tears were rolling down her cheeks, a silent cry that tugged at him, but she was so close, *so close* to breaking. She just needed a little more.

"Do you think that's the only way for you to submit? To be some hole, some object, for their use?" He grabbed the sides of her face when she tried to turn away from him, and he was more than aware of the chill on her skin as she absorbed the heat of his palms. "I know you think that's hot. I can *see* that you get turned on by it – but what happens when they're done, little one? What happens when they're done with you? When they leave?"

"Nothing!" she shouted at him, and tried to twist out of his hands, but he held on.

"Exactly. So, you want someone to use you? Treat you like you're nothing? I can do that. A *lot* of Doms can do that," he corrected, trying to pull himself out of the discussion so he didn't box her in further. She was too tempting to claim, to make his. "But you deserve someone who is going to pick you up after, and remind you that you're precious."

"STOP!" Sienna screamed, and it was loud enough that people beside the tank stood up, and he felt Garreth moving closer, but then she started crying hard and he had to bite his cheek to keep from smiling at the victory.

This was what he'd been waiting for.

"What is it, little one?"

Pulling at the restraints holding her to the chair, she whined and turned away from him, and he let her. Releasing her to step back as she let out muttered curses between quiet sobs.

"Tell me what you want."

"I don't want to feel this!" she shouted, and he shrugged.

"I know. It's what you've been avoiding." Alexander traced his fingertips down her arm, shifting to her ribs to continue down the curve of her waist, the swell of her hip, and then across her thigh. "Figured out what you actually want yet?"

"I don't know!" The torment on her face was stunning. A kind of pain that didn't exist at the end of a belt, or a crop, or a whip. This was all mental – his favorite game to play.

"Then tell me, do you want pick-up play for the rest of your life, or do you want something real? Something that's going to last more than a single fuck over a bench?" He leaned closer, his eyes tracing the furrow between her brows, the way she pressed her lips together like she was swallowing words. She was thinking, but he was too. Remembering his last girl, the one who hadn't been able to handle this side of him. The side that liked to push, to punish, to break. She'd wanted something real with him, but she'd wanted it with a sanitized version of who he was. A version of him that was only the softness, the sweetness, with none of the rough.

And Sienna was the opposite.

She fought the caring, the kindness, the gentle touches – and craved the abuse. The harsh words, the humiliating commands, the demand of submission. It had Alexander captivated. "Tell me what you want, little girl."

"I want something real," she whined, collapsing back against the chair, and he slid his fingers between her thighs, stroking at the silken wetness that was still there.

So wet.

"You have to let someone in to have something real, Sienna." It was difficult to focus with his balls aching, his mind so determined to have him buried between her sweet thighs that he was switching between looking at her body, and the plain, dark wall, just to retain his sanity. "Say it out loud, say what you want, little girl."

"I want someone to use me, I want someone to treat me like I'm nothing…" Those words seemed to be painful for her to speak, and he knew they were true, but the next phrase was far worse for her to say aloud. "And then I want them to take me home. I want them to want me around. I want them to ignore me so I can feel what it's like to be wanted again!" She almost screamed the last words, breaking into a sob.

It was perfect. *She* was perfect.

"Good girl," he whispered, leaning down to kiss her again, and she parted her lips quickly, her tongue reaching for his hungrily, and he found himself moaning against her mouth as his fingers pushed in to tease her.

Fuck, he wanted to be inside her, but he needed to get her ready. To build her back up so she was present.

When he finally managed to pull back from the kiss, he knew he was breathing just as hard as her, her eyes dilated so wide that he almost couldn't see where the black ended and the brown began. "What's your favorite color?"

"What?" she asked, a tone of shock in her voice, but he just laughed.

"I'm so proud of you right now, so damn proud, but I still want to know about you, little one. Open up for me. What's your favorite color?"

"Green," she answered, staring at him like he was insane. *And maybe he was, but he needed to get them both on track before he fucked her, and there was no doubt in his mind that he was going to have her before the end of the event.*

"Favorite food?" he asked, prying himself back from her to stand near the railing of the tank so he wouldn't rip her free of the chair and bend her over it.

"I don't know! French fries?"

"My kind of girl, little one." Alexander smiled, steadying himself. "Favorite movie?"

"Um…" A tiny furrow appeared between her brows as she thought, her breasts rising and falling as she took quick, deep breaths.

"Tick tock," he teased, lifting the remote for the chair, and she instantly stilled.

"You wouldn't dare."

"I don't think that's a movie title, is it?" He grinned and pressed the button, hearing her gasp for air just before she was inside the water again, but he was gracious, and only counted to three before he pulled her out again.

"Son of a bitch!" Sienna screamed as she was returned upright, a fresh rush of water running off her body, and the chair, to soak the floor where his shirt was a ruined mess.

Covering her mouth, he pressed his fingers in hard to her cheeks, giving just enough pain to make her focus again, the submission over-riding her irritation. "I have a deal for you, little one. Answer three questions about yourself in a row without pausing, and I'll give you so many orgasms you'll *beg* me to stop."

The second he lifted his hand she flicked her delicate tongue over her bottom lip. "What happens if I mess up?"

"I dunk you, isn't that obvious?" Alexander laughed when she stared at him, her mouth dropping open to tease his cock with the memory of what her lips had felt like wrapped around it. "Ready?"

"You're evil."

"Sir," he added, and she glared at him.

"You're evil, *sir*."

"I've been called worse." Shrugging he tried to play it casual, which was a challenge with his erection tenting the slacks he'd barely managed to button as she'd been underwater. "Favorite movie?"

Panic flashed across her face and then she sputtered out an answer, "Titanic!"

"A little pessimistic aren't you?" He chuckled as she rolled her eyes. "Don't think I didn't catch that, little one. I can still spank you as soon as you're off that chair."

"Yes, sir."

"Alright, favorite vacation spot?"

"The mountains," she answered fast. "Sir."

"Very nice." He drummed his fingers on the railing, and then he smiled up at her. "Favorite band?"

A low whine escaped her lips, her wrists pulling at the soaked cuffs, but as soon as he lifted the remote, she shouted, "The Civil Wars!"

"I have no idea who that is," he replied, giving her a questioning look.

"That was an answer, you have to count it, sir." Sienna argued with him, actually argued, and it made him happier than anything else that evening. *Well,* almost as happy as having his cock in her throat just before he'd made her sob.

"Good, girl."

CHAPTER 5

She felt breathless, wrung out, as he reached under the chair and pulled something that let out a metallic *clunk* just before he turned the chair around, away from the tank. "Am I allowed to get up now?"

"Not at all, little one." Alexander grinned down at her and picked up the vibrator. "I promised you orgasms, didn't I?"

"Yes, sir."

"Well, it'll be so much easier to make you come over and over if you can't squirm away." His voice had that edge to it again, that low growl that made her stomach tighten, her thighs tense, and that only got worse when he rested the vibrator on the chair and ran two fingers between her lips. Bringing them to his mouth he ran his tongue over them and she stared, open-mouthed, as he tasted her. "Fuck, you're delicious."

Sienna was speechless, again, as he leaned forward and kissed her, dipping his tongue between her lips so that she could taste herself, and him, in a heady mixture that had her melting against the chair. Then, she heard the vibrator kick on and she squeaked against his mouth as he pressed the powerful little device directly to her clit.

Her nerve endings were raw, put through so much that it took almost nothing to bring her back to the painful horizon where she knew she could fall apart if he would *just* allow her. "Please," she begged into the kiss, and he smiled as he pulled back enough to see her face.

"You know what I want to hear, little girl."

"That's humiliating," she whined, and he laughed.

"I thought you *liked* humiliation," Alexander taunted. "Let me care for you, little one. Give yourself over to me. You just have to say the words."

Glaring at him, she thought through everything he'd said. The promise of using her like he had when he'd fucked her throat, the strict discipline he'd enforced when he'd made her answer his endless questions. Time after time he'd put her in the water, edged her, taunted her with all the power and control that got her off with Doms the rest of the time – but he promised the other half too. The after-care, the time to make her feel right again. The warmth that she'd been missing when she watched Doms leave Overtime, comforting herself with the lingering bliss of subspace.

He wanted to use her like an object, and then care for her like she was someone worthy.

That's what a Daddy does, little one.

His words echoed in her mind. A promise, an offer, and while Sienna was quite sure she wasn't going to start calling everyone Daddy, she knew she could do it for him. He'd earned it.

Licking her lips, she lifted her eyes to his, and finally said what he wanted to hear, speaking softly, "I want to come, *Daddy*. Please, let me come?"

The fierce growl escaped him just before he kissed her again, hard enough to bruise her lips, but the vibrator was back, focused on her clit, and she found herself rocking against it in a matter of moments, wishing her hands were free to hold onto him. "Come for me, little one, let go," his words, hissed against her lips, were the key she hadn't known she needed – and everything shattered.

Sienna slipped over the edge, gravity releasing her once more, until she was nothing more than warm, sparkling light that raced along her nerves. Somewhere outside of herself, she could hear her gasping his name, his soft laugh as he slid two fingers inside her and used his other hand to hold the vibrator in place, urging her higher in her bliss. Further into the white noise that blocked out the world.

The threat of another orgasm hung in front of her, painful and glorious, and then his mouth closed over her breast and he pushed her into it. She half-screamed, tumbling into another release, the heat inside her crushing any lingering chill on her skin. This was a kind of escape she'd never reached, loosely tethered to her body at the point where he pumped his fingers, but otherwise she was free. Weightless and glowing, suffused with pure fulfillment.

Is this what he meant?

Her body wanted to rest, wanted to pull back, but he wasn't stopping. Whimpering, she twisted in the cuffs, pleading as he only intensified his efforts. Stroking her g-spot with his fingers, aligning the vibrator to rest *just right* over her clit, as he teased her nipple with his tongue and teeth. Soft and then hard, painful and then pleasurable. "Please, please, please..." she begged, but there was nothing she could do as he pressed her, urged her forward.

"Just one more," he lied, and she fell at his command. Pure bliss for just a moment, a golden haze that wrapped her in relief, but then he was drawing her back. Teasing her to a new edge, a new horizon, and she tensed against the cold metal of the chair, her body aching, but Alexander managed to bring her over.

Again, and again, and *again* until every stroke became more agony than satisfaction.

Too much.

"Please, Daddy!" she begged, desperate, and that made him still. The secret code to Alexander – unlocked. Sienna was practically delirious with orgasms, her mind in some sort of whirlwind, and he chuckled as he slid free and traced his fingers over her lips.

"Open up and taste yourself, little girl." With his words, she obeyed. Sucking his fingers clean, tracing her tongue along them until *he* groaned. Finally, he pulled free of her lips and she saw him check his watch with a smile. "It's not even ten o'clock yet."

"Impossible," she whined.

"Totally possible, which means we have *not* made it to the end of the night. Don't you want to win?" he teased.

Sienna laughed, a little insanity edging into her voice, but Alexander kissed her again and all was right with the world. Suddenly, gravity took her back, reality returned, and she felt aware of the agonized heartbeat behind her clit. "You're going to kill me, *Daddy*..."

* * *

ALEXANDER HAD to step back from her so he wouldn't come in his slacks like some teenager. She was using the phrase like a weapon, but he didn't even care. That was his kink, and hearing the word in the sweet, post-orgasmic tones of her voice was his kryptonite. "If we want to do something else, we have to spin for it. You know that, right?"

Whining, Sienna nodded. "I just want out of this chair."

"Alright, little one. Are you okay with me spinning for you?"

"Can you do that?" She lifted her head, damp, dark strands of hair plastered to her cheeks, highlighting the blush, and the swollen pout of her lips. *Fuck, she's beautiful.*

Turning around, Alexander found Garreth standing between them and another couple playing in the area, amidst the various voyeurs who had been watching Sienna suffer and then come over and over. As soon as he caught the dungeon monitor's eye he waved him across and the man stalked towards them with a grin on his face.

Someone had been having fun monitoring the evening's events.

Garreth paused at the base of the stairs, leaning on one of the railings as he looked over Sienna, but it was a clinical assessment, not a leer. "What's up? You guys okay?"

"More than okay, but Sienna seems to think she can't handle any more orgasms in the chair right now." Alexander grinned when he heard her groan and drop back against the chair.

"You're a real asshole, Reed."

"So I've been told." He shrugged, and then got to the point. "Anyway, I don't want to untie her yet, but we wanted to pick something other than the water tank. Can I spin for her?"

"If she says it's okay." Garreth glanced over at Sienna, and Alexander pinched her thigh to get her to pay attention.

"– the fuck?" she growled, lifting her head again.

"Two spankings," Alexander noted as he raised two fingers into the air. "Be polite to the dungeon monitor, little girl. He wants to know if you consent to me spinning for you."

"If it gets me off this chair, he can spin whatever he wants."

Garreth chuckled and looked back to him. "Alright, you can spin for her. Chase is near the stage, just make sure he witnesses."

"Will you watch her?" Alexander asked.

"Of course."

Before he left, Alexander turned on his heel and kissed her hard, feeling the hum of her moan against his lips. "Be right back, little girl."

"Thank you, *Daddy*." She added a bit of exaggerated emphasis to the term again, but it still sent a thrill down his spine, making him adjust in his pants before he faced Garreth again.

'Daddy?' Garreth mouthed at him, and Alexander just grinned and shrugged as he walked past the man.

* * *

"ALRIGHT, Sienna. Check in with me. You okay?" Garreth stepped up to her, moving behind the chair to squeeze her fingers, which she immediately gripped back to prove she hadn't lost circulation.

"I'm fine, sir, I promise."

"Mmhmm…" He made a noise as he turned to grab one of her ankles, squeezing her toes. "You're cold, can you wiggle your toes for me?"

She laughed and flexed both of her feet. "I'm *cold* because the fucking water is cold, and I'm naked, if you missed that."

Garreth arched an eyebrow at her as he stood. "You really think I missed that?"

"No, sir?" she answered, turning it into a question as she smiled.

"Right. And the water is cold because it's fucking February. I told those guys that a water tank was a poor choice, even if they *did* want to deal with the heating bill this month. Do I need to pull you out of this scene?"

"No, sir, I'm okay." Sienna gave him a confident smile to try and convince him, but he kept his face stoic as he leaned against the railing to the platform. Behind him the sounds of some intense sex struck up, and she strained to try and see, but she couldn't see where the noise was coming from on the floor.

Garreth glanced back for a second, mostly uninterested, before he spoke again. "So, it seems like you and Reed are getting along just fine."

"Reed?"

"Alexander Reed," he tilted his head back towards the stage where Chase was talking to the man in question. "I was worried earlier. That scream..." he shuddered. "I didn't know what he'd done."

"I was just frustrated."

"I'd hate to see you pissed," he countered with a chuckle.

"True. You would." Sienna grinned, and realized that she was having a full conversation with him, without any of the normal anxious butterflies making her feel panic.

"How are your joints? You've been cuffed in this position for about an hour now." The question was clinical, and she couldn't help but feel a warm and fuzzy sensation inside at how careful they were being with the subs. Pretense of suffering submissives or not, this club had its shit together.

"I'm sore, but I've been struggling a lot. My own fault. Nothing a hot shower in the morning won't fix." *That* was based on experience, because she'd been tied in predicament bondage or suspension stuff for longer than this and been fine. "Hey, is Terry around? He's the one who suggested I sign up."

"Are you kidding?" Garreth laughed and pointed across from her where she had to really strain to see, but then she caught sight of the huge guy near another wall. "He's been walking over here all night, I keep having to flip him off and tell him to watch *his* stations."

"He said he would keep an eye on me."

"Well, you should have seen him when you screamed earlier, I thought he was going to punch Reed." Garreth shrugged a little and returned his eyes to her. "You and Muscles a thing?"

Sienna burst out laughing, unable to control it as wired as she felt from the aftereffects of so much adrenaline and so many orgasms.

"Um, no way. He's a monitor at Overtime, and he convinced me to sign up for this event on the basis that he'd look out for me. We've never played."

"Well, I'm watching too. Nothing is going to go wrong, okay?" Garreth smiled. "Anyway, you handled the water-based breath play like a champ. I was waiting for you to safeword the fifth or sixth time he put you under, but you just kept going."

"It wasn't so bad," she lied, trying to ignore the panic she'd felt as she held her breath under the water. It had really only been tolerable because she'd been so irritated with Alexander that she'd wanted to prove to him she could handle it.

"Sure, if you say so. Oh, shit..." Garreth started laughing, loudly, and Sienna lifted her head to try and see where he was looking. "Good luck, Sienna!"

As the man walked down the stairs, Alexander walked up, and his grin was dangerous. "What is it, sir?" she asked.

"We spun the absolute perfect thing for a wet little girl like you."

"What?" Her eyes looked over the collection of wires in his hands, connected to other *things*, and she felt her stomach tense.

"Electrical play."

"You've got to be fucking kidding me!" Sienna jerked at the restraints. "There's no way."

"Want me to bring Chase over? He can confirm." Alexander leaned close, lining up his blue eyes with hers. "Don't worry though, I turned down the car battery."

"They did *not* offer you a car battery."

He grinned. "Guess you'll never know, since I picked the TENS unit."

Sienna searched her mind for the term, trying to remember exactly what it was, but then she saw him attaching components to a small, black box. Including something that looked *very* much like a medium-sized vibrator, only there were shining, silver stripes on either side of it. "Sir, *Daddy*, I –"

"Little girl, that term is for respect, not manipulation. If you start using it with me to get your way, I'm going to finish with this TENS unit, and then as soon as they declare the event over, I'm going to paddle your ass. Roulette wheel be damned, got it?"

"Yes, sir," she answered softly, dropping back against the cold, metal chair. Her skin was still damp all over, her hair soaked, and she'd come so much that she knew her pussy was dripping. Electricity seemed to be like some joke from the universe.

How much more did he want to break her down? She was already questioning everything about herself, her kinks, her life.

"Have you ever played with a TENS unit before?" Alexander asked, wrapping his hand around the vibrator shape, before turning something on the black box. His slight jerk made her eyes go wide.

"No, Daddy." The response had come naturally, the term only fitting him, but she was far too nervous to add any snark at the moment.

His eyes were heated when he turned to her. "Ready to play a little more?"

Nodding, she watched as he moved to the end of the chair. Slowly, he pushed the black vibrator-like thing inside her as she lifted her hips off the chair a little. It wasn't very big, but she was aware of it, especially with the wires extending up to the black box in his hands.

"Say yellow if it's too much, alright? We *do* still want to win." Even Alexander seemed nervous as he turned the dial, and she felt a low *thump* of a shock in her pussy. It was barely enough to make her gasp, but she tensed. He watched her carefully, and then did something else to the box, and the next snap of energy made her clench tight, twisting as it pulsed through her, until it finally released her.

"Fuck..." she gasped when it stopped, her ears still buzzing, her pussy tingling and twitching around the invader. Underneath the surprise, she realized it had felt like riding the line between pleasure and pain, that humming space between the two that she normally only got to enjoy just before she fell. Slowly, she smiled. "That was fun."

"Naughty little girl." Alexander grinned and adjusted something, and then the thing buried in her pussy fired off again, sending a sharp jolt that felt like a pinch for a moment, but as it continued Sienna felt like she was floating on the edge of an orgasm once more.

So close, so close.

"I have to admit, this makes your body do some delicious things. I think I need to invest in one for my playroom." He grinned, turning the device a little further. "Hold on to something, little one."

"AH!" Sienna yelped, unable to hold it in, but the sharp spike lulled for a moment into a low thrum inside her, and then spiked again, and she was reaching for oblivion, fevered with the strange pulses of energy humming through her. "More, Daddy, more, please?" she begged, half-aware of herself.

"Oh, Sienna, you're perfect." Alexander's voice was a wanton groan just before the next peak amplified, and somewhere amidst the mixture of confusing pain and buzzing pleasure, she cried out and came. Ecstasy. Warm and sweet and flooding through every inch of her, pushing back the aches in her joints, the tension in her back, to replace it all with tingling light that had her mumbling his name like a prayer.

Heaven had nothing on kink.

She descended back to earth like a falling feather, gliding – and then everything was painfully tense for a moment, the sensation somewhere outside the spectrum of description, but she was caught. He turned off the TENS unit and she instantly collapsed back to the chair, not even aware that she'd arched away from the bindings. Limp and exhausted.

"Little one?" Alexander's voice had an odd note to it as he came close, his hands cupping her face, bringing her head upright again. "Sienna? Baby? Are you okay?"

Snapping out of her daze, she opened her eyes and pulled in a long breath. "*Whoa*, yes, sir. Daddy, yes. I'm fine." She nodded, but there was concern all over his expression.

"We're getting up, and I'm getting you warm. If they forfeit your month, I'll fucking pay for it."

"Sir, no! I'm fine!" Sienna tried to argue, but he was removing the cuffs from her limbs, and the sudden *whoosh* of her blood flowing more freely made her a little dizzy, which did *not* make her claims very convincing when he looked back at her face.

"Hold on, little girl." The last few straps disappeared and he lifted her like she was weightless, holding her against his chest as he walked carefully down the steps.

"Did something happen?" Garreth's voice appeared behind her head, and she angled it back to see him, upside down.

"I'm fine," she tried to answer, but Alexander spoke over her.

"She got faint with the TENS unit, do you have a blanket?"

"Of course," Garreth answered, and then he rushed off just as Alexander settled them on a couch with her curled up on his lap.

Pushing at his chest to try and relax the iron grip his arms had on her, she whined, "I'm *fine*, I promise."

"You fainted," he accused, and she grumbled.

"I did *not* faint. I came, and I was resting." Sienna struggled to sit up. "That's normal!"

Alexander caught her cheek, turning her face to his, and she saw the sincere worry in his eyes. "It scared me, you just collapsed."

Heat flushed her cheeks, and she shrugged a little. "It was an intense orgasm?"

"Dammit..." he sighed, holding her against him even tighter, and then she heard the rapid steps of Garreth returning. Without a word exchanged between the two men, she found herself covered in a blanket, the edges tucked around her tightly.

"I'd like to check her pulse, look her over. See if she's in shock." Garreth cursed under his breath. "I *told* them the water event shouldn't be held in winter. It's too fucking hard to keep the subs warm enough."

"I AM FINE!" Sienna shouted, throwing the blanket off her shoulders as she sat up in Alexander's lap. Both men stared at her as she looked between them, huffing that she'd even had to shout – and then she was stunned that she'd been *able* to shout.

Who was this person that had taken over her body?

Alexander wrapped one arm across her legs, holding her on his lap. "Are you sure, little one? I think our dungeon monitor friend would feel a lot better if he was able to verify you're alright."

Rolling his eyes, Garreth added, "Right, because I'm the *only* one worried about you right now."

"Sienna, are you okay?" The low voice of Terry came from behind the couch, and Sienna let out a little screech of frustration, raising her arms to try and stop the onslaught of concerned Dom attention.

"Would *one* of you just listen to me? I'm fine. I had an orgasm, after a *lot* of other orgasms, that came after a lot of intense play. I was just tired. I did *not* lose consciousness!" She pointed at Garreth. "I did *not* faint." Then she looked at Alexander, and shifted to look up at Terry. "And I definitely did not safeword. I am perfectly fine. Sirs. All of you."

The three men exchanged glances over her head, having some sort of ancient, manly, non-verbal communication about her, but they all seemed to come to the same conclusion that she had already voiced several times – she was fine.

"If you have any change of symptoms, call me over," Garreth said as he nodded and walked back to another scene still in progress.

"I'm still here, Sienna. If you need me, just ask." Terry gave Alexander an intense stare, and then turned to hulk his way back to his post.

Then she was left sitting on Alexander's lap, looking at him and waiting to hear *his* comment. "Well?" she asked.

"You look incredibly hot when you come, little girl." He grinned, and she laughed as he settled her further into his lap. "Honestly, I think Chase might have rigged the wheel in my favor."

"What?"

"Why else would I have been the one to end up with you?" he asked, and the sincerity in his voice plucked a chord deep inside her that she wanted to ignore.

"You don't mean that." Sienna laughed quietly until Alexander suddenly grabbed onto her still wet ponytail, and forced her down to the arm of the couch.

"Excuse me, little girl?" His voice was *anything* but funny, and she swallowed hard as his eyes bored down into hers. "Say it again."

Shaking her head, she found that her voice had run for the hills again.

"Are you telling me no?" Alexander lifted his brows in a clear threat, but she couldn't get her voice to work, and in another flip of her perspective she was over his lap, her ass over his thighs, and then a single resounding *smack* seemed to echo around her. The vibrant sting of his palm connecting with her ass made her wiggle.

The second made her gasp, but the third, fourth, and fifth had her whining and grabbing at the leather cushion in front of her. "Please!" she begged, and he paused.

"Repeat what you said," he demanded, and she had to swallow to summon her voice again.

"I just meant that you aren't that lucky ending up with me, I mean there were some *gorgeous* women here and –" A hard swat from his hand right at her sit spot had her bucking off his lap, the warmth spreading until it joined the steady throbbing between her thighs.

"There's no *and* to that sentence. That sentence is bullshit." His palm ran over the places he'd swatted, alternating between squeezing the flesh and rubbing. "Do you really think I'd have you in my lap right now if I didn't want you here?"

"Sir..."

He ignored her interruption and continued, "Do you think I would have taken you off the chair? Or made you come, if I wasn't interested in you at all?"

Guilt surged through her as his fingers slid between her thighs, finding their mark as he pushed two of them inside her to tease that focal point. Sienna groaned, spreading her legs wider for him.

"Answer me, little girl. Do you really think I don't care?" His other hand ripped the tie he'd used in her ponytail free, letting him grab a handful of the soaked hair to strain her neck back.

"Daddy..." she whined, and sprawled over his lap she couldn't help but feel the weight of the trouble she was in for her off-handed comment.

"Alright then." Alexander sounded frustrated, just before he tightened his grip in her hair and slid his fingers free to deliver a series of hard swats to her ass and thighs. Landing them randomly so she could never predict where the next would fall, but eventually she felt her entire backside glowing, pulsing, and she was squirming in his lap.

Her thighs parted of their own accord, and she lifted her ass so that his next swat landed even sharper, but Sienna moaned softly against the leather of the couch. "Daddy, please..."

"What do you want, little one?"

"Fuck me?" she begged, and the frankness of the request stunned her, but Alexander seemed to appreciate it, because he pulled her up by her hair, turning her so he could kiss her. The moment his tongue tangled with hers, she knew she was going to be his, even if she hadn't noticed the hard press of his cock against her ass.

He slid her off his lap, standing up beside the couch to toe his shoes off. With a grin, Alexander pulled out his wallet and plucked a condom wrapper from it. "You know, you act like you weren't the one I was hoping to spin." His voice was a purr as he pushed her back to the couch, dropping his boxer-covered hips between her thighs. Miming a thrust against her like they were teenagers making out.

"Did you want...?" Sienna whispered the unfinished question, her doubts reappearing even as his erection rubbed against her center through the fabric.

"Of course I wanted you. You're *exactly* my type." He nipped at her neck as he rolled his hips, teasing her. "I've got a thing for brunettes with wide, innocent eyes."

"My eyes are *not* innocent," she argued, but it was difficult when he slid one hand between them to stroke at her, brushing her clit with his deft fingers.

"Not anymore, that's for sure." Alexander grinned down at her, and then he freed his cock from his boxers, tearing the condom wrapper with his teeth so he could roll it on. She watched his movements, hungry and mesmerized, because she'd wanted to feel his skin against her since he'd first kissed her. "You sure about this," he asked, one elbow braced beside her on the couch.

"Please," she whispered, rocking her hips up to meet his and he groaned against her shoulder, lining up, and then he thrust inside her in one powerful stroke. Their moans were almost simultaneous, a chorus of satisfaction as he filled her and settled his weight against her to start moving. Each slow, steady thrust was stoking the fire inside her, creating a new glowing possibility that she wanted to reach – but she could tell he was holding back. Tempering each movement. "I'm not breakable," Sienna whispered against his skin, and he chuckled.

"You're wonderful, that's what you are." Alexander groaned as he thrust deep again, and she wrapped her legs around his hips.

"More, Daddy," she begged and *that* was it. He drew back and his next drive was harder, more powerful, and the pleasure was a thrumming ache between her thighs. Somehow, even after everything that had happened that night, she found herself inching closer to another orgasm. It didn't matter that her body was tired, that every inch of her was sore for one reason or another, with Alexander Reed moving inside her, she only felt the pleasure. The promise of another blissful escape hovering just beyond her fingertips. "Oh God, yes," Sienna hissed, and he started to fuck her harder.

No mercy, no holding back, and she loved the way his fingers dug into her hip, holding her still as he slammed home. It was demanding, and hot, and her clit pulsed along with each thrust, edging her nearer to her own completion. "I want to feel you come, little one," Alexander growled, and she closed her eyes to focus on the pleasure now that she had permission.

Everything else in the room dissolved. There was no chatter, no random voyeurs watching them, it was just her and Alexander, and the bright, glittering haze that was slowly overwhelming her. Between one breath and the next, she came, her body squeezing him tight, drawing him in, and he groaned above her, his hips working until he joined her in bliss. It was somehow less than the first explosive release she'd had, but simultaneously better with his weight above her, his heat against her skin, the stretch of him filling her so completely. Their soft moans clashed together in her ears as her body shimmered, shattered, and then reformed just as Alexander drowned her breaths in kisses.

"You are incredible – perfect – wonderful…" he whispered the words between kisses, his hips locked against hers as the spiraling aftershocks slowed.

Sienna was floating somewhere between consciousness and a hazy dreamland, but it fit her completely as he grabbed the blanket from the floor. Sliding to her side, he turned her into the couch so he was at her back, before draping the warm, thin cloth over them both. With his arms around her, she felt like she could do anything, could *say* anything, and still be safe.

After a few, peaceful moments of silence where their breathing evened out, Alexander shifted so he could whisper against her ear, "I want you to work at my office."

"What?" She asked, confused, twisting under the blanket to look up at his eyes, and he smiled down at her, tracing a finger down the line of her nose.

"I want you to apply to be the stenographer for our depositions. We have an open position, and I want you to have it."

Sienna groaned and dropped her head back to her arm, avoiding his eyes. "No."

"Excuse me?" He asked, pulling her hip back against him, but she just shook her head again.

"I'm not going to work for you as some glorified sex-bot." Sienna was frustrated that he'd even suggest it. Their night hadn't been perfect, but it had been wonderful. It had made her second-guess some of her decisions, re-think how she chose to play, and *now* he wanted to make it all some kind of sex-based job interview? Just the idea of it was making her angrier by the second.

"Sex-bot," Alexander repeated, and she could hear the laughter in his voice from just behind her head.

"I *have* a job, remember? Two of them." She growled. "Tonight was about trying something new, which I have. Several things actually. But it was *not* some opportunity to whore myself out for a job."

His fist in her hair made her hiss air between her teeth, the grip sharp and biting, which was only distracted by the way his other hand dug into her hip, painfully tight. "First of all, little girl, I do *not* think you are a whore. Second of all, had you bothered to *ask* instead of making assumptions you would have learned that applying at my firm would put you in front of quite a few people, but *I* would not be one of them. Ever. I'm not involved in hiring."

"I –"

"Last, I only offered because it would make me very happy to know you weren't killing yourself working two jobs to make ends meet, when you could have *one* job at my firm, which I happen to know pays quite competitively – and then you'd be fine." The fierce pressure of Alexander's fingers had only grown while he was talking, and she tried to nod against the fist in her hair.

"I understand, Daddy. I misunderstood."

As if he suddenly became aware of the strength he was using, he released her completely, instead moving his arms to hug her tighter to his front underneath the blanket. "Dammit, Sienna... I just want you to be taken care of, even if you won't let *me* take care of you."

Alexander pressed a lingering kiss to her shoulder blade, squeezing her until she struggled to draw breath, and then she felt him roll out from under the blanket to stand and she turned to catch his arm. "What are you doing?"

His eyes looked shadowed, his expression dim, as he used his free hand to grab his slacks from the floor. "Event is pretty much over, you don't have to spend any more time with me."

Just as Alexander spoke, Chase was on stage again and the audience members scattered across the room started clapping, some of them cheering, but Sienna just tightened her grip on his arm as the ex-model started calling the event to a close. "I don't give a shit about the event," she growled.

"Okay." Alexander nodded and tried to pull away from her again, but she held on and let him drag her to a sitting position.

"Wait! I want you, Daddy," she whispered softly, but he flinched.

"I told you not to use that –"

"Unless I meant it, and I do. I'm not sure if I'll ever be into that scene the same way you are..." Leaning down she picked up the bow he'd tucked into her hair that had fallen when he'd ripped the ponytail free, and she held it out to him. "But I get it. With *you* I mean. You treated me like a person even though I didn't want you to. You made me recognize that I wasn't happy just being an object, no matter what I'd told myself."

"Right." Alexander sounded unconvinced, and when he turned again he managed to tug his arm free of her grip.

"Terry told me the same thing!" Sienna was desperate not to let him walk away, and he turned back to her with such a look of confusion that she knew she had him for at least another moment. "At

Overtime. He approached me after I played a role in this couple's scene, and he said some of the same things *you* did, but I didn't believe him. I didn't believe any of it until *you* said it, until *you* showed me that I wanted more. That I *could* want more than I had, and that someone like you could give it to me. That a Daddy could give me what I really needed."

"Sienna..." he sighed, and she winced, shifting to her knees on the couch, still completely naked and not caring a bit for the people watching her as she formed into a kneel.

"I want you. As my Dom, my Daddy, my Sir, my Master – whatever you want me to call you, I'm here and ready to use it. *Respectfully*." She whined, wishing she were better with words as she struggled to think of what would convince him of what she already knew. "I suck at this, I'm not good at talking, but I know that you're the only person that's ever made me feel like a person and not an object."

Tears sprung to her eyes, and the words he'd said to her earlier in the night came back loud and clear, so eloquent, so perfectly put, so full of almost supernatural observation skills that she was still stunned by them.

"You had every right, and every opportunity, to simply use me tonight. To do whatever you wanted within our activity, and be done. But *you* decided to talk to me, you made *me* talk, and if you expect me to just forget that, to go on to someone else and not think of you – well... well, fuck you!" Sienna slapped the arm of the couch beside her, trying to push back the tears, wiping her cheeks furiously so they wouldn't show. "So, why don't you talk now! You tell me if you were lying, if all of that shit was just part of the game!"

Alexander, for once, seemed stunned. Speechless. He pushed a hand into his hair, the only clothing on him his boxers, and his socks, as he stood beside the couch and surveyed Black Light. He stood in silence for so long that she felt something new and fragile inside her fracturing, breaking with each moment that passed – but then he turned to face her. "Come to my place. Tonight."

"What?" she asked, confused, but then he moved to his knees by the couch so that they were almost eye-to-eye.

"I want you to come home with me. I want you in my bed so I can watch over you, so I can make sure you're okay, and then I want to take you to breakfast before work." Alexander reached up to interlace their fingers. "And then it would make me very happy, little girl, if you would obey me and apply for the damn position at my law firm, so that you'd have more time to see me after hours. I wasn't lying, little one, I just didn't want to corner you."

"Really?" she asked, her voice wavering.

"Yes." The strength in his voice should have been confirmation enough, but with all of her arguing, all of her bratty behavior, she needed more.

"Are you sure?"

"Absolutely."

"What if you don't like me tomorrow?" she asked, that small piece inside her still shaky, but he started laughing.

"Little girl, you haven't seen me coming home from a bad day in court. I'm a fucking nightmare." He placed his hands on either side of her face, holding her gaze to his blue eyes. "But no matter what, I want the opportunity to show you that you deserve having someone take care of you, having someone at your back, and someone to be there when you need them. And whether you put up with me for one week, or thirty years, I don't care. I just want the chance. Just a chance. Will you give me that?"

Smiling, Sienna felt the warmth blooming at her core, that new and fragile thing becoming a little more solid just behind her ribs. "I think as well as we did at roulette tonight, that games of chance just might be our thing."

"Is that a yes?" he asked, grinning.

"That's a hell yes." Sienna wrapped her arms around his shoulders as he kissed her again, and while she *still* didn't believe in destiny, or karma, or any of that hoopla – she had a feeling that roulette wheels might just be her new religion, and Alexander Reed might be just the man to convince her that faith could bring her everything she'd ever wanted.

THE END

ABOUT THE AUTHOR

Jennifer Bene is a *USA Today* bestselling author of dangerously sexy and deviously dark romance. From BDSM, to Suspense, Dark Romance, and Thrillers—she writes it all. Always delivering a twisty, spine-tingling journey with the promise of a happily-ever-after.

Don't miss a release! Sign up for the newsletter to get new book alerts (and a free welcome book) at: http://jenniferbene.com/newsletter

* * *

You can find her online throughout social media with username @jbeneauthor and on her website: www.jenniferbene.com

ALSO BY JENNIFER BENE

The Thalia Series (Dark Romance)

Security Binds Her *(Thalia Book 1)*

Striking a Balance *(Thalia Book 2)*

Salvaged by Love *(Thalia Book 3)*

Tying the Knot *(Thalia Book 4)*

The Thalia Series: The Complete Collection

Dangerous Games Series (Dark Mafia Romance)

Early Sins *(A Dangerous Games Prequel)*

Lethal Sin *(Dangerous Games Book 1)*

Fragile Ties Series (Dark Romance)

Destruction *(Fragile Ties Book 1)*

Inheritance (Fragile Ties Book 2)

Redemption (Fragile Ties Book 3)

Breaking Beth Series

Breaking Beth

Damaged Doll

Scarred Siren

Daughters of Eltera Series (Dark Fantasy Romance)

Fae *(Daughters of Eltera Book 1)*

Tara *(Daughters of Eltera Book 2)*

Standalone Dark Romance

Taken by the Enemy

Imperfect Monster

Corrupt Desires

The Rite

Deviant Attraction: A Dark and Dirty Collection

Appearances in the Black Light Series (BDSM Romance)

Black Light: Exposed *(Black Light Series Book 2)*

Black Light: Valentine Roulette *(Black Light Series Book 3)*

Black Light: Roulette Redux *(Black Light Series Book 7)*

Black Light: Celebrity Roulette by Various Authors

Black Light: Charmed by Jennifer Bene

Black Light: Roulette War by Various Authors

Black Light: Unbound by Jennifer Bene and Lesley Clark

Black Light: Roulette Rematch by Various Authors

Standalone BDSM Ménage Romance

The Invitation

Reunited

UNMASKED

A Black Light: Valentine Roulette Novella

by

Lee Savino

CHAPTER 1

eah, her clit was definitely broken.

Chessie laid down her phone and sagged back against her pillows with a sigh. Muffled sounds from the porn clip she'd been watching continued to play until she picked her phone back up and stabbed the screen with a finger, silencing the video 'Sexy Secretary II'.

Goddammit. She was an educated, intelligent, and successful woman, with a grad degree in poli sci, working in D.C. as a lobbyist – for women's rights, no less. Yet she was frigging her clit to a clip of a naked woman kneeling in front of a man in a suit.

Not her finest feminist moment.

Pussy throbbing, she scrolled for another video. She'd gotten off work early for a networking dinner, and, having beat the rush home, she had a precious hour alone without her roommate, without distractions, just her and her cellphone and an internet full of porn.

Bring on the self-loving.

But seriously, she deserved it. Other than this stolen hour, she had one night off for the rest of the month – and that was dedicated to her and her roommate's annual 'anti Valentine's Day' celebration. Most years they celebrated by eating chocolate out of cheesy heart-shaped boxes, drinking wine, and comparing stories of their worst dates. Best story got to choose the restaurant where they ordered take out. Chessie wouldn't be winning the contest this year. She hadn't had a date since... before the primaries. Way, way before.

Which brought her back to her current quest for an orgasm.

She clicked another link and watched a dick saw in and out of a woman's mouth.

"Yeah, baby, that's it. Suck it. Suck it hard."

It wasn't like she'd ever do this in real life. It would never be her on her knees, big doe eyes silently begging a man to use her. Settling back, Chessie cradled the phone in her left hand while her right index finger moved frantically against her clit. Her abdomen tightened, a tendril of arousal curling through her.

"You're just a whore," a male voice growled. On screen, the dick pulled out of the woman's mouth and started slapping her face.

Chessie jabbed her cellphone screen, stopping the video with a sound of disgust, and whatever arousal that had been building faded away.

Maybe it was time to give in and download that erotic novel, the really smutty one with the five cowboys who kidnap one woman. The last time she'd read it, she'd cum over and over to the scene of them tying their captive up and dominating her. Afterwards, she'd deleted the book from her e-reader in shame.

Desperate times called for desperate measures, and she hadn't cum in a really, really long time.

A reminder popped up on her phone. 'Speaker Dinner 7pm'.

"Crap." Chessie swung out of bed. Stretching the cramped fingers of her right hand, she fished through her closet with her left. Usually she was more organized than this, but her pussy's annoyance was taking over her brain. She'd just spent sixty minutes scrubbing her clit, swiping through pictures of celebrities, sports stars, heck, even old boyfriends. Nothing excited her until she saw the picture of the woman on her knees. But she didn't really want that sort of thing... did she?

Her phone chimed its reminder again. She silenced it, and closed all the porn and sexy book links even as her pussy wailed in protest and the last of her arousal died a sad, quavering death. Her lady garden was going to wither like a neglected houseplant if she didn't get some action, soon.

Maybe this February she'd talk her roommate into going out of town, get some privacy. She'd buy a vibrator, download a nasty novel, and spend a romantic weekend all by herself.

Happy Valentine's Day to her.

* * *

HALF AN HOUR LATER, Chessie wove past round tables filled with power people and their aides at the hotel ballroom. She'd missed the early networking, but with her lack-of-orgasm frustration, that was probably a good thing.

On her power walk to her seat, she caught a few rubber neckers. In addition to her usual 'uniform' – that's what her roommate called it – of black on black shirt and slacks, she'd added a pair of patent leather red pumps. The fuck-me pumps were her roommate's, and a bit racy for D.C., but Chessie was in a mood.

The admiring looks lasted only until the men caught sight of her resting bitch face. Fine. If any man hit on her tonight, she'd probably bait him into a conversation on wage equality just so she could snarl at him.

Servers were laying down appetizers as Chessie found her place. She was the first at her table to arrive, so she circled it to read the names on the place cards to see if she recognized anyone. D.C. was just a small town, after all. A small town filled with bigwigs – or smallwigs who thought they were important. When she'd first come here, she'd been dazzled by every judge, ambassador, and elected official. Now she was just tired of the boring suits – most of them assholes really, scrambling to get their slice of the power pie.

God, she really needed to cum...

At her table, the most prominent guest was a senator. Senator Peyton B. Kane III. She ran through her mental files, trying to place the name with a state. One of the southern ones, Georgia maybe. Another white man with a charming drawl and enough of daddy's money to send him to law school and launch him into a career pandering to the other rich, white men who told him how to vote in the back rooms of their country club.

Welcome to politics.

"Ma'am? I think you're at my seat." She turned, place card in hand, and looked up at the most incredible pair of blue eyes.

Oh, mama, this one was pretty.

Even with her in fuck-me heels, the senator stood a good six inches taller than her. She was right on the money, too – by the looks of him this one came from lots of it, old money. Preston Kane the Third was white, and male. Pale skin, patrician features. The only thing that threw off this picture of fine breeding was the mouth – a tad too lush – and the tips of his sandy hair – a tad too long and curling into boyish, blondish curls.

He didn't look that much older than her – though he was probably closer to 35. He stood politely with what looked like a bevy of aides at his back – all young, fresh-faced white men.

"If you'd be so kind, I think the speaker's about to begin." Just a faint trace of a good ol' boy southern accent, but it was there, two-stepping with the polite words he learned at his mama's knee.

"Of course." She recovered and set the place card down before stepping to her seat half way around the table. To her surprise he followed her, and pulled the appropriate chair out for her to sit. Usually she brushed off charm school manners as cheap and over-bearing, but as the senator took care to guide her into her seat, something in her woke up and paid attention.

The forty-five minute talk on the transforming power of women in leadership, delivered by a Rwandan politician and rape survivor, should've captivated Chessie. Instead, every cell in her body was tuned into the tall blond senator across the table from her. He ate little and kept his attention on the speaker, his tall frame relaxed yet focused. His aides often leaned in to whisper some unknown piece of commentary to each other, but his attention never wavered, except to thank the servers in a low but clear murmur. From the blush on one of the young lady server's cheeks, Chessie wasn't the only one taken with his old world charm.

When the talk ended, the waiters served coffee and dessert, but everyone lingered for the real purpose – the meeting after the meeting. During the talk, the rest of their table had streamed in, which, in Chessie's opinion, was unspeakably rude, but unfortunately common in a city full of self-important people. As soon as the applause faded after the closing remarks, the latecomers vied for audience with Senator Kane, who entertained them while his aides continued their whispering and Chessie picked at the bit of dairy fluff on top of a sliver of dry chocolate cake that served as dessert. As far as networking went, this evening was a bust, so she just sat and stared at the beautiful man across the table from her.

Her peaceful contemplation ended when she heard a buzzword from her job.

"Sounds a bit like Affirmative Action for feminists to me," one of the aides said to the others. "Requiring thirty percent of government seats to be filled by women. People should vote for who they want to vote for."

"Next thing they'll want is an all-women government." The aides guffawed and Chessie couldn't stop herself.

"Why not?" she muttered loudly enough for the smug aides to hear. "We've had an all men one."

The men regarded her and she gave her best fake smile.

"You really think a minimum quota of women leaders is something that will work here?" The aide who spoke had produced a toothpick from some pocket and was working it between his teeth.

"Why not? It had an amazing effect in Rwanda. I know one country isn't a large enough sample size –"

"Of course it's not, sweetheart," he cut her off and exchanged smirks with his buddies.

"Don't call me 'sweetheart,'" she snapped with enough force that the rest of the table stopped talking and paid attention.

"I was just –" the aide started.

"Now, Boyd, let the lady make her point." Senator Kane's drawl was more pronounced giving gentility to what was otherwise a firm order. "I'd like to hear her side. Ms. Jones." He inclined his head.

Chessie flushed. One, he knew her name – he must have read if off her place card. Two, he defended her – which irritated and satisfied her at the same time.

"I acknowledge that we don't have enough data to know if legislating a minimum quota for women representatives would be beneficial. But studies show that companies with diverse leadership are more successful. And so far, the same could be said of governments."

"Interesting point." The senator moved to her, offering his hand. "As much as I'd like to continue this healthy debate, we really must be going. A pleasure, Ms. Jones."

She took it, ignoring a flash of heat that leapt between them. Those pretty, pretty eyes. Was that a hint of a real smile in the corner of his sensual mouth?

His attention left hers and the table started to put on their coats to leave.

Chessie let herself be carried along by the press of people, her hand still tingling from the touch of the senator's.

Outside the hotel, she paused a moment to take a breath of cold, clear air. D.C. could be so beautiful at night – the statues and Capitol building all lit. Not as lovely as spring when the cherry trees bloomed, but still.

Tugging her coat around her, she started the brisk walk home, detouring through a private space between two buildings that was half stone walkways, half garden. There were two men in dark coats ahead of her, but the place was lit enough she wasn't worried. They were probably guests from the same speaker dinner.

"And what'd you think of that pretty piece of taffy?" The voice drifted back to her, echoing between the two buildings.

"Fine, very fine," came the reply. Chessie almost missed her step. That was Senator Kane's voice.

"Uppity, though." In the building's reflection, Chessie saw the speaker – the aide who'd sucked on toothpicks right at their table. He had one in his mouth now and was working it around his teeth as he spoke.

"Give the lady some credit," Senator Kane said. "She was just defending her corner."

"Uptight, too. Someone needs a session with the Kane," Toothpick guffawed.

Chessie's face went hot, then cold. Were they talking about her? The only reason she didn't call out and make the idiot choke on his own toothpick was that she wanted to hear what Kane said next.

"Naw," the senator drawled. "The Kane's too advanced an implement for a beginner. Just a nice session over my knee... and then a good hard fuck. Always sets a lady straight."

Chessie missed a step and almost fell and cracked her face on the pavement. She caught herself just in time, only to have Senator Kane glance back at her. His baby blues pinned her.

Despite the anger stiffening her body, she shivered. The aide was still walking, blabbing, but for a moment only she and Kane existed. She raised her chin. If she had any guts at all, she'd march forward in her harlot heels and slap the senator right across the face.

Instead, she detoured between the buildings, and made her escape.

"Asshole," she whispered as she ran lightly down the alley, the senator's voice still ringing in her ears.

She slowed down for a moment to google Senator Kane on her phone. Yep, there it was: thirty-seven, the youngest senator out of Georgia. Unmarried. Daddy was big in business, while his mama was a former model and a debutante. Scrolling, she clicked for an image of the tall senator and got quite a few, including one stepping out of a car with a Miss Georgia pageant winner.

She took the steps up to her apartment two at a time.

"Mina?" she called, and listened, but didn't hear anything besides the rumbling in the radiator as it prepared a blast of Death Valley heat. Her roommate wasn't home. She was alone.

Tearing off her coat and kicking off her shoes, she rushed to her bedroom, flopped down and spread her legs. She found a close up image of the senator – wearing a suit and a handsome, half smile.

Transferring her phone to her left hand, she slipped her right in her pants and... hello. Wet and slippery, just as she'd suspected. Her fingers moved tentatively.

Images flashed through her head – the good senator talking, his casual drawl as his eyes flicked up and down her curvy form. Only this time, he said the phrases she'd only read in the raunchiest erotic stories.

"Strip," he'd say. "On your knees." And then the more hardcore images – her sucking him, stroking her body at his command. Her body tightened at the thought of submissively lapping at his balls, taking his cock and... more... doing what he ordered. He'd pull his cock out of her mouth and trace her lips, smiling like a shark as he told her, "These belong to me."

"No." She wrenched her hand away, even as her whole body quivered on the edge of orgasm. This was wrong. So wrong. Thinking about the senator like that, with her on her knees like a naughty intern. What the fuck was wrong with her?

The front door to the apartment slammed, interrupting her shame spiral.

"Chess? You home? How did the dinner go?"

"Fine!" Chessie scrambled to fix her clothes. Mina had the energy of a chihuahua on speed – and just as little concept of personal space.

Mina stuck her head into Chessie's bedroom a second later. "Just fine?" Dark, straight, shoulder length hair and too-big glasses, Mina looked like Marcy from the Peanuts cartoon. Except this nerd had quite a mouth on her. "You look as tired as a street walker on Saturday night."

"Thank you. Thanks for that."

"Seriously, what's wrong with you? You've been looking forward to this dinner for ages."

What had the speech been about again? "Uh, it was really good." Chessie wracked her brain and came up with a memory of the senator sitting across from her at the table, one long finger absently stroking the white tablecloth. "Inspiring. I was just stuck at a table with some senator's people."

"Huh," Mina said, and popped out of Chessie's room again, only to shout across the apartment two seconds later, "What happened to my shoes? Looks like you ran a Tough Mudder in them, and left them in the Potomac."

"Sorry," Chessie winced. "I'll buy you a new pair." With great reluctance, she deleted the pictures of the senator off her phone before Mina bounced back into her room.

"Well, I'll forgive you, if you do me a favor... no," Mina corrected. "Do yourself a favor." She held out what looked like an invitation, printed on black paper.

"What's this? Another speaker dinner?"

"Nope. Ticket to your wildest dreams."

Chessie snorted but plucked the paper out of her roommate's hand. "Black Light's Valentine Roulette? What's this?"

"You know Club Runway – the one where Cash Carter played a few months ago?"

"Is that the hot night club in Georgetown? The one opened by the famous threesome?"

"Yes... but wait, there's more." Mina waggled her eyebrows. "Guess what they built under the music venue."

"A basement?"

"Yes. Oh, wait...I have to swear you to secrecy first. You must tell no one what I am about to reveal to you – that under the hottest club in town is... wait for it...a sex club."

Images of the club owners – a very hot, very out threesome made up of two guys and one lucky girl – spilled through Chessie's head.

"A BDSM sex club." Mina enunciated each word as if they tasted like candy.

"What? No." Chessie tried to hand the ticket back, and when Mina wouldn't take it, she sputtered, "Why would I be interested in that?"

"Because. Oh come on, Chess, I've seen the porn you look at. I wasn't spying –" She held up both hands when Chessie stiffened. "You handed me your phone to look up a recipe and I saw your search history."

"That was... research." Chessie felt her face redden. "For a white paper on... uh... exploited sex workers."

"Suuuure it was. Those naughty, naughty sex workers getting paddled in their school uniforms."

"What!? I never..."

"Looking at spanking pictures isn't a crime. Neither is getting off to it. And this I do know – you haven't been on a date for three years. Maybe longer – since college. You need to get off, girlfriend. I'm dying to use the ticket myself, but I can't because I'm off for three months for the Chapman internship."

"You got it? Mina, that's great!"

"Yep. My dream internship, but I leave tomorrow. I gotta hurry up and pack." Mina all but ran to the closet by the front door and dragged out a suitcase larger than her – along with half the detritus in the closet. Chessie rushed in to keep the avalanche from engulfing her petite roommate.

"Okay, okay, slow down."

"I can't! I need you to hold down the fort, and go to the club. Experience, explore. Maybe bag a big bad Dom and bring him back here."

Chessie frowned at the piece of paper in her hand. It was beautiful, black with gilt lettering and a sort of shimmery code on it. She wasn't sure whether to frame it or burn it. "Mina... I don't know."

"Do it for me."

"You want me go to a sex club for you?"

"When you put it like that..." Mina paused her flurry of motion to gnaw on her lip. "I promised one of the employees that I'd go. They need more subs that night, for this Roulette thing they're doing. Oh – I just remembered, you have to sign a privacy thing, an NDA."

"This is too much."

"Chessie, I promised. I already sent them an email telling them I had a replacement. If you go... and do the Roulette... I'll pay your share of the rent for three months."

"Seriously?"

"Yes," Mina said with the satisfaction of someone who knows they're about to win an argument. "The internship gave me a huge stipend for housing, but I'm staying with a friend. So I can cover rent for three months. But," she held up a finger, "you have to go and –" She held up a second finger, "You have to get off." She met Chessie's glare with a shrug. "You've been so cranky, I can tell the closest you've gotten to sex is listening to Gangbang every night."

As if on cue, the radiator started clanging. Mina had christened the fifty-year-old radiator 'Gangbang' because it 'sounded like a bunch of guys with giant tools'.

"Oh my god, Mina." Chessie threw her pillow with half-hearted force. "Fine. I'll do it." Three months rent would be worth it.

"Awesome. You can borrow an outfit. Just... when you do bring a guy home... don't have sex on my bed." Mina disappeared with a wink.

CHAPTER 2

"Three months rent, three months rent," Chessie chanted as she entered the club. She'd clutched the invitation like a weapon, showing it to the doorman at the super secret entrance to Black Light, wondering how in the hell life had lead her here. Only Mina could talk her into something like this night out of her wildest fantasies. In addition to the monetary bribe (not to mention the promise of potential orgasm), Mina had pulled out the big guns and dared her, practically called her a coward. And Chelsea Wilhelmina Jones was no coward...at least, not last night, when Mina had gotten in her face. Right now, she was trying not to shiver as she descended into the opulent underworld.

Black Light was basically one large room, with a few curtained off areas lining one wall, offering some privacy. Various equipment dotted the floor – tables, stocks, wooden structures for strapping subs to, even a hot tub and – oh God – a stage in one corner for public displays.

This was such a mistake. Shifting uneasily in her knee high boots, Chessie resisted the urge to pull down her short black dress. On Mina, it fit perfectly. On Chessie, it was a tad too tight, the hem hovering scandalously at mid thigh. The fabric hugged her curves, making her cleavage pop so that she didn't need a bra, not that she could've worn one under the sheath.

For her journey to the club, she'd covered the whole ensemble with the longest coat she could find, finally surrendering it with her purse and cellphone in the locker room, but based on the looks she was getting from the men in the club – and some of the women – she had no reason to hide. So far she blended in with the well-dressed patrons. There weren't any naughty school girls, or subs in head to toe fetish leather, or beautiful slaves naked but for a collar...

...yet.

"Excuse me, are you here for the Roulette?" A dungeon monitor moved her politely, but firmly, towards the line of subs waiting to go on stage.

Relax, Mina had said. *Everyone's nice and professional. I've made friends. If you let yourself, you'll have a good time.*

Forcing herself not to fidget, Chessie surveyed the club. On the other side of the giant wheel they would spin to begin the night's activities, a line of men waited. Some were chatting, and others observed the line of subs across from them, much as Chessie was doing. When their gaze swept over her form and stopped to feast, she felt heat spill from her cheeks into the rest of her body. Tonight, one of these men would claim and command her. Hate it all she wanted, she couldn't deny it turned her on.

Mina had given her pointers: be yourself, use your manners, and call the dominants "sir" and "ma'am" unless they tell you otherwise. One of the Doms – a tall, burly man with muscles straining to pop out of his black t-shirt – crossed his arms and leveled a look at her. Chessie had to fight to keep from dropping her eyes automatically under the overpowering gaze. Instead, she looked away, swaying on her heels a little.

What had she gotten herself into?

"It's all right," one of the subs beside her whispered.

"What?"

"You look as if you're about to faint. New here?" At Chessie's curt nod, the sub continued. "All the dominants are really, really good. Experienced. They'll respect your safeword. And there are dungeon monitors who will stop play if anything gets out of control. So it looks intense, but it's actually pretty safe."

"Thank you." Chessie tried to call up some inner poise and channel it onto her face.

"They'll probably get rid of your mask first thing, though." The sub gave her an almost pitying look, and Chessie touched the stiff black satin molded to her face, the only piece of her armor she had left.

"Most Doms won't like you hiding any part of yourself from them," the sub prattled on. "But it's not like you'll be paired with someone you actually know."

Biting back the urge to tell the oh-so-helpful sub to mind her own business, Chessie merely nodded and turned away, just in time to meet the perusal of pretty blue eyes.

Fuck. Oh no. Oh no, oh no. Not him.

Senator Kane stood in the line next to the muscled Dom. He must have just arrived – a faint tinge of pink on his cheeks lingered from the outdoor cold. Otherwise, he looked much like he had at the dinner a night before, tall frame encased in a fine tailored suit. Blue-blood good looks softened by a good-ol' boy smile as he spoke with the man next to him.

She trembled even as she reminded herself she wore the mask. With all the people he met, the senator wouldn't remember her anyway. At least, she hoped he didn't.

Worrying about this was enough to make her zone out through the club owner's opening remarks. What if the Roulette paired them? Would he recognize her? They'd be up close and personal, scening intimately for up to three hours. His elegant hands touching her, guiding her. He'd start by tracing her collarbone, dipping to explore her cleavage.

You've been a naughty girl, he'd whisper in her ear, so close she could inhale the clean scent of his aftershave, or touch her lips to his jaw. His hands would rest on her tiny waist and glide along the flare of her hips, appreciating her hourglass figure. *You need to be punished.* He'd grip her ass, hard, and smack her bottom.

"Hey, that's you," the sub's harsh whisper propelled her forward.

"What?" The sub pushed Chessie a few steps forward before she realized the MC was calling her name.

"Ms. Jones! Her hard limits are electrical pain play, blood play, needle play and water sports."

Next to the wheel, the giant Dom glared down at her, and all moisture left her mouth. This was her Dom for the night? He looked like he popped steroids for breakfast and washed them down with nails. If he whipped her, she'd probably end up bloody.

The MC handed her a white ball and motioned for her to drop it on the roulette wheel that would decide her fate. "Ms. Jones, toss your ball in."

Fear and acid taste in her mouth, Chessie obeyed with jerky, hesitant movements, body like a robot out of her control.

"Sybian Orgasm Torture!"

Torture? What the fuck? And what was a Sybian? She wracked her brain for Mina's explanation, like a student who'd crammed all night before the test.

This had to be a nightmare.

Teetering on her heels, she faced her new Dom. Black t-shirt, bulging arms – add a whip in his hand and a shivering, naked sub on a rack and Mina would dub him 'The Torturer'. Except Chessie was going to be that poor, helpless sub.

The Torturer crooked a finger at her.

As she waited next to him the glare of the stage lights fried her brain, and whited out any of the action in front of them. The club safeword ran through her head over and over again.

Once the Roulette wheel had spun for the last time, the Dom gripped her elbow and dragged her off the stage. Finding a seat, he dropped into it and pointed at his feet.

"Kneel, Ms. Jones."

Here? Now? Around all these people?

"Um…" When Chessie hesitated, his scowl turned fierce.

"Little sub, if you don't want me to start your orgasm torture with the worst caning of your life, you need to kneel at my feet. *Now.*"

Caning? After her little run in with the senator, Chessie had looked up pictures of women getting caned. Advanced implement, indeed. She could tell by the red lines, raw and angry, sliced onto supple thighs.

Fuck three months rent.

Darting back as if he'd reach out and grab her, Chessie whispered, "Red."

With a disgusted sigh, the Dom rose like a mountain before her, grabbed her arm, and pulled her across the floor. Half walking, half dragged, Chessie went without a fight – until she realized where the Torturer was taking her.

"No." When she tried to dig in her heels, the huge Dom gave her a tug that sent her flying forward – straight into Senator Kane's arms. The senator had been sitting talking to his sub for the night – a stunning blonde in a barely there dress – but he somehow got to his feet and caught Chessie with an arm around her waist. Sagging in his firm hold, Chessie found her feet and stared back at her would-be torturer for the night.

"What's going on?"

"She safeworded," the Torturer explained to the Senator, "but I don't want her to flunk out so quickly. She just needs a different Dom."

Chessie found herself dipped back in the senator's strong arms, like they were dancing.

"Sounds like you're mine now." A smile tipped the senator's lush lips. Up close he was even more beautiful. "Unless you want to safeword out of the whole thing."

She licked her lips to wet them, only to have Kane's gaze sharpen on them like a hawk's.

"You're going to get us all disqualified," the blonde said.

"I'll run it by the Dungeon Master. Besides, the senator will cover our fees if that happens." The Torturer winked, a strange look on a terrifying man, but Senator Kane didn't speak.

"Have fun," the blonde waved as the other man led her away.

Slowly, he righted her so she stood on her own. "Shall we begin?"

She jerked her head 'yes.'

A twitch of the sculpted lips, and he said, "Try again, and address me properly."

Just like that she was wet, even though her answer came out hoarse. "Yes, sir."

"Good girl."

Liquid heat poured through her, arousal and embarrassment swirled together in a confusing cocktail. Why did two condescending words make her feel so good?

The senator laid a finger on her lips, and everything in her focused on the light point of contact. For a moment he just regarded her. Chessie wondered if he was going to kiss her. When he broke contact and stepped away, she could've cried at the loss.

Did Doms not kiss their subs?

"Follow me, two steps behind, now." He walked on without a backward glance, leaving her to scramble behind him, wondering if she'd done something wrong.

Throughout the club, couples were starting to scene. One tall dominant actually grabbed a handful of his sub's hair and pulled her towards the pool area. Chessie didn't realize she'd slowed to watch until Kane loomed over her.

"If you cannot obey a simple order, I can leash you."

Her spine stiffened. He didn't think she could obey? "Forgive me, sir," she murmured, her voice a sultry caress.

He raised a brow, but seemed satisfied. When he moved on, she dogged his heels as gracefully as she could.

Kane led the way to one of the semi-private rooms. He snapped his fingers and pointed to a spot on the floor for her to wait while he went inside and laid out his implements.

Frustration built as she waited. She'd signed on for a night of make-believe, whips and chains and kinky fun. Not to be intimidated by scary men who spent too much time at the gym, or to be treated like a dog.

The fact that her pussy dripped like a faucet when he did was neither here nor there. She deserved respect. *Be yourself,* Mina had said. Submissive or no, she wasn't a pushover.

But she'd already safeworded once, and fate led her to the senator, the one Dom she itched to scene with. Whatever he asked, she'd do. Her whole being wanted to serve him.

Returning, Kane walked around her slowly, and his examination, like she was a car on the lot, only made her stiffen further.

"Name?"

"Ms. Jones," she responded.

He paused a beat. "Remaining anonymous, are we? Very well." He sang a few bars of 'Me and Mrs. Jones' in a low, confident tenor as he removed his cufflinks, stripped off his jacket, and rolled up his sleeves. A pleasant hint of muscle in the taut forearms made her hope to God she got to see the rest of him.

"Eyes down, sub," he murmured, as if ordering someone to look where he told them to was perfectly natural. Worse, she immediately obeyed, glaring hard at the tip of her boots while he finished getting ready.

She was back to the internal chant, 'three months rent'. If she wasn't careful, her inner bitch would break out and tell him to 'Fuck off'.

At least it was obvious he didn't remember her from the night before. Of course he didn't. The amount of people he met on a daily basis... why should he remember the girl in red shoes he wanted to 'spank and then fuck hard'.

She was relieved, really. They'd scene and she'd wear the mask, because she damn sure wasn't taking it off for him. It was all very good for a white man who wore power like a suit coat to flaunt his identity here. Not her.

"And so we begin." Kane had returned to stand not a foot away. She felt his heat melt her body, like strong arms wrapping around her, promising a night of adventure, of sensuous comfort, promising everything would be okay.

He reached for her mask.

"No," Chessie darted her head away. "The mask stays. I will safe-word and leave if you take it off." Three months rent be damned. She'd safeword again – he knew she'd do it. She wasn't risking her career for an orgasm, even at the hands of this supremely fuckable man.

Yes, security was paramount at Black Light, filled with world famous celebrities and politicians getting their rocks off in the kinkiest ways. But she didn't need protection from the paparazzi. She was more worried about meeting the powerful people she might meet later in the real world, petitioning them as a lobbyist. People who would judge her for her submission, even while they didn't bother to remember her name.

People like him.

"You seem to have a chip on your shoulder, Mrs. Jones," he murmured, as if reading her mind.

"Ms.," she corrected, and defied his order to meet his gaze head on. Her satisfaction at the flicker of annoyance in his face drained away when the air between them turned to stone. Kane's gaze went hard, his body still as a predator preparing to pounce. A second of silence passed, and he seemed to grow taller, assuming a mantle of power right before her eyes.

She was about to say something when his hand shot out, collaring her throat lightly.

"I think that," he said in a dangerously calm tone, "you need a reminder of who's in charge here." His other hand dropped to cup her breast, squeezing gently, possession in his touch. Her pussy moistened at his casual claim of her body.

"Kneel," he ordered, releasing her neck. His touch made her so weak it was a wonder she didn't fall to the floor on the spot. Still, she hesitated until he gripped the back of her neck and applied gentle pressure to ease her down.

"Good girl."

Again her heart rate fluttered at the endearment, even though she was kneeling on a club floor in a nice dress in front of a man she barely knew. Her body was coming alive, pulsing like there was an electric shock running through her. Her thoughts skittered through these facts as Senator Kane paced another circle around her.

He prowled back into their semi-private room and returned with a pair of shears. She couldn't keep her eyes on the floor when he snapped the scissors thoughtfully.

She opened her mouth, but he spoke first.

"From here on out, you do not have permission to speak unless I give it."

"Excuse me?" she spoke aloud before she realized it.

"You heard me, sub. Push me and I'll gag you. Now, choose a hand signal as your safeword."

Gaze still locked in a battle with his blazing blues, she didn't have to think before she extended her middle finger.

Instead of losing his temper, he nodded. "Your protest is duly noted. Now, choose something more respectful, please."

CHAPTER 3

ane watched his 'submissive' seethe on the floor. She was obviously new here. A regular at the club, he'd clocked her as soon as he'd come in – the feisty beauty from dinner the night before. No wonder he'd wanted to engage with her last night; he'd picked up on latent submissive tendencies. They were deep but they were there. He'd hoped his 'turn her over my knee' comment would encourage her to approach him, but instead she'd turned and run away. Away from him, away from what she obviously desired.

Now she was here, and she was still running.

He liked scening with newbies, but submitting was the last thing on the delectable Ms. Jones' mind. It wasn't him she was fighting so much as herself, her need to obey and give over control. Perhaps she was ashamed of her desires. He'd have to work her through that while he put her through her paces in tonight's play.

The rules of the night dictated they spend three hours together, and at least half an hour in the kink the Roulette chose for him.

Around them play was starting. He preferred a little more time to learn his sub, get an idea of what she liked and disliked, the way her breathing changed when she answered his questions. Once he learned more, he could lead her with the subtle leash of dominance. He'd obviously made a mistake and assumed she had some ideas of the basics. He'd come off domineering, and now she had her hackles up.

Time for a change of pace.

She looked startled when he reached out again and stroked her hair. He respected a woman who would submit to him. Submission was a treasure he could never deserve, only handle with care when it was in his hands.

"Ms. Jones, I'm waiting for a hand signal safeword."

She raised two fingers in the Victory sign. He suppressed a smile.

"Thank you." She looked surprised again, as if she didn't expect he would use his manners. Of course, being polite didn't mean he wasn't going to lay out the rules. "I won't be calling you Ms. Jones. I asked your name as a courtesy. I prefer 'slut', 'sub', and 'slave'. If one of those bothers you to the point of distress, you may safeword and go home. Understood?"

She blinked and nodded.

"When asked a direct question you will answer *yes, sir* or *no, sir*. You're earning quite a punishment for your lack of respect." He added the last part mildly, and was rewarded with a slight intake of breath on her part. The thought of punishment turned her on.

Good.

"I'll ask again, slave. Do you understand the terms of our arrangement tonight?"

"Yes, sir."

"Good girl. Now take off your dress."

He snapped the shears in warning and it was enough to have her scrambling, pulling the stretchy fabric over her head.

The sight of her naked on her knees was definitely worth pushing through her power games. Without a bra, her breasts bounced slightly as they were freed. Lovely orbs, high and firm on her chest, soft curves juxtaposing the strong, supple elegance of her back. Her ass was perfection, or would be, when he removed her panties. He had a use for the shears, after all. He could buy her a new pair in the morning – and he had no doubt he could keep her as long as he wanted. She'd already obeyed his commands, responding without realizing why. The right mix of dominance and tenderness would coax the resistance from her; a few orgasms would blast any lingering doubts away. Once she lay pliant in his arms, he'd touch every inch of her, claim her body as his own. Forget three hours – they'd be here all night. In the morning, he'd take her home in his car.

His dick, hard enough to punch through the fine fabric of his slacks, approved of his plan.

Shears in hand, he snapped them in warning. "Hold very still. Mistake, wearing panties into this place." Bending, he watched her chest rise and fall with pleasing distress as he snipped off the lacy scrap. He noted the cream on the gusset before folding them carefully and putting them in his pocket. She wouldn't be getting those back.

"Walk to the couch, retrieve the cane and crop, and return them to me." He'd laid a number of implements on the couch, but she didn't hesitate. She'd done some research, and she was clearly intelligent. Just untrained. He kept firing commands, testing her. "Offer them to me on your knees. Head bowed, palms flat so I can lift the implements."

When she obeyed, genuine pleasure colored his voice. "Good girl." Another subtle quiver went through her at the compliment. So much fight up front, a bluff to hide the depths of her desire. How many times had she busted a man's balls, testing to see if he had what it took to lead her?

"I am Master Kane. This is one of my implements of choice. This is the other. I tap and issue a command, you move, instantly, sub. I can tell you're new at this." He used a condescending tone, knowing that would set her teeth grinding. Tell a high-powered woman they're not good enough, and they'll work fifty times harder to please you. "You're mine tonight. And I'm going to make sure you have the time of your life. Sit up straight." He used the crop to tap her back until she arched as prettily as he liked. "That's it, show off those lovely breasts. The perfect handful, aren't they?" Reaching down, he fondled them, ignoring her rushed intake of breath. "Very nice. Sensitive too." He pinched a nipple, then swatted the whole globe so it jiggled. "Beautiful. I could have some fun with these." He glanced at her face. "Could do without that glare, though."

He had a thought. A quick interlude with a dungeon monitor brought him the gear he needed.

"If you want to stay masked, Miss Jones," he put emphasis on the 'Miss' to be a dick, "then you wear the one I choose. This night, everything you do or say is on my terms." He handed her a black leather hood, one with holes for her eyes and her mouth. "You may stand and go into the room to put it on."

By the press of her lips he knew she was biting back her response. There was that delicious resistance, the inner fight. Her last stand, if he guessed correctly. Once she surrendered, she wouldn't wrestle control back. He'd keep things moving too quickly for her to miss it. Deep down, she knew she needed to be overpowered for a night, forced to her knees by someone stronger. Someone she could trust to protect and guide her, usher her into the sanctity of her deepest fantasies. She wavered on the threshold, desire and reluctance warring on her face, and he knew the moment when desire won.

She took the hood, rose and went to the semi-private room to change. He enjoyed the sight of her hips and soft buttocks swaying, ready for his lash.

God, he loved being a Dom.

When she returned, he noted how her shoulders were tense, a little wary, but her gaze was on the floor. The mask was humiliating and comforting at the same time. It reduced her to a beautiful body, a mouth and pair of eyes, but offered her privacy. No one could see her expression, not even him.

He checked the fit and tightened the laces in the back. She'd done it up as much as she could, anticipating his moves, still trying to stay in control. He finished straightening the hood, making sure he could see her beautiful eyes and kissable lips through the holes in the mask.

"Can you breathe all right, sub?"

"Yes sir." There was a slight tremor in her voice. She was affected.

"Good. If that changes I expect you to safeword. You look beautiful in your hood, sub." He rose up over her and studied his slave for the night on her knees, naked except for a hood over her face. "You have permission to thank me."

* * *

SHE WAS GOING to break a tooth from grinding them. The hood wasn't uncomfortable, but she hated the feel of it wrapped around her face, enclosing her into her own private world. Somewhere in the club, a woman was protesting something, but Chessie couldn't hear more than angry sounds muffled by the leather covering her ears. Chessie wanted to turn her head and see what the argument was about, but the mask was as effective as a hand wrapped around her face, reminding her that her attention, her very senses, belonged to this tall asshole who owned her for the night. She had to trust that if there was an emergency, or something she needed to know, he'd tell her.

He leaned down and spoke near her ear. "I'm waiting, slut."

Prick. If anyone talked to her this way in real life, she'd deck them.

How can you stand it? she'd asked Mina in their heart to heart last night. *How can you let go and submit to someone like that?*

It's pretend, Mina had said. *I just play the game and have fun.*

If this was the game, Kane was a master player. Every word and action made her solar plexus tighten. Her nipples tingled. If she wasn't careful, she'd leak down her thighs.

She hated it, and she craved more.

"Thank you, sir."

"Hmmm." He circled, still holding the crop. Was he really going to use that vicious looking thing on her? How would it feel? Did she really want to know? "You don't sound too thankful. Maybe this will help."

He busied himself out of the line of her sight, and then – blackness.

"No!" She seized his pant leg, wavering on her knees.

"Yes." He finished tying the blindfold and rose. She felt like flailing, looking for... anything. He'd hooded her as if she were a horse, a prize filly who might startle.

"I don't – please, take it off." It was too much, too humiliating. Her heart raced like she'd run a mile.

His clothes brushed her naked flesh as he bent and took her hand, his touch warm and comforting.

"Listen to me. Take a deep breath. That's right, focus on me, and only me."

He was close, very close, leaning down or maybe even kneeling next to her. She turned to him like a flower gravitates to the sun. She did as he commanded and loosened her grip, but he shifted his and caught her wrist, affirming his control as he kept up that mesmerizing whisper.

"I own your world." His other hand touched her breast and she twitched in surprise. He cupped it, stroking so her nipple ruched even more tightly. The ache spiraled down to the cradle of her hips. "Do as I say and this will be the best night of your life."

She sighed when he took his hands away.

"One more thing. Open."

She did and groaned when he placed a ball in her mouth.

"See why you should thank me next time? No matter what I do to you, you should be grateful. It can always be much, much worse. Whatever it takes for you to learn your place. Now, rise."

Even as he barked an order, he helped her obey it, lifting and steadying her with a hand on her shoulder and forearm. His arm slipped around her, like they were lovers at a dance, except she was totally naked and barefoot. A slave.

His fingers blazed a trail over her skin, finding their way unerringly to her labia, dipping between them.

"You're already wet. What caused it, I wonder? The hood? The promise of what's to come?"

She grunted softly.

"Can't understand you. It doesn't matter. Your mouth can lie but your body tells me what I need to know." He traced a finger down her spine. "Do you know what orgasm torture is, sweetheart?"

When she shook her head, the drool started to leak from the sides of her mouth; she felt it hit her breasts. He didn't seem to care, he kept talking, kept stroking between her legs, little touches that didn't quite hit her clit, driving her mad.

"I tie you down and make you orgasm so much you'll beg me to stop. And you know what I'll do then?"

She was almost afraid to shake her head. He leaned so close, his lips must have been touching the hood.

"I won't stop."

Only the confident movement of his fingers kept her from grabbing the hood and ripping it off. He kept it up, brushing her labia, spreading her juices around until her world tilted on its axis, revolving around him and his rasping voice...

"Now." He took his hand away. She would've fallen but he captured her arm and propelled her forward instead. When she stumbled a little, he bore most of her weight, completely supporting her while holding her off balance at the same time.

Barefoot, she felt the difference in their height more acutely. His body engulfed hers. Next to his superior height and muscled frame, she was petite and feminine.

He dropped into a seat and she found herself flailing over his knee.

"Shhhh." Again, he steadied her. "Calm down, sweetheart."

His hand passed over her bare bottom.

"Time for your punishment," he said, and she shivered.

She could always safeword, she reminded herself. How bad could it be?

* * *

DAMN BUT HE could live with this woman over his lap. If she was his full time slave, she wouldn't go much more than an hour without him tormenting her delectable body, just so he could reward her with pleasure and cuddle her afterwards.

"This is for your disrespect earlier. I'm in charge here. You'll remember that or come morning, your ass will be raw."

He let loose a flurry of swats and watched the globes dance under his palm. She squirmed, resisting, and he secured her hands in the middle of her back. "Relax and take it, or I get a paddle. You don't want wood stinging your ass this early in the night, trust me."

He continued spanking her harder, faster.

Throughout the club, play was picking up. The dungeon monitors swarmed, making sure everything was satisfactory. Earlier, one sub had thrown a fit, snarling her outrage before stomping out on her Dom. At any moment the enigmatic Ms. Jones could decide to do the same. He'd take it as a testament to his skill that she hadn't already, except there was something deep down holding her here.

Kane returned his attention to the quivering buttocks before him. His thumb teased her rim, noting how she tensed. Anal virgin, perhaps?

He was going to have fun with this one.

* * *

THE SPANKING STUNG, but oddly enough the longer it continued the more she relaxed and let the pain flow over her. She was drooling, and dripping, but the arousal pulsing through her put her past all caring.

He stopped at times to touch her, and her pussy practically sucked his fingers in. She was a slut, wasn't she? Getting turned on by a spanking? Her cheeks burned, making her almost grateful for the hood.

At last he swung her down between his knees, removed the blindfold, and unhooked the ball gag. She worked her jaw, relieved when he offered his handkerchief to clean her mouth. His hair was a little mussed from their play so far. After having been denied it for a few minutes, she drank the sight of him in before remembering his order to keep her gaze on the floor. His shoes were so shiny.

"Tell me about your last orgasm. You have permission to speak."

"I... don't remember." Panicked, she almost forgot his title, so added quickly, "Master Kane, sir."

"How do you usually orgasm?"

Fuck.

She shrugged, hoping he wouldn't push the subject.

"That's an order, sub. You will tell me," his voice sharpened.

"I don't." Her own voice broke. "I can't. I get there and... I just can't."

"Can't or won't?"

"A little of both."

"Thank you for your honesty." He touched her breasts again, circling the nipples with his thumbs.

"You're a damn beautiful woman."

She leaned into his worshipping fingers.

"Hands behind your back, offer yourself to me." His soft commands threw her. The harsher he was, the more she wanted to defy him, but now, she arched her back as she obeyed, hoping her form was pleasing to him.

"Perfect." He toyed with her a moment. "So, you say you can't orgasm. I think we're going to fix that tonight."

He rested a hand at her throat, collaring the sensitive skin there, reassuring her before he rose.

"Come."

He led her across the floor, and she followed, docile as a trained pet. The protest in her head had quieted, and she wasn't nervous any more.

He stopped to watch one couple, and she waited with him. The man had his submissive tied to a spanking bench. He applied a paddle and a stingy looking whip to her naked rear. The woman cried out with each strike, but under the red marks on her ass, the tops of her thighs were shiny.

Chessie swayed a little and Kane secured her with an arm just under her breasts, pulling her so she molded against him, his front to her back. "I want to mark you, tonight." He murmured, his lips pressed to the leather covering her ear. "I want you to wake up in the morning and know you're mine."

The man in front of them set down the paddle and the whip, and picked up a cane. After one strike, two faint lines appeared on her pale buttocks. The woman howled.

Chessie whimpered, and Kane held her still, forcing her to watch. The caning continued, each stripe looking more and more wicked. Would he give her a taste of it tonight?

"When you try to orgasm what do you do?" Kane's arms tightened around her. "Don't think, just answer."

"I, um, touch myself."

"Touch what, your clit?" One of his long arms slid down across her body so he could touch the place in question, a brief glide that still made her wobble.

"Yes."

"Any penetration?"

"No. Not when I'm by myself."

"Forgetting your manners again? Maybe when this couple finishes here I'll have you take her place."

"Sorry, sir."

"Good girl."

Two words of praise and she melted into him. He was training her, like a pet. Only instead of treats she'd get orgasms. At least she hoped so.

Kane led her on, past more scening couples – subs in the depths of torment looking like they were in the heights of ecstasy. Nothing made sense anymore, but it didn't have to. Chessie scuttled along in the shadow of her Master, grateful for his confidence. She felt small and defenseless, but safe.

When Kane stopped in front of a spare device; a long iron bar sticking straight up from the floor, taller than her and affixed to a stand on the ground. She started to move, to anticipate where he wanted her. He caught her arm.

"No. Follow my lead," he murmured.

So she stood ready and pliant, and let him place her so her back was against the iron bar. Her hands he cuffed behind her back. He cuffed her ankles at the base, too, with her legs slightly more than shoulder width apart. Her stomach did somersaults at the vulnerable pose. She was dripping and everyone could see.

"There we go," he murmured as he worked. "All secure. No escaping anything now, slut. I can hurt you." He pinched one nipple as if to emphasize his point. "Or I can make you feel good. My decision, my rules. Say 'yes sir'."

"Yes, sir," she whimpered, and he pinched the other one. Pain zinged through her to detonate between her legs.

"Oh yes, you like that."

She wanted to protest, but it was true. However he touched her – good, bad or indifferent – she responded.

"You're so beautiful. There are men watching you right now. They want to fuck you, but you're mine tonight, sweet slave. All mine."

One thing about politicians: they all loved the sound of their own voice.

He left for a moment, returning with another pole on a stand, similar to one that might hold a microphone, except fixed to the top was a white vibrator almost as long as her forearm, with a bulbous head. She recognized it as one of the most powerful vibrators money could buy.

Kane kept talking as he set the smooth head of the vibrator between her labia. "I noticed you when I first came in. You looked so pretty. Elegant. A woman used to wrapping men around her little finger, but that's not how it's going to be tonight." He finished setting up the vibrator firmly between her slippery lips, and gripped her chin. "You need someone to put you in your place, little slut. And that someone is me."

How was it possible for her to be close to climaxing based on dirty talk alone?

Kane replaced the blindfold.

"For a chance to win a free membership, we need to stay in the scene for at least half an hour. I didn't make the rule, sweetheart. A half hour of orgasm torture... starts now."

He turned the Hitachi on. Chessie would've jumped if she hadn't been tied up. As it was her hips twitched back and forth, rocking as far as she could go.

Oh, god, she was going to come. Ten seconds and she was going to
—

Kane stopped the vibrator.

"I forgot. I owe you for your earlier insolence."

"No, please," she started to protest, and a swift smack to her bare breast silenced her. It didn't really hurt, but the force was enough to chastise.

"Excuse me, slave?"

"I'm sorry, sir. It's just... I was about to cum."

"You're not cumming tonight without my permission. Understand?"

"Yes, sir."

"Punishment for talking out of turn." She felt a leather flap cover her nipple a moment before it snapped against her vulnerable flesh. She cried out.

He remained close, so she could hear his voice, a murmur through the mask. "Now the other one, for good measure."

She sucked in a breath, chanting 'ow, ow, ow' in her head.

"What do you say?"

"Thank you, sir," she hurried to obey.

"Good sub." He turned the vibrator onto a low setting, a steady vibration, not enough to cum, but it felt lovely. She relaxed all the way to her bones.

"A nice pair of marks for your breasts. I'll add a few more to your ass you can take home as souvenirs."

"Yes sir," she sighed.

"Good girl, such a good girl." His voice was smooth as good bourbon, and just as potent.

She imagined him stalking around her, swishing that crop through the air, and viewing her bound body from all directions. Warm heat closed over her breast and she jerked in surprise. Kane's clever tongue flicked her sharpened nipple and she moaned.

"Shhh, I just want to enjoy my beautiful sub. These breasts belong to me for the night."

Relaxing, she arched her back, pressing as much as she could into the heat of his mouth.

He took it away and the next thing she felt was the sting of the crop on her ass. Pain washed into pleasure and pushed back into pain.

"The night isn't complete without a few cane marks. What do you think, sweet slave?"

A few minutes ago – or was it an hour? Time had no meaning anymore – but she would've protested the cane. Now, she pushed out her breasts, dying for some stinging pain to take the edge off the overwhelming pleasure. Sometimes, when she worked towards orgasm, she would pinch her nipples and imagine a Dom like Kane clamping them, punishing them. The thought always pushed her closer to the edge.

Her master pressed the long wooden dowel to the tops of her breasts, letting her feel the implement roll over her flesh before flicking it on her tits. She let out a shriek at the line of fire.

"What do you say? Remember your manners or you'll get more."

"Thank you, sir!"

"Good girl." She felt a cloth around her mouth, wiping away the drool. The old Chessie would've felt shame at being reduced to a mouth in a black leather hood, but not her. "Such a good girl. You've earned a reward." The Hitachi buzzed to life, its vibrations biting into her soft flesh. "You may not cum yet. Hold off from that."

Noises escaped her throat, little pants and sighs as the vibrations grew stronger and backed off. Kane was merciless as he edged her, ramping her up to the heights where she could see the pinnacle, could almost tip over the edge, and then shutting the vibrator down to the lowest setting so whatever pleasure had built dissipated into thin air.

She found herself gasping, mouthing nonsense words, begging silently even though she knew that it was useless, that this stern master was implacable, and held her fragile pleasure in his strong, capable hands. He knew just when to increase the vibrations, and when to take them away. He seemed to enjoy her desperation.

"This is almost more fun than orgasm torture. Perhaps I'll play with you all night and won't let you come at all. You'll go home, dripping and needy. Before you go, I'll set you on your knees and use your mouth 'til I cum. Spurt in your face, make you rub it into your skin. Send you off with the smell driving you wild. Would you like that?"

"Please," she whispered. Her orgasm was so close, she could almost reach for it. Her muscles tightened deep within her, her body readying itself for the final, shattering sensation.

"The correct answer is 'Whatever my master wishes'. Isn't that right? Because I own you tonight. And I'm going to enjoy every minute that you are mine."

* * *

KANE CHUCKLED to himself as his sweet submissive squirmed on the Hitachi Orgasm Tower and made desperate pleading noises. She wasn't asking permission to come; she hadn't been trained for that yet. He watched her carefully, noting how she struggled, wanting the orgasm but obeying him. His plan was to make her push off pleasure until she forgot her assertions that she couldn't cum, forgot her attitude, forgot everything including her own name. She was a woman too used to thinking, to being in control, and he would push her past all that, fill her overactive mind with pleasure until she was a gooey, sated, submissive puddle on the ground. Then he'd pick her up, clean her off, strap her down, and force her to cum again.

He tried not to think too much about the way his cock jumped at the prospect of cuddling her close. Usually he scened and didn't become too attached, but this defiant little beauty was proving different than any sub he'd ever had the pleasure of dominating. So reluctant to surrender, even though it was obvious she craved it. Her hands squeezed into fists, as if subconsciously gripping the invisible corner of control. By the end of the night those hands would be open to him, just like her body and mind. He wouldn't be satisfied with anything less, and if she made him work for it, well, he'd always loved a challenge.

The moans escaping his hooded slut's lovely throat were getting louder. She'd blush if she knew how many people in the club could hear her, but at this second she was in her own little world. "Good sub. You may cum," he said, and pushed the vibrator on high.

* * *

CHESSIE'S EARS rang with her screech. She'd cum, thrashing against the pole securing her, flopping like a rag doll. Now she sagged in her bonds and Kane pressed himself against her, holding her up, grounding her.

After a moment, she realized the vibrator was off and Kane was crooning to her.

"That's it, sweet one. Good girl."

Kane removed the blindfold and she blinked, feeling vulnerable and yet strong. He set a water bottle to her lips, and wiped her mouth for her when she was done. He hadn't unbound her.

"I didn't know it could be like that," she said as soon as she found her voice.

He smiled but said nothing. Only when he returned from putting the water bottle away and she tugged impatiently at her bonds did his grin widen.

"Oh no," he said. "You're not done yet."

Panting from the pleasure that had made her weak, she couldn't think of an answer.

The Hitachi started to shake against her numb skin.

"No," she twisted, trying to get her vulnerable bits away from the overwhelming buzz. "It's too much. You can't!"

"I can." He turned the vibrations higher.

"NO," she protested, and received a sharp swat to her butt cheek from the crop. That alone almost sent her over.

"You forget who's in charge." He smacked her ass over and over, varying the intensity of the hits so she never knew if the leather tongue would lap at her bottom or sting it like a bee. Her ass must have been peppered with red marks by the time he was done. And the insistent rumble of the wand between her legs mounted pressure on her brain, a rising wave of sensation so mind numbingly powerful, she didn't know whether it would hurt or feel good.

She grunted and twitched, fighting it. Kane stepped closer and stroked her flesh, squeezing her sore bottom, whispering sweet, dirty nothings in her ears through the hood, even licking and kissing her bare chest while he slipped his fingers inside her. Little words and touches warmed her up, distracting her so she wouldn't fight her impending orgasm. Once she realized it had started, she couldn't stop it if she tried. Kane's teeth caught her nipple and sent her flying down that slippery slope. Not just slippery – she had enough wet between her legs to drown a man, or set his cock swimming.

Someone in the club was screaming at the top of their lungs. As her orgasm struck like twenty lightning bolts at once, she realized that someone was her.

* * *

"PERFECT, LITTLE ONE." Ears still ringing from the air splitting shriek, Kane mopped sweat from his sub's flushed chest. She hung in her bonds, trembling a little. Motioning for a dungeon monitor to help him, Kane undid the restraints and caught her when she slumped into his arms. He held her until she found her feet, nodding to a Dom across the club who met his eye and gave him a thumbs up. Regulars tended to be cautious of newbie subs, avoiding them in case they carried baggage. This one had baggage in spades. But Kane noticed she didn't have her fists clenched anymore.

Poor little subbie. She had no idea what she was in for tonight. They were only getting started.

"All right, sweetheart," he whispered, "Now that you're warmed up, it's time for the Sybian."

* * *

TIME FOR THE WHAT?

The words drifted through her pleasure fogged brain. The senator cleaned her off and steadied her on her feet before tugging her forward.

She wished she could take off the hood. Why was she wearing it again? Oh, right, her identity. Her job as a lobbyist. Those normal, everyday things that seemed light years away.

Kane guided her gently across the club floor, to what looked like a large black box, covered in supple leather.

"Let's try something new," he said. A dungeon monitor helped him affix a dildo attachment.

Chessie eyed it with some confusion.

"Up you go. Sit on the cock, there's a good sub." His hands gripped her hips firmly and set her down on it. She nearly spasmed on the spot as the dildo filled her.

"So wet." Kane put his mouth close to her head so she could hear his murmur. "I could slide a torpedo up there. Now that's an image that will get me through the next Homeland security budget talk..."

He stepped back and studied her as if waiting for her to make a witty comeback. But Chessie couldn't think of anything at all beyond how full her pussy felt with the hard plastic cock stretching her wet hole.

"Do you know what a Sybian does?"

"No," she started to reply, and then Master Kane turned it in on. The whole leather box she was mounted on started vibrating.

"No, no, no –"

"I think this time I'd like you to be quieter."

"– no, please, turn it off –"

"Your last orgasm, I bet they could hear you at the Capitol." He fixed her with a stern look and waited a beat, but try as she might, she couldn't keep from gasping loudly as the Sybian's vibrations increased again. It was like riding a bucking bull at a rodeo, only instead of a crazed, bucking motion, it was a constant, tickling vibration, focused directly on her sensitive bundle of nerves.

Grinding down on the wide base gave her some relief and spread the vibrations through her legs and buttocks, but she couldn't stop her sharp gasp of panic when the cock bumped a pleasurable spot deep inside her…

"Turn it off, turn it off –" she pleaded even as her hips rocked wildly.

"Naughty sub, talking without permission."

Kane walked away and returned with a gag. This one had a small phallus. Kane slid it between her lips, an eager light in his eyes as her mouth accepted it.

"Suck on that. Pretend it's my cock."

Mustering the last bit of fight in her, she ground her teeth down on it.

He laughed. "Bad sub. I guess you haven't quite learned your place. Maybe this will teach you…"

The Sybian increased its vibrations. A crowd was forming, watching the senator torture her, but Chessie didn't care. Her clit felt numb, overstimulated, and desperate for more, all at the same time.

"Let's make this more interesting." Kane's attention was hers, and hers alone. He didn't so much as glance towards the people gathering around. As far as he was concerned, it was only her and him in their own little kinky world.

That gave Chessie a warm, satisfied feeling. Try as she might, she could not push that back.

Tiny claw-like pincers pierced her nipples, and she yelped, warm haze broken. She stared down at the evil looking pincers.

"Those are pretty tame, as far as nipple clamps go. If I were you, I'd be grateful to your kind master for showing mercy."

"-ank -oo," she garbled around the gag.

"Still breathing all right?" he leaned close to ask.

She nodded.

The world went black as he blindfolded her again. It was cruelty, leaving her without any senses but the merciless vibration between her legs. Her breath hitched in her throat as it increased.

She felt the senator hovering at her shoulder again. "Why don't you suck that cock." The words sounded twice as filthy in his normally polite drawl. "Lick it real good, show me what I have to look forward to. Show me what a good girl you are."

That shameful appellation – good girl. She'd do anything to hear it. Her mouth went to work, slurping and sucking on the fake intruding phallus. Her tongue stroked it lovingly, and all the while her pussy dripped even more at the submissive service.

Kane turned up the buzz, higher and higher, until it reached a level she hadn't thought was possible without breaking her in two. Mouth still busy sucking, she careened towards another soul-shattering climax.

"Wait for it," Kane ordered, hovering close. "You look so beautiful, pleasuring that fake cock. Such a lucky piece of plastic. I can't wait to replace it with my own giant member."

She almost gasped a laugh. Of course he'd use that adjective to describe his phallus.

"You doubt me? You'll pay for that." He increased the juice, until she was almost crying. Her much abused clit was going to explode, it would fall off, she would never be able to have an orgasm again.

"I'll put you on your knees and have you make it up to me. You're going to come on the count of three. One...two..." On 'three', he ripped the nipple clamps off her aching tits.

The orgasm blew up around her, closing in like a giant's fist. It wasn't until she stopped thrashing that she realized Kane was holding her, keeping her caged and safe.

Beyond him, the sound muffled by the mask, she could hear faint cheering. The audience?

Kane eased the gag from her lips, and removed the blindfold.

"Ready for another?" he asked gently.

"No," Chessie sagged her head in defeat. "Please. Please, I'll do anything."

"Anything?" Kane put an arm around her waist to steady her as lifted her from the Sybian. For a second she was weightless as he carried her away from the machine. When he set her down on her feet she clutched at him, but he was already there, his arms under hers, supporting and guiding her to the floor.

"On your knees, sweetheart."

She sank down, grateful for the padded floor. The place between her legs felt raw and thoroughly used, her nipples sore from his attentions, but at least he'd put her down on a cushioned mat. She'd be grateful for small mercies.

The sound of a zipper met her ears, and she tilted her head, opening her mouth with a sharp sigh.

"That's it," he murmured above her. He took a handful of her hair, tilting her head back further, taking over control. Limp as a doll in his hands, she was happy to give to him.

"Do I need to get a gag to hold your mouth open?"

She started to shake her head before she remembered the proper answer. "No, sir."

"Good girl." His tone warmed her through and through, as did the gentle fingers on her jaw, cradling it.

"Open wide, darling. Give your master some pleasure."

His cock touched her tongue, and at the first taste of his pre-cum, she hummed happily.

Blowjobs she could do. Her first efforts to be submissive, she'd learned as much as she could about pleasing a man. Her first clue she was submissive.

Flicking her tongue against the head, she arched her neck to take more of him down, and stopped at the sting in her scalp.

"You're not in control. My pace."

She moaned at that, but let him guide her, letting her lick the tip, the head, the upper part of his shaft. Finally taking him down further and closing her mouth around him. He was long, but also thicker than he'd let on; a delicious mouthful. She hummed a little as she licked and sucked, trying to find the spots he liked, the pressure.

"Oh, yes. You were born to serve cock. My cock."

He rocked a little in and out of her mouth. "If you were my permanent slave, I'd get your nipples pierced. You'd always be topless in the house, and I'd lead you about by a chain dangling between them. Would you like that?"

Her 'yes sir' was garbled by the rod in her mouth. He chuckled. "Can't understand you, sweetheart. And it doesn't matter anyway. You'll take what I give you, for my pleasure. Hold still now."

She tensed her neck, waiting. He loved to talk, he loved control. She could imagine what would happen next.

The first thrust brought him into her mouth a bit more, shallow. The next went deeper. He held her head tenderly, but gave no quarter as he slammed his cock forward in rhythm. She sucked as he fucked her face, trying to relax, to soften her jaw and her throat. The next invasion tapped at the back of her throat and she choked a little, tensing. He pulled out, reaffirming his grip on her hair.

"You like taking Daddy's cock?"

He said it with such a deep southern drawl, she nearly laughed. His member hit her cheeks in chastisement.

"Naughty one, laughing at me."

Instead of answering, she opened her mouth, weaving her head a little to catch him. No shame in being a cock hungry whore. None at all.

Kane's fist tightened, pulling her hair and bringing tears to her eyes – and more wetness to her pussy.

"Deep breath, sweetheart, and wait for it."

She stilled. Both hands steadied her head, and he began to slam into her mouth, going deeper each time, beating down the back door of her throat. She gagged a little at first and clenched her fists in protest, but then numbed herself to it. She would take it, had to take it. She'd wanted this. She owed him for the orgasms he'd given her. How many times had she come for him – a hundred? A thousand? She'd spend her life on her knees to repay him.

"That's it slut, take my cock." He pushed in and held it all the way, making her gag a little before resuming his timed thrusts. "Earn my cum. Good girl." He groaned as she swirled her tongue on the underside of his cock, working to please him even as he treated her like his own personal toy. "Such a good sub."

She couldn't help the corners of her mouth turning up at his praise.

"I'm going to cum, darling, and you better take it all," he warned. "Or I'll whip your tits until you'll beg for me to cut up your dress instead of letting you wear it out of here."

She gurgled.

He paused, readying himself for the last rally. "Hold it in your mouth, don't swallow. You get to taste your Master. Your reward for being such a good girl."

As if there wasn't already a puddle on the floor, Chessie felt wetness sliding down her thighs. She didn't bother squeezing her legs together. She was a slut, everyone could see it. From her red nipples to her wet cunt, she'd own who she was, and if anyone said anything, Master Kane would be there. He would protect her.

He slid in for his last assault. This time, she relaxed her hands, and tried to stay as open as she could for him. He beat against her mouth, squeezing handfuls of her hair, working her head just how he liked it. Tears squeezed from the corners of her eyes, even as she felt a rush of pleasure stir through her, starting from her pussy and spreading through her body, tingling through her breasts.

Holy hell, did she just cum from a face fuck?

Kane buried himself deep in her mouth, and she focused on him again, moaning, humming, swirling her tongue. He pulled out and she tasted his ejaculate, a mild flavor that was not unpleasant. She quivered with pleasure at being able to serve him. At the last second she remembered not to swallow, but tipped her head back and kept her mouth wide open, showing him his cum.

Every part of her arched and aching to please him.

"Good girl," he rasped, and she felt triumph that he wasn't unaffected. "Such a good girl. You may swallow."

She did, and he didn't even have to prompt her next words.

"Thank you, sir."

* * *

DAMN IF THIS wasn't one hell of a sub. She knelt before him, chest heaving, pussy weeping, pretty eyes glazed as they fixed on his face. He wanted to tie her up again and do bad things to her. He'd fuck her pussy, her ass, her mouth until she was filled with the essence of him, and only him. He wanted to ruin her for all men, and keep her forever.

One thing at a time.

She had cum without permission. During face fucking no less, the magnificent creature. She probably wasn't even sure what had happened. If he took her home, he'd bind her so she spent the whole weekend on her knees.

The whole weekend, now that was a thought.

Now she waited, docile, without a peep.

"Good girl," he told her again, and just to see how far he could push her, grabbed a handful of her hair. "Crawl now, darlin'. Hands and knees."

Instantly she was on all fours, moving on wobbly limbs to heel. He'd train her to crawl too, but for now her ungainly scrabbling was beautiful, because she struggled to obey him.

They moved across the club towards the next station he had in mind.

"Up." He helped her to her feet and placed her hands on the bar of the stocks. She jerked back when she felt them. He waited.

"Sir –"

A sharp smack resonated and made her bottom wobble. "Did I give you permission to speak?"

She shook her head. "Permission to speak, sir." Her chest heaved.

"Denied." He started strapping her in. "We're not done. The rules state the minimum time we need to remain in the scene is thirty minutes. I haven't tortured you for thirty minutes straight. Not even close." He'd enjoyed teasing her too much, controlling her responses and making her beg. She'd resisted each orgasm and fought beautifully, but he wasn't satisfied with mere surrender. He needed to break her.

Her legs shook a little as he secured her to the wooden frame.

"There you go." He left and returned with the Hitachi still soaked with her exertions. He placed the stand close to her. Just to be mean, he turned it on so she could hear, but not feel it.

* * *

CHESSIE GASPED and threw herself forward, before she remembered she was bound to the stocks and couldn't get away.

"No, no, no," she sobbed, writhing her bottom in useless protest.

"Yes sweetheart," Kane's voice was sweet and patient, even as he turned the hitachi buzz higher in promise of what was to come. "You can do this. You want to please me?"

She shook her head, but the answer was yes. She did. She would do anything for him.

"You have a safeword. You can admit defeat at any time. I'll make you kiss my shoes first, but then you can go."

She kept shaking her head and this time she meant it.

"Safeword? You may answer."

"No sir. Please, just... help me. "

"I will, sweetheart."

The Hitachi switched off.

She sensed he'd left the space and she waited for his return, shifting slightly from foot to foot. Her poor clit was so numb and abused, she couldn't possibly orgasm again. Kane had led her to a bottomless well of pleasure; she didn't know if she would drink or drown. All she knew was that he was the one holding her up, guiding her, keeping her from losing it.

Something cool touched her lips. "Drink baby. That's it. You've been so, so good for me."

She finished the glass and waited for him to finish the statement.

"One more round and I'll take you into the next room and cuddle you to your heart's content."

She nodded and hung her head in defeat.

He took away the glass and returned but didn't turn on the torture device right away. Instead his hands softly stroked her arms, waist, rubbed her tense biceps and shoulders. The massage made her relax, but the kiss on her neck overcame her.

She let out a sob, tears leaking behind the leather mask.

"You can do this. I'll be so proud of you. I'm already proud of you. Free membership awaits. Just a little bit more."

Free rent, free membership. She'd forgotten these far away, insignificant details. She'd forgotten everything but him.

He turned on the Hitachi again for a mere second and she tensed, but didn't beg. She would do this for him.

Another layer, another layer. He stripped her defenses away, one by one. What would he do when he found she didn't have any more to give?

The wand switched off. "Good girl. I'm going to help you." His touch glided down her spine. Head and wrists bound in the stocks, Chessie was bent forward with her legs straight and stance wide. Trapped, helpless.

Again he placed the bulbous head of the Hitachi wand between her dripping folds, pressing it snugly against her clit.

"I have the remote, so be good for me." His voice floated to her but she was already gone, in her own world ruled by her arousal and his touch. Falling, falling into that black well. Far away from the usual angry traffic in her mind. A beautiful, easy mental space.

At least, until something cool was spread between her ass cheeks.

"Unk," she choked.

"Relax, subbie. I'll stretch you out, nice and easy. Fingers first. I'm going to train this ass for me." His fingers followed, doing what he'd promised. Pushing and probing until her back hole burned with the stretch. "My cock is long but not so thick. It'll fill you, though."

His fingers twisted into her, and she moaned long and deep, letting her head sag further.

"You like that? You're dripping on the floor." He clucked in mock disapproval. "Naughty subs lick their messes up. But you're not naughty. You're a good girl. You want your Master to fill you."

Hanging in her bonds, Chessie panted and tried to keep from shouting her outrage, not sure if the invasion of her tender hole mortified her or felt good. Probably a healthy dose of both. Her face was flushed under the leather and her nipples were hard as he probed her. It was so wrong, so taboo.

So why was she so turned on?

"You're so sweet and pliant. Under that fighting facade, there's a spirit that wants to submit." The fingers popped out of her ass, but before she could sigh in relief, the vibrator came to life. Kane kept up his steady whisper. "Let go, girl, let me take care of you for a little while."

The hitachi ground against her raw skin. Electricity pulsed through her, gathering, promising a climax, a pinnacle higher than she'd ever experienced before. It didn't make sense anymore – was it pain or was it pleasure? It was pain past all pleasure, pleasure past all pain.

On and on Kane whispered his soft litany, a lullaby lulling her to the heights, his voice the only thing tethering her to the world.

The hitachi turned on high.

Again, her own cries filled her ears. Now she was begging.

"Stop, please, stop, I can't –"

"You may cum," he told her, and she did, crashing to the ground and almost immediately starting to ascend again.

"It's too much, it's too much." Her whole body clenched, fighting the climb. The vibrations between her legs pulled her up and threw her off the summit again.

"God, please," she groaned. "I can't – "

Not even Kane's voice could reach her now. It was too much. The bracing buzz between her legs didn't touch the cacophony in her own head. Her body felt hot, and cold, and her stomach turned. She was frozen, she was on fire.

She came again and again, sputtering. Her eyes, nose and mouth were dripping, clogging the leather, making it hard to breathe. She coughed and couldn't stop coughing.

The vibration stopped, but she kept shaking. Her arms were released, and a strong, warm body cradled her.

"Enough, sweetheart. Enough. I've got you."

"Kane." She clung to him, breathing in his perfect scent.

"Here." The mask loosened, and peeled from her skin, and just like that she could breathe.

"There you go, darling. Drink this. I've got you." He cradled her and tipped a water bottle to her lips, then wet a handkerchief and cleaned her face as if she were a baby.

She shivered, curling into him. He'd carried her into the semi-private room and cradled her on the couch.

"Permission to speak," she croaked.

"Scene's over, baby. Talk as much as you like."

"Did... what happened?"

"You hit subspace, and went away."

"But...did we win?"

"We did. You did. You did so good for me. It'll be okay."

"I wanted... to be good for you."

"You were, baby, you were." Someone waved to him from outside the room, and he frowned. "One second, baby. Stay here and drink this –" He handed her a water bottle. "And I'll be right back."

"Okay," she sniffled. Before he left, he wrapped a giant blanket around her shoulders. "Thank you."

She gazed after him hungrily, drinking in his long form as he went to speak to the dungeon monitor. He still looked as poised and cool as at the beginning of the night, while she was a naked, dripping, drooling mess. Deep in conversation with the club employee, Kane angled his body to gesture back at her, and she saw the rather impressive hardon tenting his slacks. The senator wasn't completely unaffected by the night's events.

But when was he going to fuck her?

Dismay hit her body harder than the bout of trembling. Was he going to fuck her? Should she ask or offer? Was it even done? Maybe he didn't want to fuck her. Maybe she wasn't good enough, wasn't pretty enough. Maybe if she asked, he'd decline.

Ms. Jones, he'd say in that polite tone of his, *thank you, but I must regretfully decline...*

Now there were two men speaking with the senator. One she recognized as the club owner. Was she in trouble? Kane had said something about the month's free membership.

Oh God, she'd safeworded at the beginning. Maybe she'd messed it up for him. What if the only reason he'd come tonight was for the free membership and she'd ruined it for him?

Where five minutes ago there had been perfect peace, the thoughts poured into her head and wouldn't stop. Something else nagged at her. She didn't realize what it was until she'd finished the water bottle and set it down, and her hand hit the mask.

The mask! He'd taken off the mask. She lifted it with trembling fingers. All her anonymity, carefully preserved. Ruined in an instant. Her status as a lobbyist, totally destroyed. She could see it now – she'd knock on a senator's door, try to gain entrance with an aide, and Kane would be there, and he'd smile a knowing smile...

"How was it?" The sub from the stage stood beside the curtain, smirking at her. "He's good, isn't he?"

"What?"

"He sent me to give you this." The woman handed her a water bottle. "And I'm not surprised. He usually doesn't do much aftercare, which is kinda strange, seeing as he always goes for the newest subs."

"The newest subs?" Chessie repeated in the daze. The pieces of the night were coming into focus, combining into a picture of terrible clarity.

"Yeah," the sub said. "Sucks though. I scened with him once, when I was new, but only once. After he takes a sub and breaks her, he tends to drop them." The woman shrugged. "At least you got one night, right? I'll never forget the taste of the Kane. And I don't mean the wooden one." With a wink, she was gone.

The shivers overtook Chessie despite the thick blanket. Kane always went for the new ones. Until he broke them, the sub had said. Well, he'd definitely broken her. There were pieces of her soul lying all over the club floor.

Oh God, she had begged him, cum for him, even crawled for him.

She rose and started pawing through his things, looking for her dress and boots, blinking to clear her vision.

She'd thought she was special. He'd made it sound like they had an extra connection, that she could trust him.

'It's all a game', Mina had told her from the beginning. Kane was a master. She just wished she had been an equal player and not just a pawn in his hands. She should have known once he reached the core of her, laid her bare, all the challenge, the mystery would be gone. Puzzle solved, he could toss her aside as easily as he discarded her mask.

CHAPTER 4

"I don't mean to argue, I just wanted to point out the rules," the dungeon monitor said. "I watched you take your sweet time getting into the play, and didn't say anything, bt now you're monopolizing a semi-private room. The point of the Roulette was to play out here, in the open, where people can see."

Kane channeled his cool and resisted the urge to tear his hand through his hair. He had a weary sub waiting for him and wanted nothing more than to go wrap his arms around her. Instead, he was debating with a stupid dungeon monitor who wanted to make sure the audience got their money's worth. As if he, Senator Kane, and his beautiful sub for the night, were trained monkeys.

"I understand that," he said through gritted teeth. "She's new to the scene. I wanted to ease her into play. Help her explore, and learn what she likes."

"That's another thing. She rolled Sybian orgasm torture--you didn't get her there until almost forty-five minutes after your scene started--"

"Are you auditing our scene?" Kane couldn't help but raise his voice, put force into his tone. An asshole move, but he was two seconds from just walking away from the conversation. He had to get back to his helpless, quivering sub. She might need him. "I'm the dom,

I got a new play partner for the night. I wanted to see to her needs. Not titillate some crowd."

"Master Kane, is everything all right here?" It was Jaxson, thank God. The owner of the club saw that he was about to lose his cool.

"Tell your employee that as a Dom in this club, the safety and care of my partner for the night is my highest concern. Not whether or not we're putting on a good show." Kane kept his words civil, but the bite to his tone made the overbearing employee's blood run from his face.

"I only wanted to make sure he knew the rules. He also shouldn't be spending so much time in a private room – those are for everyone, and the Roulette players are supposed to keep their scenes on the floor –"

"Yes, thank you. I'll make sure Master Kane understands the rules. Could you check to see if they need any help at the stocks?" Jaxson said, dismissing the man.

Kane unclenched his fists and tried to relax. It didn't help that he had a hardon the size of the Washington Monument trying to break free of his slacks. That wasn't a testament to his size, just a fact any red-blooded American male would be facing after a couple of hours with the lovely Ms. Jones.

Damn but he had to learn her real name...

"You've really got a thing for this one, don't you?" The teasing lilt in his friend's voice had Kane clenching his fists all over again. If Jaxson didn't watch it, he was going to get a black eye.

A sub Kane knew strutted by, and to distract himself he turned and caught her arm. "I have a sub in the semi-private room. Can you bring her another water bottle and tell her I'll be right there?"

After the sub left, Kane faced Jaxson again. The club owner studied him with a shrewd look on his face. "What's going on? I've never seen you this close to losing your cool. Not even when your bill was defeated and you convinced three subs to spend all night taking your cane."

Kane gave in to the urge to run his hand through his hair, and gripped the back of his neck to still his nervous gesture. "It's this sub. She came in with all these walls, and I've broken through. I want to see her again... but there's a reason she came in wearing a mask. She doesn't want me to know who she is."

"I can't tell you her name, man. Confidentiality."

"I know that. She went through three rounds of orgasm torture. Is there a chance you can offer her the free membership?" Kane lowered his voice. "I know Master D and I broke the rules, swapping subs so early in the game. Technically, Ms. Jones safeworded. But even if we didn't win the free membership, I was hoping you could find an excuse to offer it. I'll pay for it myself."

Jaxson's eyebrow went up. "Paying for her? Didn't you just meet her tonight?"

"Yes, and you know as well as I do what it feels like when you've found the one." He met his friend's gaze. Jaxson stared right back, but Kane didn't back down.

Finally, Jaxson broke into a smile. "Well, shit. I didn't know it was like that." He clapped Kane's arm. "I better not keep you any longer. If you want her, go get her."

The surge of triumph lasted as long as it took to stride back to the semi-private room. He sent a glare in the dungeon monitor's direction, then stopped short at the entrance, heart stuttering to a halt as he took in the empty room.

No Ms. Jones. No dress or boots either. Just an empty water bottle and two pieces of black plastic that broke apart fully when he lifted it.

The mask.

HER BODY WAS BROKEN. The orgasms had broken her. That was the only explanation. Halfway home, her body had started shaking uncontrollably. The taxi driver probably thought she was on something. He'd noticeably bit back a comment when she'd fumbled the fare out of her wallet, but he'd taken her money and driven off with only a, "Take care of yourself, ma'am."

It took all the strength in her to climb the stairs to her apartment. Once inside, she dropped her purse and stripped off her boots, but left on her dress. She still clutched the blanket from Black Light in a ball around her chest. No one had made her hand it over, and she'd forgotten it until now. Her one souvenir from the night.

God she was a mess. She didn't want to get into bed – didn't want her stink on the sheets. She should shower, but couldn't quite bring herself to move any further. Darkness curled on the edge of her vision and there was a faint ringing in her ears. Her own panic was threatening to deafen and blind her, more effectively than any mask or leather hood.

"You're safe, you're safe," she chanted, but found herself sinking to the floor. Still clutching the blanket, she crawled the last few feet into her closet, and curled into a ball.

* * *

KANE CAUGHT the arm of the sub he'd sent in with the water bottle.

"Where is she? Did you see her?"

"Who?" the woman asked.

"Nancy Pelosi, who do you think?" Kane snapped and almost growled at the look of confusion greeting his sarcasm. "The sub I asked you to help." It was all he could do to keep from shaking the woman. As it was, his fingers bit into her arm with a little warning force.

"Stop – you're hurting me!" The woman wrenched her arm out of his grip. "Help!" she raised her voice.

Jaxson was at their side in an instant.

"What's going on?"

"Ms. Jones is missing," Kane explained through gritted teeth. "She's in no condition to leave on her own. I worked her over pretty good. She'll need aftercare."

"And you'd know all about aftercare, wouldn't you," the woman sneered. "You beat and fucked me three months ago, remember? I gave you my phone number and I haven't heard a word since."

Kane felt his eyebrows try to crawl into his hairline. "Ma'am," he said in the coldest drawl he could muster. "I never made any promises to seek you out afterwards. In fact, I distinctly remember thanking you for the night and making it clear that I don't often scene with a sub more than once."

"So why are you so worried about her?" the lady snarled, lunging at Kane. Jaxson caught her, strong arms caging the woman as she screeched with outstretched claws.

"Go –" he said to Kane, containing the struggling sub. "Find your Ms. Jones. Make sure she's all right."

"Are you looking for your sub, Master Kane?" Another club employee rushed to help Jaxson. "I think I saw her leave. She didn't look too good –"

"So you just let her go? You didn't try to stop her? Christ, I'm surrounded by incompetence."

"Preston, get it together," Jaxson snapped. "You can't intimidate my staff; I don't care who your daddy was."

Kane opened his mouth, and thought better of it. He was picking a fight with his friend, and, worse, his friend's employees who'd done nothing wrong.

Ms. Jones had affected him more than he'd realized.

"Kane, go," Jaxson ordered, and, for the first time in his life, Preston Kane the Third obeyed a dominant's order.

"My apologies," he bit out and dashed for the door.

Stupid, stupid. He'd been too cocky. He'd over-estimated his ability as a Dom. Breach a woman's defenses and carry her into the deepest levels of submission all in one night? There was only so much a sub's mind could take. Ms. Jones was a strong, intelligent woman, but she had her limits, and even if he used all his skill as a Dom to push her past them, there was always a price.

He only hoped it wouldn't cost him everything.

Grabbing his wallet and cellphone from the locker, he thought about badgering the doorman to ask where Ms. Jones headed, but one look at the beefy fellow and he thought better of it. Pushing out through the back entrance, he emerged onto the street.

Think, he had to think. She's alone, and feeling out of her depth, maybe even already experiencing the effects of sub drop, when her brain, high from the endorphins her body had released that night, finally crashed. Even if she wasn't going through a drop, her body would be weak and shaky from exertion, needing water, rest, and care. Needing him.

Dammit, he'd let her down. So much for being her permanent Dom. He didn't even deserve to scene with her for one night.

He couldn't just stand there. He picked a direction – towards the heart of Georgetown – and started walking. As he moved, he called his most resourceful aide.

"Jameson? I need an address." What sort of excuse did he have to be meeting with a lobbyist this late? If he didn't watch it, it'd be all over the Hill. People pretended they didn't know who was fucking who, but it was the most popular source of gossip. "A lobbyist who works for a women's rights firm. Last name 'Jones'." What had been the first name on her placecard at the speaker dinner? "First name begins with a C... no, I am not fucking kidding you. I'm willing to call in whatever favors we have to get the info. Fuck!" He narrowly avoided tripping over a trashcan. He was almost to the busy street where he could find a waiting cab. As his aide dithered on the other end of the line, Kane realized he'd been charging down the sidewalk so fast that the drunks and homeless got out of his way.

'Way to not call attention to yourself, asshole,' he scolded himself. For once, looking calm and poised didn't matter. Not with his Ms. Jones out there, possibly hurting, possibly alone.

"I've got a lead," his aide said, and paused a moment. "Wait. Isn't this the lady we met at dinner last night?"

"Yes," Kane said. "Yes, that's her."

It took longer than he'd liked, but a few phone calls, and a short Uber ride later, Kane stood outside Ms. Jones' apartment. Not the best part of town, but not the worst, either.

There was a man standing on the stoop, smoking. Kane drew himself up to his full six three height and turned on his full good ol' boy drawl.

"Evening, sir. Did you see a woman enter here? Lovely gal with dark hair?"

"Yeah, man, she went up to her place in 2B. Looked real bad. A nasty trip or something, you know what I'm sayin'?"

"Indeed I do. Thank you." Kane took the steps two at a time.

Apartment 2B. He felt a moment of trepidation – what if she was fine, and didn't want to see him? He decided he'd insist. He'd at least make sure someone capable was with her and could spend the night. He owed her that much.

His dismay lasted as long as it took for him to reach her door, where it turned to cold fear. The door was ajar. No lights were on inside or out. Her keys were hanging from the lock.

Not a good sign.

He knocked lightly and the door creaked open further. "Ms. Jones? Chelsea? It's Senator Kane. From the club. You left the keys in the door." He pulled them out and held the doorknob so he could knock harder. "Ms. Jones, are you there?"

If she didn't answer, he was going in, one way or another. Thank God he had gotten here first. Someone could've broken into the apartment, taken advantage –

A loud banging from inside nearly sent him out of his skin. Without thinking, he pushed inside the dark apartment.

"Ms. Jones, is everything all right?"

He hit the light and found the source of the horrible clanging – a large radiator belching forth waves of heat.

No sign of Chelsea, but she had to be here. He stepped further into the tiny apartment, and kicked a pair of boots lying in a forgotten pile on the hardwood floor. One heel was broken.

As the radiator sound died away, he heard a low sniffling sound. Only a short hall separated him from an open bedroom door.

He locked the door behind him before he started towards the source of the crying.

His shoes creaked on the hardwood, and he prayed Ms. Jones didn't carry a weapon, and that she'd forgive him for breaking and entering.

"Mina?" came a small voice. "Is that you?"

"Ms. Jones, it's Preston Kane." He winced as he realized they hadn't been properly introduced. "I don't mean to intrude. I just wanted to talk to you. You ran off before I could make sure you were okay."

He flicked on the light in the bedroom and heard another whimper. The room wasn't a real bedroom, he realized, but a tiny parlor converted into one. The bed took up most of the space. His sub was hiding in the closet.

Flicking off the light, he crossed the room in two strides and turned on a bedside lamp. "It's me, darlin'. Master Kane, from the club. You left your door open and I was worried. I have your keys." He laid them with a clink on the bed. "I'm here to make sure you're all right."

Moving slowly, and modulating his voice to a soothing tenor, he crouched to peer into the closet. "You left so quickly, I wanted to make sure you were okay."

As he got closer, she moved, and the soft glow from the bedside lamp illuminated a pair of liquid brown eyes.

"Master Kane?" She huddled in the closet, her arms around her knees. Black makeup ringed her eyes as she shivered.

"Yeah, baby." Kneeling, he pulled off his coat to wrap around her. "It's me. How you doing?"

"I d-don't know." She pushed a heel of her hand in her eye, smearing her makeup further as another sob shook her.

"Oh, darling. I'm so sorry," he couldn't stop the drawl as his heart plummeted straight to his feet. "Come here. Let's get you warm."

He sat fully on the floor in the soft nest she'd made from the club blanket and piles of clothes, and pulled her into his arms. She clutched his arm like a lifeline.

"I don't know what's happening to me."

"Shh, you're all right." Her small frame shook, breaking his heart further. He closed his eyes, inhaled the scent of her hair, and tried to match his breathing to hers.

"There's something wrong with me."

"No, baby, this reaction is normal. Your brain got overloaded in the club, and you need some aftercare. I'm here now. I'm going to take care of you."

That undid her. She leaned into him and cried.

"That's it, baby, let it all out. You're going to be all right. I'm here." He kissed her hair. "You're just fine."

He kept crooning to her until the shaking subsided. He was just about to ask if she had some orange juice in the house, something to boost her blood sugar, when she spoke. Her quavering voice barely broke the dark.

"I don't know why I'm like this. I wish I wasn't."

He stayed quiet, resisting the urge to tell her she was beautiful and perfect, that he wouldn't change a thing about her.

"I've had men touch me. Cop a feel in the metro. Shout catcalls as they drive by. I hate that. I hate being treated like an object." She angled her body to look at him. "But when you did it, I liked it. The more you did, the more I liked it."

"There's a difference. Consent. You can stop play with a safeword."

"It's messed up though." She turned away again. "To want what I want. To orgasm –" She covered her face with a hand for a moment.

"Is it wrong to know what you want and go after it?"

She shook her head, but he knew she wasn't agreeing with him.

"You said you had trouble orgasming." He tried a different tack. Wrapped around her body in the small space, he kept cuddling her and hoped the intimate position made her feel safe enough to spill her secrets.

"I didn't tonight." She gave a small, brittle laugh.

"Maybe all this time, you just needed to be forced. Not actually forced," he clarified, "but in a safe, carefully monitored environment where you've given consent first. You needed someone to push you past your boundaries. Break down your walls."

"I don't know," she said. "I don't like this part of me that wants to be hurt, degraded. I'd cut it out of me if I could."

"Amputate a part of yourself to fit some norm? That's not very kink positive now, is it?" He let his tone turn light, teasing.

"You don't understand. I'm a feminist."

"What's more feminist than getting a guy to give you fifty orgasms in a row?"

"Oh my God." She covered her face with her hands again, but this time he knew she was smiling.

Lifting her hair, he gave her neck a small kiss. "Come on." He scooted back so they both could rise. "You need sugar and liquids. Chocolate, if you have it. If you don't have any, I'll go out and get it."

"Fifty orgasms and now you give me chocolate," she murmured. "You're too good to be true."

But she clutched the club blanket to her, keeping a slight distance even as she swayed a little on her feet. She still didn't trust him.

"Point me to the kitchen, sweetheart, and I'll get everything. Do you have loose comfy clothes you can change into?" He kept his manner confident, clinical.

Once his little sub was in pajamas, sipping juice and tucked into bed, he sat to take off his shoes.

Her eyes, which had been drooping along with her head, got wide again. "What are you doing?"

"Getting ready for bed." He stripped to his undershirt. "Unless you have a boyfriend or significant other? Someone who might barge in and find us, and shoot me?"

"No."

"Good." He kept on his slacks and undershirt, and placed everything else in a pile.

She frowned a little as she watched him. He was crossing a line by staying, but he sensed that she needed him to. He'd be damned if he'd leave her alone tonight, even though he was sure she'd fight him, insist she could take care of herself, if she wasn't so tired.

"I have a roommate though."

"I know. She left a note on the fridge reminding you to water the houseplants while she's gone." He climbed into the bed and helped himself to one of the chocolates with a satisfied sigh. The bed wasn't large enough for him to lay beside her without touching, but he kept talking, movements friendly and matter-of-fact even as he enjoyed the warm curves of her body against his much taller one. "She also told you to – and I quote – 'Call me after the Roulette, you kinky bitch.'"

Ms. Jones blushed a little. "Yeah, that's my roommate. She's... got a mouth."

"Her name is Mina, right? I think I've met her at the club." He took the moment to thread his arm through the pillows, around his Ms. Jones shoulders. She stiffened for the briefest moment, and then relaxed into his warmth. He couldn't keep from bending his head and breathing in the sweet scent of her. His dick didn't thank him. It was back to screaming for release. He ignored it.

"I know we're not scening now, but can you do one more thing for me? Close your eyes and just rest. It'll help."

"I don't even know you," she said even as she obeyed.

"Preston Kane the Third. I work ninety hours a week and beat women on the weekend."

"Typical man."

"I only beat women consensually."

"I stand corrected." Her mouth curved into a lazy smile. She was half asleep, but still, he counted it as a win.

He put both arms around her, and suppressed the surge of glee at being in bed with a beautiful woman who could hold her own in conversation. One who got off on his particular brand of punishment.

God she was perfect.

"Why did you come after me?" She was still fighting sleep, fighting him. "Woman said you didn't do aftercare."

"Woman?" he asked as soon as he remembered the sub he'd sent in with the water bottle, the one who almost attacked him. "She didn't know what she was talking about." Anger coursed through him and he was careful not to let it through his voice. "She misunderstood."

"She said you always look for the new subs."

"I've scened with new submissives before, but I don't look for them." He took a chance and squeezed her tighter. "I looked for you."

"You remember me?" She tipped her head back, and he saw her expression, hopeful, anguished.

"I do. Ms. Chelsea Jones, from table nine."

"You told your aide you wanted to turn me over your knee."

"That I did. I wanted to see your reaction."

"You knew I'd heard you?"

"Of course. Watched you turn tail and run. Thought I'd read you wrong, until you showed up tonight. Close your eyes, now. We can talk more in the morning."

"Okay," she sighed. Sweet and obedient, as he knew she could be. His balls were way past blue. It was going to be torture, holding her all night, but he wasn't about to let her go.

"Chessie," she said sleepily.

"Hmm?"

"My friends call me Chessie. I like it better."

"Chessie." Soft and unique, like her. "Go to sleep, beautiful."

* * *

CHESSIE WOKE IN AN EMPTY BED. For a moment she wondered if anything had happened last night, or if she'd just scored some bad weed and fallen asleep to the director's cut of Fifty Shades of Grey. When she moved, she felt the soreness in her core and legs, and little chocolate wrappers fell off her bed.

Not a dream, then.

Last night had been amazing. And hard. She still didn't know what she thought about it all. She wanted to talk with someone about it, but a part of her was relieved that Master Kane – Preston, or Senator Kane, or whatever the hell she was supposed to call him in a normal setting – was already gone.

A part of her was pissed... and disappointed.

Mincing across the floor to the bathroom, she realized she was walking funny and almost laughed out loud. Her inner thighs ached, though a quick peek in the mirror proved that her bare mons was a little red and inflamed, but none the worse for wear. Her ass cheeks and breasts had a few fine marks. She wouldn't be rubbing one out anytime soon, but once she had a hankering for an orgasm – and her pussy had recovered – she had plenty of masturbation material ready. All she had to do was close her eyes and think of the Kane...

A clanging sound made her jump. It wasn't Gangbang, the overactive radiator. It came from the kitchen...

She rounded the corner and stopped in her tracks at the beautiful sight of Senator Kane, barefoot in black slacks and his white button down shirt, wiping her counter with a sponge.

"I broke an egg." His lush lips broke into a heart-stopping smile, and her pussy woke up all over again. A frying pan sizzled angrily on the stove.

Silently, she padded to the tiny breakfast nook, moved a pile of junk mail and Mina's magazines, sat down, and watched Senator Kane cook her breakfast.

"You sleep okay?" he asked over his shoulder.

She nodded. "You?"

He wrinkled his nose. "That radiator is really loud."

"Yeah."

"Warm though. What do you like in your omelet? I found eggs, tomato, cheese – I figured you wouldn't mind if I went ahead and raided your fridge. You need protein."

Her brain scrambled. "Um, everything but cheese. Thank you."

"I would've made coffee but couldn't find your filters."

"We have a French press. I'll get it." She rose, happy for a chore that would wake her up a little. After all the awful and wonderful things Kane had done to her, being in the kitchen with him was a little disconcerting. "French roast okay?"

"Egg-cellent," he purred and it was so ridiculous she laughed.

"Puns will get you tarred and feathered around here."

He bumped her hip lightly as she stood beside him. "Maybe I'd like that."

"Kinky," she teased. "Can I jump in the shower real quick, before breakfast? I just want to rinse off. I'll be out before the coffee brews."

"Sure. I'll keep these warm." He caught her hand before she walked away. "Come here."

Trepidation flickered through her, followed by a sense of peace at his confident touch. He brought her to stand in front of him, his hands on her shoulders. Not an intimate touch, but it still sent butterflies through her stomach, even as it calmed her mind.

"You doing okay?"

"Yes," she ducked her head. "Um, I'm a little sore, but in a good way."

"Good." His gaze dropped to her lips and for a wild moment she hoped he'd kiss her. Instead, he drew her in for a little hug. "Last night was everything I had hoped for, and more," he said. He pressed his lips to her hairline for a brief second before he released her. "Go get your shower. When you come back, we can talk."

Knees weak, it was a wonder she made it to the bathroom, where she stripped and rinsed off in record time. God, but she wanted him. She didn't have any doubts about that, anymore. She really hoped he'd stay.

What if he didn't want her? What if he did?

It took her as long as the walk to her closet to make a decision. Kane had spent the night and given her a hug. She'd spent too long denying herself. It was time to go for what she really wanted.

When she returned to the kitchen, she wore a short, silky robe, and nothing underneath. Kane's eyes lit at the sight of the robe – at knee length really not much more than a negligee – but he said nothing at first. Instead, he served her eggs and coffee, waiting for her to taste them before grabbing his own plate.

"You're spoiling me."

"I believe in treating a lady like a queen. Unless she wants otherwise."

"About last night." Chessie cleared her throat. "How did you know what I needed?"

He shrugged. "I just tried to read you, see what turned you on. I tried things and if you enjoyed them, I went a bit further. I actually need to apologize. I may have gone a bit too far."

"I liked it though." She felt that wistful uncertainty again. "I don't know why I like it. I used to think something was wrong with me."

"What if we thought about this a different way? You're a successful lobbyist. An intelligent, educated woman. You probably have a to-do list a mile long."

"Ten miles long."

"So, it's simple physiology. Your frontal lobe is too engaged during sex."

"The what-?" she asked before she recognized he was talking about areas of her brain.

Leaning forward, he tapped her forehead. "The reasoning part of your brain. You need to turn this off, and get to the primal part of your brain. That's where your orgasms live. And having someone take control during sex is just the thing you need. If I were a doctor I'd prescribe it once a day and twice on Sundays." He sat back with a Cheshire grin.

"But... last night, I had the shakes... what was that?"

"Sub drop. Endorphins flooded your system, and when they left your brain went through withdrawal. You crashed."

"Like from a drug."

"Yes. A totally natural self-induced drug. You know why marathoners run?"

"They like pain?"

"The body's response to pain. The runner's high. It's addictive. That's why there are crowds that flock to a big race, and a line outside Black Light's door."

* * *

KANE WATCHED his sub sit curled in her chair, her beauty framed in the soft morning light. Her brain was working, that overactive hamster spinning in its wheel, running the maze, and coming to its conclusions. She'd either agree and say something brilliant that summed up all his blathering in one eloquent phrase, or call bullshit and kick him out on his ass. He really, really hoped it wouldn't be the latter.

"That makes sense," she mused. "It's like skydiving. It's dangerous, but with the right instructor, I'll reach the ground safely, and on the way down, let go and fly."

She took his breath away.

She pinned him with her gaze. "But what do you get out of it?"

"Assisting you with the high. Serving you. Controlling your responses. What does a man get out of driving a Ferrari?"

"He gets laid."

"Bingo." He couldn't resist leaning forward and tapping her nose to break her dry expression. She had a few freckles there. "There are a lot of things I get – including a high akin to subspace. Different part of the brain. I have a folder of research I can send to you."

"Ooh, research. Careful, senator. Talking data with me is like foreplay."

Her elegant foot stroked up his calf.

He closed his hand around it, stopping its ascent but keeping it in his lap. He kneaded it a little as she looked out from under her lashes at him.

"So I just have to say 'randomized, double blind study' and I can have my way with you?"

Her head tipped back and her laugh bubbled out of her, natural; the sound made him complete.

"Scientific dirty talk," he mused. "I can handle that."

"Can you, senator? I was under the impression that your political party doesn't even grasp the basics of ecology, not to mention a woman's anatomy. Unless they're groping it." She pointed a finger. "If you say 'not all men', I will shishkabob you with my roommate's shoe."

"Ooh. No thanks, love. Anal penetration is one of my hard limits."

She laughed again, but then got serious. "So it can be like this? Sitting around, talking, playful banter?"

"Honey, it can be however you want." The wistful look in her eye twisted his heart – and gave him courage. "Now I need you to do something for me."

She gave a him a curious look.

"Lose the robe. Sit with your feet apart. I want to see that pretty pussy while I clear the breakfast dishes."

* * *

AND SO IT BEGAN.

Heat flared into her cheeks, but she immediately did as he asked. She let the robe skim down her back, suddenly feeling alive.

He didn't look at first, but cleared the dishes while she waited, his arrogant expectation that she'd obey him turning her on even more. Two days ago she couldn't orgasm, and now she was sitting, soaking wet, in the breakfast nook.

"Mmm, now that's a sight I'd never get tired of."

He was back, seated and sipping a fresh cup of coffee as he regarded her like a work of art he'd just purchased. She sat up a little straighter, emphasizing the curve in her back, thrusting out her tits.

"You are perfect, Ms. Jones. If I had my way, every time we dined you'd be naked and sit just like that."

"Typical chauvinist fantasy," she couldn't help but murmur.

"Exactly. And when I was done enjoying your intelligent commentary I'd gag that smart mouth. Hush now, let me look at you."

She blushed even more under his gaze. Good thing she'd moved the magazines; her pussy was leaking. She didn't just feel objectified, though. She felt admired, cherished. Desirable.

A thought crossed her mind, and she frowned before she could stop it.

"What's wrong, Chessie? I need you to be honest, if this is going to work."

"Last night... you didn't... you didn't fuck me." God, it hurt to be this vulnerable.

"As a Dom, I will take a woman in every way I wish... but there has to be consent. You dropped into subspace so quickly I didn't have time to talk it out with you. Sex requires a level of trust and consent I didn't feel you'd given."

"But..." She licked her lips, wondering how to articulate how hurt she'd been. How unwanted and used she'd felt.

"If you'd woken up and known I'd taken you in that state, how would you have felt?"

"Confused. Maybe violated," she admitted.

"Exactly. There was a chance you wouldn't have been able to separate it out from all the feelings, and I wouldn't risk that. I'll do unspeakable things to your body, but never ever violate your trust."

"Will you... will you fuck me now?" She could barely look at him. If he said no, he could crush her. That was the agony of letting herself want something that only another could give. They could take it away.

"Is that how you address your Master?"

"No, sir."

"Ask properly and I'll consider it."

If felt so natural to let her body soften and slide to the floor, to her knees. His eyes widened a little, perhaps he wasn't expecting that level from her, but his legs spread to accommodate her. She fitted between them like she belonged.

"Master, please, will you fuck your slave?"

"Hmmm, depends. Are you prepared do what I say, exactly how I say it?" His thumb and finger caught her chin and forced her to look at him.

"Yes, sir. Please..."

"No back talk?"

She hesitated. "Depends on how good you are?"

"Naughty sub." He gave her head a little shake, and released her chin to pinch her nipple instead. His voice dropped an octave. "Are you wet for me little one?"

"Yes, sir."

"Mmm. If I asked you to rub yourself on my pant leg would you leave a damp spot?"

She whimpered at the thought of doing just that.

He caught a fistful of her hair, using it to pull her to her knees in front of him. His grip stung and felt so right...

Kane's lips skimmed her temple, her cheek, her throat as he turned her head this way and that. "This is what you need, isn't it? To give yourself to someone. To give up control."

"Yes," she breathed, eyes closed, body awash with longing.

He reached down and fingered the cleft between her legs. She made a small noise and shifted as he touched her tender folds. His grip in her hair tightened.

"Be still." He waited, and when she obeyed, his fingers fluttered over her labia, the gentlest butterfly kiss. She sighed.

"Yes, that's it. You won't give yourself orgasms; you need someone strong enough to take them. Someone like me."

Pushing his chair back further, he pulled her up over his lap. She teetered on tiptoes, grasping for balance as his hand caught the underside of her bare buttocks in three sharp swats. He held her easily in place so his fingers could keep exploring, gliding now over her quivering bottom.

"No bruises from last night," he mused. "Pity. I was hoping you'd wear my marks for the rest of the week, and remember who spanked you."

"How could I forget?"

He smacked her harder.

"Ow! Sorry, sir."

"You're not in trouble," he chuckled. "I just wanted to see these pretty cheeks bounce." He kept swatting her, alternating, changing the pace. At first she fought the pain, tensing and trying to anticipate it, but after a minute or so, she surrendered. The sting became a hazy blend in her mind, she hovered above it, taking pleasure in pleasing her Sir.

"That's it. You love it. You need it, don't you? Answer me, sub."

"Yes, sir," she said dutifully, and added, "I don't like the pain though, not really."

"This is good pain." His hand worked her buttocks, squeezing them. The massage made the ache disappear. "The type that heightens pleasure, turns it into a drug you crave – a natural one your own body creates."

"Endorphins."

"Yes." He pulled her up and helped her straddle his lap. They were still in the scene, somehow, even as he talked her through her concerns. "Do you trust that I'll never try to cause you pain, other than the good kind? The kind that opens the door to pleasure." He pinched her nipples as if to demonstrate.

She gasped and arched her back, a silent plea for more. "Yes, sir."

"Good girl." He grinned and she caught her breath at how lovely he was. His gaze was on her breasts, his hands alternately torturing and worshipping. It felt incredible to have every iota of his attention on her.

"Naughty one." Setting his hands on her hips, he lifted her. "You creamed all over my pants. You know what that means?"

She froze, uncertain at his sudden glower. If his frown wasn't real, it was very convincing.

Before she could offer to pay for dry cleaning, Kane rose and tossed her over his shoulder in one fluid movement. He was halfway to her bedroom before she could get so much as an "Oompf!" out.

He flung her down on the soft comforter, laying her out like a sacrifice on an altar before him. In a thrice, he'd stripped off his clothes and climbed onto the bed, rising over her breathless body, a muscled god come to claim his offering.

"I fuck you. Hard." Sliding her legs over his shoulders, he did just that.

* * *

AFTERWARDS, they lay entwined, wearing nothing but lazy smiles.

"My apologies. I couldn't hold off any longer," Kane said in a normal voice. "I was going to eat you out, but I figured you might be too sore."

"No apology necessary. I just wanted to be fucked." She hadn't orgasmed, but the stretch of his cock inside her had felt divine.

"Next time I'll make it up to you."

"Is that a promise or a threat?"

"Both." He rolled, pulling her under him again so their bodies pressed together, inch by delicious inch. His cock stirred against her, rising to half-mast as they kissed.

She broke away first, and he could tell by her slight frown that she was thinking too much. "So where do we go from here?"

He lay back down beside her, so he could touch her face and toy with a strand of her hair. "I want to own you."

Her eyes narrowed slightly, but she didn't pull away, so he asked, "What's the first thing that jumps into your head when I say that?"

"That I'm lucky I'm good enough for you to own."

He grinned. This one could be taught.

"Yes, dear slave. I only possess the best." His hand dropped to caress her breast.

She rolled her eyes. "Typical one percenter. Full of capitalist pride."

"You bet your ass."

Her gaze dropped to his hand groping her. "Just my ass?"

"All your lovely bits. But especially the ass. In fact –" He sat up, his hardening cock jutting out from his body. "Let's see that ass now. Hands and knees, facing away from me. I think I need to fully inspect my property."

* * *

THREE MONTHS LATER...

The line outside club Runway stretched around the corner, but the bouncers moved the cord the moment Senator Kane approached with his date.

"Senator," they acknowledged him, and so it went all the way through the club, to the secret entrance to Black Light. Once he and Chessie were inside, Preston helped her off with her coat before removing his and placing them both in the locker.

He fixed the black collar around her throat, brushed her lips with a kiss before attaching a short lead to it. Testing it with a tug, he bent and whispered into her ear, "Two paces behind me, sweetheart," before stepping back and swatting her bottom, hard. Her eyes never left his, and a contented look never left her face.

"Yes, Master," she said, and smiled.

THE END

ABOUT THE AUTHOR

USA TODAY BESTSELLING AUTHOR LEE SAVINO is an author and a mom and a chocoholic.

I've written a bunch of books, all smexy romance. Smexy = smart + sexy. Check them out!

If you liked *Unmasked*, Lee recommends you read her novella *Devil Dog*, nominated Sexiest Story by Gravetell Reader's Choice Awards.

Visit www.leesavino.com for a free book.

OTHER BOOKS BY LEE SAVINO

The Berserker Saga
Sold to the Berserkers
Mated to the Berserkers
Taken by the Berserkers
Given to the Berserkers
Claimed by the Berserkers

The Rocky Mountain Bride Series
Rocky Mountain Dawn
Rocky Mountain Bride
Rocky Mountain Rose
Rocky Mountain Romp
Rocky Mountain Rogue
Rocky Mountain Wild
Rocky Mountain Ride

Other Books
Pearl's Possession
Rescuing Regina
Innocence in the Underworld: Mafia romance Trilogy

The American Alpha series
Devil Dog

UNRAVELED

A BLACK LIGHT: VALENTINE ROULETTE NOVELLA

by

Addison Cain

CHAPTER 1

*S*pencer had tolerated a great deal from Maxine Torres in the last week: her lurking—and lurking was a kind way to describe the unwarranted visits downstairs—her cold-eyed assessment of his staff, and her supercilious references to Black Light's lacking service quality. Twice she'd slipped her concerns into a weekly oversight meeting before their boss. And today she'd dared to slide a piece of paper across the conference table, motioning for him to pick it up.

"You need your own Noah, someone who grasps how to run the team behind the bar. I've known Klara Eriksson almost twelve years. She's a career bartender, fast, and not one for idle chitchat. Believe me when I say, she'd be a good fit for Black Light. You'd be lucky to have her."

Glancing down at the resume, Spencer infinitesimally lifted an eyebrow. He read over the page, mentally preparing his rebuttal. "If she is so wondrous, why didn't you hire her yourself?"

Maxine dared to cock a smirk. "I tried. Klara has a good thing going where she is now. Runway was unproven, there was no guarantee it would have drawn a crowd. Which is why I'm going to warn you, you're going to have to make her a ridiculous offer to tempt talent like that away from Jack Varens' nightclub."

The idea that Maxine thought to get her hands in his business deserved a cold response. Spencer deadpanned and gave her the same stare he would have offered any enemy in the field... right before he'd killed them. "Is that so? The last thing I need downstairs is a squeamish woman squinting at our patrons. If she's not into kink, it won't work."

"My only concern is maximizing Black Light's business. Whether I like it or not, our clubs are symbiotic. Your quality of service reflects badly on us all." Maxine put her hands on the table and gave Spencer's dark Armani suit a once over. "Klara's got ice in her veins. Hire her and you'll have a professional employee heading the bar who won't blink an eyelash at the floor show. Your hair's gone grey enough in the last weeks, Spencer. Don't look a gift horse in the mouth."

The budding rivalry between his two General Managers, the constant bickering, Jaxson had had enough. Spencer was his friend, his good friend, but the ex-Navy Seal's personality sometimes leaned towards stubborn in the extreme.

Jaxson cleared his throat, less than pleased with the pair of them. "Spencer, bring Ms. Eriksson in for an interview. If she's willing to sign the Non-Disclosure Agreement, fresh blood downstairs wouldn't hurt. There have been complaints."

Maxine was wise enough to keep her expression even. Spencer, on the other hand, ground his teeth, slicing her a glare that promised retribution.

* * *

WITH A LAST NAME LIKE ERIKSSON, of course she'd be Swedish. Hell, she could have been a model. She'd worn a suit with a modest pencil skirt, seamed stockings, and python pumps. Sexy secretary meets stone-cold bitch. Maxine was right. One look at the blonde and anyone could see Klara was not the warm, cuddly type.

Pin straight blonde hair, tan skin, minimal makeup. The sorry state of her fingernails told a story of a hard worker. They were uneven, unmanicured, and short. Those were hands that spent the night washing pints, picking up broken glass. The rest of her though, it was annoyingly perfect.

Even her handshake had been firm.

When he'd brought her through the secret back entrance from Runway to Black Light, she had not stammered out questions or hinted any surprise at the clandestine nature of the club's entrance. She'd kept her mouth shut, her eyes forward, and willingly waited while he'd led her to a closet, tugging the handle of a mop to reveal a secret door. She'd even walked first down the dimly lit narrow stairs when he'd gestured for her to precede him.

This was a woman who wouldn't stutter when a senator ordered a scotch. There would be no wide-eyed gawking, or a submissive down turn of the eyes... something unfortunately lacking from his current squad.

With Black Light closed during the day, he'd kept the lights turned down, the sprawling room's only illumination the pendant glowing above the bar. That's what had her attention, just as Spencer had intended. When he'd sat her down at one of the club's lounge tables, she'd held his eye. Even with his size, the quality of his clothing, and his equally unsmiling face, Spencer had not made her nervous in the slightest.

Instead, she was eyeballing the shelves, honey eyes darting from bourbon to scotches, over tequila, to rum. It was difficult to know her thoughts, for that face gave nothing away, but Spencer had a suspicion she found fault with what she'd seen.

Interested in getting this over with, he began the interview. "Mrs. Torres is a personal friend of yours?"

"Maxine? Yes, she is." Posture straight, one ankle crossed over the other, Klara spoke with an even, resolute manner. "Over the years we've grown very close... close enough to share the occasional three-some with her husband. And before your jaw hits the table, she encouraged me to disclose that information with you despite my... reluctance to broadcast my personal life to a stranger. She swore to me that, if I were to trust you, it would never go beyond the two of us or be mentioned again. Like me, Maxine is a private woman. I'd be disappointed to learn she was wrong."

His jaw had unhinged, barely. With one statement the Swede had placed herself on higher ground. Klara sat there unshakable, no blush to her cheeks, no nervous breaths, but he knew she had been uncomfortable making her stone-faced, completely unprofessional confession.

Unsure what to make of it, Spencer leaned back into the plush leather chair, and looked her over again. He crossed an ankle over his knee, superior and unfortunately intrigued. "You've offered a provocative character reference... as Maxine intended."

"And she refused to tell me why sexually harassing you, Mr. Cook, was imperative to a potential job offer. In fact, her *mysteriousness* on the subject is the only reason I considered this interview." Klara offered her first hint of a smile. "She has a way of... hooking my interest."

The last thing he wanted was a friend of Maxine's down here, telling tales to the ball-busting wench upstairs.

Ex-Navy Seal, Dungeon Master renowned in the community for his control and attention to detail, Spencer had gone up against far worse than a thirty-something bartender with cool composure and flashy shoes. "Black Light is an ultra-exclusive private club for those whose sexual tastes lay outside the mainstream. Are you familiar with the term BDSM?"

"Who isn't since Fifty Shades of Grey made masochism the latest buzz word?" Klara did not miss a beat, but her eyes had finally left his face. Peeking over her shoulder, past the size of the bar to take in the layout of the room, her icy façade altered minutely. At her back was a room set up with all the trappings of a medieval dungeon. With the lights down, it was hard to see exactly what was what, but the more she looked the more her brows drew together. "The things that go on here, are they legal?"

Smug, Spencer knew he'd won. He didn't want her there, and now she would walk out all on her own. "All participants are consenting adults. We have monitors and security in place should a situation arise. I am the Dungeon Master."

Her eyes went right back to his. "I walk with five-hundred dollars, cash, on a typical Friday and Saturday night. If this place is exclusive, I cannot imagine your clientele would have the numbers to meet my quota."

Spencer frowned to see she had not risen to her feet with a hasty goodbye, that she spoke as if the venue was in question, not her qualifications. "Strangers will be fucking in front of you. Scenes will play out on these stages. Just last night, a woman was tied to the chair you are sitting in and tormented with orgasm denial."

He'd seen it with his own keen eyes—Klara had pressed her legs together, and it wasn't out of unanticipated sexual excitement. She was a prude, the story about Maxine most likely a lie.

Sorely tempted to laugh right in her face, he decided that if she were unwilling to bow out gracefully he'd bring her onboard and watch her implode. He'd make an example out of Klara. More importantly, Jaxson would learn a lesson about allowing Maxine to meddle in Black Light business. "As head bartender of Black Light, what benefit would you bring?"

Klara turned again to the bar, blonde hair slipping over her shoulder, stick straight and shiny. She was in no rush to answer, cataloguing the booze on the shelves, the layout of the glassware. "Let me guess, when you ordered this selection of liquor you only invested in what you like to drink—which would be Scotch. You're unfamiliar with alcohol trends; you'd have to be to serve that brand of vodka to high-end clientele."

He could hardly believe her nerve.

"Is there only one kind of white wine by the glass?" She had hit the nail on the head, stretching up just enough off her seat to see what was chilling in the fridge. "There it is. Pinot Grigio, off brand, and nothing else. Your liquor reps are taking you for a ride if they convinced you to carry this stuff." Klara scooped up a cocktail list bound in leather with a beautifully rendered Black Light logo branded right in the center. One look and she smirked, but not at Spencer, her smile was for the expensive creamy paper printed with a terrible drink list. "Do the men order drinks for the women? Do the women pretend to like them as part of the game? I bet they complain when they get home and the leather comes off."

A muscle in his jaw ticked. "Excuse me?"

"I can renegotiate your deals with the liquor reps, and if we order some inventory in tandem with Noah upstairs, I have a strong feeling it will cut costs. Furthermore," she turned the menu so it faced Spencer, tapping a finger at one of the listed libations, "appletinis are out of fashion. Half of these drinks will have to go. This is the age of the craft cocktail."

Oh, he was going to enjoy picking her apart. Klara wouldn't last longer than three weeks, less if she dared to speak to Jaxson with such presumption. Maxine's little stunt was going to blow up in her face and Spencer's point would be made without lifting a finger. "You're hired, Miss Eriksson. I'll pay you ten dollars an hour. If you do not meet your tip quota on Friday and Saturday nights, I will supplement your cash to the amount of five-hundred, but you have to sign our Non-Disclosure Agreement immediately and start tonight."

Klara cocked a smirk, a spark shining in her honey eyes. "What's the uniform? A mesh thong?"

An instant image of the long-legged Swede dressed only in red scraps of lace flickered between Spencer's forming plan. She'd be as pretty under those clothes as she was in them, but what did that matter? Every last woman he'd invited to work in Black Light was attractive. More importantly, every last one of them had manners this woman lacked. "This is a professional establishment, not a strip club. Dress accordingly." The last thing he wanted was to see her show up, tan skin swathed in something sexy and red. Spencer narrowed his eyes as he added, "All black."

CHAPTER 2

*S*he'd returned a few hours after signing the final page of the NDA, dressed in skintight black from head to toe. The fabric of her slacks was something stretchy that would be easy to move in. The swell of her ass, the line of her thigh, her calves, everything was there to be seen, ending in an ugly pair of black non-slip athletic shoes. One look at those shoes and he almost sent her home, choosing to glare at her feet to avoid her low cut top, and the generous display of ripe tits.

"Are you going to introduce me to the staff, or would you rather I do it?"

His eyes skipped right over her breasts and straight to her mouth. He'd told her to wear black but her lips had been painted bright crimson.

As if she knew what he'd noticed, Klara attempted a joke. "It's a trick of the trade. Grown men are terrified of a woman wearing red lipstick. It makes cocky guests easier to manage."

This woman was so far out of her scope that Spencer could not help but scoff. "You are not here to manage our guests."

"What exactly is it that you think bartenders do?" A blonde eyebrow cocked, Klara made light of the exchange. "When someone's butt is in my chair, I am running their show... whether they know it or not. I tell them what they are going to drink, how much they are going to enjoy it, and make each and every last patron think they are happier for it. But you are right, boss. I'm here to manage your bar."

"Girls," Spencer called to the women prepping for the night. "This is Klara Eriksson, Black Light's new head bartender."

And that was all the introduction Klara was given. One last glare at her shoes, and Spencer gave her his back.

Watching her from the security footage in his office, Spencer observed her exchanges with the collection of scantily clad women wiping tables and cutting fruit. For the next two hours before opening, he watched her criticize almost every last thing his staff was doing.

They weren't cutting the fruit properly.

Constrictive corsets were not acceptable work clothing.

Every last bar tool had to be set up differently. The arrangement of the well was altered.

Klara had overwhelmed every last girl, his staff frazzled by the time the night's first guests arrived.

By then Spencer was back on the floor, a crisp white dress shirt on, a blood red Turnbull & Asser tie hanging in a double Windsor knot at this throat. His fresh suit was impeccably pressed, and his tapered hair had been combed, not that even a strand of salt and pepper had been previously out of place.

He'd monitored scene after scene, glancing repeatedly to the bar where Klara was rushing back and forth to serve the swell of thirsty patrons. The rest of the staff stood back, deer in the headlights as one woman ran the whole fucking show.

As much as he'd hated it, Spencer had smiled and shook the hand of Senator Kane while the man commented on how much he'd enjoyed the new bartender's suggestion of bourbon. Who knew Utah could produce something so smooth?

It wasn't a bottle Spencer had ordered. But there it was on the shelf... and it could not have been there unless Klara had brought it downstairs.

At the end of the night he'd cornered her and made her explain herself.

Without pause, she'd said, "I shopped from the better inventory upstairs. Maxine was fine with it. I'll restock what I borrowed when I place Black Light's next order." And then the woman who had smiled at every last guest at her bar dared to keep her expression stony, handing him a sheet of paper with pencil notes scribbled across it. "This is the early list of all the things wrong with your bar."

After hours of work with no break, Klara's red lipstick had worn off, her nose and forehead had a slight sheen, but her hair was still pin straight and smooth. It was so smooth it hung over her breasts when she put a casual elbow on the bar between them to walk him through her bullet points.

When Klara had gone home after his gruff silences, Spencer found that damn paper in his hand and read over it point by point, having no recollection what on earth she'd said. All he could remember was that there were exactly three freckles on various parts of her face, one on her neck, and a small scar above her left breast.

She'd smelled of Chanel Coco Mademoiselle.

* * *

HEARING NOT one but two unwelcome women in his club, Spencer stood back in the shadows, eavesdropping with no shame.

"Maxine, you know I'm taking a huge risk for you here. Giving up my place with Jack Varens—which pissed him off, I might add—coming to a bar where my regulars can't follow me. I can lose a lot of ground if this gig flops. And its crystal fucking clear Spencer Cook does not want me on his staff. The man hates me."

Maxine was ready to make the hard sell. "He needs you. He just doesn't know it. Without you, Spencer doesn't have any actual service talent down here. The guests might come to play, but if their other needs aren't met, Black Light might not remain as elite as Jaxson desires. If this place goes south it will ricochet to Runway. Get their shit straightened out, train the staff. You don't have to like him, Klara. I get it. He's an asshole. Worst case scenario, you get them set up for success and then I'll bring you in upstairs."

Klara put that famous Swedish snap in her voice. "I don't want to work at Runway. I told you that."

"I am asking you as my best friend to trust me. Black Light means less hours for the same pay. You'll have more time to spend with—" Maxine's cell began to ring, the chirping ringtone signaling it was Noah calling from Runway. Stern, she popped her lips and changed gears. "I've got reps upstairs. We'll have to talk later."

When Maxine pushed off to attend to business, Klara had a parting of her own. Her grumbles were in Swedish, and from their harsher edge, were definitely an unladylike string of curses.

By the clink of heavy glass and the constant shuffle, Spencer figured Klara had chosen to take out her frustration by cleaning. He was right. Rounding the corner he found her wiping down bottles, making ticks on an inventory sheet, and just as ice cold as the day he'd met her.

Even if her time was being used to benefit Black Light, Spencer wanted her to know she was not welcome to come and go as she pleased. "Your shift doesn't start until eight."

He'd surprised her, Klara jumping a little before she glanced over her shoulder at the man in the dark grey suit. "Inventory has to be done so I can calculate spillage and prep tomorrow's orders."

"Shandra is responsible for inventory."

"Well, she's never done it right. Your liquor costs are three times what they should be." Klara offered the stapled register and looked Spencer dead in the eye. "If I ordered according to these figures you'd end up with three cases of mezcal and no vodka—the base liquor in half of your cocktail list."

Her tone was not appreciated. Spencer narrowed his eyes, warning, "It's your job to design a new cocktail list."

Klara brushed off his gruffness with a wave of the hand. "Another reason I am here now. Take a seat. I'll whip up a few of my ideas and you can tell me what you like."

Lips curled in a contemptuous grin, Spencer growled, "I don't drink on the job."

She froze, and in the mirror behind the bar, Spencer could see her unpainted lips thin. A heartbeat passed and Klara was right back in motion. Grabbing bottles, bitters, juices, syrups, she poured and stirred, finishing off the first silky creation by pouring the golden drink with flare into a coupe.

He ignored the glass, his hand on the bar before it, his blue eyes locked on hers.

His lengthy silences annoyed her, he could see by the slight flare of her nostrils no matter if her eyes remained flat. There was no sip, he wouldn't even try it. That didn't stop Klara from making another drink, and then another, until there was a line of beverages waiting to be sampled on the bar.

Her cold façade was cracking. "I spent all morning making these syrups, squeezing these juices. Don't you want to know what they taste like?"

"No."

"I do!" A bubbly voice came from the entrance, Emma Fischer smiling. Behind her walked Chase, and he was not smiling at all. In fact he was staring... at Spencer.

The smile Klara never bestowed on her boss was immediately set upon the pair. She even sighed under her breath, *"Oh, thank God."*

Spencer sat in stiff silence while the pair of Jaxson's lovers went drink by drink through the alcoholic smorgasbord. After much laughing and a few noises of disgust, five were chosen to grace the new cocktail list. Three were rejected utterly.

"I had an idea about making a second list of drinks, exotic mock-tails. Fruity or creamy drinks, seasonal flavors, people could sip on all night without worrying about intoxication... or just if they needed a sugar boost." Honey eyes went to where Spencer sat like a silent stone, Klara adding, "What do you think?"

Emma opened her mouth to wholeheartedly agree, only to be silenced by Spencer's immediate, "No."

"You're right." She might have verbally agreed with him, but Klara challenged his verdict by simply adding. "One thing at a time. We can discuss it again after the staff gets comfortable making these."

An hour later, Spencer caught Klara huddled over her compact in the corner, painting on her crimson lips. By the time they were open for business, the bar was clean, Klara was once again unflappable, and patrons were approaching, calling for her by name.

CHAPTER 3

$\mathcal{I}$t had been a week since Klara's arrival at Black Light. Five whole nights where he'd been repeatedly distracted from his role of Dungeon Master to deal with some issue her presence inspired. By her third night she'd made two staff members cry. By her fifth she'd vocally reprimanded a senator who was trying to wrangle a third drink from one of the meeker cocktail waitresses.

The ensuing argument, and her complete disregard for the scenes playing nearby, drew attention from more than just those near the bar.

Spencer could not fault her for enforcing the two drink limit. He could fault her for her tone in dealing with a patron. In the privacy of his office, he'd dressed her down with great enthusiasm, and she'd stood there and took the entirety of his temper. He was sure he'd finally scared her off when just for a moment her mask slipped. It was not fear or anger peeking from the cracks in her icy stare, it was concern.

Victory.

And then she said, "Okay, boss. Tell me exactly what you want me to do."

His cock twitched. Spencer ran a hand through his silver hair and eyeballed her with distaste. "If a guest is causing you or anyone in the bar trouble, you come and get me. I'll deal with them."

"You want me to leave my station and go out onto the floor?" Klara's distaste with his mandate was not concealed. "What if you're *participating* in something?"

Oh, he'd be participating in something alright. When this meeting was over he planned to decompress and forget about the irritating blonde's icy stares with some good, clean play at the stage nearest where she might see. "Do you have an issue with anything I may or may not be *participating* in?"

"I have an issue abandoning the bar when there is no one competent on staff to pour more than a glass of water. Managing the bar is my job. If I have to run to daddy every time there is a hiccup, then I cannot do that effectively. Why hire me if you want to handle all the work yourself?"

She had a point. Spencer trilled his fingers while he regarded the unsmiling woman. He took up a great deal of his chair, broad-shouldered and bulk no matter the tailored cut of his suit jacket, but it was Klara who took up the whole room. And she did it by doing nothing but standing there.

Skintight black, always skintight black. No color save those ruby red lips.

"Klara..."

For a moment, just one single moment, she put a hint of pleading into her voice. "Just tell me what you want from me, Spencer."

What he wanted was her gone. "No more distractions. I want it to be as if you're not even here."

It didn't show on her face, but Spencer could sense his words had stung. With a voice lacking all inflection, Klara said, "I can do that."

But she couldn't, and as the month passed Spencer saw her more, watched her more, and found fault with every last thing she did.

* * *

FEBRUARY 7TH

It had been a busy night, complications having arisen in several scenes that either himself or his Dungeon Monitors had been busy attending to. But finally he'd had a break, standing beside the St. Andrew's cross, training an eager dom in the art of the bullwhip.

Owen, his shibarist Dungeon Monitor was waving for him to step down from the stage. Abandoning the scene, Spencer leaned forward so the man might whisper in his ear.

Immediately he pulled back, snarling, "What do you mean Adele is crying in the bathroom? Can the guests see?" Catty bullshit was not something Spencer had time for. Another crying bartender, another issue since Klara had barged in. "What did Klara do?"

"I don't know."

Klara was rushing back and forth to make drinks, oblivious to the Dungeon Master and his monitor's weighty stares. He was on her in a minute, taking her by the arm to pull her away from where guests might hear.

He backed her into the wall, his body a shield from prying eyes.

She'd bit her tongue until Spencer had set her arm free, ready to defend yet another ridiculous scenario. "Look, if this is about Adele crying in the bathroom, I snapped at her, it's true, but she was trying to serve coconut rum to Miss Younge. Miss Younge is allergic to coconut and this point has been discussed in lineup many times. Adele could have sent one of your guests into anaphylactic shock. Not only does she suck at her job, but she endangers your clientele with her stupidity. I know you like to play with her, that she's everyone's favorite sub off the clock, but when she's *on the clock* she needs to be focused on her JOB not incessantly making eyes at you."

That she would think to speak to him in such a tone made Spencer far blunter than he should have been. "Why must I deal with nightly tears and complaints of bullying from the staff, Klara? You're a brat and I don't have time to give you the constant attention you seem to think you deserve."

She wasn't having any of his unfair criticism. "Most nights I work without so much as taking a bathroom break. Every night I split my tips with whoever you put on the schedule—the schedule that as head bartender I should be writing. My efforts go into the pockets of women who spend their time staring at the room without even a side glance towards their guests. Several of them have disappeared mid-shift, only to reappear... *from some dark corner.* Until you enforce it, they won't differentiate work from play. Why should they?"

There was an edge to his smirk. "You think I don't punish them when I hear all your complaints? Each one of them has felt the consequences."

"Don't twist my words into one of your kink things." Klara had heard enough. "You know what's hard? This job. If those girls don't toughen up, they are never going to survive your shitshow rodeo down here. The Valentine Roulette party is in a week, and unless they get their asses in gear, they are going to be up to their elbows in weeds. For fuck's sake, all they do is whine. Their quality control is laughable. Half of them make your signature drink and serve it in different glassware with different garnishes. Do you understand why that's bad? The bar in your fancy perv club is a joke."

Face going red, Spencer felt a muscle tick in his jaw. Voice unnaturally level he said, "You did not just call me a pervert."

"It was a poor choice of words on my part. I'm sorry. It's not like I haven't been spanked during sex or tied up. Everyone has." Speaking over him, Klara's hasty apology was merged into her previous argument. "My point is—"

He'd heard enough. He sliced his hand through the air between them, cutting her off with a growl. "Your mouth, your language, are one-hundred percent unacceptable."

Klara let out an extremely agitated breath and attempted more professional speech. "Adele has to go. She is only in the way and slowing the rest of us down. Move her to coat check, have her hand out condoms and lube, just get her the fuck out of my bar."

"She stays..."

"I know you're new to this business. I know you think I'm some horrible dragon, but this isn't personal. She could have killed someone, Spencer. Any bartender worth their salt would say the same thing I'm saying to you right now." Substituting the word perv for something her boss might find palatable, Klara continued. "Your clients might come here for the show, but they won't stick around if the front of house service sucks. And just to be clear, I'm not talking about sucking coc—"

"Stop!" He could see it, back behind that honey-eyed stare, she was purposefully trying to get a rise out of him. The busty mouthpiece was goading him on purpose because they both knew she believed she was right. Spencer had no issue turning the tables. "Every last girl working *my* bar lives the lifestyle to varying degrees and plays here on their off hours. Then you prance in, vanilla, condescending, and yes you're good at your job. But I bet every last one of them is a lot better at sucking cock. Which do you think our paying guests prefer?"

Murder was in her eyes. "What did you just say to me?"

"You want to throw grownup taunts around, little girl, I will too." Spencer lowered his voice, made it satin and growly, employing the exact tone that made his subs cream their panties. "A perk of staff's compensation is free membership. We encourage everyone to play off the clock, but no one makes anyone do anything here that isn't consensual. They love it. You, you just stand on your soapbox and judge."

"The only thing around here I judge," she swept her gaze from his shined shoes to his immaculately combed grey hair, "is the quality of the team you have behind the bar. That's the job you hired me for. I have ten girls with no experience and an inability to handle even an ounce of pressure. They also know that if they go running to you, if they muster up some tears, that I am the one who's going to get in trouble. I'm doing my best."

Klara was disheveled, her hair mussed and her cheeks red. Spencer stared down, noting even as she was, her eyes never once wavered from his. She would never be a sub. There was not a single fucking submissive thing about her.

He was raw and hungry, with no interest in furthering a confrontation with his head bartender where guests might hear. "Then get back to work."

CHAPTER 4

She'd made it five weeks. Five weeks in a job she should never have taken. There was not enough liquor in Runway for Maxine to comp that would make it better.

Klara had fucked up and she knew it. Cash came in hand over fist this time of year at Jack Varens' club. She should never have taken this job, have risked her livelihood, or endangered her family's wellbeing.

Elias wanted to go to space camp; she'd promised him she'd find a way to make it work, and here she was, right on the cusp of ruin. His tuition alone cost almost as much as she made in a year. Without his good grades and the subsequent financial aid, her brother would never have been able to enjoy the opportunity of D.C.'s finest private high school. Unlike her, he was smart as a whip. And he was such a sweet boy.

And none of the pressure or her personal condemnation was being let up no matter how many shots of vodka Klara had swallowed.

"This is the first time I've managed to get you to come in. And you sit there sulking. It can't really be all that bad."

Klara pushed her glass towards the handsome bartender, frowning and unwilling to talk. "Shut up, Noah."

Night after night she'd worked amidst the sound of screams, moans, and dirty talk so foul it would make her grandma roll over in the grave. Sitting up in Runway, Elixxir's music pounding loud enough to drown out even the nearest small talk, Klara found she preferred the less abrasive noises down in the basement.

Not that she would ever sit at that bar as a patron.

Black Light had all the makings of a bartender's dream job: gracious clientele she did not have to shout at so they could hear her, less mayhem since very few people managed to get drunk, but the last thing a wise bartender did was drink where they work. Pity, for it hadn't been hard to chat with the BDSM crowd, meet their eyes, and pointedly ignore everything going on past her corner of the room. They were all pretty nice. Shift after shift she had run her ass off, she had talked her voice hoarse trying to explain for the thousandth fucking time the difference between a Collins and a rocks glass to her incompetent coworkers, and even with Spencer's complaints, most nights hadn't been too bad.

At least at first. They had gotten progressively worse, and now it was only a matter of time before the ax dropped.

Hand cold from the frosty martini shaker he'd used to chill her drink, Noah reached over the bar and gently slapped Klara's cheek. When she stopped moping and looked up, he cupped the side of her face and smiled. "Wanna crash with me tonight? It would be like old times. I'll even rub your feet."

When you worked all night, almost every night, the pool one socialized with was almost always industry folks. Everyone knew everyone. Everyone slept with everyone else. It was an incredibly incestuous circle. Klara had hooked up with Noah many times over the years… he was gorgeous.

Having a warm body next to hers didn't sound like such a bad idea.

Klara was tempted… except her eye was on someone else.

There was another man at the bar who fit the bill better than sweet Noah might. Pointing with her honey gaze towards an actor known for his brooding both on and off screen, she let her friend figure out what just might tempt her to smile.

Noah had known her long enough to get the point, even laughing impishly. "Well… aiming for the stars, are we? I'll make the introduction, but first you might want to clean up your smeared mascara."

Swiping her thumbs under her eyes, Klara made quick work of turning the mess into a half-assed attempt at a smoky eye. "Any other pointers, kid?"

"Smile. You look miserable."

Turning on the charm was instant. Shit, she'd been bartending for fifteen years. Charming the pants off strangers was her best well-honed talent.

Within an hour she had the arms of the next James Bond around her waist. Klara smiling up at a man everyone knew and no one knew at all. Martin Goodchild, a special guest of Runway, hadn't been nearly as unfriendly as he looked. In fact, his mouth was on hers by their second drink, and he kissed like an eager teenager, all tongue and teeth.

There was no reason to explain herself, no reason at all that she should not sigh at his attention and enjoy it. But the elevator dinged and near the hall that led to Jaxson's private suite, a silver-haired mountain of judgment appeared. Unlike when she'd pointedly ignored him doing freaky things to her worst bartender week after week, unlike when Klara had not blinked an eye, he got one look at her doing nothing but kissing, and Spencer Cook froze.

When their eyes met, she even imagined he'd snorted like a bull.

She dismissed the unwelcome voyeur, lowering her smudged lashes and reaching down to cup Martin Goodchild's jeans right over his throbbing erection. One touch and she decided his cock was big enough, his fingers were smooth enough, and though he was a bit young for her taste, the famous actor would serve just fine as a one-night entertainment.

* * *

ENOUGH WAS ON THE DOCKET, but here they were arguing over a single employee. Again. Jaxson already had a headache. He was glad Emma and Chase were not there to see his bad mood today. And he was equally annoyed they were not there to ease his stress once the meeting concluded.

The Valentine Roulette party was the biggest event Black Light had attempted, and it was happening in a week. Lists needed to be discussed, staff, security, background checks, continuing to build word of mouth in the community, and it was almost impossible to get his team to focus on the task at hand.

Klara. They were endlessly arguing about Klara.

Spencer had sat silently through Maxine's meeting, but now it was his time, Black Light's time, and he was having no more of this mess. "I saw her with Martin Goodchild last night. She practically mounted him atop your bar, *and* was seen leaving with him. The last thing I need is Klara's face in the papers with a string of Runway VIPs or angry boyfriends storming in to cause trouble."

Maxine flat out laughed, the idea completely ridiculous. "One? She doesn't have a boyfriend. Why would you think she did? And two, who cares?"

Speaking over her, Spencer refused to back down. "The guests downstairs need to have faith that our staff is discreet."

Eyes sparkling, roving over Spencer's greying temples, Maxine teased. "Let me guess, she shot you down. Too bad you've been such a hardass. Klara's always had a thing for older men. You'd have been just her type."

Spencer's face grew an angry shade of red from the jab. "It's inappropriate for her to be seen leaving Runway with celebrities. She's an employee—."

"Not of Runway!" Maxine defended her friend, sneering. "And it's a bit hypocritical for *you* to be commenting on *her* sex life. If she wanted to sleep with any patron or performer from my club, that's her business."

Spencer looked ready to lay into her.

Before he might blow his top, Jaxson banged his hand on the table. "If Klara is not working out, Spencer, that's your call to make. I can't have you two in here arguing over one member of staff every single time we sit down."

The look in Maxine's eyes when she turned to her boss... it was as if he'd sold her out.

She had no choice but to try and smooth it over with Black Light's Dungeon Master. "You need her, Spencer. Don't blow it because she's focused on her job and doesn't kiss your ass like the other girls. Your numbers have improved dramatically. I know your guests must like her. Everyone does."

It had already been decided. Spencer's eyes were unforgiving, his voice gruff. "She can be replaced."

"What's your plan? Gonna take out an ad on Craigslist for bar manager, *only submissives need apply?*" Maxine was not above looking at him like he was crazy. "This is about you and me. Leave Klara out of it."

That's not at all what it was about. "I'm firing her tonight, Maxine. It's a personality issue. She doesn't fit in with Black Light."

There was no reason for her to sit in further on their meeting. Not when she was tempted to lean over the table and strangle Spencer Cook with her bare hands. Rising from her chair, Maxine sneered. "You're a prick."

CHAPTER 5

*T*he light was on in his office and the door sat ajar. With Black Light open for business, there was absolutely no one who should have dared enter that room. Even Spencer rarely ventured off the floor during business hours, but today he'd arrived downstairs after dinner with Jaxson at a later hour than usual.

Only to find this...

Ears pricked, he listened in on Klara.

Her muffled tone was as abrasive as usual, the woman speaking on the phone. "Did you really think you were going to get away with it? I can't believe you would even consider pulling this kind of shit with a new business. Your markup is ridiculous."

A pause and she continued. "Yeah, well fuck you very much, Jamal. You are going to give me everything I've asked for, and throw in a case of good champagne, or I'll see that this account is transferred to Carroll. I'm sure she'd be more than happy to rake in the easy commission."

There was another moment of silence, and then Klara giggled. She actually fucking giggled. "If you think taking me out to dinner is going to get you back in my good graces, you better pick a pretty spectacular restaurant. And, I'll be expecting one or two good bottles of wine. The expensive kind."

The grumble of a male voice hummed through the other end of the receiver before Klara agreed, "Yeah, maybe a movie too. But, not tonight, I'll be getting off too late." She added sweet as pie, "I'm free tomorrow, you conniving motherfucker."

Both participants in the exchange were laughing until Spencer shoved open the door.

Klara lost her smile, eyes almost wide as her boss stalked forward to loom over his desk.

She said one more thing, "Alright, eight o'clock," then hung up.

Before her, spread out on the desk were invoices from their main liquor distributor, several lines marked with red pen.

She knew what he was looking at, and cut him to the chase. "Why haven't you been showing me these? Jamal has been taking you for a ride. Don't worry. I fixed the problem."

That was not Spencer's greatest issue at the moment. On the desk, to the right, under her elbow, was a manila folder with a sticker placing it as one Klara Eriksson's background check. There was a discarded newspaper over it, but if she'd been snooping, there was no possibility she had not found it.

Like most days, Spencer had been looking through it earlier and had not thought there was a need to put it back in the locked filing cabinet.

She must have seen it. She must have seen it on his desk, noticed how the pages were creased from having been handled repeatedly. Had she seen the photograph Jaxson's PI had taken? The one where she was smiling and comfortable? The one where she was in a polka dot blouse with sunglasses on her head? Had she opened that file and seen his notes?

Spencer wanted the conversation to be focused. He wanted her eyes on him. "Is that how you talk to our liquor reps?"

"I've known Jamal for six years. I know everyone at Nation Wine & Spirits. Believe me, that conversation was tame." She seemed proud of herself, less cold, more temperate. "Meanwhile, I got two-hundred bucks knocked off our next order."

"And a date for tomorrow night?"

"Uhhh..." She seemed unsure how to answer. "Taking out a client is pretty par for the course."

"What about going to the movies? That par for the course?" Spencer rounded the desk and walked right up to where she sat in his chair, staring down at the little growing wrinkle between Klara's blonde eyebrows.

Just as he'd intended she turned in the chair, and met his hard stare.

The file was at her back, nowhere near her line of sight when he asked, "Are you sleeping with him?"

He'd pushed too far, Klara snapping. "Are you sleeping with Shandra, and Adele, and Margaret, and Ling? Yes, you are. You are sleeping with your entire female staff."

Crossing his arms over his chest, deeply thrilled to see her ruffled, and equally pissed off at having found her in his office, Spencer said. "I don't *sleep* with them."

She snorted. "Call it what you want."

Spencer smirked, certain she was not at all welcome to sit in his chair and use his things. "What are you doing in here?"

"This is the only phone on this floor. Where did you think I placed the orders from, my apartment? That would violate your very thorough NDA."

So she'd been in there before. How many times had he left her file out? How had he not noticed the smell of her perfume? "I come to work to find we have a packed house and you are in here chatting on the phone? Considering your complaints against your coworkers, that seems ironic, Klara."

"If I had called Jamal before nine it would have gone straight to voicemail. After seeing these invoices, I knew I'd need to corner him. Otherwise there would have been weeks of back and forth while he milked your business on each transaction. And can you really compare my behavior to theirs? Shandra slipped away mid-shift last night and came back half an hour later with cum in her hair. I had to remind her to wipe it off and wash her hands before she touched anything!"

She'd buried herself with that last comment and now Spencer had more than enough ammo to get what had to be done, done. "Those invoices were in my locked file cabinet."

Honey eyes hardened. "It wasn't locked."

"It always is. You'd have known that since you've used my phone previously without permission."

Klara confessed. "I asked a friend at Nation Wine & Spirits to send me your backlog. Without bothering you it was the only way I could do my job."

Spencer had relished every second of catching miss perfect in a lie. It would make the next part so much easier. "You're fired, Klara."

He'd thrown her for a loop. An array of subtle reactions passed through her expression moving from shock, a moment when she looked like tears were possible, and straight into anger. Lips thin, nostrils flared, Klara asked, "What? Why?"

"You are not a good fit for Black Light."

Hoisting from the chair, unwilling to push it back to make room, she stood close enough they were almost touching. Lip in a sneer and her breath coming hard, Klara gave him a nonverbal fuck off. "Good-bye, Spencer. Have fun running this place into the ground."

She marched out and he gave her the courtesy of not calling security. Once she was gone he picked up her background check, the file with every one of her completely untawdry secrets, and dropped it in the trash.

CHAPTER 6

"*He* made her cry," Emma said, demure in her approach towards the table where Black Light's owners, and her lovers, Jaxson and Chase, had just settled in. "I don't know why Spencer's so hard on her."

Jaxson cracked a wry smile, having seen the woman in question throw her purse over her shoulder and leave moments before. He knew she'd been fired, and it was probably for the best. "Women like Klara don't cry."

Men could be so oblivious, even Emma's sweetheart. "I heard her in the bathroom. She was in the stall, but I know it was her. She's the only girl who wears tennis shoes inside Black Light."

Emma was obviously upset, so Jaxson crooked a finger and called her to his lap. When she settled in, he took her face in his palms and kissed pouting lips. "I know you liked her, but Spencer made a call to let her go. I have to trust him."

"It's a pity." Chase had his own view of the issue, the man thoughtful as he said, "I'd never seen Spencer so focused on one woman. I thought with time he'd figure it out."

Jaxson could see that neither of them were happy with this alteration, but could not help but think they were mistaken. "You can't honestly imagine Spencer was pining for Klara. He's disliked her from day one."

Lashes downcast, tucking her head under Jaxson's chin, Emma dared to softly disagree. "I think you're wrong, sir."

This was another complication Jaxson didn't need right now. He'd come here to relax and it was becoming more obvious lately that owning Black Light brought more stress than it relieved. That had been his whole motivation to allow Spencer to manage as he saw fit. Jaxson didn't want to micromanage the club, he wanted to play here.

Patrons enjoyed the scenes. As a Dungeon Master, Spencer was unparalleled, but the service staff had one complication after another. Obviously the DM could not be two places at once. Waitstaff needed a manager—training them, directing the front of house—and Klara had failed that task.

Caressing the soft skin of Emma's upper arm, Jaxson thought it over. Maybe he should have become involved before it came to this. Deferring to his DM's judgment, he'd given Miss Eriksson a wide berth, disinterested in participating in Maxine and Spencer's tug of war. And yes, he had noticed a few of the girls backtalk to Klara and pout when she called them out... the same subs Spencer liked to play with.

"I'm never going to win the bet now," Emma said, her fingers toying with the hair at Jaxson's nape.

She was cute when she was forlorn, Jaxson couldn't help but smile, kiss her nose, and ask, "What bet?"

Chase answered for her. "We made a friendly wager on how long it would take Spencer to ask Klara out."

An amused, chesty laugh came with Jaxson's scoff. "He doesn't date his subs."

Chase raised his glass to him. "But Klara is not a sub... at least she isn't one yet. A woman like that, I'd imagine she'd enjoy learning to give up the power and let it all go. Or she would have if given the chance."

Emma sighed again. "I feel bad for Klara. She doesn't understand what's going on. And I feel bad for Spencer because he's totally blind."

* * *

HUMILIATED, angry, Klara sat on her couch, the television flashing some action movie her brother had chosen, and glared down at the laptop warming her thighs. There was a wineglass on the coffee table where she rested her feet. Beside it sat an empty bottle. Having downed the whole thing, she wasn't exactly the best role model for her brother Elias. But, heck, he was almost fifteen. He was probably already sneaking sips when she was at work.

"Come on, Sis, you're not even paying attention to the good parts. You love Die Hard."

She wasn't paying attention because she was too busy staring at the splash page for Black Light's Valentine Roulette party. Spencer had not yet revoked her membership and online access when he'd fired her, and for three days Klara had considered... doing something crazy.

The day after she'd been fired she'd gone straight to Jack Varens and begged for her old job. That bridge had been burned when she'd jumped ship with no notice. He didn't want her back. In fact, one look at her, and he'd blacklisted her from the nightclub.

Rent was due, Elias's tuition was due, the electric bill, cell phones... she had to work. Even if it meant going to some stale Irish pub full of twenty-one-year-olds who couldn't hold their liquor and gave shit tips. But instead she was sitting on her couch, drinking, and very worried she'd blown the whole fucking shebang.

Glancing towards her baby brother she put on a brave face. She'd raised him since he was three, working two, three jobs, whatever it took. Through all of it he'd never known how hard it had been for her to keep all their shit together. She'd never been mommy material. Elias deserved better, and none of this was his fault.

God, she loved that kid. "Don't you have homework?"

Elias offered his best teenage eye roll. "It's Friday night. Sheesh."

"I stand corrected."

Valentine's Day was Tuesday. Klara was running out of time to decide. In fact, it was probably already too late to register for the Roulette party. She had to choose.

Fingers flying over the keyboard, she filled out the application for submissives, ready to make a statement that might win back her job.

And because she was still pissed and could not wait to see the look on his face, where the form gave the option for a sub's chosen safe-word, Klara typed *Spencer*.

CHAPTER 7

"*B*efore you is the final guest list." Jaxson motioned for Spencer and his team of Dungeon Monitors to look over the paperwork. "As you can see, there have been a few last minute alterations on the page of submissives participating this evening. Mina Wu has been replaced with Chelsea Jones, and—"

All these changes Spencer had already approved, the information old news until his eyes scanned down. He choked on a breath. "Why is Klara Eriksson's name on this list?"

And why the hell had she listed her safeword as *Spencer*?

There was no overt reaction to his friend's shock. Jaxson calmly explained, ready to move on. "Klara's application was submitted Friday. After speaking with her Saturday afternoon, I decided she was an interesting addition."

Nearby, Chase sat with a silent Emma. As Master of Ceremonies he was already making notes, everyone acting as if the monumental adjustment was normal.

Spencer, cynical to the core, glanced back and forth between them. "I'm asking you not to do this."

Jaxson met his friend's eyes, direct and expecting answers. "Why?"

"I'll be distracted. She'll need more looking after than the rest."

He could lead a horse to water but Jaxson couldn't make it drink.

"All of our participants have differing levels of experience, but several of them have yet to visit Black Light. Klara has at least experienced the club. She's talked to the guests. There is nothing she hasn't seen. I don't believe she'd sign up on a whim." If he had to strong arm his friend, he would. "Now that she is no longer a Black Light employee, there is no conflict of interest on her end. We're short on subs and she wants to play. Everyone wins."

The Dungeon Master disagreed. "She doesn't know what she's getting herself into."

Dismissive, Jaxson said, "If it's too much for Klara to handle, she can safeword. After working here for almost six weeks, she's seen enough scenes to have a general idea what to expect."

Spencer, hardass ex-Navy Seal Spencer, looked nervous. "I would consider it a personal favor if you were to find someone else. The waiting list..."

Jaxson shook his head, cutting off his Dungeon Master's protest. "Half the subs on the waitlist are staff. Tonight will be busy. Everyone is expected to be on the clock."

The almighty Spencer adjusted his tie, glaring at the paperwork as if some miracle on that page might relieve his discomfort. "I fired Adele. She could step in."

Everyone had heard Adele bawling from Spencer's office when he'd called her in at the start of her last shift. Unlike Klara's silent departure, Adele had made a scene. Jaxson was not having another one. "I read your closing report about the incident. After speaking with Miss Younge, you'd confirmed Adele almost served her an allergen. You cannot imagine her inclusion would inspire our patrons' faith that we put their safety first. Your disagreement is noted, but Klara stays. As you said, the reason for her termination was a personality issue, not a competency one. And, Spencer, you don't have to interact with Klara Eriksson. She's going to be playing with somebody else. Chad, Owen, Garreth, or Terrance can monitor her progress through the scenes." Jaxson's eyes left his friend's angry face, going right back to the paperwork they all needed to go over. "Now, on to page seven."

* * *

Spencer had been looking forward to Black Light's Roulette party... until now. Jaxson was pulling something. He knew his friend well enough to see that plain as day. When he'd tried to corner Black Light's owners after the final pre-event meeting, he'd been brushed off so Jaxson might have some alone time with Chase and Emma before the big event.

He was stuck with this mess.

The party had begun. The sheet with Klara's details and hard limits was in his hand, paper distorted from his tight grip.

Safeword: *Spencer*. Oh, he'd get her to say his name.

Her listed hard limits—fisting, needle play, blood play—were not that surprising. What was surprising was her fourth hard limit, anal. She'd struck him as someone who would have enjoyed it. And with that thought came an image he could not shake: the Swedish siren strapped down, ass up, a ball gag in her mouth while being mercilessly fucked in the ass.

Sweat was gathering near the salt and pepper hair at his temples. Fuck, he was even growing hard.

Wool slacks were not going to hide his arousal, and this was one time, he could not make his cock just lay down out of sheer willpower. Covertly adjusting himself, Spencer was glad no attention was on him. Everyone else was too busy mingling, gathering around the stage, and sipping the fancy champagne Klara had finagled out of Jamal.

His irritation with the situation was only eclipsed by his frustration when a woman dressed in fiery red stepped into the room. For all intents and purposes, the cocktail dress was cut demurely at both breast and thigh. It was in the way it wrapped her curves that screamed *fuck me*.

Why did she have to wear red?

Why did she have to be beautiful?

With her blonde hair caught up into a French twist, she looked polished. Just like the first time they'd met, her makeup was minimal and her lips were a soft shade of pink. Her dom would have no crimson gloss to smear around her mouth. She would not leave a mark on him either.

Pink lips... innocent.

She was anything but.

Despite the crowd, Klara found the man in the dark grey suit, the man wearing a tie as red as her dress. If she'd held any trace of hesitation, it vanished the instant their eyes met.

Klara crossed the room in a beeline for him, almost tall enough in her heels to equal his height.

When she was close enough for Spencer to hear her, she said. "Jamal is gay, flamboyantly gay, so no, I'm not sleeping with him. I wasn't hitting on your business contact. *That would be unprofessional.* I was negotiating with a friend."

Several people glanced towards her outburst.

"Come with me." This was not to be a conversation for public consumption. Spencer dared touch her for the first time since they'd met. His hand resting on her lower back, he hurriedly led her through the throng, past the bar, and into the privacy of his office.

Once the door was closed, the two of them alone, he threw professionalism out the window. Backing her against the wall, he growled, "Explain yourself."

Boxed in by bulging arms, Spencer's fingers drumming against the wall with impatience, Klara refused to back down. "I need this job."

He had not been expecting that—just like he had not been expecting Jaxson to be party to her mischief. Eyes on her mouth, Spencer breathed hard, and said nothing.

Misreading his silence, Klara blurted again. "I *need* this job. You think I can't fit in here, you make assumptions. But, if I win tonight, I'll get a free month's membership... which means I will come back here every day until you hear me out. And, if I win, you'll have to admit that I am..."

He cut her off, hissing, "That you're what?"

Klara wasn't sure exactly what he needed to hear. "That I can be valuable. That I'm not afraid or disgusted by the floor show just because I keep my work and private life compartmentalized. Besides, I think we both know you'll enjoy watching me get smacked around."

More than he'd ever admit aloud. "My job is to keep things safe, sane, and consensual."

Klara spoke of the doms gathered around the club's stage and argued. "I am giving consent. One of those guys out there is going to fuck me. I don't even care which one it is."

"That's not the only thing they are going to do to you." Spencer could not help but imagine a multitude of scenarios, each one tightening the knots in his stomach until his sack began to ache. "You won't make it through one scene, Klara. You're not a submissive. Whoever spins your name will be disappointed."

There it was again, that flash of hurt he'd inspired so many times in the last six weeks. "You don't know me, Spencer. You've never even taken the time to talk to me. You never gave me a fair shot. All you have ever done is undermine my hard work and boss me around."

His palms had been flush to the wall beside her face, but they'd begun to inch towards Klara's neck. "I am your boss."

"You *were* my boss. Tonight I'm your guest, and if I remember the policy correctly, the first drink for newbies is on the house. I'll take a vodka. When I win, I'll have a glass of champagne. You can put that on your tab too."

His fingertips diverted to her shoulders, large hands curling around as if he wished to grab her and give her a good shake. He squeezed, and in unison his thumbs stretched to trace the line of her throat from the underside of Klara's earlobe all the way to her clavicle.

The look on her face changed, bumps on her skin rose. Before she might stop herself she shivered.

There was only a hairsbreadth between them. All Spencer would have to do to close that space was ease forward, and then she'd be trapped between his hard body and the wall. And she'd be soft in the right places, and warm...

He was so fucking tempted that he swallowed, exhaled, and had to force himself to step back.

There was a slight flush in her cheeks, a dilation to her pupils; Spencer saw it and hated himself for it.

"I'll take that vodka now." Klara had grown flustered, her hand absently reaching for the doorknob. "Maybe you could use one too."

Hoarse, Spencer muttered, "I drink scotch."

With that, Klara chuckled, threw her shoulders back, and walked out.

* * *

KLARA WAS NOT THERE to enjoy the pageantry. Chase was a nice enough guy. The few times they'd chatted, he'd entertained her as much as she'd entertained him, but Klara hardly heard a word of his greeting to the gathered guests or his speech outlining the rules of the events. She already knew them by heart. She even recognized many of the subs. Several she had served, joked with at the bar, comforted when they were down. A familiar petite brunette had welcomed her up to the stage, as if she was one of them, but Klara had been unable to do more than smile back, offer a stiff hello, and get back to the job at hand—winning.

She had her eyes on the prize, and it did not involve making flirty glances at the waiting doms or enveloping her body in shyness and nerves like many of the other subs who'd volunteered for the festivities.

This party was really for them.

Klara was the intruder, and she was fairly certain it was stamped on her forehead. Or it could be because Spencer had come up behind her. And though she had not glanced over her shoulder to acknowledge him, she was certain his arms were crossed over his chest, and that he was projecting his normal don't-fuck-with-me vibe.

To think the doms hadn't noticed would be stupid.

Spencer was a big guy, it was impossible to miss him in a room, larger still standing behind a line of women. It should not have bothered her, after all, every other Dungeon Monitor was on or near the stage, but his placement was off-putting.

And she knew he was doing it on purpose.

Chase was charming, the audience, the participants, all cheering and laughing when they should. The first dom was asked to approach the wheel and spin. He was partnered to a tall woman who projected an aura of strength as she crossed the stage to go to him. As expected, she spun for her scene, all of it only half absorbed by Klara.

The tingle scratching up her spine from Spencer's nearness was distracting, uncomfortable, and by god, Klara just wanted to spin on her heels and tell him to back off. On it went, minutes dragging by while sub after sub was selected, Klara one of the remaining few. Spencer had not budged an inch, though the gathering of submissives was growing sparse.

"Klara!"

Her name had been called. Hearing it snapped her out of impending trouble. Just like that, she was once again a contender.

The dom who had spun her waited, watching as if he'd already known which one she was in the lineup.

He was certainly something to look at.

Maybe this wouldn't be so bad. Klara liked a man in a suit—one with style, clean cut, broad shouldered, and stern. His skin was a deep shade of black, his shirt hinting at lavender and contrasting well with the intense plum of his tie. When her eyes landed on the rich brown of his, the whole night looked a lot better.

There was a murmur at her back before her heel could hit the step. "He's a hardcore sadist, Klara. He's going to hurt you."

She felt a devious little grin, and offered her own low spoken whisper in exchange. "Maybe I'll like it."

Spencer's voice dropped, introspective and unhappy. "Maybe you will."

Will Coleman had spun her. Will Coleman held her card with her four chosen hard limits in his hand. Will Coleman was waiting, silently, for her to approach and belong to him as Chase stated the dom's rather tame hard limits: oral, pet play, latex, and anal.

It was so much easier to do than Klara had expected. She even accepted the ball to spin her first scene with a smile. Focusing on the wheel as he spun it, she released the little marble to clatter and jump slot to slot.

It landed, Chase announcing, "Whipping!"

Klara had no strong feeling one way or the other, though she did cut Spencer a snarky glance.

"Good evening, Klara." Her name flowed like honey, Will's deep timbre slow, controlled, and enhancing every syllable. He'd spoken the moment her spin ordained their first scene to be whipping. In fact, he'd done more than speak. The heat of his palm had gone to her stomach, pushing Klara to take an awkward step backward. "We will wait for the stage to clear before we begin."

She took another step, tempted to look behind her, not confident in heels, nervous he was going to push her too far and she would fall right off. He must have seen the internal conflict, felt the muscles of her stomach tighten, yet did not waver in pushing her all the way to the edge.

She let Will do it because Spencer was glowering at her, and she'd be damned if she was going to *disappoint her dom* in the first five minutes.

Will pinched the fabric under his hand to halt her backward progress. "Step down. One at a time. There are five steps total."

Sliding her toe back, she found the lip of the stage and hoped to God he was not going to let her topple if she missed. The step was there, just as Will had said it would be, and then another, and another, until her feet were on carpet and there was no more stage to worry over.

She'd been absorbed in paying attention to his non-verbal commands, absorbed in meeting his eyes, and scrutinizing the minutia of his expression just as she would any guest she was feeling out.

"Do you always look at men this way?"

Hearing him speak again, seeing that he had not altered his expression no matter her obedience, was almost startling. "What way?"

"Klara Eriksson, you will address me as Sir."

Of course, there were rules to these exchanges. Klara obeyed. "What way, Sir?"

He did not answer her, and Klara suspected that Will Coleman considered ambiguousness would make her analyze her actions far more than if the dom had spelled out his observations. He wanted her to think, and that seemed strange considering the point of Roulette was for her to do as she was told.

"Sir, I don't really know what I'm doing."

The man crooned, a hint of a smirk on his full-lipped mouth. "Noted."

"I have to win tonight."

"Did you expect that you'd bat your pretty eyelashes and I'd go easy on you?" Every word had been said so gently it was threatening.

And just like that, Klara was nervous again. "No."

"Princess, you are in for a surprise."

Being referred to as princess made Klara cringe. She'd heard it all from behind the bar: slave, pet, bitch, cunt, any of those designations would have fit the scenario. Princess? She'd never been anyone's fucking princess. No, in order to get by, she'd always been the dragon.

He knew she wouldn't like it, just as Will knew reaching up to take the pins from her hair, pulling apart her effort to appear stylish, controlled, would be met with another look of poorly veiled distrust.

Klara had spent over an hour on her hair, she'd borrowed the red dress, worn her only nice pair of shoes; she'd even bought new lingerie. Everything had been selected for a purpose, and only with her hair falling loose did it strike her that, inevitably, of course it was going to be removed.

The statement had really been for Spencer anyway. He'd seen it, so it shouldn't matter that Will's hands were combing through her hair, that it would be kinked where the pins had mashed the stray bits down. But, it was still an awkward sensation.

"I want you on your knees now."

Will remained standing even though a comfortable leather chair was behind him. Were she to kneel, she'd have to crane her neck back to meet his stare. These were the first thoughts to go through her head, as was a witty reply to tease him into doing what suited her better.

That's not how subs were supposed to behave, so she bit down on her tongue and did as she was told.

They'd only just begun and already Klara could see that Spencer was right. She wasn't submissive, inadvertently wasn't doing it right, and Will could have noticed.

Insecurity had never been Klara's weakness, but it was rearing its ugly head once carpet dug into her knees and her heels were awkwardly tucked under her rump.

"Now, you will tell me, Princess, why Spencer Cook was speaking to you by the stairs."

Klara didn't hesitate, she told the truth. "He dislikes me, Sir, and would like to see me fail tonight."

"Why?"

And that was not a question Klara could easily answer. She didn't know exactly why Spencer disliked her, she could only guess. "I'm not entirely sure."

At last Will settled his body into the leather chair. Chin in his hand, regarding her posture, expression, and tone, he asked. "What did he say?"

"That you were going to hurt me, Sir."

The man offered a single chuckle, a spark of amusement glittering in his dark eyes. "The role of a dominant is to give his submissive what she needs, and in doing so fulfill his own desires. It is not a selfish exchange. But for some reason, I feel you are being very selfish right now, Princess."

Unsure what he meant, Klara thought to make her position clear. "I'm going to do whatever you want."

"...Sir." His warning was offered in a smooth timbre. "I will not verbally correct you again."

"I'm going to do whatever you want, Sir."

"Crawl closer to me." He watched her slide cat-like over the carpet, her long legs and toned arms sleek. "Place your hands on my knees, and stroke upward towards my cock."

The use of coarse language didn't faze her in the slightest. Doing as she was told, Klara found her body between his spread thighs, her hands slipping up the fine wool of his trousers. Under the fabric he was hard, his flesh muscular and athletic.

When her painted nails neared their destination, Will struck out for her wrists and had her in a grip of iron. "That's enough, Princess."

Unsure why he was restraining her, Klara tore her attention from his lap and met his eyes. His hold was too tight, it hurt, but she was distracted from the discomfort when he issued her next order. "You're going to unzip my slacks with your teeth, reach in for my cock, and lick it from base to tip."

A lightbulb clicked, Klara refusing. "But, Sir, oral sex is on your hard-limit list."

Which was exactly his point. She was not going to do everything he wanted. That would break the rules. "So you were paying attention on stage after all."

"Sir, your hard limits were oral, pet play, latex, and anal... which is also on my list." And Klara could not help but think it was a pity she had not picked something like watersports instead. The fact that they shared a hard limit only knocked seven things off the board. Also, what man in his right mind didn't like a blow job?

From the way his cock tented his trousers and twitched each time she'd looked at it, she was certain he would have enjoyed her lips wrapped around whatever was hidden behind his zipper.

And then it hit her. She smirked, feeling crafty as she teased, "You are playing a deeper game than I am."

Reaching behind her head to begin gathering her hair in his fist, Will pulled, arching her throat, and bringing a sting to her scalp. "Are we playing a game?"

She was bowed back, Will barely visible over the apples of her cheeks. For some reason, his rough handling was not exactly unwelcome. Klara was even smirking. "You would prefer steering the wheel to more extreme play."

His free hand lightly circled the front of her throat. "You forgot to say sir."

Klara could not help but feel something tighten below the waist over thoughts of what Will Coleman might do to correct her.

His chocolate eyes slipped from her face to take in what waited at her back. Leaning forward, Will pressed his lips to her ear. "It would appear the stage has been cleared. I believe it is time I showed you how bad you have been."

CHAPTER 8

There had been scenarios on the roulette wheel Klara had been hoping to avoid. Whipping was not one of them. How bad could it be? In the weeks she'd worked there, no sub at Black Light had ever been truly hurt. Even better, she was able to face the wall and avoid making eye contact with anyone watching.

Will had slowly stripped her naked, unzipped her dress and had her step out of it, unhooked her new racy bra and slid the matching thong down her hips. Before too many people might gawk at her nudity, her wrists were strapped to a wooden whipping post, and spectators would only be able to view her ass. As far as she was concerned, all of them could kiss it.

Especially Spencer, who had taken it upon himself to hover and monitor her scene. He'd even been the smirking bastard who'd prepared the equipment on Will Coleman's direction.

Klara had expected as much. Fortunately, it was much easier to tolerate the unwelcome Dungeon Master with Will running the show. Her dom for the evening was overwhelming despite his soft-spoken voice and languorous movements. It was more than the height of him, his bulk apparent when he pointedly stripped off his suit jacket, tie, and lavender button down. When he was shirtless, the crisp line of his tailored slacks riding low on his hips, Klara let her eyes linger over the insane definition of his musculature. The man was an Adonis, smooth and hairless, moving with a panther-like grace as he slid his hands to her hips. He turned her away from Spencer's eyes and towards the wooden pillar, his every movement as drawn out as his speech—the grip on Klara's wrist as he stretched her arm upward and cuffed one limb then the other above her head, deliberate yet lingering.

When she was bound the way he desired, Will pressed his chest to her back. He was large enough to surround her, warm hands running over her belly, weighing her breasts. It was all long strokes, no pinching of her nipples, no teasing of the trimmed blonde hair above her sex. He was petting her like a cat, fingertips to shoulders, flank to hip, over and over until Klara felt the strain on her wrists from wilting.

The moment should have been between only the two of them, even Klara was willing to pretend they were somewhere else, intimate under different circumstances, but an intrusive voice crashed into her headspace.

"You understand that you can safeword at any time. Just say it once and this can all be over." Spencer had circled the stage, standing right in front of the whipping post, directly in her line of sight.

Yes, she understood, and she didn't appreciate being interrupted or talked to like a child. "Yes, Spen—" Klara caught herself before she said her chosen safeword, gritting her teeth to complete the sentence, "—yes, boss. I understand."

There was a grumble from the man at her back, though his hands did not waver in their warming strokes. "Princess, were you just rude to Black Light's Dungeon Master?"

There was no apology in her reply. In fact she was still glaring at the man in question. "Perhaps, sir. It's open to interpretation."

Will stepped away, his body heat fading with him as he purred, "I'm starting to think you don't want to win after all."

Klara had never seen him pick up an implement, but before Will's last words had left his lips there was a whoosh through the air. Something fell with a snap across her shoulder blades, something that felt like it should have been soft, but stung with a vengeance.

The first strike had been so unexpected that Klara squeaked. When the second blow came she'd locked her grunt behind her teeth, but tensed and pulled against the restraints. Three fell in quick succession, no longer peppering her upper back, but scathing dots of fire from her ass to thigh.

Spencer was still watching her, observing every time her body jumped, the way she had screwed her eyes shut and breathed too shallowly.

There was no rhyme or reason to Will's tempo, no way to count through it or breathe in time with his strikes. There was only pain.

Klara tried to tell herself that Viking blood ran through her veins, that she was better than this. She tried to think of anything but where she was or why. It was impossible.

Will gave her a few seconds of reprieve, probing, "Why are you really here, Princess?"

She had yet to catch her breath, struggling to pant a reply she thought he'd want to hear. "To please you, Sir."

He brought his implement down again, hard. Even his voice, that voice that had been velvet, turned sharp. "Why are you here, Princess?"

Fuck, it hurt. It hurt bad. Klara turned her head, needing to see Will's face so she might find the answer that would make him stop.

Spencer interjected when Will drew back his arm, a black deerskin flogger ready to crack down on the place that made her squeal loudest. "Don't tense up, Klara. Relax your muscles."

Her head swung around to find the familiar voice had come closer. Spencer waited, arms crossed over his broad chest. A vein bulged at his throat, and his eyes burned when she finally met his gaze.

The first thought in her brain was so bizarre Klara wasn't sure if she'd gone loopy. It was Spencer's red tie. In that instant, she realized it was the same one he'd worn the day they'd met—when he'd sat her down for that five minute sham of an interview.

Honey eyes were on it when the next blow landed. From shoulder to shoulder she was on fire yet shivering from cold. Klara knew there were silent tears on her cheeks, but what she didn't know past the shock was that Spencer saw it all.

Accusation, anger, and frustration, all twisted up in grief, and it was directed right at him. One look laid all the blame at his feet.

Spencer uncrossed his arms, shifting his weight. "Say your safe-word, Klara."

The second he challenged her to do it, stone-cold resolve took over. A switch flipped, Klara relaxed as he'd suggested, closed her eyes, and tried her best to let Will hurt her without making another noise.

She had to win.

The world was against her, all the weight bearing down on her shoulders. Pain, responsibility, culpability for every time she'd failed Elias. Klara was drowning in it, could feel it pool like sewer water building up around her toes. It crashed against her legs, scorched up her thighs, and twisted where for some reason she'd grown wanton and thirsty.

Another volley of quickly fired stings landed across her buttocks.

God help her, she moaned. And then the hurt twisted into something more—calm amidst the shower of pain, her breath leveling into slow, even breaths. The next time she heard the whoosh of her dom's impending blow, Klara opened herself to it.

"Good girl, that's right." Will's strong body was at her back once more, the man curved around her, his touch instantly pressing up between her legs. He was careful there, one hand's fingers pumping smooth and slow into her pussy, the other hand swirling deliciously over her clit. Half of her body burning, the other half cooled from sweat, he blended all she was and was not, deliciously.

It built like a spark of electricity from the roots of her hair, jolting through a pounding heart, to crash like thunder in a fluttering belly. Sex had never been like this, it had never drawn out animal noises. It had never shaken her to the point her beginning and end were one.

She came on a deep inhale, toes curling, the world nothing like what it was supposed to be.

Lips soft, full and tempting at her ear, again Will asked, "Why are you here, Miss Eriksson?"

He gripped her hair, pulling enough to send a ripple of sensation through her scalp. Turning her head, he demanded honey eyes meet deep chocolate brown.

She could barely manage a whisper. "Because I need it."

"Yes, you do." For a moment Will was as gentle as he'd been at the start. "Let go."

Just like that, whatever high she'd indulged in was over. There were too many things in the way. Too much she had to do. "I can't."

His thumb pulled her bottom lip to the side, smearing her juices all over her mouth. He looked unmoved by her resistance, leaning down to press a kiss to her forehead. "Then I'm going to have to hurt you until you can."

Will backed away and spoke louder. "Mr. Cook, hand me the Loopy Johnny."

Klara had no idea what that was, or why Spencer seemed to disagree with her dom's choice of tools. It was not as if the Dungeon Master had vocalized dissent or even hesitated to retrieve the flogger Will had chosen. But there had been something in his mannerism Klara had seen before.

Spencer had gone from swaggering to grumpy.

It should have made her nervous. Instead it gave her a thrill. Enjoying her momentary, silent rebellion, Klara sighed, closing her eyes and resting her forehead against the whipping post.

Behind her the men, their gathered audience, admired what had been done to her body. Will's blows had been well-placed, avoiding delicate internal organs, and spread out to maximize discomfort. Klara's round ass was cherry red, stripes crisscrossing in a pleasing array. The pattern across her shoulders was just as lovely, angel wings spanning her ribs.

But he had only just begun.

A whistle of air preceded Will's chosen toy.

When it landed, the strike was more precise and the sting far more intense. Klara screamed. Whatever Will had struck her with before was child's play; she'd been foolish to think that she'd known pain. Three more snapping strikes and her thready composure crumbled into nothing.

Wailing, Klara began to cry. She cried as if her mother was still alive and might be there to comfort her. She sobbed as if Elias's father had not been a deadbeat who'd smacked around her baby brother until Klara had found out and taken the boy away. She wept as if she had not given up a scholarship and any kind of future she'd imagined for herself to raise him. She cried until there weren't tears or hiccups or screams.

Limp as a rag, she hung from her restraints and grew empty. The subsequent blows still hurt, but over time each kiss of the Loopy Johnny began to feel almost good. Before she knew it she was nearly swooning, purring out nonsense groans, unsure why her pussy throbbed in time with the welts on her ass.

CHAPTER 9

*a*fter a heavy male sigh, the scratch of curtains pulling across their rod sounded, and a soft spoken argument filled the semi-private enclosure. "You took it too far."

"I respectfully disagree. Look at her. She's flying." Gentle fingers brushed back the sweaty hair stuck to Klara's forehead, a low rumble staking claim. "She may have entered subspace sooner if you hadn't been distracting her, Mr. Cook. Don't spoil Princess' lesson by drawing her out before she has fully enjoyed it."

Ice cold water was at her lips, Klara sipped, half-awake and comfortable.

She was draped over someone's lap, wrapped in the softest of blankets and unwilling to move anytime soon. From toes to fingertips her skin tingled, muscles loose and drowsy. Klara had never felt so contented or so disconnected.

Spencer was still mumbling, though he had lowered his voice as if not to disturb her. "It was her first time sceneing."

"I am aware." A hint of annoyance colored Will's deep timbre. "And she did very well. Every moment of pain was good for her."

Disagreement raised his whisper to a hiss. "Klara is complicated. You're not the type of dom she'll learn from."

"From one sadist to another, you're out of line, Spencer. You shouldn't even be in here right now. These moments should be about her, not you." Will gathered his dozing sub closer, rocking Klara gently until she smiled softly. "If you need your turn at the whipping post, I'll be happy to see to your issues later."

A low growl preceded, "You might be Dungeon Master back in L.A., but I am in charge at Black Light."

A flap of fabric and quiet stole in. With Spencer gone, at last Will had Klara all to himself.

* * *

SPENCER WAS LOOKING for an excuse to disqualify them, and having a prominent member of the community all but accuse him of unfairness right to his face had been... frustrating. It didn't change the way he felt. There was something wrong with him, how he'd stood by and salivated watching another man undress Klara before her scene. There had even been a stifled groan in his throat when red fabric had parted and the tattoo right in the center of Klara's back was exposed.

A knotted ouroboros—a depiction of a serpent swallowing its tail, rendered with Nordic influence—delicate yet stark.

It was the sexiest fucking thing he'd ever seen. Or it had been before he'd seen the trimmed wisps of blonde on her mound. Even if she'd grown it out, Klara's pubic hair would never be a thatch. It was shiny and sparse and looked downy soft.

One glance and Spencer's fingers had instantly formed a fist. Because, in truth, he wanted to reach out and touch it.

He should have sent Owen to monitor Klara; he should have known Will Coleman would push her right to the limit in her very first scene. There was something about the guy. Deep down Spencer didn't trust the man. Not when it came to Klara. He knew her better. The nuances of her stubbornness only he could interpret.

Spencer didn't believe she would safeword if she needed to—not when she was trying to make a point.

If he didn't watch, she could get hurt. Furthermore, how could he resist?

In pain, Klara's face had been perfection. Watching her unravel...

he'd never grown so hard. If he'd glanced down even once to see her naked breasts jolt with every strike, his aching cock would have spurt a mess in his slacks.

Which is what brought him to the men's room the second he'd left Klara and Will alone in the semi-private booth.

Behind the isolation of the stall door, Spencer did something unthinkable. He reached into his pants, hard dick caught in his hand. It took less than three manic pumps of his fist before he'd come, biting back any noise, filling his palm with creamy white.

Teenage boys had more control.

Staring down at the slimy palm of his hand, he sighed. The orgasm had been unfulfilling but at least his dick was starting to go limp.

After a few minutes of collecting himself, Spencer washed his hands, smoothed his hair, and walked out of the restroom and into a new fresh hell.

Klara was on stage, and she'd spun Breath Play.

* * *

BREATH PLAY. Klara didn't even know what that was.

Choking? Was that it? One guy she'd dated back in her twenties had wanted to try it. It hadn't really done anything for her, but Will Coleman was not the kind of man who was going to be squeamish about it.

Considering the praise and massage he'd just lavished her with, the care he'd taken explaining how she was feeling and why it was okay, she was willing to give him a go.

But she did not know him well, and even with the lapse of thirty minutes, she wasn't one-hundred percent normal. Truth was, she felt drunk... and it was kinda nice.

Warm and fuzzy even though Will had taken the blanket away so all who saw her might enjoy his handiwork, she smiled. For some unknown reason, naked in front of the room, Klara was even proud of herself. She'd made it through one intense scene. The rest of the night would be a cake walk. After all, what could be worse than being whipped for thirty minutes straight?

After sneaking side glances at other scenes and moaning couples, Klara had to admit she was surprised by how much everyone seemed to be enjoying themselves... even the subs being tormented. It was a revelation. And yes, her back stung, yes, she was drowsy, but she also felt powerful for the first time in weeks.

If she was going to do this, she wanted to experience it all the way.

Klara wanted to come screaming like the girl in the stockade. She wanted to test her bravery and see if this good feeling might expand. Mostly, she wanted to make Spencer eat every last mean word he'd ever said to her.

Unlike their last scene, Will was not leading her to the stage. Instead he'd chosen a place near the corner where massage tables were available for use. In all her weeks at Black Light, Klara had never seen those tables used for an actual massage. He was going to fuck her on one... at least that's what she hoped.

Even after the orgasm he'd given between strikes on her back, she was horny. Ridiculously horny, and Will was ridiculously hot. From the look of the bulge in his pants he was most likely ridiculously well-hung too.

The fact she was even slightly excited about having sex in front of people she knew made the whole thing *ridiculously* insane. That didn't change how much she wanted him inside her.

Klara was pretty certain from the wicked look Will had just shot her that he could read her mind.

Around them congregated several Black Light party goers who'd come to witness a scene suiting their tastes. Since the table was not on a raised platform they seemed more a part of the moment when they gathered around, and Klara was not sure she liked it.

"Pay attention, Princess." Will patted the end of the massage table, motioning for Klara to take a seat. "The nature of Breath Play is very advanced. You may not be able to safeword if you want out."

All her cocky self-assurance evaporated with that one comment from her dom. "Sir?"

"The first round, I went easy on you. Pain was nothing but a fleeting sensation. Your issues were here." First he tapped her skull, then he smoothed his fingers down from her forehead, over the slope of her nose, her lips, pinching her chin. "Our next scene will be less mental and much more physical. Think about that before you commit." For the first time in the night, Will pressed a lingering kiss to her mouth. His tongue dipped between her parted lips, and the moment she began to kiss him back he pulled away, warning, "I want you to know I am going to use you."

Voice thick, Klara hesitated. "What do you mean?"

"What did I tell you about the dominant's role?"

She had to think about it, but quickly recalled, "To give the submissive what she needs."

Will cocked a brow, offering a chance for Klara to amend her statement.

She was never going to get her part in this right. Frustrated with herself for forgetting again, she quickly amended, "To give a submissive what she needs, Sir."

"Mr. Cook was right to warn you the moment I spun your name. Obedience is not what I'm looking for, Princess."

When he honeyed his words and manipulated the deep velvet of his voice, Klara could not help but like it, warning or no. "What do you want, Sir?"

Will Coleman gave her a roguish grin.

It was the first time she'd seen him more than mildly smirk. Teeth white against such dark skin, he was devilishly handsome even if the smile was hard and there was something unsavory underneath it. "Lay back on the table. I am going to put a red foam ball in your hand. When our play reaches its pinnacle, you won't be able to speak. That red ball is your safeword. Drop it and the scene will end immediately. Now, repeat everything I said back to me."

Klara did as she was told, stretching out on the padded table. Laying prone, pretending that those who'd gathered to watch were not inching forward and crowding her.

"Close your eyes, Princess. Do not open them. You are to breathe in and out on counts of four. No matter what, you may not come unless I give you permission." Gone was the soft-spoken gentleman. In his place was a commanding authoritarian who grabbed her by the hips, dragging her body down the table until her legs dangled precariously from the edge.

Surprised by the sudden movement and how it made the welts on her ass sting, she'd gasped, eyes flying open.

"Close your eyes!" Will was not messing around. He was not smirking or playful. "Do not open them again."

Klara obeyed, nervous when his hand came to her chest and he pushed her back down.

"Breathe in, deep." The musical croon was edged with darkness. "Breathe out."

He had taken her left foot. Kneading her arch with both hands, he pushed her knee back, and opened her leg at an angle. Unsure what he was up to, Klara exhaled on his count then yipped at the feeling of another pair of hands on her right ankle.

Someone else was mirroring Will's actions until she was obnoxiously spread—the new player taking it a step further by drawing her big toe into a wet mouth and sucking.

Already she'd broken the pattern of breath, and Will was ready to correct her. But, there was one major problem. His voice was coming from a distance. Neither person handling her feet, neither stranger bracing her legs so her pussy was on display, was her dom. "For every time you fail to breathe on command, I will make you wait another full minute until you can come."

This was getting out of hand and Klara was much less keen to continue. She'd opened her mouth to complain when another pair of hands fell on her body. Wrists taken in a gentle hold, her stiff arms were hinged at the shoulder until stretched back, spanning the table above her head. This was not a hold partnered with soothing massage or a dirty mouth. It was pinioning, a strong grip much more intimidating than cold shackles.

Was it Will?

Klara didn't know, and before she could decide the game abruptly progressed.

A pair of ravenous strangers fell upon her breasts. Nips and gnaws pinched the hardened tip of her left nipple. The man, woman, Klara wasn't sure, on her right far more interested in suckling and circling the flesh with their tongue.

There were five—five people holding, rubbing, touching, licking, spreading her body as if it was theirs to do with as they pleased.

This was not what she'd intended. Klara broke rank, wriggling under the onslaught of too many hands and tongues. "Stop."

Will's baritone breath was right against her ear. "Saying stop will do nothing, screaming won't make this end. Yellow, safeword, or drop the ball, Princess. Otherwise get back to breathing on four counts as I ordered."

She'd said stop and he'd refused, and she'd never been more turned on, or mortified, in her life. Klara was growing embarrassingly wet, certain anyone standing with a view of her spread legs could see her pussy was pink, swollen, internal muscles twitching over and over.

Five unknown strangers had their hands all over her body. Two of them were licking her tits as if they were covered in ice cream. So much was going on at once, Klara writhing both against and away from fingers and lips, that when the next participant joined the fray, she began to struggle manically against the hold on her arms.

Will had told her not to come, but it was too late. When out of the blue, a tongue slithered between her labia, delving upward to strum her clit, she spasmed, shuddering, fighting against the hold of so many as waves of unwelcome orgasm twisted every muscle and stole her breath.

"Bad, bad, girl."

Panting, mouth wide open, Klara tried to focus less on what others were doing to her, how someone was eating her out like no one's business, and pinpoint where Will's voice was coming from now. "Oral is one of your hard limits, Sir..."

Chuckling, Will agreed. He was twisting the rules, and not the slightest bit sorry. "But not one of yours. Someone else is licking your pretty little cunt, someone who is enjoying your squirming very much."

It wasn't fair!

Under her back the sting of her welts against the table was

inspiring an overwhelming tingle to creep around and edge ever closer to where her pussy clenched to deny a probing tongue.

Who was doing this to her while two others held her legs splayed open? Klara could not bring herself to open her eyes, not when her first thought was that it might be Spencer. The shame of envisioning him, his silver-haired head tucked between her thighs, made her whimper and nearly come again.

Will pressed a kiss to her mouth. "Deep breath, Princess. Hold it until I say let go."

She obeyed, and the second her chest had expanded fully, fingers pushed inside her pussy.

Klara was going to burst.

Warmth encircled her throat, the lightest of pressure distracted, and the edge of orgasm ebbed away.

"Exhale."

Every nerve on her skin sang with the release of that breath.

Unknown partners working in unison seemed to know exactly what kind of pressure, suction, massage, or bites to apply to steal her momentary control. It was a perversion of the worst sort, made all the worse when Klara's mental reluctance seemed to enhance every tingle.

Despite her protests, her flesh came alive.

Shameless in her wriggling, unwilling to come to terms with how much she loved the feeling of Will's hands around her throat. Klara fought all the harder. His light pulsating grip was her only lifeline in the chaos. His deep voiced commands to inhale, hold her breath until her lungs burned and her head swam, the worst kind of decadence.

She had crossed into a world that was so wrong it was right.

Sensation began to meld together, the growing crescendo out of her control no matter Will's edicts. It was as he'd claimed; her mind was shut off, muted in favor of automatic response.

Adrenaline spiked when whomever gnawed her clit pulled away. Nipples burning from even the lightest brush of slathering tongues, joints aching from the resistance of strong bodies bending them at will, Klara's sudden urge to break free was exploited as the perfect distraction.

Will had said he would use her, and before she could throw off a single pair of slithering hands, a new pressure grew between her spread legs. A condom covered cock drove in.

An oomph, and some of her held breath escaped, Klara's body jolted by the suddenness of unyielding entry.

Immediately she went still, practically panting as if she'd climbed a mountain.

Hands back at her throat, Will growled. "Hold your breath. Behave and I might let you enjoy it."

Had a man talked to her in that tone in any other situation, Klara would have verbally ripped off his dick. Being growled at now, every part of her body under the maestro's control, set her clit throbbing and her eyes rolling back behind closed lids.

Every commanded breath in, he pulled out. Each exhale and Will fucked deep into her belly. Caught up in the cadence, following the Master as he did his work, Klara grew light headed from over oxygenated cells.

He was having her breathe too deep, too fast, and it was glorious.

The noises he made were music to her ears, each grunt, each growl, heady. Closer and closer she came to exploding all over his cock, and knew without a doubt she was powerless to stop it.

Where he held her throat, his hands began to squeeze. Unlike the first times he'd playfully strangled her neck, it no longer distracted from her need for release. It enhanced it to a point she was bowed on the table and spasming in the grip of her captors.

Will never held longer than she could tolerate, no matter how red-faced she grew or the choking sounds forced from parted lips. In fact, had she been able to speak, she would have been begging for more.

It was debauchery at its finest.

Pleased with her enthusiasm, Will began pounding her pussy, squeezing harder until her attention went down to a pinpoint—his cock, how much it stretched her, how greedy it was, how she was certain her pussy was choking down on it as if it might breathe the air her lungs were denied.

She could feel the rush of blood in her head, her face as red as the ball she squeezed in her hand.

If Will stopped fucking her she was going to die.

Klara was so close, so close to something she hardly understood, and then it was taken away.

She was still being fucked, the smooth jerk of Will's hips delicious, but the tension around her throat disappeared. Lungs aching, that first breath was sucked in by a body out of her control. With the shock of feeling a body where moments ago she'd been pure energy, Klara unwittingly opened her eyes.

It was not the man pounding away between her hitched thighs that waited to be seen.

It was Spencer.

All along, he had been the one pinioning her arms, his mass leaning over her so he might watch each subtle reaction cross her face.

It had never been him sucking her clit, and unlike the others, he had not sought to bring her torturous pleasure, but he had been the most intimate observer of them all.

Crystal clear baby-blues made all the brighter by the silver of his hair, stared down, they beckoned.

As oxygen flooded her system, a sense of relief inspired the strangest fulfillment. It didn't matter who was sucking her toes or massaging her feet. The pair of dark haired strangers fondling her breasts and twisting her nipples were unimportant. Even Will, with his glorious cock and expertise in wielding it had all become background noise.

But Spencer was not her dom, he was her adversary.

The dark hands around her throat tightened again, beautiful euphoria riding hard on the noises of her choking gasps.

If it was possible, Klara felt the thing shoved deep inside her expand, opening up her cunt in ways unknown. Fight or flight returned, the struggle to angle her hips into that freight train of cock as confusing as her need to wrap her free fingers around Spencer's forearm and hold on for dear life.

One command blew her world apart. "Come."

Klara, mouth agape, saw white, and in it, in the maddening jerks of a body orgasming beyond belief, found the world empty of all things but the silent encouragement of gloriously blue eyes.

Her throat was set free. Blood rushed through her jerking body, Klara croaking when a scream was unmanageable.

Fear twisted in her pleasure, enhanced it, burned away reason and just when she thought she'd drop the red ball, the cock tucked deep in her belly kicked.

Will had used her exactly as he had promised.

And he was not the only one.

A first splash of warm semen landed on her belly, dazed honey eyes traveled to where warm goo pooled near her navel. She noticed the others then. The men who'd sucked, stroked, touched... were still hovering near, standing around the table jerking their cocks.

They were looking at her like she was meat, watching her splayed and spent as their fists moved up and down swollen, purple shafts.

Limp, her body felt like an alien thing. She didn't feel as if she was completely inside it, but someone still was. A dark skinned man was reaching between them to pinch a condom in place as he pulled out of flesh still twitching in the aftershocks of a dangerous orgasm.

"Will..." That was his name. His name was Will.

More spunk landed on her tits, shot from the man fondling her nipple.

Klara didn't like it. In fact, it was disgusting. Muttering, she pushed to sit up. "Yellow."

It was one thing having the hands of strangers entice her nerves into Will's mind-bending game; it was another having their body fluids shot upon skin that was so sensitive even the slightest droplet stung.

"Back off, gentlemen." Helping her scoot back and sit up, Will offered reassurance. "Princess, the scene is over."

She didn't care if half the participants groaned in complaint. She wanted them away from her. "I need a towel."

One was under her nose immediately, and only then did Klara realized she was sitting hunched forward, her eyes on the carpet, the sounds of wet fucking, raw moans, and harsh grunts all but tuned out over the rushing of blood in her ears.

The hand that presented the fluffy cloth did not have black skin. Instead it was tan, rough, tattoos starting at the wrist and moving up a muscular forearm.

It was Spencer's arm. He'd rolled up his white shirt sleeves. "Are you okay?"

He was still clutching the white cotton, using it to wipe her stomach and breasts when she was having a hard time reaching for it herself.

Every pass of the terry cloth sparked nerves that had been overused. Fumbling, she pushed him off before dropping her head in her hands. Her throat was sore, it felt slightly swollen, and a headache was beginning to pound away behind her eyes.

"Put your head between your knees, Klara. William will brace you. You won't fall forward."

Calm reassurance saturated every word, and automatically Klara obeyed. The crown of her head rested on Will's hard stomach. Even with his dick hanging right before her eyes, smelling of sperm and latex, it was immensely comforting having a wall of muscle to lean onto. Her arms found their way around his waist and she was clinging to him as if he was the only thing to hold onto in the vortex blazing through mind and body.

Will's fingers were in her hair, stroking gently. "The dizziness will pass. There is nothing for you to be afraid of."

That was exactly the word for it. Klara was afraid... after something so beyond an orgasm had ended, it finally sank in that she should be. The marks on her back stung, her nipples had been sucked raw, every inch of her skin was buzzing, and someone she'd only just met had literally held her life in their hands.

Spencer crouched down, low enough to meet Klara's eyes. "You're overstimulated. Your nervous system needs a moment to recalibrate. No one is going to let anything bad happen to you."

She wanted to giggle considering Will's huge schlong was right next to Spencer's face but something else came out of her mouth. "When did you take off your tie? I like that tie. Don't lose it."

Ignoring her bizarre sass, he took her wrist, put his fingers to her pulse point, and stared down at his watch. "You need to rest and drink water. You're not allowed to spin until I give you clearance to do so."

But she'd come so far, Klara was not going to give up now. "I'm fine."

Spencer grew gruff. "If you argue with me, Klara, I'll disqualify you now. I thought you wanted to win."

"And I thought you wanted me to fail." The retort couldn't be bitten back, not with how strange she was feeling.

For a moment it looked as if Spencer was ready to bark at her, but he shut his mouth and considered for a moment. His sharpish concession did not come easy. "I underestimated you."

"That's the nicest thing you've ever said to me, boss."

He was at a loss, pushing to his feet to leave her in the care of someone who might comfort her where he could not.

CHAPTER 10

*T*he glass in her hands was frosted with a crust of ice, the vodka within chilled to the point it was almost tasteless. Will had been gracious in offering her a drink, in sitting with her in a quiet corner. He'd even ordered a snack, feeding Klara toast points smeared with camembert topped with glazed figs.

Around them new alluring scenes progressed, a show for every appetite on display. Participants, party goers, everyone possessed the glazed look of euphoric delight. The room was high on sex, pain, lust, pleasure, decadence, even humiliation.

Klara was high on... a sick sense of disordered fulfilment. Part of her felt very bad; her body ached in strange ways, the enduring cottony feeling of a passing headache lingered. But beyond that nagging ick, she was incredibly satisfied and equally confused.

Will sat on the couch, having placed her on the floor between his spread legs. The degrading position didn't bother her as she thought it should. Klara felt safe there, shielded with his strong thighs supporting her head, where she could press close and see only his torso if she wanted. It was like her own warm little haven.

He toyed with her hair, petting her like a dog, but cautious of touching her skin. He knew she wasn't ready yet, though Klara had not said a word. He just knew.

Will knew many things she didn't know.

Klara was certain he even knew exactly how she felt inside.

Was it like this with all experienced doms? Would Spencer have spoiled her with quiet, safety, and soft touches?

No. She'd never seen him lavish any of his play partners with this kind of attention. At least he'd never done it in front of her. Almost six weeks working at Black Light, and Klara had noticed even his brand of aftercare appeared monotonous and cold. Subs who played with him knew not to expect an emotional connection —water, a blanket, a quick cuddle, a place to cry—that's all he would provide.

He was unfailingly polite to the girls he fucked... nothing more.

Spencer Cook would have never made her feel safe like this.

He'd seen her come, held her down in a scene, and walked away.

Across the room the man who knew just how to get under her skin had already returned his red tie to his neck, rolled down his shirt-sleeves, and currently sported his suit jacket as if nothing unusual had taken place. He did not even spare Klara a glance. Instead he was all business, observing a different couple's scene, and doing it without involving himself.

So why, twenty minutes prior had he looked Klara dead in the eye and watched her writhe in unmitigated lust? Why had he held down her arms and participated in a scene to an effect that felt inevitable, and intimate, and wrong—wrong in a way that had made her come with such violence that she could still feel echoes of twitching plea-sure down below?

She should not have liked it. She should not be staring at him now...

Knowing she was ridiculous, Klara tried to engage with the dom who deserved her attention and ignore the one who'd made her life hell. She turned her head up and smiled at Will. "Handsome, shirtless men hand-feeding me... there might be something to this submission thing after all, *Sir*. But, I feel like I might be taking advantage. Shouldn't I be the one waiting on you?"

"Not right now, no." In mirror of her self-indulgent playfulness, Will smirked. Another bite was prepared. He told her to open her mouth, watched her chew, and rumbled approval. "Your shivering will stop once your blood sugar levels out."

"I am already feeling much better, Sir. Thank you." She had to keep her eyes off Spencer; Will deserved that regard and more. She shifted a hip, settled against Will's opposite thigh, putting her back towards the Dungeon Master. "But I don't see the other subs—"

Brow cocking dangerously, Will dropped the smile and cut in. "Princess, it would be good for you to trust me and submit to what I say is best."

There was no doubt he'd behaved better than she had. Klara put an arm around his middle, closing her eyes as she settled into his weight. "Sir, I've benefited from your patience and experience. You know best. If I've been difficult, I apologize."

A hand rested atop her head, Will's fingertips rubbing against her scalp. "And you are trying so hard to behave: remembering to say *sir*, behaving demurely... I wonder what brought about this sudden change?"

Guilt had. Klara felt as if she'd wronged the dom with her behavior. "The last scene. I don't think Mr. Cook should have been a part of it."

"A monitor needed unrestricted access to observe your face. It was to assure your safety." Will trailed his fingers to her neck, running a feather-light touch over soft skin.

Klara sighed, unsure what to say or how much to tell. "But it shouldn't have been him."

"He objects to your being here?"

A stifled laugh caught in her throat. "That's one way to phrase it."

"Phrase it another way. Explain yourself, Princess."

And there it was, that milieu of discontent Klara had been anticipating from the dom all night.

She opened her eyes, her cheek to his thigh, and confessed. "He told me whoever spun my name would be disappointed. I figured, if you didn't know my *background*, sir, that you would enjoy yourself more. From my end, I was happy I didn't recognize you."

He took her chin a bit too hard, making Klara raise her head so she might see his unnerving expression. "The Dungeon Master doesn't speak for me, Princess, and neither do you. I will form my own opinions."

She lowered her lashes, guilty. "Have you been disappointed, Sir?"

"No."

Maybe clarity was the best course. "What do you want to know?"

"Whatever it is you didn't want to mention."

Still crouched between his thighs, chin caught in her dom's hand, Klara said, "I worked here. I was fired, a week ago today."

"By Spencer?"

She frowned. "Yes."

"What did you do?"

Rancor bubbled up, days of resentment unmitigated by all the feel-good chemicals floating around her bloodstream. "I did my job, that's what I did. I did my job every night Black Light was open while working for a man who..."

A husky growl grew in Wills timbre. It was not the purr of encouragement, but one of caution. "Who what?"

"It doesn't matter, Sir." She was making a fool of herself. Daring to meet Will's eyes again, she confessed. "You were right. My reasons for participating were thoroughly selfish. I signed up to make a point."

"Your choice of safeword was interesting." He nodded, still holding her jaw, and tucked a wisp of her hair behind her ear. "I believe your point was made. But you didn't answer my questions, Princess. You said, 'while working for a man who'. Who what?"

She didn't want to talk about it. These feelings were private, just like her sex life and her family situation. But on this one subject, after what they had shared, Klara acquiesced. "Who treated me as if I were disposable. Who criticized my efforts even though they consistently improved his business. Who asked me to be invisible while on the job so he would not have to look at or speak to me. Spencer Cook is an asshole."

His focus had been on her face, as she watched Will listen closely. But once she was done he'd glanced over Klara's head, addressing another. "Now you know how she feels."

An intruder had approached the couch where they lounged and had heard her tirade. Klara didn't need to turn around to know who it was. Humiliated, she locked accusing eyes on Will and felt her jaw tick.

The dom had led her right into speaking her mind in front of the man she despised.

Spencer didn't balk, he spoke formally, politely. "Miss Eriksson, it's been thirty minutes. Are you feeling better?"

Was she supposed to turn around and look at him? She couldn't bring herself to do it, not when she was red-cheeked and mortified.

Klara yanked her chin from Will's grip, tipping back her vodka and swallowing the whole thing in one go. Forcing out a thick breath, she swung her head around. "I would have said it all to your face. You should not have hired me, allowed me to put my career in jeopardy by quitting a great job to work here if you never wanted me as part of your staff. What you did, the way you treated me, was wrong. You're an asshole, Spencer, but I don't have to like you to work for you. As far as I am concerned, our differences were never an issue."

Spencer didn't so much as blink an eyelash. He was deadpan. "I asked you about your throat. Answer me."

Klara swallowed, found her fingers encased the front of her neck. "It's... a little sore."

"Are you lightheaded?"

"No."

"Nauseous?"

"No."

"Hmmm." He looked her over, eyes narrowed as if they might catch something unseen under the blanket. "I'm adding ten more minutes to your recovery time before you can spin."

Insulted, Klara growled. "Did any other subs get extra time?"

Spencer narrowed his baby-blues. "No."

"I shouldn't get special treatment. That's not what I want."

Quiet, gentle as death, Spencer muttered. "I am not going to rehire you, Klara."

Klara pushed to her feet, unwilling to kneel before her antagonizer. Face to face with Black Light's Dungeon Master, a pair of matching tears tripped down her cheeks. "You will."

CHAPTER 11

"**W**hy did you do that?" Klara's eyes flashed, her lips thinned, and she spun to stare down Will Coleman the second Spencer was out of earshot.

The dom took the edges of the blanket and tightened it around her, yanking her into submission like some tantrum throwing child. "You've earned a punishment for forgetting to address me as sir."

She'd stumbled, foot caught on his ankle, and fell across Will's lap just as he'd intended. "What?"

A hard smack landed right on her ass. Klara was shocked that he'd dare ignore her protest, that he'd humiliate her before her former boss, that he'd hit her for no reason. "Stop it! What the hell!"

The other cheek was smacked even harder, the blanket doing little to muffle the sting. And then the blanket was gone, Will easily wrestling it away from her. The man spanked her with gusto until Klara stopped screeching, until she stopped fighting, until she lay limp and seething with rage.

The commotion had drawn eyes to the woman pinned over the knee of an indomitable dom, to her bright red ass and thighs—to her complete embarrassment. This wasn't a spanking for scene or sexual stimulation, it was a punishment for God only knew what.

Klara pressed her face to the couch, panting from the effort it took not to scream fury. Spencer was looking, she knew he would be, and she could not face him.

"Be my good girl." Will lay his rich timbre over her ear, pouring warm and sweet to soothe the wound.

My good girl. Is that what she'd done wrong?

He gripped the burning flesh of her ass, the pressure soothing and equal uncomfortable. "Say you're sorry."

For what? She ground out two words. "I'm sorry."

A cracking slap bounced her ass cheek. "I don't think you meant it, Princess."

The welts on her ass were throbbing, her heart was racing, but her temper she held in control. "I will be your good girl."

A finger traced from her tailbone, up Klara's spine and neck, to tease her ear. Will leaned over her, his words only for them. "But you want to be a bad girl."

"Aside from snapping at you, sir, I don't know what I did wrong." And he'd been the wrong one for betraying her into saying those things within Spencer's earshot.

That deep voice dropped low. "And, now you are lying to me..."

Sniffing, Klara turned her head enough to peek up at Will through her hair. She whispered, "Why, though? Why encourage me to say those things in front of my boss?"

"Transparency is best. That's why."

"You don't understand. If I can't get this job back, I can't pay for my brother's school. I need it, Sir. And, Spencer didn't need more reasons to refuse."

Will softened his hold, rubbing the hair off her flushed cheek face. "You'd be fooling yourself if you think Mr. Cook was unaware of your opinion of him. Hearing you voice your reasons made him personally accountable for his part in it."

"Sir, that's manipulative."

He cocked a handsome brow. "Don't you want your job back?"

Klara could not tell if Will was genuinely trying to help her, if he was punishing her, or what his endgame might be. All she knew was that she had a growing sense of unease. "May I please get up, Sir?"

Thoughtful, Will settled his frame against the back of the sofa, trilling his fingers on her back. "You have ten more minutes. You will stay exactly where you are."

Red ass up, legs hanging twisted from Will's lap. It was not only uncomfortable, it was embarrassing. "Yes, Sir."

* * *

AT THE SOUND of the first crack across Klara's ass, Spencer's ears pricked, his head had turned. Captivated, he watched the flesh of her globes jiggle under each punishing smack.

She'd fought her dom tooth and nail under the volley of slaps, her skin flush with anger from her ears to her toes. It had been a fine performance on Will's end, Spencer feeling the sting in his own hand with each satisfying smack pinkening Klara's ass and thighs.

There was one problem. He should have been the one to yank her over his knee. Instead, Spencer had been trapped again, deferring control of the woman to another man. And there was nothing he could do about it.

He would never get to enjoy feeling her squirm on his lap, not after the way he'd treated her.

It would take a fucking miracle before Klara Eriksson would ever submit to him.

Spencer would just get the scraps—he'd observe her scenes, maybe get lucky again and have the chance to pin her arms above her head. If she tasted like cotton candy, he'd never know. Skin bumped under his tongue, he'd never feel.

And it was his own damn fault.

She wasn't supposed to be real in this world. The sexy Swede was supposed to stay behind the bar and out of his fantasies. Now he'd be stuck jacking off for months to the image of her held down, choked, and fucked to blistering climax.

So beautiful.

And she was walking, eyes downcast, right towards him.

Will Coleman was the culprit—the blonde's hair caught up in the dom's fist, her body controlled as if she were his puppet.

Klara would not meet his eye, and didn't see the look of annoyance

Spencer shot towards Will.

The dom had an agenda. "Do you have something to say, Princess?"

She kept her eyes fixed on Spencer's tie, cheeks flushed, and expression compliant. "I'm sorry, boss."

"Klara, I—"

"I'll have to stop you right there, Mr. Cook. Princess is not allowed to say anything else to you. That should end any potential complications to the remainder of your evening."

Before Spencer might cut in, Will yanked her away, dragging the naked beauty to the steps of the stage.

Klara let him do it; the spanking had done its job. The fight was out of her.

When Will had her before the roulette wheel he unhanded her hair, smoothed it down as if she were some doll, and put the white sphere in her hands.

Chase spun the wheel so she might earn her next scene, Jaxson's lover openly frowning when the pill landed and Klara hung her head in her hands. Whatever the token had landed on, Klara was already shaking her head no.

"Watersports!"

* * *

STARING down at the white ball slotted neatly in its new home, Klara felt her skin crawl. Gone was the excitement from the earlier victories... any lingering hope was sucked right out of her bones.

Watersports.

There had only been four hard limits a sub might choose out of the myriad potential scenes. Klara had played the odds. It was a fucking one in a million shot that the ball would land on the one thing she had almost put on the list in place of blood play.

Seeing it now, she'd rather have Will hold a knife to her throat.

Rubbing a hand over her face, Klara let out a shaky breath. There was no use in even pretending she was happy with the outcome.

Will had her by the elbow, pushing her reluctant feet towards the steps of the stage, all the while gloating. "It seems the stars have aligned."

Against her. They had aligned against her.

Dumbstruck, she followed Will's lead as if marching to the gallows. It was not like her preparation for the whipping when determination and lack of fear had steeled her backbone. The moment shared no similarities to her confident strut to the tables before breath play. Klara was shaken.

Dragging her feet, Will steered them towards the tiled co-ed shower area set aside for more... unsanitary kinks. "I don't want to do this."

Unmoved, Will smiled. "We don't always get what we want in life, do we Princess?"

Shoulders up to her ears, Klara, pulled on his arm. "Please, Sir, I can't do this scene."

"You don't know that." Will stopped, looked her in the eye, assuring, "Pain, pleasure... both did you good. Humiliation will be no different. This is not going to hurt. You might surprise yourself."

Throughout the evening Will Coleman had kept her from sinking, but she was starting to doubt he would continue bearing the brunt of her inexperience. In fact, by the shark's grin he'd given her when the ball had landed where it did, she worried he was looking to exploit it.

Will didn't want her submission, he wanted something else. Even Spencer had warned her against the dom. What if the warning had been genuine?

The watersports area was cleared for their scene, a crowd gathering to watch the couple's finale. Cold tile under her feet, a drain nearby, Klara was told to kneel. The smell of disinfectant tickling her gag reflex, imaginings of horrible things brought a sour taste to her mouth, and stiffened her legs.

Her body physically rebelled, refused to kneel. But, she was here for Elias; she'd sacrificed everything for that kid. What was this last shred of pride?

"Kneel, Princess."

Swallowing down the taste of bile, she scanned the crowd as if someone in it might help her.

For the first time in the night, Spencer was not her monitor. Owen stood by, deadpan, waiting for Klara to obey. They had never been friendly. In fact, not a single Dungeon Monitor at Black Light had said more than hello and goodbye to her.

Out of deference to Spencer.

Who was not there as he'd been for whipping, the breath play...

She'd been abandoned.

Will was eager, happy enough to force her down. "Kneel!"

Klara pushed back against him, crumbling under his greater strength. Panicked, she asked, "And then what?"

"Release your bladder."

That's it? She just had to pee on the floor. No... there would be more. Cutting a glance to the crowd Klara observed the line of men eager to be a part of what was coming. She knew what happened on these tiles.

Her voice was unsteady. "I don't want to."

"You have a safeword, Princess."

Squatting over the drain it took her an eternity to make her muscles let go. A splash came. There had been no bathroom breaks all night, a thing that had not occurred to her until a warm flood pooled around her toes. It didn't run down the drain as fast as she'd hoped, the yellow puddle growing until it reached and enveloped the tips of Will's patent leather shoes.

"You disgusting girl. Look what you did!"

Her flesh went cold. Will was into it. This was his kink and he wanted to play. She knew he was a sadist, knew what that meant: the more she hated it, the more he would get off. She was screwed.

Klara whispered the words, "I'm sorry, sir," between shaking breaths.

"Lick them clean." He took her by the hair, pulling her forward until she'd slipped from her squat, falling hard to her hands and knees.

Fingers wet with urine, feeling the cold tile leach away any warmth, she sobbed a single protest. "No!"

"Princess won't obey," Will barked to the swarm, singling one man out. "You. Show her what happens to bad girls."

There was a zip before warmth splashed her back. Klara cried out, trying to back away from the stream of piss. Will held her by the hair, blocked her retreat with his grip.

It was dripping down her back, between her butt crack, tricking over thighs, calves, Klara gagging between shouts of, "Stop!"

More men were invited to join, and they took no time saturating her until it was dripping in her hair, running in her eyes. Mouth pressed tightly closed, Klara found she could hardly breathe. She could smell it, taste it, and was going to throw up right there.

Everyone has their breaking point, and hers was reached the second Will threw her head back and ordered, "Open your mouth."

He had his cock pointed right at her face, aimed, ready to defile her.

Eyes wide, she panicked the second a few drips dribbled from the tip. Klara fought him off in earnest. "Red! RED! SPENCER!"

It stopped with such precise timing, the room gone deathly quiet— all that could be heard was Klara's dry heaving turning to sobs as she huddled over in the puddle. She had her hands over her ears, shaking so hard she couldn't make her legs push her away from the mess.

"Help her up." It was Owen. Who he was speaking to Klara didn't know.

The instant she felt hands, she shrieked, cowering away. "DON'T TOUCH ME!"

"Give her a moment." A new pair of shoes showed up in her line of sight. They were brown, scuffed, and clashed with the yellow piss on the tile. Whoever it was laid a towel over her back.

Gathering it around her like a shield, Klara bawled, unable to lift up her head.

* * *

EVERYONE HAD HEARD her scream *red*, scream his name. Every remaining scene had stopped as per protocol. But, he had not been able to get to her before she'd scrambled from the floor, bolting towards the women's locker room.

It was Owen who Spencer unleashed his wrath upon. "What happened?"

The Dungeon Monitor frowned. "The scene escalated quickly and Klara safeworded."

"Escalated quickly?" Spencer swung his head towards Will, eyes flared, teeth showing. "What did you do to her?"

Tucking his dick away, Will zipped his fly and shrugged. "I broke her. Looks like we lose."

Spencer saw red, lunging forward only to be caught by Owen's full weight.

"I observed the whole scene. Mr. Coleman was aggressive, but he didn't break any rules. Neither did any of the men participating."

There were others standing on the tile, others who had lined up and added to the mess on the floor.

Growling, Spencer pushed Owen off, and fought the urge to crack a fist into Will's jaw. "You saw how she reacted when the men in your last scene ejaculated on her body. How could you invite strangers to urinate on her? You knew it would push her too far."

Will dropped the casual façade. "Spencer, I've not exactly enjoyed playing the third wheel to your unrequited crush. Why you put that woman in a position to fail, yet follow her around like a lost dog, I can't say. What I can say is that it was you who pushed her into something she wasn't ready for. You're the reason she didn't safeword the instant the ball landed on watersports. She had to learn play is not about *winning*, it's about self-discovery. And you have to live with the guilt for not teaching her that yourself."

"You don't know what you're talking about."

He knew far more than Spencer might like. "Without this job she can't pay for her brother's tuition. Did you know that? She was whoring herself out tonight for him. It might have been safe, it might have been consensual, but it wasn't sane. You drove her to do it, Spencer."

Spencer ground his teeth. "Do not call her a whore."

Standing his ground, Will crossed his arms over his chest. "She only just told me before the scene. Had I known, I would have never agreed to partner her. This was a lesson for you both."

"Don't think this is over, Coleman." Spencer shoved past, heading straight for the women's locker room. "I'll deal with you later."

CHAPTER 12

Spencer could hear her crying from behind the shower curtain. He'd invaded the women's locker room, shooing off the few inside as if he had a right to be there. He didn't, but he couldn't stop himself at the sound of Klara's grief.

They weren't the tears earned by a whipping, they were the whimpers of a traumatized woman. Pulling back the curtain, he made out the shape of her body in a thick cloud of steam. Klara was standing under the spray, the water turned all the way to hot. Arms wrapped around her body she had her eyes screwed shut, shaking like a leaf.

Pulling off his jacket, he let it fall on the floor behind him, and called to her. "Klara..."

Her lip was trembling, and though she opened her eyes, she didn't say a word.

Fully dressed, he walked into the water with her, reaching around her body to adjust the spray from scalding to warm. She shielded her breasts and met his eyes, but it wasn't in defiance. It was in surrender.

She'd been reduced to nothing. She had lost.

White dress shirt sopping wet, Spencer ignored the water and reached for the shampoo dispenser on the wall. He filled his palm and brought it to her head.

While she cried he washed her hair. "There is nothing wrong with you, Klara. You are not unclean."

The lathers smelled of lavender. Spencer worked it into her scalp, standing under the weight of her projected distrust.

Teeth chattering, Klara muttered. "Your shoes are getting wet."

A smirk came to the corner of his lips. It was so like her to mouth off.

Spencer moved closer, the back of her head cradled in his hands, and pressed his lips to Klara's forehead. "I'm sorry. I am sorry for everything."

"You'll catch a cold." A hit of annoyance colored her complaint.

"Klara, I don't give a fuck about my clothes being wet." He was smiling, forceful and gentle all at once. "Tilt your head back so I can rinse out your hair."

She obeyed, closed her eyes, and let the stream of water sluice the bubbles down her body. Spencer was very thorough, taking his time to massage her scalp until the tears stopped and a bloom of color began to return to her cheeks. When her hair was clean, he attended the rest of her. First he cupped her cheeks, using his thumbs to stroke her skin, rinsing soap away with a soft touch. He washed her neck, shoulders, working downward until he had to take her wrists and pull them from her breasts.

She let him do it, let him expose her chest, but started crying again the second he moved to wash them.

"Shhh. Come here." He pulled her into a strong embrace, Klara sobbing on his shoulder clinging to the wet cotton of his shirt. While she purged he soaped her back, taking time to massage the welts and forming bruises. "You were so brave. I was the coward, Klara. I need you to be brave a little bit longer."

Hopeless, she whimpered. "I didn't win..."

Untangling her clinging arms, Spencer met her eye. "You won the moment you walked in the door."

It was as if she hadn't registered he'd spoken, Klara desperate to be heard. "Jack Varens won't take me back. He made calls to his friends. No good bar in D.C. will hire me. I don't know what else I can do to show you I can belong here. Please..."

"Take a deep breath, sweetheart." He nodded when she complied. "Good. Another one."

Lips shaking she did everything he told her to, calming a little more with each heartbeat.

Taking her arm, he lathered from shoulder to fingertips, mirroring the movements on the other side, all the while softly smiling down at her.

The flat of her stomach he stroked in large foamy circles, her hips, buttocks, going so far as to kneel at her feet so he might soap up each one of her legs.

A large bruise was forming under her right knee—one Spencer knew she had not received in any of the other scenes. He put his lips to it, felt her stiffen, and glanced up like a penitent child.

"This was my fault."

She shook her head. "Will pushed me down."

"It was my fault, Klara. I should never have fired you. I should never have said the things I said to you." His face was one of utter shame. "You're right. I was a jerk from the day we met. You weren't supposed to come in and be beautiful and wonderful and funny... not when I couldn't have you. I acted like a child denied a toy."

He'd gone to kissing the soft skin near her navel, kneading his thumb from her knee to her hip. "Will you forgive me?"

"No."

He was undaunted by her petulance, smirking again as his fingertips trailed closer to her inner thigh. "How about now?"

The last thing Klara should have been feeling was arousal, the twinge and her subsequent gasp when he'd ghosted a touch near the place between her legs, too nice.

Spencer purred the words like butter melting over hot bread. "Klara, you're a very bad girl, and I like you that way."

Will Coleman had wanted a good girl. A Princess. It had not fit her at all.

Having heard Spencer say *bad girl,* her pussy fluttered, her clit thrummed, and Klara all but moaned.

Spencer stood in a fluid motion, urging her back through the spray until the warm wall met her back. Broad chest pinning her where she could not get away, he smirked down at the wide-eyed troublemaker and promised, "I'm going to show you how to be bad, when to behave —I am going to punish you and reward you, and you're going to like it."

"You're an asshole, Spencer."

Leaning down, he breathed over her mouth, "I know," before setting claim with a hungry kiss.

There was no civility in the way he devoured her mouth. Hands claiming flesh, pulling her hips flush to the growing erection in his trousers, Spencer growled into her mouth that she was his.

When his fingers hitched her thigh upward, so his groin might rub against the place his cock longed to be, Klara threw back her head. Tearing at his belt, yanking down a stubborn zipper he stood there half dressed, soaking wet, cock in hand.

Brushing the slippery mouth of her cunt, he hesitated. Vasectomy aside, there was no condom. He'd have to leave her there to get one, forfeit the moment he might never achieve again. The only way to own her was to finish what they'd started. "I want to fuck you. Klara, tell me I can."

She was breathless, impatient, bearing down on him without thought.

She'd sunk halfway down his length before he found the will to groan, "I don't have a condom. You need to give me permission." Gripping the flesh of her breasts, he pinched her nipple hard enough she stilled, adding, "Or I can make you come by other means."

Her complaint was immediate. "If you're going to call me a bad girl, then you are going to fuck me. That should be the first rule."

One hint of her sass and he drove home, stealing her breath and growling, "Bad girl."

She was putty in his hands, Spencer meticulous thrust by thrust. He knew exactly what would make her eyes roll back, clawing at her breasts while gently rocking in and out of her pussy. This was a woman that fed off both hard and soft. She'd want to be challenged and cuddled.

There would not be any other way to keep her attention.

Leaving her mouth, he licked and bit down her neck. At her ear he began to describe how her pussy felt squeezing tight around his cock, how he'd imagined it, the things he wanted to do to her in filthy detail until she began to come, scratching at his back when her knees buckled.

It was a fulfilling, perfect orgasm—not blinding or burning through her, but nurturing the places that were raw and lonely. Spencer let go, joining her the second he heard her cry out his name. From the base of his spine glorious tension gathered, shooting from his tight sack right down his throbbing shaft, until he was spurting white hot come deep inside his *bad girl*.

He was panting, forehead to the tile, Klara trapped between his shuddering body and the wall. "Klara, will you go out to dinner with me Friday night?"

Soaked through and through, Spencer still deep inside her, Klara began to chuckle. "Can I pick the restaurant?"

"No." There would be no negotiation once she consented. He would take her out, dress her in red, and show her all he could offer. Spencer kissed her breathless, demanding, "Say yes."

Giggling, she teased. "I'll have to ask my boss for the night off. He can be pretty unreasonable."

Grumbling a lust drenched warning, Spencer cautioned, "You have until the count of three to say yes. One."

It was her turn to kiss him. Arms around his neck, it was softly done with a whispered, "Yea, boss, I'll go out with you."

"I would have tied you up and thrown you over my shoulder if I had to." He met her eyes, running his thumb over her lips. "Now I'll save the rope for after dinner."

THE END

443

ABOUT THE AUTHOR

USA Today bestselling author and Amazon Top 25 bestselling author, Addison Cain is best known for her dark romances, smoldering Omegaverse, and twisted alien worlds. Her antiheroes are not always redeemable, her lead females stand fierce, and nothing is ever as it seems.

Deep and sometimes heart wrenching, her books are not for the faint of heart. But they are just right for those who enjoy unapologetic bad boys, aggressive alphas, and a hint of violence in a kiss.

WHERE TO FIND ADDISON CAIN:

- Website - http://addisonlcain.com
- Facebook - https://www.facebook.com/AddisonlCain/
- Goodreads - https://www.goodreads.com/AddisonCain
- BookBub - https://www.bookbub.com/authors/addison-cain

OTHER BOOKS BY ADDISON CAIN

The Alpha's Claim Series:
Born to be Bound: Book One
Born To Be Broken: Book Two
Reborn: Book Three

The Irdesi Empire Series:
Sigil: Book One
Sovereign: Book Two

Anthologies:
The Dark Forest: A Collection of Erotic Fairytales

Historical Romance:
A Trick of the Light

Available Summer 2017:
Alpha's Control Book One

UNBROKEN

A BLACK LIGHT: VALENTINE ROULETTE NOVELLA

by

Maren Smith

CHAPTER 1

*A*bby knew how late she was, not because she couldn't stop checking the time, but because the nearest parking garage was completely packed. The local joke was Congress must be in session. Having spent the day shuttling back and forth from the airport to various hotels in the area, she knew it was going to be a busy conference week. Great for her paycheck. Not so great when it came to trying to find a parking spot.

"Come on, people," she muttered as she wended from one level of the underground garage to the next. "Take a freakin' cab, already."

She checked her watch again. Runway wasn't open tonight and Black Light's Valentine's event wasn't advertised to start for another fifteen minutes. She still had time, but crap, crap, crap! She was going to have to run the half block that separated this garage from the psychic shop that fronted as the entrance to tonight's BDSM club of choice. She never should have taken that last pickup. Airport runs always took longer than expected, but regardless of her holiday plans, it was hard to turn down a paying fare when she didn't yet have next semester's full tuition in the bank.

She wasn't the only late arrival cruising up and down the sloping aisles in search of a vacant spot. The headlights of a big black SUV lit up her side mirror as it crept around the corner, slowly cruising down as she was coming up on the opposite side of the garage.

"I see you, you big jerk," she said under her breath. She knew that SUV. She knew the driver too. Frankly, she didn't like either one of them.

The SUV sped up just a hair and Abby's reaction was instantaneous. She hit the gas, reaching the end of her aisle a good ten seconds before he did. That's when she saw it: a narrow wedge of a parking space between two oversized trucks, one of which hugged the passenger-side line while the other's rear driver's-side tires were slanted a good four inches over.

"Ha!" She stomped the gas, romping it around the close corner and sliding—tires squealing as she hit a patch of black ice—into the waiting space just a car's width ahead of the black SUV, which promptly slammed its brakes to keep from running into her. Safe, sane and always play-by-the-rules Newton hadn't been going as fast as she had and so didn't slide, but before she grabbed her purse off the passenger seat, unbuckled her belt and stepped out of the car, his window was rolled down.

"Seriously?" he demanded, hooking his elbow out the window. Gripping the top of the steering wheel, he frowned at her. It was winter. Although only a quarter to eight, the sun had long gone to bed and the sky was black, but the dim amber of the overhead lights lit up the disapproving frown that pulled at Newton's mouth. "Packed as this place is, and that's how you drive?"

"Cabby," she reminded as she locked her doors. "Scaring the shit out of people with our driving since 1897."

"The recklessness is only half as scary as your attitude. I wonder if you'd still think it funny if you hit something... or someone."

Slamming the door, Abby walked the length of her car towards his. "Did I take your parking space?" she asked, not bothering to disguise her mocking tone or hide her grin. "Is it the last spot in the whole parking garage? Is it the last one?"

His right hand on the steering wheel flexed, the long fingers stretching outward before he re-gripped the wheel. He said nothing, which only made her smile widen. Handsome as Newton was, she saw no point in trying to be nice to him. He didn't like her; had never liked her. Well over two years ago when she had first been vetted as a Crucible member, he'd taken an instant dislike to her. When she'd been vetted into the Overtime Club, it was the same. But even now after Terry—better known as Muscles among the other DMs—had helped her obtain one of Black Light's discounted new sub rates, for some reason, Newton still glared. To this day, she had no idea what she'd done to offend him, but she couldn't remember a time when he'd looked at her without wearing that same stern frown.

Like he was her Dom, and she was a particularly rotten submissive.

Except that he wasn't; and neither was she. She was a damn-fine submissive. And these days, she no longer wondered what she'd done to irritate him way back when. Oh no, these days, she went out of her way to earn his disapproval. Irritating the hell out of certain people was the spice that made life worth living. Just like now. With one hand resting on the tailgate of the pickup truck parked beside her and her other knuckled against her hip, and the frigid February wind blowing through the garage and up under her black winter coat, she gave him her best 'suck ass' grin.

"I guess one of us is going to have to find another place to park." Her grin widened, showing a bit of teeth. "There's another garage three blocks down the street. Near the park. You know, the one that's filled to the concrete brim with about a bazillion winter birds. You'll be digging your car out with a shovel by the end of the night."

"Yes," he said, gritting his teeth. "I know where it is."

"Have a nice walk."

His frown deepened. Pulling his arm back in, he found the button to roll the window up.

"Loser," she called helpfully, just before the window closed. "Move along."

She shooed at him, but he had already shifted into forward gear. His giant black SUV crawled around the corner and continued down the slope toward the exit. She waved, but if he looked back, she never saw it. Hopefully, he didn't look back, because Murphy's Law ruled her life and if he did, then it was probably at that exact moment when her foot found that same slick spot her tire had and, skidding out from under her, down she went. She set off the theft alarm on the car she used for balance while she got her feet back under her.

The parking garage amplified the sound. She could still hear that alarm seven minutes later when she finally made it down the block, across the street to the row of buildings that harbored the psychic shop.

"Hoodlums," she told Luis when the door unexpectedly opened and he stuck his head out to check the street.

"Uh huh." He gave her a knowing look, but held the door wider so she could slip past him and come inside.

Abby flashed her membership card to gain access to the cold tunnel that led down to Danny at the security desk and the locker room, and then the dungeon beyond. A shot of pure giddiness bolted through her, raising all the fine hairs on her body. Without exception, Valentine's Day was the worst holiday on the face of the planet. She never had a date. Between work and college, her social life outside of study groups—and the two nights a month that she squeezed out of her budget so she could get her kink—on was practically nil. But this particular Valentine's Day was different.

She shivered, weeks' worth of building excitement sizzling through every part of her at once. She'd been looking forward to this night from the moment she found out her recruit application had been accepted. No, she wouldn't get to pick her Dominant tonight. In fact, she wouldn't even know who he was until he spun her name on the giant roulette wheel, like the one pictured in the header of the email that had been sent to every member on the mailing list. That seemed a small drawback compared to what else this night promised—three solid hours of fun-filled, no strings attached, anything goes scening. So long as she didn't safeword out, the night would even culminate in a prize: a fully-paid, thirty day membership. Abby shivered again, thrilled at the very thought of being able to come here every single party night for a full month—so long as she wasn't working. The new sub discount was great, but it was still money out of her pocket. As it was, she was struggling to afford one night a week.

The burly security guard looked up from the short stack of papers he was studying when she exited the tunnel into the security room. "You made it," he said, by way of a greeting.

"As if I'd miss out on any part of tonight." She was so close to the dungeon now she could smell the leather and wood. She shivered all over again. Something Danny must have noticed as he assigned her a locker for the night.

"Nervous?" he asked.

"What could I possibly be nervous about?" she scoffed, handing over her membership card.

"You don't pay tonight." Danny handed it right back. "I just need to log you in and assign a locker. So... not nervous at all, huh?"

"Nope." She stubbornly refused to think about the four hard limits she'd listed on her application—all of which Jaxson had assured her would be strictly upheld—and, perhaps more importantly, the two remaining ones which hadn't made the cut. If she rolled them on the wheel, her only choice then would be to either do it, or to safeword out. Unfortunately, while safewords were always an option, taking that option meant failing the competition. Failure simply was not an option. Not for Abby.

The palms of her hands grew clammy before she banished the unpleasant thought. There were more than thirty kinks on the roulette wheel the Black Light administrators had designed. Only two terrified her to the point of cold sweats and panic. Both were on her list, but already her stomach was rolling. She pressed her hands over the worst of it, as if holding it hard enough might still the unease. "Am I the last to arrive?"

"The last submissive," he confirmed, tapping at his iPad. "As soon as Newton gets here, then we'll have all our Doms too."

"How did he make it into this event?" she grumbled.

"How did you?" Danny countered, with a pointed look.

Abby didn't know if Danny was an actual Dom or not. She'd never seen him play, and just because he worked here on party nights, that didn't necessarily mean he was into the lifestyle. But if he wasn't, damn, he had that look down.

"I guess it doesn't matter," she said, more to herself than him.

"Once I'm partnered up, I'll be so busy having a good time that I won't even notice he's here."

"Unless you're matched to him."

"Bite your tongue!" She laughed as if the very thought of that didn't make her stomach flip-flop all over again. Not that she was concerned. Fifteen pairs had been signed up for this event. Fifteen Doms, which gave her a one-in-fifteen chance of rolling the dud, which also gave her a fourteen-in-fifteen chance to roll literally anybody else. Her heart quickened, thudding against her ribs in a cadence of new-budding excitement. "This is going to be a good night," she said, rubbing her hands down her winter-coat-covered thighs. "It's going to be the best night of my life. Not scary at all."

Studying her, Danny set his iPad down on his desk. "Are you sure?"

She rubbed her thighs again, every trace of confidence within her suddenly turning false in the time it took to meet his steady gaze. She tried to laugh, but it came out faltering and nervous-sounding. "Of course, I am. Why wouldn't I be?"

"That depends."

"On?"

"What you're trying to prove and to whom."

Abby stood in front of his desk, unable to break her stare from his and suddenly feeling every bit as cold as she had been walking down that cold tunnel outside. "I don't have anything to prove," she heard herself say. She didn't know how she managed it. Her lips felt oddly numb and uncooperative. Like they were someone else's and she was borrowing them to talk through. "I've got every right to be here, if I want…"

"I didn't say one word about rights." Danny planted his hands on the edge of his desk—he had huge hands; Abby could remember thinking that once before, but the realization struck her again now and with it came the most absurd urge to circle around this suddenly too small desk and let the burly security guard pull her into a strong, secure hug with those massive hands of his—he leaned towards her. Arms braced, he brought himself right to her eye-level.

"If you think Terry wouldn't tell us something as important as this before you were accepted as a new recruit, you can think again," he said evenly. "That man beat you up—"

"I'm fine."

"Hog-tied you—"

She tried to laugh again, but only because she had to do something and covering her ears and singing 'la-la-la' at the top of her lungs really wasn't an option.

"Assaulted you," Danny brutally continued. "Strangled you. Threw you in the trunk of his car, drove you out to butt-fuck nowhere, and left you for dead in the middle of the night in an Amish corn field."

She spread her arms. Everything inside her felt shaky and cold. "And yet, here I am."

"Yes, you are."

"I survived," she insisted, as if such a thing required proof above and beyond standing here in front of him.

"Yes, you did."

"I'm fine." She had to insist that too, and she hated that her voice squeaked when she did.

He arched an eyebrow. "How many plates and-or screws did it take to put your jaw back together again?"

Twelve.

Her mouth tightened, letting her feel with heightened awareness the two points where her teeth still didn't meet up quite the way they had... before. She cleared her throat. She also stiffened her spine, standing as tall and as straight as she could. "I'm not here to prove anything to anyone, Danny. I just want what everyone else here tonight wants: to have a good time." She thought about it. "Preferably with someone who isn't a giant asshat." She blanched when Danny cocked an eyebrow. "Uh... I didn't mean you."

A corner of his mouth quirked into a very small, very crooked smile. "No, I know you didn't." He arched both eyebrows at her now, giving her a look that—despite that smile—held an even greater level of severity than normal. "Terry has his eye on you tonight. You know how you get when you're starting to panic but too stubborn to call it, and now so do all the DMs. The second any of them suspect that's starting to happen tonight, you won't need to safeword. They'll call it for you. Got it?"

She caught herself before she actually stomped her foot. Folding her arms across her chest, she demanded, "Did Terry do that to any of the other submissives?"

"For," Danny emphasized. "Not to, and none of the other submissives went through what you did. This isn't up for debate. Either you agree to his terms and be aware that he's going to be watching you closely all the way to midnight, or you turn your little ass around and take a walk. Which would be a pity since I suspect—" Danny deliberately dropped his stare from her eyelevel to her chest. "—beneath that thick, black, scratchy-ass wool winter coat, you're probably wearing one of your cute little cock-tease outfits, and lord knows I'd hate to miss out on how you like to flash me before you go inside."

Her turn now to cock an eyebrow, Abby struck a pose. She also untied her waist belt, plucked the buttons undone from chest to hip, and whipped her coat open. It was her favorite part of the night: the Great Reveal. She'd spent more time on her outfit tonight than normal, and from the way Danny's eyes lit with hungry approval, she knew every minute of that time had been well spent. This particular little black number she'd picked up at the mall. Made entirely of black lace netting, the babydoll cut gown was see-through from top to bottom, showing off her barely-there thong panties and complete lack of a bra. She wasn't wearing stockings tonight. Hell, as soon as she was in the main room, she wouldn't be wearing shoes. Letting her coat drop to the floor, she stood before him knowing she looked damn good.

"Hell, yeah," Danny said appreciatively.

Abby turned around, showing him the equally transparent view from the back, and cast him a knowing smile over her shoulder. He was staring at her ass, shaking his head and not bothering to hide his approval.

"Victoria Secret, eat your heart out," he said.

"It's not my heart I want eaten tonight." Very deliberately, she bent over, taking her sweet time in retrieving her fallen coat. "Spankable?" she coyly asked.

"Among other things." His voice had lowered, thickened, become that soul-shivering growl that she loved to hear her Doms use.

She looked back over her shoulder again. "Want me to twerk it a little?"

"I'd rather be able to do my job without the added embarrassment of a full-on woody. No, thank you."

"Be nice to me," Abby said with a smirk, "and I'll tell you where to get this exact dress for your girlfriend."

Abby had hooked the collar of her coat but was still completely bent over when the door to the secret passage yanked open, letting in a gust of extremely cold air and an almost as cold Newton.

"Je-suh—" Halfway over the threshold, he stopped both mid-step and mid-exclamation when he saw her. The heavy metal door swung shut, bumping his back hard enough to nudge him the rest of the way over the threshold. He never once took his eyes off her upturned and mostly bare ass.

Straightening slowly, Abby fought back the urge to strike another pose. She folded her coat over her arm instead. Now he was staring at her tits. She let him too. An odd tingling sensation lit up her belly, spreading goose bumps up her back, down her arms, reaching into the valley between her breasts to pepper its effect across the halves of each exposed mound.

"Do you like what you see?" she asked.

At first, he didn't seem to hear her. But then she saw him visibly startle and at last his gaze snapped all the way up to lock with her eyes. He didn't say one word. Nor did the stark somberness of his expression change, although she was amused to note a slow flush of color rise to stain his winter-ruddy cheeks. It might have been the cold, but she much preferred to think that blush a result of having just been caught with his eyeballs in the titty jar.

"It's okay." She took two sultry steps closer to him. "I don't mind if you look. Here."

Shifting her coat away from her body, she turned in a single, slow circle, letting him gaze his fill. However, when she finished and once more stood facing him, his gaze remained stubbornly locked on hers. In fact, she'd have sworn it hadn't moved. The tingles in her stomach morphed into the sinuous fluttering of a dozen butterfly wings, all of them tickling at her in ways that made her silly heart flutter and her pussy twitch along in time. Especially when she saw his jaw tighten and his throat swallow.

"Very nice," he finally said, his tone was every bit as expressionless as his face, but Abby wasn't fooled.

For the second time that night, she let her smile grow teeth. "Yeah. Too bad 'look' is all you'll ever be able to do. Because this right here, is the closest you'll ever come to touching me. Tonight or any other night. Not without violating consent."

At last. His coffee-brown eyes darkened even more, ever so faintly narrowing on her words, though he made no attempt to respond in kind. Still, any reaction out of a disapproving ice giant like Newton was, in her opinion, as good as victory. The lower simmer of temper lurking just under that handsome frown was proof enough that she was getting to him. That right there was almost enough to make her whole night.

"Come anywhere near me tonight and I'll scream consent violation so loud that the Runway regulars will hear it. And considering Runway isn't open tonight," she smugly pointed out, "that's loud."

Turning on her three-inch-high stiletto heels, Abby put all the sultry wiggle into her strut toward the lockers. It would have been perfect too, if only she hadn't stepped on the hem of her own coat. Like a submissive on a too-short leash, she stumbled, tottering on her high heels and ruining her own snark-exit from the conversation. She caught herself after only one faltering step, quickly yanked the hem of her coat out from under her foot, and found her balance. Balling up her wayward coat, Abby tugged and smoothed her dress back down into place and stole a quick look behind her to make sure no one was laughing. Arms folded across his chest, Newton hadn't cracked so much as a smile; Danny had a hand over his eyes. Not her best walk away, but no one was making fun of her, so…

"Nailed it," she said under her breath. Head held high, she walked away as if her face wasn't burning and her hands weren't shaking. Not that she had anything to be embarrassed about. This wasn't the first clumsy thing she had done in front of Danny and, to be honest, it wasn't likely to be the last. As for Newton... well, who cared what he thought? He didn't like her and she was long past caring why. No way was she going to base the success of her night on his opinion of her or anything she did, especially since she probably wouldn't see him once the event got started. Give her someone with a stern but steady hand, someone she could sink into the right headspace for and Newton could start his scene right next to her and she'd never notice him.

That suited her just fine. Stuffing both purse and coat into her assigned locker, Abby left Danny to finish checking Newton in and pushed through the heavy door that guarded the pleasurable wonders of Black Light's dungeon. As it always did, Abby paused just inside to drink it all in—the evenly spaced play stations, the dark dungeon décor, the multicolored track lights that lit up each stock and cross and spanking bench enough for those getting their kink on to see what they were doing... and for them to be seen by those who liked to watch. The bar was already open, tables and chairs provided pockets of comfort for all those who would not be participating in the main event, and up on the stage, two massive roulette wheels had already been set up. Her name would be on one; the other would be sectioned out in a variety of potential kinks.

Her stomach tightened. *Be strong.* She rubbed her hands on her thighs again, the damp of her palm soaking into the transparent lace. *You can do this.*

That one awful day two long years ago was not going to rule the rest of her life. Tonight... tonight she was going to break another paralyzing tie.

"Excuse me."

Abby quickly stepped aside, letting Newton pass her with his giant black suitcase of a playbag rolling along behind him. He headed straight to the Roulette stage and the contestants already gathered there.

This was it. Time to take her place among them.

With one last steadying breath, she pressed both hands over her stomach to stop its nervous fluttering before weaving through the crowded tables to join them.

It was going to be a good night.

CHAPTER 2

*F*uck. His. Life.

Newton stood frozen on the stage as the roulette wheel turned in one direction, the white marble spun in the other and—thunk!—dropped with a bounce into a named slot. Just over half the waiting submissives had already been chosen and now stood to one side next to their assorted Doms. Of the remaining ones, however, he only knew two by name: Abby and Marcy the Crier. God help him, but he would put up with anyone, including Marcy, to avoid spending the next few minutes, much less hours of scening, with Abby. But no. The damn ball wobbled to a stop and in that moment, every nerve in his body bounced wildly between the culminating buzz of weeks' worth of heightened anticipation and this curious prickling, crawling sensation that seemed only to intensify the longer he stood frowning at the black pie-wedge with Abby's name on it.

"Abby," Chase announced, removing her name from the wheel and handing a corresponding index card to Newton long enough for him to glance over the hard limits she'd listed: Medical play, fine with him. Confinement of any kind—so, no locking her in the closet until she promised to behave; more's the pity. Masks and gags—damn—and rope—double damn; he loved rope. It wasn't a lot to memorize, but once he had, he dropped the index card with her name and limits onto the discard pile with those who had already been picked.

At this point in the process, the other subs had ventured onstage to join their newly selected Doms and spun the roulette wheel that designated their first scene of the evening. Stepping back from the wheel, Newton glanced expectantly across the stage. In that cluster of waiting submissives gathered before it, Abby wasn't hard to pick out. She looked stunning. She always looked stunning, but apart from dropping her head back to cast her 'why me' glare at the defenseless tracklights above, she wasn't moving. That stung a little.

"Lucky," someone behind him whispered. "I was hoping for her."

"Want to swap?" Newton replied without looking to see who it was. He was too busy trying to decide how irritated he was—enough to drag her up onto the stage by her hair… or to quit the event before it had even started.

"Abby?" Chase said, beckoning her to come up on the stage. "Come on. You're holding up the line."

Dragging her head up, Abby looked right at Newton. Everyone in that room could feel her unspoken disappointment. That included Chase, who crooked an authoritative finger at Abby and summoned her up onto the stage as easily as, well, a Dom with a short-leashed sub. And Abby came, although she did it dragging her feet and scowling.

"There is no swapping partners without one hell of a damned good reason, and that reason is approved only by the DMs," Chase told them both, sternly repeating what they both already knew. The rules had been printed on the applications both had agreed to back when they each registered for this event. "You can choose not to participate, but should either of you leave the premises, or fail to scene, or not complete the minimum time requirement for your scene or scenes— no less than thirty minutes if you choose three smaller ones or one long scene at no less than ninety minutes—or call 'Red' before you've met the full ninety-minute requirement outlined in the terms of your applications, then you will both be declared forfeit."

He gave them each a stern and, to Newton's eye, oddly paternal 'Are you going to mind me, or do I have to spank' frown. He knew

Chase and very much liked the man, but looks like that tended to slither up a man's spine and set his teeth on edge. A dominant soul, he didn't need or enjoy being told what he already knew he had to do. Oddly enough, that same look had a much different effect on Abby. Her face lost some of its glowering mutiny, her shoulders drooped and her gaze fell to the floor.

"I want verbal acknowledgement that you both understand the terms of this event," Chase persisted.

"I understand," Abby muttered.

Newton folded his arms across his chest, gritting his teeth to keep back the sarcasm. He still liked Chase and he understood why MC felt the need to say this—it wasn't a secret how he and Abby felt about one another; by now, most of the newbies in the audience tonight had likely picked up on it. Chase was right to address it now before it became an issue, but Newton still didn't like being talked to as if he were three. It took effort to keep his tone light and civil. "So do I."

"Do you plan to proceed?"

For his part, absolutely. Black Light was one of the newest BDSM dungeons in the whole of the D.C. area and yet, it was already touted as being one of the best. It was big, it was spacious... it was still a money pit for the owners, but it was rumored that, unless something catastrophic happened, the dungeon space would be completely paid off and running in the black much sooner than it took most new businesses to either succeed or fold. That was a huge achievement for any club and virtually unheard of when it came to BDSM-oriented ones.

"I do," Newton said.

Abby nodded as well, though she had to take a deep and bracing breath before she could make herself do it.

The stern MC gave them each another dark look before, content that his warning was being taken seriously. He motioned Abby toward the submissive's roulette wheel. "Take your spin."

Accepting the marble from Chase, she waited for him to spin the wheel before dropping it onto the track. She stepped back, almost bumping into Newton. "Do you actually know how to use the things you carry about in that suitcase of yours?" she muttered at him out the side of her mouth.

"Better than you're going to wish I did," he replied the same way.

The wheel spun vigorously. Across the stage, an entire soap opera was silently taking place among the other paired partners. A pretty boy switch was trying on his Dom-y pants with a submissive who liked to top from the bottom. One submissive had already run for the door, sparking an impromptu capture scene when her Dom chased her down and dragged her back. And if that wasn't bad enough, unless the wheels of fate aligned themselves with this particular roulette wheel, there was a very real chance that the happily divorced Mastersons might actually get stuck playing with one another.

Newton looked at Abby again, but no. The prize for the most unlikely couple here still went to them.

"I just want you to know, I'm a big girl." Abby watched the marble and wheel spin, the force of both slowly beginning to diminish. She folded her arms across her chest. She probably thought it made her look tough, but all Newton saw when he looked down at her diminutive five-foot-four-inch height—and that included those potentially ankle-breaking stiletto heels—was a woman eight inches shorter than he was, a good eighty pounds lighter, and shy any kind of personality that he'd have found appealing. "I can take care of myself."

"I never said otherwise." Newton fought to stifle a sigh.

"Bullshit," Abby scoffed.

He frowned at her. "I beg your pardon?"

"You did so too say otherwise."

"Tickling!" Chase announced to the room when the marble finally dropped into a scene slot.

"When?" Newton demanded.

"Now," Chase started to reply, but stopped when Newton held up a staying finger.

"When?" he demanded of her again.

"Oh, like you don't know," she hissed back. Mouth snapping shut, her eyes narrowed and her nostrils flared. Like she had any right to be upset when he'd been putting up with her snarky ass for years!

His teeth ground. "If I knew, I wouldn't be asking because I'd already know. And knowing is half the battle. G.I. Joe taught us that."

One of the already partnered subs giggled at that.

Up until that moment, Newton hadn't known that Abby could deliver her snarkiest comments without ever saying a word, but the look she turned on him said everything she no longer had to. "I didn't come here to argue with you. I came to have a good time."

"So did I."

"So did everyone else, frankly," Chase tried again. "So if you guys would just take your place over—"

Newton snapped up that silencing hand again. He also took his last deep breath and, just like his subsequent exhale, let it all go. "Look," he told her, extending his best proverbial olive branch. "We both want the same thing. It's just one night. There's nothing to be gained by this constant antagonism and I don't know about you, but I could use a 30-day free membership."

The blonde lines of her eyebrows beetled and the flatness of her mouth twitched. "Are you suggesting we put aside our differences long enough to win the prize?"

Newton inclined his head. "I promise, you can go back to hating me for no good reason tomorrow."

"I don't hate you," she snipped, twin spots of color rising to stain her cheeks. "And I have a *very* good reason."

Now it was his turn to scoff. "Like hell you do."

Her arms unfolded; her fists snapping down straight at her sides, fingers so tight that even her knuckles flushed with anger. "Like *hell* I don't!"

"Not that the audience isn't enjoying the drama, but…"

Ignoring Chase's attempt to get the event moving again, Newton gave Abby his complete and beginning-to-get-annoyed attention. "Like what? What could I possibly have done, except be an incredibly good sport about the way you badger, mock, and insult me every chance you get?"

"Who insulted who?" she shot back, eyebrows arching in outraged surprise. Somehow she pulled that look off well, too. No one knew better than he did how often he'd bled to the cutting edge of her very sharp tongue over the years, and yet he was almost convinced she didn't know what he was talking about.

"If you two aren't—"

Newton spun around. "Shush," he snapped, with just enough irate Dom in his tone to startle the MC silent. "Now you look here," he growled at Abby next, unsure whether to be pissed when she promptly knuckled her fists into her hips and growled right back at him, or be endeared by that appalling unsubmissive-like behavior. Not that submissives couldn't be feisty; he'd known more than his fair share of those, and he adored them—the fire, the sass—but usually when a Dom's temper flared, a submissive's backed down. Not Abby. No part of her was backing down and he found that at once highly aggravating and, worse, faintly arousing. He absolutely refused to be aroused by anything this woman did. "I have never in my life *ever* blindly insulted anyo—"

"The first time we met," she challenged, not letting him finish.

Newton stopped, trying to think, but coming up with nothing that could explain two long years' of enmity. It wasn't that he couldn't remember their first encounter. No one could have walked in on the scene he had and ever forgotten the sight. He remembered huge, muscular Terry—a DM at both Overtime, and now Black Light as well, but back then he'd been just another Dom competing for play partners. The large man had been picking up short, scrawny, battered Abby—her face covered in a mottle of old, ugly yellowish-brown surgery bruises—and flipping her like a pancake before slamming her to the floor.

"Don't interrupt my scene again," was all Terry had growled back then when Newton voiced a very loud and startled objection.

Even then, when Abby had looked at him, she'd looked at him with fiery dislike. She'd also picked herself up off the floor and thrown herself at Terry again, and again, and again. Fiercely. Inexhaustibly. She did it punching, kicking, screaming, and even head-butting. She did it repeatedly, with Terry pinning her for her troubles each and every time. And he didn't just pin her, sometimes he hit her back: cuffing her upside the head; slapping her—her shoulder, her hip, the back of her leg, whatever part of her that he could reach as she scrambled to find her footing; and then grabbing her by the hair to drag her around the playspace. He split her lip that night. That might have been by accident, but nobody got out of that kind of scene without bleeding a little, and God knows she drew enough of Terry's blood to make the single Kleenex she held to her lip look inconsequential in comparison.

The brutality of that scene had been appalling. It had almost reminded him... well, of an attempted rape. Every single time Terry had thrown her down, pinning her while she'd bucked and kicked and screamed until finally, eventually, every single time she wrenched a hand free to strike back, break free, and scramble up far enough to attack him all over again. It had been disturbing to watch. On so many levels, some of which bothered him so much that to this day he dared not examine them too closely.

Long hours after that horrible scene had ended, Newton remembered running into Terry in the dungeon's kitchen area. Having left Abby to recover while wrapped in a blanket on a well-used mattress in the Aftercare room, better known as the Suck and Fuck, he'd been fixing a plate of protein-heavy snacks, a few cookies, and two bottles of water from the fridge.

"What the hell?" Newton had demanded then.

"I didn't ask your opinion," Terry had told him bluntly. "Nor do I need your permission."

"No?" Newton had shot back, his temper sparking in defense of what had, at that time, been a newbie given the worst of all possible introductions into the kind of things they did. "What were you doing to her?"

"Giving her her power back," the battered Dom had replied. Then, with plate and waters in hands, he'd ignored the 'No food in the play area' rule and taken both back to Abby.

That had been almost two years ago. Now, as he stood on Black Light's stage and stared into Abby's accusing eyes, Newton had no trouble remembering any part of that night. Including the way she had glared at him when she'd finally come out of the back room, so exhausted that Terry had to help her walk to the changing room. He'd probably helped her re-dress too, Newton thought, then had to wonder where in hell *that* had come from. Not only had that been *two years ago*, but even at the time Abby and Terry had been nothing to one another but play partners. In fact, between then and now,

Newton was hard pressed to think of a Dom in this room that Abby hadn't scened with at least once.

...except him, of course.

"I am so terribly sorry," he said slowly. "It wasn't my intent to disrupt your scene, but I can see how that might be construed as insulting. In my defense, I was a little surprised. Most people come to these parties to get beaten with canes or paddles. I just... I hadn't seen anyone opt for fists before."

She looked at him as if he were an idiot. "What?" she demanded, her voice rising in both tone and volume.

"What?" he echoed back, openly bewildered.

"And a one, and a two, and..." Chase sang out, conducting the crowded room with two fingers as if they were an orchestra. And right on cue, the entire room cried back, "What?"

Newton and Abby both jumped, startled. He looked at Chase, who thumbed to the wheel. "Tickling," Chase said again. "You want to take your place with everyone else so we can continue this?"

As one, Newton and Abby looked at the wheel. Sure enough, the wheel was stopped and the marble was lying squarely in the red pie wedge marked: Tickle Fetish.

Abby studied that for a long time before, arms swaying, head tipped, her expression as close to smugly triumphant as he'd yet seen it—and Newton could have sworn by now he'd already seen every variance of that out of her—she turned on her hip to smile at him. "Good luck with that."

It was the smirk that got him, and before he could stop himself, Newton fired back, "Why? Because you're not ticklish? Or because you think I don't know how to get around that?"

Her smirk vanished and gradually relocated itself onto Newton's lips.

"I pay attention, sweetheart," he said, gesturing for her to precede him off to one side where the others had been assigned to wait until all participants had their partners.

Her chin hiked. "If that were true, you wouldn't have just apologized for the wrong thing."

It took everything he had not to swat her ass when she walked past him, head held high. His palm itched to deliver one smack —just one; it would so be worth it—where it would do her the most good. And who knew, if he spanked hard enough he might actually remember what she'd no doubt have him apologizing for two years from now. Laughing, not really finding it funny, he followed in her wake.

The remainder of the spins passed much quicker. Or maybe it only seemed that way because time moved differently when a man paid more attention to the annoyingly hostile woman standing next to him than anything else going on in the room. It was a relief when it was over and everyone filed off the stage to start their scenes. It was fun seeing which submissives rushed to find a play place and which, like Abby and the ex-Mrs. Masterson, dragged their feet like condemned prisoners bound for the gallows.

All the best stations were taken by the time Newton retrieved his playbag from the table where he'd tucked it so no one would trip over it. He lost sight of Abby in the hustle and shuffle, but spotted her again when she arched up on tiptoes to wave him out into the crowd of seated onlookers. It was an open section of floor near the rear wall, away from the other event participants, which Newton liked. On the one hand, a lot of people were going to get a bird's eye view of Abby as she challenged his authority at every step. On the other, they were going to get a bird's eye view of him putting her back in her place, too.

"How about here?" Abby asked, gesturing around them. "I doubt we'll need a lot of room for tickling."

"It's not the tickling that takes room." Newton motioned with one finger for her to turn around.

She folded her arms across her chest. Eyes narrowing, she didn't obey. "Why?"

"Because I said so."

She cocked an eyebrow.

"All right, look." Newton set his playbag upright and squared off against her. "If you don't have any intention of following the rules of the game tonight, then—"

Dropping her eyes, Abby raised both hands in instant surrender, but he wasn't about to let her off that easy.

"—don't waste my time. All I have to do is walk out of here and you lose too."

She surrendered a little higher. "You're right."

"So let's set a few ground rules right now. We both want to win tonight, but more than that, I think we both came here hoping for a night full of fun and maybe an experience or two we wouldn't ordinarily have thought to try." Newton thought about it. "Like tickling. I don't know about you, but this will be a first for me."

"It usually starts like this." Abby struck a pose, fingers curled in what she probably meant to be playfulness. But she was still a little pricklish, so the effect came out with her fingers looking more like claws. "Kitchee, kitchee koo."

He pointed at her. "Now see. This is what I'm talking about. I didn't come here tonight to argue with anybody, much less you. I came here tonight to play. So you've got one choice and I'll thank you to make it right now. You're the sub, I'm the Dom. You either do as I tell you, when I tell you, or just safeword right now. I'll go get a beer and probably have a wonderful time somewhere else. But I'm not going to put up with one more argument out of you. I mean it. One more, and I'll safeword. We can both go home. What do you say?"

Drawing a deep restraining breath, her lips flattened together. "You're right. I came here to have a good time. Just because you're a jerk doesn't mean—"

Grabbing his suitcase, Newton snapped about on his heel. He whistled through two fingers, signaling Terry from out among the nonparticipating guests where he'd found a spot from which to watch all the scenes currently taking place.

"All right, all right!" Abby hissed. She ducked around him, slapping both hands against his chest in an attempt to stay his leaving. "You win, damn it! I'll behave."

"Yeah. Like that was convincing."

Terry was coming towards them now, wading his way through the tables of onlookers.

Abby checked his progress. Newton could see 'oh crap' written all over her face right before she swallowed it—swallowing her pride along with it—and turned back to him. "I'm sorry. I don't want to call it an early night. What can I do to make you change your mind?"

"Is there a problem?" the DM asked once he'd reached them.

"Not sure," Newton said.

Her face colored and her eyes flashed, but she kept her mouth shut. Cocking his head, Newton studied her. He doubted she'd be able to maintain her angry silence longer than it took Terry to walk away again. Still, if she was willing to try... A slow smile tickled at the corners of his mouth and her eyes narrowed at him. Defiance darkened the blue of her eyes to that of a stormy sea—a submissive silently threatening to overtake him with the fury of her swells unless he did as she wanted.

And she wanted to play.

Maybe it was time she learned who was in charge and who only thought she was.

"Fine," Newton said aloud, surprising himself almost as much as he'd apparently just surprised her. "Time's a ticking. Let's do this."

Leaving his bag where it was, he approached the nearest table to swipe a vacant chair. "Is anyone using this?" he asked, and once he received a confirming 'no', he dragged it into the middle of the open spot of floor they'd secured. Positioning himself to face the audience, he dragged his suitcase over and laid it on its back directly behind the chair. Unzipping the main compartment, he dug through the neat assemblage of sorted plastic containers until he found his sensation kit.

"What is that?" Abby grudgingly asked.

Removing the lid, he selected two items—the twin of the black glove, which he left in the storage container, and a stainless steel rod, crowned by a wheel of toothy spikes. "If you have to pee, I suggest you do it now."

When he looked up, her eyes were glued to the Wartenberg wheel in his hand.

"I already told you," she tried, and for a moment he wasn't sure if she actually stammered or if it was a trick of his ears in what was rapidly becoming a noisy room. Most of the other contestants were already getting started with their scenes, but Abby wasn't distracted by them. She stared straight at him and never once looked away. "I'm not ticklish."

"That's what you said all right." Closing his playbag, Newton stood up long enough to seat himself on that waiting chair. He beckoned her to him. "Come here, Abby."

She didn't move. "Why? I mean… if there's no point, then…"

She stopped when Newton smiled.

"There's all kinds of points," he replied, and beckoned again. "Especially since, as I already told you, I pay attention."

"It's either comply or safeword and forfeit the game," Terry said implacably.

If she considered that option, she didn't give it more than a second or two before, jaw clenched and lips pressed tight, at last Abby obeyed.

CHAPTER 3

"Take your panties off," Newton said, already rolling up his sleeves. The vampire glove was draped over one strong shoulder. The metal handle of the Wartenberg was sticking out of his back jeans pocket and, God help her, the sinewy bunch and release of his muscular forearms as he freed his arms for a wider range of unencumbered motion was far more impressive than she cared to admit. It set her nerve endings humming, particularly those already prickling into wakefulness all across the surface of her bottom.

She opened her mouth, the argument—'It's a thong'—springing readily to her lips, except no more arguing, he had said. Not one more word, or he'd call the scene himself. Then they'd both lose. Much as she wanted that free month's membership, that wasn't what made her shut her mouth and keep it that way. She didn't want to lose. She refused to be seen as weak.

She was *never* going to let anyone see her like that again.

Instead of his forearms, now she stared at his hands. They were a lot like Danny's—big, blockish, with thick blunted fingers that all too soon finished fussing with his sleeves and dropped down to rest upon his jean-clad thighs. She shook herself mentally. Dropping her gaze to the floor—commercial carpet, in a dungeon; obviously, whoever came up with that bright idea wasn't in charge of after-party cleanup—Abby swallowed the last of her pride. She also dipped her hands up under the lacy hem of her babydoll negligée, hooked her thumbs in the waist of her thong panties and skimmed them down her legs.

Heat flooded her face. It took root in the middle of her chest, a tiny burning lump of shame no bigger than a kernel of corn that she could feel like a meteor embedded up under her sternum. She couldn't really say why it was there, either. It wasn't like she was completely nude and she had been before—completely nude—right here in this dungeon. What she hadn't been, however, was any kind of undressed in front of Newton. Around him, sure. But not in front of him, as if she were doing it *for* him.

"Good girl," he said approvingly as she stepped out of her panties, leaving them in a puddle of black cloth on the floor. "That wasn't so hard, was it?"

Avoiding his stare, she kept her head down and her hands clasped tight over her mons. She regretted wearing see-through lingerie. On any other night, it would have been fine, but not in front of this man. Not when he was seated where he couldn't help but see right through the lacy hem to the shadowy triangle not quite hidden behind her hands.

"Come here." He patted his thigh. "Bend over my knee."

Her gaze snapped up to his at last. "Why?" Nervous as she was, that came out sounding much harsher than she meant it to. Too late, she tried to cover her mistake. "What does that have to do with tickling?"

"You aren't in the proper headspace," Newton replied. "I could tickle you all night long and you would never respond correctly because—"

"I'm not ticklish?" she finished for him. That came out harsher than she meant it as well.

"Because you aren't in the proper mood to submit," he corrected. "Look, if you don't want to do this, then you know what you need to say. Perhaps we could try again another night?"

As if there were any way in hell she'd consent to scening with him if she weren't being forced. Rules of a stupid Valentine's Day game were hardly a gun to the head, but still...

Abby glared, as cross with herself as she was the rest of the situation. "No," she muttered. "No, it's fine."

Newton patted his lap again. "Come on, then. Right over. Let's see if we can't sweeten our grumpy baby's sour disposition."

She glared.

He cocked an eyebrow back, and the longer she stood there and the longer the silence between them stretched endlessly on, the more she began to feel exactly like that. Petulant. Childish. She had come here tonight with such high hopes and now here she was, the only submissive in the place not having any fun—except for one maybe, a submissive across the room loudly resisting the pet play activity the roulette wheel had chosen for her; already Terry was excusing himself from watching their scene to go handle the situation. So, at least there was one silver lining in this mess.

This wasn't how she'd wanted the night to go. This was just the kind of behavior that could pin a good submissive with a bad label and guarantee, even if she was invited back to play again, that no other play partners would scene with her. At least not the ones who knew what they were doing. And not just at Black Light, either. Large as the BDSM community seemed at times, it wasn't so large that gossip on bad play experiences wouldn't spread through it faster than fire through a paper factory.

Her stomach tightened. So did the tangle of her own fingers, clenched tight before her. She really, really didn't want to be the focus of that kind of gossip. She didn't want to be someone no one wanted to play with.

Abby stared at his lap, the tangle of knots in her nervous stomach growing in both number and tension. What was the worst that could happen? He'd smack her ass a few times, maybe grope and fondle a bit. She could fake a moan if she had to. Faking a laugh would be harder, but unnecessary. The requirement of the scene was that he tickle her. Whether she laughed or not was completely irrelevant.

She could do this.

Bending, Abby let her hands rest on his knee, instantly trying to tell herself that the sensation she felt rolling over her was the crawl of disgust and not the sinuous tingle of awareness waking up her nerves because she liked the solid feel of his muscles or the scent of his after-shave. She laid herself across his lap and her nipples tightened, loving the soft scrape as her heavy breasts moved underneath the gossamer flow of her negligée. One could hardly blame them for not recognizing disgust when she felt it. Nipples could be easily confused like that.

"Nice." The heat of Newton's hand settled warm against the back of her thigh. His other swept the back of her skimpy outfit up, baring the round curves of her bottom.

There went that rolling wave of disgust again, prickling up her legs to center beneath his palm and sweeping out across her back, wrapping her middle, crawling her ribs, confusing her breasts to make the beaded tips tighten even more.

"Let's see if we can't put you into a more compliant mood."

Abby stiffened like a plank when his hand moved from the back of her thigh to rest, as if it belonged there, on her ass. That prickled now too. The whole surface of her left bottom cheek, all the soft flesh beneath his open hand, prickled and tingled and ached to be touched.

"Are you nervous?" Newton asked, tracing an almost comforting circle upon the tense summit of her ass.

"No." Hands braced upon the floor, Abby stared at a spot of carpet between them.

"You're trembling," he pointed out.

"No, I'm not."

"Liars get spanked."

She rolled her eyes. "Since it's going to happen no matter what I say, it doesn't really pay to tell the truth, does it?"

He swatted her and Abby's whole body startled in response. The clap had been loud, seemingly louder than any other sound in that crowded room that also included one couple arguing with Terry and another DM and thirteen other scenes taking place. It must have been her vantage. Maybe having one's head closer to the floor somehow helped sound find her ears, or the carpet amplified the crispness. Either might have explained the heightened sound, but it didn't explain how much more crisp the blow itself felt. It made her catch her breath and in the involuntary convulsion that followed, somehow her hands left the floor. She grabbed both the chair and his leg instead.

"Lovely," Newton said. "I've seen you scene off and on for two years and I never knew you colored this nicely. How about you? Are you feeling more subservient yet?"

She glared at the carpet. "Fuck you."

He swatted her hard enough to make her jump all over again.

Ow, she mouthed, stubbornly refusing to give him the satisfaction of hearing that aloud.

"How about ticklish?" he inquired. "Are you feeling ticklish yet?"

Craning her neck, Abby glared at him now too.

"I'd say that's a big no." His lips twitched, as if he were fighting back a laugh. "Well, I suppose I ought to put at least a little effort into this, hadn't I? After all, the clock's a-ticking."

The heat of his resting hand abandoned her, and Abby tensed so hard that her toes curled. Her hands fisted, gripping both his ankle and the chair leg tight, and she grit her teeth to keep back the cries she just knew he was going to delight in beating out of her. He might have deserved it, but she hadn't been very nice to him over the years and now was his chance to get even. She knew this. In every cringing inch of her, she knew it. Except that it wasn't his spanking hand that she felt next.

The pinwheel spines that crowned the Wartenberg wheel rolled its needle-tipped caress up the back of her thigh. Jolts of sheer sensory panic zipped up her spine and down into nerve endings that took each sharp poke and delightfully misinterpreted them. The prick of each metal tooth sparked an instant writhing reflex. Abby opened her mouth to shout, but what came belting out was three hard barks of involuntary laughter that she'd have just as soon cut her own throat before emitting again.

Clapping a hand over her mouth, Abby reared up on his lap, fighting to break free of his restraining arm and get well out of reach from that wheel. "Oh my God!" she gasped, every inch of flesh the Wartenberg had traveled now humming in heightened sensitivity. "What the hell did you just do?"

"I'm not the only member of Black Light who used to attend other dungeons. In particular, I'm not the only one who remembers last year's Beat in the New Year party at Overtime."

Abby's stomach lurched in tight and hard. For a moment she wasn't sure she could breathe as she felt his hand—bare fingers now trailing up the back of her leg, following the same path the Wartenberg had forged all along the undercurve of her left bottom cheek—before he cupped the no-longer ticklish flesh and squeezed, molding her ass in the palm of his warm hand.

"Eight Doms," Newton reminded her, while the nerves in Abby's stomach flipped and twisted until the giddiness almost overwhelmed her. "All of them taking turns with you, one after the other, after the other, with canes and straps and floggers, leaving no part of your body untouched. And none of them elicited the same reaction you gave when ol' Marcus put on his finger claws and began to rake you with them. I've seen a lot of women scream and moan and squirm under the scrape of those claws. You're the only one I've ever seen who laughed… and writhed…" He curled his fingernails under, hooking tender flesh that seized when he scraped and sent those awful races of ticklish glee zipping through her nerves.

Abby threw her head back, erupting in kicks and helpless squeals. She bucked, the full force of his weighted arm pinning her across his lap while his nails raked the tender line between her buttocks and thighs. She vaulted backward, fighting to get up. "Let go! Let go, let go!"

He didn't. Instead, half a heartbeat after his scraping hand vanished from off the backs of all her firing sensory nerves, the flat of his palm came cracking down again. All vestiges of ticklishness were smacked out of her with a jolt that hit harder than anything she was prepared for. And yet, as far as spankings went, it was so anticlimactically mild that for a moment, Abby couldn't process it. She'd been expecting brutal. She'd been expecting a hardwood paddle or the Lexan stinger that Newton kept in the main pocket of his suitcase playbag. The one with the holes that for more than a year now, she'd watched light fires and leave bruises on every submissive to lay herself across his lap or bend over a spanking bench and offer herself up to its biting sting. She'd expected Newton to take his revenge on every mean little thing she'd said or done to him over the years, and there were more than one or two. If she didn't already know he'd deserved every bit of it, she'd almost regret that right now.

Except that he'd said he hadn't meant to call her weak.

'Liar,' her gut instantly spat.

He swatted her again, as if she'd said that part out loud instead of deep in the privacy of her own head. And it still wasn't the vindictive assault she was expecting, but it did make an impressively loud clap as he flattened her ass cheek under his palm. It even stung a little. Okay, more than just 'a little', but it wasn't brutal or harder than she could take. He swatted her again and she tensed, catching her breath. This definitely wasn't a child's game of pat-a-cake, not by any means. The force of his next spank, as well as the three or four others that followed—right cheek, left cheek—in steady rhythmic measure, shot through her. The sting made her catch her breath, but even she knew as far as spankings went, this was a warmup. With a warmup's delicious sting and that bloom of wanton heat sparking under the jubble of her flesh and the bounce of his hand. Newton's hand. Her skin should be crawling, but God help her, though she had every reason not to want it to, her belly still picked up that burn, absorbing the molten glow and turning it into something so much more.

She felt his arm move and tensed, ready to reject the next traitorous smack as heat and the pleasurable burn slowly filled up inside her. What she was not prepared for was another pass of the Wartenberg, rolling up her sensitive thigh, over the curving hill of her buttocks and the small of her back.

Abby threw back her head, erupting into squirms and teeth-gritted squeals of laughter she was helpless to bite back. Her feet drummed the floor, toes digging into the thin carpet while she twisted. Newton held her easily, letting the sharp tips of the pinwheel spines discover, torture and tickle up and down her back, playing along her ribs, down her sides to wander the rounding of her hip and back to her bottom again. She wanted to shout; she laughed instead, high-pitched and frantic, thrashing over his knees like a landed trout, every bit as incapable of breaking away.

And that sensual pulse that blossomed low in her belly moved lower still. Steady thumping need took root, growing in the bare-shaven shadow of her tightly clenched legs. She didn't want this erotic hum swimming through her veins, following in the wake of Newton's toy, filling up her breasts until they swelled, picking up the pulse of that carnal song until her nipples throbbed along in time. She didn't want this from Newton, and yet all she could do was laugh. Like the voyeurs around them were laughing—her shrieking giggles and their infectious guffaws—until Newton abruptly shifted the Wartenberg to his other hand, and then he was spanking her again.

Harder this time. Abby's giggles became an instant moan, the most mortifying loss of self-control she'd allowed herself to suffer since that awful night two years ago when she'd awakened in her own bed to the weight of a stranger falling on top of her, his hand clamping over her mouth so hard that the inside of her lips cut against her own teeth.

Don't think about it. She reared back, fighting to get up as if that physical escape could put equal distance between herself and those ugly unwelcome memories. At once, Newton's arm across her back became a steel beam pinning her down. He shifted, sweeping one leg out from under her to capture both her kicking ones in a scissoring vise.

"No!" she gasped, but *yes* was in the heaviness of the hand he now spanked her with. Harder. Faster. A harsh, demanding cadence that grabbed all her attention and brought it crashing back into the here and now of pure physical surrender. He didn't need a paddle—wooden, Lexan, or otherwise. He didn't need ropes, either. He held her down with immeasurable strength. A Dom who knew how to conquer and control, to counter the growing frenzy of her struggles because he'd done it before. And like him or not, the submissive inside her responded to that surety, that strength, that inescapable burning pain that mentally calmed and centered her within herself until the franticness of her struggles abandoned her, leaving her to wallow in the growing burn.

The blossoming pulse.

The lust and the need that soothed her masochistic soul with the promise of peace once the pain was overcome.

Prickles—not the Wartenberg wheel this time, but so many more —caressed her throbbing ass, sending those battered nerves to singing and Abby to helplessly laughing once more. She bucked and thrashed, unable to hold still. Her long hair flew about her. Her toes stubbed the floor, sending shocks of pain up her leg to get lost among the tickles and her high-pitched shrieks of laughter.

"What is that?" she squealed, humping her ass against his knee. No matter how she twisted, there was no escaping the wandering tickling caress of what felt like dozens of sharp little tacks.

"Vampire glove." His hand smoothed down the backs of each leg in turn, sending her overstimulated nerve-endings into spasms of unre-quited humor. He tickled her thighs, her feet, what parts he could reach of the backs of each knee. He tickled with the prickling pads of his gloved fingertips, scraping up the insides of both her legs as once. He prickled her sex, cupped it, scraped it, held it as if he owned it with tack-like spikes that rested on and in and against her inner and outer folds, against the heat of her molten core, against the throbbing of her desperate clit which only begged harder for the promised bite of each tiny metal tip.

Her laughter died abruptly. Abby gasped, panting. Jesus, she was sweating. She was trembling too.

"Stop," she croaked, suddenly hoarse in a throat that now felt too tight to breathe through, much less laugh.

Newton's fingers flexed, not drumming exactly but applying gentle biting pressure against her needy sex.

"What are you doing?" Her voice cracked. Now, when sounding too harsh could only have served her well, instead she came out sounding as if she were on the verge of panic.

With gentle pats, he let her feel all the pricks and spines hidden in the finger pads and palm of his black leather glove. "What does it feel like I'm doing?"

Even knowing he wouldn't let her, Abby tried to get up, but froze when his fingers scraped along her slit, abandoning her pussy to scratch back up the curve of her bottom. For a moment, she was terri-fied he was going to spank her again, this time with the glove on. Her relief when she felt him take the glove off, however, only lasted until the heat of his fingers and palm cupped her sex once more. His thumb wandered, caressing a single pass along the crack between her buttocks before stopping directly on top of her anus.

Her pussy tensed. That awful drumbeat of desire pulsed continuously now and his fingers weren't helping. One had taken up new ownership over her clit. It alternated between idle petting and circular strokes that only made the pressure build, becoming thumps so maddeningly strong that she could feel the heated tugging of her greedy cunt regretting its emptiness all the way up to her womb. Her thighs squeezed closer but with his hand already wedged between them, there was no keeping him out now.

"I think you're taking advantage of me," Abby stammered, her eyes wide and fixed, staring straight out into the crowd at nothing and nobody in particular. Why was he doing this? She was tingling, the whole of her body, everywhere he both had and hadn't scraped her with either the pinwheel or the vampire gloves. Her pussy tingled. Her clit, swelling with unrequited need beneath his touch, hummed. Her back, her belly, breasts, legs... her ass. God, her ass. The sting of only a moment ago had dwindled into a pleasant, throbbing heat. Taking notes from his fingers, his thumb now circled her back passage, rolling all around the darkened rim and now and then even dipping in, and she could feel the tickling slip of moisture slipping along her labia in anticipation of more. He hadn't pierced her, not yet. But with each circle and every caress, he was stoking her body's awareness of him from the flickering of an uncertain match-flame to that of a raging wildfire.

"Taking advantage?" he echoed, finger and thumb both increasing the pressure. Her clit reveled in being forced down, pinned flat within the heated wetness of her folds, but that was nothing compared to the sheer exhilaration she felt when his thumb increased its press that last iota more and she felt the tense ring of muscle behind her at last yield. "Are you saying you came to an 'anything goes' BDSM party expecting no sexual contact to take place?"

Her toes curled against her will. No, she definitely hadn't come thinking that.

"It wasn't on your list of hard limits." Slow and steady, his thumb penetrated until he was lodged as deep as the second knuckle and the abutment of his palm would allow. She shivered, hating how much she loved the feel of him pulling out only to penetrate her all over again, just as slow as before, just as disinclined to stop. Newton or not, like him or not—her body accepted his touch like that of a long-lost lover and her pussy flooded his fingers in response.

"My, my." The flat of all four fingers increased their pressure, pressing in until she grabbed his thigh with both hands—not so much an attempt to rise as to process the unexpected pleasure as her clit was mashed and rubbed. "I don't recall. Was penetration on your list of hard limits?"

Abby clamped her lips against a muffled squeak as, without seeming to, he opened his fingers enough to catch her clit between them and then clamped down tight.

"Was fucking?" he asked, soft as the lover her body wanted him to be, a demand nonetheless.

Hands clenching into fists in the minor wrinkles of his jeans, Abby shook her head.

"Use your words, please."

What the fuck were words? Abby floundered. "N-no."

"No what?"

Frustration reared its ugly head. "No," she snapped, "fucking was not one of my hard limits."

"Speak to me again in that tone of voice. I double dog dare you."

Abby's belly twisted and quivered at how easily he could sound at once both amused and yet deadly serious. He patted the whole of her pussy, a warning that he was not afraid to spank. Just the thought of being spanked there, in that most vulnerable of all places made her belly quiver all over again. "I... I'm sorry."

"Quite all right. I can understand how having to repeat certain words or phrases might be embarrassing for some submissives. Was it difficult for you to have to say that, considering where my fingers currently are and how deeply my thumb is stuck up your ass? Does saying things like 'fucking' when I'm touching you like this embarrass you?"

Her face burned. Her pussy pulsed and throbbed, drooling more than enough lubrication to keep every woman in this room fuck-ready for hours. That it was happening was bad enough. That he was feeling it drip and roll down his fingers made it far worse, and yet neither of those things were half as terrible as having to talk with him about it.

"Yes," she admitted. "It does."

"Since ours is a strained acquaintanceship, at best, I suppose you'd rather not be forced to tack on the usual forms of respectful address? No 'thank you, sir, may I have another' or 'please, sir, fingerbang my ass because I obviously enjoy it'?"

Abby closed her eyes, the burning in her face and stomach becoming stovetop hot before she could swallow. "Yes."

"Yes, you'd rather not say that, or yes, you need a good finger-fucking? Because I could believe that. As tight as you are, something tells me it's been a while since anyone has held you facedown by your neck, permitting you to plead, cry and wail your submission into the pillows while your asshole took a hard pounding."

Her pussy dribbled; her ass convulsed around his thumb. If her face flared any hotter, she was going to melt into a puddle of pure mortification right here on his lap.

"No," Abby groaned through gritted teeth. "I really would rather not have to say any of that."

He grunted. She couldn't see it, but she could almost hear the smugness of his nod. "Well, isn't that just too damn bad? Because, personally, I enjoy communicating with my submissives, particularly when I know there can be no chance of misunderstandings. So, here's how this works, when I ask a question, I expect all the specifics to be repeated back to me in your answer and your answers should all be punctuated with the appropriate terms of submissive respect."

"Or what?" she growled, eyes narrowing to thin slits. She could only wish she were either half as angry as she sounded or half as horny. "What are you going to do if I don't, shove another finger up my ass? That'll teach me."

"I doubt it," he said mildly. "I'm thinking dropping you on your ass right here, quitting the contest and walking out the door might have a greater impact."

"I have done everything you've asked," she seethed.

"No, you haven't."

Abby stiffened, and for once it didn't have anything to do with the pressure of his fingers stroking her clit or his thumb as he caressed in and out of her. She stared at the floor, hating how easily he'd just manipulated her. She didn't want to quit the contest. She needed this and, disaster though it was to be paired to him of all men, she needed him not to quit the contest too. They both had to cross the finish line. Afterwards, if they never spoke again, then fine, but for now...

Abby closed her eyes in defeat. Bowing her head, she schooled herself until she was sure she could keep a civil tone. "Thank you, sir..." She almost choked. "...for explaining the rules. I will do my best to follow them, sir."

"Are you being sincere?"

She ground her teeth. "Yes, sir."

"Shall we test that?"

Just as soon as she won this contest, she was going to kill him. "Please test me, sir."

"All right." His thumb sank deep inside her again, then stilled. He cupped her pussy, holding but no longer rubbing. Abby caught her breath, tucking her chin against her chest until she was sure she wouldn't react. Until that moment, she hadn't thought anything short of Newton actually using his cock on her would have been worse than rubbing and finger-fucking. She was wrong. After what he'd been doing, no stimulation at all was much, much worse. "Answer honestly: Did you not include sex as a hard limit because you were hoping to make it part of the evening, or..."

"I ran out of room," she snapped. "We were only allowed four limits." Belatedly, she added, "Sir."

The suddenness with which he pulled his thumb out of her ass made her gasp. Abby caught her breath when the heat of his palm abruptly vanished from between her legs, but that gasp was all she could do before the painful breadth of his hand came clapping back down again. He caught her pussy squarely. He caught her swollen, pulsing, aching clit, and Abby jolted over his knee, back arched and head thrown back in a shout of pure pain and disbelief... and relief.

She writhed, spasming convulsions seizing hold of her sex, shaking her from the inside out.

"Try again," Newton urged. "This time with a little more respect and a lot more honesty."

Abby fought to calm down, to hold herself obediently in this bent position across his knee. Her pussy throbbed harder, burned hotter, stung fiercely in every shadowy part where his hand had swatted. And that was everywhere. Big as it was, his hand had covered all. She gritted her teeth, eyes closed once more albeit for different reasons now. Her embarrassment was still high, but the heat pulsating through her now-wounded sex was unignorable.

"I don't have a problem with sex, sir," she eventually managed. "Had I been paired with someone I liked, I wouldn't have objected if he'd wanted t-to..." she faltered into awkward silence.

"Dominate you sexually?" Newton asked. His hand folded over her pussy again, his thumb slipping back between her blushing cheeks to once more circle the dusky rim of her anus. "Order you head down, ass up? Bite the pillow and do as Daddy commands? This is going to hurt you more than it does me, but I'll bet I can make you come in spite of it?"

Her chest was tightening. With each subsequent suggestion he made, she could feel it growing harder and harder to breathe. But it wasn't until his thumb began again to apply pressure, pressing in until the tight ring of muscle there yielded, that she realized how very breathless she now was.

"Do you want to safeword?" he inquired when she did not answer.

Yes. Only Abby didn't say that. She shook her head instead. With his thumb lodged inside her, now it was his restless fingers that began to wander. She bit her bottom lip when they skimmed over her clit, parting the folds of both outer and inner labia, and immediately became immersed in the slick heat sheltered in between.

"Answer honestly, sweetheart." Twin fingers slipped into the softness of her yielding flesh, sliding into a silken in and out motion that her hips immediately, humiliatingly, unstoppably began to rock to. "When I put you over my knee, you thought I was going to beat your ass in revenge for all the snarky things you've said and done to me over the years, didn't you?"

Both his thumb and fingers sank in as deep as they could go.

Abby pressed her lips tight against the inadvertent mewl that tried to escape. "I wouldn't put it past you."

"You wouldn't put it past me," he echoed, his voice like warm velvet, and his fingers and thumb filled up her insides. He flexed them, both sets finding one another through the thin membranes of her passages and sending shocks of pure pressure and delight zinging to her womb.

"No!" Her hands fisted against his leg again. Her belly flinched. Tiny, trembling convulsions, a prelude to something much bigger, reverberated off the tips of his lightly tapping fingers. The vibrations tremored the length of her clit. Somehow caressing it from the inside. "No, God!"

She clamped her lips, rolling them tightly together again.

"No?" he asked, flicking his fingers and sending another radiating jolt into her clit. "No what?"

"Stop!" Abby hissed, horrified by the pure physicality of her body's response to him. Her heart thundered in her chest, pushing the fiery pulse of her wanton desire through her veins. She could feel it— thumping in her nipples, thumping in her sex, thumping deep down in her twitching womb where the rawness of her need was building. If she didn't stop him, he was going to make her come. Newton, of all people, was going to make her orgasm.

Abby threw herself backwards, fighting with all she had to scramble off his lap and failing so catastrophically that she barely budged his restraining limbs.

"God, damn it!" she exploded, only belatedly attempting a laugh to mask her growing aggravation. It didn't work. Not only was Newton not stopping, but now the DMs were looking their way. She lowered her voice, something damn near impossible to accomplish with the fluttering of his fingers, tapping out a seductive morse code against her g-spot. "You c-can't do this!"

"Can't I?"

"This isn't our scene!" Her back arched as both his fingers and thumb began to thrust. Her toes scraped the carpet.

"Our 'scene' started the moment you became my submissive for the evening and it won't end until either you call the safeword or we complete the contest. If, however, by 'scene' you mean our roulette wheel designated activity, then we were only required to do that for thirty minutes to get credit for accomplishing it. I tickled you for thirty-one, but it's not really my thing, so I stopped. This, however..." Two fingers abruptly became three, winning a full-throated shout from her as he shoved them deep inside. When he pinched fingers and thumb together, she groaned. "This is exactly my thing. No revenge required."

"Bullshit!" she spat, her brain in full revolt but her hips—oh!—and her pussy grinding down on him, riding his hand as if he were the love of her life. "You ass! You absolute ass! You know what? Fine! I didn't just *think* you were going to take your revenge out on me, I *knew* it! And I wasn't wrong, was I? You've been an absolute dick, just as expected! Are you happy now?"

"Not particularly, but what did you expect?" He slammed his fingers deep, twisting his hand around, searching until he pressed and every muscle she owned suddenly seized up in a convulsion of pleasure too intense for her to bear. Newton smiled at the gutturalness of her groan. "You've gone out of your way to make me miserable practically from the day we met."

She arched up, twisting back as far as she could to shoot him a scathing glare. "You're damn right, I have! What do *you* expect after what *you* called *me*?"

"What I *called* you?" His hand stilled between her legs, then his eyes narrowed. "What did I ever call you?"

"As if you don't kn—" Abby broke off with a shout when his fingers suddenly lashed out, flicking that same spot inside her again. The jolt was near electrical, a pleasure so brutally intense that it felt as if he'd just whacked her funny bone. Only it wasn't funny, and that wasn't where she kept her elbow.

"Try again," Newton said in a tone that would brook no disrespect.

"You called me weak, *sir*!" she spat. Her stomach flipped, but her pussy—already so lost in a confusion of feelings she never should have felt for this of all Doms—convulsed when she twisted back far enough to see the fierceness of the glare he locked on her.

"I. *Never!* Said th—"

"'Gee, Terry!'" Abby erupted, casting his voice in as deep a tone as she could muster and she did not skimp on the audial retardation implication. "'What are you doing? She's half your size!'"

"Number one, I don't sound like that," Newton fired back. "And number two, I don't say 'gee' or 'golly' or 'wowie kazowie' or whatever other Scooby Doo phrases you're about to put in my mouth next."

Abby forgot about the crowd of tables around them, or the people watching the argument unfold with, no doubt, all the same amusement they'd use later when they repeated her words for the entertainment of every kinkster not present to hear all of this themselves. She forgot everything except the heat in her bottom, and in the palm of his hand as it mashed against her labia, and in the blaze of awareness that laved her clit from the inside out in a wash of sensation every bit as tangible as a physical mouth. Just not Newton's mouth. Because he was an ass, and they didn't like each other, and as soon as she got up off his lap her pussy was going to remember that fact and stop this stupid, empty, aching, maddeningly distracting throbbing!

"The words you used don't matter. You *said* I couldn't handle it," she accused. "That means the same damn thing!"

Furious, she reared, shoving backwards off his lap, and he was just startled enough by her outburst that she almost got her feet under her. But in a flash of piqued temper, his left arm hooked around her waist and his right hand grabbed, missing her leg altogether and catching hold of her pussy instead. When she lurched back, he heaved forward, and down she went in flailing arms and kicking feet that he quickly locked down. Back went her legs into the squeezing vise of his thighs. He caught her free arm, wrenching it up against the small of her back when she slapped at him.

"Ow!" She bucked and thrashed, but he was bigger and stronger and she simply could not find the leverage to break free.

Angry as he was, Newton held himself frozen, letting her fight until exhaustion drowned out her revolt. Eventually, she collapsed under the fury of her own struggles. Panting, swearing and glaring at the floor, she lay drooped over his knees while she waited for his inevitable argument.

"You're right," he said, startling her instead. "I don't remember saying it in those words, but you're right. That's what I was thinking. I didn't believe you could handle fighting off someone Terry's size and if it had been me Topping you that night, that scene absolutely would not have gone the way it was when I walked into the club. However—" The weight of his arm across the small of her back disappeared. Catching her wrist, he pulled her up to sit on his knee. "—I wasn't the one Topping you that night, I wasn't part of that scene, and I had no business saying or doing anything that might have been construed as me passing judgment over you. So for that, I am sorry."

Except for the raggedness of her breathing, Abby didn't move. He had one hand braced upon his thigh while his other burned heat into the small of her back. Ass though he might be, Newton had sexy hands. She tried not to look at them. The last thing she wanted was to feel mollified enough to forgive him or worse, find any part of him sexually attractive.

When she refused to answer, Newton caught her by the chin and forced her gaze to his. Unsmiling, he leveled a stern look on her. "I interrupted your scene," he said again. "I made a rude comment, but I *never* thought of you as weak."

Unsure if she believed him, Abby looked away. He chased her chin, catching it between fingers that smelled strongly of her own feminine arousal.

"Truce?" he coaxed.

Her mouth flattened in stubborn defiance. Ever so slightly, his curled into the smallest of smiles.

"All right," he agreed, a steely-edge creeping ominously in among his words. "Either we agree to a truce right here and now, or—"

"Or what?" Abby countered, hiking her chin a little higher. "You'll give up like the quitter you are and walk out on me?"

Something in Newton's dark eyes changed, growing, heating, vanishing in a blink before she could get a solid bead on exactly what she'd been seeing. She touched a hand to her stomach, unsure why it suddenly felt as tight and hard as a brick.

"Or," Newton continued with exaggerated patience, "I can put you back over my knee and paddle your bare ass until you scream your surrender to the ceiling rafters."

And just like that, Abby realized what had been lurking in the hardening of his stare. It had been intent—the iron-clad will to do what he thought needed doing without any regard at all to how she would hate him for it later on. She sat stiff and unmoving, barely breathing, upon his knee, and in no part of her being did she think he was lying. Or joking. Or even exaggerating. Oh no, as she stared soul-deep into his threatening stare, with one of his hands heavy on her back and the other braced against his own thigh, in every fiber of her being Abby knew he meant exactly what he'd said: either she gave in, or he'd bust her ass until she did. And she had no recourse but to take it.

Or call 'red' and prove to everyone, including herself, that she really couldn't take it. That everything she had done these past two years had been a joke. That she really was not just weak, but useless too.

"Truce," Abby said through gritted teeth.

Just like a jackass to try and rob a girl of her best grudge right when she needed it most.

CHAPTER 4

"*H*ere you go," Newton said with all the cheerfulness he could muster as he handed her a plastic water bottle, followed by a plate of sandwich meats and cheeses. "The menu isn't varied, but they do have protein."

Swaddled in a soft blanket, Abby set the plate on the cushion beside her and went back to hugging her knees. That she kept hold of the water bottle surprised him a little, but she made no move to drink from it. Instead, huddled in a corner of the couch exactly where he had parked her, she picked at the blue and white label and refused to look at him. At least she wasn't shouting anymore. He took that as a good sign, though she was still angry. In fact, the longer he stood watching her the more certain he became that she was deliberately hanging onto her anger. As if it were the only available lifejacket on the sinking ship this evening had become. Despite his apology, she clung to her long-standing grudge as though her life depended on it. As though she needed it.

Maybe she did.

Snagging an available chair from the nearest table, he thunked it down in front of her. She quickly moved her toes when he sat so they wouldn't accidentally touch. He noticed, but said nothing. A master at picking his battles, Newton got comfortable in his seat before marching head-on straight into her preferred war. "You going to drink from that bottle, or just pick it apart?"

Her mouth twitched, a grimace rather than a smile tugging at the corners. "I'm not thirsty."

"I'm not playing with a dehydrated submissive," he said flatly.

"This isn't my first play party," she answered in the same tone. "I've been hydrating for this for two days. Thank you for the water, but I'm fine."

"You were over my knee," he reminded her. "You were kicking, fussing, thrashing, working up a sweat and leaking down my arm like a damn faucet." The alluring musk of her could still be gleaned from the fingers he held up for her as a reminder. Her face flushed when she saw them. She flushed even brighter when he, tempted beyond his inclination to resist, sampled her lingering flavor. "Tasty," he murmured, just to watch that play of mortification dance across her features before she slapped her angry mask back into place. "If you want to give up now, that's fine. But if not, then stop acting like a naughty brat and drink your water."

"You're not my master, my Dom, or my father," she muttered, still picking at the label. "I might have to listen to you out there on the floor, but I don't have to do a thing you say when I'm sitting on this couch."

He sat back, eyebrow arched, half tempted to laugh. "Is that so?"

She met his gaze evenly, neither frowning nor gloating, and sure as hell not drinking. Just staring at him and waiting. 'For him to react,' gut instinct whispered. Every inch of her was set in the familiar mold of a rebellious submissive, pushing and prodding and working tirelessly to provoke a disciplinary response. Submissives like that were exhausting. And yet, while Newton had seen more than enough of those to recognize the one squaring off in front of him now, something about Abby's defiance didn't quite fit that overall bratty mold.

He studied her through narrowed eyes, carefully picking through a minefield of verbal responses. "Do you want me to make you? Because to be honest, in all the times I've watched you play, I've never seen you do this with any of your other partners."

"The night's half over, so don't worry. You won't have to deal with it for too much longer."

Something in the way she said that struck him like a challenge. He had to lock his jaw to keep from chuckling. God knows, the last thing he needed was for her to think he was laughing at her. "Do you think I can't deal with it?"

"Oh no, you're doing great so far." Sarcasm. Definitely a challenge, then.

"You remember what I said about how much I enjoy making my submissives give me extensive verbal affirmation about the things I make them do and say, right?" he countered.

"Stop threatening me," she snipped back.

"If you don't like it, then stop asking me to threaten you."

She snapped her mouth shut, frowning.

"Oh no, no," he told her, pointing a stern finger right at her. "Stop right there. You started this. In the interest of honesty, I'd like to set the record straight now. I'm not your master. Personally, it's not my favorite role. Twenty-four-seven, all year every year is a helluva lot of responsibility. I've done it enough to know which aspects I like and which I don't, and that while I am a very dominant presence in my personal relationships, I don't want a slave. I am, however, a very good Dom, and Daddy Dom is right up my alley. I suppose because it tickles so many of my own private triggers. Like, for instance, extensive verbal affirmations. Would you like to see first hand just how hard I get off on having Babygirl stand before me, blushing and stammering while she struggles to get through her punishment phrases? Daddy, please spank my naughty bare bottom. Daddy, I've been a bad, bad girl. Fuck my bottom, Daddy. Teach me to be good again. Daddy, please, please punish my ass with your cock, hurt my naughty bottom, and I will drink my water and eat my protein and be a good, good Babygirl for you." Unblinking, he held her gaze. "Do you want to say that to me, Abby? Do you want to say it over and over again, first while I spank and then while I sodomize you? Do you want me to hurt you so you can be free to kick and fuss and cry, and maybe... just maybe, finally let all this festering anger go? Because I can do that. I can make you take the pleasure and the pain. I can make you take as much of both as you can bear, until you just can't anymore. If that's what you want. Or what you need. Is it?"

Newton held her stare and neither one moved, apart from each of their breathing. Hers, he noticed, was a little shallower and faster than normal. It was the only glimpse she allowed him of what real emotion lurked under the faintly scarred mask that her too-pale face had become. He took her silence as an answer.

"Are you sure?" He braced his elbows on his knees and leaned in closer. "Because there is no phrase half as beautiful to me as those three little words: Daddy, hurt me."

Her breath actually caught a little. He could see the pulse of her heart beating in the hollow of her throat.

"Drink your water," he ordered, his voice soft and silken but an order nonetheless, "so I know your body is replenished for our next activity. Eat your food. You need protein to keep your blood sugar from bottoming out. Those sorts of things don't have anything to do with you liking me or me liking you. It has to do with playing as safely as any play in a BDSM dungeon can get."

Her mask slipped. Newton caught just a glimpse of the vulnerability that lived beneath before unscrewing the top off her water bottle, Abby downed half the bottle. She ate too, but something told him she did it so she wouldn't have to look at him. Easing back in his chair again, Newton hid a smile behind his own sips of water and he watched until she'd emptied her plate.

"Do you need to use the bathroom?" he asked, taking both her empty bottle and the plate from her lap.

"No." She frowned. "I'm not three. I don't need reminder cues as though I were."

"Suit yourself." Stretching sideways, he left the remnants of their meal on a nearby table to be picked up by someone from the bar. "Let's go spin the wheel again. Maybe this time we'll get something really fun."

As they crossed the dungeon toward the stage, he saw her gaze drift over the roulette wheel and in a rare moment of agreement, she said, "Flogging, maybe. Are you any good at fireplay?"

"Not bad," he said modestly. "Unfortunately for you, you made me walk three blocks from the overflow parking. I'm rooting for water-boarding."

One foot on the bottommost step, her hand on the stage steps rail-ing, Abby stopped long enough to snap him a look. She didn't start walking again until he swatted her butt and thumbed for her to climb the stairs. He waited until her back was to him before smiling. She'd given him enough shit tonight. Let her wonder a while if he was joking or not.

"Ready for another scene?" Chase asked as Abby stepped up to the wheel. "I saw the tickling. Got to admit, I've never seen it done with spiked gloves before."

"Whatever makes the submissive ticklish," Newton said, more cheerful than he was defensive.

"I'm not normally," Abby added. "Ticklish, I mean."

Chase passed her the ball and gave the wheel a spin. "Here's to hoping your next scene is more to your liking, then."

As she gave the ball a gentle spin on the roulette track, Newton bent down to whisper for her ears alone, "Come on, waterboarding. Oo, or butt stuff. If we draw butt stuff, I'm going to make it last the rest of the night."

Abby elbowed him in the gut. A touch of red stained her cheeks though and he could see her breasts rising and falling in that fast, shallow pattern again, so Newton let the elbowing go. He chuckled as the ticking of the wheel slowed even more. It was hard to hear over the low murmur of whispering voyeurs and the off-tempo cracks of multiple impact tools finding their targets. Newton didn't look. His attention was caught on the drop and bounce of that little white ball as it finally came to a rolling stop within a labeled activity slot.

"Cell popping," Chase announced. "Have you ever done it before?"

"Yes," Newton admitted slowly, staring as the wheel crawled into its last complete turn but mentally poking through the contents of his playbag. "I haven't done it in a long time though. In fact, I'm pretty sure I don't have my kit in my bag."

"We put it on the wheel. We've got a kit on standby. Find a station," Chase told them, already signaling to one of the patrolling dungeon monitors. "I'll have someone get it for you."

"What is cell popping?" Abby asked when Chase left them to relay his request to the DM.

"Microbranding. The Devil's Fire. You haven't seen it done before?" But even as he asked, he knew the answer. Judging by the wideness of her eyes, he could tell she hadn't, but she did catch onto at least one word.

"Branding?" she echoed, a very small but very real glimmer of unease lighting up the backs of her eyes.

"Well, not quite," he hurried to reassure. "Do you have any tattoos?"

Abby shook her head, then admitted, "I have thought about getting one, though."

"It's like that—both in pain level and in the pen used, which is close in size but much less scary looking than any tattoo artist's needle. It's also temporary. Depending on how well you heal, cell popping designs don't normally last longer than, say... six weeks, tops." Looking around the busy dungeon, he spotted absolutely no suitable stations free. He'd have preferred a spanking bench for this, but none were available. Their space at the wall was open, though, with several available chairs scattered throughout the crowd. "Looks like our favorite spot is open. Grab a couple chairs, I'll meet you over there in a minute."

For the first time, Abby offered no argument. She simply nodded, stepped off the stage and wove her way through the watchers in obedient search of vacant seating.

And hell hadn't frozen over yet.

"Huh," Newton grunted, for a moment just watching her go.

"How's it going?" Terry asked, handing over the microbranding kit he'd brought for them to borrow. "Ready to pull your hair out yet?"

"Ah, it's not that bad," Newton demurred. "We had a rough start and she's still pressing buttons, but overall I think we can make this work. Although I confess, it's nice to know I'm not the only one."

Arms folded across his chest, the DM blinked at him. "Only one what?"

"Only one having trouble with her," Newton clarified. "You just said..."

"I was being sympathetic," Terry cut in. "It's part of my social butterfly routine. One has to do that when one is working events like this. Trust me—" Clapping a hand on his shoulder, the muscular DM offered a commiserating pat and a grin that didn't quite reach as far as his eyes. "—she's golden with everyone else. It's just you she doesn't like."

"Thanks," Newton called after Terry as he walked away. "Thanks a lot."

The DM never turned around, but he did flash an unrepentant thumbs-up back over his shoulder.

Newton let that go too. But only because he didn't want to get thrown out of the club this far into the event.

Abby had two chairs set up at what he was quickly coming to think of as 'their' section of wall. He snagged a third one, dragging it over to play as a table for his borrowed equipment, all of which came neatly packed into an old metal Scooby Doo lunchbox.

"Damn," he said, turning it over in his hands. It was scuffed, dented and the paint was chipped in more than a few places. "You know, I had one of these when I was a kid. If it were in better condition, it might be worth something."

"You think so?" she asked, giving the old lunchbox a dubious look.

"All these old metal boxes are. Some more than others, admittedly, but I remember reading an article in the paper about an old lunchbox like this going for thousands on eBay. Sadly, none of mine survived my childhood." He thought about it. "To be honest, even if they had, they likely wouldn't have survived three years ago. So, I guess it's a moot point anyway. Can you hand me the first-aid kit out of the end pocket in my playbag?"

"Sure." She looked around. Someone must have moved his suitcase while they'd been near the bar, getting drinks and snacks. Although he remembered leaving it in this general area after the end of their first scene, it now stood flat against the wall, with the Wartenberg wheel and his vampire gloves resting neatly on the top. Abby spotted it just before he did and dug into the end pocket in search of the first-aid kit.

She handed it over, and then sat when he motioned her to. "So..."

She watched as he popped the lunchbox open. "What happened three years ago?"

"I started my business." Digging through the box, Newton pulled out a brand new cautery pen. Self-heating. Unlike the ones he had used before, this required no lighter or blowtorch to get the tip hot enough to scar. "Perfect."

"You own your own business?"

Newton barely glanced at her. She wasn't asking because she was curious. Her face was guarded, her eyes shuttered. She didn't really want to get to know him, but as long as she was trying to be polite, the least he could do was reward her for it. "I do. Sole owner and operator of my very own online fitness channel. One-point-two million subscribers as of last Friday."

"Wow." She wasn't at all subtle about the way she looked him over, though she did keep her opinion on his physique hidden behind her expressionless mask.

"That's okay," he mock whispered, then winked. "I know I look good."

She caught herself mid eye-roll, but wasn't quite as quick or as successful at catching the wayward smile that made her lips twitch.

"I saw that." He half-smiled too.

She folded her arms and quickly banished all traces of amusement. "You're easily the most arrogant person I know."

"No, I'm not. The word you're looking for is funny. I am easily the funniest person you know, to which I would probably have to agree." He paused, the medical pen in his hand only half unwrapped from its sterile plastic. "Which would also make me arrogant," he realized out loud. "Well damn."

There went that twitch of a smile again, pulling at her lips. Funny, how such a little thing could so completely transform Abby's face into that of an attractive woman. Newton gave himself a mental shake. That was the last thing he needed to think about. He finished unwrapping the cautery pen, then pulled out the alcohol and sterile swabs.

"Anyway," he continued. "What I also was back then, was broke. I worked two jobs, ate a lot of beans and rice and learned how to pinch a penny until it squealed for mercy. Believe me, if I'd had a lunchbox worth thousands, I wouldn't have had it for very long. Now, keeping in mind that I'm not a world-famous artist, what kind of design would you like and where do you want me to put it?"

She shrugged. "Dealer's choice, I guess."

"A small design on your shoulder okay?"

"Sure." She tugged the ribbon bow loose between her breasts and shrugged out of the spaghetti straps, hugging the sheer black cloth of her babydoll dress to her chest as if for modesty. But there was nothing modest about her state of dress and surely she had to know it. Even when she wasn't standing where the colored dungeon track lights could shine right through it, the gossamer fabric was transparent. There wasn't any part of her that he couldn't see. The jut of her nipples, curve of breasts and the dip of her waist. She wasn't wearing panties either, those had also ended up on top of his suitcase, just under the vampire gloves, and though the hem of the alluringly short garment was just long enough to cover her crotch in front and most of her bottom in back, when she stood to turn and straddle the chair, for a brief moment the smooth-shaven 'v' of her pussy was right at his eye-level.

He wasn't a saint, nor was he in the habit of depriving himself of enjoyable views. The temptation to let her know exactly what he could see so he could also watch the creeping realization turn her face bright red was the strongest he'd yet encountered all night, but Newton kept those comments to himself. Saying anything would probably bring Sulky Abby back into the game and he was only just getting comfortable with Cordial Abby. He wasn't ready for things between them to turn prickly again.

Sweeping her wavy blonde hair over her other shoulder, he prepared its twin, cleaning the area and filling the air around them with the pungent scent of rubbing alcohol. He took a moment to consider his limited design choices, before settling on something simple. He pressed the button, letting the tip heat until it glowed and was just leaning in to rest his hands on her shoulder when she said, "Strawberry Shortcake."

He paused. "What?"

"My lunchbox." She turned her head toward him, though not quite far enough to see him over her bared shoulder.

He arched his eyebrows. "You were a Strawberry Shortcake kind of kid?"

She snorted. "No. I got in trouble for stealing my brother's lunchbox all the time. His was Return of the Jedi."

He chuckled, and she smiled. There was no talking after that. Although the rest of the room remained active, a kind of quiet settled between them. Enough for him to hear the sizzle and the pop as he touched the cautery pen to her skin, burning a series of tiny dots into her shoulder. She caught her breath a little at the first steady touch, but the tension in her body didn't last beyond the fifth small burn. After that, she relaxed beneath his hands. That he liked feeling her do that was almost as surprising as how much he liked the smell of her. Beneath the stink of the alcohol and the burning of her skin as he worked, now and then he caught faint whiffs of soap and lotion and the soft underlying fragrance of a vanilla-based perfume that reminded him strongly of cookies.

"I'm going to have to get some on the way home," he murmured, taking care to make his first curve as round and as perfect as he could without a stencil.

She looked back at him again. "What?"

"Don't move."

"Sorry."

"No need to be sorry, just don't move." He waited until she'd faced forward and settled herself to endure the rest of the process.

"I didn't hear what you said."

"Just making a mental grocery list," he said with a rueful smile.

"Oh." There was that prickliness again. "Sorry I'm not more interesting."

"I didn't say that, but it is your fault. You're the one who came here smelling like cookies."

"Oh," she said again, softer this time. And just like that, the prickliness was gone but he could feel the tension creeping back into her shoulders.

"Relax," he told her, liking again the hesitance with which her smaller body eased beneath his fingers. "If you want to talk while I do this, you can."

Her hands, lightly resting one on top of the other on the back of the chair, tightened. "About what?"

Newton shrugged. "You said you're thinking about getting a tattoo. What style are you considering?"

She started to shake her head, but caught herself. "I don't know," she evaded, looking away.

For the sake of their new-found companionship, he ought to have let it drop, but he didn't.

"Dragon on your boob?" he coaxed. "Bugs Bunny on your butt? Exploding Death Star tattooed around your navel? Give."

She wasn't quite fast enough to catch and kill the soft bark of her laughter that jerked her shoulders. Too late Newton pulled the pen back, but his attempt at a straight line was ruined by a single dot well out of place.

"Did I or did I not tell you to hold still?" he said in his best Dom voice.

"You're the one who made me laugh!"

Setting the pen aside, Newton stood up. "Stand," he commanded, glad she wasn't looking at him now or she'd have seen his grin.

She stood, granting obedience without hesitation. He swatted her, his hand landing half on thin cloth and half on the naked curve of her ass.

"Sit," he ordered, and she immediately dropped her bottom back onto the chair. But she was giggling as she did it, and God if the urge to sink his teeth into her naked shoulder, wrap his arms around her and pull her back against him while he whispered a husky 'good girl' in her ear wasn't almost more than he could squelch.

Picking up the cautery pen, he reluctantly went back to work instead.

"I really don't know yet," Abby offered before that companionable silence could once more settle around them. "I look every now and then, but I haven't found something... I don't know... good enough."

Newton cleaned up his line as best he could before returning to the top of his half-finished design. He began another curve. "Good enough for what?"

She was quiet for so long that he was halfway into his second line and more than half certain she wasn't going to answer, when she did. "To remind me."

"Remind you of what?"

"It's silly." She avoided looking at him with the same dedication that she avoided the question.

"All tattoos have their own reasons and none of them are silly. Give," he said again, once more having to clean up his line. This time he couldn't blame it on her. Painfully aware of his artistic limitations, he took his time completing the design.

She sighed.

"Give," he drawled.

She sighed louder. "To remind me not to be weak again."

There was that word again. Newton lowered the pen. "You know, I think you are the only person in this room who would ever use that word to describe you."

"Only because nobody in this room knows me very well," she muttered, just not quietly enough for him not to hear it.

Now he put the pen all the way down. He braced his hands against his thighs, letting the full disapproval of his stare burn into her back, but only because she wasn't looking at him. The fire poker set of her shoulders told him she wouldn't even if he ordered her to. "I don't quite understand why you're determined to be like this, but when you verbalize it that way the urge to put you over my knee and bust your butt is, I've got warn you, making my palm itch like crazy. Why don't you try again?"

She shook her head. "Forget it."

Newton was on his feet before he realized he wanted to be. Grabbing the back of his chair, he marched around her, thunked it down where she had no choice but to look at him and sat. Close enough now for their knees to touch, he ordered her, "Talk."

She pulled back, but he moved faster, catching a fistful of hair at the back of her scalp and dragging her startled face so close to his that they could not help but share each other's breath. Hers was shaky; his was annoyed.

He kept a rein on it. He kept himself cool and under tight control. "There are only two kinds of people who do take-down scenes as brutal as the one I walked in on the day we first met," he told her, forcing her with her own hair to keep eye contact the one time she meekly tried to withdraw. He waited until she stopped fighting before he continued. "Those who harbor rape fantasies... and those for whom it was anything but a fantasy. What exactly do you think we don't know? Do you think anybody here somehow missed seeing the bruises? The cuts? The stitches that put you back together again? There is not a person in this room who would *ever* describe you as weak. I am not your Dom, Abby. But if I ever, and I do mean ever, hear you say that word again, I will personally spell out the meaning of 'consequence' as you have never had it done to you before. Do you understand?"

Her head canted at an awkward angle because of his grip, she swallowed hard. He held her so sternly she only managed the smallest of nods. Grudgingly, Newton let go of her hair and for a while they sat, simply staring at one another.

"Do you want to see what I put on your body?" he finally asked.

Rubbing her hands against her own thighs, Abby managed another nod.

From the bottom of the lunchbox, he withdrew two compact cases. Handing her one, he popped the other open, circled behind her chair and obligingly held the mirror up at about design level. He pretended not to notice the trembling in her hands as she angled her compact mirror until she caught sight of her back reflected in his.

"It's a heart," she said, sounding pleasantly surprised. Her shaking eased a little and she held her mirror higher, angling for a better look. "It's very red."

"It's going to be. I burned you."

"It looks very nice."

"I'm glad you like it." Newton set the mirror down on the table tray that had been provided for them. "It's also supposed to be a penguin."

Her eyes widened.

"Just kidding," he confessed and took her mirror before she could hit him with it. "It's a heart."

An unwilling smile breaking across her face, she hit him with her hand instead. "Big jerk."

He chuckled.

CHAPTER 5

*T*he roulette wheel spun, its rapid ticking marking the turns in ever de-escalating clicks until the whirring of the ball lost the last of its momentum and dropped with a bounce into a worded slot.

"Violet wand," Chase read out.

Abby's stomach hit her toes. She wasn't a fan of electrical play. The only reason it wasn't on her list of hard limits was because it didn't scare her as badly as the thought of being gagged, bound, or confined. Nor did it hit her squick button quite as hard or as fast as medical play, but there was nothing about violet wands that she liked. They looked like medieval torture devices. They sounded worse, and just the thought of writhing beneath the zapping attentions of a buzzing, crackling glass node left her shuddering.

"Let's see if we can avoid the wall this time," Newton muttered, turning in a full circle to survey the room. "Oh!" He caught Abby's arm. "Get my playbag!"

He hopped the stage steps and sprinted through the crowd, narrowly reaching the suspension rig before another couple. Abby followed in his wake, detouring just far enough to gather his suitcase full of implements and neatly packed kits and wheel it around the corner to the narrow alcove where Newton was holding onto the giant suspension hook with both hands.

"Yeah, it sure is crowded tonight," he told the other Dom, much too cheerfully for anyone to mistake as apologetic. "Still, there's plenty of other stations available and I got here first, so... Hey, as it so happens I know where there's a really nice section of wall just around the corner."

He gave the submissive a wink, the frowning Dom a smile, and held onto the suspension rig until both walked away in defeat.

"Sorry about that," he apologized once Abby was close enough. "I was thinking a cross or cage might be good for us until I remembered this. I love the way my little subbies look wriggling around on this thing." Her misgivings regarding the latest and last activity must have shown on her face, because as Newton bent to take his playbag from her, he did a double-take and stopped. "What's the matter?"

Her stomach twisted, a sickly churning that made it difficult to pull her thoughts together. "I don't like getting shocked."

Newton tipped his head, studying her carefully. "Don't like it as in you want to call it an evening?"

She looked away, uncomfortable with how much he might be able to read if she wasn't careful.

"No," Newton said, and damn it if he didn't use that tone that made the knots in her stomach tighten that much more. It was an odd feeling, to both not and somehow like it when he did that. But not knowing how she felt made her uncomfortable too, and that sensation only intensified when he let go of the rigging to catch her chin, forcing her eyes to lock with his. "No, don't look away. Talk to me."

"I'm not calling anything," she snapped, because that was what being uncomfortable did to her. All she felt now was defensive.

"Why not?" he countered evenly. "Does this have to do with the scene itself or with your perception of being weak again?"

Damn it. How could he read her this well? Abby didn't answer. She folded her arms across her chest and kept her lips tight, preferring instead to pretend not to notice how that thread of suspicion in his gaze turned dark with warning.

"You can either talk to me," he said, slipping half a step closer until he loomed over her, seeming in that moment so much bigger and physically more powerful that all the knots in her stomach turned somersaults. "Or I will call the scene. Whether you like it or not, part of my job is knowing ahead of time exactly what potential problems I might face with each and every submissive I play with. If this is going to trigger you—"

She stiffened when he caught her chin between firm and yet gentle fingers. "I'm fine."

"You're not fine. Anybody looking at this can tell you're not fine. I can tell it. Now, if this has something to do with what happened to you—"

Jerking her chin out of his hand, she spat, "Don't! It doesn't have anything to do with that. I... I just don't like getting shocked, that's all. I don't like the way those wands look, or how they feel or the sound they make. I just don't like it, and I'm allowed to not like it without it having anything to do with what *happened* to me!"

She was over-reacting and she knew it. Safe, sane, and consensual play meant he had a right to ask his questions and to expect her to answer openly and honestly, and she knew that too. But knowing that didn't make her any less uncomfortable, nor did it make the sudden itch of trepidation crawling through her skin easier to ignore.

"All right," Newton agreed. "If that's how you feel, we won't use the wand."

That didn't make her feel better. "We have to do the scene or we forfeit the game."

"Oh, we're going to do the scene," he assured her. "We're just not going to use the wand. Well, we will, but we won't."

"How—"

He held up a finger, shushing her. "Trust me. Big bad Daddy Dom has a plan."

"Big bad Daddy Dom?" she echoed, nowhere near as upset as she wished she could be. As she had been, mere seconds before. "When do I get to play with him?"

"Ha ha," he deadpanned. "Just for that, now you get to take all your clothes off."

For two years now he'd seen her playing with other Doms, not just at the relatively new Black Light, but also at other local dungeons. For at least one and a half of those years, he'd seen her playing with her clothes off, so part of him had to know she didn't mind being naked in a scene. And yet, there was a difference to be naked in front of anyone else and being naked in front of Newton. He saw more of her than any other Dom had in the past. As she began to pluck the ribbons that kept the front of her babydoll lingerie closed down the front, Abby felt a touch of heat bloom in her already tense belly. As she let the straps fall off her shoulders, the heat rose up through her chest to touch her face, burning her with the kiss of embarrassment. The all-seeing Newton must have noticed that too. Folding his arms across his chest, he watched her shrug out of her skimpy dress with a smile.

His gaze stayed with her until she'd folded the garment and set it aside. Then and only then, while she was looking back at him did he deliberately drop his gaze, boldly admiring first her breasts and then her neatly shaven pussy.

"Very nice," he said, turning the heat of embarrassment up a notch within her.

Her pussy twitched, tiny tickling drops trickling down through the folds of her sex, dampness spreading to her thighs.

"All right." Hanging from a length of thick black electrical cord near the wall was the button box that operated the suspension motor. Newton went to it, pushing his thumb against the top button to lower the hook to within her easy reach. "I remember ropes are a hard limit," he said as he motioned for her to step under the hook. "I also know you don't like to be confined, but how do you feel about bondage cuffs, handcuffs, Velcro, duct tape? Scotch tape?"

"I've been trying to get comfortable with leather restraints," she admitted.

Pulling his bag over to the wall, where it would be out of the way, Newton hunkered down to unzip the top. He shifted aside a small plastic tub filled with cracker packets and mini candy bars, several lengths of coiled rope in a large Ziploc bag, a hard plastic grade-school pencil box that sounded as if it actually had pencils in it, and a Disney's Frozen lap blanket before digging a hard black case out of the bottom of the playbag. He set that aside to unzip a side pocket, from which he plucked out another large Ziploc bag stuffed with different styles of restraints, lengths of chain and a whole assortment of clips kept neatly together like keys on a large silver o-ring.

"How do you feel about these?" he said, opening up his bag and handing her a pair of black leather restraints, linked together on the same clip and lined along the inside with hot pink faux fur. "Velcro tabs," he told her while she examined them closely. "Quick release, very beginner stuff. All you have to do is twist your wrists or—since I intend to use the hook—let your weight hang, and you'll pop right out."

She didn't realize she was holding her breath until she had to answer. Nights like this were all about doing things outside of one's comfort zones. "I'm okay with this," she said, handing them back.

"Are you okay with ribbons instead of rope?" he asked. "In your hair to be specific?"

She blinked twice. "I think so," she cautiously agreed.

"Hm." His eyes narrowed again, but in a way she was beginning to recognize as a playful rather than an angry look. Digging back down into his suitcase, he pulled out a red velvet bag with a pull string top. He untied it. "How are you about this?"

When he pulled out the shiny metal anal hook, the whole of her insides tightened deliciously. A pulse of desire reverberated through her clit.

"I think I'm okay with that." She immediately cleared her throat and hoped he didn't notice how breathlessly she had made that admission. Amusement glittering in his dark eyes.

Yeah, he'd noticed.

He dug back into his bag, unzipping a side pocket to withdraw a wad of markers banded together with a red rubberband. "And these? They're washable."

What in the world was he planning? Her clit thrummed, her sex pulsing in arousal. Her lips needed moisture, but her mouth was too dry. She nodded. "And we're not using the violet wand? How are we going to win if we don't use the wand?"

"Don't worry, we'll be in compliance with the rules." Newton stood, the markers in his hand. "I'm not going to ask if you trust me, Abby, but I want you to anyway and I'm willing to promise that I will do nothing tonight to betray that trust."

Her thighs felt wet. Beads of moisture tickled her, caressing her vaginal lips like the tip of a hesitant tongue. Unable to speak, she nodded instead. Coming to her, Newton took the Velcro restraints from her hand and slipped them onto her wrists.

"Reach for the stars," he told her, already extending her arms. Having already lowered the hook, it dangled right above her head and the short clip between her cuffs slipped easily over the end. "If for any reason you need to stop this scene—and I don't care what it is—just give a yank and the cuffs will come off. No safeword required. No quitting or weakness involved." He gave her a look. "Agreed?"

"Are you going to call the scene if I do?"

"Long enough to find out what the issue is. Depending on what it is, I might feel the scene needs to end, but that's my decision and you will abide by it." His look grew even sterner. "If you get uncomfortable for any reason, I expect you to do what I told you and get free. Do you hear the command in my voice?"

Abby stared up at him, his hands still holding onto her wrists, feeling absurdly, inexplicably safe.

Although he gave plenty of time for her respond, when she didn't, he said, "Abby, if you choose to disobey what I just told you and I ever find out about it, and we ever play again, I don't care if it's six months or six years from now, you will be one very, very sorry little girl."

He really was a Daddy Dom. Abby wasn't a Little. She didn't understand the fetish and didn't have the patience for it, but in that moment, with him looking at her like that, Abby felt all of three feet tall and four years old.

"Yes, sir." She nodded for good measure, and he stepped back to the button box to retract the hook. Afraid she might accidentally get out of the cuffs, she held onto the j-shaped curve with both hands, her arms slowly dragging upward until she was fully upright. A little higher and she would have been forced onto tiptoes, a little more slack and she could have unhooked her wrists herself.

"Comfortable?" he asked.

As much as she could be. She nodded, adjusting her stance so her feet were a little further apart and her weight was more balanced to endure whatever was coming next. What was he planning? He said he wouldn't use the wand, but at some point he was going to have to in order for the scene to count. They'd be disqualified otherwise. Her heart rate picked up and so did her breathing, something she didn't realize until Newton laid the flat of his hand upon her chest. The heat of his palm seared into the valley between her breasts. Her nipples tightened. That heat shot straight to her groin where it took up her heartbeat in rhythmic pulses of warmth and wanting.

"Relax," he said, his tone slow sensuality incarnate. "Deep breaths. I want you to close your eyes until I say you can open them."

"Why?"

He didn't answer and his expression never changed, but his hand did move, abandoning the valley for the rounded hill of her right breast. His fingertips circled her nipple and her whole body shivered when she felt the brush of his other hand skimming her hip, following the dip of her waist up over her ribs and along the rounded underside of her left breast. Her breath caught when he captured both nipples at once, plucking, gently stroking, before a joint pinch and twist brought Abby dancing up onto her tiptoes with a gasp and a mew that she quickly muffled behind tightly pressed lips.

"What did I tell you?" he asked, patience exaggerated.

Humming her pain, she closed her eyes and kept them closed. He released her nipples to burn and throb in the absence of his disciplinary touch.

"Good girl. Keep them closed." His hands didn't leave her. He kept at least one on her as he circled around to her back. The heated glide of his fingers touched everywhere—caressing across her bottom, smoothing up the ladder of her spine to her shoulders, combing through her medium-long hair, dragging it all back over her shoulders, drawing on her head until she had no choice but to let it lean all the way back while he let his hands run through strands, over and over again, massaging her scalp, combing out any incidental tangles he encountered. She almost forgot herself and opened her eyes when she heard him ask, "Assist me?"

Abby didn't recognize the owner of the consenting grunt that followed, but details like that hardly seemed to matter when both his hands now combed through her hair, stroking, massaging, gathering all her hair together and twisting it back in a ponytail behind her. Someone must have handed him a hair tie, but she didn't open her eyes to see who, she just enjoyed the sensation of his fingers. Newton's fingers, of all men. Never in her wildest dreams would she have believed her body would respond to any temporary play partner the way it was to Newton.

Oh God... She felt the brush of three long ribbons spilling down the small of her back and into the crack of her buttocks. He tied them around her ponytail, weaving them into her hair as he braided the length all the way down to the very ends of the ribbons. She knew what was coming next. Her skin prickled, all the fine hairs standing eagerly, anxiously up on end as air bubbles burbled out of a mostly empty gel bottle being squeezed of the last of its contents. His hand came to rest over the divide of her buttocks, two fingers dipping in to smear the cool wet lubricant directly to her anus, and she tightened. An involuntary reaction first to the intent and then the cold.

"Have I told you yet that you have a fantastic ass?" Newton said as those magical fingers began to rub, tracing all around the puckered rim in preparation of entering her. "Nice and tight," he said while her knees turned to rubber and her thighs began to tremble. "The kind of ass—" Abby caught her breath as he applied just enough gentle pressure to sink one fingertip inside her. "—that ought to be fucked often and hard. Isn't that right?"

Did he want her to agree? Hell, did she want to agree? Anal wasn't her most favorite thing, but she didn't mind it. Particularly, she didn't mind when it was used to make her feel the vulnerability and totality of her submission. She loved the mortification of it, of knowing her body held no secrets from her dominant partner. That her current dominant partner was Newton was a fact becoming less and less important the further this night wore on. Proof of that lay in her quivering belly, her molten sex, the niggling certainty that if Newton unzipped his pants to let his cock follow in the wake of his gently probing fingers, she would not object. Not beyond the sultry whisper of 'no' that her naughty side so thrilled to say, especially when it was ignored. Because no was not a safeword, it was just the word she would utter to make him re-enforce his grip and continue on, leaving her either to enjoy or endure the act from start to end.

The cold of the anal hook touched her back, and she sucked a startled breath. The room wasn't that cold. Why did it feel like ice?

"Isn't that right?" Newton repeated, his voice dipping low in warning.

"Y-yes," she stammered, mortification searing her from the inside out while his finger withdrew. It was two that pieced her now, the longer middle fingers of his right hand easing in to fill her with the unexpected girth of a working man's hand.

"Then what do we say?" he reminded, just when she thought her arousal and humiliation couldn't possibly grow any hotter.

His fingers fucked her slowly—in and out, exploring her, touching everywhere. Her breath caught.

"Y-yes, sir, m-my ass needs to be fucked... o-often and... and hard."

"Yes, it does. Yet another point on which we agree. Does it make you feel like a good girl or a bad girl when you take it in the ass for Daddy?"

"Both." She shuddered as the cold of the hook moved down her back, the smooth hard ball at the end slipping into the crevice to follow the curve of her buttocks down and under. Her breath caught all over again when he took his fingers out of her.

"A bad girl who needs to be taught to be good?" Newton seductively asked, pressing the cold ball snug into place, letting her feel the size against her nethers. Pressing almost hard enough to penetrate her, just not quite hard enough. "Or a good girl being very naughty?"

Abby clung to the suspension rigging, shaking now, terrified if she accidentally let go the cuffs might break and he'd think she wanted to stop. She didn't want this to stop. It was shocking how badly she wanted Newton to continue this, to keep touching and talking to her, whispering these naughty seductive things just behind her ear.

"Both," she repeated. Confession might be good for the soul, but when followed by the icy end cap of an anal hook that pressed for entrance until she gave it, it brought Abby arching up onto her tiptoes with a gasp and a squeak.

"Take it," he told her, inserting the hook to its fullest extent. "My cock is bigger than this. Be grateful I'm not going to make you take that."

What tiny pinch of discomfort there was, was there and gone before he had it all the way in her. It was the cold she found difficult to relax for—the cold and the alien hardness of the J-shape as it settled flush in between her buttocks, pulling her even higher onto her toes as he dragged her head back by the ribbons woven into her braid. Tying it to the hook, he pulled it so snug that she could only find relief by leaning her head far back. Her neck couldn't take that backward angle for long, but then neither could her pelvic girdle take the pressure of being split up the middle.

"Comfy?" he asked, knowing full well she couldn't be and wouldn't be, not until he allowed it once again. Her breasts swelled, heavy and aching with neglect. Chuckling, he patted her bottom just to watch the contortions of her body as she tried in vain to ease the pressure caused by her jostling. And the worst of it was, at any moment she could have let go. She'd never had someone give her that option before. She wasn't sure she liked having it.

"Let's begin."

Her belly tightened and the hard, cool foreignness of the hook embedded in her bowels prodded that much deeper and pulled at the back of her scalp that much harder. She tipped her head back to ease the pressure. She tried not to open her eyes, but she couldn't resist. His back was to her now as he hunkered down at his bag again. Unable to see through her arms or below her shoulders, she couldn't tell what he was doing. She thought she heard the plastic rattle of the markers knocking together, but then he stretched his arm and she caught a glimpse of a long black cord smoothing out between his hands.

Was he going to flog her with a cord? Her stomach somersaulted all over again, only this time due more to nerves than arousal.

"What is that for?"

"This." He held up the violet wand. With no glass electrode set into the end, it looked like a thick black headless Hitachi, right up until he plugged the black cord into it.

She jerked, gaffing herself on the hook before she remembered not to move her head. Still, it wasn't the hook or the minor awkwardness of her restrictions that put that thin note of panic into her voice. "You said we weren't going to use that."

"We will," he reminded her, "but we won't. See?"

She really had to crane her neck in order to see it when he strapped the holster around his waist and dropped the black handle of the wand into it. It might not be in his hand, but that didn't make her feel better. It was going to have to be used, she knew. Whether she liked it or not, if the violet wand was not the focus of the scene, then they would lose the competition.

Abby swallowed hard, barely noticing the hard flat plane of Newton's stomach or the bunch and flex of his shoulders as he pulled his shirt off over his head and tossed it aside. At some point, she was going to have to pull up her non-existent big girl panties and just do it.

Or call the club safeword.

God, she hated electrical play.

Right up until Newton set up a footswitch, turned the wand on, adjusted the setting down low and then picked up the end of the body cable he'd plugged into it. With his eyes on her, quite deliberately, he tucked the conductive end into the waistband of his pants, pressing it snug up against his hip.

"I'm not going to touch you with the wand," he said, showing her both empty hands. Then, just as deliberately, he reached for her. As if in slow motion, Abby watched his finger extend as the distance between his hand and her breast closed. He never actually touched her. He didn't have to. He only had to come close enough for the spark to jump from the tip of his flesh to the stiffened peak of her nipple.

Her whole body jolted, though the shock was little more than she would have received after scuffing her socks across the carpet. She caught her breath all over again, her hands gripping tight to the rigging as Newton trailed his fingers, dragging a prickly spider-crawl of static zaps along the under curve of each breast in turn. "Oh shit," she breathed, her belly flinching, her skin still crawling long after he took his hands away.

Newton's smile was pure evil. "That's the lowest setting and I'm content not only to keep it there, but to turn it off now and then and give you a nice, gentle, perhaps even easy ride all the way to the finish line. However..." He winked. "...where's the fun in that?"

"Oh shit!" Abby yelped again, fists squeezing tight on the rigging, the anal hook jabbing as deep as it would go as she cringed inward and Newton let both hands trail her sides, not quite touching, his fingertips just close enough to let the electrical current of the wand leap from his skin into hers. She could hear the spidery crackling, the hum of the wand, and every inch of her arched and writhed at the static crawling that followed his caress into the dip of her waist, across her stomach, over her hips and down her thighs.

"Absolute obedience," Newton said as his hands came drifting back up between her legs. "That's what you're going to give me, because each time you don't I'm going to turn the setting up. Can you bear it?"

She forgot about the anal hook only until she tried to nod. She groaned instead.

"Good girl. Let's test that, shall we? Close your eyes. And this time —" He winked. "—keep them closed if you know what's good for you."

Her body was humming, throbbing. Everywhere he had touched her, the nerves were awakened and buzzing. She didn't want to close her eyes, afraid of how much stronger the sensation might be if she couldn't see it, brace for it, before he touched her. And yet, she could feel the wetness growing between her legs, as well as the giddiness with which her pussy eagerly absorbed everything he did.

Humming—half nerves, half anticipation—Abby obeyed him. Clinging to the suspension hook, she trembled while she waited for the next shock, the next caress, the next command.

The heat of his breath brushed her cheek. If not for the hook and the constant pressure pulling on her hair, she'd have raised her head, turned toward the source of that breath, made herself available for the static kiss that was sure to follow. Except that Newton didn't kiss her. She heard the click of the floor switch before the wand ceased its threatening hum, and then he whispered, "Keep your eyes closed. Concentrate. You're going to feel the tip of a marker touch you on the back. It's going to write something and I want you to tell me what it says. If you can, your reward will be one full minute of absolute delight. If you can't, you and I are going to writhe and shriek our way through sixty long seconds of hell. Do you understand what I've just told you?"

"Yes," Abby quavered. God help her, she still wanted to kiss him. Newton! And yet in this moment she couldn't for the life of her think of anyone she'd rather have whispering this same bewitching threat.

"Here's the marker," he warned, but even knowing it was coming when she felt the tap of that narrow touch just below her right shoulder blade, she still jumped. "Easy, sweetheart. You can do this."

The heat of a gentle hand covered her left breast, cupping, holding, lightly plucking at the tip, teasing her with back and forth passes of his thumb that sometimes touched and sometimes didn't, and God if her nipples didn't ache for the lack of more. The way her lips still ached, tingling in the same hyper-electric way her hips tingled from the caress of his spidery hands.

"Concentrate," Newton reminded and all of Abby's nerves locked on the tip of the marker as it moved over her skin. She felt the squiggle of an 's' or maybe a 'b', but whoever was writing did it faster than she was prepared for and her senses were so fractured, quivering and caught between the anticipation of what had already happened and what was yet to come. How many letters had been drawn? Was it four, five maybe? Was punctuation involved?

"Slut?" she guessed, opting for what she hoped was a safe guess. Over the years, she'd seen a few of these types of scenes and 'slut' was almost always involved. Her pussy tightened, liking the idea.

"Not even close," Newton replied.

The marker, Newton, all sense of 'other' touching left her. She heard the click of the footswitch, the aggressive hum of the current as he turned it up two notches and though she braced herself, drawing two quick deep breathes, she lost all her air in one startled shriek when he zapped both her jutting, tightly budded nipples at once. Her eyes flew open, but seeing it coming didn't help her bear it any better. She kept hold of the suspension hook, but only just. She jerked and stamped, and twisted, wrenching her hips, her breasts, her legs backwards, forwards, convulsively from side to side, anywhere and everywhere she might escape the next biting jolt of electricity his tapping fingers sought to impart, and finding no avenue of escape anywhere at all.

He left no part of her unmolested. Hell, he'd called it, and certainly that's where he took her as he raked his fingers down her body, dragging the dancing, crackling sparks of electricity over her hips and buttocks and down the backs of oh so sensitive legs. He tortured her feet and she howled, but nowhere near as loudly or as emphatically as her shrieks became as his fingers began that slow drift back up her body, across her knees, up the inner slope of her thighs to the slick wet drips of lubrication that gathered up all those tingling jolts, dispersed them through the moisture and shot them all the way into her sex. Up into her clutching, spasming womb. All through the inner and outer nerves of her overstimulated clit. She tried to climb the suspension rigging up into the rafters, until her feet went out from under her and she flopped and floundered on the hook while he rolled his fingers all around her clit, zapping but not touching, no matter how she moved.

"Time," he proclaimed, shutting off the wand and cupping her mons, his fingers attempting to soothe all the places he had just sparked, but there was no reprieve. Her body was a live wire, sparking now in all her tiniest nerve endings. Buzzing in the calming cocoon that Newton made of himself when he took her into his arms. "Shh, shhh," he lulled. Until that moment, she didn't even realize every breath came with its own mewling-whimpering sound. "What color are you, Abby?"

They hadn't talked about either the color or number systems, but she had attended enough dungeons and played in enough scenes that when he asked she automatically answered, "Green."

"Where are you, one to ten?"

"Seven," she panted, the pressure on her hair and head too heavy to raise. "My neck..."

Without letting her go, he reached around her and plucked the ribbon free of the hook. The pressure eased immediately and she dragged her head up in relief.

"Slow breaths," he said, taking hold of the back of the anal hook.

Resting her head against his shoulder, she did as he told her. Her sex protested the loss as Newton eased it from her ass. His fingers circled her rim, but that only made the ache of emptiness within her that much harder to ignore.

"Here comes the marker," he murmured against her cheek, and Abby opened her eyes. He hadn't let her go, not one time, so that meant he must have passed the anal hook to someone else. She stared into the crook of his neck, knowing she'd be mortified about that part of it later because right now, every sense she had zeroed in on the tip of the marker that had just come to rest on the small of her back. Right above her buttocks.

"Two minutes of heaven if you get it right; two minutes of torment if you're wrong." His hands smoothed her hair down her back before moving lower still, catching her by the hips and holding her steady. "Concentrate."

Body humming, barely breathing, this time Abby felt a few stick lines and then that same squiggle again. What, was it a phrase? The same as before, or a different one? Wait, that was a 't'? So, some stick lines, a squiggle and a 't'...

"'I'm stubborn'?" she guessed. What were the chances? After all she'd done to him these last two years, 'stubborn' was the kindest thing she could think of to describe herself.

"Nice try, but incorrect."

Abby's stomach fell when she heard the click of the footswitch reactivating the violet wand. Two minutes of hell. Not one this time, but double what she had already endured. Her eyes were huge when Newton stepped back from her.

"Can you take it?" he asked, but her heart stumbled, her sex pulsed, and that look on his face said he already knew she wasn't going to quit. No matter what he did, she wouldn't. She refused.

"Let go if you need to," he reminded a half second before the zap of his fingertips came back into sharp contact with her nipples.

Her pussy wept.

Big, dumb jerk.

CHAPTER 6

*H*er areolae were swollen with desire, making them seem twice their normal size. The nipples were tight beads, lost among a sea of goose bumps that covered her breasts, belly, and legs. A sheen of feminine wetness coated the inner slope of her thighs, dripping from swollen folds to create a dark damp stain on the carpet under her. He didn't know whose bright idea brought carpeting into a place like this, but if there was justice in the world, that person would be responsible for cleaning the floors before the next party.

"Time," a man in the audience quietly said, and Newton immediately shut off the wand.

Once more, he closed the distance between them, wrapping his arms around her, lending her the strength her badly shaking body needed just to remain standing and filling his senses with the intoxication that the cloud of her arousal had left in the air between them. Pleasure and pain were too closely interwoven for her right now. He could see it in the dazedness of her eyes as her groaning moans calmed to pants and mews, and ragged gasps for air that seemed incapable of filling the deletion inside her.

God, she was beautiful. Newton held her, rocked her, moved with her dwindling undulations until she fell into step with his gentle back and forth swaying like long-lost lovers dancing heart to heart. Never in his wildest dreams would he have thought Abby—snarky, sarcastic Abby, the bane of his dominant existence at least as far as party nights went—capable of responding to him like this. Never in his wildest dreams would he have thought he'd have this much fun—good, clean, honest fun without a single dip into harsh payback—playing with her, either. But he was. More than fun, this was exactly what he had come to Black Light for tonight and he was riding high in topspace, playing her body better than David Garrett ever played a fiddle, depriving his own the sweet release he never once suspected he would desire to achieve with this of all submissives, of all women.

Abby.

She melted against him, panting, gasping, rolling her hips and probably mindless of the high salute his cock was giving her behind the confines of his zipped fly. She was flying in subspace. Soaring so far above and beyond herself that he could have done anything, suggested any kink or depravity and she'd have followed him into it. Newton folded his arms around her that much tighter, danced with her that much slower, grateful for her that he wasn't that kind of man. Whatever else happened by the end of this night, Newton could already tell he wasn't going to leave this party quite the same as when he'd come into it.

"What color are you?" he asked, soft as a kiss against her cheek.

Her shaky breath caressed his own. "Green," she whispered.

"One to ten, what number?"

"Five," she breathed.

Yeah, she was soaring in subspace all right. Flying so high with her endorphins pumping so wildly through her that he could see the euphoria in her eyes. But then, he could also see the trembling in her hands as she barely kept hold of the suspension hook. He could see the exhaustion in her as easily as he could see the sweat shining on her skin, and the arousal shining brighter, a beacon luring him to tease and touch and even to taste—what would it hurt?—once, just once before bringing this scene to its definitive end.

He checked the clock: eleven minutes left before he could successfully call the scene. He checked Abby next, sending the time-keeper for a bottle of water and holding it for her while she drank. Slow sips.

He wiped her brow and her body—as if the conductivity of the violet wand were his paramount concern, rather than dragging out the time —and then he signaled his helper out in the audience—a middle-aged submissive in a Little pinafore and pigtails—from her Daddy's knee. She came forward eagerly, marker in hand though she waited to uncap it until he motioned with a tap where he wanted her to write. He mouthed the same phrase and she nodded before stepping in close enough to comfortably write down the length of Abby's spine.

"Five minutes," he warned, feeling how Abby's breath caught and her body tensed when she felt the first touch of the marker on her back. "Pleasure or pain. Close your eyes."

He felt the flutter of her lashes against the side of his neck as she obeyed.

"Concentrate."

She curled into him. Did she even realize she'd just done that? Probably not. This was Abby, after all. He brushed a kiss across her forehead anyway and held her tighter before motioning the Little to write. She went slowly, each letter big enough to be read even from across the room and he could feel Abby's tension as she struggled through the fog of subspace to match the letters in her mind.

"I'm straight?" she murmured.

Newton lost his composure to a smile. "That's up to you, darling, but that's not what's on your back."

She was so close to being done. He could see it in her eyes, mixed in behind the weariness and the arousal and the rush of groggy confusion that was subspace. Someone with a love for electrical play could have done more and gone much longer, but Abby wasn't one of them. This wasn't her kink and it was taking a lot out of her. Were this any other day, any other submissive, he'd have called the scene. But this wasn't any other day, and more importantly, it wasn't any other submissive. This was Abby, and their time was short. By eleven measly minutes... ten now. He eyed the clock, in the back of his mind weighing what he knew he should do with how he knew she would receive it. Were she anyone else, he wouldn't care—literally anyone else would be reasonable. But Abby...

She had made his life miserable over one misunderstood comment made two years ago. If he called the scene now, over ten minutes, Abby would not take it gracefully. She might even take it personally. Another brick added to the guilt and mortar wall she had built up in her mind for why something so awful had happened to her. Not because she had fallen prey to the advantages of a predator, but because of some continuous perceived weakness.

A good Dom knew when to call a scene.

A good Dom also made damn sure the injuries he or she inflicted were always the consensual kind.

"No," she moaned, as if she could read the direction of his thoughts. Or perhaps because she could feel him already reaching for the wand. He turned the setting all the way down, knowing in this state the next five minutes were going to take everything out of her that she had left, no matter what.

"Sorry, sweetheart," he said, feigning cheerful regret while he checked her pupils and then her pulse, the slight tremble in her hands, and finally made his decision. "Rules are rules. You wouldn't think much of me if I failed to enforce them."

"What makes you think I think much of you now?" she slurred, but he recognized the attempt as exhausted playfulness rather than a real insult. "How much longer?"

So damned stubborn.

"Nine minutes," he said, glancing at the clock on the wall.

She nodded, wearily adjusted her grip on the hook and then her stance, and then she raised her eyes to his. When he didn't immediately descend on her with wicked wand at the ready, a touch of bewilderment lit in the fogginess of her gaze. "What? Don't hold back with me. I'm fine."

How could any man, dominant or vanilla, not admire that? Newton shook his head. Any other submissive... Any other time or place...

Tapping the footswitch, he turned the wand back on and then he took her back to hell. On the lowest possible setting, he spared her everything he could but left no inch of her untouched. From the sensitive bottoms of her kicking feet and tightly scrunched toes, to the backs of her knees where she howled, laughed, and howled all over again. He sharpened the contact across her ass, making her dance and wobble every bit as energetically as if he were wielding a cane instead. And God help him, in those last failing seconds of the final minute as he narrowed the focus of his torment down to that glistening pink pearl trapped within the aromatic folds of her fully aroused sex, he'd be damned if he didn't make her come. The sharp bow of her back, the bending of her knees, the full guttural shout she made as her hips shook helplessly under the relentless spasms—they were the most satisfying accomplishments he could, in this lost moment, ever remember achieving.

It was in those spasms that Abby lost her grip on the suspension hook. Newton caught her as she began to sag. He shut the wand off, his helpers from the crowd jumping in to assist him. The Little rushed to throw her own My Little Pony blanket over Abby which Newton helped tuck in around her without ever letting her go. Her knees were buckling in and out, and she shook wildly.

"Guard my stuff," Newton told the time-keeper, even as he started gathering things together. "I'll be right back."

"No problem," the man returned. He moved Newton's suitcase of a playbag up against the nearest wall, neatly stacking his toys and tools on top as he cleaned up the station. The night was almost over, but just in case someone decided to switch stations, it was the polite thing to do.

Grabbing her slinky nightie and shoes off the floor, Newton half-walked and half-carried a barely responsive Abby through the crowd to the semi-private spaces against the far wall that veteran members had long ago christened as Black Light's answer to suck-and-fucks. The biggest kink in any BDSM club would always be voyeurism, but not everyone was an exhibitionist and to that end, the owners of Black Light had built several curtained off alcoves barely big enough for the beds they housed. It wasn't ideal; there was no knowing who had used this bed before them, but everything looked clean and Abby needed rest now more than anything else. He laid her on top of the blankets, propping her up with pillows and nestling her in securely.

"How you feeling?" He checked her eyes—dazed. He checked her pulse—a little fast, but steady. Her response was slow to come though.

"I'm… fine…" Her teeth chattered just a bit. "D-did we w-win?"

"Three minutes over," he assured her, tucking the blanket the Little had given her in around her chin. "Are you thirsty?"

She nodded.

"Okay, don't move. I'll be right back." Newton left her lying on the bed long enough for him to fetch a bottle of cool water and a plate of little sandwiches from the bar. He snagged a couple green olives from a dish near the pickles and chips and was still munching on them when he ducked through the thin bordello-red curtain that offered all the semi-privacy that rooms in dungeons like this were allowed. It took his eyes a second to adjust to the dim recessed lighting, but it took his brain a half second longer to register that the bed was empty.

Both Abby and the blanket he'd wrapped her in were gone.

Newton backed out of the tiny closet of a room, double-checking to make sure he got the right one. But no, of the private rooms available, this was the one in which he'd left her. Abby had vanished.

Turning in a full circle, Newton swept the room for sign of her and, failing that, tapped the shoulder of a woman seated at the table nearest to the closets. "Did you see a woman come out of this room?"

"You mean Abby?" Nodding, the woman twisted around far enough to point at the stairs. "She just left."

Left? Newton stared at her, the plate of little sandwiches now forgotten in his hand.

Well… shit.

* * *

ABBY STOOD with her back to the mirror in the ladies locker room, her transparent babydoll nightgown hanging forgotten in her hand, and didn't move. For the longest time, she simply stared, head craned far enough over her shoulder to see her reflection and in specific, the three-word phrase written on her.

I am strong—all in caps across her shoulder, down the ladder of her spine, and strongly reminiscent of a tramp stamp just above her ass.

I am strong. Abby didn't know how to feel about that. She didn't know how to feel about Newton having put it on her. She didn't know how to feel about the way her body still hummed, still tingled, still ached to the phantom caresses of his fingers and hands. It was ridiculous to think that one night spent with the man could so thoroughly change her opinion of him, but it had and to be honest, she didn't know how to feel about that either. How did one go about looking a man she had so badly misjudged and mistreated for two long years in the eyes as if she had the right to feel the fondness that had over the course of this night taken root for Newton inside her? She was so embarrassed. She was so ashamed.

And she was so strong. It said so. Right there in black felt marker in three bold places on her back.

She wanted to cry, but she hated crying. She wasn't big on it and never had been, but if she didn't get out of here and fast, that teary eye-stinging need was going to swell up bigger and faster than she could evade its swamping grip, and then she'd start bawling right here where someone was bound to stumble upon her, and God if they asked her what was wrong, then she'd have to explain it, and she'd be damned if she could explain it even to herself right now!

Hands shaking, she got dressed as swiftly as she could. Her legs still felt like rubber. That last scene had taken a lot out of her. She felt weird—dehydrated, and the way she sometimes got when her blood sugar bottomed out. She had a juice box and a HoneyStix in her car. She just had to get to it before someone—Newton—stopped her and started asking questions she didn't know if she could answer.

Leaving the My Little Pony blanket where she hoped its owner might find it, Abby grabbed her coat and purse and ducked out of the locker area. She kept her head down, weaving her way along the wall and past what few people were gathering their things to leave a little early, making her way to Danny's security desk.

Danny barely glanced up when he heard her approach, but he promptly did a double take. "Whoa, somebody had a good time."

Her hands went to her hair. After all the thrashing she'd done tonight, it was inevitable that she'd walk out of this place looking freshly fucked… whether she had been or not. She spared a moment of regret that she hadn't made herself more presentable in the locker room, but she could fancy herself up once she had her purse and was safely in the car. She had to get out of here first and all of her limbs felt as strange as the pit of her stomach, still fluttering over those words 'I am strong' as they danced through her head. "Can you help me with my coat?"

"Sure." He held it for her while she shrugged into the sleeves. She was just pulling the two halves tight around her and buttoning down the front to conceal her state of undress when he handed her a folded over slip of white paper. "He left this for you."

Abby froze, her hands on the second to last button, staring at that piece of paper as if it were a coiled and hissing snake. "He?"

"Newton," Danny specified. "He said it was important that you get it and if you refused to take it, I was to hold you down and read it to y—"

She snatched the paper from Danny's hand. Trying to pretend as if her own weren't trembling, she opened two folds and silently read the note. Just like his playbag, Newton's penmanship was very neat. The missive was also blunt and so very to the point that it made her chest hurt.

If you subdrop and have no one to call, don't go through it alone. Call me. Abby let her finger trace over the cell number he'd left below before she noticed, written at the very bottom of the page, almost like an afterthought: *You did great tonight.*

Abby crumpled the note in her hand

"You okay?" Danny asked, those knowing eyes of his gazing into her much too deeply for her comfort. He was too much like Newton in that regard. What was it with the men here tonight?

She tried to smile. "Yeah, I'm fine."

She also tried to throw the note away—her life was suddenly much too complicated with it—but somehow, that crumpled ball ended up in her pocket where it promptly began to burn a hole through her clothes, into her leg and her consciousness.

Call me.

"Want me to have Luis walk you out?"

Digging out her keys and her mace, Abby shook her head. "N-no. No, that's okay."

"Are you sure?"

She nodded.

"Okay." He looked dubious. "I'll see you next time."

Her answering smile felt brittle, but it must have been good enough for him because Danny buzzed her on through the door into the secret passage and she was off, retreating back through the passage that eventually emptied out into the psychic shop, and then the street.

She'd forgotten about the ice and was so rattled that halfway across the street she nearly went down on her butt. She barely caught her balance. More importantly, she made it the rest of the way back to the parking garage without falling or getting run over. Pulling her collar up higher, she made her way down the stairs to her parking level and the far corner where she'd left her car.

All night parking garage lights meant city birds kept late hours and it wasn't like Abby couldn't hear the chirping masses right from the moment she'd exited the stairwell. But the significance of the loud chirping and their proximity didn't dawn on her until she was rounding the corner and suddenly spotted her car.

"Holy bird crap!" She stared in shock at what had been her car. Realistically, it still was her car. It was just parked under a splattered blanket of white-and-seed droppings, lovingly delivered by the massive flock of birds that had decided to ostracize the parking garage three blocks away and instead spend the night in the concrete nooks, crannies and rafters that filled this corner of the garage. Only a hint of the red paint color could be seen around the back fender. The windows were completely covered and she couldn't even find the door handle.

The truck that had been parked beside her was gone now. She still eased in by her car, keys in hand but was unsure where to start digging for the lock. She bent down and was just thinking about using her driver's license as a scraper when a flash of yellow lighting fell over her. A familiar black SUV pulled partway into the vacant spot beside her car. The driver's door eased open. The shadow of a head, barely seen beyond the glare of the headlights, poked out.

"Not to be creepy or stalkerish," Newton called, "but I thought I'd stick around long enough to make sure you got to your car okay. And now, seeing it… Would you like a hand?"

This was probably the most disgusting thing she'd ever dealt with, and she couldn't believe she'd actually wished this on someone else. Not just anyone else, but on Newton. This was karma, that's what this was. A big ol' steamy pile of karma and birdseed all over her car.

She deserved this. But then, as was written all over her back, she was strong and she could also handle it.

Forcing a smile, she shook her head. "No. I've got it."

He nodded, seeming unsurprised by that response and was about to withdraw back into his SUV when she both stopped and probably even surprised them both. Certainly, she surprised herself. "Hey, Newton?"

He stuck his head back out of the car. "Yes?"

"I don't suppose you…" She hesitated, feeling stupid. "W-would you like to go for coffee… with me… sometime?"

She tried to shield her eyes, wishing she could better see his face beyond the glare of the headlights.

"There's a coffee place right around the corner," he suggested. "How about now?"

She almost couldn't see it for the brightness of his headlights, but when he smiled it did terrible things to the cluster of knots tangling up her insides. Terrible and delicious things. A pulse of heat. A latent shiver that had absolutely nothing to do with the cold.

"Yeah, how about now," she mused, already stepping towards his vehicle and starting to smile now herself.

Big, dumb—she smiled to herself—jerk.

THE END

ABOUT THE AUTHOR

Fortunate enough to live with my Daddy Dom, I am a Little, coffee fanatic, administrator at two of my local BDSM dungeons, resident of the wilds of freakin' Kansas (still don't know how I ended up here) and submissive to the love of my life. An International and USA Best-selling Author, I have penned more than 160 novels, novellas and short stories, and am the author of the Masters of the Castle series.

I also write under the names of Denise Hall and Darla Phelps.

WHERE TO FIND MAREN SMITH:

- Website: http://MarenSmith.com
- Facebook: https://www.facebook.com/AuthMarenSmith
- Follow her on Twitter: @authmarensmith
- Friend her on Instagram: maren_smith

OTHER BOOKS BY MAREN SMITH

The Red Petticoat Saloon Series:

Jade's Dragon

Warming Emerald

Masters of the Castle Series:

Book 1, Holding Hannah

Book 2, Kaylee's Keeper

Book 3, Saving Sara

Book 4, Sweet Sinclair

Book 5, Chasing Chelsea

Book 6, Owning O

Book 7, Maddy Mine

Corbin's Bend:

Last Dance for Cadence (Season 1, Book 8)

Have Paddle, Will Travel (Season 2, Book 7)

A Few Other Titles:

B-Flick

The Great Prank

Jinxie's Orchids

Life After Rachel

The Locket

The Mountain Man

Something Has To Give

Black Light: Valentine Roulette

Black Light: Roulette Redux

Black Light: Celebrity Roulette
Black Light:

BARED

A Black Light: Valentine Roulette Novella

by

Measha Stone

CHAPTER 1

"Riley!" Her name rang out over the crush of people. "Riley." The booming announcement called for her again, magnified by the mic.

"Riley, get your ass up there." A friendly voice chided her from the sidelines.

Snapping to attention, she found Sydney standing among the spectators and shot her a solid glare over her shoulder. "I'm going. I'm going," she muttered, and made her feet start moving toward the stage, leaving behind an obviously upset Veronica Masterson behind. If she'd been paying attention, she probably would understand why Veronica was irritated, but as it was, she'd been in her own head and missed most of the previous rolls.

The tension among the submissive players around her mirrored her own feelings. She'd been fighting her nerves about the play event all day, and once she arrived at Black Light she'd finally settled herself down enough to get through the check in process.

Entering the psychic shop had been easy enough, but once she handed her invitation over to Luis at the first checkpoint, her stomach began to twist. Sydney all but shoved her down the steps and into the well-lit, but chilled tunnel to get them to Black Light on time.

The decision to join the Valentine Roulette party hadn't come easily for her. She'd been bouncing the idea around since she'd received the emailed invitation. Valentine Roulette offered a chance to play with something new, and someone new. Not having had a good session in a while, she'd decided to throw herself into the mix.

Maybe she'd meet someone who wouldn't mind her wanting just a bit of casual play. A lot of the Doms said they were cool with just doing a scene, but too often she ended up having to pull them from her leg as she walked out. She would have thought men with as much power and prestige as those she played with would have more pride.

It probably didn't help her cause to stick with such newbie Doms but any attempt to make something work with the more experienced ones ended badly before it even started. Besides, none of them could hold a candle to the one who'd brought her into the lifestyle in the first place – but she wasn't going to think about him.

Riley made her way to the stage, smoothing out the black skirt she'd slipped into for the evening. Nothing too tight, so if her partner wanted to spank her on the bare, he could easily yank up the skirt. She'd donned a thong for the evening's event as well, so all her bases were covered. Very rarely did she disrobe in the club during play. It generally gave her partner too much hope for anything other than the spanking or flogging she wanted from him.

"Nice of you to join us," Garreth muttered as he offered his hand to help her navigate the steps. Ignoring his hand, as she had all of his other advances toward her, she stepped up onto the stage and took a deep breath.

It occurred to her as she finally looked over at the two large roulette wheels that she hadn't paid any attention to which Dom had spun her name.

Sensing she'd taken longer than what was acceptable to get on stage, she hurried over to Chase, the evening's emcee. He gave her a playful smile and a curt nod. After acknowledging him with her own grin, she finally looked over at the Dom. She'd been so deep in her own worry, she hadn't heard a word Chase said prior to calling her name.

"You?" she muttered, unable to hide the shock in her voice.

Dane Stellar stood ten steps away, portraying a look of light annoyance laced with amusement. She swallowed back her initial reaction of shock and tried to keep a soft smile on her lips. She'd seen him in the club once or twice, but she didn't think he'd be on stage during the Roulette game. His cheek twitched. Was he annoyed because he remembered her, or amused that she'd shown up for the game?

His membership to the club wasn't a surprise. There were few clubs for those in the lifestyle to have such freedom and autonomy as with Black Light. She'd seen him play a few times since the club opened, and envied the submissive every second she'd mentally drooled over the scene. Not that she would admit that to him or anyone else. And now he was standing in front of her.

More than that, he'd apparently spun her name.

He was going to be her play partner for the evening. Being matched up with an ex wasn't exactly what she'd had in mind when she had decided to give Valentine Roulette a go. The chance that she might be matched up with him hadn't even entered her mind. Why would he need to play the game? Surely he had a full-time sub by now? It's what he'd always wanted. Wasn't that why she'd left?

Chase grinned, "So, I see you two have met. Let's give the wheel another roll, shall we?"

Chase pointed to the wheel before her lined with play activities. Glancing over them she only noted two of her hard limits. If the ball landed on one, she could re-spin. The reassurance did little to squash the nerves over having Dane so close.

Dane's stare bore into her as she opened her hand for the ball. His harsh features reminded her how his severe determination played into his scenes. She'd watched him play more times than she would admit, and during his scenes, the murky green of his eyes would darken, while his sculpted jaw tightened, leaving no doubt about where his concentration lay. Though at the moment his features suggested a balmy attitude. Even his hair, which was usually kept trimmed high and tight, seemed longer, more relaxed.

Realizing she was staring at him, she looked down at the little white ball in her hand. Had she just heard him chuckle? Great, the first time they stood in such close proximity to each other in years, and her brain was addled.

"I'll spin, you drop the ball when you're ready." Chase explained. "If the ball lands on an activity that either of you have deemed a hard limit, we'll spin again. Okay?"

She took in Chase's handsome features for a brief moment, wondering why her toes didn't curl for him like they did when she merely glanced in Dane's direction.

"Yes. I understand." She nodded, and he gripped the wheel.

"Then here we go." He flashed her a wicked smile and spun the wheel.

Her hand hovered over the spinning activities, and she tried to see the words as they flew by her. The murmurings of the crowd around them melted away.

"Riley, you have to drop the ball," Chase whispered when she still hadn't moved.

She nodded, gave one last glance up at Dane who was now smiling with obvious amusement, and sent the small sphere spinning in the track. Around and around she watched it roll, tensing a fraction when Dane stepped closer as well to get a better look. Of course, he was just as interested, it was his activity as much as hers.

As the wheel slowed, the ball began to makes its descent onto the grooves. Hands fisted at her sides, she watched it bounce until it finally settled in one groove and remained motionless as the wheel slowed to a stop. Her breath hitched and her muscles tightened. Both excitement and terror ran through her as they battled to dominate her insides.

"Humiliation!" Chase called out with a clap of his hands. "Not on either of your lists, is it?" He checked his list. Dane had moved even closer, and was now standing beside her.

"No." Without turning her head, she glanced over at Dane.

"No." His hand snaked into hers, their fingers lacing together. A familiar calm seeped into her. "We're good with this."

Humiliation play. Her eyes darted from the wheel to him. "Yeah.

Good." She slowly nodded. Her darker side hadn't allowed her to mark it on her limits list. It was that side that made her sign up for the game. Her dark desire longed to be in a scene involving it, but never had she asked for it, never had she allowed her top to think she was into that. It was one thing for her to enjoy a spanking, or a flogging, but quite another for a partner in one of the top law firms in D.C. to crave being humbled and humiliated. But she hadn't marked it as off limits. And now she was being led off the stage with the one man who haunted too many of her waking moments, and most of her fantasies.

Dane pulled her along with him to stage left to wait for the final couple to spin. The sub who had looked irritated when Riley left her to go on stage, was down-right pissed now. Apparently, her ex-husband was the only Dom left, which meant they were teamed up, and Veronica wasn't shy about how she felt. Jabs went back and forth between the two until they finally rolled their activity and every couple was paired off and ready to go.

"And that concludes our pairing ceremony. I thank all of you who are participating and also, those of you here to observe. You may all get started with your first kink." Chase sent them all on their way to begin their evenings, and Riley still hadn't wrapped her mind around having been paired with Dane.

Again, she found her hand being pulled until she started walking, following Dane off the stage and through the new crowd of couples starting to get ready to play.

Riley caught Sydney's smile as they passed her in the crowd. The little wink didn't go unnoticed, by either of them.

"Looks like she approves," Dane said as he walked them over to the bar area.

"Yeah," Riley mumbled. Sydney had made it clear she didn't understand Riley breaking it off with Dane, and she now looked more than just approving, she looked damn near thrilled. If only Riley could dredge up the same excitement. Dane had a way about him, a way to shine light on her darkness and make it look okay. For the past several years, she'd hidden that spot of hers, not letting anyone get near it and now she would be diving into one of her dirtiest secrets with Dane.

"Let's get a drink and talk for a minute before we begin." He waved over the bartender. "Two waters," he ordered for them. The bright neon lighting of the bar accentuated his strong features, giving him a serious look.

Riley took the bottle he handed her and twisted the top off, pressing her back against the bar to keep her eyes on the crowd of people sorting out their seats and play stations.

"You seemed surprised to see me." He broke the silence between them, motioning for them to move to a high-top table a few feet away from the bar.

"No, I mean, yeah, but not really. I knew you were a member." The real surprise had come when she'd seen him the first time at Black Light. Over the years, she'd lost track of his whereabouts, until then she hadn't known for certain he was even still in the D.C. area.

She put the bottle of water down on the cocktail table, watching as the condensation dripped down the rippling of the plastic onto the table.

"I've seen you, too, but we never seem to be free at the same time."

Glancing up at him, she took in his casual expression. He leaned his forearms on the table. The tribal band tattoo on his left arm had faded over the years, more blue than black now, but his biceps hadn't changed. He was still in top physical condition.

"You still like to run every morning?" She grabbed the bottle again and concentrated on taking a drink. Her heart was starting to ramp up with him so close.

"Five miles." He nodded. "I heard you were a DA for a while. Haven't seen your name in the paper lately though. Things change?"

"Yeah. Private practice now." She wiped a drop of water from the table and rubbed her hands over her skirt. "You? Probably high rank by now."

"E7 when I got out." His jaw tightened at the mention of his army rank.

"I didn't realize you were out. I figured you'd stay until retirement." She swiped a chestnut brown hair out of her face and tucked it behind her ear.

"That was the plan." Another nod. "Ended up getting stationed in South Carolina: Fort Jackson."

"Fort Jackson? Isn't that boot camp?" Riley asked. Sydney's brother had recently enlisted and had been shipped there for basic training.

"Yeah." He fixed his stare on her. An unsettling calm came over his features. His military career had always been a worry of hers. The idea of him being deployed and shipped halfway across the world had weighed on her. "Decided to stick to what I do best. Training. I was a drill sergeant for the last five years of my time."

"Hey, you two!" Sydney's voice penetrated their locked gazes.

"Sydney," Riley groaned.

Behind Sydney walked Tate, a dominant Sydney had been mentally drooling over for the last six months. He didn't look particularly pleased to be led over to their table, but Riley figured he'd work that out with Sydney soon enough. She was highly into discipline scenes, and more than likely she was setting the mood by being a little bossy.

"Dane." Tate extended a hand once they reached the table. Dane turned slightly when he reached for Tate's hand, and Riley saw the scar. A long scar ran down the back of his neck, disappearing into his shirt.

"See who's sharing my table?" Sydney pointed to her chest, indicating the man standing behind her.

"I do." Riley acknowledged with a nod.

"We're going to have our own little fun while we watch. Nothing like you're going to have, though. I'm still jealous I didn't get my application in before you." Sydney leaned over to whisper into Riley's ear. Not soft enough though; Tate raised an eyebrow at them.

"And I see who spun you." The woman was alight with giggles. To hear how giddy she was, no one would believe she was one of the top DAs in the city. "How exciting."

"We'll see." Riley glanced over at Dane again. He was watching her while Tate was talking.

"Okay, Sydney. Let's go. You've wasted enough of their time already." Tate snagged her hand.

"Talking to my friend isn't wasting time," Sydney pouted. Tate released her hand and covered her mouth with his hand, using his thumb to pinch her nose closed. Sydney's own hands went to his large paw.

"You should understand right now, I don't fuck around. If we're going to share a table, there will be no pouting, no talking back. Do you understand me?"

Riley watched with fascination as her usually headstrong, bratty friend nodded and put her hands down to her sides.

"That's my good girl." He peeled his fingers away from her nose, letting her take in a breath. "Breathe. Good. Very good." A red handprint stood out against her pale complexion. "Now. It's time to let these two finish their talk, and get you over to our table. I think you've earned a little spanking before the shows begin. Naughty girls get spanked."

"I was naughty?"

"Are you talking back again?" Tate asked.

Riley doubted Sydney understood that the hard tone Tate gave her wasn't play-acting. He didn't like bratting, and if Sydney had stopped drooling long enough to have actually watched him some time, she would have known that. But it looked like she was about to find out.

"Okay, I'm coming," Sydney huffed. A sharp slap to her tight, skirt-clad ass had her changing her answer. "I mean, yes, sir." Sydney flashed a grin at Riley before following Tate toward the tables.

"Sydney hasn't changed much." Dane shook his head and took a sip of his water.

"No, not at all actually." Riley pulled the hem of her skirt down. If she'd known whom she'd be playing with, she might have rethought the outfit. Though the mysterious, dangerous thrill of not knowing which Dom she was dressing for was part of what brought her here on Valentine's Day in the first place.

"And what about you?" He leaned forward, placing his hand on hers. "Have you changed?"

How the hell was she supposed to answer that question? "It's been eight years, Dane. I'm sure I have."

"But not here you haven't." He gestured to the play areas where couples were starting to get into their scenes. "Here you are just like always. Nothing too serious, nothing that might get you out of your comfort zone."

"Are we going to start up where we left off?" She released a heavy sigh, crossing her arms over her chest. "Maybe if you ask Chase nicely he'll let you spin again. Get someone else." Without another word, she started to stalk off.

He caught her around the middle before she could get three steps away. His tight grip around her stomach hurt, but struggling only made him tighten his hold.

"No fucking way." His mouth pressed against her ear as he spoke the words, sending a shiver through her. "Unless of course, you don't think you can handle the evening." He eased his hold, but didn't release her.

Spend the night at the mercy of Dane? After all the years of regret and wondering? If she walked away now, again, how would she spend the rest of her life?

"No, I'm good." She twisted in his grip.

He let her go, taking a step back and dragging his fingers through his hair, leaving it to stand on end in places. "Good."

"You've seen me here, but never tried to look me up?"

He flashed her his grin. The same one that had melted her resolve years ago. "Who said I didn't? Now. Anything not on this card I should know about? I know we were only allowed to list four hard limits, but if there's a trigger I should know about, now's a good time to tell me. Humiliation isn't cut and dry like flogging. If I don't know where the triggers are that will cause damage, I can't avoid them." He rolled his shoulders back, like he was getting ready to pounce.

"No, nothing I can think of. Nothing's changed in that area." Not even her level of experience or her ability to explain her desires. Playing with men who don't challenge you will keep your submission stagnant like that.

"Good. Let's go." He grabbed her hand and started marching off through the crowd towards the locker rooms. "Time to start."

* * *

RILEY'S HAND gripped his as he pulled her through the large crowd of people. Spectators were starting to take their seats to watch the scenes unfold around them, and the last couple stepped off the stage. Everyone was paired up, and he had Riley.

After eight years, Riley was his again. At least for the night.

Letting her go had been so hard, but he couldn't make her stay and he couldn't chase her down, either. After she made it clear she wasn't interested in anything more than a slap-and-tickle session now and then, she had stopped taking his calls. After a few dozen voicemails went unanswered, he accepted the invitation to go to Fort Jackson and became a drill sergeant. Doing that course was a trip to the zoo compared to trying to hold on to Riley who fought him every step of the way.

Now he was stalking across an elite dungeon, filled with women that would willingly fall at his feet with a simple snap of his fingers, and he had the one unwilling submissive in his hand that could deny them both their desires. No, not totally unwilling. She still got off on a solid paddling, from what he'd seen of her play in the dungeon. But he also saw her calling all the shots during those scenes, and looking damn miserable afterward.

"Where are we going?" She tried to pull back from him.

"Just over here." He nodded toward the stage where several couples were still milling about. When he reached his destination, he released her hand and spun to face her. "I want you to undress."

She glanced around with wild eyes. Nudity wasn't on her hard limits, not even her soft limits, yet she hesitated.

"Here? There's people—I'll go to the locker room." He grabbed her arm when she tried to turn and spun her back to him.

No time like the present to set the mood for the evening. He caught her around her middle again, pushing her over his arm, and raising her ass in the air. She shrieked but that didn't stop him, and no one would get in the way either, unless she started screaming her safeword.

"Dane!" she called out, but he wasn't giving in.

With his right hand, he flipped the skirt up over her ass until the beautiful round globes he remembered were staring up at him. She'd put on a little weight since the last time they'd been together, and she looked better for it. No time to waste admiring the deliciousness of her ass though; work needed to be done.

"Dane!" She yelped again as his hand made contact with her lush cheek. The impact pressed into her flesh, which bounced back immediately, making him want to groan. Another swat to the other cheek, and she stomped her foot.

"Can't have that, now can we?" He aimed his swats lower, down her thighs, peppering them to her knees and then back up to her ass, where he delivered half a dozen to each cheek. She squirmed, which probably resulted in even more pressure on her belly, but that was for her to fix, not him.

Once he was finished, she was gulping for air but was no longer sputtering for him to stop, or release her. "Now. The topping from the bottom stops." One last slap to her already pink ass, and he flipped her skirt back over the mounds, and put her back on her feet.

Although her face was flushed, she was nowhere near tears. He hadn't been that hard on her. He'd seen her take a good spanking, and solid canings, too. She could take more than a simple hand spanking, but to have been flipped over like a naughty girl? That she didn't have experience with. Which explained the dilated eyes, and the red cheeks.

He ran his hands over her head, smoothing down the flyaway strands. Her soft brown eyes found his. Her lips formed a perfect pout. Running his thumb over her bottom lip, he massaged away the frown. "You still fight for control."

"I—"

"It's okay. But I'm not letting you have it tonight. Tonight, you'll obey, or you'll be punished. Tonight, you'll submit and take everything I give you, or you'll be punished. Use your safewords if you need to, but it's only going to get us kicked out and stop me from giving you what you need, what you want."

"Those are big words."

Still full of snark, but he could see past it and into the lingering desire laced with the same fear she'd had years ago. The woman was afraid of her own truth, still even after so many years.

"Can you trust me?"

She eyed him silently, not pulling away from his touch, but in fact leaning into it. Her lips were supple beneath his fingers, her skin silky just as he remembered.

Framing her face with his hands, he brought her closer to him, leaning down to bring his lips near hers. Almost touching, almost feeling the heat forever carved in his memory when chaos broke free behind him. He sighed when she jerked out of his hands and looked around him toward the noise.

A small crowd of people surrounded a yelling woman. Owen stood center of the mess.

"I wonder what's going on." Riley stepped away, toward the scene. Always the curious bystander, she still couldn't resist watching drama unfold.

"She probably used her safeword. It's being handled." He recognized the Dom being talked to by the DM, Congressman Masterson. Whatever had transpired left him without a sub, but the DM seemed to be soothing the irritation of the situation away.

Dane watched Riley rush off toward the crowd and didn't bother stopping her. She'd be back once her curiosity was fulfilled, and then they could talk about her error. She still held as much charm and beauty as ever. No matter what situation she found herself in, she always emitted confidence. He had been the lucky bastard to see beneath the layer of steel resolve, and if only that hadn't scared her so terribly maybe things would have been different between them.

He rolled his head to one side, rubbing away a tenderness in his neck. Even with all the training and physical therapy he still had residual tension.

"Sorry." Riley gave him a tenuous smile when she returned to his side. She stood an entire head shorter than him, but that never seemed to concern her.

"Uh. Huh. And what did my Nosy Nelly find out?" A strand of hair stuck to her bottom lip, so he gently dragged his finger across her cheek to remove it. She stiffened at his touch, but didn't pull away.

"Apparently, she wasn't into pet play, I guess. I don't know, but she didn't like having to crawl and eat out of a bowl, so she screamed her safeword and went about having a fit. Owen gave the guy some free membership time." She gave a shrug.

"And do you think it was polite to run off and leave me here while you went in search of the gossip?" He put on his Dom voice for effect.

"Well, no, probably not." She sighed. "Sorry." She shrugged and nipped at her bottom lip.

He laughed. "You just can't help yourself, can you?"

"Help myself what?"

It was his turn to shrug. "Nothing. Never mind. Now, I think we were discussing your state of dress."

"I don't really like getting undressed in the dungeon. Can we go to the privates?" She gestured to the semi-private rooms across the way.

He shook his head. No way. This was a perfect opportunity, and he wasn't letting it slide. "Was public nudity a hard limit you chose?"

She twisted her hands together. Still giving away her thoughts, not much really had changed in the last eight years.

"No. I didn't mark it."

"Then either take off your clothes, or safeword. Make a scene if you'd like—easiest way to win the free month for me. I could use the freebie." Not really. His civilian work as well as his gym did more than keep the home fires burning.

Her slender fingers toyed with the buttons on her blouse until finally she started to undo them, working her way down the row until the material opened up and gave him his first glance at her breasts. How could he have not committed the sight to memory? He wouldn't make that mistake again.

With the shirt easing off her shoulders, he unclasped the hook of her bra nestled between her breasts. The little birthmark hidden by her bra and that she'd always been subconscious about was exposed. While she finished working the clothing off, he traced the birthmark with his fingernail. She trembled, but didn't stop in her movements to rid herself of her skirt.

He stepped back to enjoy the sight as she pushed the skirt over her rounded hips and shoved it toward the floor. "Panties, too. Although, there isn't much to them is there?" He raised an eyebrow when she looked ready to give him some lip. She could be snarky, and he loved it, but at the moment he wanted her complete obedience.

Once she was completely nude, she bent over to scoop everything up and held it in front of her, as though the pile of material could shield her from his eyes.

"Tell me something. Did you wear the skirt and thong because you figured you'd just have your top lift your skirt and give you your spankings? No need to show him all the goods?"

The blush told him he'd hit the mark.

"You figured you'd let him see that perfectly round ass of yours, but keep yourself completely off limits. Is that right? Even though tonight's completely different than every other night you've played here?"

"I didn't know who I'd be playing with or what we'd be doing." Her chin rose in a small act of defiance.

"Hm. I've seen you play, Riley. You tease the tops here. You pick the newer ones, the ones you can manipulate into giving you exactly what you want."

Fire lit in her eyes. He was definitely getting somewhere.

"You stick with a little spanking or flogging here and there because if you were to really open yourself up, you might actually find the truth lying in the center of all of it."

Her nostrils flared as she started to breathe heavier.

"You have turned into a tease, Riley." With one quick motion, he snagged the pile of clothes from her. "Stand with your arms behind your back." He didn't wait for her to obey before he quickly marched off to the stage, grabbed his toy bag and shoved her items inside.

When he returned to her, bag in hand, she stood with her arms straight at her side, her glare fixed on him. Well. So much for going easy on her.

"Looks like you're a disobedient tease. Is that right?" He grabbed her arm and pulled her toward an empty chair he'd seen. Dragging it out to where he wanted, he pointed to it. "Stand up here."

"Dane." She looked around to see if anyone was watching.

"Now, Riley." He didn't bother warning her what punishment she would get for not obeying.

"Fine." She slammed one foot onto the chair and pushed herself up.

"Hands." He gestured to her arms. "Behind your back, like I taught you. You remember that, right? The correct position?" He'd never forgotten those lessons he'd taught her. The hours of playtime they'd shared while he showed her how much she truly enjoyed being submissive and letting go of the control she harbored so closely throughout her day. It was in those moments that he saw the true Riley, saw her bare her soul to him, only to lock it up again when she herself realized how close she'd gotten to the truth. Unfortunately for them, her fear had outweighed her desire. He could only hope the years had softened that fear, at least a little.

Looking out over the crowd's heads, she moved her hands behind her, grasping each elbow with a hand.

Standing close to her brought her breasts even with his mouth, but he didn't touch her. Not yet. Her desire wasn't hot enough.

"Fuck, you're beautiful." He could smell the softness of her body wash. She never wore perfume, or much make-up. It was one of the things he found so damn appealing in her. Her beauty came naturally, nothing plastic or painted, everything raw and out there for him to see. She used to tell him that she didn't bother with all that foundation and fluff because she didn't want to waste precious sleep time with putting on makeup every morning.

"How have you not been snatched up?" He looked up at her eyes, surprised to find her looking down at him from her perch. "How many hearts do you think you've broken over the years?"

"Hearts? None. I may have left a few blue balls though." Her cocky grin wouldn't last long, but for the moment he enjoyed it.

"That's not true, Riley. If you think walking away from me—away from us—didn't leave behind some pain, you're not as smart as I gave you credit for." He continued before she could absorb his words. "I'm going to get ready. You remember the color system, right? Use your colors if you need me to slow down. But don't forget red stops all play, and we lose."

"Okay."

He pinched her thigh.

"Yes, sir!" she amended. "Can I ask you a question before you go?" Her voice lowered, the hard edge she'd been forcing eased off.

"Of course." He rested his hands on her hips, enjoying the feel of her smooth curves beneath his touch. The sensation of having her right in front of him, after all the years of playing the 'if I had her back' game, raged in his mind. But touching her, feeling her right there, everything calmed for him. The only thing that mattered was her.

"When you saw my name on that wheel, when you spun my name, were you disappointed? I mean, are you angry to be stuck with me?"

He narrowed his eyes. "If you're asking me if I'm going to use this playtime as a way for getting back at you for walking out on us, the answer is no. And I'll try not to be offended you'd even entertain that idea. If you're asking if I'm disappointed to have spun your name instead of someone else's, fuck no. I've watched you, Riley. I've watched you chew up and spit out at least a dozen Doms. But you can't chew me up, you won't spit me out, and I sure as fuck am not giving up this time." He sealed his vow by pulling her down, keeping her steady on the chair, as his mouth crashed against hers.

Her hands didn't stay in position, instead they settled on his shoulders. Not to push him away, no, she leaned into the kiss, parting her lips for him when his tongue brushed against them. Fuck. She still tasted like vanilla cream, same as always. She moaned when he dug his fingertips in her hips, but she leaned further forward.

When he broke the kiss off, he helped straighten her back on the chair.

"Hands behind your back. I want you to stay right where you are, no moving. People are going to stare at you, see you standing here waiting, and I want you to keep quiet." He ran his hand over her hip. "You can do that for me, right? You can be a good girl until I'm ready?"

"I can manage, sir." She smiled.

"Now, a question for you. Why did you sign up tonight? You don't play outside your comfort zone, so why pick this party?"

She studied him silently for moment, then let out a breath. "You were right. When you told me how afraid I was to find my full submissive side." Her bottom lip wavered, but she took a deep breath and looked away, gathering herself back up. "It's one night. A few hours. I can handle a few hours."

"Well, we'll see." He leaned forward and kissed the birthmark between her breasts and went about getting his bag ready, keeping an eye on her to be sure she was planted solidly on the chair. He was within two steps of her, easily able to get to her quickly if she needed him. He wasn't letting anything go wrong; Riley was back in his hands, and he wasn't going to blow it this time.

CHAPTER 2

A few hours? She could manage a few hours? What the hell was she thinking? She was barely holding it together as it was, and they hadn't even started yet.

Having Dane's eyes back on her in that way of his, the I'm-watching-and-memorizing-everything way, set fire to her nerves. Having him press his lips, his thick, beautiful lips to the birthmark between her breasts created an inferno.

People milled around the room, most too occupied with their own fun to pay any attention to her. Which suited her just fine. Body shame had nothing to do with it: she simply didn't like being so vulnerable. If others could see her submissive side, how could she continue to deny it to herself? Dane crouched down and unzipped his black duffel bag. As he dug around, she got another look at the scar sneaking down his shirt. After he'd filled the pockets of his cargo pants with whatever he'd been digging for, he walked over to her.

"What happened to your neck?" she asked once he was close enough to hear her.

His eyes widened at the question, and he paused momentarily in his movements. "I broke it." He crossed his arms over his chest and looked her over, absorbing her, committing the moment to memory. She could only imagine the pain and terror that had to go along with such an injury. Dane never looked vulnerable, never looked as though he could fear something, yet just before he gave his answer, she'd seen both of those emotions cross his features.

"That's why you didn't stay on active duty?" She watched the flicker of something dark in his eyes.

"Yeah. Something like that."

"You were so army strong, I'm sure that was hard for you." Her shoulders were starting to ache, but concentrating on him took her mind off the discomfort.

He settled his hands back on her hips. "Not my favorite memory, no. But everything happens for a reason, and it all worked out fine. I'm not active anymore, but I'm still working with the military, just as a civilian. Military Training Liaison. And there's my gym."

"You work in a gym?" The news shouldn't have surprised her. Just looking at how fit he'd become, how toned and hard his body was, told her he spent a good amount of time there.

"No. I own it." He gestured for her to step down, and helped her get back on solid ground. "What about you? No more DA?" He scooped up the chair and moved it a few feet to the left, directly beneath a light coming from the ceiling.

"The cases were crap." She looked away from him, toward the other couples already in full play mode. This was easy with him, talking and getting ready to play. Comfortable even, except for the nerves in her tummy.

His warm hands were on her, running up and down her arms in the soothing way she remembered. She caught his gaze and had to fight the urge to melt into his chest. No one ever looked at her with such true concern. The other men she dated weren't exactly looking for a real attachment. It was D.C. after all. If she didn't come with a tradeable commodity, her worth plummeted. And the men at the club were more distraction than relationship material. With a larger population of Doms than subs in the club, she didn't have trouble finding someone to scratch her itch when needed. Dane was the only man who could look at her and just know her. He could always sense her tension, feel her pain, and soothe it away.

Deciding to give up the DA position had been heart-breaking for her. She'd failed, and she'd had to sit in that failure alone because she didn't give the one man who had always been able to carry her through the shit and muck a chance to make a real thing from what they played at. She had thrown it all away because she was too afraid to be loved, too scared to trust in someone besides herself.

"That's partially true, I'm sure the cases were bad, but I think there's more. A lot more, and over the next few hours we'll get through it. All of it. Everything you've hidden from me, from yourself, it's all going to be bared for me." He cupped her chin, pulling it higher and brushing his lips over hers. Not enough of a kiss to satisfy her need for him, but enough to whet her appetite.

"It's just a scene, Dane. That's all we're doing here." Each word made her chest tighten. Her hands flexed and fisted behind her, her toes followed suit.

"That's all we signed up for, yes." He released her chin, sliding his knuckles down her jaw and sinking his fingers into her hair, yanking her head back more than was comfortable. "But there's more here, and it's time you started to see the truth of everything." His lips pressed against her throat, then moved to her collarbone, and he kissed his way up to her earlobe. "You wanted to be a tease? You wanted to get what you wanted and use the newbies for your little games? We'll start there, explore that for you. Now get back up on the chair."

Without letting go of her, he helped her back up on the chair. She released her elbows to help maneuver her body, but quickly put herself back into position.

A breeze blew over her naked body as a group of people rushed past them, making her nipples harden. He didn't let the opportunity pass him, and pinched one budded peak. "Do you understand what I'm saying to you, Riley? I'm in charge, and I won't allow bratting, topping from the bottom, or the slightest disobedience."

Her breath shuddered. "I'll try."

The pinch intensified. "Not good enough, girl. Try again." His eyes were wide and dark, his jaw set firm. There would be no denying *this* Dane anything. *This* Dane wasn't timid with his dominance; he embraced it and celebrated it.

"Yes, sir!" She gripped her elbows tighter, bowing her back to alleviate the burn of his fingers tweaking her nipple.

Without warning, he opened his fingers, letting her breast bounce slightly and a new heat rushed through her.

She sucked in her breath when her head was jerked back again, the tug on her hair relentless. "Yes, I understand!" She called out, hoping that would get him to relent. It had taken her several different salons to find the hairstyle she liked, if he pulled much harder, all that hard work would be in his hand instead of on her scalp.

With a light shove, he let go of her hair and stood in front of her, again appraising her. "I've always loved your tits, Riley." He cradled them in his hands, assessing the weight of them. "Nice and heavy. Do they take a nice beating?" One more thing on the list of things he'd wanted to try, but she'd been afraid. What if she had liked it? What would that have meant for them? "I asked you a question, girl. Answer me." He slapped her hip.

She caught herself before losing her balance and glared at him.

His response to her expression came swiftly. "If you get off the chair, you'll get a whipping. In front of everyone. You'll have to tell them all you didn't obey, you didn't listen and ask them to watch your punishment. That's what's going to happen if you don't follow directions."

"You almost knocked me off," she snapped, righting her position to get her balance back.

His arm wrapped around her while he positioned himself to her side, keeping her front side exposed but secured on the chair. A volley of hard slaps to the front of her thighs had her dancing in his grasp and yelping. "Your job is to stay put. If you can't do that, then you'll be begging for an audience to watch your belting."

"Okay!" She squeezed her eyes shut and calmed her breathing. No way she could do that. Having an audience for a punishment was one thing, having to handpick that audience would be too much.

"Good." His palms ran over her thighs, soothing away the burn. "Now. Teasing. That's your favorite thing, so we'll start there." He plucked a black marker from his back pocket and uncapped it. "Don't worry pretty girl, it's washable. I wouldn't want to mark this beautiful skin for too long."

The chilled tip of the marker pressed into her skin. Dragging the marker one way then the other across her chest, she had a good idea of what he was doing. But he didn't leave her in the dark either.

Once done, he stepped back and looked at his handy work. "Perfect." He didn't recap the marker though. "Do you want to know what I wrote?"

"No, sir." She swallowed. Hearing him say it, confirming it, wouldn't make it easier.

"Sure you do, but you're afraid. No worries, I'm going to tell you anyway." He pressed a fingertip to the marking and checked his finger. "All dry." A grin pulled at his lips. "T-E-A-S-E." He traced each letter with his fingertip as he spelled out the word. Her chest constricted, her breath caught, but she managed not to physically flinch.

Riley noticed a few girls walking past them pointing at her. They smiled, and the tall blonde in the middle giggled. Heat crawled up her neck and over her face. Calling her a tease was one thing, but now he'd labeled her – tagged her for everyone in the dungeon to see.

* * *

FUCK, she was hot. The new blush covering her neck and face only ramped up his libido, as if it needed any help at all after seeing her name pop up on that roulette wheel.

He was going to push, and she would resist. He counted on that, but in the end if everything he'd ever felt about her was correct, she'd find herself and accept who she was, is, and always will be. They would both benefit from that.

"Now, I want you to open your pussy for me." He took a few steps back to assure her he wasn't going to be helping her, she would be doing this all on her own.

"What does that mean?" Her eyes didn't quite connect with his, but he'd get to that soon enough.

"I mean, pull back your lips, and show me your clit. Show me what I've won for the night." His thumb uncapped and recapped the marker while she stared at him, as though if she remained still long enough he might change his mind. "Now, girl. Or do you want to add *Naughty?*" He wagged the marker in the air.

She shook her head, her dark wavy locks falling in front of her face. That wouldn't do. He stepped forward, and flicked the hair back behind her shoulders. He wanted to see everything, every grimace, every blush, every hesitation.

"My patience is wearing really thin." He warned her and nodded toward her pussy. The small line of hair, just a thin strip of runway leading to the plump lips of her sex, begged to be touched and pulled, but not yet. Sometimes controlling his own actions was harder than controlling his sub, and at the moment, with the glistening of her juices showing, it was proving to take much more discipline than he might possess.

After a heavy sigh, she finally moved her hands. Her shoulders were probably sore from holding her position for as long as she had, but he tried not to look empathetic to her plight.

His tongue ran over his lips while her fingers moved to do his bidding. The discomfort in her features didn't dissuade him. Pushing her out of her comfort zone, and making her see the true depth of her submission, wouldn't be helped by any coddling on his part.

The perfectly self-manicured fingers of hers pulled back the hood, exposing her swollen and ready clit. When she tried to look away, he called her attention to him. "Eyes on me," he instructed but he hadn't looked up at her. No, the greedy little clit held him captive.

He pressed his body to her side, wrapping an arm around her waist to steady her. With the tip of one finger he pressed down on her clit, closing his eyes to enjoy her sharp breath. Fuck, that's what heaven must sound like. Sliding his finger lower, he gathered the juices there, and toyed with her nub again. Running the pad of his finger in circles and pressing harder as he went around, her hips started to press outward, her chest began to heave, and her eyes were closed. He should technically reprimand her, but he knew his girl, and if her eyes were shut, she was fucking close.

He rubbed faster, sinking his middle finger into her heated

entrance while still managing to stroke her clit. She groaned, but held fast to the lips of her pussy.

"Doing good." He pressed a kiss to her breast. "Keep those fucking lips open, you hold that clit out for me." Moving in front of her, he crouched lower, bringing her sex even with his mouth. He inhaled her scent, promising his cock everything in the world if only he could hold on a little longer.

Taking his finger off her clit, but still thrusting inside of her, he flicked his tongue over her.

"Oh God!" she yelled out, her fingers tightening on herself. He hadn't told her she wasn't allowed to come without permission, but that wasn't really relevant at the moment.

Her thighs trembled, her clit tightened beneath his tongue, and her pussy gripped his fingers, pulling him in further. She began her familiar chant, nothing coherent, and just as he felt her about to erupt, he stopped everything.

Dark eyes flew open and found him. "No!" she yelled down at him. "No!" She stomped her foot on the chair. He couldn't help the chuckle that escaped. The pouting lips, the narrowed eyes, she looked every bit the child who didn't get her way.

"What? Did you want to come? Did I make it seem like you were going to get what you wanted, only to pull it away at the last second?"

Understanding dawned in her eyes. "I never did that to anyone," she muttered, a soft hue of red starting to cover her cheeks again.

"Sure you did. Maybe not as blatant, but you did." His fingers went back to rubbing her, teasing her, and he nipped at her nipple. "You don't get to come, Riley. Not until I say, and don't bother asking, I'll say no. You'll only come when I give permission."

"That sucks," she said with bold irritation as she lifted her chin in a small measure of defiance.

He laughed. "Maybe for you, but I'm going to enjoy myself immensely."

"Bastard," she whispered and looked away, probably thinking he wouldn't hear. But he did.

"Such a naughty girl." He shook his head, pulling out the marker again. "Stand still." He ordered and dragged the tip of the marker over her skin, right below her breasts. "N-A-U-G-H-T- Y." He announced each letter as he wrote.

"I am not." The indignation rang clear in her statement.

He gave her a heated look. "Should I add *liar?*"

She sucked her lower lip into her mouth and shook her head.

"Admit it to me then, admit that you've been a naughty girl." He'd never get tired of the blush on her face, or her neck, or how it was starting to creep down over her chest.

The corner of her bottom lip disappeared into her mouth while she mulled it over. She'd had the same expression while studying late into the night for the bar exam. Her hair had been longer then, tied up in a messy bun on top her head, two pencils, always two, lodged into the concoction, and a cup of tea nearby.

"I was a naughty girl." The whispered confession barely made it to his ears.

"What was that?" He stepped back and cupped his ear.

She huffed, but complied just the same. "I was a naughty girl!" she nearly yelled, maybe to spite him, maybe because of the burst of energy from the humiliation she was experiencing. Whatever the reason, all it gained for her was a few more people stopping to look their way.

"I know you were, says so right here." He scratched two nails over the word, delighting in the tautness of her stomach, and the shiver that ran over her muscles. Her surprised yelp amplified his pleasure.

"Tell me more about leaving the DA." His lips pressed against her navel, he could smell the scent of the marker on her skin.

She hesitated, straightening her shoulders, but answered with a quiet voice, "It was too much."

Rolling his middle finger over her clit, he stood at his full height and dragged his gaze to meet hers. "More." He nuzzled her neck. "Don't let go of your pussy, you keep yourself exposed."

She groaned, a familiar sound. The way she used to sound when he ordered Chinese for the third time in a row and she would rather have had pizza.

"The cases were getting more violent. Oh, God." She rolled her head toward him, pressing against his hand while he ran his tongue over her nipple.

"Keep going, girl." His teeth nipped her skin.

"Aaah." Her hips pushed back, away from his touch, but one quick swat of his free hand, and she was back in position. "I can't think like this!"

He responded to her complaint by thrusting two fingers into her slick passage. Her hot, tight flesh clamped around his fingers.

"This better?" He nibbled her shoulder.

"Fuck no." Another hard swat to her ass. "No, sir," she amended.

"You were saying the cases were getting harder?" he supplied for her when she looked as though she'd forgotten what they'd been talking about.

"Violent, not harder. Murders... ah fuck... oh God... kids killed... Dear God, Dane!" She was pressing her nails so hard into her own flesh, he worried she'd mark herself.

He pulled his hand free of her and stepped away. "Let go of yourself, slut, everyone's already seen your clit."

The look of death she shot him made him grin and gave him an even harder erection.

CHAPTER 3

The cases weren't just violent, they were unrelenting. Closing one only meant she was able to start the next one. Putting the SOBs behind bars offered short-lived victories. Loopholes, overcrowding, connections within the D.C. elite saw too much of her hard work washed away as the assholes were released well before their sentences were complete.

She peeled her fingers away from her lower lips, and straightened herself up, feeling a new blush form when she caught a few people staring at them from the spectator tables. They were really getting their money's worth with her and Dane right in their sights.

Dane moved in front of her, drawing her attention from the voyeurs. "So, now what? You draw up divorce papers? Small claims court?"

She didn't miss the tinge of disappointment laced in his voice. "No, but it's probably not ranked up there with a superhero like you. Training the army elite? Liaison between the military and government? No, I doubt I rank up there with you."

His eyes narrowed, and he pulled the marker back out. What the hell was he going to write now? He surprised her by holding out the marker for her to take from him.

"Take it," he said when she remained stoic on her chair. "Take it and write on your left arm what it is you think you are. I want you to put on your arm one word that describes you."

She reached out a shaky hand and took the marker from him, and she swallowed. She knew what word fit best, but to write it, inscribe it onto her flesh would make it known to everyone else around them.

"Now, Riley. And be honest. I'll know if you're making it up." He folded his arms over his chest, but his eyes never left hers. Those dark, demanding eyes that had the capability of seeing things inside of her no one else could.

He unfolded his arms and plucked the cap off the marker. "There. Now write." He yanked her left arm outward, holding it straight out, giving her a clean canvas.

She could lie. She could put any word she wanted, but that would defeat the purpose of the party for her. Outside her box, she reminded herself. She wanted to start easing out of the comfort zone that was no longer comfortable but suffocating. Dane was with her, after all, and he'd protect her from her own demons. He'd shelter her from the worst storms. Funny how the confidence she'd had in him the whole time she was without him hadn't bothered to manifest while she had been his.

Dragging the felt tip of the marker down her arm she wrote, spelling out the word that best described her career, her relationships, and her pussy-ass attempts at exploring her submission.

"Failure?" His eyes softened, and the crease in his brow intensified.

She handed the marker back to him, refusing to wipe her eyes. If she was going to cry, so be it, but she wasn't going to hide anymore.

"Because you quit the DA?"

"No, because I've quit everything. I quit us, I quit the DA. Every time it gets hard, it gets messy, I quit." She heaved a great sigh of relief. Her lungs expanded, then collapsed as a heavy weight lifted from her chest.

"That doesn't make you a failure. That makes you a work in progress." He snapped the cover back on the marker and went back to his bag. When he returned with two clothespins in his hand, she leapt off the chair. Not a hard limit, but it should have been. Damn her for being so intent on having new experiences when she filled out the forms for the party.

Dane's first expression was of shock. She'd blatantly jumped off the chair, not even thinking about it being exactly the thing he'd said she couldn't do. The surprise morphed into borderline amusement, quickly wiped away by annoyance.

"Didn't you just say you quit too easily?" He pointed back at the chair.

"Those things." She pointed to the clothespins in his hand. "They scare me." Honesty would have to do for the moment, as she had no other worthy defense.

"And did it occur to you to use your words?"

"My words?" Oh, those. Dammit.

"Well." He sighed and tucked the clamps in his pocket, turning back toward the bag. When he was once again facing her, a thick leather strap was in his hand. "Let's go." He grabbed hold of her upper arm and dragged her toward the spectator tables. "Remember what I said. You'll beg these people to come watch your whipping. And we won't get started until five people have agreed. So, you better hope the first five aren't already busy watching something else."

"Dane. No. I can't."

He stopped and glared down at her. The heat in his glare should have warned her how serious he was. He hated to be defied, she remembered that clearly. It was one of the things she had liked about him. It was also one of the things that had scared her.

"You can. But more importantly, you will."

She yanked and pulled, and did everything aside from trying to bite him to keep him away from those spectator tables, but he wouldn't let up his grip.

Three people sat at the first table he dragged her to stand in front of, two young men and an older woman. From what Riley could make out, the two young men were wearing similar leather collars and were hardly dressed, while the woman wore a full-figured dress.

"Dane." The woman spoke first, her voice advertising her amusement.

"Silvia." Dane's tone held no levity whatsoever. He really was pissed. "This girl has something to ask of you, but feel free to decline." He yanked Riley to stand in front of him, pulling both arms behind her, and pushing her chest out.

Riley fidgeted, lowering her chin, and wishing her hair was long enough to cover more than just her face, but her chest as well. She could feel the eyes of the men on her, the icy glare of the woman, their Mistress, bore into her. When she remained silent, Dane shook her, hard. He'd never been so rough with her in the past. Not even when she'd frustrated him and broke every one of his rules, not when she had continued to pretend she wasn't made for being a full time submissive, and not when she'd said her goodbyes.

"Now, Riley. Unless you want me to make it ten people?"

She lifted her head, finding the woman staring up at her from her seat at the table, her hard glare replaced by a skeptical grin while her hands petted the heads of the men flanking her.

"Would you please come witness my punishment?" she asked through gritted teeth.

Silvia stood up from the table and leaned over, squinting to see the words written on Riley's body. "Tease? Naughty?" Her deep red painted lips curled over her teeth. "You enjoy teasing your dominant?"

Riley wasn't sure how to answer, so she remained silent.

"She's working on it, but it was an issue," Dane answered for her. Thank goodness for small favors.

"Ah. And what sort of punishment are you going to be getting that you want me to witness?" She kept her eyes on Riley, who continued to stare just over her shoulder. "And I'd prefer if you looked at me while you talked with me." A suggestion it was not.

Riley moved her gaze, looking into the light blue eyes of the Mistress and wishing she could find somewhere to hide. "He's going to whip me," she spat the words out, not a good decision she figured, after the Mistress raised her perfectly shaped eyebrows.

"And you don't think you deserve this punishment?"

"I think he's overreacting." Honesty sometimes should be toned down a bit, but Riley hadn't really learned that yet.

"Oh?" Silvia moved her gaze to Dane.

"Tell her all of it, Riley. Go on." Dane shook her again, and she wanted nothing more in that moment than to kick him in the shin.

"He told me if I got off the chair, he'd whip me." She shrugged as best she could with her arms pinned behind her. "I got off the chair. But it was because—"

Silvia's hand in the air stopped her excuse from falling from her lips. "Your reason isn't valid, whatever it is." She spoke to Dane. "You'll be whipping her at the post?"

"A belting, yes."

"How many lashes for the chair, and how many more for her pitiful display here?"

Riley wanted to shrink inside of herself. They spoke like two parents deciding the best punishment for their disobedient child.

"Ten for the chair, five more for now. She needs five people, so if she continues like this, she may be up to twenty strokes before we get to the pole."

Oh, God, she had to find two more people. She'd have to do this all over again.

Silvia nodded. Her blood red lips twitched, but didn't fully form into a grin. "I'd like her to beg appropriately, if you will allow it."

What the hell did that mean?

"Of course." Dane maneuvered Riley around the table until she was standing before Silvia. The men scooted out of their chairs and stood behind their Mistress.

"Down on your knees, girl," Dane commanded. With a harsh shove, he pushed Riley to her knees, his hands still holding her arms.

Her stomach soured at the distance she heard in his voice.

The Mistress's instructions came next. "Face down, cheek on my boot and then you may beg me. And make it pretty. Stick that ass up in the air, too. My boys like to see a nice pussy." If Riley hadn't known she could feel even more humbled than when Dane took that marker to her chest, she knew it now. The two men shuffled around her and took position behind Dane, who was squatting beside her, still holding her arms. She would have kept them in place, but having his touch on her helped her survive the unbearable.

"Yes, ma'am." Riley took a few calming breaths, reminding herself she could safeword, this didn't have to happen, but when Dane moved one hand to the back of her head, to guide her into place, the idea vanished.

She moved forward until the scent of Silvia's leather boot signaled she was close, then she turned, pressing her cheek to the cool material. Dane's hand moved, sliding down her back, and resting between her shoulder blades. He didn't apply pressure. She wasn't being held in place. He was simply with her in that moment.

Time didn't move. The sounds of the room quieted, as though everything just stopped while she gathered her nerve. Dane didn't press her, and he didn't leave her either. She licked her lips and gave him what he wanted, what she had offered when she signed up for the party.

"Ma'am, I disobeyed sir, and he has promised me a belting. I beg you to come watch him deliver my punishment, if you wish to do so." There, that wasn't so bad.

"I'm sure you can do better than that." Dane rejected her attempt. "And put your ass up higher, the boys over here can't see your pussy very well."

She groaned, but did as he commanded, arching her back slightly. He actually wanted other men to gawk at her? Had he turned into a fuck 'em and leave 'em guy? But then again… did she really want more than the party with him?

"Try again, Riley."

Riley cleared her throat and gave it another try. "Ma'am, please watch my punishment. I was a naughty girl for my sir. Please witness him taking his belt to my ass." She expected to feel crushed, to have her pride twisted, yet she found a sort of calm. Dane hadn't left her, wasn't ignoring her, she'd followed his instructions, and she was still in one piece—so far. Even the heat of her cheeks seemed to lessen.

"Better." Dane patted her bottom, pulling one ass cheek to the side. The men behind her whistled and a fresh horror rocked through her, only to be soothed by Dane's chuckle.

"I think I can manage to watch your little punishment. No doubt my boys will enjoy themselves immensely. You've a nice ass that will bounce under the lashes." Mistress Silvia pushed Riley up with her foot. "You got spit on my boot!" She pointed to a small droplet on the tip of the boot.

"That was rude, Riley." Dane whispered in her ear. He pointed to the little drop. "Lick it off."

Wanting to get out of the situation as quickly as possible, she obeyed without hesitation, swiping her tongue over the tip of the boot. Licking it off made a bigger mess, but neither Dane nor Silvia seemed to care about that.

"Very good." Dane helped ease her back to her feet. "Now, we need two more. There." Dane pointed to the next table over where a young couple was watching them with wide eyes. The man at the table had his hand halfway up the woman's skirt and even from where Dane and Silvia were standing, the flush in the woman's cheeks was visible. "Get back on your knees and crawl over there, come back with their answer." The flat of his hand slapped her ass.

"I knew her ass would bounce like that." She heard one of Silvia's boys whisper.

* * *

WATCHING Riley's ass sway as she crawled the few feet to where Samuel and Jeri were sitting nearly killed him. She'd done so much better than he thought she would with Silvia. He owed his friend a drink, she'd played her part perfectly, and with no prompting.

"That's the girl, isn't it?" Silvia nudged him with her shoulder. "The one that walked away, or got away, whatever the saying."

Dane didn't take his eyes off his girl as she knelt up at the table and pleaded her case. He probably should have gone with her, but he wanted to see how well she could behave on her own. Would she obey and continue to beg, or would she take the opportunity to stray from the rules? From what he could see, she was all in. The pout of her lips, and her frown as she continued to talk told him she was obeying. She was begging, and although Jeri had already nodded, Samuel seemed to be giving her a harder time. Bastard. He loved humiliation as much as Dane did, and he was having himself a really good time over there.

"Yeah. That's her."

"She back for good?"

Dane looked over at his friend and snorted. "I'm trying."

"Does she deserve you?" The seriousness of the question sank into him. For many years, he had thought it was him that had been lacking, she'd walked out on him after all.

"She's trying." Dane nodded and turned back to find his girl crawling back to him with a triumphant grin and Jeri and Samuel walking behind her. Even in the moments when she should be at her most vulnerable, he saw her strength. The woman couldn't be further from a failure, but that lesson would have to wait. At the moment, teaching her obedience, and teaching her to love her submissive side was foremost in his mind.

"I hear this naughty girl has a belting coming her way?" Samuel nodded toward Riley, who had moved to Dane's side and was kneeling with her hands flat on her knees.

Such a good girl she was becoming, and so quickly. "Yes. I assume the girl begged prettily enough for you to get off your ass to be a witness?" Dane eyed Jeri who was smiling from behind her husband.

"Oh, yes. She did a great job." Jeri nodded with a big grin. Jeri was a humiliation slut if he ever saw one. The woman loved degradation, and lucky for her, Samuel enjoyed the play even more. "I asked her about her teasing, will you be punishing her for that, too?" The damn sparkle in her eyes made Dane laugh.

"Isn't there some unspoken rule that you subs should stick together?"

Jeri shook her head and leaned against her husband.

"She hasn't had a solid spanking since her surgery. She's trying to live vicariously through the subs here tonight. That's why we came."

"Oh, shit. I'm sorry, Jeri. I forgot all about that." Dane grimaced. Samuel hadn't brought Jeri to the club since her full hysterectomy not long ago. "You sure you're up to this?"

Dane reached down to Riley, and ran his fingertips over her hair, almost smiling when she leaned into his touch.

"Yes, thank you. I'm fine. Just no play for a few more weeks, is all."

Samuel wrapped a protective arm around his wife's delicate shoulders. The surgery had been hard on her emotionally as well as physically. Dane could kick himself for having forgotten the bleak situation of his friends.

Silvia stepped around Dane and stood in front of Samuel and Jeri. Dane couldn't hear what words were exchanged, but once Silvia had enveloped Jeri in a warm embrace he had a good idea.

"I'm going to take the bad girl over to the crosses. If you'll give me just a few minutes to get her positioned, we can begin." Dane stopped stroking Riley's hair and sank his fingers into it, clasped a clump by the roots, and pulled her upward.

She yelled, and tried to pull at his hands, but he only tightened his fingers. "Up we go." Once she was on her feet, he laughed at the glower she tried to shoot at him. "That will only get you extra. Now walk." He moved so he was in front of her, and lowered his hand, making her bend at the waist. He marched her through the play areas in that position. He could hear her groans, her little shrieks when he pulled harder on her hair, but he didn't let any of that change his trajectory.

Lucky for them, one of the St. Andrew's crosses was available. Front and center on a raised circular platform, perfect for the spectators to be able to see everything clearly and no waiting. He yanked her up to stand at her full height and released her. Her hands flew to the top of her head, rubbing away what he could only assume was an irritating burning sensation. A snap of his fingers and he had her attention again.

"Against the cross, arms up, feet spread." Her throat worked as she swallowed, her eyes washing over the wooden apparatus before them. "Now, girl."

"Yes, *boy*."

He was on her in a flash, grabbing a fistful of her hair, and dragging it back against him. His chest pressed into her back, while her head leaned on his shoulder. Her hands grabbed for him, but he managed to slip his arm around her, gripping her throat.

She could breathe, not comfortably, but her air hadn't been cut off.

"I call you girl because that's what you are. A teasing, naughty girl. I'll decide when I use your fucking name and when I won't, but you, *girl*, will call me Sir and that's it. Do you get me, or do we need to have a longer chat before your audience shows up?"

Her hands came up to his forearm, but she didn't pull at him. A tear slid out the side of her eye, and he turned to catch it with his tongue. "Answer." He tightened his grip in her hair, and moved his fingers higher on her throat. The muscles there clenched as she tried to swallow.

"Y-Yes, sir."

He released her and spun her to face him. Wide eyes found his, fully dilated and focused on him. "Good. Get in position now." He pressed a kiss to her forehead and took a step back, adjusting his steel-hard cock in his pants. No way she didn't feel it when he'd been pressed against her.

Her bottom lip sucked back into her mouth. Some wouldn't find her sexy in that moment, she did look a little silly, but he craved her more at those moments, when she let her guard down, than any others. Sensing her apprehension, he moved closer to her. He pulled her lip out and ran his thumb over the wet flesh.

"I'm right here, and I'm not going anywhere. You've earned this, you know it, and you want it. If you can't admit it to me, and to them, at least admit to yourself. Start there." He used two fingers to tap against her forehead. "For now, this moment, I want you to admit it in here that you want this, that you've craved true discipline, that you've dreamed of submitting. By the end of the night I'll have your verbal affirmation, but for now, start here."

Her eyes widened, but no refusal touched her lips. The fear he'd seen all those years ago waned.

Once he saw the war inside her start to calm, he nodded toward the cross. "Go on. Face the cross, and arms up. I'm going to light your ass on fire." A little wink and pat to her hip and he turned away from her, letting her know he didn't need to watch every move she made to know she'd obey him.

Dane was surprised to see one of Silvia's boys carrying his bag and strap. "You left your strap at our table." He held out the leather. "And Mistress told me to get your bag for you, as well." The young man, no older than drinking age, held out the bag for him.

"Thanks." He took the items and gestured for him to go back to his Mistress, who had a broad smile and open arms waiting for him. Silvia liked her boys young, and she never once broke her stern resolve for absolute obedience, but she was more than generous in the affection department.

Dane dropped his bag out of the way, and turned to the spectators. "Fifteen lashes." He toyed with the strap, feeling the soft, supple leather run between his fingers, knowing it wouldn't feel so soft to Riley once he began. He almost wished he'd worn a belt that evening, so she could watch him unbuckle it and pull it out of the loops. She'd love it, oh, she'd hate to love it, but she'd love it all the same.

From that moment, their audience would remain captive to the scene, and he'd keep himself fully invested in Riley. He wasn't going easy on her, she needed a real punishment. Even if she couldn't say the words, he knew what was coming would be cleansing for her.

CHAPTER 4

*B*egging hadn't been as hard as she'd made it out in her mind. Samuel and Jeri toyed with her a bit, but they'd relented.

Her head still stung from Dane's last grab at her, but she couldn't fault him. She'd pushed. In her embarrassment at having been led to the cross like a piece of luggage in his hand, she'd lashed out.

The heat of his fingers around her throat lingered. She should have been frightened, shocked, outraged at his actions. But she wasn't. It had been humbling to be held like that, as though with one hard squeeze he could take her air away. Like she was nothing at that moment but a disobedient girl who had crossed the line. Underneath it, beyond the embarrassment, she trusted. Dane wouldn't hurt her. Dane would protect her—even from herself.

And now she had to get through the strapping. He'd proven how unrelenting and stern he could be, and she didn't see any sign of reprieve coming from him.

She'd taken spankings, paddlings, and even had a belt used on her, but she'd been in control of those tops. She'd said how hard, how many, and where. Very little doubt resided with her that Dane would allow such things.

Dane was all control. All authority. Hearing that he'd gone the drill sergeant route didn't surprise her. He loved teaching and training, and he was all about rules and regulations. She'd figured him for a lifer, but she'd never really considered he could get hurt. A broken neck? Her heart clenched at the very thought of what could have happened.

A scream coming from the water sports sector tore Riley from her own thoughts. She turned in a flash, looking for the person. Too many people mingled, she couldn't see anything past Dane and their own spectators.

"Shh. It's okay." Dane's comforting fingers were back on her, trailing down her spine. "It's okay, that's Alexander's sub, she's fine. He'll keep her safe."

Riley nodded. If Dane wasn't worried, she wouldn't be either. He knew more people in the club than she did, and if he trusted the Dom with the woman, Riley would take him at his word.

"Now get in position." He waited without touching her again for her to move her body where he directed. As she stepped up to the cross the overhead lighting shone down on her, putting her in a soft purple spotlight. Looking down at herself she could make out the black markings on her chest, and saw some of the same on her stomach, just below her breasts. Their implications weighed heavily on her.

Reminding herself again that she'd signed up for the party because she wanted to try something new. Stepping out of her comfort zone had to be done, and the fact that it was Dane standing behind her with that strap made it all just a little bit easier.

Sliding her hands up the smooth varnished wood, she stretched her arms out over her head and spread her legs until her feet nearly made it to the ends of the cross. Her short stature didn't help her fit into such equipment, but she doubted that would delay Dane.

Soon enough his body pressed against her back, pushing her chest uncomfortably into the wood. If only she were a few inches taller, her breasts would be completely over the cross beam and hang loose between the two extensions.

"Fifteen lashes. If you need to use yellow, use it, but if you aren't saying it, you keep your mouth busy with counting. If I stop, you'll beg me to continue, ask me to finish punishing you."

She had a good idea of what he had in mind. More begging, more pleading, and more putting her pride on a shelf.

His hands started on her shoulders, and ran up her arms until he clasped each hand in his. "You'll show me how good you are by keeping in place. Grip the cross, but don't turn, don't jump away. Be my good girl, show me how good you can be for me." His lips were pressed against her ear and she wanted desperately to turn and wrap her arms around him, to feel his warmth and his strength. "You've already done so well, but I want more. And you want to give me more." A quick kiss to her cheek, and he pulled away from her, the chill of the room washing over her now uncovered back.

Her fingers curled over the edge of the wood. Wouldn't it be easier to just bind her in place? Of course it would, which is why he wasn't going to do it. He wanted her to admit it to herself, that's what he'd said. And it didn't seem that difficult anymore. She did want this. She wanted him to take the strap to her for disobeying, she wanted his discipline, and his dominance.

Stepping off that chair had been blatant and now she would pay the price. It didn't scare her like she thought it would. Could that be because it was Dane holding the strap? When other Doms had tried to punish her, or even tried play punishment, she cried off or ended the scene. She was a tease. He'd been right about that as well.

A warm hand splayed across her back a split second before a fiery strike landed across both her cheeks. She pushed up to her tiptoes but managed not to jump away.

"One!" she squealed when his nails dug into her skin. Another lash, just a hair higher than the first. She called out the number and gulped in some air. He'd never spanked her so hard, no Dom had, but that had been her doing, her calling the shots. Dane wouldn't do that with her, he wouldn't let her get away with that. It was that determination in him, that sternness that anchored her to him.

The third and fourth stripes were laid with little time in between, leaving her breathless and hurting.

His hand never left her back, but she could feel him turning toward the spectators. "Doesn't her ass bounce fucking great?" Oh, no, he was going to provide commentary for the audience. Could he make things more embarrassing? She'd just managed to forget they were there solely to witness her punishment.

Riley recognized Silvia's voice, but whatever she said was blocked out by another scream somewhere in the dungeon.

"Do you have something you'd like to ask me, Riley?" His words were whispered close to her ear, not leaving any misunderstanding of what he wanted.

She took a deep breath, and pressed on. She had to give this her all. He deserved that much from her. "Please, sir, will you please continue my punishment?"

"Hmm... why should I?"

Damn him. "Because I was naughty. I stepped off the chair when you told me not to."

"Yes, that's right. Why did you step off?"

Oh, hell! "The clamps you had in your hand scared me." Honesty would be the only way to shorten the interrogation.

"Did it occur to you to speak up? Say yellow, or just tell me it frightened you?"

She tilted her head to the side, resting against edge of the cross, unable to say what he wanted to hear. Not yet, she just couldn't go there yet.

His heavy sigh blew a strand of her hair onto her cheek. "Eleven more." The leather tapped her ass, and she braced herself.

Nothing could prepare her for the hot pain of the next lash, or the one after that. He wasn't giving her time to call out the counts, as he continued to rain down the leather. She hopped onto her toes, but forced herself to stay where she was.

A chill brushed her back when his hand left her. Turning her head, she watched him move his position, dropping one end of the strap to lengthen it.

She swallowed hard, catching a glimpse of the small crowd behind her. Her five spectators had increased. Past play partners now mingled with her invited guests, satisfaction written all over their faces.

"You aren't begging." The warning came right before a heated lash crossed her back, over both shoulder blades.

She cried out, bowing her back.

"Nine." She whispered the number and clenched her eyes shut. She didn't want to see the next wind up.

"No. That was for not begging. Now beg."

Opening her eyes again and looking behind her, she took in the gleeful expressions of one particular Dom in the small gathering. Jason. She'd joked with Dane about leaving blue balls in her wake. Jason had been a real victim of the condition. Seeing a strap taken to her had to bring him some level of gratification.

"Please, sir." She choked back a sob. "Please continue my punishment. Help me be a good girl for you." The pleas weren't hard anymore. Sincerity rang through them now. She wanted, needed, desperately to give him the good girl he wanted from her. To be what she was, without worry or censorship.

Without a word, he continued the strapping. Tears rolled down her cheeks unabashed as she tried to keep up with the count. Every inch of her ass, her back, and the tops of her thighs had been touched by the fire of his punishment. Only the areas too dangerous to strike were spared. Her fingers ached from curling around the cross with such fierceness, and her thighs shook with need to slam shut and protect herself.

"Fourteen!" she screamed out, and felt the nails of his hand drag up her back to press her further still between her shoulder blades. The sharpness of his nails cut through the heat of the strap, dragging the pain to a higher level, and making her body more awake to his presence.

"Last one. Ask me pretty please." His tongue ran over her jaw, licking off a tear before it dripped off her chin. To an outsider, the scene would look cruel and heartless, but to her, standing inside of it, feeling his connection, his pride for her obedience, it was everything.

She took a shaky breath and nodded. "Pretty please, sir. I was naughty, disrespectful, and a tease and I want—no—I need your discipline."

His forehead pressed against her temple. "Fuck, baby," his harsh whisper preceded a soft kiss, a quick peck really, to her cheek. "I've waited years to hear those words." She didn't need to see his eyes to know what he was feeling. She'd waited just as long to say them. To him. Only to him.

"Please, Dane, sir. Please finish." She wanted to wrap her arms around him, but she knew better. He hadn't told her she could move yet.

"Anything for you, Riley." Another kiss, this one closer to her lips, but still too far away.

She closed her eyes and waited. His hand trailed back down then up again, soothing her, relaxing her muscles and then he struck. An upward lash that crossed both cheeks on the undersides. She yelped and let out a curse, but managed to stay exactly where she had been put.

Rolling her head to rest on the cross, she felt his lips on her shoulder. "Stay right here in this position." He draped the horrible strap over her shoulders, like he would a scarf and turned to their audience. "Take deep breaths, baby."

She nodded, at least her head moved in a nodding fashion. He kissed her cheek again and ran his fingertips down her back to her ass, where he squeezed. "You did so fucking good. So good." He kissed her shoulder blade. "I'm going to step away for a minute. Just stay right here for me. I'm just behind you. If you need me, you call my name."

The fire in her back and ass kept her warm when his body no longer did. She heard him thanking the group and talking for a moment with Samuel before he returned to her. Both hands trailed over her ass.

"You really do have a nice plump ass now. I love it. And it marks fucking great." Fingertips trailed over what she assumed would be welts, and she hissed when he pushed hard on them. He pulled her arms down to her sides and turned her around.

She looked up at him, feeling the tears heating her cheeks, unable to stop them from falling.

"So beautiful." He whispered and wiped them from her face. "So fucking beautiful."

And then he kissed her. No peck, no brushing of his lips, but a breath-stealing, mind-bending kiss.

* * *

HOLY FUCK, she tasted like ambrosia. Every memory of ever touching her flooded back to him, more vibrant and alive than before. His body pressed against hers, his hands wandered through her hair, over her shoulders, he couldn't get enough of the feel of her beneath his touch.

When he finally pulled away, giving her a chance to breathe, those dark eyes of hers were wide, dilated. Tears stained her smooth features, her eyes held a tinge of red. She'd never looked so fucking beautiful.

Something changed with her punishment. Not just the glossed expression, or every telltale sign that she was aroused, but something in her expression, in the way she leaned into him now without the tension she'd had at the beginning of the evening.

He'd have to tread carefully, losing her to her fears now would break him.

"You spank harder than before." She broke the silence between them with a wobbly grin.

He laughed. "I've had more practice, and the little boys you've been playing with wouldn't know how to really handle you."

She nodded. "You're right on that point. I don't think I even knew what I was doing, not really. Somewhere in my head I probably had it all figured out, but I just kept thinking I was laying out my limits." Her eyes wandered down to her arm, to where that ugly lie was written. *Failure.* He wanted to strap her all over again for even thinking that about herself.

He grasped her wrist and held up her arm. "This is bullshit. Being afraid is not failure. Staying inside your comfort zone because you don't trust your partner to walk with you outside of it, isn't failure. Quitting a job that gives you nightmares and makes you question if there's any good left in humanity isn't failing. All of those things you did, you did to protect yourself, to take care of yourself, because you didn't have anyone there to do that for you or with you."

She opened her mouth, ready to argue, but then closed it again. She was listening, finally listening to him.

"Topping from the bottom, that shit doesn't make you happy and you know it. Just now, when you did everything I asked, when you took the strapping, did the begging, it didn't just make your pussy wet." He reached down with his free hand and swiped his finger through her folds, collecting her juices and rolling his wet fingertips over her clit, delighting in watching her lose her composure enough to let her eyes roll back and her lips part. "And it does make your pussy wet. Fuck, Riley."

Pulling his hand away from her, he laughed at her little pout, and when she started to complain, he shoved his fingers into her mouth. Her lips wrapped around them, and he could feel the suction of her mouth. It was his turn to groan in sexual frustration. If he didn't get his cock in her mouth or her pussy soon, he was going to burst in his jeans.

"Enough of that." He yanked his hand out. "I have something else for you to suck, then we can continue this conversation. On your knees." He pushed on her shoulders until she was kneeling in front of him.

She placed her hands flat on his thighs and looked up at him, mouth wide open. Fuck him, he'd never last. At least their audience had gone back to their tables. He really wouldn't last if he watched Riley suck him off with a crimson blush covering her face.

Undoing his cargo pants in record time, he pulled out his cock, stroking himself and bringing it to the brink of her mouth.

"How do you ask, Riley?"

"Pretty please, sir." Even her tone of voice was sexy, heavy with lust, matching her expression perfectly.

"Ask that way and you'll always get what you want." Before she could retort, he shoved his cock past her lips, over her tongue and to the back of her throat. Her hands flew to his thighs, pushing him, but he held her in place by gripping her hair and holding her down.

"Aggh, fuck!" He finally released her and gave her a second to sputter and gasp before he shoved right back in and began to fuck her throat. "Open your mouth, wider, relax... oh fuck... relax your... ah, yes, like that." Her throat muscles gave way and further down he went, her teeth lightly scraping him at the base of his dick.

Her fingers pressed into his thighs, but she wasn't fighting him. Again, he pulled her off, and drool slipped down her face and toward the floor, making a mess. He clenched his hands tighter in her hair and pulled her right back on him, fucking her face even harder and praising her for taking it so well. "Oh fuck, Riley."

Finally, he yanked her off, holding her head back so she was looking up at him. All wild-eyed and red-faced, her own spit covering her chin, dripping downward.

"What a dirty girl you are." He grinned, using a free hand to gather up her drool and smear it across one cheek. His cock twitched at the flash of arousal in her eyes. He took up more in his palm and ran it over her mouth and her other cheek. By the time he was done painting her with her own spit, her face was completely covered.

He crouched down, bringing himself to her eye level. "Tell me, Riley. What do you feel right now?"

Her lips clenched together and her eyes narrowed. "Now?"

"Right now, with your drool all over your face, my cock having just pounded your throat, what do you feel? Anger? Resentment? What?"

She swallowed a few times, her throat would be sore for a little while after he'd been so harsh.

"None of those things." She put her hands back on her thighs and straightened her back, looking the proud slut he'd always known she wanted to be for him. "Something new, something I can't explain."

"All these people just saw me face fuck you."

"Good." She smiled. Actually, grinned at him, a devious little upturn of her lips. He needed to fuck her, really hard, and at that exact moment.

"Is fucking good with you?" He hated that he had to ask. He hadn't thought to check that earlier, it wasn't planned. A blow job or hand job fine, mutual masturbation maybe, but not fucking. But he hadn't planned to spin her name either.

"Oh yeah." She laughed.

"Not here. I want you to myself." He stood up, pulling her up by her arm. "Do not wipe your fucking mouth." He ordered when her hand started to head that direction. He marched her to the semi-private rooms, completely oblivious to all of the scenes going on around them as they walked past.

CHAPTER 5

Saliva dried on her face as she was escorted into the semi-private room. Once the curtain closed behind her she realized how loud her surroundings had been up until that moment. She hadn't noticed any of it, the whippings, the cries of ecstasy or pain, all of it just blended into white noise behind Dane. Even now, everything just hummed beyond the curtain.

He'd quickly become the center of her focus. The more devious, the more humiliating the activity, the more he became the only person in the room. Everything else faded into the background. If someone had told her signing up for the party would lead her back into Dane's arms, she would have burst out laughing. Yet, there they stood, in the room all alone.

The sudden image of him walking away across the parking lot to his own car and away from her flashed through her mind and her stomach twisted. Everything felt different, but what if nothing had really changed? What if after the party was over, he just kissed her cheek and said *see ya?* She couldn't lose him, not when she'd finally come to her senses.

"Someone's over thinking." His charming grin pulled at his lips as he leaned against the wall. "What's got you scared?" He made no move to close the distance between them, or touch her, and she wanted his touch.

"I was just thinking about when tonight ends." She shocked herself with her admission, not having meant to actually spew that out here. But now that it was out, she couldn't take it back. His eyebrows raised towards his hairline and his lips parted, but he said nothing. "I'm killing the mood, I'm sorry." She looked at the floor.

"And your thoughts about what happens after tonight?" His soft question came laced with a hint of insecurity. Could he be just as nervous as her about how they'd ended things?

It wasn't her nakedness that made her feel vulnerable in that moment. No. This was the moment she would have to admit she'd fucked up by walking away from him all those years ago. That she'd been searching for him, or a version of him, and always came up short.

"I- I don't know." She shrugged.

"That strapping didn't make much of an impression on you, I guess." He pushed away from the wall and stalked over to her, grabbing her hair and pulling her to him.

His mouth crashed down over hers, knocking the breath from her. One hand held her in place, while the other ran down her arm, coming to rest on her breast. Her nipple became his target as he pinched it and twisted.

"Agh!" She tried to yank away, but he wasn't done with her. He lowered his head and took the now sensitive nipple into his mouth, grazing his teeth over the nub until she sucked in her breath with another wave of discomfort. Her breasts had always been super tender. He knew that and was using it to his advantage.

"Fuck, still so responsive." Wrapping his arms around her waist, he hoisted her in the air and carried her to the long, padded table in the center of the room. So many uses, but for the moment, she only cared about one.

He plunked her down on the table, and she scrambled back until she was completely on it, leaning on her elbows and watching him as he shucked off his clothes. The shirt flew across the room, and his cargo pants were forgotten on the floor as he climbed onto the table with her. So many more tattoos than she remembered from years ago, and a few more muscles to boot. And scars. She didn't remember his skin being so marred.

"Lie back," he ordered, and grabbed her knees, spreading them apart. "Fuck." He groaned. "Fucking perfect." He scooted himself down, until his legs were dangling off the table, and his face lingered over her wet sex. He inhaled deeply. "Intoxicating." He grinned.

She looked down the length of her body at him, while nibbling on her lower lip. Too long since a man had been in that vicinity, and she wasn't sure how long she could hold out if he touched her.

"Just for the record, I already know what's going to happen after we are done here tonight." Using his thumbs, he pulled apart her lips, revealing the swollen clit to the cool air of the room. The tiny breeze alone sent shivers through her body, when he leaned further down and licked her she cried out. "Been a while, has it, Riley?" He laughed and went back to licking her entire sex. From entrance to clit, then sucking on her enough to drive her mad. Arching upward toward him with such need she almost didn't hear him chastise her.

"Down, girl." He slapped her pussy hard when she didn't immediately obey him. How could she? She was dying, and he held the life raft out of her reach. "You're so fucking wet, Riley." His fingers trailed her sex again and she clenched her hands into fists, telling herself to let go, to leave it in his hands.

When she looked back down at him he was grinning, and when she opened her mouth to ask what he found so amusing, he thrust two fingers into her passage. Her hips bucked up all on their own, because she could no longer control the need to have him inside of her. "Dane! Please." She moved her hands, gripping the edge of the table.

"Almost, Riley. Just a little more." He bent lower again, and his teeth grazed her thigh as he nibbled his way back to her clit where he sucked it into his mouth. She squirmed and squealed but he continued his relentless torture. Thrusting his fingers in and out of her as he licked and bit at her clit.

Her orgasm teetered before her, but if she let it happen, let herself steal what wasn't hers anymore, he'd punish her. It's what she needed from him, and what he needed to give her. It was their new dance.

"Dane. Please, I can't wait." She reached down grasping for him, but coming up short as he shifted again. His lips far from her mound, but his fingers still drawing her closer to an edge he wasn't going to let her fall over yet.

"Almost, baby. You can do this, you can wait for me, right? You can be my good girl now? Just a little more."

"You want to torture me." She pouted, sucking in air as he curled his fingers inside of her, teasing a never-before stroked area that nearly spiraled herself out of her body.

"Yes." He grinned, the right side of his mouth upturning higher than the left. "I do. And you want me to." The wickedness of his words, of his tone, didn't help keep her orgasm at bay. If anything, it pushed it closer to her, teasing her, tantalizingly just out of reach.

"Oh, God. Please Dane! Please." She tried to scoot back, away from his sensual touch, but he had only to lay his hand on her stomach to keep her in place.

"Remember this word?" He reached up to dig a nail into the NAUGHTY written on her stomach. "You don't want this one to be true right now, trust me." And he winked. Winked!

Her breath came too quickly. Her throat was starting to dry out from all of the heavy panting he was causing with his delicious fingers.

"Oh, God! Oh, fuck!" She was almost there. Almost. There. The pressure was building until, permission or not, she was going to burst!

"Nope. Not yet." And just like that his fingers were gone.

* * *

If RILEY COULD SEE the pissed off expression mixed with shock that covered her face, Dane had no doubt she'd find it to be as amusing as he did. However, he couldn't blame her. Poor girl had been just about to explode with what he figured was going to be an earth-shattering orgasm. But he couldn't have that, not yet. Not without his cock buried deep inside her when it happened.

He snagged the condom he'd laid on the table when he climbed up earlier and went about tearing open the package and rolling the latex over his cock. Just the feel of his own fingers running over his steel-like rod almost made him lose his control, still inhaling the scent of her beautiful, pink, wet pussy wasn't helping matters either. He'd been reduced to a virginal teen in a matter of seconds.

Running his middle finger through her slit once more, he gathered more of her juices to smear over the head of his cock. He pressed the thick, sensitive head against her opening, she arched up at him, her tits bouncing from her movement. He'd never taken so much time thrusting into a woman before, but the waiting, the increased arousal, only made his girl hotter for him.

"Dane. Dane, please." Urgency, the pleading he wanted to hear rang loud in her plea for him to give her what she wanted, what she needed. She'd been so good for him all night. Shedding some of her fears, opening old wounds for him to help heal, every moment of their time together had started to heal their past. If she was worried he'd walk away from her once the party ended, she was wasting her time. After finally getting her back, having her kneel at his feet, hearing her call him sir, there was no way in hell he was walking away.

"How do you think you should ask?" He forced sternness into his voice, taking a moment to regain some fucking semblance of control.

"Pretty please, sir." Not a second of hesitation. Fuck, he was a goner.

He grabbed her hips, pushing her thighs open wider with his elbows and leaned forward, plunging into her with one swift, hard thrust. She cried out, throwing her head back, her hands coming up to his biceps and digging her nails into his flesh. Ah, fuck! He withdrew until he was almost out, and plunged forward again, groaning when his balls slapped against the curve of her heated ass.

"Oh fuck!" Her nails bit into him more, but it only drove him further.

"God damn, your pussy feels so good. So hot, so fucking tight. How the fuck are you so tight?" He didn't care about her answer, he just wanted to keep going, letting her muscles grip him and drive him closer to insanity. Any ideas he had of making this last any length of time, quickly evaporated when she looked up at him with tears brimming her lids.

"Please, Dane. I can't wait. Please, let me come? Please, sir. Pretty please?" The softness was there, the desire to please, the urgency to seek his permission. She'd hold as long as he demanded, but she'd held on long enough.

"Such a good girl. When you're ready, let go."

He pulled back and slammed into her again and again, grinding his hips into her pelvis, making sure her clit never wanted for attention as he took his pleasure and thrust hers into her grasp.

"Good girl, my good girl. My girl." He thrust again harder. "My girl. Mine." With that word, he slammed into her. She cried out, her nails dragged across his arms and she screamed his name. The pulsations around his cock pulled him in further and with one more thrust he found his own release. His body melted into hers as his mind blanked, his vision blurred, and everything that could possibly be wrong in the world wasn't even a speck on his radar. All that existed for him in that moment was in his arms, beneath him, gasping for breath and holding onto him as though he were the only thing in the universe for her, too.

Finally, he came back to reality and collapsed on Riley, careful not to crush her, but not able to do much else than that.

Her chest heaved against his, her breath washed over his shoulder as she tried to regain her own composure. After several silent minutes, he pushed up on his elbows, staring down at her.

The spit from earlier was dried on her face, a new trail of tears stained her cheeks, and her eyes were looking at him with such sincerity and such openness he thought he'd lose himself in her forever.

"Good tears or bad?" he asked, kissing them away.

"Good, I think." She shuddered beneath him.

"You ready to get up, or you need another minute?" He nuzzled her neck. She could be covered in horse shit and still smell like a princess to him.

"Where are we going?"

"Showers." He slipped away from her, hopping off the table to take care of the used condom. When he came back from the trashcan, he found her wiping down the table. "I'll do that." He tried to take the cleaner from her, but she was already finished. He shoved his legs into his pants and tossed his shirt over his shoulder just before he scooped her up into his arms. "Let's go, girl. You're filthy."

CHAPTER 6

*B*ack in the dungeon, some of the crowds were starting to thin out. Riley could hear more scenes coming to a close, more moans of sexual release than snaps of whips. She snuggled closer to Dane as he carried her. Everything in the last three hours had been intense, more so than she would have thought she could handle. But nothing was regrettable. Even if he said goodbye to her now, if he walked away, she would not regret a single moment of their time together.

A loud cry caught her attention, and Dane's, as he paused in his step to turn around. Over in the stockades, a woman yelled out while the man behind her fucked her—hard. If her own body wasn't sore from her own intense pounding, she'd be jealous of the woman. As many of the spectators had to be, as much of the dungeon paused to watch the intense scene before them.

Dane chuckled. "That would have been you if I hadn't been selfish and took you in the semi-private," he told her and maneuvered to open the door to the men's locker room. "Wait right here." He disappeared inside for a brief moment. "It's clear," he announced when he reappeared and pulled her into the locker room.

Again, they were alone. Dane slipped her onto the bench and went to the shower to get the water going. When he returned, his clothes were already gone, and his cock, standing at half-mast drew her attention.

"Give him a few minutes, then he's all yours again." He grabbed her hand and pulled her to the shower.

The water ran warm, not too hot to have any steam—she hated steaming showers—not cold enough to unman him either. She stood under the waterfall and let the water wash over her skin. Sore didn't quite describe how her muscles felt, but she didn't care. It was the best ache she'd felt in years.

Dane pumped some soap into his hands and lathered them up. "I think we can take this off now," he said as he moved his hands over the word tease. Just as he promised, the washable, black marker smeared then ran off her body. "And this one." He moved lower to the word naughty. "Although, I'm sure it still fits." He winked at her. Her heart hammered beneath his touch. After the shower, they'd be done. The party would be over, and she'd head back to her apartment alone. He'd head back to his bachelor pad, ready to move on with someone else. Someone who wasn't so scared of herself, one that could give him everything he deserved.

He picked up her arm and frowned at the word. "This one you'll wash off." He took her other hand and wiped some of the suds into her palm. "Go on," he urged.

"You don't think public litigation is a step down?" she asked with her lathered hand hovering over the word.

"Not if it's what makes you happy. If it keeps you safe, and keeps you from having to see the horrible shit in this world that you can't stop, then no. I don't think so."

"And, us? I failed there. I failed you." She paused, looking up at him wishing she could read his mind. "I failed me."

"You failed to face your fear and try. That's not being a failure, that's just failing at one thing. And now, you've faced it. You came tonight and put yourself in my hands and you did more than I ever thought you'd consider. So, no. You aren't a failure. Now wash that fucking word off. It pisses me off to see it." The heat never reached his eyes, but she knew he meant what he said.

She wiped the soap over the word, scrubbing until it was all gone.

"There." She smiled up at him, the genuine feeling of pleasure filling her chest as his lips curled at the edges.

"Perfect." He kissed her, a deep possessing kiss that made her want to sink her hands in his hair and beg him never to walk away. To forgive her for giving up on them, but he broke the kiss and flipped off the water.

He grabbed a towel from the hook and handed it to her, watching as she wrapped it around her body. Having her body shielded from him somehow felt wrong, as though it had just closed the door on their evening.

After drying himself off quickly and throwing on his own clothes he pointed to the door. "I'll go get your things. Did you have a bag with other clothes, or you want that skirt you had on?"

"You didn't like it?" She'd meant for it to be a tease, but his dark expression wiped away her smile.

"Oh, I fucking loved it, but it's cold out there. And if the wind picks up, you'll be flashing the parking lot. You have other clothes?"

She sighed. "Yeah. Jeans in my bag. Pink and black bag by the stage."

He eyed her for a moment in silence. "You're worried about what happens now."

"It's okay. Don't worry about it, Dane." She could feel the heat back in her cheeks and hated it. The bright lighting of the room didn't shield her embarrassment – and not the erotic sort of embarrassment that wet her pussy and made her yearn for his touch.

"My neck." He stuffed his hands into his pockets and faced her. "I broke it two years ago, going after a recruit that couldn't get off one of the towers. Freaked out once he hit the top and couldn't get himself down. I went up to help. As I was getting him in position to climb down, he freaked out again and starting flailing. Knocked me off the rig. I fell straight down, him right behind me. I broke his fall and my neck."

Riley's hand covered her mouth. Of course, he'd get hurt helping someone else.

"Oh my God," she whispered.

He took a step toward her. "Do you know what I was thinking as I fell, what thought kept spinning around in my head?"

She shook her head, unable to speak.

"You. I kept thinking I should have chased you down. I should have made you stay." His toes touched hers. "As I lay there hearing everyone barking orders at the recruits, heard the ambulance coming, I just kept thinking about you. I knew you'd made DA, and I wondered if you were happy, did you have someone new? Every moment of my physical therapy was painful, more than any flogger to your ass could ever be, but every time I wiggled a toe, took a fucking baby step, or managed to get myself to the bathroom without help, I saw it as one more step to getting back to you. The first time I saw you here, I just about exploded with relief. And every time I saw you play with some-one, saw you hold yourself back from what you really wanted I got so pissed, but I couldn't confront you."

Her face heated even more. "Dane—" he put his hand up to stop her from continuing.

"When your name hit on that roulette wheel," he took a shaky breath, "it was my turn, my chance to make you see yourself, your real self. Fuck, Riley, I was so scared."

"You? Scared?" She reached for him, touching her fingertips to his jaw, then his lips. "I was terrified you'd hate me forever. That you'd walk away after tonight, and we'd go back to seeing each other but never talking."

He yanked her into his arms and held her fast to him. She could smell his musky aftershave, and tried to memorize it. "Never. I can't let you go now."

"Don't. Please, never."

"You're mine now. We'll give this a real chance, a real shot."

He pulled away to look in her eyes, and she could see the vulnera-bility there, the fear in his own expression that mirrored hers.

"I'm yours?"

"Yeah. Mine."

* * *

DANE LEFT her to get dressed once he brought her the duffel bag and waited outside the doors to the women's locker room. She needed a minute to her own thoughts, and so did he. She wasn't running away screaming with her hands over her eyes.

If she was afraid, he was terrified. Everything could go wrong again. She could tuck tail and run, but this time was different because he knew the signs, and he would chase her. He wouldn't let her get away. Not after spending the entire evening playing with her dark side and seeing how she blossomed.

"Is Riley in there?" Sydney stepped up to him.

"Uh, yeah, just changing." He jerked a thumb toward Tate who stood several feet away eyeing them, but not looking like he was going to be joining them. "What's with your guy there?"

She didn't bother looking over her shoulder. "He's not my guy. He made that perfectly clear. Not his type, too much for him, whatever. Is she almost ready? She's my ride."

Dane looked over at Tate. He didn't look like he was quite finished with Sydney, but she seemed done for the night. "Uh, should be just a second. Are you sure that's what he said?" Dane scratched the back of his neck. The scar tissue still itched like mad some nights.

"That's what I heard." She huffed. "I'll be at the car. Can you tell her?"

"Sure."

Sydney stopped mid-turn to look Dane over. "You two do okay?"

"We finished the game, if that's what you mean." Dane looked back over at Tate. "How'd you guys do?"

She ignored his question. "So, you get her to pull her panties out of the wad they've been in since you two broke up?"

"Sydney!" Riley stepped out of the locker room with a glare. "Shut up."

"Whatever. I'm going to the car."

Dane watched Tate as Sydney sauntered past, and shook his head. Whatever she'd heard, isn't what that man meant. He did not look at all pleased to see her walking away.

"She's a little hard to handle. I can see why it didn't work with Tate, he's a bit sterner than her bratty side can take."

"Uh, huh." Dane shook his head. Tate had his work cut out for him if he was going after that wild beast, but Dane wasn't going to get in the way. He had his own happily ever after to chase. "I was going to offer you a ride, but she said you're hers. You want me to follow you?"

"Home?" She laughed. "I can manage."

"My number's the same, you know." He pushed a stray curl away from her face. "Never changed it."

Her eyes widened. "Really?"

"Yeah, just in case."

She sighed softly. "Me too."

He laughed and pulled her into a hug. "I'll at least walk you to your car."

"Fine. If you must." She wrapped her arm around his waist and didn't even protest when he took her bag. "What about your bag?"

"I'll come back in for it. It'll be fine. How's your back and your ass?"

"Tender and sore, but in the best possible way." She grinned up at him.

They walked through security where she gathered her cell phone from the lockers and headed to the tunnel that would take them back out through the psychic shop. The cool air of February embraced them once they were outside. Sydney was leaning against Riley's car, smoking a cigarette.

"Text me when you get home." He pressed a kiss to her temple.

"You going to start micromanaging already?" It was a tease, but he wouldn't let it get out of hand.

"I just want to know you got home safe. We're going to ease into this, Riley. No fast track, no list of twenty rules and protocols. This is just you and me, getting to know each other again."

When they got to the car, Riley unlocked it and Sydney scrambled into the front seat, slamming the door once inside.

Riley sighed. "It's going to be a long ride home."

"I guess no bragging about what an awesome time you had." He tweaked her nose.

"I did. I had an amazing time, Dane. Even the scary parts, the hard parts, and the painful parts were the best parts."

Her lips were too tempting, he leaned in and kissed her. The blaring of the horn broke their moment.

"Shit. She must be really pissed at him." Riley laughed. "I better go."

"Text me. And if you're available, how's lunch tomorrow?"

"Lunch sounds good. Real good." She sucked in her lower lip. "Best Valentine's Day in years." She laughed and turned to her car.

"Best spin of the wheel." He patted her ass and stepped aside for her to open the door.

The car roared to life and she slowly backed out of the space as he watched her. He didn't take his eyes off her car until she waved out the window and turned onto the main street.

Best Valentine's Day indeed.

THE END

ABOUT THE AUTHOR

USA Today Bestselling Author Measha Stone is a lover of all things erotic and fun who writes kinky romantic suspense and dark romance novels. She won the 2018 Golden Flogger award in two categories, Best Advanced BDSM and Best Anthology. She's hit #1 on Amazon in multiple categories in the U.S. and the U.K. When she's not typing away on her computer, she can be found nestled up with a cup of tea and her kindle.

WHERE TO FIND MEASHA STONE:

- Facebook: https://www.facebook.com/measha.stone.5
- Twitter: @measha_stone
- Instagram: @meashastone
- Blog: https://www.meashawrites.com/blog

OTHER BOOKS BY MEASHA STONE

Ever After

BEAST: A Dark Beauty and the Beast Retelling (Ever After Book 1)

Tower: A Dark Romance Rapunzel Retelling (Ever After Book 2)

Red: A Dark Romance Red Riding Hood Retelling (Ever After Book 3)

Owned and Protected

Protecting His Pet (Owned and Protected Book 1)

Protecting His Runaway (Owned and Protected Book 2)

His Captive Pet (Owned and Protected Book 3)

His Captive Kitten (Owned and Protected Book 4)

Becoming His Pet (Owned and Protected Book 5)

Windy City

Hidden Heart (Windy City Book 1)

Secured Heart (Windy City Book 2)

Indebted Heart (Windy City Book 3)

Liberated Heart (Windy City Book 4)

Standalones

Daddy Ever After

Kristoff: Blaire's World

Black Light: Cuffed

Until You

Until Daddy

Black Light: Suspicion

Redemption: A Christmas Romance Novella

Anthologies

STRIPPED BY SOPHIE KISKER

A Black Light: Valentine Roulette Novella

by

Sophie Kisker

CHAPTER 1

"Why do you always wear that collar on your neck? And what does the tag hanging from it say?" The question was out of Sari's mouth before she could bite it back. Apparently, all it took to erase her internal filters was one beer.

Apollonia raised an eyebrow and stared at her from the other end of the beat-up couch. The music of the basement party surrounded them, thumping and bouncing off the walls, making their discussion almost a shouting match. "I'm not really sure you want to know, Miss 'Farm-Girl-from-Ohio.'" She raised a tattooed hand to take a sip of her own beer.

Sari frowned. "You're making fun of me. I'm not as sheltered as you think I am."

Luny laughed. "If you weren't sheltered, you'd know what this is! All right, it's a collar that shows I'm in submission to a dominant man. The tag says, 'Property of Paul.'"

Sari sat up. "What?"

"I've agreed to submit certain areas of my life to a man I trust. I serve him and obey him. In return, he makes decisions and cares for me, and sometimes spanks me."

If she thought Sari was going to run screaming from the room, she was wrong. "But, isn't that the same thing that happens when you get married?"

"What are you from, the 1950s? Fuck, no!" The music stopped abruptly, allowing her exclamation to ring out in the sudden silence. More than one person turned to look in their direction.

Luny ignored them. "Marriage is about being equal partners! Besides, for me, this is a sexual thing, not a lifetime commitment thing. If either of us are unhappy, he uncollars me and we move on to other partners. We negotiate what the rules are, and when he has control, and what happens if I disobey him."

Something squirmy was happening between Sari's legs, and she tried to ignore it. "So, he spanks you when you don't do what he tells you to?" she whispered, never taking her eyes off of the collar.

Luny shrugged. "I get punished. Sometimes he spanks me, sometimes he whips me, and sometimes he ties me up in an uncomfortable position and leaves me there for a while."

Sari wasn't sure, but at the words 'spank', 'whip', and 'tie', she thought something squirmed *and* twitched. "But why?"

"Because it makes me happy. Because I get my kicks out of kneeling and serving him and doing what makes him happy. Because I get a wonderful, floaty feeling after he punishes me. I don't know why, but there's a lot of people like me."

"Will you show me?" Sari didn't know what the hell she'd just asked, but it was too late to take it back now.

Luny raised an eyebrow again, but didn't say no, and Sari knew she was about to explore something that would rock her world.

* * *

LUNY SHOWED HER. Oh, yes. Sari had been captivated and repelled, fascinated and appalled, all at the same time. She hid her head in her hands the first time she watched a paddling, the woman secured to a St. Andrew's cross. Before the paddling was over though, she was peeking through her fingers. She was at a club in a suburb of Washington, D.C., dressed in a tiny little skirt and a tiny little shirt that showed way too much boob, but was way more clothing than most of the other women wore. And she was kneeling next to Luny, who had suddenly transformed into something called a 'domme'. The collar was gone, and her tone of voice was one that Sari didn't dare disobey. She didn't *want* to disobey.

Sari saw people dressed in leather with tattoos from head to toe, and people who looked just like her co-workers. There were friendly people, and some real bitches, and a few bastards that Luny warned her never to play with. She saw female subs giving their masters blowjobs under the table while the men talked business, pausing only long enough to fill their pretty subs' mouths with cum. She saw male subs crawling along beside their mistresses, their poor cocks in little cages. She watched shibari demonstrations and wax play. She saw orgasm torture on a Sybian machine, the sub bound to it as she came over and over without relief, and screamed and begged to be let go. And when Sari was about to run to the woman's aid, she learned what a safeword was, and why it was the key to everything.

And then, one day, Luny told her it was time for her to play with someone instead of watching. Sari was petrified, but the guy had been nice, and her first spanking was so relaxing she'd sheepishly begged him for more, which he laughingly gave. She'd gone back to play with him a few more times before he went home to Nebraska.

Then, Luny told her about the Roulette event. She herself couldn't go, but thought Sari might be interested.

"But... it's with doms I've never met!" Sari re-read the description on the website.

"But you never play with a dom more than a few times, anyway! Look, I know it's been hard for you since you got hurt."

Sari nodded and chewed on her bottom lip as she studied the screen. A dom who'd known nothing about rope play had suspended her with her hair pulled back by a rope, but the other ropes were slipping and her head was being pulled back so hard she couldn't breathe. He was distracted by another scene, not noticing her struggle to yell, or when she dropped the ball from her hand that was supposed to be a signal that there was a serious problem. A dungeon monitor had spotted her just before she'd passed out, and gotten her down. She hadn't really trusted anyone since then.

"I guarantee that an event like this will be so heavily monitored you'll be totally safe. It's just one night, and it's at a club that you and I will never be able to afford!"

"Then *you* go."

"Yeah, well, love to, but my manager's a prick. That's a huge night for the bar and he's already said everyone is working, no exceptions."

"All right. Fine. But I doubt they'll take me. I'm too new. There's lots of more experienced subs out there."

"Promise you'll just fill it out. I gotta leave to get to work now."

"I promise."

* * *

ONCE SHE GOT past the legal documents and the non-disclosure agreement, she saw the list of possible activities. She had to choose four things she wanted to try. No, wait, that wasn't right. She could pick four things she *didn't* want to try, and the rest of the list was fair game. Whoa. She saw a few that would be fun, a few that were 'meh' and a couple that were on her 'no way in hell' list.

Those were easy to pick. The first was at the top of the list, and she clicked it immediately. She scrolled down the list, but before she was done the front door of the apartment banged open, announcing Melissa was home early. Sari closed the lid and turned to greet her roommate, hoping her cheeks weren't too red. She'd have to finish later.

* * *

MELISSA FINALLY DISAPPEARED into their shared bedroom, and Sari opened the laptop again. The list of hard limits was still showing, so she selected the remaining three absolutes. The rest she was going to have to cross her fingers and hope she wouldn't get. She finished and hit 'submit' without hesitating, afraid she'd lose her nerve if she slowed down.

Melissa appeared in the doorway of their shared bedroom just as Sari logged off.

"What are you doing?" She shuffled through the living room to the kitchen.

"Nothing! Just looking at something for work." Sari made a production of yawning. "Let's head to bed. Early day tomorrow and they're saying maybe some snow."

"Great."

CHAPTER 2

*A*dam Quinn hit 'submit' as he leaned back in his chair and let the soothing rhythms of jazz music wash over him. He didn't know if this game was the right way to get back into the scene after so many years out of it, but it was only one night, so what the hell. He'd had too many years of stress and worry to even think about letting that side of him out of the closet. He wasn't even sure his inner sadist was still in there.

"Daddy?" The little voice from the door startled him. He swung around to see Hannah in her My Little Pony pajamas. He held his arms wide and she shuffled over to his embrace. "I had a bad dream."

"I'm here, kiddo. Nothing is going to get you while I'm on the job, remember?"

She nodded in his arms. *This* was the reason he'd pushed aside everything else in his life. He'd fought his ex-wife hard in order to keep Hannah, while trying not to let the battle ruin the little girl's life. He'd won custody a little over a year ago, and was finally starting to relax.

He picked the seven-year old up and carried her upstairs to her bedroom where he tucked her back into bed.

"Daddy, I need a monster search."

"A monster search? How would a monster get past me to get to you?" He faked indignation.

"Monsters are tricky, daddy. They go through walls," the little girl solemnly assured him. Adam knew this was mostly for play; she hadn't really truly needed a monster search since she'd finally left her mother's apartment and came to live with him full-time. *Thank you, Tricia,* he thought with sarcasm.

"Hmm. Is it in the closet?" He threw open the door.

"No!" the little girl declared.

"How about the dresser?" He opened the drawers one by one but she shook her head each time.

"Maybe he's under the bed, daddy?"

He got down on his hands and knees and peered into the darkness, but the only thing under there was her missing pink barrette. She grabbed it and squealed. "Thank you, Daddy!"

"Okay, kiddo, time to calm down. No monsters here."

"Yeah, I think they went away." She slipped down under the covers again, and he settled on the floor next to her bed. He turned out the light and held her hand until he heard her breathing slow and steady, and then he crept out of the room.

* * *

AN HOUR later he stretched and groaned. If anyone had told him he was going to spend as much time in the FBI on paperwork as out in the field, he'd have walked out of the job interview. Every year it got worse.

His ringtone interrupted the silence. He knew it was his friend Colin before he glanced at the phone, and he was right.

"I did it, all right? I sent it off an hour ago."

"Good. 'Cause if there was ever a dom in need of a wet and willing sub, it's you. Time to get back in the scene, man."

"Yeah, well, we'll see if they think so too. These last few years I've buried it so far down and deep that *I'm* not sure it's still there."

"Are you fucking kidding? It isn't a shirt you take off, man. It's who you *are.*"

Adam chuckled. "That 'me' was long ago, before a certain sub snagged me."

"Snagged you? You're being way too generous. She tricked you into marriage and fatherhood, ran off with another guy when she realized your government paycheck wasn't going to increase nearly as fast as her ambition, and then tried to get custody just for the child support payments."

"Yeah, well, I'm just glad it's all finally settled. I don't know what I'd do if I'd lost Hannah. I've become rather fond of tying little pink ribbons in her hair," he chuckled.

"Maybe you should try out age play then."

"Fuck no. I'd be looking at the sub and thinking of my daughter the whole time. I've already put that on my off-limits list."

"You ever made up a limits list before?"

"No," he chuckled. "Doms are usually the ones who come up with the ideas, or at least veto suggestions made by subs. Walking into an activity where I don't have a choice, if I want to win the prize, is a weird feeling. This must be what a sub feels like."

"You can do it!"

"Says the man who doesn't have enough balls to try it himself."

Now Colin chuckled. "Damn right! I'll be watching you squirm from the sidelines."

"Fuck you, Colin, and good night." He smiled as he disconnected.

CHAPTER 3

S ari climbed out of the car, staring at the imposing two-story glass entrance to the dance club Runway. She absently closed the door behind her and the Uber driver sped off, leaving her alone. Black Light was supposed to be underneath Runway. But Runway was dark, and she was alone on this stretch of street. She moved under a streetlight to read the address on the email confirmation.

She'd been more than a little surprised when Black Light had accepted her, and sent an email with the QR code she needed to get in. She'd opened it while Melissa was in the shower, and had just enough time to notice she'd been accepted and the presence of an address before hearing Melissa turn off the water. Sari had printed the email in haste and thrust it into the bottom of her purse. She'd assumed she was supposed to come to Runway, and the Uber driver had known where that was, so this was the first time she'd unfolded the paper since it was printed.

Crap. She was actually supposed to go to some psychic's shop that had a back entrance into the club. She sighed and turned right towards the light, clutching the paper in one hand, and pulling her coat tight with the other. The lightweight trenchcoat, much classier than her winter parka, was not as much protection against the cold

February wind as she needed. And considering how little she had on underneath, it wasn't surprising that she was shivering. Adding to her list of unwise choices was the pair of bright red stiletto pumps she'd spent way too much money on, which were going to give her blisters before the night was done.

Her nerves grew as she reached the corner and turned left. Here, there were people and stores - Abercrombie, Michael Kors, Urban Outfitters, and more. She paused to look in the windows, wishing she could dress as stylishly as these mannequins. But interns at the National Weather Service, even those who had risen from GS-5 to GS-7, made so little money that she stuck with a few inexpensive basics that were well-worn after two years. She turned back to the sidewalk, only to see several women give her openly hostile stares. She frowned, realizing that with her shoes, bare legs, and absence of any visible hemline under her coat, she looked pretty much like a hooker. She glared back at them and scurried the last dozen yards across an alley, stopping in front of a building with a brown awning. It proclaimed 'Psychic Reader - Card and Palm Reading, and reassured her that walk-ins were welcome. Feeling even more uncomfortable than when someone thought she was a prostitute, she pushed the door open.

A middle-aged woman in a flowing dress and hair down to her knees greeted her with a smile. Sari was at a loss, so she just held up her paper. The woman nodded over her shoulder in the direction of a curtained doorway in the back of the shop.

"You see Luís."

Sari gave her a tentative smile in return and ducked through the curtain. On the other side, a muscular man with hair so black it was almost blue, and a visible scar on his weathered right cheek, stood silently in front of a door.

Sari held up her paper in supplication, noticing for the first time that it was crumpled from being clutched too tightly. 'Nervous?' she thought wryly. He took the paper and smoothed it out, looking it over carefully.

"May I see your ID, please?"

Sari fumbled in the pocket of her coat and held out her driver's license. He looked at everything thoroughly, handed it all back, and opened the door.

"Welcome to Black Light. Go down the stairs, follow the hall, and through the door."

She found herself at the top of a well-lit but chilly staircase. With a last glance at Luís, the guard-slash-bouncer-slash-muscle, she turned and descended into the cold. At the bottom was a narrow tunnel. Her sense of direction said she was headed back towards Runway so she kept walking and in just a minute came to another heavy door. Heat greeted her as she opened the door and stepped into a small room. Rows of lockers covered the walls on both sides. Music leaked into the room from a door just ahead, and between her and the music was another large muscled guy, standing behind a tall counter in the middle of the room. This one smiled as she approached.

"Here for Roulette?"

She nodded, then remembered her manners. "Yes, sir." She held out the paper again, chagrined to realize how wrinkled it had become. Something caught her eye.

What? She hadn't looked at the paper since she'd printed it, and she now realized it included her limits list. But there were only three limits listed. The most important one was missing. She remembered getting interrupted by her roommate as she was choosing them. *Shit.*

"Miss?" The security guard was still holding out his hand.

"Um, there's a mistake. The limits list. I forgot to pick one of them. Can I fix it?"

He cocked an eyebrow. "Kind of late to do that. But it's not my call. You can talk to Spencer. He's the Dungeon Master. Tall man in a suit."

She gritted her teeth in frustration as she handed the paper and her driver's license to him. She was always in a hurry and rarely stopped to double check things.

He scanned the code and nodded.

She heard a locker pop open. He handed her ID and the paper back and pointed off to the side. "All electronics, phones, and watches, in there. You can put your coat there too, if you want."

She was glad to finally take off her coat in the overly warm room. Or was that nerves that made her so hot? She stuffed everything in and shut the door. He took her wrist and stamped it with something almost invisible, except that in the strange purplish light of the room she could just make out a design. He pushed a button on his desk and the door to Black Light released.

"Have a wonderful time."

She pushed the door open and entered, her eyes wide and her heart pounding.

CHAPTER 4

*A*dam sat at the bar, nursing a drink and watching the room. Being here, in this place of pleasure and pain, should have felt like a homecoming. Instead, he felt a close kinship to a fish out of water. Almost eight years it had been. Eight years since his cocky just-out-of-college self had strutted around a room like this, sure of everything and everyone. With an ego the size of Alaska, it was no wonder he'd been flattered when the pretty young sub named Tricia had latched onto him. Everyone warned him about her manipulative ways, but he didn't listen, and after two months of dating she'd announced she was pregnant.

With a lavish wedding, a new career at the FBI, and a child on the way, it seemed prudent to keep their playing more private. And after Hannah had arrived, Tricia never really wanted to play again. Two years later she disappeared with another guy.

He finished his drink and set the glass back on the bar. The bartender looked at him with a raised eyebrow.

"Just club soda." He'd had one drink, to help him calm the jitters, but he had no intention of playing tonight with anything less than a clear mind. He glanced around the room, noting the arrivals as they entered. Several couples occupied one set of couches, the doms sitting back with drinks in their hands, their subs kneeling on the floor at the side. A domme in a red dress and tall black boots approached, and they rose to greet her. She dropped the leash that was attached to the male sub crawling behind her, and kissed the cheek of each of the men. As she settled back on the couch, she motioned to her sub, who crawled over parallel with the couch. She lifted her legs up to drape them across her living footrest, and motioned to a pretty server who wore nothing more than a tiny apron, a thong, and a smile, to bring her a drink.

He saw several other men - doms, by their self-assured manner - arrive without a partner, and wondered if they were also part of the Roulette event. His knew his friend Colin would be by later tonight, more than likely with his wife. Anyone not playing would just be spectators, though. The only people playing tonight were the participants.

Several women arrived, alone. He smiled. He knew he was beginning to relax by the way his gaze had become predatory as he roamed over their figures. They were all attractive enough, though he was always a man who preferred less makeup and less fussy hair on a woman.

A few minutes later another lone woman entered the room. He studied her as she took in the surroundings. She was tall and curvy. He liked curves on a woman. She wore a dress with a sheer bodice and a neckline low and wide that revealed luscious creamy cleavage. There was a diamond pattern in the fabric that obscured the otherwise see-through material, the pattern strategically placed to cover her nipples and make the dress just barely acceptable in public. The solid black skirt, though, was anything but decent. It covered her ass but didn't go an inch longer, and it fluttered as she walked, revealing a tiny black thong underneath. Her shapely legs were completely bare, right down to her red stiletto heels. And best of all was the mane of unrestrained chestnut curls that fell down her back, almost to her waist. His hand itched with a desire to gather all that hair up in his hand and twist it around until she was pulled to her knees in front of him, head arched backwards, and dark red lips opened wide...

He shook himself. There were a lot of subs here tonight, and for all he knew she was meeting her dom and didn't plan on playing with anyone else. Except, she was peering around the room with wide, almost innocent eyes, clearly here for the first time, and as astonished as he was at the surroundings. Her eyes lingered for a long moment on the cages set up on the stage, before moving on to the rest of the room. She wore a collar, but it didn't look like anything more than a ribbon with a round metal ring at her throat - nothing that screamed 'off-limits'. His cock twitched for the first time in so long he hadn't been sure it was still a functioning part of his anatomy. He watched her chew on her lip as she looked around and finally set off in the direction of a tall, serious man in a suit. She got about three steps towards him when someone else caught the man's eye and stepped between them. She stopped, chewed on her lip some more, then turned around and walked away.

She wandered in the direction of the row of small rooms used for scening that ran along one wall. The privacy curtains were pushed to the side, and she ducked in one, looking back at the room, probably wondering if anyone was watching. Then she sank to her knees in the classic submissive's pose with her hands placed face up on her knees. Her eyes closed and she took deep breaths, and he could almost feel her shoulders relax. She stayed utterly still. The tall man she'd approached before walked past and paused to look at her, before nodding and continuing on. Adam felt a flash of irritation that he was spying on her, before chuckling with the realization that *he* was doing the same thing.

Eventually she opened her eyes and smiled to herself. Then she looked up and Adam didn't look away fast enough. She caught his eye and grew red. He raised his glass to her in acknowledgment, then turned away to give her the privacy he should have given her before. When he glanced back a few minutes later, she was gone.

CHAPTER 5

*A*s Sari had entered the dungeon, she'd spied the man she needed to talk to. He was tall and stern-looking, and her courage weakened as she started in his direction. A dom and his sub stepped in front of her and began talking to him. She stopped. Honestly, she was more afraid of telling this man about her mistake, than bowing out and losing the free month if she had to safeword. She doubted he'd let her fix something, anyway. And it didn't look very responsible to admit she'd not paid attention to something so important.

There were twenty-something activities. The odds of landing on the one she hadn't chosen was very small. She shook her head. She would just cross her fingers.

That decided, she needed to find somewhere to be quiet for a moment, to meditate and reclaim the submission that she kept at bay during her regular life. A row of small rooms, with privacy curtains that were fastened open for now, faced out into the large room. She chose an empty one and settled to her knees, breathing deep and feeling peace descend across her tense shoulders. When she finally opened her eyes, she realized a dom at the bar was watching her. Their eyes connected for just a moment, and then he raised his drink at her, and turned to the side so fast she didn't have time to get flustered.

She studied him for a moment. He was tall, with curly black hair in a civilian crew-cut. His red shirt, red and black tie, and black trousers didn't reveal a lot about his physique, but he didn't look like a body-builder. Just someone who kept himself in reasonable shape. His clean-shaven face wore a guarded expression, as though he wasn't entirely sure this was where he wanted to be tonight. She wondered if he was a member, or here for the game, as she was. He sipped his drink, holding the glass in front of his face and staring through the clear liquid.

The crowd was beginning to gather in front of the stage, so she forced her gaze away from him, and rose to her feet, ready - mostly - for whatever the night held. A group of very nervous-looking women were grouped to one side, and she assumed they were the other submissives. She headed in their direction. It would feel good to be in like company for a few minutes.

As she reached the group she did her best to hide her shock. She was absolutely sure one of the women standing there was Khloe Monroe. She tried not to stare. Seeing the actress in a group of submissives would have been the *last* place Sari would have expected her to be. Khloe had the reputation of being a drama queen, and Sari would have pinned her for a domme instead.

She shook her head and forced herself back to her own situation. She was about to be paired up with a complete stranger and do any number of things she hadn't tried before. What the hell was she think-ing? She had zippo experience in so many of the activities on the list for tonight. Was it too late to leave? She glanced around, seeing the same deer-in-the-headlights look on several other faces. She hoped she was up for this. Which dom would own her for the evening? There were several cruel-looking guys that made her shiver. A few looked friendly enough, but rather stern. She hoped she'd find one that smiled, at least, and wasn't annoyed at her inexperience.

The emcee took the stage, introducing himself as Chase Cartwright, one of the owners of the club, and welcoming everyone to the event. Sari resisted biting her nails to shreds as she listened. She just wanted to get this over with.

The first couple of pairings went smoothly, but when Khloe's name was called, the woman took off running in the opposite direction. A collective gasp went up from the crowd as the dom she'd been paired with ran after her. Sari couldn't see what was happening because of the other people blocking her view, but the couple returned a few minutes later, hand-in-hand, to the stage, ready to roll for their scene.

Several spins later, the cruel-looking men were paired off, and she sighed in relief. As the list of unmatched doms grew smaller, her nerves returned. Her gaze was fixed on the stage and she suddenly realized the buzzing had quieted, the audience clearly waiting for someone to respond. She looked around, hoping to see a sub walking forward, and when one didn't, her face grew beet red. Oh, lord, had she—?

"Sari?" Chase read the name again. She looked at the stage and realized that the dom who had witnessed her meditation from his seat at the bar was on stage. Relief at seeing him up there swept through her. She smiled weakly and tentatively waved her hand, wondering what to do next, until he crooked a finger at her. She scurried to the front. A man standing at the bottom of the stairs held out his hand and she was so flustered she almost missed it. She let him assist her up the stairs, and hand her off to the man who would be her dom for the night.

"Sorry, sir! I wasn't listening!" Dammit, her first communication with him was an apology. This wasn't the right way to start off the night. She had also completely missed his name, and there was no way she was going to ask him right now.

He raised an eyebrow. "I see that. Are you fully present now?"

She looked up into his eyes. They were piercing, and dark, and made her shiver. "Yes, sir, I am."

Chase handed her the ball and spun the second roulette wheel. She counted to three and tossed the ball in. She watched the options flash by - *needle play* - *water sports* - *whipping* - *suspension...* Her brain was going around in matching circles. As the wheel slowed she saw one of her limits approach and she tensed. It passed by and stopped on 'wax play'.

"Well, we have our first assignment. What do you think?"

She was still focused on 'wax play' and looked up, startled.

"Am I going to have to repeat myself all night?" he frowned.

"No, sir. I, um, hope not. I'm just a little scared."

He leaned forward so his lips were near her ear. He smelled really good. "Are you in over your head?"

A ripple of fear, not entirely unpleasant, rolled through her. *I hope not.*

CHAPTER 6

*B*efore she could reply, he pressed on her back to guide her away from the roulette wheel and towards the back of the stage where several couples waited. A few had left the stage already. As she walked in front of him, he snagged her wrists and pulled them behind her back, holding them gently but securely in his hands. She shivered as he turned her around to face out into the audience, his hands still holding hers captive. "Still scared?" His voice in her ear made her jump.

"Yes, sir," she whispered. "A little more now than before, to be honest." She kept her eyes glued on the emcee, trying to calm the roiling sea her stomach had become.

"Good. But you didn't answer my second question."

She struggled to remember what questions he'd asked. They'd barely had two minutes together and she'd missed something else?

She felt his soft breath on the nape of her neck. It tickled, and she hitched her shoulder up and tried to pull away.

"No. Stay right there. Don't move, and don't make a sound."

She drew in her breath and struggled to relax. He didn't move, but breathed in and out, the air drifting against the skin of her neck and driving her out of her mind. Her wrists tugged in a futile effort to bring her hands up to rub away the tickle, and in response he gripped them even tighter. And, predictably, the junction between her legs developed an ache that seemed to steal all the blood from her brain.

Being up here on stage, mildly restrained, with all those people looking at her – she suddenly had the feeling of being on an auction block …*a slave, just sold to the highest bidder, facing an unknown future. Would her new master be harsh, or kind? Demanding? Just? No matter; she'd have no choice but to obey...*

She had a rich and full fantasy life, that was for sure. She shivered again, bringing herself back to the present.

"Is it my breath that causes you to shiver? Or some fantasy you see in your mind?" He was still right by her ear. She opened her mouth to reply, when chaos broke loose among the four remaining participants. She didn't understand all of what was happening, but gathered that a dom and his ex-wife had been paired up, and that was *not* ok with the ex-wife. They rolled pet play, and Sari understood the look on the woman's face. Pet play was not the worst thing that Sari could think of, but it ranked right up there.

The quarreling pair quieted down for the moment. Chase thanked the crowd and dismissed everyone to start.

Her temporary dom – how had she missed his name? – kept her wrists pinned as he guided her off the stage over to a couch. He let them go and sank down in it, but did not invite her to sit.

She fidgeted, unsure what to do. After a moment, she realized he was studying her. She forced her hands to her sides and let him finish his inspection.

He nodded. "That's better. Would you like a drink?"

"Um, no thank you, sir."

"So, what would you like me to know about you for tonight? Besides that you're scared?"

"Me, sir?" She couldn't recall a dom asking her that before. The good ones asked about her limits, but never about herself. "I haven't had a lot of experience?"

"Are you asking me or telling me?"

"I'm telling you, sir."

"Then say it like you're sure of yourself. Inexperience is nothing to be ashamed of."

She chuckled. "Sir, I am not very experienced."

"I might push you tonight. How do you feel about that?"

"You're asking me, sir?"

"I'm asking you to tell me how you feel about the idea. I didn't say I was going to go easy on you."

Zing. She went from damp to soaked between her legs in less than a second.

"I like that very much," she confessed.

"Good. Then we'll get along fine. Now, what would you like to ask me?"

Oh, thank god, he gave me an opening. "What is your name, sir?"

He raised an eyebrow. "You missed that, too? Do you ever pay attention? You could just call me 'Sir.'"

"Well, sir, there are a lot of 'sirs' here tonight. How will you know if I'm talking to you?"

"Because my gaze will be on you the whole night, and yours on me. Understand?"

"Yes, sir." She forced herself to look him in the eyes. It was unexpectedly hard.

"Adam."

"Sir?"

"My name is Adam. I want you to call me that. Not Master Adam." Something passed across his face.

"Yes, sir. I mean Adam."

"Any other questions?"

She thought furiously. "Why did you ask me if I was in over my head?"

His smile disappeared.

"I'm sorry, sir! I shouldn't have asked." Shit, that was the second apology, and a very intrusive question she had no business asking.

He took a moment to answer. "No, you have every right to ask me that. There were times when someone was less than honest with me, and I regretted getting involved. But I'm sure tonight will be different." He cleared his throat. "Any medical issues or things I should know about? No trouble with your jaw? No joints that give you problems? Any triggers or past experiences that would give you trouble tonight?"

She hesitated. "Actually, sir, I had a really bad experience a few months ago. A dom wasn't watching me and I was having trouble breathing. A dungeon monitor saw me and got me down."

His mouth tightened. "Was the jerk dealt with?"

"I think he was banned for life, actually."

"Good. There's no excuse for that. None. And I can promise that nothing will happen to you tonight because I will never let my attention wander."

"Thank you, sir."

"Please give me your underwear."

It took her a moment to realize they'd started. She hurried to pull off the thong, frankly glad to have it pulled out from between her butt cheeks. He took it and stuck it in his pocket. "If you make it the whole night, you can have them back. If you safeword, you forfeit them. Now, I saw you get into your submissive head earlier. I liked that. But I want to establish something between the two of us as well, before we start, and there's nothing like a spanking for that." He crooked his finger at her again and she squirmed with secret delight at being directed that way. He patted his lap. She lay down across his knees with her head and arms on the couch. She felt his hands slip the tiny skirt up, and felt the cool air settle on her skin. Her pussy contracted in anticipation. She loved being spanked more than almost anything else in the world.

His warm hand caressed her skin with long strokes and gentle squeezes. She made little noises of appreciation. Her legs relaxed and fell apart. He must have taken that as inspiration, for his hand dipped between her legs, cupping her smooth mound. She breathed out a sigh.

"I hope to get to know this pussy better by the end of the night," he whispered. She tensed without meaning to and then made herself relax, hoping he hadn't noticed. But, apparently, he did pay close attention.

"Why the fear?"

Because... "Because I'm just a little nervous, sir. I've mostly played with people I knew well. This is new." *Liar, liar, pants on fire...*

"I understand. We'll go slow." He began to lightly spank one cheek over and over, the impact only warming the skin with a nice sting. She wiggled a little in thanks. He moved to the other cheek and repeated. Then he came back to the first one. "I like to spank one at a time. I like the woman's anticipation when one cheek is red and sore, and she knows I haven't even begun on the other one yet. What do you think of that?" He increased the strength of his spanks, peppering the same spot over and over until her moans became sharper. He paused and she knew he wanted an answer.

"I think it's devious but it's also not my decision, sir!"

He laughed. "You're honest, but you know your place." He resumed, and now the spanks were raining down fiercely. She desperately wished he'd move to the other cheek to give this one a break, but he smacked the same spot over and over and over until it felt like it was roasting. By now she was squealing and struggling.

He stopped. "Color?"

He wanted to know if she was okay. "Green, sir."

"Good." He switched to the other cheek. It was only a minute or two before she was wishing he'd switch back to the first one. She clenched her jaw and tried not to tense up. Most doms wanted subs to stay relaxed because it showed an acceptance of the pain. She suddenly discovered it helped if she clenched the cheek of the one that *wasn't* being spanked, but left the targeted one loose. She approached the point where she was contemplating 'yellow', when he finally, blessedly, stopped.

But then she heard him reach into his bag and she un-relaxed.

"Sari, how many times did you miss something because you weren't listening?"

Shit. He'd noticed. "Three times, sir."

"So, three on each cheek." A moment later something hard and wooden smacked down on the tender redness of her left cheek. She squealed and threw her hand back without thinking. He grabbed it and pulled it high up on her back, once more immobilizing her.

"Oh, no. You resist a punishment, and it starts over. Got it?"

630

"Yes, sir!" His voice seemed less easygoing right now, as though she'd triggered something. Before she could form another thought, the implement crashed down again. She wailed out loud, but managed to mostly stay still. He waited only a moment before he smacked the same spot twice more in rapid succession. Her cry spilled out again, muffled by the crook of her arm where her face was pressed.

"Color?"

"Yellow, sir."

"Can you do the other side?"

She nodded. He tapped her sore cheek, wanting a better answer.

"Yes, sir."

He rested the cool paddle on her hot right cheek. The moment she felt it lift away she tensed. She was prepared when it hit, letting out only a short exclamation. He wasted no time in repeating it twice more and this time she barely let out a peep despite the incredible sting.

"Good girl." He helped her off his lap and she sank to the floor on her knees in front of him.

"Eyes." She looked up. "You okay?"

She smiled. "Very okay, sir."

"It's been a while since I did that. I forgot how much I enjoyed it. So, we've used ten minutes and one of the monitors is giving us the evil eye to get going. Ready?"

"Yes, sir."

"Wrists."

She paused for a moment before thrusting her arms straight out towards him. He turned to his bag, where he rummaged for a moment before coming up with a pair of black leather cuffs. He buckled them on and she relished the feel of the tightness around her wrists. It was a comforting sensation, one that she'd first realized she enjoyed when she'd buttoned the long sleeves of a dress around her wrists as a girl.

He hadn't told her to put her arms down, so she remained still as he sat back, her eyes locked on his as ordered. At last he nodded and stood up.

CHAPTER 7

The floor of Black Light provided a large variety of equipment for play. Tables with plentiful restraints were scattered around the room. There were two spanking benches, and a set of stocks, rigging for suspension play, a St. Andrew's cross, and a large hot tub. He could see the equipment for medical play in an alcove across the room, and next to the stage was a large wooden door that led to a dungeon. Around the perimeter were couches and tables for those who chose to watch the scenes.

Now that he was here, Adam wanted to explore all the opportunities. He was confident he would last the night. He hoped Sari would. He hadn't gotten a good measure of her yet.

He led her over to the table for wax play, covered with a dropcloth that hung off the edges. There was another drop cloth below that covered the floor out to either side. A small table held an assortment of burning candles and a few other interesting things. On the floor was a bucket of water, and a fire extinguisher. Sari didn't need to dwell on safety issues surrounding open flames, so he pushed her against the edge of the table and bent her over. He lifted her skirt and caressed her reddened ass, and reflected that as beautiful as an ass was *before* a spanking, it was even more beautiful *after* a spanking. The skin looked like a fine rose wine, with a few dark spots like raspberries. He slipped his hand between her legs and was rewarded with a moan as his fingers slid through her folds, slick and swollen. She didn't need to know that his real purpose was to check to make sure she was clean-shaven, because he intended to have some fun with hot wax in that tender area. Catching and pulling stray hairs was not on the agenda. At least tonight.

"Keep your eyes closed," he whispered. She nodded.

He gathered her glossy hair in his hand and twisted it just enough to make a thick rope, and tugged her back to a standing position. He draped the hair over her shoulder and then let it go so he could grab the tab of the zipper at her neck. He pulled it down, leisurely following the curve of her back until the dress split open in a wide 'V'. His hands slipped under the fabric. He guided it over her shoulders and down her front, stopping to caress her breasts on the way down. She had her head thrown back and was making little noises of pleasure as he tweaked her nipples. A small audience had gathered around and was watching her disrobing. He let the dress fall to the floor and puddle around her feet, while he continued to cup and squeeze the soft globes, just big enough to fit perfectly in the palms of his large hands. She was even curvier-looking out of the dress, and he slid his hands down, enjoying the solid grip of her hips. He turned her around to face him. She still had her eyes closed.

"Sari, step out of your shoes and climb up on the table. Spread your knees all the way to the edges. You can open your eyes."

She hesitated only a moment when she opened her eyes to see the number of onlookers gathered around. But she lay back as instructed, letting her knees fall to the sides. He bent over to pick up her dress and shoes, placing them out of the way on a chair.

"I'm going to restrain you now." He fastened a quick-release snap to her left wrist cuff, then raised her arm to stretch it over her head and clip it to a hook at the top of the table. He placed a rope around her left knee, and another around her left ankle, and fastened them with the snaps to more hooks on the very edge of the table, then moved to the other side to repeat the actions. She was spread wide, her most delicate tissues bared to him. She followed him with her eyes as he worked. He flashed her reassuring smiles, which she didn't return. He sensed her wariness, but she didn't object.

He placed a small amount of oil on his hands. "This will make the wax come off easier. Another time and place I might want it to stick – that's an entirely different experience, I promise – but not today." He rubbed his hands together to warm the oil and began spreading it in firm circles across her stomach and sides. He moved north to her breasts, spending an extra minute massaging the oil into the soft mounds with their crinkled brown areolas. She showed her appreciation by closing her eyes and letting out a breathy moan as he paid special attention to her nipples. He moved back down her body to her mound. At his touch, her eyes flew open with a scared look, perhaps not comprehending until now that her most intimate parts would also be a target for the wax. He massaged the area and was rewarded with a soft sigh, and eyes that closed again in bliss. He spread the oil the rest of the way down her legs to the cuffs on her ankles. He skipped her arms - they were too close to her face and he wouldn't be putting any wax on them.

"If at any time you feel like the wax is burning you and not cooling, you just say 'wax' and I'll remove that spot immediately. What's the safeword?"

"Red, sir," she responded immediately.

"And what's the 11th commandment?"

She frowned. "Sir?"

"'Thou shalt not damage thy submissive.' I promise."

"Thank you." She forced a smile at him.

Her eyes tracked his every move as he picked up one of the pillar candles. Pillar, jar, and votive candles were generally okay, especially white and unscented. Colors or scents could raise the temperature quite a bit. But he would never pour the wax on her without testing it himself first. He held the candle above his wrist, closer than he would hold it to her, and dribbled it onto his skin. The pleasantly hot sensation, nowhere near to burning, told him this was safe to use. He repeated the test with the other candles, finding them all comfortable. Sari watched him closely.

"Ready?"

She nodded.

He moved over her stomach, raising the pillar about a meter into the air. "It cools as it drops, so I start high, and then get closer depending on how it feels to you." He tipped the pillar and saw her muscles contract in anticipation. A small stream of wax spilled over the edge and down, splattering in little white dots on her stomach.

"How did that feel?"

"I hardly felt it, sir."

He smiled and lowered the candle halfway. "How about now?" Another thin stream poured out onto her skin. She made a small noise of surprise.

"A lot warmer, sir, but very comfortable."

He lowered it a bit more. This time she sighed.

"Too much?"

"No! A nice hot feeling but not burning. I liked it!" She smiled, looking more relaxed now.

"Then we'll keep it here for now." He began pouring a thin stream over her stomach in a circular pattern. The wax ran in rivulets across her stomach and down her sides; it ran into her belly button and he let the little dip fill up little by little until it was level. He was careful not to let it run into her pubic area, though he placed a small puddle right on her mound, which made her gasp. He began moving it a little lower and then a little higher, varying the temperature. He moved towards her breasts, her eyes glued to his face as she chewed her lip. He grinned as he raised the candle a little and dribbled wax right onto one nipple.

"Oh!" she exclaimed, and bucked up.

"Too hot?" he asked. He was still learning her tolerances and was checking in more than he would with someone else.

"No!" she declared. "Perfect! Though..."

He raised an eyebrow and waited.

"If it pleases you, sir, I think a little hotter might be even nicer."

This was working out better than he expected.

CHAPTER 8

S ari saw Adam's eyebrows go way up before he broke into a grin.

"My pleasure." He put the candle down, then peeled the small dollop of wax off her nipple. "But first, I'm going to do something that will make everything feel more intense."

He placed a blindfold over her eyes, securing it behind her head. He was right – everything suddenly became more intense. She strained to hear where he was, to anticipate what he was about to do. There was a sudden warmth across the cooled wax on her stomach. The warmth moved back and forth this time, instead of in circles, so when it dripped on skin that was bare she felt a sudden flash of stinging hot pain, and then a lingering, dwindling heat. He'd clearly moved the candle closer to her. She let out her breath in pleasure. Then she felt the wax move down her legs in a zig-zag pattern. It dribbled down onto the tender skin of her inner thighs. It was delicious. It was about one degree away from being too hot. She wiggled a little as she squealed, and the restraint of the ropes only intensified the sensations.

"Oh...oh...please..." Her mind drifted away again. *The slave struggled in her bonds as her master tormented her. He took great delight in her cries, and her soft pleading only increased his desires...* She felt herself sliding almost into a state of bliss. Nothing else existed except these sensations.

The wax moved back up her body, circling over her stomach, before heading again towards her breasts. This time, instead of heading for her nipple, she felt it circle the base of her breast. Around and around in a spiral, it climbed slowly upwards. Her breathing grew rapid as she anticipated the arrival of the hot stream at the summit. Just before it arrived, the heat went away. A moment later, something hotter than the sun touched her nipple and she sucked air in and bucked up as far as the ropes let her. And then – it was gone. There was no sensation of heat left at all. She squirmed in confusion. And then, as something cold and wet trickled down her breast between the spirals of wax, she understood. He'd touched her with an ice cube, instead of the heat she'd been prepared for.

"Sir!" she breathed out.

"Shh."

She struggled to figure out what he was going to do next. This was madness. The wax was intense – but the ice took it to a whole new level. Now she not only didn't know where he would strike next; she didn't know what kind of sensation to expect.

She didn't have to wait long. An icy wetness suddenly hit her other nipple and before she could do more than gasp, intense heat dropped on top of it. This heat lasted and she felt rivulets of wax spill down the sides of her breasts. She cried out in pleasure. The heat built and built as more wax dropped on top. She groaned and struggled to keep breathing with the pain. At last there seemed to be no more increase in heat there, but the icy wetness returned, the water also spilling down her breasts, and running down her sides, leaving her gasping and twitching with the cold and tickling trails of water.

The first nipple was still bare. A sharp heat hit squarely in the center, making her gasp even though she was prepared for it. Her mind was a dark kaleidoscope of heat and cold, of pain and pleasure, and she was in ecstasy.

The sensations alternated all the way back down her chest, and then stomach. She tensed as she felt the heat near her sensitive folds. There was a pause, and then a burst of heat at the top of her slit that made her cry out. She felt the wax dripping down, through her slit, and braced, but it had cooled enough by the time it reached her inner skin that it was merely warm. The heat of her arousal right now was ten times hotter than the heat of the candle. She moaned and strained at her ropes again, lifting her hips in supplication. She felt one hand on her skin, pulling her folds open to either side, exposing her clit. She held her breath. The wax hit her clit, the heat bursting across it like fireworks, and she almost had an orgasm from the intensity. She let out a guttural cry and panted, straining to close her legs and increase the already-fading sensation. She felt it hit again, the heat this time muted from the layer of cooling wax already there. She tried to twist and pull, part of her wanting to escape the intensity, and part of her trying to increase it. At last the sensations stopped.

She felt his fingers lifting the wax away from between her legs, her juices much too slick to allow it to stick. The cool air once more rushed over her clit and the change in temperature was too much.

"Please, sir, please let me come!" she begged.

"I'm going to get some of this wax off of you first. I have a little game before we're done."

His hands pried at the wax covering her breasts. It came off easily thanks to the oil, and as the cool air hit her nipples she felt them crinkle into hard points.

He put something circular on her left breast and then suddenly the hot wax burst over her nipple again. This time, though, it didn't run down her breasts, and she realized that he held some kind of ring meant to contain the wax. She felt him pour a little more on top before lifting the ring off and repeating the same thing on her right nipple.

"Hold really still."

She felt something being pushed into the softened wax on the left side, and then again on the right.

"You have one small votive candle anchored onto the wax on top of each nipple. They've been burning for a while, so any movement is going to cause hot wax to dribble over the side. Do you understand?"

Oh... "Yes, sir." She scarcely breathed for a minute or two. She willed herself to relax. She could do this, no problem.

Until she heard the unmistakable sound of a Hitachi vibrator turn on at the foot of the table.

"Sir? What are you doing?"

His quiet chuckle told her almost everything.

"No, sir! Please!"

"Are you scared, Sari?" The lilt in his voice suggested he was enjoying her predicament, like any good sadist would.

"Yes, sir. No, sir. I don't know!" She mentally crossed her fingers for luck. "I'm fine, sir."

She heard the vibrator come closer, and when it finally touched between her wide-spread legs, she jerked. She felt a hot drop splash onto her left breast. A quick sizzle of pain flashed on, then off. But suddenly her focus was not on the wax on her breasts. It was all between her legs. Her needy, swollen, wet cunt. She groaned as the vibrations buzzed through her. She desperately needed this release, but this was predicament bondage at its best. To get the release she craved, she would have to accept the hot wax spilling down her tender skin. She had to accept that her pleasure could only come with pain. That thought did it, and whether she wanted to or not she catapulted over the edge into an enormous orgasm, shuddering and jerking. She felt rivulets of pain slide down her breasts and she screamed with pleasure. When the Hitachi turned off, she continued to shudder, the wax still splashing and finding bare skin, sending little flashes of hot pain through her fading arousal.

By the time the wax had cooled his fingers were on her breast lifting it away. She felt a cool cloth wipe over the heated skin. She was liquid and languid, drifting in some sort of in-between world. After he removed the blindfold, she forced her eyes open and smiled at him. He was busily lifting away large sections of wax from her skin.

"This will take a few minutes. Just relax."

"Yessir," she slurred, and closed her eyes again.

By the time he'd finished and unclipped her arms, she was fully awake. He eased them down to her sides and then helped her sit up. She swung around to perch on the edge of the table, blinking at the light. He put a blanket around her shoulders and after a minute she hopped off. He picked up her dress and shoes, then led them back over to the couch.

"Good?" he asked with a twinkle in his eye as he pulled her down next to him on the seat. He picked stray bits of wax off her body.

"Oh, yeah. Good," she assured him. "Thank you, sir." It was the best time she'd ever had, to be honest. This was a man who knew what he was doing, and she blessed the roulette wheel for pairing them up.

CHAPTER 9

"Okay. Let's go see what's next." Adam smiled as he stood up and held out her shoes.

She groaned silently at the sight but slipped them on, wishing for an absurd moment that guys were turned on by ballet flats as much as by heels. "Sir? May I put my dress back on?" Her feet protested as she stood up.

"No, you may not. Stand up straight, shoulders back, hands clasped behind your back, and walk up to the stage with me. You're beautiful and I want to enjoy looking at you."

This was tough. She wasn't an exhibitionist by nature, but she took a deep breath and nodded.

"Good girl." He took her elbow and escorted her back up to the roulette wheel, where Chase still stood guard. The dom gave an approving glance at Sari. She felt her face grow hot and decided to stare at his feet while the two men exchanged brief pleasantries. Adam handed her the white ball, Chase sent the wheel spinning, and she tossed it in.

This time the wheel assigned 'Whipping'. She'd been whipped a few times, but Adam didn't look thrilled.

"Chase, I have no objections per se, but it's been a few years since I did this, and I'd rather not have my sub be marked all over as I practice on her." He clearly meant it as a joke, but her breath caught in her throat as her pussy clenched. Another fantasy ran through her mind - *the slave who was used as target practice for a master learning how to wield a whip. She'd be tied tight, and he'd make mistakes, and she'd cry out and scream as he perfected his aim...*

"Sari? You okay? You disappeared again." Adam's concern inserted itself into her daydream.

"Fine! Sorry, sir!" She gave him a bright smile and ignored the clenching going on between her legs.

He turned back to Chase. "Anyone here who could give me a refresher?"

The emcee peered around the room. "There's Master D and he looks like he's in between scenes. He's the best around." He motioned to the dom who was escorting his rather satisfied-looking sub to a couch. Master D murmured something into her ear, and came over. The three men introduced each other, and then Master D and Adam moved off to the side. Sari stood awkwardly, hands fidgeting nervously, until they returned.

"Master D has agreed to give me a refresher. And, since I saw how you stared at those cages when you came in, I'm going to put you in one of them so you don't wander off while I practice."

Oh... "Yes, sir!" she said, more eagerly than she intended.

"You're my captive slave, awaiting your punishment, watching me warm up as you sit in your nearby cage." He snagged her wrists behind her back again as he led her across the stage to where the cages sat, all in a neat row.

He let go of her wrists. She slipped to her knees and crawled into the cage without being told. It was small, and she was forced to remain kneeling with her head bent, her high heels making the position awkward.

He closed the door behind her. "Let's make sure you don't run away once you see the whip." She heard the lock click. *Slaves are locked in cages to await their masters' pleasure and pain.*

She watched from between the bars as Adam and Master D had a lively conversation, Adam using his hands to describe something she couldn't hear, and both men chuckling from time to time. Master D grabbed a pillow from one of the couches, and Adam produced some bondage tape, and they secured the pillow to the cross, just below where the two pieces of wood crossed, and roughly where her ass would be placed in a few minutes. Her breath caught as Adam pulled a meter-long whip out of his bag. It was long enough to have some real bite, but not too long that it needed extraordinary skill to use. The two men talked more, turning the whip around, the more experienced dom showing the other different ways to hold it. Finally, Adam took up his position and with a flick of his wrist, sent the whip snapping into the pillow.

Her pussy pulsed and she groaned. The strange thing was, once she was tied to the cross and awaiting her first blow, she'd be petrified, contemplating calling her safeword before they even got started. And after the first blow, and the second, the pain would be overwhelming, and she'd be crying out and begging him to stop. And then it would be over, and she'd recover from the experience, and remember the wonderful parts of it, and count the minutes until she could do it again. That was the strange dichotomy of S&M.

It only took a handful of strikes before Adam was hitting in the center every time. He moved around a bit, trying from different angles, and getting suggestions from Master D. Finally, he nodded. The two men shook hands and Master D returned to his patiently-waiting sub. Adam removed the pillow, now a little worse for wear, and turned towards the cage.

Sari's breathing grew short and erratic. It was her turn.

He helped her out of the cage and led her down to the cross. Without pause he had her arms and ankles secured to the polished wood. To her surprise, though, he wasn't done.

"I need you to stay as still as you can so I don't miss." He wound several lengths of bondage tape around her waist and the wood, right where the boards crossed. Her waist was pinned, and she couldn't move from side to side at all. Her delicious fear increased. *Slaves can't wiggle to escape their punishment...*

He gathered her hair and pulled her head back. "Ready?"

"Yes, sir," she whispered, already falling down the rabbit hole of submission. He moved her hair over one shoulder and stepped away.

Her sense of hearing was acute, picking up the little noises he made behind her. Still, she was completely taken by surprise when the first blow landed on her unprotected backside. She grunted, then panted, letting the familiar pain flow through her body. It felt as though it had landed perfectly.

She was still dealing with the first when the second one arrived, stealing her breath and making her struggle against her bonds. This was always where she knew she was an idiot for offering herself up like a sacrifice to the goddess of pain. This is where the fantasy always fell apart. This fucking *HURT*. She gasped and shook as number three landed, this time on the other cheek. Holy hell, this man hadn't forgotten a thing about whipping. She wished he'd forgotten a little more. Number four yanked a cry out of her, a gasping sob that lasted for long seconds. Her hands pulled futilely at the cuffs.

"Please, stop!" she cried. The fifth blow didn't fall.

"The safeword is red, Sari."

"I know! Please, please stop!"

She hoped he realized that she had to plead and beg, to give voice to the anguish she was suffering, but she didn't really want him to stop. He must have understood, because the fifth blow fell and she cried out long and loud.

"All right, Sari, you're doing fine."

She didn't feel fine. She was lost in a world of pain. Subspace, the place she'd been in during the wax play where she was relaxed and experiencing pain as pleasure, always eluded her when it came to intense pain like this. This was simply endurance, for the sake of pleasing her master. That reason alone was enough to make her push through, though her safeword sprang to her lips as the sixth strike fell.

She screamed, then dropped her head, once more panting to deal with the pain. He paused, waiting for her to give him a sign to continue or not. She took a deep breath, lifted her head, and nodded.

"Good girl, Sari. Two more and we'll be done. Can you do it?"

Could she do it? Oh, God, she wasn't sure! But her dom was asking her to try, so she would. She nodded again. Blow number seven was the most painful so far. It wrapped around her hip and she heard him curse at his mistake just before the pulse of white-hot pain reached her brain. She let out a keening cry and pulled hard on her bonds, trying to bounce away the awful sting. He was at her side in an instant, gently rubbing the pain away, and she was grateful. The doms she'd played with before had rarely acknowledged their mistakes, and almost never soothed them. She lifted her head and smiled.

"Thank you. I'm okay."

He stepped away and she braced herself. "Last one," she heard, just before it hit. This one landed across both cheeks. She knew there'd be a mark there for a long time, and she opened her mouth to give a low scream. She shook uncontrollably.

He was at her side in an instant, rubbing her skin again.

"You did so good, that's right, I'm proud of you," he murmured as he unwrapped her waist and unlocked the cuffs, and she fell backwards into his arms. He picked her up and carried her to a couch, where he eased her down and then sat beside her. Despite the pain of the whipping, it was only marginally tender to sit on the area. They sat in silence for a few minutes, and just as she knew it would, the experience became a magical and arousing memory.

"Thank you, sir. I liked that a lot."

"I did, too! I was worried at first that I was going to mark you up horribly for life, but it seems I haven't lost as much aim as I thought I had. Sorry for the one bad one, though."

It's my pleasure to be marked by accident, by my master.

He laughed. "So, my temporary sub has some intense fantasies, does she?"

Sari sat up abruptly. "Did I say that out loud?"

He grinned and nodded. "I'd like to hear more."

She colored. "Don't we have to see what our next assignment is?"

He pinched her nipple hard and she squealed, but kept her hands in her lap.

"I decide when we're ready, and I want to hear one of your deepest, darkest fantasies. And based on what I've observed, they involved cages, and being whipped by your master."

Her hands fidgeted in her lap. "Yeah," she admitted.

"Capture fantasies?"

She nodded.

"Torture fantasies?"

"No! I mean, that's too far."

"But perhaps taking what I want, when I want, and punishing you if you resist?"

He'd just bared her soul, in one single sentence. She fixed her eyes on her tightly clasped hands, unable to answer him.

"Sari." He placed a finger under her chin. "Eyes." She struggled to lift her gaze to meet his. "It's okay."

She opened her mouth to reply, when shrieks of laughter broke out. She swiveled her head to see Master D carrying his sub, sprinting around the room, while the woman laughed out loud. It made her smile. But it also broke the moment.

Adam chuckled. "I'd like to talk to you more about this sometime. But you're probably right; we need to pick our next activity before we get disqualified." He grabbed her hand and pulled her off the couch.

CHAPTER 10

*B*ack at the wheel, Chase handed her the white ball and set the wheel spinning.

She crossed her fingers as she tossed the ball in, remembering that the odds of the ball landing on the one activity she hadn't marked were very small. The wheel spun round and round and when it finally slowed, her heart skipped a beat.

"Vaginal sex with condom."

What? No! No... Why? The one thing she didn't – couldn't – do! She swayed on her high heels and Adam caught her arm.

"Sari? You all right?"

"Sir? May I go to the restroom, please?"

"Of course. You want me to walk with you? You're a little pale."

She forced a smile. "I'm fine. Just kind of hungry."

"Take a few minutes to eat something. We don't want a sub safe-wording from hunger," declared Chase.

She nodded and murmured a thank you, and fled as fast as her high heels let her to the women's locker room. The door closed behind her and she fell into a chair, hissing at the contact of the hard chair on her new welts. She dropped her head in her hands.

Shit shit shit. What was she going to do? She wasn't going to let it happen. She couldn't. She was going to have to face the fact that she was going to leave here and never be able to come back. She was sorry that Adam would lose, though. This was not fair to him.

She kicked her shoes off and reveled in the freedom to bend her toes. Suddenly she needed to wash her face. She spied towels near the showers and grabbed one, then spent a few blissful minutes with her face planted in a hot, wet towel. When she finally looked up into the mirror, the only thing left on her face was her waterproof mascara.

What the fuck are you afraid of? He's a nice guy! He'd never hurt you. In fact, he was head and shoulders above almost every dom she'd played with so far.

Her mind flashed back to the hayloft on her parent's farm, to a warm summer evening, with a boy… and the laughter that turned to tears, and the begging and pleading that finally turned to despair… and then to the accusing voice of her best friend telling her that no one would marry a girl like her. She'd left for college soon after, but things were never the same again.

She'd stayed aloof from guys, protecting herself. Sex was never a part of any scene she'd agreed to after she started playing in clubs. *Maybe this is the best way. A one-night stand. Someone you'll never see again, to get you past the speed-bump that's been looming over you for so long.* She chuckled at the mixed metaphors.

She trusted him.

She was tired of living with fear.

An idea began forming in her head, one that had more than a little appeal to it…

* * *

ADAM GRINNED as he adjusted the belt around his red velvet tunic. He'd been surprised when Sari had asked if he would consider including an elaborate scene with costumes in this next game. He was even more intrigued when she'd told him it was related to the fantasy she'd shared earlier. He was delighted to grant her wish.

Under his tunic was a reddish-gold shirt, and on his feet were high black boots. The little submissive kitty in platform boots who ran the small but well-stocked costume closet had tried to get him to put on the black hose that were part of the original costume, but Adam had drawn the line at that and retained his own black pants. He also declined the small crown that would have completed his transformation into a look-alike of Prince Humperdink from *The Princess Bride.* The curly black hair on his head hadn't helped mute the image whatsoever.

It was better than the woman's first choice. Someone here had a sick sense of humor, because he'd been presented with a replica of the famous puffy shirt from the *Seinfeld* episode of the same name. Replica, hell. Knowing the guys who bankrolled this place, it might be the original. Nonetheless he'd declined it, and now sported an entirely different look. He fingered the blunt dagger thrust into the belt and let his imagination consider the possibilities.

Sari emerged from the tiny dressing room, having transformed into a princess. She had on a long, ice-blue gown, which contrasted with her chestnut curls perfectly. It had a scoop neck and long, tight, sleeves, and a carefully concealed velcro strip closing the tight front of the bodice. The kitty had not been very submissive in her warning to Adam. "Don't you dare rip this dress open all the way down!" He'd given his promise to be careful. The dress fell into a full, floor-length skirt. On her feet were matching blue ballet slippers, and her smile as she walked told him she was silently blessing whoever had thought to include flat shoes as part of the costume. As she approached, she fell into a deep curtsy that she held until he told her to rise.

He could get used to this.

He offered his arm and they received more than one approving glance as they made their way over to a high-top table. He placed a glass of water and a small triangle turkey sandwich in front of her and they talked while they ate.

"So, tell me more about this idea?" He smiled as he bit into his own sandwich. She looked less pale than when she'd run to the bathroom, but since they were talking for a few minutes anyway he'd ordered her to eat something.

She blushed bright red and swallowed. He watched as she struggled to put into words a fantasy she'd probably never told to anyone - or hardly admitted to herself.

"You, um, capture my kingdom and take me hostage. You want to marry me to become legitimate, but my father is hiding, and so you try to get me to tell you where he is..." She stared at the table as she continued talking, avoiding eye contact.

He liked the idea. It was also becoming obvious that he liked this woman. She was refreshing and honest, and, well, innocent. It was a strange word to use about someone who clearly loved domination and submission and wasn't a complete novice to BDSM, despite her statement earlier. She was everything his ex—.

Stop, dammit. He had to stop comparing them. That was a different time, and he was a different man. And this interesting, innocent woman was making herself vulnerable to him. He wanted to give her the best time he could come up with.

He asked her a few questions, and probed for any triggers. They agreed that 'mercy' would be the signal that things were getting a little too intense. It wouldn't interrupt the mood of the scene like 'yellow' might. They discussed the entire scene right up to the end to make sure they were both on the same page, and by then she was squirming in her chair. He held out his hand and she placed hers in it, smiling shyly, and he led her in the direction of a couch.

CHAPTER 11

$\mathcal{T}$he prince surveyed the woman kneeling before him, trembling but defiantly looking him straight in the eyes. He'd cure her of that. "What is your name?" he demanded.

She said nothing.

He lightly slapped her face and she glared at him.

"Look, my dear, your name is a small thing to tell me. I could always call you 'slut'."

"My name is Sari," she growled.

He nodded. "Sari. Daughter of the King?"

She said nothing again, and he reached forward to grab the mass of hair that flowed down her back, and yanked it hard. Her head snapped back and he spoke softly, his mouth only millimeters from hers. "There is only one Sari, and she is the daughter of the King I've defeated. Tell me, are you that daughter?"

After a moment of silence, he tightened his grip on her hair. She yelped and her hands flew up to grab his wrist. He let go of her hair long enough to capture her wrists in one hand, and then grabbed her hair again. She whimpered but remained silent.

"Are you the daughter of the King?"

"Yes!" she finally yelled.

He smiled, his inner sadist enjoying the banter. *This one is going to be fun to break.* He didn't let go of her hair. "Where is your father?"

"Why would I tell *you?*" She couldn't quite cross the line to call him a name, but he could hear it in her voice.

"Because," he leaned close to her face again and was gratified to see her eyes go wide with a touch of real fear. "I could just murder him, and claim this kingdom. But if I can convince him to let me marry his daughter, I'll have a legitimacy I wouldn't have otherwise. And... I promise not to kill him. I'll just keep him safely tucked away for the rest of his days." Adam chuckled to himself. He was definitely playing a romance novel villain here; a real villain wouldn't think twice about slitting the old goat's throat.

"I will never marry you!"

"I don't need your permission, or even participation. According to the laws of your country, all I need is your father's blessing. You could wear a gag to the ceremony and it would still be legal."

He could see in her fiery eyes that she felt the outrage as keenly as if this had been real. Time to deepen the scene. He stood and yanked her to her feet. He grabbed a length of rope he'd laid out and expertly secured her wrists together, leaving a length of it that he used to drag her from their couch over to an unoccupied pole in the center of the room. She sputtered and protested the whole way, and he noticed they were getting some interested looks from guests. Once at the pole he lifted her wrists up and tied the tail to a ring high up, forcing her to stand on her tiptoes. She pulled hard on the rope to test her limits while she continued to glare at him.

"So, let's continue. Let me lay down the rules. You *will* speak politely to me at all times. Disobedience will be punished. You will call me My Lord. You might as well get used to that now, because after we're married you'll be kneeling at my feet every day while you address me in that manner."

That was too good a line for her to resist. "Kneel at your feet, you bastard? Never!"

Adam was sure he heard a small gasp go up from those watching. He doubted Sari even realized they had an audience. He moved around behind her, and in a flash his dagger was unsheathed and at her neck. She caught her breath and whatever insult was on the tip of her tongue vanished.

He spotted his friend Colin lurking on the edges of the crowd, an approving grin on his face. Adam flicked his eyes towards his bag on the couch. Colin nodded and retrieved it.

"My Lord?" he murmured with a grin as he arrived. Adam gave him a half-smile at the title. Sari was glancing back and forth like she was afraid Colin was about to become part of their scene, but that wasn't in the plan.

"Would you please pull out a gag, a paddle, and the red ball?" Adam asked. Sari tried to protest but he pushed the dulled knife harder against her throat. It might have been dull, but the sensation would still be a powerful one, and she quieted. He removed the dagger from her throat and exchanged it for the gag.

"I warned you. Now you're going to lose the ability to speak for a while."

"If I can't speak, how do you hope to interrogate me?" she challenged.

"This won't be interrogation. This will be fun." He pushed the ball gag to her mouth and she let it in. He strapped it behind her head. Then he reached up to her bound hands and pressed the red ball into one of them. It was her safeword while she was gagged. If she needed him to stop, she would simply let it drop. He moved back around to face her.

Her breasts rose and fell enticingly as she breathed in and out. He was glad she was out of the sexy heels, because now she was shorter than him and he could loom over her menacingly. He knew what he was going to do first. He took the neckline of her dress in his hands and pulled it apart. The velcro split neatly as planned but he must have been too eager because the tear kept going right into the fabric. The kitty in the costume shop was going to tear *him* a new one, but he didn't care. Though he'd already seen Sari's breasts tonight, when they spilled out of the torn dress, it was as though they glowed with their own moonlight. He cupped one, entranced, and she wiggled and squealed in protest. He ignored her, and bent down to take one of the rosy nipples into his mouth. He sucked on it hard as her struggles increased. His tongue caressed the suddenly hard point and her head dropped back as she moaned.

"My little captive likes having her nipples sucked." She shook her head furiously. "You tell me no, but there's one way to find out." Her eyes went wide as his hands dropped to her skirts. It was easy to get lost in one of these scenes; the emotions became very real, and that was exactly the experience sought by those who played games like this. He knew by the furious shaking of her head and her dilated eyes that her character was begging him not to raise her dress, but as long as she didn't drop the ball, *Sari* was more than enjoying what he was doing. He grabbed the fabric and began lifting it. She struggled harder as the fabric cleared her knees, and then rose to the level of her pussy. He kept going until it was bunched at her waist and she stood exposed to the onlookers. One hand held the fabric while his other hand slipped between her legs. She grunted in protest and then squealed as he slipped a finger between her folds. He was not surprised to find her dripping wet; after all, this was her fantasy. But the princess would be mortified. He held up a glistening finger and then ceremoniously licked it clean.

"Your sweet nectar does not lie, milady. You have *always* longed for a man to take you and make you his own."

She struggled in futility, and he let her dress drop.

"But, enough. I told you that disobedience would warrant punishment, and so you shall see." He picked her up by the hips, relishing the feel of her curves in his hands. He spun her around so she faced the pole. One hand pushed her hard against it, and the other hauled her skirts back up, tucking them underneath the waist to hold them up. Her cheeks were still pink from the earlier spanking, and the whip marks lay atop the redness in crimson lines. He traced one line with his fingernail and was rewarded with a squeal. He squeezed the lovely softness, then held out his hand to Colin, who handed him the paddle.

"Twenty, for insulting my mother by calling me a bastard." He grinned. He checked to make sure the ball was still in her hands. He raised his arm and brought the paddle down on her cheek, making a *smack* sound that echoed through the room. It also left an immediate red splotch on her smooth skin. She grunted but made no other sound. He fell into a rhythm on the first cheek as she struggled and whimpered and cried out from behind the gag. At ten, he paused and leaned close. "Are you ready to apologize?" he whispered. She shot him a look of pure hatred. "Very well." He resumed the blows, this time on the other cheek, not sparing her in the least. He appreciated the dark redness that grew across the soft globes. At twenty, he tossed the paddle aside and plunged his hand between her legs again. She stiffened as he thrust a finger up inside, but he pulled back out. She was still pinned to the pole by his hand on her back, her face turned to the side.

"Wetter than before, Princess. Perhaps you need to be paddled like this every day. However, if you don't tell me where your father is, I can promise you far more than a mere paddling."

He saw the resistance in her eyes, though she couldn't do anything more than grunt in frustration and pull at her bonds.

"But perhaps the princess is immune to pain? Perhaps something else might convince her to talk?" This time her eyes widened and her brow furrowed in confusion. "I think it's time to find out."

CHAPTER 12

*A*dam – the *Prince* – unhooked her bound hands and tugged her in the direction of a massive wooden door. There was little question that it led to a dungeon. She flicked her eyes back and forth between the door and her still-bared bottom, torn between worrying what was behind the door, and desperately wanting her dress to be lowered. She pleaded with him through the gag, the sounds coming out unintelligible.

"Nope. That beautiful red ass stays bare for everyone to see."

It was one of the many contradictions of domination and submission, that she could be paraded naked across a room and feel less humiliation than when she was fully dressed, but had some part of her body exposed. She had no doubt the red of her face matched the red of her ass.

The door swung open and he tugged her into the dim room. On one wall a second St. Andrew's cross hung like a giant, silent warning. There was a flat wooden table with all sorts of tie-down points for doing wicked things to willing subs. A cabinet stood with its doors opened, filled with all kinds of toys to cause both pleasure and pain to any sub lucky enough to be dragged in here. And near the center of the room was a set of stocks.

He escorted her to the wooden structure where he unbound her hands to place them in the lower half. He pressed on her back, forcing her to bend over. She had an internal struggle – once more, Sari wanted to obey, but the princess was defiant. Sari won. The top closed over her neck and wrists, and she was pinned. Her bared ass faced the door from where she heard the murmurs of spectators. The drool that had gathered in her mouth leaked out in a long string, down to the floor, and her humiliation was complete.

Adam came around to her front and knelt. He traced his finger over her lips, around the red ball gag. "Such beautiful, sensuous lips. I can't wait for them to be wrapped around my cock."

She jerked her head away.

"Aww, princess, you don't like my touch? That's too bad. Because after we're married you'll belong to me. Every inch of you will be mine to do with as I please. I will stroke your soft skin. I will suck on your nipples before I pinch and torment them until you cry. My hands will stroke your folds and invade your most private places. My cock will bury itself in the depths of your throat, and if you resist me I will whip you." He placed his hands around her throat. "And I will place a collar around here just tight enough to remind you every moment of every day that you belong to me."

She glared at him again. He laughed.

"That look on your face is going to be very different in a few minutes. And since I want everyone to hear you the moment you surrender to me, this will have to go." He reached behind her head to unbuckle the gag and the ball popped out, more drool spilling onto the floor until she moved her jaw around and could close her mouth.

"Go to hell," she spat at him.

"No more talking, Your Highness, or this goes back in."

She dropped her eyes and stayed silent. Adam asked someone off to the side for a spreader bar. Her mouth opened to protest but at a look from him, she cut it off. He stood up and disappeared.

A moment later she felt his hand on her ankle. "Spread," he ordered. She didn't move. A painful swat between her legs changed her mind.

"Ow!" she yelped. She shifted her legs. He nudged them wider and she struggled to obey. She felt the cuffs of the bar wrap around each ankle, spreading her wide for all to see from behind, and removing all barriers to invasion. His hand dove between her legs once more. To her utter humiliation, she heard the wet sucking sound of her arousal. He pulled his fingers out. Then he was kneeling by her head again.

"Clean my fingers."

Her mouth remained tightly closed.

"Clean them or I'll whip your little cunt. And don't bite me. I can still spank you for the remaining thirty minutes of this evening."

She raised an eyebrow but opened her mouth and took his fingers in, sucking and licking. She noticed the bulge in his pants and couldn't resist a smile around his fingers. He smiled back.

"Now, Your Highness, you're going to tell me where your father is."

She shook her head.

Still smiling, he yanked his fingers out of her mouth. "That's what I hoped you'd say." He disappeared.

She jumped when his cool hands touched her backside. She felt a finger trace the pucker of her asshole in little circles which made her wiggle and squeal in a very un-princess-like manner.

"Perhaps we shall explore this tight sweet hole soon?"

She closed her eyes at that image, already imagining it. Then she heard the unmistakable sound of a vibrator. *Oh, hell.*

"Where is your father?"

She shook her head. "No!"

The vibrator was thrust against her clit. It was too strong, too fast. She stiffened and shrieked. She wiggled in a desperate attempt to escape it.

"Dance for me, princess."

And dance she did, crying out and begging for him to stop. And then it stopped as suddenly as it had started.

"Your father?"

She shook her head. She heard the vibrator turn on again and braced herself. This time, though, he placed it lightly against her folds. She groaned in pleasure. He kept the pressure steady, changing the angle slightly from time to time. Her lower belly twisted and tightened, like a black hole pulling everything inside. She could feel her nipples hanging from her swinging breasts, begging to be touched, begging to be part of the action. She shivered and panted, torn between pulling away from the constant buzzing, and longing to jam her aching slit hard against the silicone head. She was dimly aware that he had wrapped his arm around her hips, pinning her tight against his body and preventing her escape from the overwhelming pleasure. An enormous orgasm rose up like a geyser and exploded out of her body. She was helpless to prevent the screech that was torn from her mouth as she strained against the unyielding wood that held her prisoner.

And still he held the vibrator in place. Suddenly the pleasure turned into something much less pleasant.

"Stop! Please! I can't – it's too sensitive!" She tried to wrestle her hips from his grasp.

"Then tell me where your father is, or beg for mercy!" He didn't move it a millimeter.

"No!" Her knees buckled but his grip held her in place. She wailed in distress, she struggled, and she fought, but it didn't matter, and before long the second orgasm exploded out of her. The vibrator still didn't move.

"Your father, or mercy!" he repeated.

She begged and pleaded for him to stop, and he showed not the slightest bit of mercy. He held her tight through a third orgasm, and a fourth, repeating the question each time, and she answered him only in pleas and cries. But as the rush of the fourth one faded and he kept the vibrator firmly planted over her overworked clit, it was too much. She surrendered.

"Behind the forge!"

CHAPTER 13

"hat?" Adam was caught off guard by the sudden confession.

"My father is hiding behind the forge, there's a hiding place under the floor, oh, please stop...!" She was sobbing now. He turned off the vibrator. Colin and another dom were at her side almost immediately, lifting the board off her neck. Adam, who had never let go of her hips, lifted her to standing and steadied her against his chest while the other men released her ankles from the spreader bar.

She was flushed, with tear tracks down her face. He thought she looked beautiful and as he carried her out to a couch and sank down, he placed a kiss on her forehead. She smiled up at him.

"Holy shit," she murmured. "Give me just a minute, sir?"

He handed her a bottle of water and she sat with her head resting on his shoulder. She started to speak twice, but stopped.

"Sari –" His sixth sense was prickling him.

"Sorry. That was one of the most intense scenes I've ever done. And knowing there was a crowd..." She put the bottle of water down. "So now, evil prince," she chuckled. "Now that you've forced the location of my father out of me, what will you do next? He'll never give his consent, even to save his own life." She started to pull away from him but he grabbed her dress and hauled her back.

The princess had returned, and the game was on.

"You're so sure of that?" He stood and lifted her off the couch in one movement, grabbing his toy bag and carrying her across the floor to one of the semi-private rooms. He could do this out in the open, but somehow it seemed more fitting to fuck the king's daughter with a pretense of privacy. But he wouldn't pull the curtain, because her loyal followers were gathering, hoping to witness the defiling of their princess.

He deposited her on the low, backless couch and looked down. She'd resumed the character flawlessly; her look of fear would have won an Oscar.

"So, princess, there's only one way to make sure your father gives his blessing to this marriage." He raised his eyebrows.

"No! Please, Sire, no!" She tried to scramble backwards but he pounced on her. He bound her arms and secured them over her head to a hook on the end of the red velvet couch. He replaced the gag between her lips, holding back his groan at the sight. She performed her part well; she fought him hard even after she was secured. But he pressed the ball in her hand and her fingers closed around it firmly. When he stood up again she was breathing fast and was more than a little disheveled, her curls sprawled out underneath her and her face flushed. If this had been real, he would have had a seriously hard time holding himself back.

He hadn't secured her legs, so when she began kicking, he yanked her dress up past her knees and then straddled them, pinning them down with his weight. She struggled and fought, but the red ball stayed put.

"You may beg and plead, but it won't make a difference. I'm going to take your maidenhood now, and then your father will have little choice but to yield to my demand." He freed his cock, not a hard thing to do since it had been straining the zipper for some time, and rolled a condom on over the stiffness. He stroked it while he watched her, enjoying the sensations both tactile and visual. Her eyes flickered back and forth between his hand and his eyes, but she'd stopped struggling. He lifted himself off her legs just enough to grab her ankles before she could yank them free, and pushed her knees to her chest. Her pussy was so wet and swollen it was practically begging for his cock. She was breathing fast, and her hand with the ball was squeezing and relaxing. He checked in one last time.

"Mercy?" he asked softly.

She shook her head and closed her eyes.

"Very well then, milady." He lined up his cock with her entrance and gave a push forward. She gave a little grunt and a frown as he reveled in the surprising tightness of her tunnel. She was exquisite. He let out his own groan as he sheathed himself all the way to his balls. He looked down at her, but her eyes were still closed. He pulled out, relishing the tight slide, and then plunged back in. She opened her eyes briefly and gave him a quick smile, then retreated again. He let his sadist loose just a notch, setting up a steady rhythm in and out, the pleasure growing inside him quickly after almost three hours of teasing. The orgasm erupted out of him as he pushed deep inside, and he held himself rigid as he cried out his release. His cock jerked and spurted his seed into the condom barrier.

At last he drew in a breath and forced his eyes open to check on Sari. He was relieved to find her looking up at him with a neutral expression. He pulled out, rolling off the condom and tossing it in the garbage. He reached behind her head to loosen the gag and gently pried it from her mouth.

"Now, Milady, you belong to me, forever."

CHAPTER 14

Sari responded automatically with the words the princess would have used. "I have no choice now but to become your wife, Milord." A single tear, not faked at all, appeared in the corner of her eye and slid down her face. She felt a strange sense of detachment.

"You will be my wife, and when you disobey, I can promise you swift correction. But if you obey me, you will have a reasonably pleasant life. I can promise you that."

She nodded. Suddenly, she needed to be done. "May I sit up, Adam?"

She saw the observers drift away. He released her hands, helping her up, and then he sat down beside her.

"How are you doing?"

"I'm okay. That was incredible. Intense. So... real. Thank you." She managed a smile at him.

She heard a small beep.

"Well, it's eleven o'clock, and we made it. I hope you enjoyed it as much as I have." He smoothed her hair back from her face.

She nodded and stood up, wobbling on her legs. She had an overwhelming urge to get out of this place as fast as she could, and wasn't sure she ever wanted to see it again.

He sprang up to support her. "Hey, go slow."

"I need to get dressed. I have to work in the morning." She pulled out of his grasp and started for the main room. He caught her hand.

"Sari, what's wrong?"

"Nothing," she said a little too brightly. *Please just let me go.*

"Sari, something's wrong. At the very least you've got some serious sub-drop going on. I'm not letting you leave yet."

"Yes. I'm leaving. I had a wonderful time, Adam. Thank you. You, this, it was everything I could have ever hoped for. But it's over now." She pulled from his grasp and turned towards the room again, only to find herself so dizzy she dropped to her knees. In a flash he had her in his arms again, laying her back on the sofa. He motioned to someone passing by.

"She's not feeling good. Can you bring something to drink?" The monitor nodded and disappeared.

Sari resigned herself to his care. The thought of managing the stairs out of here in her heels had suddenly become overwhelming. But she needed to contain the emotions rising up in her and threatening to erupt. Emotions she hadn't expected, and wasn't sure how to deal with. Emotions she couldn't let him see.

She didn't regret what they'd done. But she needed to be alone to think about it and come to terms with what it meant.

He rubbed her hands, and when the bottle of juice arrived he helped her sit up again. She took a sip, and then the tears started. She couldn't control them; they just flowed out suddenly and silently, and there was no disguising them.

"Sari, what did I do wrong?" His worried face searched her eyes. She shook her head.

"Nothing, Adam. I promise. It was everything I'd hoped. I think I had a better time than almost anyone here."

"Then something triggered you."

She shook her head, staring at the bottle. He put a finger under her chin and lifted it up. "Sari, eyes," he said sternly. She heard the dom in his voice and managed to lift her gaze up to his.

"I *know* what I'm seeing. What is it that you didn't tell me? What has set this off? Did you have a bad experience with sex before?"

She was so tired. She closed her eyes. "No. I didn't have a bad experience. Because this was my first time."

There was silence for so long that she was compelled to look. He sat next to her, his mouth in a straight, hard line. "You were a virgin?"

She looked down at her lap and after a moment, she nodded.

"Holy hell. I wondered why you were so tight. You didn't bleed, though."

"I was terrified of that happening. But not every girl bleeds. That's a myth."

"Why the fuck didn't you tell me?"

"Because you didn't need to know! This was my decision. I wanted to have sex; you got to be the lucky guy. But there's no long-term commitment here, so what's the big deal?"

"What's the big deal?" His voice rose in disbelief. "You manipulated me into taking your virginity! *I* did not consent to it!"

"Would you have agreed if I'd asked you?"

"No! Absolutely not!"

"Why? It's no big deal! The first time – the fiftieth time – there's no difference! It's not like anyone expects a virgin on their wedding night anymore!" *At least, not here. Back home...*

He stood up. She started to rise, too.

"*Sit. Down.*" He yanked the curtain across the opening, closing them off from prying eyes. "I will give you reasons why. First – if you've never had sex, you'd have *no* idea how rough I was going to be. You asked me to do a *rape* scene with you! You had no idea what doing that might feel like, or whether you could handle it or not. I might have hurt you, emotionally, for the *rest of your life*. You say this was no big deal, so why are you sitting here crying? Eyes!"

She forced herself to look at him through the blur of tears that wouldn't stop.

"If this had turned out really bad, do you realize the position you put me in? You go home to your roommate and cry on her shoulder, perfectly innocently, and she misunderstands and calls the police, and bam! I'm arrested for rape, and lose custody of my daughter, and lose my job, whether it's true or not!"

She stared at him in horror. "I'd never do that!"

"And then word gets out in the community about what happened. Sure, those here tonight would know the truth, but the truth has a funny way of being altered until it is unrecognizable. No club would ever have me back, and no sub would ever trust me."

"I never thought about that," she whispered. "I'm sorry."

"And you know what the most important reason is? Because every woman deserves to have her first time be something special. I know for a lot of women it isn't, but if I'd known, I would have given you an experience that would give you good dreams, not nightmares! But you didn't fucking give me a chance!" He put his head in his hands. "I enjoyed tonight a lot. I was hoping we could play again. But I spent years with a bitch who managed to manipulate me every which way from hell, and I'll be damned if I'm going to get involved with another one." He picked up his bag and pulled the curtain aside.

"Adam, please! Please don't go like this. I'm sorry. So, so, sorry."

"Why?" He was still facing away, but he'd paused. "Why was tonight so important? Why did you want to do it this way?"

"I didn't plan to do this tonight. Sex was supposed to be on my limits list, and I don't know what happened. But when it came up on the wheel, well, I spent a few minutes in the bathroom thinking maybe this was the opportunity I needed. Because there's been no other way I could think of to get past the first time. I'm too chicken to just get in bed with a guy and do it. I was raised to believe that women shouldn't have sex before marriage, and even though I've thrown off almost everything else about my childhood, I couldn't get past that one, and I really wanted to get it over with so it would stop hanging over me like a millstone. You know, 'go big or go home'. And I can't go home again, so..." her voice broke in a single sob that she stifled. She wasn't going to manipulate him with pity.

He came back over to her and sat down. "Why can't you go home again?"

"I didn't mean it literally. I can go visit, but it'll never be the same. See, girls in my town – we get married and have babies. We're not supposed to want to go to college, and don't usually go far from home. There was a boy, and we'd planned to be married eventually. He was nice. But when I told him I'd gotten a scholarship to college, we fought. He pleaded with me not to go, and finally told me that he wouldn't wait for me, and he would never consider moving somewhere else if my career needed it. Even my best friend didn't think I should go away. My parents were actually the most supportive once they got over the shock, though they were sad to see me leave."

"Pretty conservative?"

"That's an understatement. I love my home, and my family, but I've always wanted to go to college. When I was a child I used to stand in the meadow and watch a storm build overhead, and long to know more about what made it happen. So, I secretly applied to a small college not too far away and got a full scholarship to study meteorology. I wanted to be one of the people on the radio who warned us when we needed to move the animals inside, or when we needed to go down to the storm shelter. I used to find the National Weather Service site on the computer and study the weather radar for hours." She smiled at him and was relieved to see a smile back.

"How did you stumble into this world?" he gestured towards the dungeon on the other side of the curtain.

"That's a long story. I met a girl who plays here sometimes. She introduced me to the lifestyle in person."

They sat in silence for another minute.

"Adam, I'm so, so, sorry."

"You betrayed my trust in a big way."

"I know."

"How are you feeling?"

She looked inside herself and was a little surprised. "Actually, a whole lot better than a few minutes ago. How are you?"

"Tired." He chuckled.

"You have a daughter?"

He nodded. "Yeah. Her mother and I were married until Hannah was a toddler, and then she left. I've been fighting for full custody ever since. That's why I wasn't playing for a long time. A custody battle puts your life under a microscope, but it's over now."

"And I could have ruined that."

He said nothing.

"I'm sorry. I know there isn't anything I can do to change what happened, but I wish there was something I could do to try to make up for it."

He reached over to her hand and squeezed it, taking her by surprise. "I did enjoy tonight, and I'd like to play again sometime."

Her eyes bulged. "You would?"

"Yes. Would you?"

"Yes, I would."

He stood up and grabbed her hand, pulling her off the couch and through the curtain, over to Chase, who was saying goodbye to another couple. The dom turned and smiled. "You two get everything worked out? It sounded kind of loud in there for a while."

"Yes," replied Adam. "We did." He turned to Sari. "Kneel."

She looked at him, taken by surprise, and then stumbled to her knees.

"Chase, did we win the free month?"

"You know you did."

"Is there any limit on the number of days we can be here?"

"No, but we're closed Mondays and Tuesdays."

Adam turned to Sari. "Eyes! Every time I have to tell you that from now on there's a penalty, understand?"

"Yes, sir!" she replied automatically.

"Sari, you will report here every Wednesday and Saturday evening, promptly at 8pm, for the next four weeks. When you arrive, I will strap you to the spanking bench and paddle your ass until it's bright red. I intend to make you think about what you did every time you sit down for the next month. Is that clear?"

Was that clear? A delicious wave of dread swept through her. "Yes, sir, that's clear."

"Do you have anyone who might object to this arrangement?"

She held back a grin as she realized he was fishing to find out if she had a boyfriend, or another dom. "No, sir. No one."

"You will not play with anyone else, at any club, this month. And I'm keeping your thong for now."

Gulp. "Yes, sir."

"If you can follow through with this, no matter how unpleasant it may get to be, then at the end of the month we'll talk about where we go from there."

He smiled as he helped her stand, and the kiss he placed on her lips was gentle and tender. She dared to hope that there might be something in the future for them.

But first… she had to be thoroughly punished.

Her heart and her pussy both pulsed in anticipation.

The End

ABOUT THE AUTHOR

For years before I became a USA Today Bestselling Author, I wrote and hid stories in the computer, convinced that no one would be interested in the twisted musings of my mind. When the internet showed me that there were others who shared those twists, I decided to come out of the closet.

My men are strong, even when love makes them tender. My women are fierce and independent and will not surrender until they are respected. My stories are about negotiating the sometimes-dark dance between the two, until he claims her heart in the end.

Right now, I split my time between being mother, wife, over-worked employee, and servant to the cat's every need. Most evenings will find me hiding in my office cave to write, where I only care about my internet signal and the strength of my coffee.

WHERE TO FIND SOPHIE KISKER:

- Facebook: http://www.facebook.com/SophieKisker
- Website: www.sophiekisker.com

OTHER BOOKS BY SOPHIE KISKER

Finding Home: An Erotic Tale of Slavery, Love, and War

Odyssey

Sanctuary

Refining Fire

Midrosian Slave Chronicles

Memories of Surrender

Longings of Surrender

Tears of Surrender

BDSM Erotic Romance

A Captive of Fear and Desire

The Punishment Tour

Black Light: Valentine Roulette

Revenge Served Hot

Nectar for the Gods: Owned

Nectar for the Gods: Claimed

Nectar for the Gods: Saved

And He Shall Rule Over Her

BLACK COLLAR PRESS

Black Collar Press is a small publishing house started by authors Livia Grant and Jennifer Bene in late 2016. The purpose was simple - to create a place where the erotic, kinky, and exciting worlds they love to explore could thrive and be joined by other like-minded authors.

If this is something that interests you, please go to the Black Collar Press website and read through the FAQs. If your questions are not answered there, please contact us directly at: blackcollarpress@gmail.com

WHERE TO FIND BLACK COLLAR PRESS:

- Newsletter: http://bit.ly/2JY23Wi
- Website: http://www.blackcollarpress.com/
- Facebook: https://www.facebook.com/blackcollarpress/
- Twitter: https://twitter.com/BlackCollarPres
- Black Light East and West may be fictitious, but you can now join our very real Facebook Group for Black Light Fans - Black Light Central

GET A FREE BLACK LIGHT BOOK

Enjoy your trip to Black Light? There's a lot more sexy fun to be had. All of the books in the series can be read as standalone stories and can also be enjoyed in any reading order.

Get started with a FREE copy of *Black Light: Rocked* today. Your fun doesn't need to end yet!

BLACK LIGHT SERIES

Did you enjoy your visit to Black Light? Have you read the other books in the series? They can all be enjoyed as standalone books read in any order.

Season One

Infamous Love, A Black Light Prequel by Livia Grant
Black Light: Rocked by Livia Grant
Black Light: Exposed by Jennifer Bene
Black Light: Valentine Roulette by Various Authors
Black Light: Suspended by Maggie Ryan
Black Light: Cuffed by Measha Stone
Black Light: Rescued by Livia Grant

Season Two
Black Light: Roulette Redux by Various Authors
Complicated Love, A Black Light Novel by Livia Grant
Black Light: Suspicion by Measha Stone
Black Light: Obsessed by Dani René
Black Light: Fearless by Maren Smith
Black Light: Possession by LK Shaw

www.ingramcontent.com/pod-product-compliance
Lightning Source LLC
Chambersburg PA
CBHW052338020726
47503CB00001B/21